Fawcett Crest Books
by Günter Grass:

DOG YEARS

THE FLOUNDER

LOCAL ANAESTHETIC

The Flounder

a novel by

Günter Grass

FAWCETT CREST • NEW YORK

A Fawcett Crest Book

Published by Ballantine Books

Copyright © 1977 by Hermann Luchterhand Verlag
English translation Copyright © 1978 by Harcourt Brace
Jovanovich, Inc.

ISBN 0-449-20349-2

This edition published by arrangement with
Harcourt Brace Jovanovich, Inc.

An excerpt originally appeared in *Playboy*.

Selection of the Quality Paperback Book Club

Printed in Canada

First Fawcett Crest Edition: November 1979
First Ballantine Books Edition: February 1983

For Helena Grass

Translator's note

It must be evident to anyone who has ever fished in the North Atlantic or browsed in a fish market that the fish depicted on the dust jacket of this book*, described on page 39, and eaten on pages 518-519 is not what is commonly called a flounder. He's too big, stout, and pebbly. I call him a flounder because he is no ordinary fish, but an archetypal one, harking back to the dawn of human consciousness but first revealed to the general public in the Grimm Brothers' tale "The Fisherman and His Wife," all English translations of which concur in calling the fish (who was really an enchanted prince) a flounder. As is made clear on page 39 of the translation with some violence to the original, Günter Grass's fish is actually a turbot (*Steinbutt*). The Grimms' fish, on the other hand, is only a *Butt,* or flatfish, and the flatfish family includes both Grass's turbot and our flounder. Moreover, Webster defines "flounder" as "in a broad sense any flatfish," which puts us perfectly in the clear.

The translation of this book called for a range of knowledge that I cannot lay claim to. I am deeply grateful to the late Wolfgang Sauerlander and to Helen Wolff for their help and advice.

R. M.

---

* The Fawcett Crest cover art is an adaptation of the Harcourt dust jacket.

Contents

The first month

~~~~~~

The second month

The third month

The fourth month

~~~~~~

The fifth month

~~~~~~

The sixth month

~~~~~~

The seventh month

~~~~~~

The eighth month

~~~~~~

The ninth month

~~~~~~

The first month

~~~~~~

The third breast

Ilsebill put on more salt. Before the impregnation there was shoulder of mutton with string beans and pears, the season being early October. Still at table, still with her mouth full, she asked, "Should we go to bed right away, or do you first want to tell me how when where our story began?"

I, down through the ages, have been I. And Ilsebill, too, has been from the beginning. I remember our first quarrel, toward the end of the Neolithic, some two thousand years before the incarnation of our Lord, when myths were beginning to distinguish between raw food and cooked food. And just as, today, before sitting down to mutton with string beans and pears, we quarreled more and more cuttingly over her children and mine, so then, in the marshland of the Vistula estuary, we quarreled to the best of our neolithic vocabulary over my claim to at least three of her nine kids. But I lost. For all the ur-phonemes my nimble, hard-working tongue was able to line up, I did not succeed in forming the beautiful word "father"; only "mother" was possible. In those days Ilsebill's name was Awa. I, too, had a different name. But the idea of having been Awa doesn't appeal to Ilsebill.

I had studded the shoulder of mutton with halved garlic cloves, sautéed the pears in butter, and bedded them on boiled string beans. Even though Ilsebill, speaking with her mouth still full, said there was no reason why it shouldn't come off, or "take," right away, because she had thrown her pills down the john as the doctor advised, what I heard was that our bed should have priority over the neolithic cook.

And so we lay down, arming and legging each other around as we have done since time immemorial. Sometimes I, sometimes she on top. Equal, though Ilsebill contends that the male's privilege of penetrating is hardly compensated by the female's paltry prerogative of refusing admittance. But because we mated in love, our feelings were so all-embracing that in an expanded space, transcending time and its ticktock, freed from the heaviness of our earthbound bed, a collateral, ethereal union was achieved; as though in compensation, her feeling penetrated mine in hard thrusts: we worked doubly and well.

Eaten before the mutton with pears and beans, Ilsebill's fish soup, distilled from codfish heads that have had the hell boiled out of them, probably embodied the catalytic agent with which, down through the ages, the cooks inside me have invited pregnancy; for by chance, by destiny, and without further ingredients, it came off, it took. No sooner was I out again—as though expelled—than Ilsebill said with perfect assurance, "Well, this time it's going to be a boy."

Don't forget the savory. With boiled potatoes or, historically, with millet. Our mutton—as always advisable—had been served on warmed plates. Nevertheless our kiss, if I may be forgiven one last indiscretion, was coated with tallow. In the fish soup, which Ilsebill had made green with dill and capers, codfish eyes floated white and signified happiness.

After it presumably came off, we lay in bed together, each smoking his (or her) conception of a cigarette. (I, descending the steps of time, ran away.) Ilsebill said, "Incidentally, we need a dishwasher. It's high time."

Before she could engage in further speculation about a reversal of roles—"I wish I could see *you* pregnant some time"—I told her about Awa and her three breasts.

So help me, Ilsebill, she had three. Nature can do anything. Honest to goodness, three of them. And if my memory doesn't deceive me, all women had that name in the Stone Age: Awa Awa Awa. And we men were all called Edek. We were all alike in every way. And so were the Awas. One two three. At first we couldn't count any higher. No, not below, not above; in between. The plural begins with three. Three is the beginning of multiplicity, the series, the chain, and of myth. But don't let it tie you up in complexes. We acquired some later on. In our region, to the east of the river, Potrimpos, who became a god of the Prussians along with Pikollos and Perkunos, was said to have had three testicles. Yes, you're right: three breasts are more, or at least they look it; they look like more and more; they suggest super-abundance, advertise generosity, give eternal assurance of a full belly. Still, when you come right down to it, they are abnormal—though not inconceivable.

Naturally. A projection of male desires! I knew you'd say that. Maybe they are anatomically impossible. But in those days, when myths still cast their shadows, Awa had three. And it's true that today the third is often wanting. I mean, something is wanting. Well, the third of the three. Don't be so quick on the trigger. No, of course not. Of course I won't make a cult of it. Of course two are plenty. You can take my word for it, Ilsebill, basically I'm satisfied with two. I'm not a fool. I don't go chasing after a number. Now that, thanks to your fish soup and no pill, it must have come off, now that you're pregnant and your two will soon weigh more than Awa's three, I'm perfectly, blissfully contented.

The third was always an extra. Essentially a caprice of capricious nature. As useless as the appendix. Altogether I can't help wondering: Why this breast fixation? This typically male tittomania? This cry for the primal mother, the super wet-nurse? Anyway, Awa became a goddess later on and had her three tits certified in hand-sized clay idols. Other goddesses—the Indian Kali, for instance—had four or more arms. But these may have served some practical purpose. The Greek mother goddesses—Demeter, Hera—on the other hand, were normally outfitted and managed to stay in business for thousands of years even so. I've also seen gods represented with a third eye in their forehead. I wouldn't want one of those if you paid me.

All in all the number three promises more than it can deliver. Awa overdid it with her three boobies as much as the Amazons underdid it with their one breast. That's why our latter-day feminists always go to extremes. Get that sulky look off your face. I'm all in favor of the libbers. And I assure you, Ilsebill, two are plenty. Any doctor will tell you so. And if our child doesn't turn out to be a boy, she'll certainly have enough with two. What do you mean, aha? Men just happen to be crazy, always this yen for bigger and bigger bosoms. The truth of the matter is that all the cooks I have ever sojourned with have had one on the left and one on the right, the same as you: Mestwina two, Amanda Woyke two, and Sophie Rotzoll had two little espresso cupfuls. And Margarete Rusch the cooking abbess smothered the wealthy patrician Eberhard Ferber in bed with her two admittedly enormous tits. So let's not exaggerate. The whole thing is kind of a dream. No, not a wish dream. Why must you always pick a fight? Can't a man dream a little? Can't he?

Absurd, this jealousy about everything and nothing. A pathetic lot we'd be without projections and utopias! I'd even be forbidden to let pencil stay over white paper in three curved lines. Art would have to say "Yes" and "Have it your way" all the time. I beg you, Ilsebill, be just a little reasonable. Think of the whole thing as an idea with an inherent contradiction which, it is hoped, will give the female breast the dimensions it now lacks and produce some sort of superbosom. You must learn to take a dialectical view. Think of the Roman she-wolf, for instance. Think of expressions such as "nature's bosom." Or, with regard to the number, the triune God. Or the three wishes in fairy tales. What do you mean, given myself away? You think I'm wishing? Well, well. You really do?

All right. Admitted that when I grab at empty space, I'm always after the third breast. In which I'm certainly not alone. There must be reasons why we men are so hipped on breasts, as if we'd all been weaned too soon. It must be you women's fault. It could be your fault. Because you attach so much, too much importance to whether or not they sag a little more, each day a little more. Let them sag, to hell with them. No. Not yours. But they will, they're bound to, in time. Amanda's sagged. Lena's sagged from the start. But I loved her and loved her and loved her. It's not always a bit of bosom more or less that matters. If I wanted to, for instance, I could find your ass with all its little dimples just as beautiful. And I certainly wouldn't want it in three parts. Or something else that's smooth and round. Now that your belly will soon start ballooning, a symbol for everything that's roomy. Maybe we've simply forgotten that there's still more. A third something. In other respects as well, politically for instance, as possibility.

Anyway, Awa had three. My three-breasted Awa. And you, too, had one more back in the Neolithic. Think back, Ilsebill: to how our story began.

Even if it seems convenient to presume that they, the cooks inside me (nine or eleven of them), are nothing more than a full-blown complex, an extreme case of banal mother fixation, ripe for the couch and hardly worthy of suspending time in kitchen tales, I must nevertheless insist on the rights of my subtenants. All nine or eleven of them want to come out and to be called by name from the very start; because they have too long been nameless old settlers, or, collectively, a complex without name or history; because too often in mute passivity and too seldom with ready words (I say: dominant nevertheless; Ilsebill says: exploited and oppressed) they cooked and performed various other services for shopkeepers and Teutonic Knights, abbots and inspectors, for men in armor or cowls, in baggy breeches or gaiters, for men in high boots or men with snapping suspenders; and because they want their revenge, revenge against everyone; want at last to be out of me—or, as Ilsebill says, emancipated.

Let them! Let them reduce us all, including the cook inside *them*—who would doubtless be me—to sex objects. Perhaps from exhausted daddies they will build a man who, untainted by power and privilege, will be sticky and new; for without him it can't be done.

"Not yet, unfortunately," said Ilsebill as we were spooning up our fish soup. And after the shoulder of mutton with string beans and pears, she gave me nine months' time to deliver myself of my cooks. When it comes to deadlines, we have equal rights. Whatever I may have cooked, the cook inside me adds salt.

What I write about

About food and its aftertaste.
Then about guests who came
uninvited or just a century late.

About the mackerel's longing for lemon juice.
Among fishes I write mostly about the flounder.

I write about superabundance.
About fasting and why gluttons invented it.
About crusts from the tables of the rich and their food value.
About fat and excrement and salt and penury.
In the midst of a mound of millet
I will relate instructively
how the spirit became bitter as gall
and the belly went insane.

I write about breasts.
About Ilsebill's pregnancy (her craving for sour pickles)
I will write as long as it lasts.
About the last bite shared,
the hour spent with a friend
over bread, cheese, nuts, and wine.
(Munching, we talked about this, that, and the other
and about gluttony, which is only a form of fear.)

I write about hunger, how it is described
and disseminated by the written word.
About spices (when Vasco de Gama and I
made pepper cheaper)
I will write on my way to Calcutta.

Meat, raw and cooked,
goes limp, shreds, shrinks, and falls apart.
The daily porridge
and other warmed-over fare: dated history,
the slaughter at Tannenberg Wittstock Kolin.
I make a note of what's left:
bones, husks, innards, and sausage.

About nausea brought on by a heaped plate,
about good taste,
about milk (how it curdles),
about turnips, cabbage, the triumph of the potato
I will write tomorrow
or after yesterday's leftovers
have become today's petrifaction.

What I write about: about the egg.
About overeating through sorrow, consuming love, the nail
    and the rope,
about quarrels over the hair and the word too many in the
    soup.
Deep freezers and what became of them
when the current gave out.
I will write about us all at a table eaten bare,
and about you and me and the fishbones in our throats.

Nine and more cooks

The first cook inside me—for I can speak only of cooks
who are inside me and want to come out—was named Awa,
and she had three breasts. That was in the Stone Age. We
men had little say, because Awa had filched fire for us from
the Sky Wolf, three glowing little pieces of charcoal, and hidden them somewhere, possibly under her tongue. Next Awa,
as though in passing, invented the roasting spit and taught us
to distinguish raw food from cooked food. Awa's rule was
mild: after suckling their babies, the women of Stone Age
suckled their men until they sweated out their obsessions,
stopped fidgeting, and became sleepily still, available for just
about anything.

And so we were all of us sated. Never again, never in the
future that dawned later on, were we so sated. We were
suckled and suckled. Always superabundance was flowing
into us. Never any question of enough is enough or let's not
overdo it. Never were we given a pacifier and told to be reasonable. It was always suckling time.

Because Awa prescribed a mash of ground acorns, sturgeon roe, and the mammary glands of the elk cow for all
mothers, milk gushed into Stone Age mothers even when
there were no infants to suckle. That made us all peaceful
and created time intervals. So punctually fed, even our tooth-
less old men preserved their vigor, and the consequence was
rather a surplus of males; the women wore out more quickly
and died younger. We had little to do between feeding times:
hunting, fishing, the manufacture of stone axes; and when in

19

accordance with a strict rule our turn came, we were allowed to mount the women, who ruled by tender loving care.

It might interest you to know that Stone Age mothers already said "la la" to their babies and that the men, when called to take a look at them, said "na na." There were no fathers. Matriarchy held sway.

It was a pleasantly historyless age. A pity that someone, a man of course, suddenly decided to smelt metal out of ore and pour it into sand molds. God knows that wasn't what Awa had stolen fire for. But threaten as she would to withhold the breast, the Bronze Age and the masculine cruelties that came after it could not be prevented, but only delayed a little.

The second cook inside me who wants to emerge with a name was called Wigga and no longer had three breasts. That was in the Iron Age, but Wigga, who forbade us to leave the swamps with their plentiful fish and join in the history making of the Germanic hordes who were then passing through, still kept us in a state of immaturity. The one thing she allowed us to copy from the Germans was their coiling pottery. And Wigga made us gather the iron pots they threw away in their haste, because Wigga ruled by cookery, and she needed flameproof pots.

For all the men, who were all fishermen—because elk and water buffalo were becoming rare—she boiled codfish and sturgeon, pike-perch and salmon, roasted roaches, lampreys, finger-length sprats, and those small, tasty Baltic herrings on the iron grill that we had learned to fashion from Germanic scrap. Making a thick, strong broth by boiling the hell out of shifty-eyed codfish heads, Wigga invented a fish soup into which, because millet was still unknown to us, she stirred and crushed seeds of swamp grasses. Possibly in memory of Awa, whose image had come down to us as a three-breasted goddess, Wigga, always nursing an infant or two, added milk from her own breasts to her fish soups.

We unsuckled men were jumpy, as though infected with Germanic unrest. Wanderlust raised its head. We climbed tall trees, stood on high dunes, narrowed our eyes to sight slits, and searched the horizon to see if something was coming, if something new was coming. Because of this wanderlust—and because I refused to be Wigga's charcoal burner and peat cutter forever—I went off with the Germanic Goitches, as we called the Goths. But I didn't get very far. Trouble with my feet. Or maybe I turned back in time because I missed Wigga's mammary fish soup.

Wigga forgave me. She knew that history is forgotten between hunger and hunger. "The Germanic peoples," she said, "won't listen to their women; that's why they will always get themselves wiped out."

For Wigga, incidentally, I filed a comb from fishbone, because a talking flounder had shrewdly advised me to. Back in Awa's days, I had fished this flatfish out of the shallow water and let him go again. The talking flounder is a story by himself. Since he has been advising me, the male cause has progressed.

The third cook inside me was called Mestwina, and she, too, ruled in the region where Awa and Wigga had kept us in a state of infancy with their ever-loving care: in the swamps of the Vistula estuary, in the beech forests of the Baltic Ridge, amid sand dunes wandering and stationary. Po Morze—country by the sea—for which reason Mestwina's tribe of fishermen, who had begun to grow root plants, were known among the neighboring Prussians as "Pomorshians" or Pomeranians.

They lived in a Wicker Bastion, so called because of the fence they had plaited from willow withes as a defense against Prussian raiders. Because she was a cook, Mestwina was also a priestess. She raised the cult of Awa to perfection. And when it came time for us all to be baptized, she brewed up paganism and Christianity into a Catholic mixture.

For Mestwina I was at once a shepherd, supplying her with loins of mutton, and a bishop, for whom she cooked. It was I who picked up pieces of amber on the beach, pierced them with red-hot wire, and threaded them, while muttering appropriate spells, to fashion the necklace that came apart as she bent over her fish broth; and as Bishop Adalbert I spooned up that same codfish-head soup, into which, because a necklace had come apart, seven pieces of amber had melted, whereupon I became as horny as a goat from Ashmodai's stable.

Later on they canonized Bishop Adalbert of Prague, who was me at the time. But here I'm speaking of Mestwina, who, in striking me dead without a qualm, was merely doing a job that is ordinarily done by men. And when I told the Flounder about this incident of April 997, he scolded as follows: "That was supererogation! Look, you've more or less turned yourselves into warriors, haven't you? That killing should have been done by a man. Indisputably. Don't let them wrest the absolute solutions out of your hands. No relapse into the Stone Age, if you please. Women should devote themselves to a more inward religion. The kitchen is dominion enough for them."

The fourth cook inside me inspires fear, so I'm glad to get rid of her. No longer a Pomorshian fisherwoman ruling mildly in the Wicker Bastion, this one, now that the city has been founded, is an artisan's wife, known as Dorothea of Montau, because she was born in Montau, a village on the Vistula.

I don't want to slander her, but the talking Flounder's advice that after so much historyless, matriarchal ever-loving care I should devote myself with masculine high pressure to men's business and leave not the Church but religion to women as a second prerogative after rule over the kitchen, made a big hit with my High Gothic Dorothea. To say that though revered as a saint by the populace she was more like a witch and Satan's bedfellow is a mild enough observation in connection with a period when the plague was carrying people away right and left, and when witches as often as not doubled as saints.

Typical as Dorothea may have been of the fourteenth century, her contribution to the cuisine of an epoch noted for its revolting gluttony was quite one-sided, for Dorothea ruled by extending Lenten fare to the whole year, not excluding Saint Martin's Day, Saint John's Day, Candlemas, and the high holidays. The barley in her pot never saw fat. She boiled her millet in water, never in milk. When she cooked lentils or dried peas, no bone was ever allowed to contribute its bit of marrow. The closest thing to meat that she tolerated was fish, which she simmered with turnips, leeks, sorrel, and lettuce. We shall have something to say of her spices later on. How she had visions and baked the Sacred Heart in bread dough. What penance she found sweet and how she softened peas with her penitent knees. What she hungered for and how she enhanced her beauty. What advice the Flounder gave me. But no advice could help me; she was a witch, and she destroyed me.

The fifth cook inside me is Margarete Rusch, also known as Fat Gret. Nobody ever laughed like her: so totally. While holding a freshly killed goose, still warm and dripping, between her round knees, plucking it so strenuously that she was soon sitting in a cloud of feathers, she drowned the pope and Luther in her laughter. She laughed at the Holy Roman Empire and at the German nation as well, at Poland's crown and the embattled guilds, at the Hanseatic lords and the abbot of Oliva, at peasant louts and lousy knights—in short, at all those who in baggy breeches, in doublets, cowls, or armor, fought for what they held to be the true faith. She laughed at her century.

As she belly-laughed and plucked eleven successive geese, I, her kitchen boy and the target of her angry spoon, kept the down in the air with my blowing; I've always had a knack for blowing feathers and keeping them hovering in mid-air.

The goose-plucking cook was the abbess of Saint Bridget's, a free and easy nun who helped herself to every man she could fit into her box bed. She had abducted me, a little Franciscan monk, from Trinity Church during vespers. Fat Gret was so spacious a woman that many a noble lord got lost inside her. To her the young sons of patrician families were an appetizer: tender asparagus tips. She fattened the abbot of Oliva to death. She was said to have bitten off Preacher Hegge's left testicle. After that we went to work for Ferber the patrician, who wanted to stay Catholic and not to forgo Margret's peppery lamb tongues with broad beans. Then we went back to the Protestants and cooked for one guild or another on holidays. When King Stephen Batory besieged the city, we decided we would be safer outside the walls, cooking for the Poles. In her bed I found warmth. In her bed I found peace. She kept me under lock and key. She sheltered me with her fat.

Fat Gret, the Flounder said to me, was a woman after his wide-mouthed taste: she let the men get on with their deadly serious trade in wheat, toll collecting, guild fees, and indulgences, let them find more and more elaborate ways of slicing or pulverizing one another, or interpreting the Scriptures, and improved her health laughing at the murderous entertainment they offered. "If she had wanted to," said the Flounder, "she could have won back Awa's power at any time."

The sixth cook inside me—they're pushing to get out, and there are nine or more of them, each with a name—also plucked geese, but she didn't laugh. An oat-fattened goose when the Swedes, with fire behind them, withdrew. When the Swedes came back (punctually on Saint Martin's Day), nothing was left of all her geese but a bowlful of stirred blood, to which she added roots and sliced pears to make a sour black sauce for the boiled giblets—neck, heart, gizzard, and wings.

Directly behind the barn, under the apple tree, from which later dangled heads with upturned beaks, Agnes plucked the geese and sang little songs: weary wind-blown words that put the wretched Swedish occupation into rhyme and hovered in mid-air with the goose down for the length of a November day. O vale of tears!

That was when Agnes was still childlike and Kashubian. Later, when she became a city dweller and cooked for Möller the town painter, the Swedes with their Gustavus Adolphus were already somewhere else. Instead, four years after the Battle of Lützen, the poet and diplomat Martin Opitz, embittered by the long-lasting war, came to Danzig.

"Agnes," said the talking Flounder—though I'm not sure whether it was as painter Möller or as poet Opitz that I questioned the wise old fish—"your Agnes," he said, "is one of those women who can only love comprehensively. The man she cooks for she loves; and since she cooks tenderly for both of you, one for his swollen liver, the other for his embittered gall, you are obliged to sit down to table with what you take to be her divided—and what I call her doubled—love, and listen as the bed creaks."

To painter Möller she bore a little girl; and as for me, when the plague baked me and sweated me, she stuffed the pillow of my deathbed full to bursting with goose down. That's how kindhearted she was. But I never managed to turn out a poem to her kindness. Only courtly flattery and lamentations of various kinds. No mouth-filling Agnes-rhyme to chicken broth, calf's sweetbreads, manna grits, and such-like delicacies. I hope to make up for it later on.

The seventh cook inside me bore the name of Amanda Woyke, and when I let the whole lot of them and their daughters babble together, comparing the prices at different epochs, she's the one who stands out most clearly in my mind. I'd never be able to say straight out, "This, just this is what Agnes looked like," because Agnes always looked melancholy but in different ways, and always seemed torn between Möller and Opitz; for Amanda's looks, on the other hand, I easily find an image: she had a potato face. Or, to be more specific, in her face the full beauty of the potato could be admired every day of the week. It wasn't just the bulbousness; no, her whole skin had that earthy sheen, that glow of palpable happiness, that can be seen on stored potatoes. And since the potato is first of all grand, sweeping form, her eyes were small and lay, unaccented by heavy brows, embedded in roundness. Her lips, not fleshy red but the color of sandy soil of Kashubia, were one of nature's happy caprices: two bulges always prepared to utter such words as *Bulwe, Wruke, Runkel.** To be kissed by Amanda was to receive from the earth, or, rather, from that dry potato soil that has made Kashubia famous, a smack that was not ephemeral but filled you up, just as potatoes boiled in their jackets fill you up.

When Mestwina smiled, you beheld the sheen of willow branches in March; Dorothea of Montau's smile froze the snot in children's noses to icicles; my Agnes's smile, tinged with a yearning for death, made death tasty to my palate; but when Amanda smiled at me, the story of the triumph of the potato over millet could be spun on and on, a story as sinuous as Amanda's potato peelings—for when her storytelling took hold of her, she peeled away from the thumb. As cook at the Royal Prussian State Farm at Zuckau, she had to prepare food each day for seventy, for farm hands and house servants, for day laborers, cottagers, and retired old folks.

"She deserves a monument," said the Flounder, "because without Amanda Woyke the introduction of the potato into Prussia after the second partition of Poland, when famine was raging far and wide and acorns brought a good price, would not have been possible. Though only a woman, she made history. Isn't it amazing? Yes, amazing!"

The eighth cook inside me absolutely wanted to be a man and, in keeping with her revolutionary times, mount the barricades with militant breast; yet all her life Sophie Rotzoll,

* Pomeranian dialect for "potato, rutabaga, mangel-wurzel."—TRANS.

close as many men (including me) came to her, remained a virgin under seven seals. The only man she ever loved was Friedrich Bartholdy, the stammering schoolboy who was condemned to death for Jacobin conspiracy. He was seventeen and Sophie fourteen; in view of his youth, Queen Luise of Prussia commuted the death sentence to life imprisonment. It was not until forty years later, when her Fritz was released from the fortress of Graudenz in failing health, that Sophie, by then an old woman, or, rather, an aging spinster, saw him again. Calf's head in herb vinegar, hog belly with chanterelles, hare stewed in red wine; regardless of what she cooked for him, of all her attempts to fire his spirit, of all the lofty goals she held up to him and mankind, Bartholdy had had enough; all he wanted was to puff away at his pipe.

I knew her well. As a boy I went gathering mushrooms with Sophie in every acre of woods around Zuckau. She knew them all by name: the honey tuft, the poisonous sulfur tuft, the anise agaric, which liked to grow in a magic circle on beds of pine needles. The cep stood solitary. The word "stink-horn" took on meaning for me. Hopelessly as Sophie had ruined her eyes reading revolutionary books, she could identify any mushroom at a glance.

Later, when she cooked for Pastor Blech, the chief pastor at Saint Mary's, and still later, when she cooked, first enthusiastically, then conspiratorially, for General Rapp, Napoleon's governor, I was successively Blech, the pastor she ran away from, and Rapp, the governor she tried to depose with a dish of special mushrooms.

Sophie could fire with enthusiasm. In the cellar, on every flight of stairs, and in the kitchen she sang *"Trois jeunes tambours."* Her voice was always in the vanguard: saberthrust, whipcrack freedomthirst deathkiss. As though Dorothea of Montau were trying to discharge her heavenly high pressure on earth. "Ever since Sophie," said the talking Flounder, "the kitchen has been in a turmoil. Always revolution." (And my Ilsebill also had this *demanding* look.)

The ninth cook inside me was born in the fall of '49, when Sophie Rotzoll, the eighth, died. One might almost suppose she had wanted to pass the banner of revolution on to Lena Stubbe; and it seems equally possible that Lena, who as a young widow ran a public soup kitchen (her husband, an anchor maker, whom she had married when very young, was

26

killed before Paris in the Franco-Prussian War), dished out her soup in silence but harbored secret socialist hopes. But Lena's voice didn't carry. As an agitator she was a failure. She was never really carried away by enthusiasm. For all her intensive reading of Bebel, her spirit never rose above the gray commonplace.

When Lena Stubbe remarried she was already a mature woman; I, like her first husband an anchor maker, was no spring chicken myself, though ten years younger than she, and was, admittedly, a drinker.

She took charge of the strike fund and tried to guard it against my depredations. She endured my blows, and she comforted me when I was bowed with remorse because I had beaten her again. Lena survived me, for in 1914, when I was sent to East Prussia with the Landsturm, she was widowed a second time.

After that she did nothing but dish out soup: barley, cabbage, pea, and potato soups. In soup kitchens, in settlement houses, in field kitchens during the Spanish-flu winter of 1917, then at the Workers' Aid. When the Nazis came in with their Winter Aid and one-dish Sundays, she was as old as the hills and still active with the soup ladle.

As a boy—back again and still driven by curiosity—I saw Lena. Her white hair, parted in the middle. Her special way of dishing out soup. A grave woman who seemed to practice compassion as a trade. The Flounder thinks Lena Stubbe was basically apolitical, except for her "Proletarian Cook Book," which circulated in manuscript after the abrogation of Bismarck's Socialist Laws but never found a publisher.

"You see," said the Flounder, "that might have brought about a change of consciousness and created something new. True, there were any number of 'bourgeois'* cook books at the time, but not a single proletarian one. That's why the working class, impoverished or not, went in for bourgeois cookery. Before you 'invent' a tenth, let alone an eleventh cook, why don't you quote from the posthumous papers of Lena Stubbe? You're a Social Democrat, aren't you?"

The tenth and eleventh cooks inside me are still fuzzy of outline, because I came to know them both too well. Only

* *Bürgerliche Küche* (literally "bourgeois cookery"): "simple home cooking."—TRANS.

their names are present on an otherwise blank sheet of paper: I lost Billy (whose real name was Sibylle) in the sixties, on an Ascension Day, which is celebrated with great hullabaloo in Berlin and elsewhere as Father's Day; Maria, who works at the canteen of the Lenin Shipyard in Gdánsk (formerly the Schichau Shipyard in Danzig), is a relative of mine.

I admit it: Billy and Maria are pressing to get out. But since the Flounder advises me to observe chronological order and since I have so many cooks inside me, I shall take the liberty—especially as my present Ilsebill is kind of urging me—of making Awa's three breasts more palpable before taking up the Father's Day celebration—exclusively a men's affair—that was held in June 1963 in Grunewald, in Tegel Forest, in Spandau, in Britz, and on the shores of the Wannsee. A man clogged with so much past who finally sees a chance of relieving his constipation can't help being in a hurry to speak of Mestwina's amber necklace, even if the uprising of the shipyard workers in the Polish seaports, as recorded by the world press in December 1970, ought to be closer to him.

Old yarns. The story of millet. What did the peasant serf have left to eat? According to what menu did Fat Gret fatten conventual abbots for the slaughter? What happened when the price of pepper fell? Rumford soup for the poor. How the deadly amanita gave promise of becoming political. When the invention of pea sausage gave the Prussian army new strength. Why the proletariat was drawn to bourgeois cookery. What it means to go hungry. "But perhaps," said the Flounder didactically out of his crooked mouth, "history can teach us what role women played in historical events, in the triumph of the potato, for instance."

Awa

And if I were faced with three breasts
and were not divided between the one and the other tit
and if I were not double because of the usual split
and did not have to choose between
and were never again confronted by an either/or

and bore the twin no grudge,
and harbored no other wish . . .

But I have only another choice
and am attached to another set of tits.
I envy the twin.
My other wish is as usual split.
Even whole, I am only half and half.
My choice always falls in between.

Only in pottery (vaguely dated) does Awa
(supposedly) exist: the goddess
with the triune font,
one of which (always the third) knows
what the first promises and the second withholds.

Who expunged you, making us poor?
Who said: Two are enough?
Diet and rationing ever since.

How the Flounder was caught

No, no, Ilsebill. Of course I'm not going to tell you that
phony fairy tale all over again. Of course I'm going to
write the other truth that Philipp Otto Runge took down,
even if I have to pick it word for word out of the ashes. For
the old woman's additional babblings into the painter's ear in
the summer of 1805 were burned under the full moon between woodland pond and deer meadow. It was done in defense of the patriarchal order. Which explains why the
Grimm brothers only threw one Runge transcript—"The
Fisherman and His Wife"—on the fairy-tale market. The fisherman's wife Ilsebill has been proverbial ever since: a quarrelsome bitch who keeps wanting to have, to possess, to
command more and more. And the Flounder the fisherman
catches and sets free has to keep on delivering: the larger
cottage, the stone house, the palace royal, the might of empire, the Holy See. In the end Ilsebill wants God's power to
make the sun rise and set, whereupon the greedy woman and

her good-natured husband are punished and sent back to their wretched hovel, their "pisspot," to live. Really, an insatiable virago. Can't ever get enough. Always wants something more. That's the Ilsebill of the story.

My Ilsebill is the living refutation, which I hereby make known. And even the Flounder thought it was high time to publish the original version of his legend, to rehabilitate all Ilsebills, and to confute the misogynistic propaganda tale that he himself had so treacherously disseminated. That's right. Pulling no punches. Nothing but the truth. Believe me, dearest, there's no point in starting a fight. You're right, right as usual. Before we even start fighting, you win.

It was toward the end of the Stone Age. A day unnumbered. We hadn't begun yet to make lines and notches. When we saw the moon lose weight or put on fat, our only thought was fear. No prefigured event happened on time. No dates. Never did anyone or anything come too late.

On a timeless, partly cloudy day, I caught the Flounder. In the place where the river Vistula mingles in a constantly shifting bed with the open sea, I had set out my basket traps in hope of eels. We had no nets. And baited hooks hadn't come in yet. As far back as I can think—the last ice age sets a limit to my memory—we hunted fish in the arms of the river, first with sharpened branches, later with bow and arrow: bass, pike, perch, eels, lampreys, and, on their way down the river, salmon. There where the Baltic Sea laved wandering dunes, we speared the flatfish that like to lie bedded in the sand at the bottom of the warm, shallow water: turbot, sole, flounder.

It was only after Awa taught us to plait baskets from willow withes that chance helped us to discover that baskets could also serve as fish traps. An idea seldom came to us men. It was Awa—always Awa—who sank a basket full of gnawed elk bones in the rushes by the bank of a tributary that was later called the Radune and much later still the Radaune, so that the water might soak away the last fibers and bits of sinew; for Awa used elk and reindeer bones as kitchen utensils and for ritual purposes.

When after sufficient time we hauled the basket out of the river several eels barely escaped, but along with some small fry, five arm-long customers remained in the wickerwork, lashing and thrashing amid the smooth bones. The operation was repeated. Improvements were made. Awa invented the fish trap, just as exactly two centuries later she developed the first fishhooks from the wishbones of swamp birds. According to her instructions, and under her supervision, which seemed to have been imposed on us by fate, we plaited those baskets tapered on the open end, to which later, on our own incentive—for we were not to require Awa's tutelage forever—we fitted a second and then a third basket, so as to make it harder for the eels to escape. Long, supple willow withes forced into a complicated mesh: an early craft. Something that could be done without Awa.

Good catches ever after. More than we needed. First attempt at smoking in hollow willow trees. The words "eel" and "trap" became a hallowed pair, which I, with my obsessive drive to leave my marks wherever I went, converted into an image. Before leaving the beach after setting the traps, for instance, I would draw in the wet sand, with the sharp edge of a shell, a picture of wriggling eels behind intricate wickerwork. If instead of being flat and swampy, our region had been mountainous and honeycombed with caves, I would undoubtedly have bequeathed a cave painting of a trapped eel to posterity. In his mid-twentieth-century timephase the Flounder would pontificate, "Neolithic graffiti originating in northeastern European fish culture, related to the southern Scandinavian Maglemose drawings on bones and amber." The Flounder has always been hooked on culture.

One thing Awa couldn't do was set signs, draw a likeness. She admired the pictures I scratched in the sand and found them useful for ritual purposes; she liked my palpable representations of herself and her three breasts; but when, just for the fun of it, I drew on the sandy beach a trap consisting of five tapered baskets, she instantly forbade both the drawing and the fivefold trap itself. The basic value, three, as established by Awa and her breasts, could not be exceeded. And again I was sharply called to order when I drew a picture of the Flounder, who had been caught in an eel trap. Awa exploded in mother-goddessly wrath: she had never seen such a thing, and because she had never seen such a thing, it couldn't exist. It was mere invention and therefore untrue.

Threatening punishment, Awa and the whole council of women forbade me ever again to draw pictures of a flounder caught in an eel trap. Nevertheless, I kept doing so in secret. For, much as I had learned to dread the withholding of the breast that suckled me thrice daily, the Flounder was stronger, especially since he spoke to me whenever I wished: I had only to cry out "Flounder, Flounder." "All she wants," he said, "is constant self-affirmation. Everything outside of her is ruled out. But art, my son, refuses to be ruled out."

Toward the end of the third millennium before the incarnation of our Lord (or, as a computer has computed, on May 3, 2211 B.C., a Friday, so it seems), on a neolithic day—east wind, loosely knit cloud formation—an event occurred which later, for reasons of patriarchal self-justification, was falsified, twisted into a fairy tale that still sends my Ilsebill up the wall.

I was young but already bearded. Late in the afternoon I pulled in my thrice-tapered eel trap, which I had set out early in the morning before the day's first suckling. (My favorite eel-catching spot was on or near the site of Heubude, the popular beach resort that long centuries later could conveniently be reached by streetcar number 9.) Because of my talent for drawing, Awa, in her ever-loving care, had favored me with an extra, out-of-turn suckling. Consequently, when I saw the Flounder in the eel trap, my first thought was: I'll bring him to Awa. She'll wrap him in moist lettuce leaves as usual and bake him in hot ashes.

Then the Flounder spoke.

I'm not sure that I was any more amazed at his crooked-mouthed speech than at the mere fact of having caught a broad-beamed flounder in an eel trap. In any event, I did not respond to the words "Good afternoon, my son!" with a question about his astonishing gift of speech. What I did ask was why he, a flatfish, had chosen to force his way, through all three narrowings, into a trap.

The Flounder replied. From the very start his know-it-all superiority made him garrulous despite his categorical finalities, now nasally professorial, now infuriatingly paternal. His purpose, he said, had been to join conversation with me. He had been motivated not by foolish (or did he already say "feminine"?) curiosity, but by the well-matured decision of a masculine will. There existed, so he said, certain information pointing beyond the neolithic horizon, and he, the sapient Flounder, wished to communicate this information to me, the dull-witted fisher, kept in a state of infantilism by total female care. To prepare himself, he had learned the dialect of the Baltic coast, a language of few words, a wretched stammering that named only the strictly necessary. In a relatively short time he had mastered the speech defect that broadened all our sounds. Language, he assured me, would be no obstacle in our dialogue. But in the long run he would feel cramped in this wicker basket.

I had scarcely freed him from the tripartite trap and set him down on the sand when he said first, "Thank you, my son!" and then: "Of course I am aware of the dangers to which my decision exposes me. I know I taste good. I've heard about all the different ways your women, who rule through ever-loving care, have of grilling roaches on a willow spit, of baking eel, pike, perch, and hand-sized sole on well-heated stones, or of wrapping larger fish like myself in leaves and bedding us in hot ashes until we are cooked through, but still succulent. *Bon appétit*. It's flattering to be considered tasty. All the same, I'm sure my offer to serve forever as an adviser to you, that is, to the male cause, outweighs my culinary value. In short, my son: set me free and I will come whenever you call me. Your magnanimity puts me under obligation to supply you with information gathered in every corner of the world. We flounders, you see—and related species—are at home in every ocean and on every coast. I know what kind of advice you need. Deprived as you are of every right, you Baltic men will need my encouragement. You, an artist, able in your affliction to set down signs and symbols, a *man* in quest of enduring, meaning-charged form, must realize that my timeless promise is worth more than a few mouthfuls of baked fish. And in case you doubt my trustworthiness, allow me, my son, to divulge my motto and first principle: 'A man's word is his bond!' "

Fact: I fell for him. His talking to me like that gave me a sense of importance. Of significance. Of inner growth. Self-awareness was born. I began to take myself seriously. And yet—believe me, Ilsebill!—my doubts were far from dispelled. I'd have to put this talking Flounder, who had promised me so much, to the test. No sooner had I tossed him into the smooth water than I called after him: "Flounder! Come back! There's something I've got to ask you."

In the exact place where I had dropped him, he jumped out of the Baltic Sea and landed on my two palms. "What is it, my son? Always at your service. Even, I might add, in surf and storm."

"But suppose," I said to the Flounder, "suppose we're not unhappy under Awa's ever-loving care? Suppose we're doing all right and have no complaints? I mean it! Because we get everything we need. Yes, indeed, we want for nothing. The breast is seldom withheld, only when we're fractious. Three times a day we get suckled. Even doddering old men can count on it. It's always been that way. Since paleolithic times. Anyway, since the end of the last ice age. Breast feeding is right for us. We feel contented and sheltered. We're always kept warm. We never have to decide for or against anything. We live as we please, without responsibility. Yes, of course, we're a bit restless now and then. We get to wondering where the river comes from. Or whether something's going on behind the river where the sun rises. I'd also like to know if it's possible to count higher than we're allowed to. And then the question of meaning, that is, whether the things we do, which are always the same, might not point to something else in addition to what they are. Awa says they are what they are, and that's that. Whenever we start fidgeting and doubting, she gives us the breast. Which is an excellent remedy . . . for what? Well, for restlessness and asking questions. Whereas you, friend Flounder, make me nervous. You're so ambiguous. What is this information you speak of? Just tell me this: Where does the river come from? Is there some other place where people are allowed to make eel traps with more than three baskets? And do existing things also mean something else? Fire, for instance. All we know is that soon after the last ice age Awa brought three pieces of glowing charcoal down from the sky for us. She says fire is good for cooking meat, fish, roots, and mushrooms, or for keeping us warm when we sit around it chewing the fat. I ask you, friend Flounder: what else can fire do?"

And the Flounder replied. He told me about hordes on both sides of the river who also had their Awa, even if they called her Ewa or Eia. He told me about other rivers and about the ocean, which is much larger. Like a swimming newspaper he brought me news, reported all sorts of heroic and mythological gossip. A god named Poseidon had commented on some quotations from Zeus, and the Flounder now commented on the commentaries. He supplied glosses on female deities—one was called Hera. But even when he stuck to cold facts I didn't understand very much. He told me for the first time about the metal that can be smelted out of rock with the help of fire and poured into sand molds to cool and harden. "Bear in mind, my son! Metal can be forged into spearheads and axes."

After his crooked mouth had proclaimed the end of the hand-ax era, he told me about the hilly region, a short way inland, that came to be known as the Baltic Ridge, and assured me that small amounts of metal-containing rock were to be found there. And three days later, when as agreed I called him again—"Flounder, Flounder in the sea"—he brought me, probably from Sweden, an ore specimen, tucked away in one of his branchial sacs.

"Take heart!" cried the Flounder. "Smelt down this and more like it and you will have not only acquired copper but also given fire a new, progressive, incisive, decisive, and masculine significance. Fire is something more than warmth and cookery. In fire there are visions. Fire cleanses. From fire the sparks fly upward. Fire is idea and future. On the banks of other rivers, the future is already under way. Resolute men are making themselves masters of it, without so much as asking their Awas and Ewas. It's only here that men are still letting themselves be suckled and lulled to sleep. Even your old men are babes in arms. Like Prometheus you must take possession of fire. Don't content yourself with being a fisherman, my son; become a blacksmith."

(Ah, Ilsebill, if only that metal had stayed in the mountains!) While allegedly hunting in the hills that later became known as the Ziganken Mountains—and we did actually spear a wild boar—we found confirmation of the ore specimen the Flounder had brought me. Soon we had a copper ax, some blades, and a few metal spearheads, which we boastfully exhibited. The women shuddered and giggled as they touched the new material. I started taking orders for ornaments. But then Awa put her foot down.

She flew into a rage and threatened to withhold her breast. We Edeks were subjected to niggling interrogations. How had we, who had never before conceived a useful idea, come by this sudden knowledge? It was up to her, the supreme Awa, and nobody else, to decide what uses fire could be put to. Not that she questioned the utility of the new metal objects—among them my own creation, the first kitchen knife—but this sudden independence was too much of a good thing.

All her suspicions came to rest on me, because the other Edeks had mentioned me in their confessions. I invented accidental occurrences and didn't betray the Flounder. The women, the whole lot of them, punished me by denying me their breasts and cozy comforts for the duration of the hard winter. Metal was strictly prohibited. It was forbidden to divert fire from its proper purposes. After a stamping round-dance centered on Awa's three breasts, which I had drawn in the sand and incrusted with shells, the copper ax and the few blades and spearheads were thrown into the Radune River amid screams of abjuration. (Believe me, Ilsebill, having to go back to the hand ax was no joke.)

But when in my despair I summoned the Flounder out of the sea, he shouted above the seething, churning waves: "Nothing to get so excited about. Has it escaped your notice, my son, that despite her autocratic condemnation of all metal, your Awa, your three-breasted paragon of historyless femininity, your all-devouring megacunt, in short your mother goddess, has hidden the copper kitchen knife, which you forged, tempered, and sharpened for her pleasure, in with the elk bones she uses as kitchen utensils? She uses it in secret. Just as you, despite the prohibition, secretly draw my picture in the sand. She's a shrewd article, your loving-caring Awa! It's time for you men to cut loose! How? With the kitchen knife. Kill her, my son. Kill her!"

(No, Ilsebill. I didn't do it. She was struck down later on, but not by me. I've always been faithful to Awa; I still am.)

She stopped the passage of time. She was the sum of our knowledge. Indefatigably she thought up new ritualistic pretexts for solemn processions in consecration of things as they were, and the dimensions of her body determined the form of our neolithic religion. Apart from Awa, we sacrificed only to the Sky Wolf, from whom a woman of our primordial horde—the ur-Awa—had stolen three little pieces of glowing charcoal. Everything came from her, not just the eel trap and the fishhook.

Perhaps to deter us Edeks from further abuse of fire, or perhaps only to improve her cooking, Awa established the potter's craft in our territory. It began with her wrapping swamp birds and their feathers or hedgehogs and their quills in a thick layer of clay, and setting them down thus protected in coals and hot ashes. It seems conceivable that when the clay envelopes, with feathers or quills still embedded in them, were broken open, the possibility of using them as receptacles was recognized. In any event, Awa taught me to knead clay and to build an oven from glacial rubble. Heaping up glowing coals around its protective walls, I baked not only bowls and pots in it but also primitive little art-works. This was the origin of the three-breasted idols that have today become museum pieces.

When I told the Flounder about all this, he must have noticed the pleasure I took in modeling Awa's flesh, her bulges and dimples, in clay. "Well then," he asked me, "how many dimples has she got?"

So then the Flounder taught me to count. Not days, weeks, or months, not lampreys, snipe, elk, or reindeer, but Awa's dimples, which took me up to a hundred and eleven. I fashioned a three-breasted clay idol with a hundred and eleven dimples, and our Awa, who thereupon learned to count up to a hundred and eleven, really liked that idol—all the more so since the other women (counting became a favorite pastime of our horde) never got anywhere near a hundred. Awa (like yourself, Ilsebill) had the most dimples in her winter pillow, her buttocks, thirty-three of them.

The Flounder was triumphant: "Splendid, my son. Even if we haven't succeeded just yet in ringing in the Bronze or even the Copper Age, the hour of algebra has struck. From now on there will be counting. Counting leads to calculation. And calculation leads to planning. Look at the Minoans, who have recently taken to scratching their household accounts on clay tablets. Practice your figures in secret and the women won't be able to outreckon you later on. Soon you'll be able to measure time and to date events. Soon you'll be exchanging counted things for counted things. Tomorrow or the day after you'll get paid, and you in turn will pay, pay, pay. First with shells but then, in spite of Awa, though perhaps long after Awa, with metal coins. Here's one. Attic silver, still in circulation. I found it on board a ship that had run aground off the coast of Crete after a seaquake. But why am I telling you about Crete and sailing ships? What do you know of King Minos? You lummoxes cling to your women's tits as if you'd been bewitched and let your Awa with her hundred and eleven dimples make fools of you."

It must have been centuries after my first little arithmetical tricks that the Flounder gave me the coin. Possibly a drachma, but I'm not sure. More likely an offertory coin from Asia Minor, without currency value. One thousand B.C. seems a likely date. But what were a thousand years more or less in the light of our minimal development in the swamps of the Vistula estuary. Anyway, at some time or other the Flounder brought me a metallic coin in his branchial sac, just as earlier and later he brought me Minoan, archaic Greek, Attic, and Egyptian artifacts—gems, seals, figurines, and filigree knickknacks. Naturally, stupid as I was, I gave Awa the Greek drachma. Though the handy little silver piece amused her, she wouldn't listen to any talk about counting games that might lead no one knew where, about buying or selling. She declared a hundred and eleven to be the highest and absolute number, the definitive Awa number. Of this she was the living proof, and anyone who wasn't convinced could count her dimples. As long as exploring fingers could find no more than a hundred and eleven on any woman of the horde, a hundred and eleven remained the absolute number. Any calculation that led beyond it was unnatural and therefore contrary to practical reason. All speculation, she declared, would be punished; irrationality must be nipped in the bud. And then she ordered me to prop a hundred and eleven elk skulls on a hundred and eleven poles and place them in a circle measuring a hundred and eleven paces, so marking off a new sacrificial area—all this before the onset of winter!

You'll admit, Ilsebill, that so much ur-motherly loving care, even if it kept me warm and in innocence, was bound to become oppressive in the long run. Because there the matter rested. For uncounted centuries we were only allowed to count up to a hundred and eleven. True, some time in the last millennium before the incarnation of our Lord, we began to trade amber to the Phoenicians, who came sailing along in their ships as though the Flounder had piloted them to our remote shores. But at first we gave away fist-sized nuggets of our amber, and we had a hard time learning to barter. We were hornswoggled every time.

When I called the Flounder out of the sea, he griped and

totted up our losses. You're all a lot of Stone Age simpletons! Are you going to play the fool forever? With your amber you could supply a hundred and eleven hordes, as large and fatherless as your own, with all the bronze implements they need. Plus silver gewgaws and purple cloth for the women. If she won't let you mint coins, try at least to get it through your heads that in Sidon and Tyre your amber is as valuable as gold. I'm getting sick of you. You'll never be really men. Milksops, that's what you are!"

Just as the tale of the fisherman and his wife speaks only of the flounder or flatfish, without further identification—"And the flounder said to him . . . Then the flounder came swimming and said . . ."—so I, too, speak of *the* Flounder, as though there were only this one omniscient Flounder who advised, taught, and indoctrinated me, who raised me to manhood and told me in no uncertain terms how to keep the women folk supinely bed-warm and teach them how to suffer in cheerful silence. Actually the word "flounder" as consecrated by the fairy tale, is only a popular designation for the flatfish family, including the brill, the sole, the halibut, the plaice, the turbot, and, of course, the flounder. To tell the truth, my own flatfish was a turbot, closely resembling the brill except for the bony, pebblelike bumps under his skin.

The turbot is found in the Mediterranean, throughout the North Sea, and in the Baltic. As in all flatfish, the axis of the eyes is not quite parallel to the crooked mouth, and that is what gives him his shrewd, malignant, I might say underhanded look: he squints in quick motion. (The Attic god Poseidon is said to have enlisted him in the struggle against Hera, the Pelasgian Athene, and related exponents of matriarchy—as a propagandist.) Turbot or not, tradition demands that I go on calling him a flounder.

The whole flatfish family is tasty. The neolithic Awa roasted his fellows in moist leaves. Toward the end of the Bronze Age, Wigga rubbed them on both sides with white ashes and laid the white underside in ashes strewn over a bed of coals. After turning, she moistened the flatfish either in the neolithic manner, from her always overflowing breasts, or modern-style, with a dash of fermented mare's milk. Mestwina, who already cooked in flameproof pots placed on an iron grating, simmered flounder with sorrel or in mead. Just before serving, she sprinkled the white-eyed fish with wild dill.

He, the one and only, the talking Flounder, who has been stirring me up for centuries, knew all the recipes that had been used for cooking his fellows, first by the heathen and later as a Christian Lenten fish (and not only on Friday). With an air of detachment and a glint of irony in his slanting eyes, he could sing his praises as a delicacy: "Yes, my son, we happen to be one of the finer fishes. In the distant future, when you imbecilic men, you eternal babes in arms, will at last have minted coins, dated your history, and introduced the patriarchate, in short, shaken off your mothers' breasts, when after six thousand years of ever-loving womanly care you will at last have emancipated yourselves, then my fellows and relatives, the sole, the brill, the plaice, will be simmered in white wine, seasoned with capers, framed in jelly, deliciously offset by sauces, and served on Dresden china. My fellows will be braised, glazed, poached, broiled, filleted, ennobled with truffles, flamed in cognac, and named after marshals, dukes, the prince of Wales, and the Hotel Bristol. Campaigns, conquests, land grabs! The East will trade with the West. The South will enrich the North. To you and to myself I predict olives, refinements of culture and taste, the lemon!"

But that took time, Ilsebill. (You see how hard it is for you women to make men stop persecuting *you* with *their* ever-loving care.) Long after Awa and her hundred and eleven dimples and three breasts, women continued to rule, but they had a harder time of it. We men had tasted metal. And the Flounder kept us informed. I had only to call, and the swimming newspaper came. I heard about distant high cultures, about the Sumerians and the Minoan double-edged ax, about Mycenae and the invention of the sword, about wars in which men fought against men, because everywhere the history-hating matriarchate had been shattered and men were at last allowed to inscribe dates.

The Flounder treated me to tedious lectures. About Mesopotamian palace architecture and the first palace in Knossos. About the growing of grain—amelcorn barley spelt millet—in the Danube basin. About the domestication of animals—goats and sheep—in the Near East and the possibility of domesticating reindeer in the Baltic area. About the spade, the hoe, and the revolutionary plow.

The Flounder concluded every lecture with words of supplication: "It's high time, my son. The Neolithic, as we call the late Stone Age, has entered upon its final phase. Fostered by male vigor, a high culture has spread from Mesopotamia by way of the Nile Delta to the island of Crete, where I've seen women tilling the fields and, once the grain is grown, grinding it in stone mortars. In those regions, famines are not a fatality. They keep herds of pigs and cattle, and meat is plentiful. Stocks are always on hand. Permanent dwellings are built. Hordes and clans join to form nations. Hero-kings rule. Empire borders on empire. The men bear arms. They know what they're fighting for: inherited property. While you live in lewdness and fornication and don't even know the meaning of fatherhood. Mother screws son. Sister doesn't even know what brother is doing to her. Unsuspecting father lies with daughter. All in innocence! I know! Yes, yes, you want those tits. Can't get enough of them. Breast-fed babies to the end of your days. But out in the world the future has started blazing trails. Nature is sick of being submitted to with womanish passivity; it wants to be mastered by men. Trace canals. Drain swamps. Fence in the land, plow it, take possession of it. Beget a son. Hand down property. Your suckling time has lasted two thousand years too long, two thousand years of waste and stagnation. My advice to you: away from the breast. Wean yourselves. That's it, my son, at long last you must wean yourself!"

That was easy for the Flounder to say. Too easy. We, in any case, needed a good millennium to become men in the Flounderian sense. But then we became men, all right, as the history books bear witness: men with leather caps, helmets, and gimlet eyes. Men of wide-ranging, horizon-searching gaze. Men stricken with procreative fury, who sublimated their stinkhorns into rivaling towers, torpedoes, and spaceships. Methodical men, banded together in male orders. Thunder-hurling hairsplitters. Discoverers in spite of themselves. Heroes who would never never under any circumstances have consented to die in bed. Hard-lipped men who sternly decreed freedom. Persevering, steadfast, unflinching, grandiosely exalted, tragic, bloody-but-unbowed, come-what-may men, determined to transcend themselves and attain ultimate goals, men with principles who invented their own enemies, loved honor for honor's sake, and yet saw themselves in the mirror of irony.

Even the Flounder, who had advised us to develop along these lines, became more and more horrified and ultimately

41

took refuge—that was in Napoleon's time—in the Low German fairy tale. By then he was giving only minor advice. Then for a long while he said nothing. It's only recently that he's become approachable again. Now he advises me to help Ilsebill with the dishes and—in view of her pregnancy—to sign up for a course in infant care. "Lots of women," he says, "are quite capable of doing a man's work. Like your able Ilsebill. That deserves recognition, my son, and it has been our benevolent intention to recognize it from the very start, ever since I voluntarily forced my way into your eel trap."

And just imagine, Ilsebill, just recently the Flounder told me he means to answer those women and their indictment any day now. And he condemned the Grimms' distortion of his legend. "That fairy story," he said, "has got to go!"

Division of labor

We—two roles.
You and I keep—you the soup warm,
I the spirits cold.

Sometime, long before Charlemagne,
I became self-aware
whereas you have only perpetuated yourself.
You are—I became.
You are still wanting—I'm reaching out again.
You secure your small province—
I venture my vast project.
You keep peace in the house—I hurry forth.

Division of labor.
Come, hold the ladder while I climb.
Your whimpering won't help; in that case I'd rather cool the champagne.
Just hold steady while I come at you from behind.

My brave little Ilsebill,
on whom I can utterly rely,
of whom, to tell the truth, I would like to be proud,
who with a few deft strokes fixes everything shipshape,
whom I worship worship
while she, through inner recycling,
becomes entirely different, differently strange and self-aware.

May I still give you a light?

How the Flounder was caught a second time

I've already told you: one neolithic day he squeezed into
my eel trap. In those days women kept the lid on everything
that might have been controversial. Our pact is known: I let
him go. He helped me through the ages with his Floundery
advice. Through the Bronze Age, through the Iron Age.
Through the Early Christian, High Gothic, Evangelical, and
Baroque periods; throught enlightened absolutism, socialism,
and capitalism. The Flounder anticipated every historic
change, every shift of fashion, every revolution and relapse,
every latest truth or progress. In short, he deliberately helped
to promote the male cause. We, we at last, had our hand on
the throttle.

Until yesterday. Now he won't speak to me. Imploringly
and repeatedly I cry out "Flounder, Flounder," but no familiar "'What is it, my son?" comes in answer. Women sit at a
long table judging him. He has already started to confess in a
dilatory sort of way. (And I, too, confess, to the reasons why
the Flounder has been disgusted with me and the male cause
for quite some time.)

When, a few months before the oil crisis, I called him out
of the sea (for advice on my income-tax problems), he
denounced our agreement: "Nothing can be expected of you
daddies any more. Nothing but dodges and gimmicks. Now,"
he said as though in leave-taking, "I'll just have to pay a little
attention to the Ilsebills."

Naturally it was in the murky Baltic that he got himself

43

hooked. Tradition means a lot to him. If not in the Bay of Danzig, then at least in Lübeck Bay, in the slop that laves the eastern coast of Holstein, between the lighthouses of Cismar and Scharbeutz, barely a sea mile from the tarry fringe of the bathing beaches, he consciously consented and—as he later confessed in court—"voluntarily gave the three bored ladies a bit of fisherman's luck."

Sieglinde Huntscha, who for a time responded to no other name than Siggie, Susanne Maxen, known as Maxie, and Franziska Ludkowiak, Frankie for short, had rented a sailboat for a few hours in the coastal village of Cismar and, more often becalmed than bebreezed, were boring one another stiff with their jargon. Three hard-boiled females in their thirties (about your age, Ilsebill), Maxie in her early, Frankie in her late ones, who when speaking invariably spit contemptuously after every few sentences, who describe just about everything as shit, shitty, or at the very least crappy.

Probably because, for reasons hard to define, Siggie, Maxie, and Frankie thought of themselves as lesbians and consequently belonged to a women's liberation group, whose first commandment was radical rejection of male penetration, Siggie had taken her walking stick—a common masculine article covered with souvenir plaques—into the boat with her. This stick served as a fishing pole. A piece of plain string had been fastened to it. The hook was a pair of sexless nail scissors. Frankie busied herself folding bits of newspaper into little boats. They, too, floated motionless. Not the slightest breeze consented to rise.

Siggie wasn't even telling fishermen's jokes. They knew nothing about sailing and just drifted this way and that, meanwhile needling one another in the extravagant terms of the long-dead student movement. Everything—including Siggie's fishing—struck them as pretty shitty. "What we really need," said Frankie while folding a boat, "is an ideologically acceptable prop of our superegos." And then the Flounder bit.

So help me, Ilsebill! Deliberately taking his cue. (Later on, in court, he testified that it hadn't been so easy to get speared by that sharp but unsteady nail-scissor blade. He had had to ram it through his upper lip twice.)

It was Maxie who managed to utter the traditional cry of "Got him!" To which she added: "Pull, Siggie! Pull him in! Boy oh boy!"

And the millennial "Ah!" And the anticipation: will it be the extraordinary, the rare, no, unique and legendary fish of the ages, or only a soggy old shoe? Fisherman's luck. You just have to keep patiently quiet. Timelessly suck your tongue. Think of nothing or the opposite. Cancel yourself out until you might just as well be somebody else. Or say the magic word. Or be hook and bait yourself. The writhing little worm.

But, though bare, the scissors-hook had aroused the Flounder's appetite. The flatfish lay flat on the bottom of the boat. His upper lip didn't start bleeding until Siggie cautiously, but with what can only be termed manly courage, pulled the hook out of the bulge. The size of him! Never (except once upon a time) had so imposing a specimen been caught in the Baltic. I'm almost inclined to think that my neolithic catch was less impressive. He has grown since then. More pebbles lump and wrinkle his skin. Can it be that he, too, ages with time? That he's mortal?

In spite of his size, it was still an ordinary fish that called forth the females' amazement. Frankie called him a nifty flounder and suggested simmering him in white wine. She had seen fresh dill, so she said, in one of the many food stores that make the beach resort of Scharbeutz a shoppers' Mecca. Siggie wanted to oil him on both sides, sprinkle him with basil, and bake him for half an hour in a moderate oven.

The three lived in a farm hand's hovel rented out as a holiday cottage. Since Maxie refused to eat any fish that could be recognized as such—Ugh!—Frankie suggested filleting the Flounder, cutting him into strips, rolling him in egg, and deep-fry him, because then he would no longer be recognizable as fish.

Siggie said, "Damn it! Our Billy should have been here. She'd have sautéed this flounder in tarragon butter or maybe flamed him in cognac." And Frankie chimed in with, "How about it, Maxie? If our Billy served up the flounder with all the trimmings. What do you say? Would it still be 'ugh'?"

But Maxie didn't want any fish, no matter how it was cooked, not even à la Billy. No sooner had Siggie pulled the nail scissors out of the bulge in the Flounder's upper lip than Maxie wanted to throw him back into the murky Baltic. "That shifty, vicious look. Bound to bring bad luck. His blood is so red and human-looking. That's not what we

45

wanted to catch. That's no fish; it only looks like one." Then spake the Flounder.

Not in a loud voice, more in a conversational tone, he said, "What an odd happenstance!" He could just as well have said, "What time is it?" Or, "Who's leading in the Federal League?"

Siggie, Frankie, and Maxie were, in a manner of speaking, dumbstruck. It wasn't until later, when the Flounder started spouting, that Maxie managed to squeeze out, *sotto voce*, such exclamations as "This is a howler! Incredible! Boy oh boy! If only our Billy coulda been here!"

But Frankie and Siggie were silent. Their two minds went to work on this Sunday-afternoon episode, determined to confute the Flounder's allegation of chance, to anchor the irrational occurrence in reason and discover the rational underpinning of its innocent fairy-tale logic—for the Flounder had introduced himself as follows: "Surely, dear ladies, you are familiar with the fairy tale of 'The Fisherman and His Wife'?" These were the questions to be resolved: Who was speaking here and for what purpose? What would they have to explain first? The fact that the Flounder could talk or the substance of what he was saying? Was this a late reactionary attempt on the part of medieval Scholasticism to prove that evil could take the form of a fish? Was this Flounder a personification of capitalism? Or—an even greater contradiction—might he be an embodiment of Hegel's *Weltgeist*?

"Who are you?" cried Franziska Ludkowiak, commonly known as Frankie, breaking into one of the Flounder's involved periods and seizing Siggie's now idle fishing pole, the metal-ringed walking stick, with the evident intention of disinviting the uninvited guest. He reminded her of the films in which slightly distorted madmen peered out of cracked mirrors; she felt sure he had come from the shadow realm of the unconscious and would induce schizophrenia. (Much as she liked Maxie to tell her fortune with cards, Frankie detested all irrationality.)

The question "Who are you?" has been asked on many such astonishing occasions. Most often it has been answered in a cryptic whisper or not at all. But the Flounder didn't go in for mystery. First he asked them to pour water over him from time to time—Siggie obliged with an empty tin can—then he asked them to dab his still-bleeding upper lip with

Kleenex—which Siggie did. Then at last he explained himself without ifs or buts.

After a brief account of the neolithic situation and an objective picture of the fatherless matriarchate, he introduced me, the ignorant fisherman, and set forth his reasons for squeezing into my eel trap and contracting to serve as my adviser.

He termed me a neolithic dolt and mediocrity, incapable, because of the state of dependence in which I was kept, of seeing through the system of total care at the base of the matriarchate, let alone destroying it. "Only his artistic gift," so the Flounder went on, "only his obsessive urge to scratch signs, ornaments, and figures in the sand led me to hope that with my advice he might lay the groundwork for a gradual"—"evolutionary" was the word he actually used—"liberation of men from the rule of women. It happened, too, though in the Vistula region, with a delay of two thousand years. But even then I had my troubles with him. In all his time-phases, during the High Gothic period, in the century of the Enlightenment, he was a failure. Passionately and singlemindedly as I have devoted myself to the male cause, I now feel that there's nothing more to be gained from it. But that's the way I am; I always have to experiment. Creation cannot be regarded as complete; on that score I'm in full agreement with Ernst Bloch, the old heretic." (Here he threw in a quotation from the philosopher: "I am. But I do not have myself. Therefore we are still in the process of becoming.") "Now you will surely understand—by the way, just call me Flounder—why I've decided to usher in a new phase in human development. The male cause is washed up. A world crisis will soon signal the end of male domination. The guys are bankrupt. Abuse of power has exhausted them. They've run out of inspiration, and now they're trying to rescue capitalism by means of socialism, which is absurd. From now on I'm only going to help the female sex. Not that I mean to stay on land. Water, after all, is my element. But I feel certain that three ladies who have become hopelessly bored with the stupid old man-woman relationship will appreciate my elementary needs.

"In short," said the Flounder in conclusion, "you, dear ladies, set me free; and I shall advise you on every situation as it comes up, but also on overall policy. Let this day mark the beginning of a new era. Let power change its sex—that is my fundamental principle. Let the women take over. There's no other way of giving the world, our poor world, which has lost all hope and become the playing of enfeebled and degenerate males, a new direction—why not say it?—a feminine direction. All is not lost."

Obviously Siggie, Frankie, and Maxie did not simply cry out, "OK! Terrific! It's a deal!" Because if the three of them had taken up the Flounder's proposition without further ado, had put him back in the Baltic Sea and secured his advice with a handshake, the long story of my time-phases down through the millennia would have remained hidden; but because the Flounder, instead of being set free, had water poured on him, had his bleeding lip dabbed with Kleenex, and was finally brought ashore, everything came to light, the Vistula estuary became an exemplary place, and I an exemplary individual; because the Flounder was not set free I must make a clean breast, confess to Ilsebill, and write it all down.

Sieglinde Huntscha, who had a law degree, explained her position succinctly: "Your offer is interesting, but we can't accept or reject it without consulting the executive committee of our organization. Didn't you yourself just say that the days of masculine, in other words individual, decisions are over? You must be aware that your partial confession raises questions that can hardly be settled aboard a rented yawl. Consider yourself under arrest pending investigation. I personally guarantee that you will be well treated." To which Frankie added, "Dontcha like our company?"

The Flounder replied coldly at first but then with a threatening note. "Dear ladies! I put myself in your power of my own free will. My loyal offer to stop promoting the male cause and to support the women's movement from this moment on, to help the many desperately resolute, but also perplexed and still mommy-minded Ilsebills, stands. But should it be your intention to make a public example of my floundery existence, of an existence harking back to the primordial darkness, I shall know how to defend myself with, shall we say, masculine ruthlessness. I shall strike back without mercy. To have me as an adversary is no joke. If you decide to put me on trial, no sociological arguments or legalistic hairsplitting will get you anywhere. No human law relates to me. Yet you have every reason to fear me."

Maxie was indeed rather frightened. "He means what he

48

says." But Siggie and Frankie stood firm, for they remembered the precepts of their organization: Don't let them frighten you with threats. We know the song and dance. God the Father and that kind of stuff. Male arrogance, that's what it is!

Now, as might have been expected a fresh breeze came up. It blew them straight to Cismar, an East Holstein village with a monastery featured in the guidebooks. Back at their thatched farm hand's hovel, Frankie lodged the Flounder in a zinc bathtub and hauled several loads of sea water in oil cans. Maxie went to Eutin and bought a book of instructions for keeping ocean fish in aquariums. Meanwhile Siggie, after jotting down all the particulars, went to the village post office and made phone calls to Berlin, Stockholm, Tokyo, Amsterdam, and New York. It cost her a pretty penny, even though for the most important conversation she had the main office call her back. Naturally women's libbers of all countries were delighted to hear about the talking Flounder and his phenomenal confession, for one thing because the misogynistic fairy tale "The Fisherman and His Wife" had parallels as far afield as Africa and India.

"Wanna make a bet?" said Siggie to Frankie. "They'll set up a tribunal, and what's more—count on me for that— they'll hold it in Berlin. This thing is *meaningful!*"

With her nose in her manual, Maxie declared, "It's a common flounder. Found in the Atlantic, the North Sea, and only rarely in the Baltic. Eats algae, insects, et cetera."

His upper lip had stopped bleeding. He lay flat on the bottom of the tub. Siggie kept a tape recorder in readiness. But the Flounder was silently resting.

What about you, Ilsebill? Would you have voted for the Tribunal, for a public accounting?

Ilsebill said, "Of course not, dearest. If you must know, I'd have let the Flounder go and wished for something sensational, like in the fairy tale: a completely automatic dishwasher, for instance, and much more; and more and more."

Dreaming ahead

Careful, I say. Careful!
The weather is breaking up and our bit of reason down.
Even now this somehow feeling:
somehow funny, somehow spooky.
Words that behaved and carried meaning
have turned their coats.

Changing times.
Itinerant prophets.
Someone somewhere claims to have seen
signs in the sky, runelike, Cyrillic.
Felt-tip pens—single or collective—cry out
on the scribbled walls of subway stations: Believe me O believe!

Someone—who can also be a collective—has a will
that no one has considered.
And those who fear him batten him with their fear.
And those who have preserved their bit of reason
turn down their lamps.
Outbursts of cozy comfort.
Group-dynamic attempts at contact.
We huddle together: still with some intimation of one an-
other.

Something, a force that has not yet been named
because no word is adequate, pushes, displaces.
Public opinion thinks it has
several times and pleasantly anticipated this slipping
(admittedly, we're slipping)
in dreams: going up! We're going up again.

But a child—children, too, can be part of a collective—
cries out: I don't want to go down. I don't want to.
But he must.
and everyone cajoles him: sensibly.

How the Flounder was prosecuted by the Ilsebills

It was August when they fished him out of Lübeck Bay. He was flown to Berlin via British Airways. Early in September they rented an abandoned movie house in Steglitz, which had formerly been called the Stella and was later maliciously termed the Pisspot by the press. It took five weeks of wrangling to choose a judge and eight associate judges from among the seven (nine, after two splits) women's groups. The Tribunal met only in the afternoon and on occasional weekends, because the judges, all except the housewife Elisabeth Güllen, had jobs.

A prosecutor was quickly chosen. And since the accused waived his right to counsel of his choice, the court was unanimous in appointing a smartly dressed young person to defend him. Siggie, Frankie, and Maxie had fallen out in the course of factional squabbles, and the only one of them to take part in the trial was Sieglinde Huntscha, the fisherwoman.

The former movie house, with its burgundy-covered folding seats, had a capacity of 311. There was no balcony. All sorts of technical devices had to be built in, and no money was left for renovating the hall, which, thanks in part to the seaweed-green wallpaper, preserved something of its cozy, neighborhood-movie-house atmosphere.

Of course there was a certain amount of disorder at first, but honestly, Ilsebill, I have no intention of harping on trifles—we men aren't always so brilliantly organized, either. I'll come right to the point. In mid-October, shortly after we ate mutton with beans and pears, begot, and conceived, the bill of indictment was read; but please don't expect me to give you a formal record of the trial; in the first place I've had no legal training, and in the second place I was a party to the proceedings (despite my vacillations). Maybe I didn't make the headlines, but I was on trial along with the Flounder all the same.

There was once a Flounder. He was just like the one in the fairy tale. When one day some women who had caught him haled him before a tribunal, he resolved not to say a word,

51

but only to lie flat, mute, much-wrinkled, and old as the hills in his zinc tub. But after a while his thunderous silence bored him, and he began to play with his pectoral fins. And when Sieglinde Huntscha, the prosecutor, came straight to the point and asked him whether he had deliberately circulated the Low German fairy tale "The Fisherman and His Wife" as a means of minimizing the importance of the advisory activity that he had demonstrably been carrying on since the Neolithic era, by maliciously and tendentiously distorting the truth at the expense of the fisherman's wife Ilsebill, his crooked mouth couldn't help opening and pouring out speech.

The Flounder replied that he had only couched a centuries-long and hence complex historical development, which all in all, despite occasional abuses, had redounded to the benefit of mankind, in simple words appropriate to the popular tradition; that the Romantic painter Philipp Otto Runge had taken down this same text, but also the history-charged original version, from the narrative of a little old woman. "Can I help it," cried the Flounder, "if the Grimm brothers, in an excess of fear, burned the painter's historically faithful record in the presence of the writers Arnim and Brentano? That's why their fairy tales are the only source of my legend. Even so the story can still be and still is quoted. Take, for instance, 'My wife—her name is Ilsebill—has got a will that's not my will.'"

But when the Flounder let his philological fancies run away with him and began to reel off Hessian, Flemish, Alsatian, and Silesian variants of the story—"and oh yes, I forgot to mention an extremely interesting Latvian version"—the prosecutor interrupted him. "Why, defendant Flounder, did you give the popular version of this tale such a misogynistic twist? Why did you permit this slander of the woman Ilsebill, which time and time again has provided the propagandists of the patriarchate with a talking point? One need only quote the defamatory jingle. Ever since it was first concocted, the cliché about the eternally discontented woman who keeps wanting more and more has been rammed down our throats. The relentless consumer. Just one more fur coat. Her craving for that allegedly noiseless dishwasher. The hard-as-nails career woman, lusting after higher and higher positions. The man-killing vamp. The poisoner. In books, films, plays, we have been treated to luxury dolls, who keep their diamonds cool in safe-deposit vaults while their poor husbands pour out their life blood and age before their time. Who, I ask, has cast us Ilsebills in all these roles?"

"High Female Court!" cried the Flounder. "When during the last phase of the Neolithic a fisherman, comparable to the fisherman in the tale, caught me in an eel trap and gave me back my freedom, it seemed to me that the young man's magnanimity put me under obligation to help him with my advice. Lord, how stupid he was! Yes, there was something terrifying about the ignorance of Stone Age men. They seldom acted, and when they did, their motive was nothing better than vague feeling. Sniveling, garrulous creatures, in dread of the cold, they wanted above all to feel sheltered. No trouble at all for the women to keep their little Stone Age men in a state of idiocy. The women, for instance, were quick to discover (at the very latest when they began to domesticate animals) that elk cows, wild sows, and consequently human women did not conceive their young unaided, but had to be inseminated by a male elk, a boar, a man, and so on. But the ladies didn't breathe a word; they craftily kept this knowledge to themselves and ignored the possible rights of fatherhood. They simply kept the men in the dark, allegedly for their own good. And so for thousands of years the men remained dependent, in seeming security. In modern terms you might say, 'The women ruled because they were better informed.' "

A few members of the audience—the trial was open to the public—tittered for a moment and then stopped themselves, as though frightened at their audacity. When the laughter had died down, the Flounder continued. "Most prominent among the ruling women was a certain Awa, who had three breasts and was idolized. This Awa put a taboo on those impulses that later, possibly encouraged by my advice, led to all the manifestations we casually refer to as culture. You most of all, my esteemed prosecutor, must realize that it was necessary to counter this state of total dependence with a liberation movement. At the very least I was under obligation to help my magnanimous fisherman."

"By substituting the rule of men for that of women?"

"That," said the Flounder, "sounds to me like a leading question."

The prosecutor stuck to her guns. "Are you then of the opinion that male informational superiority, having replaced female informational superiority, should remain the norm?"

He answered irritably. "The women's historically conditioned loss of power has been widely overestimated. Since the early Middle Ages, home and kitchen, the bed and hence the realm of dreams, child rearing, Christian morality, and the all-important household treasury, have been the preserve of the female sex. And what of woman's intuition, the tyrannical little caprices, the sweet secrets, the old habit of saying no and meaning yes, the pious lies, the stylish games, those glances that mean everything and nothing, the desires so quick to sprout regardless of the season, the charming but expensive follies. Think how often a single, never to be repeated smile has been paid for with life imprisonment! In short: the women retained plenty of power. . . ."

Here the speaker was cut short. "The Women's Tribunal," said Ms. Schönherr, the presiding judge, "has heard enough of your platitudes. We have only to open a book to see that all history has been made and interpreted by men. A cursory glance at current affairs shows that all positions of power are occupied by men. It's common knowledge."

When the Flounder, visibly agitated, broke in with, "What about Cleopatra? And Lucrezia Borgia? And Pope Joan? And Joan of Arc? And Marie Curie? And Rosa Luxemburg? And Golda Meir? Or right now the president of the Bundestag?"—his list was brusquely cut off by Ms. Huntscha, the prosecutor. "All exceptions that prove the male-chauvinist rule. The usual concessions. Tell me this, defendant Flounder: did you advise the men to treat history and hence also politics as a purely male affair?"

"You could call it division of labor. The small change of politics; the so-called dirty work, as well as military affairs with all their dangers, was left to the men, whereas the women . . ."

"Stick to the point! Defendant! You have been asked a question."

"I admit that on my advice the oppressed male terminated many thousands of years of historyless female domination by resisting the servitude of nature, by establishing principles of order, replacing incestuous and therefore chaotic matriarchy with the discipline of patriarchy, by introducing Apollonian reason, by beginning to think up utopias, to take action, and to make history. Often, I have to admit, he has been too intent on power. He has become increasingly petty about safeguarding property rights. Much too reluctant to attempt
54

anything new. I tried to compensate for his abuses with my advice, but time and time again he rejected it. For in principle I stand for equality between the sexes. Always have. Always will. But when I was caught during the late Neolithic, I had no other choice. If a woman had caught me and not a fisherman, I would not have been set free—I'd have been cooked over the fire in accordance with the precepts of neolithic cookery. What do you think? Probably with sorrel and manna grits. Well, there you have it. The consequences are almost unthinkable. To tell you the truth, I could easily have been won over to a perpetuation of ever-loving care. And I'd have known how to promote it. Too bad a man had to catch me. But just supposing. Supposing you, esteemed prosecutor, had caught me not just recently in Lübeck Bay, but once upon a time in the unruffled waters of the Vistula estuary, set me free, and given me a long-term contract as your adviser? Ah, the possibilities! Who knows, who knows! History would undoubtedly have taken a different course. Possibly there wouldn't be any dates. Unquestionably our world would be—well, closer to paradise. I wouldn't be lying in a zinc tub, breathing in the nicotine-containing fug of an assembly that calls itself a tribunal. The Ilsebills of the world would all be grateful to me. But sad to say, I was caught by a stupid though not ungifted young fellow, who refused to understand whom he had caught."

Thereupon the Women's Tribunal adjourned, but not before Ms. von Carnow, the defense counsel, had demanded the appointment of two commissions, one to determine under what conditions a neolithic woman would have set the flatfish free and signed him up as an adviser, and the other to draw up a brief outline of the course human development would have taken from neolithic times to the present if the matriarchate had been retained. "If the Women's Tribunal wishes to guarantee a fair trial," cried Ms. von Carnow, "it must be willing to project convincing alternatives."

Frankly, Ilsebill, nothing much came of it. The nine Berlin women's groups met among themselves. Sketches of regressive utopias were drafted. Nine women's paradises were described. But when the drafts were compared in an attempt to work out a unified concept, war broke out among the groups. Pathetic! The League of Socialist Women refused to take seriously what they called the "sexual pecking order" of

Lesbian Action, while the liberal-extremist Bread and Roses group condemned the contribution of the "debating societies" as "social romanticism." The Ilsebill Women's Collective was accused of planning a "shitty beehive state with the queen, workers, and drones." The August Seventh Feminist Initiative Group—August 7 was the date on which the Flounder had been caught for the second time—covered itself with ridicule by predicting that thanks to certain genetic manipulations future generations of males would menstruate, bear children, and even suckle them. And when the presumably Maoist Red Pisspot faction, a split-off from the League of Socialist Women, put forward a utopian vision of radical return to neolithic conditions, its members were suspected of being CIA agents or worse.

All this of course gave the press a field day. Sardonic remarks in all the gossip columns. Ms. Schönherr, as presiding judge, was hard put to it to keep the Tribunal together and get on with the trial. In the end, her compromise formulation was approved by all the warring groups and factions. Ursula Schönbart read the succinct formulation: "In the opinion of the Women's Tribunal, any answer to the Flounder's question—how human society would have developed if matriarchy had not succumbed to the patriarchate—must perforce be hypothetical. It nevertheless seems safe to say that mankind would be more pacific, more sensitive, more creative though free from individual aspirations, more affectionate, more just despite abundance, and thanks to the absence of male ambition less hectic and more serene; moreover, there would be no state."

In any case the trial continued. The Flounder remained under arrest, but more and more his responses were limited to the one word "unwell." To spare his voice, a no-smoking rule was imposed at the behest of the defense.

After that the trial ran smoothly for three or four days. The Flounder testified quite willingly concerning my neolithic time-phase—amusing little anecdotes. The public was intensely curious about the loving-caring stratagems that Awa used to keep us men in a state of servitude for thousands of years. When the Flounder cited neolithic dishes—curds with flatbread made of acorn and manna meal, wild goose baked in a shell of clay—the pencils of those present scribbled feverishly. Awa's recipes were reprinted in the women's pages of several daily newspapers: "Mushrooms à la Awa, baked on a bed of hot ashes."

Only when the Flounder started referring more and more frequently to the three-breasted Awa, to the myth of the third breast, did his listeners grow restless. Questions were raised during recesses: "Is a third breast indispensable to the establishment of women's rule? Can it be that we women are short of something?"

The first drawings evoking the principle of three-breasted hegemony made their appearance on the toilet walls of the erstwhile movie house. (Later the mammary triad filled unoccupied advertising space in subway stations. A primordial masculine desire expressed itself with sweeping brush strokes on hoardings and walls.) When the Flounder claimed that the end of total matriarchy had been brought about not by his advice, but by the sudden disappearance of the third breast—a phenomenon that even he was at a loss to explain—it was once again necessary to recess the Women's Tribunal.

"The Neolithic era," said Ms. Huntscha, "is behind us; in the opinion of the prosecution, the Flounder's guilt has been proved. But before sentence can be pronounced, certain material still remains to be examined, especially the following allegations of the Flounder: (1) there were three-breasted women in the Neolithic era; (2) only thanks to the third breast were women able to repulse the male claim to power; (3) only three-breasted women can possibly restore the matriarchate. Furthermore, the court must determine whether or not, after the alleged disappearance of the alleged third breast, the Awa cult, as it continued to be practiced during the Bronze and Iron Ages, was able to preserve certain vestigial matriarchal rights. And lastly, the Flounder's contention that—masked as the cult of the Virgin—the Awa cult remained in force through the first centuries of Christianity, cannot be passed over in silence. On the contrary, our movement must investigate, or appoint a special commission to investigate, the question whether the third breast should be regarded as an essential feature of early matriarchy. If the answer is yes, then we must keep faith with out prehistoric past and renew the neolithic three-breast cult. Experts must be consulted. But even now shouldn't sex-conscious woman artists be encouraged to work out a modern formulation for the Awa cult? On the other hand," she concluded on a note of warning, "it's a tricky legend, and if we're not careful it will make fools of us all. Perhaps in reproducing the myth of the three breasts, we shall only be falling in with the male chauvinist's wish dream of tits, tits, and more tits. For—as you must all be aware—men have never been satisfied with two breasts."

To make a long story short, the Women's Tribunal resolved after long tergiversation—accompanied by the usual factional fights—to dismiss the third breast as a real or conceivable possibility. Ms. Schönherr (who, incidentally, is ideologically close to my Awa) cast the one unavailing contrary vote. The graffiti on the walls of the movie-house toilet were covered over with whitewash. A wasted effort, of course. Time and time again, ball points and magic markers were exercised. Flamboyant posters appeared on the market. Even schoolchildren, egged on by their teachers, seem to have daubed Awa's opulence in exuberant size and color. A baker in Tempelhof started baking Awa-shaped buns, and they sold like hot cakes.

After so much public mischief, the verdict, as read by the the presiding judge, was bound to be severe: "The Flounder is found guilty. His one-sided advice benefited the male cause alone. With ruthless single-mindedness he worked for the introduction of patriarchy. Though for many centuries his efforts were fruitless, his misogynistic purpose must be counted against him. In framing this judgment the Tribunal has seen no reason to take neolithic woman's alleged three breasts into account."

Would you have said that? Oh, Ilsebill! It was all so different. Important as breasts, two or three, are and have been, devotedly as I scratched the three-breasted Awa in the sand, kneaded her in clay, carved her in wood, scraped her out of a lump of amber, the only really crucial question was this: who, when we were shivering, who when we had only raw food to eat, stole fire from the sky?

And you, friend Flounder? Why didn't you tell the Tribunal that it wasn't any man but our Awa who stole fire from the old Sky Wolf? You don't seem to find it convenient to remember how often, in our many conversations on the sands of the estuary, I laughed at your Prometheus story. What was it again that you said? "Fire is masculine thought and action in one." Your cock-and-bull story was supposed to boost our morale. No, friend Flounder. As well you know, it wasn't a man, it was Awa who went to the Sky Wolf who guarded the fire, and lay with him. You didn't want to believe it. And now the women's libbers have put you on trial. The Ilsebills of the world are pointing their fingers at you. Tell them who brought fire to the earth, admit it. Tell them—because they don't know—where Awa hid those three little coals. Because the consequences were far from negligible. Tell them the whole story, friend Flounder. The Ilsebills need to know. Every teensy-weensy detail.

Meat

Raw rotten deep-frozen boiled.
Supposedly the Wolf (elsewhere the Vulture)
was the first custodian of fire.
In all the myths the she-cook was crafty:
while the Wolves slept (the Vultures
were deep in cloud) she hid
the coals in her moist pouch.
She stole the fire from the sky.

No longer cutting sinews with long teeth.
No longer foretasting the aftertaste of carrion.
Softly the dead wood called, wanting to burn.
Once we had assembled (for fire is an assembler)
plans kindled, thoughts crackled,
sparks rose up and names for raw and cooked.

When liver shriveled over the fire,
boars' heads were baked in clay,
when fish were lined up on a green branch
or stuffed guts were bedded in ashes,
when bacon sizzled on hot stones
and stirred blood turned to pudding,
then fire triumphed over rawness,
then we men among ourselves discussed taste.

The smoke betrayed us,
we dreamed of metal,
and that was the (foreshadowed) beginning of history.

Where the stolen fire was briefly hidden

In our early myths there was no fire. Lightning struck,
moors burst into flame on their own accord, but we never
succeeded in holding on to the fire; it always died out. And
so we ate our badger, elk cow, and grouse raw or dried on
stones. And we huddled shivering in the darkness.

Then the dry wood said to us, "Someone whose flesh is
also a pouch must climb up to the Sky Wolf. He is the
keeper of the primal fire, whence comes all other fire, including the lightning."

It had to be a woman, because the male has no pouch in
his flesh. So a woman climbed up by the rainbow and found
the Sky Wolf lying beside the primal fire. He had just been
eating a crispy brown roast, and he gave the woman what
was left of it. Before she had finished chewing, he said sadly,
"I know you've come for fire. But have you a pouch?"

When the woman showed him her pouch, he said, "I'm
old, I can't see any more. Lie down with me and let me test
you."

The woman lay down with him, and he tested her pouch
with his Wolf's member until he was all worn out and fell
asleep on her flesh. After waiting a little while and another
little while, she let his tester slip out of her pouch, tipped
him—remember, he was lying on top of her—off to one side,
sprang to her feet, and shook herself a little. Then she took
three glowing bits of charcoal from the primal fire and hid
them in her pouch, where they instantly seized on the Wolf
sperm and made it hiss.

Thereupon the Wolf woke up, for he must have heard or
sensed that the fire was consuming his seed in the woman's
pouch. "I'm too exhausted," he said, "to take back what
you've stolen. But let me tell you this: The primal fire will
make its mark at the opening of your pouch, and the mark
will leave a scar. Your scar will itch and itch. And because it

itches, you will wish for someone to come and take the itch away. And when it doesn't itch, you will wish for someone to come and make it itch."

The woman laughed, for her pouch was still moist and the glowing charcoal hadn't yet started to burn her. She laughed so hard she had to hold herself in. And, laughing, she said to the exhausted Wolf, "You old wreck. Don't make up stories about my pouch. I'll show you what else I can do. You'll be amazed."

At that she spread her legs and stood over the primal fire. Holding two fingers under her pouch to make sure nothing would fall out of it, she pissed into the primal fire until it went out. And the old Sky Wolf wept, for that spelled the end of crispy brown roasts; he'd just have to gulp everything down raw. That, it seems, is what made earthly wolves murderous and misanthropic.

Just in time the woman climbed back down to earth over the paling rainbow. She returned to her horde, screaming, because her pouch was dry by then and the glowing charcoal was burning her. "Awa! Awa!" she screamed, and those primordial sounds became her name. In a later day the scar at the entrance to her pouch, which the Sky Wolf had prophesied, came to be known as the clitoris or tickler, but it remains an object of controversy among scientists investigating the origin of the orgasm.

From then on we had fire. It never died out. Where there were people there was always a wisp of smoke. But because a woman had brought us fire, the woman kept us pouchless men in a state of dependency. We were no longer allowed to sacrifice to the Sky Wolf, but only to the Heavenly Elk. For many, many years the function and origin of the itching scar were unknown to us. For when the returning Awa had finished screaming, she told us ever so casually that the old Wolf had been kind to her, that he had roasted a hare for her over the primal fire, that roast hare is perfectly delicious, and that she now knew how to cook. She further told us that she had complained to the Wolf about how cold and dark it was down here, that of all sacrifices in his honor he preferred elk calves, that she had washed his left hind paw—which was infected—and dressed it with the medicinal herbs she never went anywhere without, that he, poor fellow, had been so grateful to her for curing his limp that he had given her three glowing coals out of the primal fire, and finally that—male superstition to the contrary notwithstanding—the Sky Wolf was a female.

That was all Awa told us. And I myself wouldn't have known a thing if I hadn't given a great deal of thought to that teensy-weensy scar and examined Ilsebill's tickler in the light of other myths. I told the Flounder, but he wouldn't believe it. He believed only in his reason.

What we lack

Forward? We're tried that before.
Why not regress, quickly
and without stopovers?
Everyone can bring something along, something or other.

We have begun to develop—
blinking to left and right—backward.
A few fall by the wayside:
Wallenstein musters regiments.
Just to be fashionable, someone deserts in Gothic ecstasy
and is overtaken (clad in brabant) by a plague year.
While the migration worries along,
a certain group (as everyone knows) splits off from the Goths.
Those who had sought their future as late Marxists
want now to be Early Christians or Greeks
before or after the Doric purge.

At last all dates are effaced.
No more talk of succession.
We are back in the Stone Age, blank and uninscribed.
But I've brought my typewriter along
and I tear giant leek leaves into legal-sized sheets.
Hand-ax technology, fire myths,
the horde as the first commune (how it settled conflicts)
and the unwritten law of matriarchy—
all want to be described,
and right this minute, though time is standing still.

I type on leek leaves: The Stone Age is beautiful.
Sitting around the fire, so cozy-comfy.
Because a woman has brought fire down from the sky,
women rule bearably.
What (the one thing) we lack is a handy utopia.
Today—but there is no today—
someone, a man, has made an ax from bronze.
Now—but there is no now—
the horde is discussing the question: is bronze progress or
    not?

Because history has started with a bang,
an amateur, coming like me from the present
and bringing his fish-eyed camera,
wants to hand us down to posterity
in color or black and white.

Hospitably from horde to horde

In any case, enlightenment was late in coming to us. If,
when I took the Flounder out of the eel trap, he had said
right away, "My son! Wouldn't you like to know where all
those children come from? Not to mention the elk calves?
And how the bees and the marsh marigolds are fertilized and
reproduce?"—I'd have said, "Yes, indeed, friend Flounder,
tell me how it's done. Awa keeps saying that she and the elk
cows do it all by themselves. With maybe a little help from
the full-ripened moon. She says we Edeks and elk bulls have
nothing to do with it."

But the Flounder didn't enlighten us in time. True, he went
on and on about the father right that we still didn't have, but
that our pestles were fraught with consequences, that the
sticky snot we and the elk bulls discharged, blindly but with
unerring aim, was called sperm and had the power of fertiliz-
ing, that it made women and cows swell up and led ultimately to childbirth, so making us men, if not individually,
then at least collectively and in principle, into fathers—of all
this he didn't breathe a single word to us for many centuries.

Was he ashamed? Was he himself in the dark? He didn't

even regale me with a little lecture about the milt and roe of the Baltic herring, things that were quite familiar to us fishermen. Instead, he brought me news of far-off cultures and abstract drivel about patriarchal property rights.

He had progress on the brain, and did he chew my ear off! "On Crete, my son, where King Minos and his brothers rule"—actually the women ruled in secret—"the bronze double-edged ax is being perfected; no haphazardly plaited huts of willow withes, but solidly built, many-storied palaces; household accounts are being kept on clay tablets; horde and clan have given way to an organized city-state. Only recently an artist and engineer by the name of Daedalus . . ." But what was that to me? That kind of thing cut no ice in the marshes of the Vistula estuary. (You know me, Ilsebill, I can't eat butter without bread.)

The one bit of lore I was able to pass on to Awa was something the Flounder treated as a mere incidental, the Minoan method of making hand-molded cheese. Of course we had neither cattle, goats, nor sheep at the time. They were brought in much later by the Scythians, those great travelers from the depths of the Russian land mass, where no Flounder propagated culture, and barbarism was never assailed by doubts.

Our cheese was extracted from elk and reindeer milk. Casually I passed the tip on to Awa, who soon learned to let the milk stand in clay bowls made by me, to let it sour, curdle, and discharge the whey under pressure, to mold the cheeses with her hands, wrap them in lettuce leaves, tie them up, and hang them on wind-twisted willow trees.

Awa took this as home-grown procedure. No whiff of King Minos and the first European high culture had reached her. And when, later, the Iron Age Wigga mixed curdled goat's and sheep's milk with codfish roe before it turned into cheese, she had without Cretan influence invented a dish that the Cretans still sell for a few drachmas and serve as an appetizer.

It was not until Mestwina's time that cow's milk and sheep's milk were processed along with mare's milk. We called our local cheese *Glumse*. Milk *glumsed*, became *glumsy*. A shepherd at the time, I became Mestwina's "*Glumser*." "*Glums*-head" is still a term of affectionate disparagement. In good times and bad, cool cellared *Glumse* was always in demand.

For Dorothea of Montau, who refused to touch so much as a shred of meat, *Glumse*, beaten with roasted barley grits, provided a High Gothic Lenten dish that she served on such holidays as Candlemas. She also crumbled *Glumse* into her leek soups.

And when, a little later, it became necessary to starve the Teutonic Knights out of their fortress not far from the Wicker Bastion, the townspeople gave body to their mockery by tossing handy little balls of *Glumse* into the besieged stronghold. That demoralized the Teutonic knights, and they surrendered.

The abbess Margarete Rusch stuffed quail and snipe with well-pressed *Glumse* and cranberries before aligning the little birds on the spit, a procedure that was said to have earned her, after guild banquets, the lucrative favor of the beer brewers, coopers, and wealthy drapers.

And the kitchenmaid Agnes Kurbiella also served the poet Martin Opitz *Glumse*, flavored with caraway seeds (of which he was inordinately fond), in the belief that it was good for his nervous stomach. (But the word *Glumse* never found its way into his iambics—no adequate rhyme for *Glumse*.)

On Sundays, Amanda Woyke, who cooked for the help at the Royal Prussian State Farm at Zuckau, served the day laborers and serfs *Glumse* and a negligible quantity of sunflower oil along with their boiled potatoes, while on weekdays she gave them bowls of dry, fatless curds, sometimes adding a few onion rings.

When Danzig became a Napoleonic republic and was consequently besieged by the Russians and Prussians, the French governor learned to prize his cook Sophie Rotzoll's brilliant idea of stirring, at the last minute, a sweet-and-sour mixture of *Glumse* and raisins into her stewed horsemeat, cut from the flanks of his Polish uhlans' expired stallions.

Lena Stubbe embellished her watery cabbage soups, which derived what little taste they had and an eye or two of fat from an occasional beef bone, with crumbled *Glumse*. Or she would make sour-milk soups and add cubes of stale bread or slices of cucumber that some charitable soul had donated to the Ohra soup kitchen. Her "Proletarian Cook Book" included a recipe for pickled herring in *Glumse*.

When Billy celebrated Father's Day with her girl friends and the world still seemed to be a cheerful kind of place, barbecued steaks and lamb kidneys were followed by Bulgarian

65

sheep's-milk cheese, which is related to our native, Minoan-influenced *Glumse*.

And Maria Kuczorra, who as canteen cook of the Lenin Shipyards in Gdánsk keeps an eye on food and food prices, also eats Polish *Glumse* off her knife as she stares silently into space.

Just as my Ilsebill, now that she is pregnant (by me), has developed a craving for curds, kefir, kumiss, and yogurt, all relatives of *Glumse*. But the Flounder told me next to nothing about the further development of our Minoan-influenced cheese industry. And he won't admit that he enlightened us too late. On the contrary, he contends, in his testimony before the Tribunal, that Awa and the other women suspected if they didn't actually know what and who kept impregnating them, and that they needed outside help to be mothers. But, he goes on, Awa didn't find it convenient to divulge this suspicion or half-knowledge, which would have lent support to the principle of paternity, if not to any individual fatherhood.

Is that right, Ilsebill? Did you know the facts and conceal them? Was it your neolithic system to keep us men in the dark? Did you exchange winks? Were you women a conspiracy even then?

I'd rather not believe the Flounder. He's always griping. Always running everything down. How unwilling we Edeks, we lazy Pomorshians, were to assert claims of fatherhood, to found families, to hand down property, to create dynasties that would bloom, proliferate, and degenerate. "Why, there's nothing to prove you ever were fathers. You never even thought of giving the handles of your clay pots obscene shapes, of documenting your culture with so much as a stone phallus. Pure waste of time, my telling you about the Minoan bull. Sure. You were as potent as rabbits, but culturally speaking, because you were unaware of your procreative power, you couldn't get it up."

That's unjust, Ilsebill. He ignores the fact that we were influenced at a relatively early date by the Minoan method of milk processing. As if *Glumse* production were not a cultural activity! As if paternity were all that mattered! As if we hadn't transmitted our *Glumse* hospitably from horde to horde.

Just as we invite people to dinner—my eggplant sprinkled with grated cheese and baked, your crisp salad—and have reason to fear return invitations to mushy hormone-fed chicken in curry sauce, so in the late days of my neolithic time-phase we also had guests. Then as now: we can't always eat stingily by ourselves, even if the nice couple next door with their eternal marriage problems aren't exactly our dream, for man is by definition a social animal.

The Flounder, you see, had already deplored our isolation and advised me to make contact with the neighboring horde, which, he assured me, had for centuries been living only a short distance inland—"Get out of these marshes, my son! Shake a leg. If you refuse to borrow anything from the Minoan high culture, if you think your *Glumse* is achievement enough, then at least make comparisons with other hordes here in your home country, so that one day you may become a clan, a tribe, and finally a nation. And if your Awa wants you to go on believing that there's nothing in the whole world but her and you, you'd better be guided by my knowledge; there's more world beyond the mountains, my son; there are people busy multiplying. You are not alone."

So I persuaded a few hunters in our horde not just to hunt elk and water buffalo in the nearby bogs, but to follow the Radune upstream and explore the woods along its banks. My fisherman's opinion—that if the eels came from up there and swam downstream in quest of the Mottlava, the Vistula, and the open sea, there must be something else up there and not just nothing—met with hesitant approval. Fear had to be cowed: "What can happen to us? We'll stay near the river. And if it gets too scary, we'll turn back."

Of course we knew the fringes of the woods from gathering mushrooms and roots and cautiously hunting the badger and wild boar, but we had never ventured deep into the dark forest; our courage extended only to the swamps and moors. But to make a long story short, as the Flounder would say, we started out. Unbeknownst to Awa, six hunters and I crept through the rolling beech and oak forests into the wooded, pond-studded section of the Baltic Ridge that later came to be known as Kashubia; and as we crept, we whistled. At that early date we learned to purse our lips and resort to the now traditional remedy for fear.

Perhaps, Ilsebill, you should know that our region was then

relatively new. It hadn't come into being until after what we like to think of as the last ice age, when, as the waters receded, the Baltic coast took on its present contours. Before that, in the Riss-Würm interglacial era, there was nothing, only time and glacier. It was only after the Würm period, when elsewhere idols were being carved and cave drawings scratched, that our paleolithic ancestors followed the receding ice. They found an inhospitable region. For in their advance and withdrawal the glaciers had planed the tops off the Kashubian mountains. Their line of flight was marked by glacial rubble and deep Eocene valleys.

On our way, we seven whistling plainsmen found crudely hewn hand axes, bearing witness to the existence of the primordial horde at a time when the Sky Wolf still kept guard over his fire, when raw food was eaten day after day and our Awa had not yet come into her own; what's more (I'm pretty sure) there was no Flounder at that time, either.

After the provisional withdrawal of the glaciers (they will come again, they always do) our region seems to have consisted exclusively of windy steppe, hills covered with glacial rubble, gurgling swamps, and restless rivers that kept seeking new beds. Only as the climate grew warmer did the forests start to grow. The reindeer, elk, and water buffalo retreated to the river deltas, which remained primordial swamp country. But in the wooded hills, apart from wolves and bears, which we knew and avoided, there were new animals to frighten us—wild horses, lynxes, and hoot owls, for instance. We stayed as close as possible to our homeward-flowing Radune and whistled more and more intricate tunes to ward off fear. Thus and thus alone, pursing his lips in response to fear, did man invent music, though the Flounder insists on the spiritual source of all the arts.

After the third day of our forbidden journey, we seven hunters of swamp and moor found ourselves confronting, a stone's throw away in the ferns, seven forest hunters. Between us: smooth beech trees; mushrooms singly or in magic circles; a busy anthill; filtered, obliquely falling light.

Believe me, Ilsebill, they were as scared as we were. (You could have heard the strangers whistling softly between their teeth, just like us.) Naturally the first thing we did as we approached one another was to compare their stone axes, spears, and arrowheads with our own equipment. We favored pieces of flint, which we picked up on a stretch of steep shore

68

bordered with chalk cliffs, later known as Adlerhorst. The forest hunters had no flint and made do with quartzite and touchstone. Though the sharpness of our flint blades seemed at first glance to give us an edge, we soon saw that the forest hunters carried heavy stone axes which were not only hewn but also polished, with handles that were fitted into a bored hole—but how had they bored those holes? We still tied our axes and hatches to their forked handles. Quite possibly our tapering flint arrowheads aroused the curiosity of the forest hunters in equal measure. In any case we showed each other our equipment and made menacing gestures but took no action, because in the absence of Awa no decision was possible. Although the impulse to bludgeon and pierce literally make our muscles quiver, we kept our distance; and our opposite numbers also fidgeted indecisively.

Well, Ilsebill, I was known as a fast runner, so my companions sent me to the coast to consult Awa, and one of the seven woodsmen was sent into the bush. As though pursued by demons, I ran through the terrifying woods, where lived not only the lynx and the hoot owl, but the fabulous unicorn as well. My adventures on the way—two wolves strangled with my bare hands, a brown bear spitted through and through with my spear, a lynx struck with an arrow between its glittering eyes (at night, what's more!), the unicorn fooled, made to ram his horn into a beech, elm, maple, no, an oak—all that is irrelevant, beside the point, for only my mission mattered.

Toward the end I jumped onto the back of a wild horse and rode the last stretch of the way. I enjoyed riding. Only when the woods thinned as I was crossing our flat country and approaching the mouths of the Radune Mottlava Vistula, the always hazy moors, the ridge of dunes, the white beeches, and the Baltic, did the mare throw me. For two days and a night I ran and rode, toward the end singing at the top of my lungs because I was on horseback, exultant.

After listening to my breathless report, Awa held a women's council from which I was excluded, came back with two women who loaded a fully packed basket on my back, and gave the horde she was leaving behind her ever-caring instructions; then off we started, she and I and her companions—two three-breasted young women—on our arduous journey.

This time two lynx frightened us. No unicorn stood shimmering in the ferns. The forest primeval was already known to me. One did not whistle in Awa's presence. I speared lying pike in the Radune. Where familiar mushrooms grew, we bivouacked. Our baggage included a small pot of fire bedded in ashes. Plump frogs, wild strawberries bigger than we had ever dreamed of. I, the guide, was well treated, suckled by all three women. When frightened wild horses rushed from a beech thicket, Awa seemed delighted; I'd have liked to show her my prowess as a horseman.

And then we came and saw: of our six men one was seriously, two slightly injured; our opposite numbers had four slightly injured, who were lying in the ferns beside our wounded. All were being cared for by the Awa of the forest horde and her women. Remedies well known to us: sorrel, nettles, and moneywort. The other Awa and her companions, who, however, were not called Awa but Ewa, also had three breasts, and like our Awa ruled by all-embracing care. The system was already well known to us.

A while ago I deplored the lack of solidarity among the women of our region (and everywhere else, for that matter). Now I have something more gratifying to report: naturally the two Awas understood each other splendidly. How they giggled as they ran their fingers over each other's dimples, how they sniffed at each other and squealed in high-pitched gutturals. Off to one side of our damaged males they held a women's council. Invitation and return invitation were soon exchanged by Awa and Ewa. No war was declared; instead hospitality was offered. That very evening we and our wounded were the guests of the neighboring horde, who had settled nearby between two lakes, water holes left over from the ice age. I was soon deep in conversation with the fishermen of the neighboring horde. In addition to traps, they already had nets. I showed them how the wishbone of the wood pigeon could be made to serve as a fishhook.

We gobbled to the bursting point. Of course the women ate separately and had special food. But we, too, enjoyed new taste sensations. While at the women's board bleak baked over hot stones was followed by steamed wild-horse liver with flatbread made of honeysweet acorn flour, we Edeks were regaled with roasted chunks of the horsemeat, also accompanied by bittersweet flatbread. I forgot to tell you that each of the Ewas and Ludeks, as the men of the neighboring horde were called, like each of our Awas and Edeks, ate singly, averting his eyes from the others. They didn't brighten up until later, when the whole horde got together for a collective shit. But I'll come back to that later on: how in our neolithic time-phase we ate by ourselves but contemplated our excrement in social groups.

After the feast Awa unpacked the basket. I was called and honor was shown me, for the women had packed my ceramics as presents—a few *Glumse* bowls, which when testifying before the court the Flounder magnanimously attributed to the bell-beaker culture. Three fireproof pots of the kind in which Awa boiled the stomach walls of an elk cow, just as today we simmer beef tripe for four and a half hours. The basket also contained eight clay figurines that had been molded around the middle finger of my left hand—sturdy three-breasted Awa, such as we used in our cult. My flounder-headed idols, which Awa disliked but had not prohibited, were not represented; nor, it goes without saying, was there a single elk's pizzle.

The Ewas petted and praised me. The potter's art was still unknown to them. The artist of the neighboring horde, a fisherman whom I later took to calling Lud, was summoned. He listened to my short lecture about pottery but showed little interest, a truculent fellow who was to become my friend off and on in the course of my various time-phases. Ah, Lud! How we drank black Danzig beer in the High Gothic era! How we argued about the sacraments! How we ate cheese with our knives in the Baroque vale of tears! And how in period after period we talked art to death! Only recently Lud died again. How I miss him! I shall honor him with an obituary. Later.

And that night the unharmed Edeks and Ludeks, as well as those who had suffered only slight injuries in their ears or noses, were exchanged. My Awa took the truculent Lud for herself, and I found a replica of my loving-caring Awa in Ewa: every bit as rich in dimples, as soft, as basic, and as radically, thoroughly, consummately head-emptying.

Believe me, Ilsebill, I'll never forget it. I will always be looking for Awa and Ewa when I'm with you. And sometimes when I lie with you I find them both. If one pushes me out, the other takes me in. I'm never entirely without a refuge. With Awa and Ewa I always have a cozy-warm home. No need to lie with strangers. That is how Awa as Ewa and Ewa as Awa enslaved me. Because just imagine: Ewa returned our visit, with her companions and a full-packed basket.

According to modern time-reckoning, they turned up three weeks later, with the seven forest hunters and the still-truculent Lud in their train.

We served them what we had on hand, sturgeon roe, manna grits cooked in reindeer milk, chunks of water-buffalo fillet spitted on damp willow sticks and roasted like shashlik. And for dessert our *Glumse* mixed with juniper berries. The meal went over big with Ewas and Ludeks. And we were pleased with their presents.

From granite-hard stone Lud the net fisher and artist had hewn (with what, I wonder) mortars and pestles for grinding acorn meal; his production further included stone axes with holes bored in them, a fish net (to serve us as a model), and various fertility idols carved in white limestone. These idols, however, represented not three-breasted Awas or Ewas, but oval, broad-lipped twats with open, deep-bored clefts. The openings had been polished smooth and were shaped like mouthpieces, so that these conveniently sized stone vaginas could serve as drinking cups for water, berry juice, mead, sour elk's milk, and other beverages, notably the skimmed, fermented, succulent, heady mare's milk that was the favorite drink of our neighboring horde, who kept herds of wild horses just as we had domesticated elks and water buffaloes. Dogs and their barking were common to both our hordes.

After this return invitation, good neighborly relations developed between the two hordes. By watching Ewa's people we learned to knot fish nets, to bore holes in stone axes, and to bake flatbread, while they learned from us to make *Glumse*, to fish with hooks, and to fashion pottery. And just as the Flounder had wished, there was communication in other repects as well. The exchange of males between the hordes soon became customary, even though it created little problems, for we Edeks, and Ludeks were not consulted; like it or not, we had to oblige.

You can see that, Ilsebill; with some of the Ewas we just couldn't do it. And our Awas came away empty now and then, too; the oldtimer just wouldn't oblige. There are early afternoons when a man would rather play with pebbles, take it easy by himself, pick his nose without a desire in the world, let his cock dangle. Sometimes a man's cock is a plain nuisance, an obtrusive stranger, a bothersome appendage between his legs. And so we experienced failure (and the idiotic shame a man feels when he's a flop). Complaints passed from horde to horde. For a time our neighborly relations were impaired. Blows were struck between Edeks and Ludeks, between Lud and myself. We had to supply them with arrowheads hewn from flint; in exchange they offered only raw material (hard rock, unpolished and unbored). Lud disparaged my ceramic articles as cute; I countered by ridiculing his stone twats: couldn't he think of anything else? Bad blood. Brawling and bellowing. But it never got to the point of war. Men continued—though less and less enjoyably—to be exchanged. Awa and Ewa saw to that. They always came to terms. What interested them most was the principle of the thing. Gradually the two hordes merged into a clan; later we became a tribe.

And on addressing the Women's Tribunal, the Flounder, too, despite his higher misgivings and critical objections to the principle of ever-loving care, called the exchange of men a sensible arrangement, because it enabled the two neighboring hordes to escape the dangers of stultifying incest.

"Of course," he declared, "men should be allowed to choose their sexual partners, but even so, my advice put an end to isolation, fostered communication, prevented degeneration, and promoted the development of a Pomorshian nation."

Three of the eight associate judges supported this view. Unfortunately, Ms. Schönherr, the presiding judge, abstained from voting, and Sieglinde Huntscha, the prosecutor, said, "Promiscuous fucking may be acceptable for men, but a woman has no business settling for the first pair of pants that comes along."

How about you, Ilsebill? What do you think? Suppose you had to do it with every man who felt like it or even half felt like it? Now that you're pregnant as a result of our free choice, you must understand my disgruntlement at the time.

Admit it was oppressive, exchanging us like that from horde
to horde, without consulting us, whenever the women were in
the mood. They called it hospitality, but really!

Dr. Affectionate

What's wrong?
Something missing?
Your breath down my neck.
Something that sucks chews licks.
The calf's tongue, the mouse's teeth.

A desire is going around the world for mumbled words
that yield no meaning.
Children lisp it, and so do old men all alone
under the covers with their thumbs.
And questioned now, your skin shrinks away from the test:
modesty, which in the darkness (when company was gone)
was not cast off.

Someone is called Dr. Affectionate
and he still lives in forbidden concealment.
Exact science classifies what's missing
as caress units,
for which thus far
no substitute has been found.

Fed

My mother's breasts were large and white.
Snuggle up to her tits.
Make the most of them before they give way to bottle and
    pacifier.
Threaten with stuttering and complexes
if they should be withheld.

Don't just whine.

Let the milk include clear beef broth
or cloudy soup of codfish heads boiled
till blinded eyes roll
approximately in the direction of happiness.

Men don't give suck.
Men squint homeward when cows
with heavy udders cross
the road, blocking the traffic.
Men dream of the third breast.
Men envy the suckling babe
and always miss something.

Our bearded breastlings
who provide for us with their tax payments
smack their lips between appointments
and comfort themselves with cigarettes.

After forty men should start being suckled again
publicly and for a fee
until they are sated and wishless and stop crying,
stop having to cry in the john—all alone.

The wurzel mother

And then the third breast disappeared. I don't know the
details—I wasn't around just then, I think it was after the
hundred and eleventh generation of Awas. Anyway, Ilsebill, it
was gone. It doesn't seem to have wasted slowly away; rather,
one day it was just suddenly missing. No, not because the
women were sick of suckling us, but because the Flounder
wanted to be God to us Edeks!

"Typical!" you say. But at that time there was a growing
need for compensation, for a bit of male divinity. We didn't
want the Flounder to be the only god, just an associate god.
And at some time or other, one of the still three-breasted
priestesses of Awa, besieged with petitions by us men,

consented: she lay with the Flounder in the rushes, or on a bed of leaves, or on a compromise bed of rushes and leaves, and came back the next day without a middle breast.

Or was it entirely different? Because nothing was happening, we Edeks thought we'd have a little fun and give the women a bit of a scare, just as I recently gave you a bit of a shock. "Oh! Something slippery-slimy! Eek!" you screamed and kicked the covers off: arm-long, in coiling beauty, it lay between us on the sheet. Irresponsible of me, I admit. Now that you're pregnant, the Lord knows what that eel in the bed might have done.

Then, during the hundred and eleventh generation of Awas, I secretly molded clay into a life-sized man, with an extra penis growing out of each buttock, so he could have pleasured three Awas at once. One moonless night we stationed this monstrosity outside the women's lodge. And the next morning (seen through sleepy eyes) my super-Edek was taken for real. In any case the women, some of whom were pregnant, screamed; but miscarriages were not the only consequence. Or did some other, comparable shock make the third breast fall off like a wart? It simply disappeared. High time.

Or it was something else again. The decisive step came much later. Even Wigga still had the third breast Pomorshian men required. We had scarcely modified our needs. Why should we have? (We were damn well off.) But when Wigga, in a series of major campaigns, had the so-called dream wurzel, a very special multipurpose root, exterminated as a public enemy, when she deprived us of the wishing weed, the plug we had chewed for thousands of years, which brightened our dreams, assuaged our fears, and appeased our yearnings, we no longer knew exactly what we desired.

The film of our vivid imagining broke off. We lost our innocence. Gone was the third breast. No longer palpable because no longer dreamed. Unsuckled, we reached into the void from that day on. Dull reality had made us poor. Believe me, Ilsebill, it was sad, though having ceased to wish (because we had ceased to dream), we could no longer realize what we had lost.

After that we grew restless. Dissatisfaction set in. Later (up to Sophie's time) we compensated for our loss by chewing fly agaric—not to mention various substances that today are kiffed and hashed, steeped with tea, or shot into the veins.

But nothing could or can equal our (exterminated) wishing wurzel.

And addressing the Women's Tribunal, the Flounder, who had never heard of our primordial drug, said: "Well, ladies, that's the way it was, the three-breasts hoax was finally exploded—during Wigga's Iron Age, to be exact. At last the men developed a sense of reality, and the fiction of the triune primal mother went up in smoke. All at once—demystified by what lightning flash we do not know—good old Wigga was standing there with two plain, ordinary tits. It may have been the ensuing disenchantment that led a few Pomorshian men to experiment with the migrations. Nothing unusual. Dreams of primal mothers had faded long before in other places. True, the Cretan goddess Hera, famous in her day as the best of Minoan earth mothers, had not abdicated, but she had been forced to marry—yes, marry!—the god Zeus, and to share her hegemony. I myself was obliged to take on the function of god for a time, in order to compensate just a little for the power of the primal mothers, who despite the lost breast went right on tyrannizing men with their loving care. I was under pressure. Despite my failures, my millennial efforts in the male cause had not been forgotten. Through a division of labor, I was put in charge of everything connected with oceans, rivers, and fishing. My role was comparable to that of Poseidon in relation to the Pelasgian Athene—I was expected to assert myself alongside the Awa cult, which continued to linger on. Naturally conflicts were inevitable—in Athens and elsewhere. As you can imagine, ladies, the replacement of mother right by the rational though in a sense fictitious father right resulted in several counterrevolutions. Need I remind you of the Bacchantes, Amazons, Erinyes, Maenads, Sirens, and Medusas? The battle of the sexes in ancient Greece was rough, really rough. By comparison nothing much happened on the banks of the Vistula. Apart from the sudden disappearance of the third breast, there is little to report. No material for tragedies, though at that very time the restless Goths were taking a rest in the region of the Vistula estuary, for, eager as they were to perform heroic feats, they couldn't make up their minds whether to return northward or to pursue their southward course. Among the Pomorshians, timeless matriarchy continued, though somewhat mitigated by me, the associate fish god. Even three-breastedness lived on, in small ceramic artifacts.

No question of a new era, or at the most this: beginning with Wigga, root plants were grown for food. She was a true wurzel mother; she even looked like a mangel-wurzel."

With Wigga farming became drudgery. As long as one of the long line of Awas dealt out loving care, there was a limit to the amount of barley, spelt, and oats grown, we retained our independence as fishermen and hunters; most of our time was spent beyond hailing distance in the reeds or underbrush, on moors or remote beaches, and though oppressed we were able to enjoy life. It was Wigga who first harnessed us to wooden plows and sent us out to the beet fields. We had to gather the seeds of wild root plants, for in her garden-sized experimental field Wigga sowed rows of charlock and mangel (*Beta vulgaris*), bred the precursors of the radish, or salsify, and of the beets with which at a much later date Amanda Woyke cooked beet and dill soup for the farm hands of the Royal Prussian State Farm at Zuckau. On hot August days it was carried to the fields and dished out to them cold.

In any case the Goths despised us as root eaters, while we called them fire-eaters, for the Goths, like those other Germanic tribes that Tacitus observed, were too lazy to bend over for roots. They preferred to dream of faraway places.

We always liked to nibble roots. I remember juicy wild roots that brought tears to the eyes and, though tough, could be softened by long chewing. In Awa's time only the women were allowed to grow them. After Wigga's first attempts to breed root plants, which did not bring results until Mestwina's time (the radish), Dorothea of Montau in her Lenten garden, the nun Margarete Rusch in the garden of Saint Bridget's Abbey and Agnes Kurbiella in her diet garden raised a root plant related to our carrots, celery, and those delicate little Teltow turnips. Still later rutabaga, bred from rape, came to us from Bavaria by mail. Amanda Woyke gave it the apt name of *Wruke*, and Lena Stubbe, in times of early capitalist famine, cooked tons of it in soup kitchens (her response to the social question). The war and influenza year 1917 bequeathed us the expression "rutabaga winter."

I have nothing against rutabaga, but here I'm thinking of its primal form, which was long and firm, covered with wrinkles and grimaces, with protuberances all around it. It tapered to a point amid curling root threads, or else a few wisps dangled from its rounded head. Where the roots grew too close together in the glacial rubble, they clutched one another with many fingers. We ate them as we found them, straight or crooked. Except when the ground was covered with snow and everything looked alike, we pulled up roots day in, day out; believe it or not, they were as long as your arm. They tasted best raw. It was the women's privilege to bite off the tip; we Edeks were given what they left, but we, too, had a privilege, however questionable: we were allowed to sample dubious mushrooms first.

Awa made a ritual out of root biting, as she did of everything that allowed of comparisons. In the sacrificial month, the women held the mangels suggestively in front of their faces. They screamed furiously as a warning to us Edeks, and then their teeth crashed down on the roots. Bundles of roots were placed in the bleaching skulls of bull elks as sacrificial offerings. Roots were used for healing. Our wishing beets ran wild. Beet lore was passed on. . . .

Once, after three hours of effort in which eleven women displayed their strength, Awa and her companions pulled a man-sized mangel out of a moraine that ran all the way down to the beach. (When at last the mangel emerged, the image of the women, knotted together and tangled in greens, had engraved itself on my mind; later on I cut it into birch bark and colored it with the juices of plants.) And the man-sized, ecstatically convulsed mangel cut so paradigmatic a figure in the eyes of the marveling horde that a mangel god (Ram)—some of the women were on the point of blurting out a name—was almost born to us. But Awa straddled the presumptive divine phallus and made her Edeks carry her around in triumph. She tolerated nothing outside of herself. The old wolf god, from whom she had stolen fire, already had claim enough to an accessory cult. (And the Edeks—so it was rumored—were trying to think up a fish god.)

As it happened, the monstrosity had a woody taste and rotted after a while. Not even the water buffaloes wanted what was left of it. But the biting of beets remained a favorite amusement among the women and inspires primordial terrors in us men to this day. To Dorothea of Montau beets were still vicarious food, as though sweet Jesus manifested himself to her in that form. And likewise for the abbess Margarete Rusch and her nuns, carrots were more than a vegetable. Agnes Kurbiella was the first to cook carrots until soft,

79

add a bit of fat, and serve them up without religious implications. But today, with the cultivation of macrobiotic garden vegetables, guaranteed free of chemicals, the root cult is on the rise again. Wherever you go, raw carrots are eaten in public. Loudly and to the terror of men, young girls bite off the ends. The advertising industry has registered the trend in large color plates: radishes and raw carrots flanked by assorted cheeses, ham, sausage, and pumpernickel. Obviously that means something, something more than affectionate nibbling. Root vegetables are still being bitten off vicariously. But fear is on the rise. . . .

During a recess in the trial—the Flounder had suffered another attack of faintness while the Iron Age Wigga was under discussion—I saw the prosecutor, Sieglinde Huntscha, biting into a radish with large, slightly yellow incisors. When I greeted her in passing—we had known each other before the trial—she took another bite, and only then, still chewing, replied: "Well, well. So they've finally let you in? You have me to thank for it. What do you say? We're making it pretty hot for the Flounder, aren't we? But never mind, he wasn't born yesterday. He'll talk himself out of anything, and if I do manage to corner him, he'll feel faint again. Like the other day when he was trying to tell us that women had a natural aptitude for farm work. From the mangel-wurzel to the red beet: that's his idea of progress. Significant contribution to the development of human nutrition. Woman's historical achievement and so on. So I sent out to the market for a bunch of radishes. Want some?"

She gave me what was left. I nibbled like a rabbit that can't help itself. Then the debate on the Wigga case was resumed. The Flounder had apparently recovered. And finally, thanks to Siggie's recommendation, I was able to count myself among the public.

Really, Ilsebill, they'd been unjust. At first they didn't even want to let me in. My contention, supported by documentary evidence, that from neolithic times to the present I had lived in a relation of intimacy with Awa, Wigga, Mestwina, the High Gothic Dorothea, the fat Gret, the gentle Agnes, and so on, was not corroborated by the Flounder—"Men" he said, "have at all times been interchangeable"—and was ridiculed by the associate judges: "Anybody can make such claims.

What is he, anyway? A writer looking for material. Trying to ingratiate himself, to latch on, to grind literature out of his complexes, maybe talk us into settling for special allotments to housewives and suchlike appeasements. But here we are not concerned with petty reforms; here we are concerned with the Flounder as a principle. The private lives and alleged sufferings of individual men leave us cold. That kind of crap is coming out of our ears."

My right to testify was contested. Some four thousand years of my past were expunged (as if I weren't still suffering from injuries incurred in the Neolithic). The proceedings were supposedly open to the public, but the public was carefully screened: ten women to each man. And even the few men who were admitted had to show affidavits from their working wives, attesting that they did their share of the housework (cooking cleaning taking-care-of-baby). ("He washes the dishes regularly.")

Finally, when I applied for the third time and enclosed two Xeroxed letters in which you express your conviction that not only my domestic virtues but also my impaired manhood were the foundation of our relationship, I was notified that my dossier was under favorable consideration. (Thanks, Ilsebill.)

Maybe I ought to admit that I nevertheless attended the trial from the very start. An electrician who from the operator's room of the former movie house regulated the lighting, the infrared lamp over the Flounder, the PA system, and the projector for documents and statistical charts, let me look into the hall through a little square window and listen in with earphones. Call it male-chauvinist solidarity. Anyway, he let me stay, though the only comment on the Women's Tribunal that occurred to him was "Wouldn't you like to be a Flounder? Some show those dames are putting on."

Then at last I was an acknowledged member of the public. While Wigga, the primordial root, the first cultivation of beets, my monotonous existence as a charcoal burner, our neighboring horde, the parasitic Goths, and my brief participation in the migration were being debated, I occupied a burgundy-upholstered seat in the eleventh row of the movie house. On my left sat an old woman with a bitter laugh. On my right a young women's libber, who was knitting an extremely long screaming-green muffler. Though I proffered greetings to the right and left, I was not acknowledged as a male or as anything else.

Before his attack of faintness—during which he floated around in his tub with his white underside up—the Flounder, to distract attention from his advisory role, had verbosely and with bold figures of speech praised the Iron Age Wigga as the goddess of roots, as the culture heroine of the beet fields, as a great woman and mangel mother. When interrupted by the prosecution in mid-flow, he was stricken with faintness, and it was necessary to call a recess. It was then that Sieglinde Huntscha sent out for the radishes, bit the tip off one of them, gave me the rest, and yakked away until a bell signal called us back into the hall.

There, since there was nothing more to be got out of beets, the debate turned to the Germanic conception of freedom, especially that of the Gothic males. Accused of instigating the migrations and persuading the Pomorshians to participate, the Flounder not only defended himself with glibly recited alliterative lines from Nordic epics, but also leapt to the attack. "Ladies, what justification have you for putting me down as a vile seducer? Would it not be closer to the truth to say that the matriarchal regime, which became increasingly oppressive after Awa, was bound to make even the easygoing Pomorshian males receptive to the free, one might almost say popular-democratic attitudes of the Gothic men? For servile they were not. The sessions of their *Thing* went on for hours on end. Everyone contradicted everyone else. Even old Gothic crones were allowed to contribute words of advice from the edge of the circle and whisper maxims arrived at by casting runes. So you see, the women were not excluded. And don't forget German monogamy. Fathers and mothers had something to say to each other, while with the Pomorshians polyandry without father right was still the rule. Objects of use and soon used up, the men lost their last spark of desire. Everything that might have amused them—thinking games, dueling, the acquisition of honors, organizations—was taboo. Small wonder, in short, that the free though barbaric life of the Germani, of whose primitive vigor Tacitus had warned the Romans, attracted the unfortunate males of the coastal horde, especially when you consider the disappearance (regardless of its cause) of the third breast, which might have slaked a male's thirst for freedom, appeased his wanderlust, and quieted his urge to act for action's sake. The only hope was to push off. Into the wide world. Into history. It's true that they soon crawled back home, these Pomorshian men, but that's another story."

While the Flounder was speaking and while his speech was being torn to shreds by the prosecutor, exposed as male chauvenist rubbish, and while the Flounder—for having praised the Germanic concept of freedom—was once termed prefascist and twice postfascist, I, at last admitted to the audience, had my eye on the second to the left of the eight associate judges who, four to the left and four to the right of Ms. Schönherr, the presiding judge, maintained the symmetry of the long, raised table.

There she sat. Every bit my Wigga. Gigantic and unwieldy, she never modified her posture. Her crossed arms forming a rampart in front of her bosom. Her radish-colored hair, as though she were determined to overtower at all costs, piled high and held in place with a hairpin, which might, however, have been one of those rusty nails that the Goths, when they finally started southward, left behind as scrap. Wigga! Her father—so it was rumored among us—had been a Goth. Hence her name, a variant of Frigga, the Germanic goddess. Hence her unwieldiness, her morose impassiveness, her calm severity. My Wigga, a Pomorshian Valkyrie, then presiding over us as the wurzel mother, today over me as associate judge of the Women's Tribunal.

Impassive, she listened to the Flounder, to the prosecutor. With that same gaze full of nothing, she might have been looking out over the Baltic Sea. Only once, when the Flounder in his carping way spoke of Wigga's attempts to raise beets as deserving but none too successful, she abandoned the rampart posture of her forearms, stopped looking out over the smooth Baltic, slowly, very slowly, with her right hand pulled the endlessly long hairpin or Gothic nail out of the tower of her hair, and (bending her wrist) scratched her back with it. Believe me, Ilsebill, just like Wigga, when I told her how I'd joined the migration. (Her father, by the way, was said to have been the Gothic district chief Ludolf, from whom my always truculent Gothic friend Ludger was descended.)

I didn't get to hear my contemporary Wigga until the associate judges cast their final vote. Seated in her large-checked two-piece outfit, Ms. Helga Paasch, sole owner of a large nursery garden in Berlin-Britz, declared: "Well, if you ask me, this Mr. Flounder is guilty. For putting ideas into the guys' heads. All this nonsense about history. Promising them heaven knows what, palm trees, cypresses, olives, lemons. Globe-trotting passed off as progress. Freedom, he called it. But all his incitement went for nothing. The Pomorshians came back. Pretty quick, too, with their tails between their legs. After which they had to plow again and grow beets. Because he was unsuccessful I say: extenuating circumstances for Mr. Flounder this time."

The old lady on my left laughed bitterly while, overcome with rage, the women's libber on my right dropped several stitches and bit into her screaming-green choker. I sat very still; I hardly breathed. But after ironically terming the mild verdict "astonishingly fair," the Flounder merely concluded, "After that bit of bungled history, nothing of interest happened among the Pomorshians for seven centuries; their only progress was in beet production."

Not a word about the dream root, or wishing wurzel. Yet it was important and explains more than the Flounder concealed. (Or can it be that he really doesn't know?) In any event, not so much as a syllable about our primordial drug came to the ears of the Tribunal. No attempt to explain the disappearance of the third breast. All of a sudden it was gone, and that was that. When as a matter of fact it owed its very existence to the wishing wurzel.

The crossbreeds attempted today—the bean tree, the tomato-potato, quota-exceeding rye-wheat—wouldn't have held a candle to our wishing wurzel. Its pointed bluish root with the faintly almondlike taste sent up a luxuriant bush from which, when it reached maturity, hung edible pods full of protein-rich beans; the leaves, rolled into plugs, were chewed by us Edeks. Pods and beans nourished us, the root was our dessert, but the leaves kept us quiet, made the third breast a reality for us, emptied our heads, fulfilled our wishes, and gave us dreams: boundless, heroically exalted, immortal, exciting daydreams.

It was not innate laziness but the wishing wurzel that stopped us from making history. And really, Ilsebill, it was Wigga's doing that we finally woke up a bit. In the course of several campaigns, she had the dream wurzel, which only in our marshy soil produced leaves and beans from pointed roots, radically exterminated. Oh yes, we protested feebly, but she had the last word with her impassively stated argument that the poison kept us from becoming industrious tillers of the soil and growing normal beets. From then on no more dreams, no more wish fulfillment. Wet, cold agricultural reality. Periods of hunger. Slowly we came awake.

And the Goths, who with us had become addicted to the weed (as a substitute for travel), woke up at the same time, found our region a hopeless bore, and started on the travels they had been dreaming of, the so-called migrations.

Wigga invited the Gothic chieftains to a starvation meal and persuaded them to go.

That was after an overlong winter and a rainy summer, when the barley rotted on the stalk and the only beets to be had were moldy. The herring and flounder had stayed away, too, and the fish perished in the rivers as if the country had been cursed: perch, bass, roach, and pike were seen drifting belly up. We would have come through the winter even so, but, accustomed as they were to sponging on others, our Gothic guests had nothing to fall back on when their cattle were carried away by a plague, so we were forced to slaughter our last remaining reindeer and water buffaloes. True, the Goitches still had horses (though they creaked at the joints), but their horses were sacred to them and were never slaughtered, not even in times of famine.

So Wigga invited the Gothic chieftains to a special kind of noonday meal. She had decided to serve her guests the only food which we Pomorshians still had and which, though in short supply, we would continue to have throughout the coming winter. The guests were Ludolf, Luderich, Ludnot, and my friend Ludger, all of them hulking fellows with a studied truculent glare. For once all four were unarmed. Possibly they were so weak that the sheer weight of the iron would have been too much for them. It had rained all summer, and now in the fall it was still raining. So Wigga had invited the visitors to her hut, where it was smoky but cozy. They all sat on sheepskins, their watering blue eyes magnified by hunger. Luderich chewed his red beard. Ludnot gnawed his fingernails. Nevertheless Wigga, before bringing in the steaming bowl, delivered a brief but instructive lecture about the one dish she had provided, which later, after it had produced its effect, we named "Wigga's Gothic mash." She spoke about manna grass and manna grits.

Now, sometimes because there was nothing else to eat and sometimes because of the pleasant taste, the seeds of manna grass (*Glyceria fluitans L.*), known in my part of the country as wild grass, have been gathered and ground from the earliest times down to the twentieth century—during the First World War, for instance, or in 1945, the year of mass flight. This local grain has been called *Schwade* or wild millet or heaven's bread, or by the Prussians simply manna.

It was not easy to gather the manna grains, because when ripe they hung loosely from the stalks. For this reason we gathered the grain in the morning dew with the help of taut, flat bags that were fastened to the ends of sticks and moved through the grass. Later on we used manna-grass combs. And in the nineteenth century, when more and more of the land was cultivated and the wild grass was rarely seen outside of marshy areas, manna-grass sieves were attached to poles that were often as much as twelve feet long. (Perhaps I should tell you that manna grain was gathered almost exclusively by men, whereas the gathering of mushrooms, berries, wild sorrel, and roots has been women's work since time immemorial. That's why the Flounder actually tried to get the Women's Tribunal to characterize the use of manna grits for emergency food as a male achievement.)

Pounded manna seeds were so popular that in the eighteenth century (before the introduction of the potato) they figured among the region's exports. Even the serfs had to supply manna grits to their owners, along with other produce. And before cheap Carolina rice appeared on the market in the nineteenth century, sweet manna porridge cooked in milk and seasoned with cinnamon was served at peasant weddings instead of the usual wedding millet. Because of their digestibility, manna grits were prized as food for the aged, and West Prussian cottagers, on retiring, stipulated a certain measure of manna grits as part of their reserved rights.

Of course we gathered other wild grasses in times of famine, wild millet (*Milium effusum*), for instance, or the red cowwheat (*Melampyrnum arvense*), from which a rather bitter but wholesome bread could be baked. And when the harvest was poor, lyme grass was used to stretch our supply of cultivated grain. But of all the wild grains that helped us to get through the winters, our favorite was manna grass, or "Prussian manna." And that was why, when Wigga wanted to get rid of the Goths, she served them a "Gothic mash" of manna grits—plenty of them, with nothing much added. Only a few sunflower seeds were mixed with the grain before it was crushed in a mortar.

The Goths didn't care for our manna. Ludolf, Luderich, Ludnot, and my friend Ludger were meat eaters. They would eat fried fish in a pinch, but as a rule resigned themselves to porridge only as a filler. True, they shoveled it in from the deep bowl that Wigga had set down in their midst, but the prospect of living a whole winter and more on grits (and woody mangel-wurzels) took their appetites away. My friend Ludger looked as if he had been asked to eat toads. To make matters worse, Wigga, in her instructive lecture about the difficulty of gathering the seeds (definitely man's work), mentioned our meager Pomorshian stocks but made it clear that the place where they were stored was secret and inaccessible.

It was my friend Ludger who humbly (all the hauteur had gone out of him) asked for advice. Luderich and Ludnot also asked what was to be done. Finally, when Wigga remained silent, Prince Ludolf, a handsome, monumental man who not only was the father of Ludger, Luderich, and Ludnot but also was thought to have begotten Wigga, asked simply and directly what this foggy marshland between rivers had to offer the Goths, apart from not enough manna grits.

"Nothing," said Wigga. And, rather harshly, "You'll just have to shove off. Either to the north, where you came from. Or to the south, where everything is supposed to be better." And she proceeded to vaunt the southland to her guests: Every day spitted bullocks and sheep. Mead awaited them in never empty pitchers. Never a foggy day. The rivers were never clogged with ice. You were never snowed in for weeks on end. And to top it all, the south promised the brave victory, honor, and posthumous fame. If people wanted to make history, she went on, there was no point in their settling down as if the beet culture were the only possible advance; no, they must indefatigably conquer new horizons. "So pack your stuff and beat it!" she cried, pointing her long arm southward.

Thereupon Ludolf, Luderich, Ludnot, and my friend Ludger shoveled in the rest of the grits to fortify themselves for the next day. As Wigga had advised them, they shoved off southward and started on their migration. The outcome is known to every schoolboy. It's true, they went far.

In our country, on the other hand, centuries went by without noticeable change. Only the weather varied. Until Bishop Adalbert arrived with the cross.

Demeter

With open eyes
the goddess sees
how blind the heavens are.

Pertrified eyelashes cast shadows all around.
No lid consents to fall and bring sleep.

Always horror
ever since she saw the god
here in the fallow field
where the plowshare was engendered.

Willingly the mule goes round and round over his barley.
That hasn't changed.

We who have fallen out of cycle
take an overexposed
photograph.

What a cast-iron spoon is good for

Adalbert came from Bohemia. All his books (as well as his crosier) had stayed in Prague. Because he was at the end of his scholastic wisdom, he decided to abandon theory for practice, that is, to convert the heathen and spread the one true faith in our country, the region of the Vistula estuary. (Today they call it "working with the masses.")

Wladislaw, king of Poland, had signed him on as a propagandist. He arrived with a Bohemian retinue under Polish protection. His actual purpose was to indoctrinate the Prussians, because the king of Poland wanted to extend his power to the east bank of the Vistula. But since the Prussians had a reputation for ferocity, his Bohemian retinue advised him to start by practicing on us, the rather dull-witted but good-natured Pomorshians. (Build up experience, inspire confidence, do good, get acquainted with the foreign economy, said the prelate Ludewig.)

They camped near our settlement. They had brought provisions in oxcarts. But before they had even launched their missionary activity, their Polish cook died on them. After preliminary talks—with both parties exchanging what they had—our cook (and hence priestess), Mestwina, offered to cook for the bishop and his retinue. Our contribution consisted of mangel-wurzels, *Glumse*, mutton, grits, mushrooms, honey and fish.

Neither Fat Gret or Amanda Woyke was the first to fold her bare fuzz-blond arms below her bosom and survey the table with a stern to benevolent look. In this same attitude my Mestwina watched Bishop Adalbert after serving up his dinner. She held her head slightly tilted, and her expression was one of expectancy. But Adalbert did not praise the dishes he liked; he ate as though tormented by disgust. He poked listlessly about, he chewed with distaste, as though every bite were at once a temptation and a harbinger of hell's torments. Not that he found fault with anything in particular or, confronted with Pomorshian cookery, missed his Bohemian cuisine; his disgust was universal. (You can't imagine, Ilsebill, what a repulsive sourpuss I was toward the end of the tenth century A.D. Because in principle I was this Adalbert of Prague, who gagged on his food and seemed to have been born without a palate.)

And yet Mestwina had fallen for the gaunt missionary. She, too, wanted to convert. When she looked over her folded arms and saw him chewing, her face flushed, and the flush rose to the part in her hair. For she hoped that her heathen cookery might give him a foretaste, perhaps not of her conversion to Catholicism but at least of her love, for love him she did—with a love that ran hot and cold.

For Adalbert she baked bacon flatbread. For Adalbert she stirred honey into millet porridge. For him there was sheep's-milk cheese with smoked cod liver. For and against Adalbert she cooked (after singeing the bristles) a whole boned boar's head with roots and morels. Then Mestwina put the head in a bowl and covered it with its broth. In the January frost the broth soon hardened into jelly. (The bishop's mercenaries had speared the wild boar in the endless wooded hills of the interior.)

And toward noon, when the bishop wished to partake of a simple meal with the envoys of the king of Poland—Wladislaw was pressing for the conversion of the Prussians—Mestwina, for and against Adalbert, overturned the bowl and dumped the boar's head on the table in such a way that though surrounded by jelly it could be seen for what it was. The famished envoys delivered it from the quivering jelly. But because Mestwina was looking on in her expectant attitude (over folded arms), Adalbert had to put a pious interpretation on their greediness: "One would think Satan in person had got into that jelly!" So the five of them vanquished Satan, and the bishop, as the standing Mestwina could see, had difficulty in displaying his usual disgust. The prelate Ludewig was encouraged to crack a joke or two about Satan's excellent flavor; but Adalbert did not laugh.

By then the zealous missionary had been with us for weeks. We Pomorshians were still heathen, though I, during my time as a shepherd, carved linden wood into handy little Blessed Virgins—who, to be sure, had three breasts under their drapery. (Take my word for it, Ilsebill; even as a missionary on the one hand and a shepherd on the other, I remained an artist.)

And once when Mestwina, who lived with us in the Wicker Bastion on Fisherman's Island in the middle of the Mottlava, was making fish soup for the bishop from five popeyed codfish heads, her necklace of uncut amber tore just as she was taking the heads, which were about to disintegrate, out of the broth. As she bent over the steaming kettle, the waxed string came open and slid unaided over the rounded nape of her neck. Though Mestwina raised her hand quickly and tried to catch hold of the open string, nevertheless nine or seven pieces of amber, pierced (by me) with hot wire, slipped into the pot, where they dissolved in the foaming soup and gave the Christian Lenten fare the pagan strength which has resided in amber since the earliest times. Its effect so transformed, nay, revolutionized, the chaste Adalbert that no sooner had he spooned up the soup than he clutched my Mestwina like a madman and kept at it all that night (which had already begun to fall) and the following day. Time and time again the ascetic penetrated her flesh with his by now utterly unrepentant gimlet. Just as a Pomorshian might have done, but with more religious zeal and dialectical contradiction, he exhausted himself inside her, all the while mumbling his Church Latin, as though he had discovered a new way of pouring out the Holy Spirit. For we of the Wicker Bastion had not yet been baptized.

That brought dependence. From then on the bishop ordered Mestwina's amber-seasoned fish soup once a week. No wish could have been easier to satisfy. Never, even in the winter, was there any shortage of fish. Along with oatmeal, barley and manna porridge, root vegetables, and mutton, fish was the staple food of the Pomorshians. That was why we had recently taken to worshiping a certain fish along with the traditional earth goddess Awa. And Mestwina—as cook and priestess—sacrificed to the god Ryb, who was flat of body, flat of head, and crooked of mouth; in other words, he looked very much like the talking Flounder.

True, there was strife among the people of the Pomorshian coast when, flouting the women's will, the fishermen put through the cult of the flounder-headed god, but Mestwina amalgamated the new cult with traditional rites. She knew of legends to the effect that every spring the flounder god shared a bed made half of rushes and half of forest leaves with the three-breasted Awa. True, said Mestwina, they often quarreled, but Awa wouldn't mind if a small share in the cult were devoted to her fish bedfellow. After all, he had been useful in his way, providing her full nets and calm seas; it was he who appeased the Vistula in time of flood, and he who had endowed amber with certain powers.

This was why the children of the Wicker Bastion carried sturgeon and codfish heads, the head of the silvery Vistula salmon, and the venerable gray head of the sheatfish on long branches cut from the willows that grew along the banks of the Radune, in a procession that followed the banks of the dikeless river mouths to the sea. And in the lead they carried crooked-mouthed, slant-eyed flounder heads. The idea was for the fish—the pike and the perch, the bass and the cod—to see the rivers and the Baltic Sea once again, and for the young god Ryb to be worshiped and appeased in his flounder form. (Even then the legend was going around that the Flounder—one had only to call him—would grant wishes and give advice, that he was especially devoted to fishermen and most remarkably intelligent.) "Flounder, O Flounder!" cried the children of the Wicker Bastion, festooned with old nets and rotting fish traps. And even after Mestwina's death, when they turned us into Christians, we continued to be good heathens. At Easter time—why not at Easter time?—after lashing ourselves with willow switches on the bank of the Radune, we showed the fish the rivers and the sea in a solemn procession, led by a priest with the cross and six choir boys with little bells. Incense was provided by ground amber, swung in bowls. Pomorshian prayers for a good catch were chanted. But also in evidence were the taut pigs' bladders that the girls tied on, three each, in memory of Awa. Only the litany was Catholic. For the dead eyes of the fish glittered unbaptized. Congealed eyes raised heavenward. Mouths ready to bite. Pectoral fins spread-eagled.

Toward evening the willow branches with the heads on them were planted like a fence in the road of logs leading to Fisherman's Island. Screaming, the children of the Wicker Bastion ran away. The gulls dove down. As far as the road they had followed the procession with shrill cries but remained at a distance. Now they fell to, starting on the eyes, and battled one another until the willow branches were bare. And once in the spring, I recall, a porpoise, a small member of the whale family, was thrown up on the beach. Its head was placed in a leather holder fastened to the end of a long pole, which two young fellows took turns carrying in the middle of the procession, right after the effigy of Saint Barbara. And later, much later, when the Old City was founded in accordance with Culm law and the Charter City in accordance with Lübeck law, and I as a swordmaker was at last admitted to a guild, the children of the Wicker Bastion—among them my daughters by Dorothea—made fish heads of colored paper, put lamps inside them, and carried them around on poles. A pleasant sight in the evening, though it always made me rather sad—yes indeed, Ilsebill—because Mestwina was no longer with us.

And because of those fish heads, which boisterous children carried along the log road and into the Christian-Bohemian camp, Bishop Adalbert, who was later to be numbered among the martyrs, flew into a rage and waxed obscene in Latin. With holy water he armed himself against the devil's artifices. The innocent codfish heads made hellish faces at him. Especially the slant-eyed Flounder, as seen by the bishop, had Satan's ironic, disruptive look. Against that look he raised the cross aloft. With a wave of his hand he commanded his mercenaries to behead the fish heads once again. Snick-snack, it was done, and that infuriated Mestwina, for from her priestess's point of view, more was hacked off those willow branches than the ascetic dreamed of. What could he know of Awa and the recent male deity who went by the name of Ryb?

Mestwina knew. She knew and suffered. Small and round as she was, she grew a little. But she said nothing. She stored it all up, Pomorshian-style. Later she drank fermented mare's milk in tiny sips. It was almost evening before she had worked herself into the right state. And by the time the ascetic came as usual to visit Mestwina on her bed of leaves, her fury had taken on body and purpose.

Her hut was walled with plaited willow withes, plastered with mud thrown from outside. A comfortable room. Adalbert came in with a pious greeting, but he also brought his dialectical contradiction. Though carnal lust lifted his cowl like a mighty tent pole, Mestwina did not appease him on a short-term basis, but for all time. He didn't even get a chance to discharge. Promptly and vigorously she bashed him again and again on his Bohemian head with a cast-iron cooking spoon, and in her fury avenged the cod and the sturgeon, the perch, the pike, the silvery salmon, the reddish bass, and repeatedly the flounder god of the Pomorshian fisherfolk.

The only sound out of Adalbert was a brief sigh. But his adversary stood unbowed, stood valiantly for its own sake. Even when the bishop was already dead and a martyr, it refused to bow down.

Mestwina had slain the subsequently canonized Adalbert of Prague, I buried the cast-iron spoon, for we had reason to fear that if found it would be elevated to the status of a Christian relic. As for the body, we threw it into the river. A little later all of us in the Wicker Bastion (and with us Mestwina) were driven by Polish mercenaries into a shallow stretch of the Radune, where Adalbert's successor, the prelate Ludewig, subjected us to forced baptism. This Ludewig, incidentally, had a feeling for art and was devoted to me. He liked my little carved Madonnas. He even put up with the Virgin's third breast (under the drapery). The honey-colored amber eyes I had fitted into the linden wood gave the Mother of God a magically compelling gaze, but that, too, he interpreted in the light of triumphant Catholicism. Perhaps it was because of my useful talent that I went scot free when Mestwina was condemned to death; as an artist, one is welcomed by all religions. And besides, as you know, Ilsebill, I haven't got the makings of a martyr.

It was in April of the year 997 that Adalbert was slain by the drunken Mestwina, that we Pomorshians were baptized and the spoon buried. I buried it not far from the future settlement of Sankt Albrecht. And there, in the exact same place, it was dug up in the fall of 1889 by Dr. Ernst Paulig, sometime rector of the Sankt Johann Gymnasium, who donated it to the Museum of the City of Danzig. "Pomeranian cooking utensil," said the little tag. Actually the spoon was of Bohemian origin. Actually Adalbert had brought it to convert the heathen with. Mestwina used it only to ladle out the mare's milk fermented for her own use; for cooking she used wooden spoons.

What else happened when Mestwina, shortly after the forced baptism, was condemned to death and beheaded by a Polish executioner will be told later on: who betrayed her, what signs and wonders befell as the sword descended, and what absurdities schoolbook history has handed down to us.

"Only with Mestwina," said the accused Flounder before the Women's Tribunal, "did Awa's rule come to an end. From then on, the male cause alone counted." But the women weren't listening. They had other preoccupations. The case of Mestwina had become secondary. Strife was the order of the day. The feminist cause threatened to lose itself in resolutions.

But one day, after prolonged tergiversation, in the course of which the opposing or tactically allied groups expressed themselves in urgent motions, the Tribunal finally arrived at its seating order, for it was not always the accused Flounder who forced recesses and adjournments. Along with the judge and her eight associate judges, the prosecutor, and the court-appointed defense counsel, all of whom had, and wished to preserve, their symmetrical seating order—the judge and associate judges upraised, before them in the pit the Flounder in his tub, and to the left and right of him the prosecution and the defense—there was a further group, which was also part and parcel of the Tribunal, namely, an Advisory Council consisting of thirty-three women who were supposed to have been seated in the first two rows of the former movie house, but were so divided among themselves that they had thus far brought forth only two resolutions: (1) that the current proceedings should be recessed, or else (2) that the Tribunal should be adjourned. The Flounder had frequent occasion for irony at their expense: "If the esteemed Advisory Council of the High Court, which has recently taken, so I hear, to calling itself 'revolutionary,' has no objection, I, as the accused, should prefer to carry on with the proceedings, because, you see, I want very much to treat of the pre-Christian episodes of Awa, Wigga, and Mestwina together, as part of a larger context, the decline of the matriarchy. That, too, was development. Or—if you prefer—revolution!"

It was only after discussion of the Mestwina case that the Advisory Council had begun to call itself "revolutionary," because the murder of Bishop Adalbert of Prague suggested parallels down to our own day. Since the thirty-three members of the Advisory Council represented groupings separated by only the haziest of dividing lines, *ad hoc* coalitions were frequent. Throwing ideological scruples to the winds, the left-wing majority, consisting of four different factions, had suddenly (and only because the Flounder had three times used the word "evolution") allied itself with the radical-democratic Federation of Women, and voted in favor not only of prefixing the title "Advisory Council" with the word "revolutionary" (which decision was carried by a bare majority) but also of the proposed new seating arrangements. They no longer wished to sit at the front of the pit, where they had to crane their necks; they wanted to be up on the stage, to the right and left of the judge and the eight associate judges, and arrange themselves in accordance with the results of the last vote. The Flounder commented, "New vote, new seating arrangement. Marvelous! That will keep the ladies moving."

And so it did. Accordingly as the Revolutionary Advisory

Council voted, the chairs to the left or right increased or decreased. And since even during the Tribunal's regular proceedings new political conflicts kept arising, the public often took more interest in the factional infighting of the feminist movement than in the cases of Awa, Wigga, and Mestwina, which are also my case or cases; after all, it was I who buried the cast-iron cooking spoon a good three feet deep.

Despite the Flounder's annoyance, he was ignored amid the passions aroused by these procedural debates. When the first two rows were evacuated by the Revolutionary Advisory Council and thrown open to the public, he protested and threatened to withdraw from the proceedings. "This is intolerable," he cried. "I can't have the public so near me. There have already been several menacing incidents. I, too, am entitled to security. Reserve the first two rows for experts. I'm expecting several gentlemen and a lady whose publications have established them as authorities in the field of archaeology or of medieval canon law. They, too, must be seated. And for myself I demand security guards."

His pleas were granted. From then on the first and second rows were occupied by various experts, two female security guards, and witnesses for the prosecution—all women who, whether destitute, divorced, working, disadvantaged, deserted, battered, or oversupplied with children, had in some way been victimized by the institution of marriage. Stammering, whispering, voiceless, or shrill, now on the brink of tears, now with malignant laughter, they gave expression to the misery of oppressed womanhood: But after my fifth child . . . Sleeping with my head next to the radiator . . . But he just wouldn't stop. . . . He even threatened my mother. . . . And the relief checks stopped coming. . . . So I took those pills. . . . But nothing helped.

Whatever sufferings the witnesses for the prosecution invoked, men were always to blame. I felt guilty at every turn. But the Flounder remained on a high plane and stuck to facts. He knew everything and the opposite. He was even up on canon law. That was why he waived his right to defense witnesses, including me, who after all was the man most intimately involved. By and large I was mentioned only in passing. Tried anonymously, I was a mere member of the public. Silent, often bored, because the factional struggles were again drowning out the case of Awa, Wigga, or Mestwina, I, in my place in the eleventh row, drew parallels.

True, I found no Awa among the judges—except perhaps for the always serene Ms. Schönherr—but I had discovered my morose Wigga in the form of Ms. Helga Paasch the nursery-garden owner. And Mestwina, too, sat facing me among the associate judges: how beautifully round everything about her was! The small head, framed in strictly ordered hair. The round, columnar neck with—really, Ilsebill—an amber necklace on it. The gently sloping shoulders. And the latter-day Mestwina—this, too, must be mentioned—also had the glazed and empty look that had betrayed my then Mestwina when she had sopped up too much fermented mare's milk.

Ms. Ruth Simoneit is obviously an alcoholic. On several occasions she disturbed the discussion of the Mestwina episode with babbling, compulsive headshaking and intermittent swigs from her private flask, and finally, when Mestwina's decapitation was brought up, with tragic sobs and loud howls, with the result that Ms. Schönherr was obliged to escort the besotted and hypersensitive associate judge out of the movie house with motherly firmness. (And later on I myself took a certain interest in the poor, unfortunate spinster.) She started before noon on Rémy Martin. And she never ate properly. And the record player was always running in her two-and-a-half-room apartment: tragic tear-jerkers, professional screamers. But she wants to become a teacher. Incidentally, Ruth is the only one of the eight associate judges who, though drunk at the time, inquired about me: "And what became of the shitass who buried the cast-iron spoon?"

Because, to tell the truth, Ilsebill, the action always revolved around me. I made messes and squirmed out of trouble with lies. I repressed and forgot. How gladly, there in the presence of Ms. Schönherr, or Helga Paasch, or Ruth Simoneit, I'd have confessed that I was to blame for everything: I did that. And that. Chalk Mestwina up to me. I and I alone am responsible. I still take the blame. Here I stand, yes, here I stand, a man, though damaged and since then intimidated by history. . . .

How I see myself

In mirror reversal, more obviously crooked.
The upper lids beginning already to sag.
The one eye tired, drooping, the other crafty, awake.
So much insight and inwardness
after all my loud and repeated
barking at power and those who wield it.
(We will! It shall! It must!)

Look at the pores in the cheeks.
I am still or again good at blowing feathers,
and like to make definite statements about matters that are
   still up in the air.

The chin would like to know when at last it will be allowed
   to tremble.
The forehead holds firm; what the whole thing lacks is an
   idea.
Where, when the ear is covered
or committed to other images,
do crumbs of laughter nestle?

The whole is shaded, darkened with experience.
I have put my glasses aside.
Only from habit does my nose sniff.
On the lips
that are still blowing feathers
I read thirst.

Under the udder of the black-and-white cow
I see myself drinking
or snuggled against you, O cook,
after your bosom hung
dripping over the fish stew;
you think I'm handsome.

Oh, Ilsebill

*Now that you're burgeoning. Though there's still noth-*ing to see. But even now my mouth is filled with intimation. I have a foretaste. We might, you and I, that is—for I am burgeoning with you—two gourds—make plans. A future for three and more. Wishes. Who hasn't got wishes? You need a noiseless dishwasher. Good. I'll buy you one. And travels, of course. Why not? To the West Indies, like it says in the folder. And right after the event—end of June, you say—fluttery dresses, the kind that wrinkle and don't drip dry, outrageous pants, sexy sweaters. Everything you want. No more dishwashing problems. And in the garden (next to the graveyard) I'll grow a gourd-vine arbor for us, like the one that throve for three summers during the Thirty Years' War on Königsberg's Pregel Island, across the way from the tavern. In it sat my friend Simon Dach when he wrote to me (Opitz von Boberfeld) in delicate rhymed verses, "Here let me live at ease amid the beans and peas. Breathing fresh air I lie. Peering through vines, as clouds pass swiftly by . . ."

A gourd-vine arbor would give us and our little boy when he gets here a place to think in without having to travel, because a gourd-vine arbor would be just perfect for you and me. And they grow quickly. And I with a kitchen knife will—as Simon Dach wrote, "I used to carve my sweetheart into the gourd"—scratch your fairy-tale name in a still-tiny (but soon, with you, to burgeon, Ilsebill) gourd. There in the twining arbor we shall read the papers to see what a mess the world is making of itself: on the Golan Heights, in the Mekong Delta, and now, too, in Chile, where there was a glimmer of hope. Thus camouflaged with gourd leaves and biblically secure, I could commit my lamentations about the rising price of copper and the Yom Kippur War to writing; just as my friend Dach wept aloud in his gourd-vine arbor when Field Marshal Tilly broke all records in the field of Catholic atrocities: "O Magdeburg, shall I keep silent now! Of all thy splendor what remains to show?" If the truth be known, the Thirty Years' War—as seen from a gourd-vine arbor—has never stopped, because a gourd-vine arbor, though—as the prophet Jonah found out—it doesn't amount to much, is nevertheless a fit place from which to see the world as a whole with all its changing horrors. That lovely vale of tears.

No, Ilsebill, no need to travel. We can stay right here and, as soon as I've bought gourd seeds at Kröger's next door and planted them in mid-April as per instructions, bring the whole world into our arbor and think it over thoroughly. The soft facts and the dreams hewn in stone.

Even the past will cast shadows as the plant shoots up, so that, while you are burgeoning along with the gourds, I shall be able to tell you about Awa Wigga Mestwina, with whom, though the gourd was then unknown in our country, I often sat in similar twining arbors: with Awa under giant ferns tied together to form a sunshade (how I counted and re-counted her hundred and eleven dimples), with Wigga under a roof plaited from willow withes (how I had to tell her over and over again about my brief participation in the Gothic migrations). And when I visited my Mestwina in her little kitchen garden, we sat among broad beans whose tendrils entwined lasciviously above us. We drank fermented mare's milk with *Glumse*, and ate flatbread and smoked codfish line. And Simon Dach lived in much the same way with his friends Albert, Fauljoch, Blum, and Roberthin in the gourd-vine arbor on Pregel Island: "Good Lord, how oft we sat up late eating choice morsels off a plate, drinking and singing. . . ."

Let's do just that, Ilsebill: eat Wilster Marsh cheese off our knives, wash down the dry rye bread with red Palatinate wine, as night falls and I squeeze a swelling gourd with my right hand and with my left hand your body. Later on I could sing to our little fellow, if it's a boy, "Pray, baby, pray, the Swedes are due today." And never again would I run out on you in the stupid way men have; no, never, because there'll be no more quarreling and no dishwashing problem, but only loving kindness creeping up the latticework. Happiness as fragile as the prophet's gourd, which God—it might also have been the Flounder—caused to be gnawed by a worm. Our happiness, Ilsebill, will last all summer. And the summer after. And every summer: we with the little fellow—he'll soon be walking—happy, at peace, shaded by the past, far from the world, and therefore seeing it as a whole with its horrors and counterhorrors, as friend Dach saw

Magdeburg—the defoliated Mekong Delta, the empty shoes in the Sinai desert, the daily terror in Chile; but grateful, because the fragility of the gourd-vine arbor protects us, and because you can safely bear the fruit that is rounding out your belly.

But you don't want to be twined with me, hedged in by me. "You and your shitty idyll!" you say. "You and your fancy subterfuges. Wouldn't it just suit you! To grab me out of the nest like a bird's egg whenever you need me. And expect me to be fascinated by your eternal comtemplation of your navel. Have I," you say, "studied like mad so I could live out here in the country with kids and cooking in a gourd-vine arbor, even if it does amuse me once in a while to shake out your pillow? No!" you say. You want to travel. The Lesser Antilles and other travel folders. Visit London and Paris and meet interesting people who have met interesting people in Milan and San Francisco. Discuss the liberation of women from top to bottom. "And besides," you say, "we need a noiseless dishwasher and an apartment in town. Gourd-vine arbor? Why not say 'pisspot,' like in the fairy tale? I'd sooner have an abortion—in London, for instance—than let you twine me in out here. It's the old male-chauvinist trick. The gilded-cage routine. What's wrong with you? Tired?"

Yes, Ilsebill. A little. Tired of times we live in. But if you say so, I'll book a charter flight. Maybe to the Lesser Antilles. And the dishwasher goes without saying. Same for the interesting people in London and Paris. About the apartment in town, well, I'll think it over. You're right, right again. Obviously the liberation of women cannot be properly discussed in a gourd-vine arbor. Just an idea of mine, because back in the seventeenth century my friend Simon Dach . . . And because you, too, Ilsebill have always longed for a little more security.

At the end

Men who with that well-known expression
think things to the end
and have always thought them to the end;

men for whom not possibly possible goals
but the ultimate goal—a society free from care—
has pitched its tent beyond mass graves;
men who from the sum of dated defeats
draw only one conclusion: smoke-veiled ultimate victory
over radically scorched earth;
men who at one of those conferences
held daily since the worst proved to be technically feasible
resolve with masculine realism on
the fine solution;
men with perspective,
men goaded by importance,
great exalted men,
whom no one and no warm slippers
can hold,
men with precipitous ideas followed by flat deeds—
have we finally—we wonder—seen the last of them?

What I don't want to remember

The word too many, rancid fat, the headless trunk: Mest-
wina. The way to Einsiedeln and back: the stone in my fist,
in my pocket. That Friday, March 4, when my hand dipped
into the strike fund. Frost flowers (yours) and my breath.
Myself as I ran: away from the pots and down the slope of
history. That Father's-Ascension Day not so long ago;
naturally I was there. Shards while washing dishes, substituted
meat, the Swedes on Hela Peninsula, the moon over Zuckau,
the man behind the gorse bush, silence, the deaf man's yes.
The fat and the stone, the meat and the clutching hand, silly
stories like this one . . .

One prehistoric day, after the usual mythological chit-chat,
the Flounder, to enlighten me at last, told me about King Minos's wife, how she lusted for her husband's white bull and
how a certain Daedalus, known for his ingenuity, made her a
disguise of cowhides, whereupon she was mightily mounted—a happening which, as we know, resulted in the Mino-
taur and other myths. And in conclusion the Flounder said:
"This must not be taken as an incident of purely local impor-

tance. Others can learn a useful lesson from it. The whole continent is concerned. Don't forget that Zeus in person took the offended King Minos (in the form of a bull) to the maiden Europa. So that Queen Pasiphaë's *faux pas* contributed to the fall from power of the Cretan women. The Zeus principle, the male seed, the pure idea triumphed. Because the bull-headed monster was a living illustration of matriarchal profligacy. The same demonstration might be made in the Baltic bogs. It doesn't always have to be a bovine; it can just as well be a white elk bull. Supposing a robust young specimen goes roaring through the bogs night after night as if he had had his fill of cranberries and willow shoots and never wanted to mount a normal elk cow again, but had made up his mind to engender a Baltic myth instead. Now here's what you must do to stimulate the three-breasted Awa. Mold clay into arm-long elk pizzles, bake them as you would pots, set them up in a circle where she can't help seeing them, and let them take their effect."

I did just as he said. The erect ceramic pizzles amused Awa and her companions. When the sun was shining, they cast wandering shadows. A new cult began with a game: the women aimed quoits plaited from willow twigs. Soon the pizzles were adorned with wreaths of flowers. Jumping over them with outspread legs became a women's sport. (How obscenely they screamed. How gross were their jokes even then. What fun they got out of my modest attempts at sculpture.)

The Flounder called me the Baltic Daedalus. On his instructions I made a convincing disguise of elk skins cut to Awa's measure. I steamed elk calves' sweetbreads for Awa. And as though under contract to the Flounder, the white elk bull roared night after night in the Radune bogs nearby.

But Awa didn't want it. She had no desire to make myths. With three suckling breasts, she was sufficient unto herself (and unto us as well). She flew into a neolithic rage when I (urged by the Flounder) attempted with prurient stimulus words to arouse her interest in the bull. No, she cried, no, thus inventing a word with a future. All my pottery elk pizzles had to be smashed. (That's why our region has yielded no phallic idols.) And for punishment I was tied to the rear end of a tame elk cow—we had domestic animals by then.

For the whole of a neolithic day I tried to prove myself. But I didn't accomplish anything. I don't remember begetting any monsters. I have no desire to recall the disgrace that followed, but I have to, because I am writing and must therefore write that Awa and her women made an annual spring festival out of my shameful ride on the elk cow. Under the full moon she and her companions (borrowing from my sartorial art) dressed in the hides of elk cows. We Edeks had to deck ourselves out with the palmed antlers or elk bulls. We were required to emit a sound resembling an authentic mating cry. The tails of elk cows were tied to the women, and under those uplifted tails they offered themselves. Can you imagine anything more bestial?

"These loathsome fertility rites!" cried the Flounder. "Aren't you ashamed of yourselves? All this mating without father right. At this rate you'll never produce a masculine myth, a Jovian head-birth."

Then he went on about the refinements of Minoan culture. He spoke of palaces with many rooms, of open staircases with dimensions appropriate to royal dignity, of water pipes and steam baths. And while he was at it, he reported the birth of the young hero Heracles. As though in passing, he deplored the fact that a seaquake (or the wrath of Poseidon) had recently destroyed the capital city of Knossos—"But King Minos was miraculously saved!"—and raved about hand-sized bronze statuettes representing men with bulls' heads and marketed as far afield as Egypt and Asia Minor.

"That, my son, is what I call lasting influence! Way back at the beginning of the first palace period, Queen Pasiphaë's offspring was bumped off by a certain Theseus. Not without the help of the artist Daedalus. Only the other day I told you the story of the ball of wool and the tragic sequel. What was the poor girl's name again? Was she left to rot on some island? Nobody remembers. But those Minoan bronzes and charming terra cottas, all with the same motif—they were paradigmatic; they set a style."

And he made me a present of a clay figurine the size of a little finger, which like his other gifts he toted unimpaired through the seas in his branchial sac. The little man with the bull's head: one more item in my growing art collection, which I kept hidden in an abandoned badger's burrow, until it was stolen by my friend Lud and hauled away God knows where. Then the Flounder persuaded me to make figurines of comparable mythical import and to perpetrate a pious fraud as a way of keeping my disgrace out of history.

And so I did. I molded seven or nine hand-sized little men surmounted by elk heads with palmed antlers, baked them secretly, and buried them near the suburb of Schidlitz, where in the twentieth century more or less fortuitous excavations were to produce neolithic finds. Unfortunately the archaeologists, two dilettantish schoolteachers, were not as careful as they should have been. All the palmed antlers, which had previously fallen off, were dug under, so that the art historians never took them into account. Misinterpretations followed. Talk of neolithic pig-men. *West Prussian Folklore* magazine spoke of surprisingly early domestication of pigs in the marshes of the Vistula estuary. Experts argued over shards that were unique in the Baltic region, for on the Flounder's advice I had made the figurines hollow, molding them around my left middle finger in the Minoan manner.

But my terra cottas did not transmit a myth. Nothing came of them but controversial footnotes and a doctoral dissertation which in the year 1936 propounded the thesis that my "pig-men" were early Slavic testimony to the existence of an inferior, degenerate, worthless race.

The odd part of it is that later on (though the Flounder doesn't know it) Awa did let herself be mounted by an elk bull. In the moonlight. Without the disguise I had tailored. All three breasts bared. Down on her knees she offered herself. Her fat rump glittered as she wagged it. Playfully he approached. A young bull with a white hide. He didn't assault her violently; his approach was more on the timid, experimental side. His light-catching palmed antlers. His hoofs on her shoulders. Affectionately at first, nuzzling at the back of her neck. Then everything fitted, nothing was impossible, it happened naturally and didn't take long. Hidden in the willows, I looked on. Heard Awa cry out as never before. I wanted to preserve the image, her three breasts hanging down into the cranberries. But I forgot, swept memory rubble (other stories) over it. I didn't want to remember, because when, after the usual length of time, no god with palmed antlers but a girl was born, she resembled Awa all right but showed indications of four breasts, the equipment of an elk cow, whereupon she was killed forthwith with a stone ax.

"No!" cried Awa and wielded the ax. "This is going too far. Let's not overdo it. Three are enough. Who knows what the little wench would do later on. No crimes against nature, if you please. We don't want tongues to wag."

And she ordered us to hunt and spear the white elk bull. We ate the young flesh crisp-roasted with mashed cranberries, as though nothing had happened. But now at last I was enlightened and started looking for a word for "father."

That, by the Flounder's time reckoning, was shortly after the Argonauts embarked on their voyage and two years before the Seven marched against Thebes. But in our country the women kept their power. Whether Awa or Wigga or later Mestwina, they prevented legendary voyages and campaigns. They survived without special emblems of power, and when we tried to make history (or trouble) they stymied us with their womanhood. Wrath gave way to quietness. They made us tread lightly. Smiling injustice triumphed. The caprice of the mighty prevailed. Enslaved by their mild forgiveness, we remained domesticated. (I stop in my flight to sue for peace over the phone. "Sure, sure," says Ilsebill. "It's all right. So you want to come home? If you behave, you can be the father. Let's forget all about it. Get a good night's sleep. Then we'll see.")

The things I can't help: drought, killing frost, rainy spells, cattle plagues, times of famine when nothing but manna grits was available and not enough of them. What I would like to distract people's attention with: how I developed the charcoal industry and invented Baltic bricks. What I could not for a long time bring myself to say, but the Flounder said: You must. What I don't want to remember: how I marched southward up the river with the Goths, leaving Wigga, who kept our horde on short rations, alone with her pots.

My first flight. (Typical male escape syndrome, still common to this day: beat it quick around the corner for a cigarette or two and never come back; gone forever.) We pushed off in May. In other parts of the world the calendar said 211. Everything was in flux. Germanic restlessness. The first migrations. Marcomans, Herulians, and our Goths with their inborn wanderlust pushed off, invaded new lands, made history. I, too, was sick of being Wigga's charcoal burner, also condemned of late to farm work, beet raising. Like the red-haired fire-eaters whose god Wotan the Flounder had taught me to worship in secret, I wanted to sit in a manly circle deliberating, to strike my shield in assent, to lower my shield in dissent, I wanted to be a man: A man consulted, a man with rights and a voice, with sons to come after him. A man exempt from daily chores and hungry for distant places. I wanted to be gone, to quit the trivia of daily life. I wanted to live dangerously, to discover, prove, fulfill myself. Weaned at last, I wanted to know the meaning of honor victory death.

"Clear out," said Wigga. She sat—a giant when seated—under the willow-withe arbor, molding small dumplings of herring roe, herring milt, and oatmeal, and dropping them into foaming fish broth. "Clear out!" She'd have no trouble replacing me as her charcoal burner and in my other functions as well. She rolled the dumplings on her flat, hard thighs, two at a time, clockwise and counterwise. Just as Ilsebill can say, "Have it your way," so Wigga, not even comtemptuously, said, "Just clear out."

But I didn't get very far, only three days' journey up the river. There, where later, much later, the town of Dirshau (Tczew) with its railroad bridge across the Vistula was supposed to be strategically important, I already had blisters on my feet, the uncouth Goths frightened me, I cast longing looks homeward and cursed the Flounder who had advised me to shove off. (To make matters worse, my friend Ludger treated me like a groom, with beastly condescension.)

I often wept while cooling my feet in the river. Without a roof over my head I felt sorry for myself. We Pomorshians were not admitted to the meeting of their *Thing*. I had to curry their horses, scour their short-swords with ashes, comb out their women's matted hair, and put up with their arrogant sulking after bouts of mead drinking. When they had chewed too much fly agaric soaked in mare's milk, they became murderously aggressive and thrashed us in place of enemies who had not yet materialized. Once I heard them deliberating under a solitary oak tree when and how they would sacrifice me and a few other Pomorshians who had run off with them to their hammer god, Thor: spitted on lances.

And when, in the place on the east bank where later Graudenz (the fortress) was to be situated, I was kicked by a horse, cut in the thumb by a short-sword, reviled by Gothic women as a "Pomorshian swamp rat," and buggered in broad daylight behind a gorse bush by a Goth (during which operation he didn't even remove his boar's-tusk helmet) who was always drunk or under the influence of fly agaric and had so few teeth that I had to chew his dried meat for him, I beat it, I lit out for home, limping and weeping, heard myself and

107

the river and the screech owls crying "Wigga," and more and more desperately, "Wigga!"

In short, I soon proved unequal to history. They could smash up Rome without me; Wigga's dumplings of herring roe and herring milt meant more to me. I was only too glad to be her charcoal burner again and take care of her brats, a few of whom were plainly by me. Let the Flounder call me a milksop; I went back mouthing apologies: Never again, a lesson to me, sincerely regret, just punishment, I'll be good, I'll never . . . But Wigga didn't scold. If she had only scolded, punished me, sent me out to the beet fields with a hoe. Her vengeance was no brief outburst, but long-lived, though after each of my public self-criticism sessions she would say, like Ilsebill the other day on the telephone, "Let's forget all about it. Water under the bridge."

For in the presence of the assembled clan—we were not yet a tribe—I had to confess my crimes: I had been unforgivably bored with charcoal burning. I had taken a treasonable pleasure in mocking the sedentary Pomorshians to the Goths. I had bartered Pomorshian charcoal much too cheaply to the Gothic armorers. Seduced by my friend, I had become addicted to fly agaric as a substitute for the prohibited and eradicated dream root. And I had betrayed Pomorshian secrets (the instructions for making *Glumse*) to this same Ludger.

Then I had to make a public statement abjuring the frivolous emotion of wanderlust. Then I had to swear to the female council of the clan that I would never again aspire to conquer or die, that is, to make history. Then I had to renounce something that I had bombastically termed "paternity rights." Then I had to report how many blisters I'd had on my feet at the beginning of the migrations, why the hair of the Gothic women is always matted, in whose honor I and other Pomorshians were to be spitted on lance heads, how young Ludger's stallion had given my left knee such a kick as to stiffen it for all time; and I had to exhibit the scar on my right thumb all around the circle. (It was my forced renunciation of the fungus poison muscarine that introduced the fly-agaric habit among our people.)

The one thing that I concealed repressed forgot was what that stammering Goth who never took off his boar's-tusk helmet did to me behind the gorse bush. The disgrace of it. The gap in my narrative. The empty speech-balloon. What I didn't want to remember: how he manhandled, chewed, and licked me, rubbed me with rancid fat, and then ripped in with his old man's war club, so deep. . . .

But Wigga knew. When I ran away from her, she sent two swift-running girls after us, and by the time I came hobbling back, they had told her the whole story in every detail. That was probably why, later on, when I lay with her, in her, armed and legged around, she would often say, "Well? Isn't this better? Isn't it a lot better this way?"

Ilsebill will soon be in her second month. Her time interval, which makes her difficult, is the only thing that counts. I (her charcoal burner) stand beside her or flee downstairs through the centuries until the Flounder, as though he were still talking to me, catches me up: "There's nothing you can do about that, my son. It's her nature, which is stronger and always right. Your fatherhood holds you tethered. The women will always have you there. As your Ilsebill knows."

Then he advises me to buy more paper. Once you put it in writing, he says, everything looks normal. "Only written matter," he pontificates, "can stand up against nature. The written law wins out almost every time. And what you don't want to remember, what you don't even want to think of again—because of the disgrace—will be as good as forgotten once you get your story in print." And, clearly wishing to be quoted, he concludes, "Men survive only in the written word."

All right. I admit it, I betrayed Mestwina, my Mestwina. But there was more ambiguity in what I did than a simple sentence reveals. For, you see, I was her (and the tribe's) head shepherd, and at the same time I was Bishop Adalbert, who had come to convert us heathen. As a shepherd I supplied her kitchen, and as an ascetic I spurned her cookery. It was I who stole the cast-iron spoon from the supply hut of the Bohemian baggage train; and it was I, the later canonized bishop, whom Mestwina slew with the cast iron. If I remember right, I was too cowardly to cut the bothersome missionary's throat with my razor, though Mestwina asked me time and time again to do her the favor. But as a bishop with a desperate craving for blows, I let myself be murdered without resistance, for even as a choirboy I had often confessed the wish to die a martyr's death and be canonized later on.

Shepherd and bishop—for the first time I sojourned doubly; I was split, and yet wholly the pagan shepherd and wholly the Christian zealot. Life was no longer as simple as under Awa's care or in Wigga's shadow. Never again, except in relation to Dorothea or to Amanda Woyke the farm cook, neither of whom allowed of ambiguities, have I been able to wear myself out so completely at one with myself: unsplit and for life. For my time with Billy doesn't count. And in Maria's eyes I'm nobody.

Maybe my present Ilsebill will pin me down, cure me of my ambiguity. "No nonsense," she says. "The kid's got to know who his father is. What do you mean, a fiction? No subterfuges, if you please!"

Anyway, I was dead as a bishop when I took my sheep smell to the main Bohemian tent and betrayed my Mestwina.

But why? It was all so well hidden. After the murder, which had gone off smoothly, with no other sound than the gentlest of sighs, she and I threw the cold, stiff, and later to be canonized Adalbert (in other words, myself!) into the swift-flowing Radune. Far downstream, on a sandbank in the ramified estuary of the Vistula, a region often raided by our hostile Prussian neighbors, the holy man's bloated corpse was washed ashore and found by Polish mercenaries who had been looking for him for the last five days. I craftily buried the cast-iron cooking spoon. It seemed reasonable to assume that the heathen Prussians had murdered Adalbert. A courier was already on his way to report the event to the king of Poland. The date given was April 12, 997. The whole episode scratched into history: one more saint.

And I like a fool had to go and testify to the truth. The Flounder advised me to expose the fraud. "My son, it's your duty to speak out. I know how devoted you are to your Mestwina, but you will have to sacrifice her. For the first time you lazy, unconscious Pomorshians, who have never done anything to prove you existed, have really taken action; with a political murder you enter history, you set a classical date— what eloquent ambiguity: he was killed on a Good Friday!—and already you're trying to wriggle back into a state of Stone Age innocence. You stand idly by while the glory goes to those barbarian bandits the Prussians. Too cowardly to confess like men. Go to them and say aloud: Yes, you Christian knights! It was one of us, Mestwina, our queen. He desired her, he lusted after her. She killed him to make our people conscious of their historic role. Make a saint of Adalbert, if you will, but we of Mestwina's tribe stand unbowed, like men. We don't want the cross. Our goddess is Awa. She is related to Demeter, Frigga, Cybele, Semele. Great figures, every one of them. Every one of them throve long before your cute little Mother of God. In short, we've got religion already!"

I spoke to the Bohemian prelate and the Polish knights as steadfastly as the Flounder had counseled, but without the provocative vocabulary. I can't remember asking Mestwina for her approval of my history-charged confession. She might have been generous enough to consent. But more probably she would have laughed at me, called me a fool, thrashed me when I talked back, and to get me out of the way sent me under guard to far-off beaches to look for amber.

Secretly I went to the Bohemian knights. They listened impassively but recorded only Mestwina's blasphemies against the crucified God and that part of my confession which showed her to be a still-active priestess of Awa. That fitted in with her drunkenness. And it fitted in with her habit of chewing fly agaric both raw and dried. After all, she had killed Adalbert, while drunk or on a muscarine trip.

The next day the Bohemian knights, presided over by the prelate Ludewig, condemned Mestwina to death by beheading. For us they ordered immediate forced baptism, but continued (undeterred by my confession) to maintain that Adalbert had been killed by the heathen Prussians. It would have been difficult if not impossible to canonize the bishop if he had been murdered by a woman, for according to the papal canonization bull, no one can become a martyr through the act of a woman. After all, the bishop's Bohemian retinue knew that Adalbert had tried several times to mortify his carnal lust inside Mestwina. The Polish knights whispered jokes about the pious Bohemian's penetrating technique of conversion. If so much as a suggestion of Adalbert's pleasures on the bed of leaves had found its way into the canonization file, we can rest assured that there would have been one saint the fewer.

In his testimony before the Women's Tribunal, the Flounder justified his bad advice with neo-Scholastic eloquence. "It was quite in the spirit of the Hegelian dialectic, dear ladies. I, too, regret deeply that in those days women were denied the right to produce martyrs. I said to myself: From a subjective point of view a certain Mestwina may have bashed the

111

bishop's head in with cast iron, but objectively, before the judgment seat of history, it had to be men, the heathen Prussians. And so, quite logically and only in apparent defiance of the facts, all the historical sources give the Prussians credit for making church history on this occasion."

It was supposed to have been done near Tolkmit. With a wooden oar, which later became a relic. Don't make me laugh.

What next, friend Flounder? It's all down in black and white: the rutting roar of false and authentic elk bulls, what the character with the boar's-tusk helmet did to me behind the gorse bush, how I sang to Christian knights. So am I exculpated? Is my guilt any lighter? And the rest of my shame? Intricately tied packages that want to be unknotted. Because after we were forcibly baptized as Christians, our sin only increased. And to Ilsebill I said, "With that Dorothea, who suffered from migraine in the High Gothic period as you do at present, I often knelt penitently on peas."

There she comes with blood on her dress. Which I don't want to remember. But I must.

The second month

~~~~~~

How we became city dwellers

At the time when Mestwina, drunk but with unerring aim,
stuck down Bishop Adalbert, the region of the Vistula estuary
was inhabited, apart from us old established Pomorshians on
the left bank and the Prussians who had settled on the right
bank of the river, only by vestiges of peoples that had passed
through: Gepidic Goths, who had been pretty well stirred together with us Pomorshians, and Saxons who had fled from
the missionary zeal of the Franks. Slavic Poles trickled in
from the south. And the Norse Varangians raided us whenever they felt like it. They built forts to ward off Prussian in-
cursions but were unable to keep the Prussians from settling
to the west of the river valley. The name of the Prussian
chieftain was Jagel, a precursor form of the Lithuanian
Jagello. And that is why, later on, when the city was founded, the hill came to be known as the Hagelsberg.

As early as Mestwina's day the Varangians had disguised
themselves as Pomorshian fishermen and murdered Jagel in
his robber baron's castle. But not until the Polish duke Boleslaw Chrobry threw the Prussians back to the right bank of
the Vistula was Varangian replaced by Polish rule. For we
became subjects soon after Mestwina slew Adalbert, whom
the Polish duke had enlisted as a propagandist, and subjects
we remained.

Boleslaw had the wonder-working corpse taken to Gniezno,
where it is held in honor to this day. Our territory was ele-

vated to the status of province and named Pomerania—Pomarzanie in Old Polish—after us, because we lived by the sea. With friendly condescension, the pious Boleslaw called us Pomorshians "Kashubs." We were allowed to appoint our own governors, who, though they all harked back to Mestwina's womb, soon learned masculine forms of authority by observing others. Their daughters and daughters' daughters continued to hand down mother right, but only in secret.

The first of our princes to become known by name was Sambor, who founded the Oliva Monastery and endowed it with privileges—exemptions from custom duties, the right to collect tithes. His son, Subislaw, was sickly and died young, whereupon his uncle, Mestwin I, became prince of Kashubian Pomerania. He barely had time to make his daughter, Damroka, an abbess, and with her at its head found the Convent of Zuckau, where just six hundred years later Amanda Woyke directed the farm hands' kitchen of the Royal Prussian State Farm, before the Danes invaded Pomerania and took possession of it for ten years, at the end of which Mestwin's son, Swantopolk, sent them home and appointed himself duke of Pomerania, which displeased the Polish duke Lesko. In truly masculine style the two dukes fought a battle to the death near Gniezno, which was won by Swantopolk and cost Lesko his life. But in the course of his unsuccessful warfare against the still-heathen Prussians, who would not yet recognize the Vistula as a borderline, the now independent Kashubian duke made the same mistake as the Poles: he, too, called the Teutonic Knights, who found themselves unemployed at the end of the Crusades, from Palestine to Kashubia. They came and made a clean sweep of everything Prussian. In the end they defeated Swantopolk several times and took his firstborn son, Mestwin II, prisoner. Set free, Mestwin allied himself with the dukes of Brandenburg against his brother and cosovereign. Thereupon the Brandenburgers dug in, and Polish help was needed to drive them from the city of Danzig, or Civitas Danczik, founded in 1236 near the Pomeranian fortress and endowed with Lübeck law.

My Giotheschants, Gidanie, Gdancyk, Danczik, Dantzig, Danzig, Gdańsk: you were a bone of contention from the very first. We Pomorshian fishermen and basket plaiters stayed in the old Wicker Bastion under the protection of the fort and went on eating grits as we had always done, whereas the new settlers, mostly from Lower Saxony, bearing such names as Jordan Hovele, Johann Slichting, lived as merchants and artisans behind the city walls and ate pork sausages with white beans.

The last Pomeranian dukes—Mestwin was childless—and the Polish duke Przemyslaw battled the margrave of Brandenburg and the Teutonic Knights, for so history ordained. In addition, the Polish governor Bogussa battled the Kashubian Swenzas until, on November 14, 1308, the grasping Teutonic Knights seized the city and occupied the fortress, from which vantage point they were able to control the city. Though the Polish Wladislaw bewailed the loss of his Pomeranian possessions and appealed to the faraway emperor and pope, he was obliged by the terms of the Peace of Kalisch (1343) to cede Pomerania.

My Dorothea to be was then three years old, and I, her Albrecht to be, though already of marriageable age, still clung to the apron strings of my Pomorshian mother, Damroka, who had married a city man. My father, the swordmaker Kunrad Slichting, raised me to be a swordmaker, too—a trade with a future. The city was growing quickly and wanted to be defended with handy two-handers.

The smooth synchronization of a German command to hold on at all costs, of the Soviet army under Marshal Rokossovski, and of English pattern-bombing was needed before the hardy product of burghers' toil, handed down from generation to generation for hundreds of years, amassed here behind grandiose façades, there in humbler dwellings and workshops, could fall a victim to a generalized conflagration that smoldered for a whole week, and before all Danzig, its angular Old, Charter, Lower, New, and Outer Cities, down to the brick walls of its big and little churches, could be leveled as though for all time. In the pictures preserved in the archives, the destruction looks total. In aerial photographs, the phases of the city's expansion in the early Middle Ages are discernible. Only at Leege Gate, near the Church of Saint John, between the fish market and Roaring Brook Street, around Saint Catherine's, and in a few other places, a fragment or two of something or other had been left standing by chance. But in the very next pictures to be taken, those shown in the memorial exhibition at the Charter City Rathaus, bricks are being cleaned, rubble shoveled off the perrons of Frauengasse, vestiges of façades on Brotbänkengasse are being propped up, and the stump of the Rathaus tower is being encased in scaffolding.

And thirty years after the fire a young man, speaking into a clip-on mike for the Third Television Program of North German Radio and Television, related how the Inner City had been eighty-percent destroyed. Pan Chomicz, the municipal conservator, is responsible for rebuilding the historical Danzig, which has now become the Polish Gdańsk.

That morning I had flown in from Berlin-Schönefeld airport on an Interflight propeller plane and landed in the new airfield, where only three years before my great aunt's Kashubian potato fields had still been moderately productive. What I had in my luggage: gaps in my manuscript, still-undocumented assertions about my earlier life in the days of the High Gothic Lenten cook Dorothea of Montau, and advertisements requesting information about the curly-headed kitchenmaid Agnes Kurbiella and mentioning Baroque allegories in which she figures. Objections on the part of the Flounder. My Ilsebill's wishes. And I also had with me a catalogue of questions, for I was planning to sneak away from the TV cameras and meet Maria, who is still canteen cook at the Lenin Shipyard. "Tell me, Maria. How was it in December 1970? Was your Jan there when thirty thousand workers sang the Internationale as a protest against the party? And where exactly was your Jan when the police fired on the workers? And where was he hit?"

When they started shooting the picture, it all became two-dimensionally present. Historical quotations—1813, the fire on Warehouse Island—became slips of paper to be thrown away. We had set up our three lamps, the sound equipment, and the camera in the restored treasure room of the Charter City Rathaus. For all his assurance about the facts, the municipal conservator stood somewhat embarrassed amid the paneled walls and the Dutch sink-of-inquity paintings. Behind him hung town painter Anton Möller's *Tribute Money,* its top forming a half circle; Jesus and his New Testament bunch are standing in manneristic agitation where in actual fact the wide Renaissance Green Gate (Gothic: Koggen Gate) should be separating the Long Market from the bank of the Mottlau. In the direction of the Rathaus, the Long Market narrows into the slightly crooked Long Street, leading to the High Gate. Möller painted this allegory against an urban backdrop immediately after his *Last Judgment;* this was in 1602, which like the year preceding was a plague year. (But no winding sheets are hanging from the windows. No overloaded carts enliven the background. No doctor is making his rounds with mask and rattle. Nowhere is straw being burned. Warning yellow is nowhere predominant.)

The conservator, obviously used to such tasks, looked straight into the camera. Neither one nor the other hand took refuge in a pocket. With economy of gestures he called Möller's painting a document, important for the reconstruction of the center of the devastated city and comparable to Canaletto's paintings, which had been helpful to the rebuilders of the old city of Warsaw. "Astonishing" was his word for the proof provided by this painting that as late as the early seventeenth century nearly all the patrician houses on the Long Market were still graced by Gothic masonry and gables, exceptions being the Artushof and the broad Renaissance-style burgher's dwelling across from the Rathaus.

The conservator was explaining with a smile why, in rebuilding, not the Early Gothic, less cost-intensive form but (shunning no expense) the elaborate Baroque façade had been chosen—when in mid-sentence our three lamps went out. A fuse had blown in the Charter City Rathaus (reconstructed in accordance with Möller's picture). The house electrician was called but did not come. Instead, unannounced and walking ahead of his party, Prince Philip of England entered the historic hall. Some regatta or horse race seems to have been the occasion for his semiofficial stay at the Grand Hotel in Zoppot. Visibly exhausted by his tourist program, Prince Philip winced at the sight of the camera. Although the prince could scarcely have been mistaken for anyone else, our sound technician, whose name was Klaus—"Hey, Klaus! Go get it, Klaus!"—wanted to put him to work as the long-awaited electrician. Before this mistake could be converted into an anecdote and make history, the prince and his escort were gone.

Later on at the Monopol café, I noted: what if Copernicus or the hoary-headed Schopenhauer had turned up and been mistaken for someone else? Ah, those great historic moments! If you've seen one, you've seen them all. Come to think of it, Peter the Great, Napoleon, and Hitler had been in the same place. Toward the end of the fourteenth century, the English nobleman Henry Derby, long before becoming a character in

Shakespeare, arrived here with his retinue to join in hunting down the heathen Lithuanians, a popular Christian winter sport at the time. From Dorothea's husband, the swordmaker Albrecht Slichting, he bought a gold-plated crossbow, and never paid for it. A story fraught with consequences. Unpaid bills wherever you go.

While waiting for the right electrician—and because television filming involves so many timeless interruptions—I toddled off down the stairs of history (all the while talking coexistence with our Polish Interpress attaché) until, in the fourth decade of the seventeenth century, I saw town painter Möller's kitchenmaid, then pregnant, coming toward me across the Long Market.

Agnes Kurbiella has bought a soup chicken unplucked. It persists in being winter, although we were shooting the TV documentary in fine late-August weather, at the height of the tourist season. In January 1636 Agnes is in an advanced state of pregnancy; King Wladimir VI has taken up residence in the Green Gate, thus lending a date to the town's history. There he is chatting with the Silesian diplomat and poet Martin Opitz von Boberfeld. The king is planning to engage Opitz as secretary and court historian. The admiral of the Polish navy, a Scotsman by the name of Seton, is also present, as are several local patricians with well-fed faces over stiff ruffs. Now that the armistice with Sweden has been extended, the king wants Opitz to negotiate a new schedule of harbor fees. Just a little while ago the poet had submitted some fresh-baked iambics praising the sovereign as a prince of peace, and it is plain that they have won the king's favor. The patricians assure the poet—recently driven out of Silesia—that here he will be able to live in peace. During a pause in the official deliberations, Admiral Seton, a Catholic well versed in letters, tells the Protestant Opitz, half in amusement, half in real concern, how his sons' tutor, a young man of the Lutheran persuasion and like Opitz a fugitive from Silesia, is sick in bed because the festivities of the hard-drinking burghers—who couldn't very well help drinking to the successfully concluded treaty with Oxenstierna's commissioners, could they?—have been too much for the young man, who is hardly more than a boy; so "at the moment he's writing bilious sonnets, proclaiming that all is vanity. His verses might
118

interest you, all the more so since young Gryphius doesn't write in Latin but in plain German."

But, worn down by the long war, Opitz is too distraught to ask for copies of the sonnets. Through the tall windows of the Green Gate, he looks out (in the perspective of town painter Möller when he painted his *Tribute Money* picture) on the wintry Long Market, across which the kitchenmaid Agnes Kurbiella in an advanced state of pregnancy is still plodding through the wet snow with an unplucked soup chicken. Now she is passing the Rathaus, where three centuries later we are waiting for the house electrician. Now she is turning onto Beutlergasse. She is planning poached chicken breast in chervil sauce with oaten porridge. Soon Agnes will be cooking light, easily digested dishes for Opitz. That summer, shortly before the departure of the recovered Andreas Gryphius, the diplomat takes up lodgings in the house of the preacher Canassius. By then he has entered the service of Sweden as well as Poland: a double agent.

When the electrician finally arrived and our three lamps, plugged into an auxiliary line, were again shedding light on the municipal conservator and on Anton Möller's *Tribute Money* scene on the Long Market, I had just left the seventeenth century with its varied religions and was back in the early fourteenth century—May 17, 1308, to be precise—watching the execution of the sixteen Pomeranian knights, all members of the widely ramified Swenzas family. One reason for my interest was that it is still uncertain whether the Teutonic Knights, as their first contribution to the history of the city of Danzig, beheaded only the sixteen Swenzases, or whether they butchered over ten thousand urban Pomorshians, all of whom lived between Saint Catherine's and the old Pomeranian castle, which soon became the castle of the Teutonic Knights. The Pomorshian part of the Old City was still known as the Wicker Bastion. For when the sixteen nobles or ten thousand Pomorshians were executed, there was still no Charter City, although the Teutonic Knights had already decided to found a new city governed by Culm law to the south of the Pomorshian settlement.

In any event, more than sixteen Pomorshian-Kashubian counts and less than ten thousand Kashubian-Pomorshian inhabitants of the Wicker Bastion were executed or otherwise slaughtered. History, to be sure, tells us with chronological precision that on February 6, 1296, the Polish king Prze-myslaw was murdered in Rogasen, but the figures for the mass slaughter remain crude guesswork; just as in recent times I was unable to find out by random questioning of resident Poles (which I kept up as long as we were shooting the television film) how many workers at the Lenin Shipyard in Gdańsk and how many shipyard workers and longshore-men in nearby Gdynia were shot in mid-December, when the police and army of the People's Republic of Poland were or-dered to fire on the striking workers. For fire they did, and not without effect. Maria lost her Jan, who, when hit, was quoting the *Communist Manifesto* through a megaphone. What ideological contradictions provide whom with dialecti-cal (in the Marxengelsian sense) entertainment when in a Communist country the state power gives orders to fire on workers, thirty thousand of them, who have just been singing the Internationale outside the party building in proletarian protest?

In Gdańsk five or seven seem to have been killed outside the shipyard entrance on Jakobswall, where the shipyard al-ready had its entrance in the old days; in Gdynia the exact number—between thirty and forty killed—has been kept secret. Details were not discussed. The whole thing was sub-sumed and deplored under the head of "December Events." And the Teutonic Knights were also quick to proceed to the order of the day. The facts and *Realpolitik* argued in their fa-vor: Pomorshian Danzig was allied with the Swenzases and Brandenburgers against Lokietek, king of Poland. On the ad-vice of the Dominicans, who were loyal to the king, his bur-grave Bogussa had called on Plotzke, the provincial master of the Teutonic Knights, for help. The Knights had sent a bat-talion, which fought its way into the besieged fortress, forced the Brandenburgers to withdraw, drove Bogussa and his Poles out of the fortress, and seized the Pomorshian Swenzases. Af-ter the Swenzases were beheaded, and after a massacre whose victims cannot be numbered, the Knights made the inhabi-tants remove the city's walls, bulwarks, and other fortifica-tions, and finally demolish their many defenseless mud huts and few frame houses. What was left of the population dis-persed and a few years later was again decimated, by the famine that raged throughout Europe. And when, beginning in 1320, the first streets of the new Charter City were laid out at right angles to the Mottlau—Brewer Street (later renamed Dog Street), Long Street, Brotbänkengasse, Holy Ghost Street—only sparse remnants of the Old City population, but large numbers of Lower Saxons, driven eastward by hunger, came to settle there. And at the same time the Wicker Bastion section, outside the new Charter City, rose up anew on the ruins of the old Pomorshian settlement.

By then no one spoke aloud of the sixteen Swenzases and ten thousand massacred Pomorshians, for one thing because a papal commission of inquiry had set its seal on the report of the Teutonic Knights' procurator. Don't forget that all the people involved were Catholics. Just as the strike and uprising of the longshoremen and shipyard workers of Gdańsk, Gdynia, Elblag, and Szczecin and the order to fire given the police and the People's Army were all of the Communist persuasion. In any case, the municipal conservator kept thoroughly silent about the events of December 1970, all the more so because no striking shipyard workers interfered with the reconstruction of the Charter City (in accordance with the plans of the Teutonic Knights).

When our lamps were functioning again, the conservator spoke into his clip-on microphone, informing the public that in the Old City only the churches had thus far been rebuilt, most recently Saint Bridget's, but that the Charter City, with all its principal streets, had been reconstructed as a self-contained unit inside the city wall built in 1343: it was bounded by the Old City Ditch on the north and the Outer City Ditch on the south, on the east by the stretch of the Mottlau extending from Cows' Gate to Hawkers' Gate, and by the reconstructed city wall to the left and right of Long Street Gate on the west.

The director of the television crew made an announcement in TV jargon: "Cut statement in front of Möller painting. Tomorrow nine o'clock sharp Saint Catherine's spires; statement. Followed by Saint John's, Hawkers' Street, artists from Vilna, and so on . . ."

I went to look at some more shooting sites and couldn't remember for sure whether the brick house of the swordmaker Albrecht Slichting, built in 1353, was on Smith Street in the Old City or on Ankersmith Street in the Charter City. When construction on the Late Gothic house was begun (most probably in the Old City, come to think of it), Dorothea of Montau, the daughter of Wilhelm Swarze, a peasant recently arrived from Lower Saxony, was just six years old. (You see, Ilsebill, I have a better memory for flights of stairs, kitchen smells, winding sheets hung out of windows, and personal defeats than for places.) Be that as it may, after bubonic plague had paid its first visit to all our streets, thus lowering the price of city lots at a time when the price of everything else was going up, I, then a swordmaker, started building my house. We stayed in the Old City, and the amiable conservator, who is rebuilding only the Charter City on the most orthodox lines, was unable to help me locate my Old City building site.

I often went to Montau on my way to the Marienburg through the country between the Nogat and the Vistula, which had been freshly diked in (after the famine years). My father, the swordmaker Kunrad Slichting, who refused to die and kept me, his eldest, on short rations, not only supplied the Danzig headquarters of the Teutonic Order in the by then rebuilt Pomeranian castle; the grand master's chancellery, whose red-brick buildings were spreading out farther and farther along the east bank of the Nogat, also preferred to give its orders to Old City smiths and swordmakers, and the orders were ample, thanks to the losses incurred during the annual winter forays into the Samland Peninsula and across the frozen swamps of Lithuania.

Bearing richly ornamented hilts for the notorious two-handers, enchased scabbards, and silver-plated sword belts, I made the journey by way of Montau, the new village on the Island. There I saw how boiling-hot water was spilled on little Dorothea, seventh of the peasant Swarze's nine children, on Candlemas of the year '53 and how she nevertheless (as though by a miracle!) retained her fine skin and blue-veined transparency, while the careless kitchenmaid got perfectly normal burns on both feet.

I fell in love with the child Dorothea then and there. Thirty years of age and not yet a full-fledged master craftsman. I should have set up a household of my own in the Charter City long before. But not only were we closely watched by the Teutonic Knights; we were also under the thumb of my grandmother, who put pressure on her daughter Damroka to stay near the Wicker Bastion, the original settlement, which kept rising from its ashes. My father, you see, had married into a Pomorshian clan. Women have always kept me on a short lead. I've always tied myself to some Ilse-bill's apron strings. And when I fell madly in love with Dorothea, whom the boiling water had left unscathed, it was no different.

Lord, what qualities I saw in that slender child, who seemed to have been cut from silver leaf. Yet her graceful little questions—Had the Lord Jesus sent me? Had I brought her a message from sweet Jesus?—should have aroused my suspicions. And when the child (grown to the age of ten by that time) wheedled me into giving her a seven-chained scourge with a silver handle (inlaid with mother-of-pearl and amber tears) to play with (it had been ordered by the abbot of Marienwerder), my only feeling was one of affectionate amusement; for how was I to guess that Dorothea drew blood night after night by flaying herself through her hair shirt. And her first verses—"Jesu, guide my litel chaine, for my flesh hath chosen paine"—struck me as nothing more than fasionable babble. Only when at sixteen she was married to me yet did not become my wife, did I, in temporary possession of her utterly indifferent flesh, feel the scars on her back and the festering, still-open wounds.

In those days flagellation was pretty much what pot smoking is today. Especially the High Gothic youth, among whom I could no longer number myself, sought out the warming stench of the bands of flagellants, the percussion rhythms that went with their litany, their terrifying descents into hell, group ecstasies, and collective illuminations.

When in the year '63 Dorothea became my wife and went to live in town, the enormous building site that was to become the Charter City was often clogged with flagellants. Quivering female penitents who had come from Gnesen (Gniezno) lay exhausted amid the rising brick walls of Saint Mary's and Saint John's, and outside the Holy Ghost and Corpus Christi hospitals. For some years after the Teutonic Knights had built their Big Mill on the recently dug Radaune Canal, which circled the Charter City, fights were frequent between the millworkers and the obstreperous flagellants, more and more of whom took to camping between Saint Catherine's and the Big Mill. When I was looking for my Dorothea, I could always find her with the lepers in Corpus Christi Hospital or with the flagellants outside Saint Catherine's. Tramps and spongers, that's what they were! Who do you thing brought us the plague!

The mill is standing there again, the interior broken up into offices while pigeons nest in its skylight. Today the Radaune Canal is no more than a stinking gutter; too many of the Kashubian water holes have been dammed up and made into reservoirs.

Max had set up the camera across from the Big Mill, behind the hoarding of the Saint Catherine building site. There stood four pinnacles ready to be mounted, and the central bulb-shaped steeple. All expensively covered with copper, which, as no precautions were taken against air pollution, had already put on an attractive verdigris color, because fumes from the sulfur wharves not only corrode the reconstructed sandstone façades, but also blacken the copper roofing of the church towers.

The director sat me down (in a "natural" pose) beside a pile of scaffolding. At a signal from him, the concrete mixer some twenty steps away was set in motion. Pan from the spireless stump of the Old City Church tower to the boarded-up towers and verdigris-green central steeple. Then I came into the picture, pronouncing the concluding words of the documentary. As soon as the big crane arrived, I said, the day's work would begin. With the Big Mill of the Teutonic Knights and behind it the churches of Saint Catherine and Saint Bridget, an architectural unit dating from the fourteenth century had been reconstructed in the Old City, adjacent to the self-contained Charter City complex. This, I declared, was a noteworthy achievement. Poland had not disavowed its history. But now an appeal to the Hanseatic spirit of the people of Lübeck was in order, for the famous chimes of Saint Catherine's were hanging in Lübeck's Church of Saint Mary but belonged here in Danzig. The cause of German-Polish reconciliation would be well served by generosity on the part of the people of Lübeck. And so forth and so on.

What I did not communicate to the tube: that when I looked over the hoarding into the sixteenth century, over there in the spot where today only the barest fragments of the convent remain standing beside the Church of Saint Bridget, the abbess Margarete Rusch had survived the hair-splitting of the Reformation with her free-ranging Brigittine nuns and was putting more pepper into her cookery than ever; that right next door, though a century later, the poet and court historian Martin Opitz von Boberfeld was living in the so-called preachers' houses, until the plague carried him away; that here, outside the Charter City wall, the millers of the Big Mill joined forces with the rebellious brewers, coopers, and other guildsmen against the patrician order, though only the brewers of Jopengasse and Dog Street had serious reason to rebel, in so far as they were injured by the importation of beer from Wismar.

In any event, seven ringleaders of the artisans' uprising were executed in May 1378, among them an Old City miller; whereas the strike and uprising of the shipyard workers in December 1970 resulted not in the arrest of the strike committee of the Lenin Shipyard, but in the dismissal of Gomulka and several minor officials and in the annulment of the projected increase in the prices of staple foods. The shipyard workers' threat to send several large ships down the ways unfinished, if not to blow up the shipyard, was heard as far away as Warsaw: state power recognized worker power. The state gave in, made some changes in personnel, and announced one more "new policy." But if we consider the workers shot in Gdańsk and Gdynia in a political light, along with the executed ringleaders of the medieval artisans' uprising, then as now little was achieved: true, the Danzig patricians dropped their plan of importing beer from Wismar, but they granted the guilds no voice in the city council or court of aldermen; and the demand of the shipyard workers for worker management went equally unheard. All the same, one thing has changed in Danzig or Gdańsk since 1378; today the patricians have a different name.

We panned a couple of times in the direction of the New City and the shipyards: high-rise buildings, low-cost housing under construction, the air pollution that goes with progress the world over. While Max and Klaus were packing their tin suitcases and unwieldy equipment, I looked for traces of my High Gothic wife, Dorothea, near one of the side doors of Saint Catherine's. All I could see to remind me of her Lenten fare was nettles and dandelions. When she betrayed the projected uprising of the guilds to the Dominicans, I struck her narrow face with my swordmaker's hand, though I, too, had my misgivings about the uprising and took no part in it.

Actually Dorothea's betrayal had no effect, for the Dominicans were at odds with the patricians because the town councilors, with the help of their Culm charter, had confiscated all the grasping monks' landed property and turned the Dominicans into mendicants.

When we rose up, even the Teutonic Knights kept their peace. Feeling threatened by the power of the patrician merchants and by the Charter City's ties with the Hanseatic League, the Teutonic Order, on the advice of the aged grand master Kniprode, founded—to the north of the Charter City and the Old City—a New City, *"juvenile oppidum,"* with its own charter and, much to the irritation of the Charter City, its own port and maritime laws. Dorothea knew nothing of that. There was no politics in her piety. After the death of my mother, Damroka, I would have liked to establish myself in the Charter City, but instead, thanks to the Knights, who paid me well, built a new home in the jagged triangle formed by Brabank, Bucket Makers' Court, and the Lime Quarry, where the canalized Radaune follows Carp Pond, roughly between the Wicker Bastion and the castle of the Teutonic Knights, within convenient distance of the New City warehouses, to take the place of our old timber-frame house. We made liberal use of brick, which even in the Charter City only the patrician merchants and a few coopers and drapers could afford. Until the city ordinance of 1451 prohibited wooden buildings, even the main streets of the competing townships of Danzig were lined with thatched frame houses, and frequent fires encouraged new construction. The quarters adjoining the Mottlau long remained swampy and almost impassable; the main pillars of Saint John's (near Hawkers' Gate), which was built on marshy, unstable ground, are still sinking.

When we set up our camera in the ruins, the municipal conservator told us how much it had cost to reinforce the pillars, which though damaged by fire still support the vault, with concrete: eight thousand zlotys apiece. The price of tradition. History must be paid for. I stood amid unsorted fragments of façades and perrons, beside one of those pillars that had sunk so expensively. "Shooting. Twelve seven. Statement: Ruins of the Church of Saint John."

On orders from the conservator, two construction workers quickly gathered up the human bones that were lying about in the rubble. "Too macabre for the television audience," he said. Might give them the wrong idea. These bones hadn't belonged to German soldiers in the recent war, but to people in the Middle Ages, whose last rest had been disturbed when bombs had shattered the stone floor of the church. The dust particles dancing in the obliquely falling light, the fluttering of frightened pigeons, the grimaces of fragmented sculptures, gave the interior of the church atmosphere enough. Hadn't Andrzey Wajda shot several scenes of his world-famous *Ashes and Diamonds* inside Saint John's? And really you don't need bones in a documentary.

Yet it seemed distinctly possible that the bones of my swordmaker father, Kunrad Slichting, were here in this heap with those of other once prosperous burghers. For, with characteristic stubbornness, the old man had bought a burial plot in the Charter City. Who lies where: Opitz, dead of the plague, in Saint Mary's, his name incised in sandstone. In Holy Trinity worshipers and tourists are standing on the slab that covers the bones of Anton Möller the town painter. So many dead. Names of town councilors whom we hated at the time of our rebellion: Paul Tiergart, Peter Czan, Gottschalk Nase, Pape, Godesknecht, Maczkow, Hildebrand Münzer . . . And hardly sweeter to our ears were the names of the Teutonic Knights who lived during my High Gothic time-phase: Hinrich Dusemer, Ludwig von Wolkenburg, Walrabe von Scharfenberg. . . . And when, in December 1970, units of the police and army fired on workers in Gdynia and Gdańsk, the name of the commanding general was Korczynski. The order to fire is said to have been given by a party secretary named Kliszko. One Stanislaw Kociolek, a member of the Politburo, arrived from Warsaw and demanded drastic measures, because of which it became necessary to transfer him. Though the Communist Party of Belgium lodged a protest with the king, Kociolek was accredited as Polish ambassador to that country. An attempt was made to convert General Korczynski into a military attaché in Algeria. Shortly afterward he shot himself in the head. Only Kliszko kept his old job. The Lenin Shipyard is still called the Lenin Shipyard. Maria, who had lost her Jan, had her daughter baptized under the name of Damroka. And the priest of Saint Mary's who, toward the end of the fourteenth century, wanted to put my wife, Dorothea, with her mania for penance and flagellation, on trial for witchcraft, bore the name of Christian Roze. But Dorothea was not destined for the pyre.

127

Next the camera turned to a Charter City artist. In his attic studio a graphic artist, one Richard Strya, showed our camera some many-layered etchings, meanwhile speaking much too softly of Vilna, the place he had left to settle in Gdańsk. His etchings, dry points, and aquatints mingle gable and tower motifs with medieval flagellants and penitents. Groups struggling with the temptations of the flesh. Ecstasy in the midst of apocalyptic beasts. Lepers whose second sight is peeling along with their skin. Knights dominant in black iron. The miraculous in diagonal composition. Twilight apparitions. A wedding while the bells are advertising the plague. And in the crowded street, amid the early revolutionary tumult, my Dorothea over and over again, in rags, twined with snakes, maddened with fever, riding naked on a sword, etched into the plumage of the griffin, woven into latticework, open, vitreous, suspended from whirling strings, kissing the Flounder, and finally immured, cadaverous, already holy, worshiping, horrible.

In speaking, Strya concealed more than he explained. While the film technicians spent their time rearranging props, preparing cutting copy, and lighting the set, we, with the help of modest sips out of water glasses, drank ourselves back to the past. Strya and I can do that. We are contemporary only for the time being. No date pins us down. We are not of today. On our paper most things take place simultaneously.

While I was sitting on the perron of the Polish Writers' Club on Frauengasse, drinking my gritty coffee, and waiting for Dorothea in the shadow of Saint Mary's, Maria came by with her shopping bag. I paid for my coffee and joined her. Yes, she said, she was still canteen cook at the Lenin Shipyard. We mingled with the tourists. I told her something about our television film. Maria said nothing. The chimes from the Rathaus tower sounded a heroic theme. Amber ornaments were on sale in the shops on the perrons. Maria didn't want a necklace or a polished pendant. We passed through Our Lady's Gate and stood irresolutely on the Long Bridge. Fried fish was being sold on a barge that had tied up between Holy Ghost Gate and Crane Gate. You could stand at narrow tables; the fish were served on paper plates, and you picked them up in your fingers. For a small extra charge they would toss a dollop of Bulgarian ketchup on your plate. Behind the counter, women powdered with flour got portions of cod and mackerel and small Baltic herrings ready for the frying pan. The Mottlau smelled stronger than the frying fish. Gulls overhead. The ferryboat-restaurant was roofed with a ragged fish net. Tired from plodding through streets and looking for subjects to photograph, the tourists ate in silence. Maria wanted cod. We ate a portion each. Foretaste of rancid fat. She had had her corkscrew curls cut off. Just tell me this, Maria. But she didn't want to talk (not even under her breath) about the shipyard workers' uprising. That was over and done with. Talking wouldn't bring Jan back to life. Yes, the apparatchik from Warsaw had been called Kociolek. Once the price increase was rescinded and their wages raised, the men had calmed down. The one thing that made them gripe was a beer shortage—there'd been one recently. The girls were doing fine. A dead father was no drawback. The shipyard canteen had been renovated. No, nobody liked the food, but it filled you up. Oh well, who can laugh these days?

And because Maria clammed up after that, I told her about Dorothea. Maybe she listened.

By Gothic standards she was beautiful. Her strength of will defeated the laws of nature. What she wished for materialized, happened, came to pass. She could walk barefoot on the frozen Vistula; when in the heat of passion I came close to her in our warm bed, she was and remained a lump of frozen meat. For our nine little children, all but one of whom died young, she had hardly a glance; yet she could scratch the scabs of the lepers in Corpus Christi Hospital with fervor. My troubles didn't interest her in the least, yet how quick she was to uplift the soul of every no-good tramp who appealed for her sympathy (and my money); oh, how sensitive, how warm-hearted and wise she was when it came to appeasing the cares of total strangers!

At first we attended guild dinners and the weddings of the young master craftsmen together. We were present in our Sunday best when Saint Dominic's Market was blessed. But she in her beauty held aloof from my guild brothers, repelled by their robust, laical merriment, vexed because her sweet Jesus wasn't always first in everyone's thoughts—when the suckling lambs were being carved, for instance. Later she refused to take part in my social life; the boasting of the men, the finery of the women turned her stomach; she preferred to clothe herself in rags and mingle with the flagellants and penitents outside Saint Catherine's, where her girlish laughter could be heard above the din of the nearby Big Mill. In the midst of this riffraff she could be silly and giggly, merry, relaxed, free. But free from what? From me, from conjugal duties, from the need to care for her dying and oncoming brood. She was unfit for marriage. What else could she do but look for compensations, and become a saint if not a witch.

My fellow guildsmen made fun of me, and the swordmaker's wife was the neighborhood laughingstock. When we joined with the Charlter City goldsmiths to form a brotherhood and installed our little chapel in Saint John's, right next to the mason's altar, I had to supply my guild brothers with ritual vessels of silver before they would admit me. If only Dorothea had been put on trial! I'd have testified against the witch: "Yes, my dear Deacon Roze, doctor of canon law. She let our children, every one of them except Gertrud, perish miserably. . . ."

Little Kathrin liked to play with spoons and saucepans, mortars and pestles in the kitchen. She would look into all the pots, and the maids had to keep an eye on her. Not so her mother, who in the period after Ash Wednesday and on all Fridays cooked her penitential Lenten soup, made from codfish heads and root vegetables and thickened with barley. As long as the fish heads and mangels were foaming in the big kettle, she knelt with her back to the low hearth, her tender knees resting on dried peas. Her wide eyes glued to the crucifix, her fingers knotted bloodless, she saw nothing, and no maternal instinct gave her a hint when her second daughter, who must have been three and a half at the time and had been baptized at Saint Catherine's, also knelt down on a footstool, this one beside the kettle, but, far from being immobilized by religious fervor, fished with a big wooden spoon for the round white eyes in the disintegrating codfish heads, in the course of which operation—to make a long story short—little Kathrin fell into the great family-sized kettle. All the child could manage was one shrill scream, not loud enough to tear her mother, immersed as she was in her Jesus, away from the penitential peas. If the maid hadn't missed the child, she might have been boiled away completely without disturbing her mother's fervor long enough for a Hail Mary.

And so the swordmaker Albrecht Slichting lost his second eldest after his third youngest daughter. When the mother stood seemingly unmoved before the steaming bundle, I struck my wife, Dorothea, several times with my swordmaker's hand.

No, Ilsebill or Maria, or whoever else may be listening to me, Dorothea did not strike back. Quiet and frail, she endured my blows; her capacity for contrition was boundless.

The next day we shot Saint Mary's from all sides. Hightowering from Long Street through the shaft of Beutlergasse. From the Holy Ghost Street end of the Long Bridge across the Mottlau, the cameraman was able to squeeze the whole Gothic-brick mother hen into the picture. In two other long shots, from the Old City Ditch and across the dam, the Royal Polish Chapel leans against Saint Mary's and enhances its proportions. And in still another, taken at the corner of Outer City Ditch and Frog Pond, the colossal church steeple and the slender Rathaus tower, rising behind the gabled roofs of Dog Street, seem to be wedded forever. Of course we also shot the familiar postcard views from Jopengasse or the shady Frauengasse, depending on the position of the sun. And next day, when we visited the state workshops on the marshy flats between Werder Gate and the Vistula, our team set up its equipment on the roof of the wrought-iron works and captured the silhouette of the distant city. "This in itself," I said to the conservator, "makes it worthwhile. The expense, I mean."

In the evening I met Maria again. I called for her at the shipyard gate. The new canteen is right behind the entrance, where in Lena Stubbe's early-socialist days the workers' kitchen already had a way with stews. Maria appeared in sweater and jeans, in roughly the spot where a few years before her voluble Jan had been shot in mid-sentence. She had no desire to stop and briefly honor his memory. "But Maria," I said, "he was so gloriously mad. To this day no one has disproved his thesis that right after the final curtain of Shakespeare's *Hamlet*, Fortinbras led his troops to Kashubia and was defeated by Swantopolk!"

But Maria said only, "Today it was pork and cabbage." She was carrying a dinner pail along with her vinyl handbag.

We went to the central station and took the streetcar to Heubude. There wasn't much doing on the beach. We headed eastward and made barefoot tracks. The usual half-hearted waves. I found a few crumbs of amber in the seaweed. Then we sat down in the dunes and spooned up the lukewarm pork and cabbage. Like the rest of the shipyard workers, Jan had this same dish, cooked as usual with caraway seed, in his belly when, on December 18, 1970, the police shot him square in the belly.

"Those idiots," said Maria, "thought they could raise the food prices before Christmas." She showed me a photo of her girls, Damroka and Mestwina: pretty. Then we fell silent, each on a different subject, until Maria suddenly stood up, ran across the beach to the Baltic Sea, and three times shouted the same Kashubian word, whereupon the Flounder jumped out of the smooth sea and landed on her outspread palms. . . .

Quarrel

Because the dog, no, the cat
or because the children (yours and mine)
are unhousebroken, making them the scapegoats,
because visitors have left too early
or peace gone on too long
and all the raisins tend to be . . .

Words that are wedged into drawers
and are hooks and eyes for Ilsebill.
She wishes for something, wishes for something.

Now I am going.
Making the rounds of the house.
Boiled beef is stringy between the teeth.
Sky Night Air.
Someone far away, who is also making the rounds of the
    house. Again.

Only the pensioner and his wife
who live in the pisspot next door
have gone to sleep without a word too many.

Ah, Flounder! Your story has a dismal ending.

Dishwashing

My glasses are afraid of Ilsebill. When, for no reason
at all, or because the weather had changed, or because I had
emptied her pickle vinegar, which she sopped up as if she
was hooked, down the toilet, when suddenly something
snapped and sent her into a cold, jellied rage—how she
trembled and what an aftertremor went through her when it
was over—and with furious hand, no, with a dry dishcloth,
swept my whole collection of glasses off the shelves, or because I had said, "The trip to the West Indies is off," because
it so happens that pregnant women are entitled to drink
pickle vinegar and a case of migraine was brought on by a
Scandinavian high-pressure zone, I, the collector, looked
calmly on as more and more of my glasses, including special
favorites, were dashed to splinters, for Ilsebill had stopped
sweeping away the entire fine-blown contents of a shelf at
one stroke with a rag, and instead, while the slanting rays of
the afternoon sun played over the shards, was picky-choosily
smashing one glass at a time, because, to spare my sensitive
glassware, I had said an unequivocal no to a Bosch or Miele
dishwasher with six control knobs and a guarantee of minimal noise. "Not in my house!" I had cried.

One more example of how firmness persists (until it is
heroically abandoned). More and more serenely I watched
Ilsebill. Because I was liberated at last from my collector's
obsession, I slipped into a speculative mood and wondered
whether apart from obvious causes—the pickle vinegar, the
trip to the West Indies, the Scandinavian high-pressure zone,
the dishwasher—there might not be other, more obscure reasons for this clean sweep, this heroic housecleaning, for it
seemed possible that Ilsebill's rage was High Gothic in origin
and had been storing up ever since I exchanged her little sil-

ver scourge—a fine piece of swordmaker's craftsmanship—
for a Venetian (Murano) goblet. This beautifully blown
piece, which would have cost a fortune today, was the last to
be shattered by Ilsebill.

"Trying to make a witch or a saint out of me, whatever
serves your purpose at the moment. This isn't the Middle
Ages!" she cried as she hurled. She was as terrifying as that
Dorothea who has been pressing against my gall bladder
since the fourteenth century, and it's high time for her to
come out, the bitch!

Freed from my glasses, I considered the purchase of a
dishwasher with a Super-55 control panel. After twenty washings the supply of special soap must be renewed. Atlantic
low-pressure fronts countered the migraine effect of the Scandinavian high-pressure zone. All you have to do is load and
unload. Not even the Bosch company can guarantee that the
purchase of a dishwasher will put an end to our dishwashing
problem. Who's going to load and unload? I? Me?

Certain kinds of glass (hand-blown) are likely to cloud after three washings. Never again, as long as my Ilsebill is pregnant, will I throw pickle vinegar down the toilet. I put all the
shards—Bohemian, Venetian, lots of English Regency—back
on the shelves. As for our trip to the West Indies, travel folders came into the house: White, unpolluted beaches. Coconut
palms. Ice-cold fruit juice. Dark-skinned people and their
carefree laughter. Happiness included in the purchase price.
And there's Ilsebill stepping out of a charter plane, and blond-
ly she moves about in the range finder of an adman's movie
camera that is blind to anything but blond.

Actually my glasses are still beautiful as shards. Even broken they are sounder than we are. And to Ilsebill I said:
"This Dorothea—if you care to remember—owned a scourge
plaited from silver wire, which, when she was still a child,
was given to her by the swordmaker Albrecht Slichting. Probably on the Flounder's advice, because at the Women's
Tribunal this High Gothic utensil, with which Dorothea approached her Lord Jesus in times of migraine, has been repeatedly characterized as an instrument of oppression invented by men and therefore typical. Do you, too—tell me
frankly, Ilsebill—sometimes feel like inflicting, let's say, moderate pain on yourself with a little silver scourge? Or does
smashing glasses satisfy you? You seemed really liberated
when you were through. Free, yet affectionate. We can buy

new ones any time. I saw two Baroque, ostensibly Danish glasses in Hamburg—sinfully expensive, but what does it matter? They were related like you and me, irregular in different ways but harmonious. What do you say?"

No, says Ilsebill, meaning yes. Both glasses are still harmoniously safe and sound. It will be some time before the next Scandinavian high-pressure zone comes around. Sour pickles are no longer in demand. At the moment it's sauerkraut, raw, and plenty of it. The extreme humidity in the West Indies is said to keep migraine away. But the claim that the dishwasher—there it is at last, running full tilt—makes next to no noise is a swindle, Ilsebill, a pure swindle. And our dishwashing problem, the sum of all problems since Dorothea, remains unsolved. Your turn and my turn refuse to become *our* turn.

"No, friend Flounder," I said later, "that Dorothea I saddled myself with in the year 1356 was an ill-tempered bitch, and her way of doing me in is still in force; for my Ilsebill, now in her second month of pregnancy, is still capable of the same infectious moods. When angry she has only to pass an open bowl of milk and it turns. She casts her shadow, and good, solid glassware cracks. Stands mutely behind our guests, whose laughter has been bouncing around the circle as gaily as a ball, and the merriment seeps away, the ball springs a leak, the children are gathered up, in a muffled, time-to-go-home atmosphere someone starts looking for the ignition key, a dispirited voice says, 'OK, we'll be seeing you.'

"Our guests are gone. Nothing is left but that bilious look. The windows cloud over. The last fly, that last bit of summer joy, drops from the wall. A Central European migraine becomes a social event. And that's how it was—believe me, friend Flounder—when on your advice—'Marriage will multiply your possessions'—I married the High Gothic Dorothea of Montau."

According to custom the wedding should have gone on for three days. Not only had the members of the swordmakers' and goldsmiths' guilds donned their finery; also, the still-rich Island peasants had driven from Montau and Käsemark, in carriages drawn by two or more horses, although they knew that even on so joyful an occasion Dorothea would serve up an Ash Wednesday menu; from her childhood on, she had been repelled by meat dishes.

To make matters worse, Dorothea had also invited several patricians, a few Teutonic Knights, and her Dominican confessor and seated them at separate tables. Trouble was inevitable. The guildsmen were offended, and not just because of the meager fare—fish, leek soup, a bit of dried meat, lots of manna grits, and no fatted steers, suckling pigs, or stuffed goose with milky millet porridge. Still, the platters had an appetizing look, for they were garnished with sorrel leaves and raw beets. There were bowls of herring roe mixed with curds and dill. *Glumse* could be dipped in linseed oil. Anyone who wished to could sweeten his manna grits with plum butter.

But the atmosphere was homicidal from the start. The Teutonic Knights boasted of how many Lithuanians they had driven to the marshes in their last two winter campaigns! The Dominican monk deplored that the peasants of the Montau region in the Vistula loop were still enjoying their rich lands in sinful freedom from tithes. The patricians told the swordmakers to their faces that in other cities the authorities kept a tight rein on the guilds and cracked down at the slightest murmur. At first my fellow guildsmen put up with the insults; then their eyes bugged out with anger; then angry words flew from table to table. And immediately after the brawl that started when a Teutonic Knight crudely tossed a radish into the lap of the patrician Schönbart's smartly dressed daughter, the wedding party broke up. Only the peasants, who understood very little of what had happened, stayed on. Thoroughly embarrassed, I cleared the table. Dorothea laughed.

"I assure you, friend Flounder, it was no happy guffawing, but a tinny bleating, as if she had escaped from Satan's goat barn, that my Dorothea served up to the bewildered remnants of the wedding party for dessert. And later on they wanted to make a saint of that cold-blooded bitch. What a laugh!"

Here the Flounder tried to comfort me. Yes, the price was high, but not really too high, and it had to be paid. Only with the help of the Christian religion had it been possible to end matriarchal absolutism, and the whole basis of the Christian religion was alternate fasting and feasting. This had made it necessary to accept the bad part, the rule of the Dorotheas over household and kitchen.

"Yes, yes," said the Flounder. "Her eternal Lenten soups are not exactly inviting, but as a guildsman you can catch up at morning get-togethers and other social functions, where nothing prevents your stuffing and swilling till your liver swells up. Besides, your Dorothea is beautiful with a beauty that calls for something more than adulation. And healthy to boot, not nearly so frail as her inner visions and heavenly copulations would suggest."

"But that's just it, friend Flounder. Her health is crushing me. When I—all it takes is a sudden change in the weather—come down with a splitting headache and fits of tears, she, even in sultry weather, stays malignantly serene and keeps her mind clear for ascetic speculations. She can fast till she's as thin as a rail; her peace of mind doesn't lose an ounce. She paralyzes my wit. She cuts down my thoughts. She undermines my health. I can't stand the daylight any more. I can't bear noise—the croaking of toads, for instance. Ever since I married Dorothea, I've been ailing. My head, impervious to the din of the most infernal smithy, threatens to burst as soon as I hear or even suspect her light step, that witchlike shuffle. And when she speaks to me in her cold, long-suffering voice and forces me into a joyless system with her ascetic rules, I'm afraid to contradict her. I'm afraid of her compulsive rhymes that connect everything under the sun with her sweet Jesus." And I quote from my Dorothea's verses: "When Jesu swet my viol boweth, ah, what pleasur he bestoweth. . . ."

At that point the Flounder, my adviser and foster father, stuffed me full of medieval Scholasticism. He gave me lessons and taught me how to interpret crooked as straight, a pile of shards as sound glassware, darkness as an edifice of light, and constraint as Christian freedom. He expected me, thus educated and never again at a loss for an answer, to force my Dorothea into the Procrustean bed of my dialectic whenever in her robust way she became insufferable.

"Don't let her develop a logic of her own," said the Flounder. "What she doesn't understand will always be beyond her understanding. As a woman, you see, she's not really entitled to logic. Devise—I know you can do it—an edifice with many rooms but reduced dimensions, in which one thing follows from another and the next from the next. If she contradicts you, or says her instinct tells her that your projected edifice lacks an entrance or an exit, you have only to reply: My edifice is logical because the rules of thought have been correctly applied, and contrariwise. And if your Dorothea continues to argue, or if she goes so far as to oppose your system with sweet-Jesus jingles, then put on your friendliest voice and say: You mustn't overtax yourself, wife. This kind of thing is too much for you. Leave the general ideas to me. You look pale, tired. Your eyelids are fluttering. There are beads of sweat on your Madonna forehead, which doesn't get its beauty from thinking. Let me apply cold compresses. Let me draw the curtains. Everyone will pad about in stocking feet. Not a single fly will be left uncaught. Because you need absolute quiet. Because you've been under a strain. Because you're sick, my dearest, and I'm worried about you."

Thus transformed into a Scholastic and master of hair-splitting by the Flounder in several courses of lectures, I went to my wife, Dorothea, and, when she couldn't follow my logic, talked until my so-called migraine transferred itself to her. After that, of course, I was less responsive to the weather and seldom suffered from headaches and weeping fits. But whether my loss of migraine—the last of men's prehistoric prerogatives to have survived—brought me any relief, I venture to doubt. And answering to the Women's Tribunal, the Flounder, after the usual evasive replies (in which he quoted the Church Fathers in Latin), admitted that while his advice that I should talk High Gothic women into regarding migraine as a female prerogative may have enhanced their beauty, it hardly advanced the male cause.

In any case Dorothea, before or after her attacks of migraine, put me through a severe grilling. True, she spoke in rhymes and images, but if they had been translated into prose (the language of my Ilsebill) she might have said, "Now where did you get that? Don't tell me it came out of *your* thick skull. Talking me blind with your shitty logic. Who told you that stuff, and where?"

Thus cornered, I finally confessed, and betrayed the Flounder to Dorothea. True, I was able to warn him in time—"Watch your step, friend Flounder! She'll be coming to see you, and she'll want something"—but his feelings were hurt, and to this day he hasn't forgiven my betrayal; "breach of trust," he called it.

"Look at all I've done for you, my son! Weaned you from your Awa. Taught you to smelt metals, to mint coins, to piece together philosophical systems, to think logically. I have set your rational patriarchy above purely instinctual matriar-

138

chy. For the benefit of you men I invented the division of labor. I advised you to marry, and marriage multiplied your possessions. Most recently I relieved you of your chronic headache, whereupon, sorry to say, you turned into a jughead, garrulous and unreliable. You gave me away, betrayed my trust, told our secret to a chatterbox. From this time on marriage will be a yoke to you. From this time on the dominant male will have to pay tribute to his domestic battle-ax, if only in the kitchen, when it's time to wash the dishes. From now on, in any case, I shall advise you only in extramarital matters. Let her come, this Dorothea of yours with her Madonna face. I won't tell her a thing, not even if she kisses me."

It must have been just two years after our marriage. I wasn't present. The particulars didn't come out until the Flounder's trial, when he himself disclosed them to the Women's Tribunal. As it happens, the prosecutor bears a frightening resemblance to my Ilsebill, and not only to my Ilsebill. Both are sisters of Dorothea of Montau: that compelling look, that strength of will, which pinpoints everything, which can move mountains even when there aren't any. They are appallingly blond (all three of them), dedicated to strict morality, and possessed by the brand of courage that always barges straight ahead, come what may.

So Dorothea went to see the Flounder. She took with her all her beauty and untarnished youth. One Friday, after simmering Scania herrings in onion broth. She was wearing her long (penitential) gown of nettles, and her hair was unbound.

I had instructed her, "You must go into the sea. When you are up to your knees, call him several times, give him my regards. Then he'll come, and perhaps if you kiss him he'll tell you something. Wish for something; wish for something."

So Dorothea went straight down the beach, making tracks with her bare feet, to the shallows where the halfhearted Baltic waves petered out. Then she gathered her gown of nettles. Up to her knees she stood in the lazy water, and her cry smelled of herring as she cried, "Flounder, cum oute, ich wol kisse thy snoute."

Then she introduced herself as Dorothea of Montau, who belonged to no man, not even to her Albrecht the swordmaker, but only to the Lord Jesus, her heavenly bridegroom.

And if, she went on, she kissed the Flounder, she would not be kissing him but her sweet Jesus in the guise of a flounder.

And just as, in all my time-phases, the Flounder jumped up onto the palms of my hands, so now he jumped into my Dorothea's arms. She was so frightened she let a fart, which along with other particulars was cited before the Women's Tribunal and duly entered in the minutes.

The Flounder said nothing but offered Dorothea his crooked mouth. Her lips were chapped from the sea wind. With her long, ascetic fingers she held his white underside and his pebbly top side. It was a long kiss. A sucking kiss. They kissed without closing their eyes. ("Upon my lips the Flunder's kiss hath ravishèd my soul from heavenly blisse," ran a latter Dorothean rhyme.)

That kiss changed her. Her mouth was twisted, though just perceptibly, out of shape. It wasn't her sweet Jesus who had kissed her. With a slightly crooked mouth she immediately asked the Flounder how many other women he had kissed before her. And whether his kiss had tasted the same to those other women. And what made his mouth crooked. And how she could explain all this to her dear Jesus.

But the Founder gave no answer, and she thought him strange and terrifying. So she threw him back into the sea and called after him, "Flunder, ichab ykist* enow, telle me then, where sitteth thy plow."

When Dorothea came home, I saw that her mouth was twisted and no longer ran parallel to the axis of her eyes. From then on she had a sardonic expression, which enhanced her beauty, though the street urchins took to calling her Flounderface.

Next day, when I went to him for an interim report—Dorothea wouldn't say a word, but spent her time kneeling contritely on unshelled peas—the Flounder said, "Your breach of trust will have dire consequences; I liked your little woman, though, even if she did smell of herring. I like the hysterical flutter of her tongue. Her way of wanting more and more. Only her questions got on my nerves."

I warned the Flounder that Dorothea would be back, but he remained unruffled: why should that frighten him? Naturally she had something up her sleeve. Women always

* "I have kissed."—TRANS.

had a compulsion to avenge their defeats—that was their nature—but no skirt was going to hook him.

And, facing the Women's Tribunal, he said to Sieglinde Huntscha, the prosecutor: "But, my good woman, of course I was aware of the risk! Wasn't I running a still-greater risk when I voluntarily fastened myself to your ridiculous hook? I've always been attracted to ghastly blond hair like yours or Dorothea's. I can't resist it. Strong-willed women like Dorothea and yourself—may I call you Sieglinde?—have always made me—what's the expression now?—lovesick. Though within reasonable limits. You see what I mean—my fishy nature."

When Dorothea went back to the Flounder, she took a kitchen knife. "Flunder, cum oute!" she cried. The Flounder jumped. They kissed. But when he again neglected to answer her questions, she, in housewifely manner, cut off his head with a single stroke directly behind the pectoral fin. She smacked the quivering flat body down on the sand, spitted the head on her vertically held knife, and, her mouth made crooked by Flounder kissing, cried wildly, "All right, Flounder. You going to talk now? Answer me, Flounder! Answer my question: do you love me, Flounder?"

Before the Flounder speaks from the vertically positioned knife, I'd better remind you how he, my omniscient, too-too-clever adviser, had persuaded me to sublimate the purely instinctual relationship between man and woman in a higher sentiment, love, because love and its corollary marriage gave rise to a dependence that was most becoming to women: "Aren't they always wanting to be told whether and how much they are loved, whether love is holding its own or on the increase, whether there's a threat of love for some outsider, whether love is sure to last." Consequently, Dorothea's question, which up until then she had addressed only to her sweet Jesus and never to me, was a dependent question; for which reason the Women's Tribunal not unreasonably denounced the "institution of love" as an instrument of male oppression (although in the turn of phrase "catch oneself a man" the bait is tossed in the other direction).

In any case the severed Flounder head spoke gruesomely from the vertically positioned knife: "Aha! Snick-snack! That's the way! Most professional! But no one can cut me

141

apart. I'll find myself again. I will always be one. I don't care for your snick-snack love. And let me tell you this: because you want everything or nothing, because my kiss that makes you beautiful is not enough and never will be enough for you, because you demand love but refuse to give love unquestioningly, because you have perverted the sublime Jesus principle into the pleasure principle, and finally because you give your husband, Albrecht the kindly swordmaker, who loves loves loves you, nothing but your cold flesh, you shall have all of me, Dorothea, and right now. For a day and a night."

So saying, the Flounder jumped off the knife, joined himself to his flat body and tail, grew before Dorothea's horrified eyes into a giant flounder, lashed her with his fins and tail across the beach into the sea, deeper and deeper; as promised, he took her in with him.

Just like that. And in his testimony to the Tribunal the Flounder made himself perfectly clear: "In short, I took her in with me." "Typically masculine," said the women in disapproval, whereas the Flounder, addressing the selfsame court, had called Dorothea's "Do you love me?" typically feminine. He furthermore admitted that with his punitive action he had wished to provide an early formulation of his fairy tale, "The Fisherman and His Wife," later interpreted as misogynistic. But what happened under water he refused to tell. "Fact is, I'm the old-fashioned sort. A woman's reputation, don't you know."

When the smooth sea released Dorothea next day, I was waiting on the beach, worried and by then quite willing to forgive and forget. Slowly she rose from the sea and made tracks past me. In horror the gulls kept their distance. It didn't surprise me that her gown of nettles and her wheatlike hair had stayed dry. Yet she had changed again. Her eyes, too, were sightly out of kilter and at an angle to her crooked mouth. She came back fish-eyed, and that is how I shall sketch her when Ilsebill sits for me.

As she passed by, Dorothea said she now knew all there was to know but would reveal nothing. And since the Flounder also kept a tight lip before the Tribunal, it has never been divulged what happened at the bottom of the Baltic Sea in the early summer of 1358 to make my Dorothea omniscient. Nevertheless, Sieglinde Huntscha, the esteemed prosecutor, displays the exact same knowing, foreknowing smile with which Dorothea from that day on descended stairs, knelt on peas, and trod the streets—once again lost in her Jesus and very nearly a saint.

The household was a shambles after that. For the first time a maid walked out on us. Unwashed dishes piled up, attracted flies, brought rats into the house, stank. Ever since Dorothea, the dishwashing problem has been with us.

No, Ilsebill, even earlier, with the kneading and molding of clay, with the baking of the first bowls, jugs, and pots, in Awa's day, when she first developed ceramics, dishwashing began to be a problem. Though the timeless question "Who's going to wash the dishes?" received a clear and simple answer: the men. Naturally that arrangement didn't last. At some time or other (shortly after Mestwina), we just dropped the nasty, greasy things. It was beneath our dignity. The male cause was getting ahead.

Obviously to have the woman standing at the sink from morning to night is no solution. In this light your dishwasher, which we men invented, which you wished for, which you (absolutely) insisted on having, can be regarded as progress on the installment plan, with a year's guarantee. Maybe it will emancipate us all. From what? From blobs of mustard on the edges of dishes? From crumbling mutton fat? From desiccated leftovers? From disgust in general?

And so we delegate our dishwashing. Never again will an Agnes caress our daily cares away with her dishpan hands. Never again will Sophie sing her rabble-rousing revolutionary songs over heaped-up cups and dishes. There will only be your next-to-noiseless dishwasher. If only such a thing had existed after the Flounder released Dorothea and she made me wear myself out over a mountain of dishes.

Elaine Migraine

Sits in the cleft of a tree
and reacts to the weather over plucked—
tweaser-plucked—eyebrows.

When the weather changes
when high pressure brings blue sky
her silken thread snaps.
We all dread the change,
flit past on stocking feet, curtain the light.
It's said to be a pinched nerve—here or here or here,
something askew inside, no, still deeper.
An ailment that began with the last ice age,
when nature went through another shift.
(And besides: when the angel came clanking
too close to her, the Virgin, so it seems,
dotted her temples with her fingertips.)

Since then doctors have been making money.
Since then faith has been practiced by autogenic training.
That cry which everyone claims to have heard—
even old people remember their horror
when mother lay silent in the darkness.
The pain known only to those who have it.

Again it threatens,
cup strikes loud on saucer,
a fly perishes,
too close together, the glasses stand shivering,
the bird of paradise squawks.
"Elaine Migraine," sing the children outside the window.
We—who have no idea—feel sorry from a distance.
But she, behind lowered blinds, has entered the torture chamber.
Attached to her whirring wire, she grows more and more beautiful.

Libber, Libber

Between separate beds
at shouting distance
the sexes are being discussed.

Finish! Let me finish.
You've had your say.
You've been talking for centuries.
We'll simply cut off your sound.
You've got no words.
You aren't even funny.

Libber, Libber! the children call
as the fairy-tale Ilsebill passes.
She has smashed what is dear and precious.
With a dull ax she has
destroyed our bit of one-and-only.
She wants to be independent, entirely on her own,
no more joint bank account.

And yet there used to be a we—you and I,
with a double Yes in our glance.
A shadow in which, exhausted,
we were many-limbed, yet one sleep,
and on a photograph true to each other.

Hate forms sentences.
How she settles accounts, does me in,
grows out of her role, towers above me,
and has the last word! Finish! Let me finish!
And stop talking about Us and We.

Libber, Libber! said the signs incised on clay tablets,
Minoan finds (Knossos, first palace period)
which for long years were undeciphered,
mistaken for household accounts
or fertility formulas,
matriarchal trivia.

But from the very first (long before Ilsebill)
the goddess was agitating.

Like my Dorothea

Whether I rub against Ilsebill until she is pregnant, or meet Sieglinde Huntscha after a trying day in court—once again the Flounder has been floating belly up in protest—for a beer and so on, or whether with the help of my portable typewriter I finally liberate myself from Dorothea, it is always the same type that makes me weak and fluttery, that I fall for, that reduces me to strictly nothing.

The other day, while the Women's Tribunal was discussing my questionable behavior in connection with the uprising of the guilds against the patricians, I took out a soft pencil and drew in my sketchbook pictures of the prosecutor, first in profile while she was accusing the Flounder of having stood foursquare behind the hegemony of the patricians, then in three-quarter view, and finally fullface, in order to provide myself with a portrait of Dorothea. But all my sketches insisted on looking like Ilsebill: always that terrifying narrow face, dominant and ineradicable, as though their fathers, instead of being an Island peasant, an engineer, and (like Gerhard Huntscha, who was killed in North Africa) a career officer, had all been diabolical he-goats from Ashmodai's stable.

And if among the associate judges of the Tribunal I recognized my morose Wigga in Ms. Helga Paasch, and in the always crocked Ruth Simoneit my mare's-milk-guzzling Mestwina, then I can also be certain that the prosecution not only is being represented by Sieglinde Huntscha (and by you, Ilsebill), but is in addition giving my Dorothea certain advantages, which to be sure are counterbalanced by the eminently fair presiding judge, Ms. Schönherr. A mother figure with no smell of the stable about her. She who with few gestures transforms a madhouse, as the movie theater often becomes, into the best behaved of kindergartens reminds me time and again of my primal mother, Awa. In any event, she admonished the prosecution when Sieglinde Huntscha accused the Flounder of "playing the lackey to the ruling class of the moment."

The prosecutor was of the opinion that the Flounder had made use of me, Albrecht Slichting the irresolute swordmaker, to sow discord in the ranks of the guilds after they had resolved to fight the patricians. According to her, it was I who at the Flounder's suggestion had termed the grievance about the importation of beer from Wismar a problem that could bother only the city brewers and, in a pinch, the coopers' guild.

Sieglinde Huntscha spoke as if she had been there. In her version, swordmaker Slichting, shaken by the Flounder, had declared: "Of course I can't speak for the anchor makers, bucket makers, pitcher makers, and blacksmiths, but I find myself in duty bound to tell you that at their guild meetings, and those of the Scania mariners as well, I discerned no great eagerness to oblige the rich brewers, who are selling plenty of their black beer despite the competition from Wismar, by marching on the Rathaus with crowbars and sledge hammers. And as for the political demand for an equal voice in the decisions of the seated council, the general council, and the nine-man court of aldermen, you make me laugh. Trust a man who has traveled widely—such an arrangement exists nowhere. Would a tailor, for instance, claim to be a master of the diplomacy needed to defend the city's interests at the Hanseatic Council in Lübeck? And who will stand up more boldly to the Teutonic Knights, to that old fox Kniprode, for instance? Will it be the patrician Gottschalk Nase, who has been traveling from Bruges to Novgorod for years on the city's business, or Tile Schulte the butcher, who is incapable of even writing his name, let alone of defending the Danzig trading post in Falsterbo and the rights of the Scania mariners with sign and seal? Why, all this agitation is only a trick of the rich coopers, who are trying to worm their way into the city council. With the help of the guilds, of course. But once they're elected, you'll see them striding through Koggen Gate more arrogantly than the patricians. My advice, in short, is to keep out of it. The charter granted in accordance with Culm law has proved satisfactory. Rebellion won't get us anything but harsher tyranny."

The prosecutor called it a "triumph of the medieval proletariat" that the uprising had nevertheless taken place, even though it was led by a profligate patrician, the wood carver Ludwig Skriever.

"Poor deluded proletariat," the Flounder scoffed. "No,

dear ladies, my protégé, the not only honest but also experienced swordmaker Slichting, was right in eschewing acts of violence. I was not the only one to confirm him in his misgivings; his wife, Dorothea, who knew nothing of politics but made up for it in instinctive wisdom, gave him the same advice. 'Don't follow like a dumb sheep.' That's what she said. And consider what happened: Barrels of Wismar beer were emptied into the street. Ludwig Skriever, motivated by thoughts of private vengeance—the patrician Gottschalk Nase had termed Skriever's daughter a 'poor match' for his son because her dowry seemed insufficient—tried to incite the rebellious guildsmen to murder the town councilors and aldermen. And the patricians, who had the bargemen and carters with them, counterattacked. Even before Tile Schulte and six other ringleaders, including a miller's helper from the Old City, were executed, wood carver Skriever decamped. Long prison sentences were meted out. But the council wisely voted against importing Wismar beer. Whereupon the journeymen brewers presented Saint Mary's with a side altar and some silver liturgical vessels. And everything was hunky-dory. I'm sorry. Especially for our prosecutor's sake. Because to tell you the truth, the patrician order was vitiated by nepotism. A little new blood would have helped, a few representatives of the guilds—in the court of aldermen, for instance."

Sieglinde Huntscha sat as though sealed up. Sickened by so much half-truth. Only intense concentration could offer resistance to so-called reality and its stinking facts. That is how it was when a gray veil cloaked Dorothea's eyes; and that's how it is when Ilsebill, whose gaze is normally greenish, suddenly, as soon as reality makes its petty demands, exchanges her optical organs for glass eyes. At such times she says, "I'm afraid I don't see it that way. Just count me out." And as for Dorothea, whenever I mentioned the enshamblement of our household, her eyes looked far into the distance and her speech reduced itself to verses rhyming "Jesu dere" with "joy ant fere." And Sieglinde Huntscha spoke in rebuttal as softly and tonelessly as if she had wanted to prove that the art of speaking with sealed lips was still an art.

"Yes, defendant Flounder, you win. All the facts are on your side. In addition to Slichting, the appeaser trained by you, there was the provocateur Skriever, who, come to think of it, seems to have been friends with Slichting. The proletariat of the Middle Ages fell for your smooth talk. The time wasn't ripe yet. And your argument, which I can already hear coming—'the time is never ripe, not even today'—is irrefutable. If we look from the medieval uprising of the artisans against the patrician order to the uprising of the Polish shipyard workers against bureaucratic Communism, we cannot help seeing that then as now the time is always unripe. And yet, defendant Flounder, you're wrong. I won't say that the ludicrous gains achieved then and now—the council's decision not to import beer from Wismar, the rescinding of the rise in the prices of staple foods—refute your reactionary pessimism; no, what sweeps away your stupid facts is the proletarian principle of hope. Hope clears away the rubble from history. Hope frees the road we call progress from time-conditioned encumbrances. Hope springs eternal. For it alone is real."

These evergreen words were not red enough for the audience. Giggles were barely repressed. Someone called out, "Amen!" And if the Flounder had had shoulders, he would have shrugged them. As it was, he only said, "A respectable, ethically tenable view. You'll find similar ideas in Augustine and Bloch, both of whom I highly respect. You remind me, dear prosecutor, most charmingly of the High Gothic Dorothea of Montau. She, too, never ceased to hope for freedom, until at last, immured in her cell, removed from the world and its contradictions, she found freedom as she saw it."

Tumult in the movie house. Catcalls addressed more to Sieglinde Huntscha than to the cynical flatfish. Ms. Schönherr cast glances of ur-motherly appeasement. She said: "An interesting argument. It's true. What would become of us women if hope did not sustain us. But perhaps we should ask the Flounder to tell us why Dorothea Slichting, née Swarze, found freedom only in a cell removed from the world. Can it be that the patriarchal invention of marriage offered women no freedom? And when the Flounder recommended marriage, was he not aiming precisely at such deprivation of freedom? Was it not the Flounder who drove poor Dorothea into the one area of freedom that was open to her, namely, religious madness? Later on, men tried to make a saint of her, but for this there were purely practical reasons; it so happened—to mention the other form of freedom then available to women—that it would have been impolitic to burn her at the stake. The Flounder's main guilt had nothing to do with his

149

part in that preposterous uprising of brewers and coopers; your principal crime, defendant Flounder, consists in what you did to our sister Dorothea. Since Dorothea men have tried either to canonize women's desire for freedom or to laugh it off as typically womanish foolishness. Before sentence is pronounced, does the defendant wish to reply?"

The Flounder abstained. The atmosphere in the movie house recovered its bounce. Only Sieglinde Huntscha seemed downcast. How listlessly she rebutted the arguments of Ms. von Carnow, the court-appointed defense council.

Before the judges had finished deliberating, the Flounder began to wobble, and it wasn't long before he turned over and was floating moribundly belly up. When the court pronounced him guilty of helping to enslave women by promoting the institution of marriage, of ruining the life of Dorothea of Montau, and of urging her immurement and canonization for the sole purpose of providing the Teutonic Knights with a propaganda pinup in their war against Poland, the Flounder maintained his protest posture and gave no sign of concern.

I waited for Sieglinde outside the former movie house. I felt sorry for her. Or, rather, I wanted something. To tell the truth, my sympathy was real, but I also wanted to exploit it. "Join me for a beer?" Sieglinde joined me.

No, Ilsebill, I am not "talking like a typical male again." She could have said no. But she needed my sympathy, and she also knew that I wanted something.

We went to the Bundeseck café and had a few beers and a few schnappses. Not a word about Dorothea. First we talked at random of current events. Then we went back to the early days of our acquaintance. We've known each other quite a while. When I first met her, I was engaged to Sibylle Miehlau. And Siggie—as Sieglinde called herself in the early sixties—had hot pants for Billy, as Siggie, Frankie, and Maxie called Sibylle. They all had a thing about lesbianism, and they shook me off. The whole thing ended tragically with Billy's death. On Father's Day, '63.

So over beer and schnapps we talked of the old days. We could see them in perspective now. "We had no political ideas. Only a suspicion that things could be done differently. We tried desperately. Today I know better. I'm still in touch with Frankie and Maxie. But it's not the same. We've grown apart. Frankie still reels off her Stalinist slogans. Maxie used to be a Sponti; now she's on an anarchist trip. And me? That kind of childishness makes me sick. When, pretty much by accident, the three of us caught the Flounder last summer, we were still all right together. It was then that things got difficult. The Tribunal came between us. Frankie didn't see how I could cooperate with a liberal like Schönherr. If you ask me, she's been doing all right so far. At least she keeps things moving. And the way she came to my rescue just now when the Flounder was putting me down was tops. The way she swept that whole shitty artisans' uprising aside and brought Dorothea back into the picture. Yes, she's married. Three children. Even said to be happy. But what about you? What are you up to? So I've heard. A big blonde? Always looks kind of frantic? Yes, I think I know her. Well, let's hope your Ilsebill can put you in your place."

We drank a few more beers and schnappses. To Sieglinde's question "What are you working on now?" I replied very cautiously: "This Tribunal interests me. The whole subject interests me, not only as a writer, but as a man as well. Makes me feel somehow guilty. Comes in handy in a way. At first I was only going to write about my nine or eleven cooks, some kind of a history of human foodstuffs—from manna grass to millet to the potato. But then the Flounder provided a counterweight. He and his trial. Too bad they turned me down as a witness. The ladies disposed of my experience with Awa, Wigga, Mestwina, and Dorothea as ridiculous, if it wasn't pure fiction. You just turned me down flat. So what can I do but write write write as usual?"

She seemed to have stopped listening. She sat hunched over, smoking as if it were required, and slipping more and more into the cell of solitude, which Dorothea was seeking when as a child she spent her days in hollow willow trees, and which still helps Ilsebill to make, express, and carry out wild decisions in no time at all. Anyway, speaking out of her solitude after a last swallow of beer, Sieglinde suddenly said, "Come on. Let's go to bed."

Sieglinde lives on Mommsenstrasse. Two hours later we took a cab to Steglitz after what I wanted of her—"You've got the key to the movie house. I want a word with the Flounder"—had popped out in two sentences. She can't have been very much surprised. "I thought there'd be a little something else. One last fart, kind of." She had no objection and called the cab. No, Ilsebill, she wasn't pissed off or disappointed.

I'd expected it to be much more complicated. An alarm system, a room like a safe-deposit vault. But with two common keys Sieglinde unlocked the doors and locked them again behind us. Then she sat down in the former ticket office and said, "I'll wait here till you're through. Got two mark pieces? I'm running out of butts."

I gave her a pack of Lord Extra Longs, said, "See you later," and stepped into the dark hall, which did not smell of males. Only two red emergency lights to the left and right of the tub showed where the Flounder was spending his night. I groped my way forward as one does at the movies when the film has already started.

"Flounder," I said. "Maybe you remember. It's me. Me again. I caught you on a partly cloudy neolithic day. Oddly enough, in an eel trap. We made a pact: I set you free, and you promised to advise me, to help men out of their dependency, to serve the male cause and only the male cause. I'm sorry they've haled you before this preposterous Tribunal on that account. Unfortunately the girls wouldn't admit me as a witness. I'd have spoken in your favor. I'd be willing any time to argue for the historic necessity of your contradictory existence. If there is a *Weltgeist*, it's you. Great, the way you told those females off again today. The prosecutor was speechless. And take it from me, it's really something to stop the mouth of Sieglinde Huntscha. But that's just the type I keep falling for. Like that rotten bitch Dorothea some centuries ago. Right now a certain Ilsebill is doing me in. The stupid piece. Never satisfied. Always wanting something. That fight the other day about the dishwasher. And now she wants a second apartment in town. And what she has she doesn't want. And what she gets she doesn't like. Sure, but we both wanted her to be pregnant, we both wanted a child together, a quick-growing gourd-vine arbor. But I haven't come here to weep on your shoulder. I admit that you warned me and I fell in love with the witch from Montau all the same. Because she attracts me with her indolent, seemingly untapped vitality. I mean my present Ilsebill. You know how restless I am. How I need a pole to revolve around. A stationary pole. But she wants to move around, too. It won't do! Same with Dorothea, never gave us a moment's peace. Always pilgrimages. What was there for me to do in Aachen or a Swiss dump like Einsiedeln! Same with Ilsebill—always wanting to go places. The Lesser Antilles! 'Can't you be pious right here?' I'd say to Dorothea. Oh no. They all want to be free and independent. Or, like Dorothea, belong to no one but their sweet Jesus. As if there were such a thing as independence. I, at all events, have always had to slave for other people. The dear kiddies, for instance. It wears a man out. Uses him up. Flounder, I'm done for. Somewhere along the way we must have done something wrong. The women are getting so aggressive. Dorothea was already that way. And when Ilsebill lifts her voice to a heroic pitch, it literally makes me sick. Gives me the gollywobbles. Say something, Flounder! Look, I'm writing a book about you, for you. Or aren't we friends, aren't I allowed to call you Father any more?"

Of course I'd meant to be a lot calmer and more collected in addressing the legendary flatfish. But I was carried away, because the pressure had been mounting of late, no, for centuries, ever since my first marriage, to Dorothea Swarze. Even when I managed to evade marriage, the pressure had mounted from woman to woman. It had to come out some time.

The two red lights to the right and left of the zinc tub sufficed to show me that the Flounder had completely buried himself in the sea sand. Only his crooked mouth and slanting eyes were uncovered. Oh, how he had used to jump—I had only to call—up onto the palms of my hands! And oh, how he has spoken, advised, commanded, lectured, instructed me, what sermons he had preached to me: Do this, don't stand for that, listen to me, watch your step, don't pin yourself down, make them give you that in writing. Your profit, your privilege, your manly duty—you must continue to find them all in the male cause. . . .

Slowly the movie house with its challenging smell grew into an empty speech-balloon. I was on the point of leaving, no, taking flight. Then spake the Flounder.

Without modifying his position of repose in his bed of sand, he moved his crooked mouth. "I can't help you, my son. I can't even offer you mild regrets. You have misused all the power I gave you. Instead of turning the rights bestowed upon you to caring, charitable use, you have let hegemony degenerate into repression and power become an end in itself.

For centuries I did my best to hush up your defeats, to interpret your wretched failure as progress, to hide your now obvious ruin behind big buildings, drown it out with symphonies, beautify it in panel paintings on a golden background, or talk it away in books, sometimes humorously, sometimes elegiacally, and sometimes, as a last resort, only intelligently. To prop up your superstructure I have even, in my desire to be helpful, invented gods, from Zeus to Marx. Even in the modern age—which for me is only a second in world history—I am obliged, as long as this all in all entertaining Tribunal goes on, to season your masterful absurdities with wit and squeeze some meaning out of your bankruptcy. That is hard work, my son. Even for the much-invoked *Weltgeist*, there's not much fun in it. On the other hand, I'm coming more and more to like these ladies who are judging me. It never bores me to listen to Ms. Huntscha, my esteemed prosecutor. In retrospect I recognize—acknowledging my error in this point—Dorothea's solitary greatness. Ah, how she cried, 'Flunder, cum oute, ich wol kisse thy snoute.' What could she do but get rid of you? What but religious exaltation could have raised her above the monotony of marriage? Another baby, and still another! And what you tell me about your Ilsebill, how she puts you down and shakes you up, I like it, yes, I like it. She's amazing. All that untapped will to power—it gives me food for thought. Give her my regards. No, my erring son, you can't expect any comfort from me. Your account is overdrawn. Slowly, a little late perhaps, I have discovered my daughters."

I sat there for another short while. I probably said something; confessions, promises to reform, the usual male self-pity. But not another word out of the Flounder. He seemed—if that is possible—to be asleep. Groping like someone who walks out in the middle of a film, I left the former movie house and its smell.

Sieglinde said, "At last! Finished shooting the shit? He's a shrewd article, all right. But I'll put him down yet."

I revealed nothing but called the attention of my friend Siggie (honestly, Ilsebill, it's not a relationship to be taken seriously) to the absence of security measures. "There's every reason for your Tribunal to go on. You haven't half exhausted the case of Dorothea of Montau. But what will you do if somebody walks off with the Flounder?"

As she was double-locking the former movie house from outside, Sieglinde promised to do something about it. "You men think of everything," she said.

Like at the movies

A woman who strokes her hair
or leafs quickly through her loves
and can't remember.
She'd like to be a redhead for a while
or slightly dead or play a minor part
in some other film.

Now she disintegrates into fabrics and cutouts.
A woman's leg taken by itself.
She doesn't want to be—but to be made—happy.
She wants to know what he's thinking now.
And she wants to cut the other woman,
if there is one, right out of the film: snippety-snip.

The action proceeds: body damage, rain,
suspicion in the trunk.
Weekends leave imprints of men's shorts.
Hairy—hairless. Limbs limbs limbs.
A slap in the face promises something that later sounds real.

Now she wants to get dressed again,
but first be born out of foam
and stop smelling outlandish.
Skinny from eating too much yogurt,
Ilsebill weeps in the shower.

Scania herring

*The dignitaries had invited themselves. On master sword-*maker Albrecht Slichting's return home from a pilgrimage of more than three years with his wife, Dorothea, and his last remaining daughter, Gertrud, their marriage relapsed into a daily domestic hell, and members of the congregation found more and more grounds for complaint: Dorothea's spells of ecstasy during Mass were becoming too frequent and tumultuous, and that wasn't all. She was making a mockery of the Eucharist with her giggling and guffawing. The uses to which she put the word Jesus were ambiguous, to say the least. She wore wreaths of henbane on Candlemas. She collected the scabs and pus of the lepers in little bottles. She had a cross-eyed look, and if she wasn't possessed she had probably made a pact with Belial, for how else was one to account for the feverish twitching of her limbs and her hours-long spells of rigidity.

At first these accusations were uttered in private, but then they began to be aired more and more openly. Everyone sympathized with her old and ailing husband. It seemed that the once prosperous swordmaker was faced with destitution, for his wife had squandered his hard-earned fortune on frivolous handouts to riffraff from God knows where. His apprentices kept running out on him. Unable to sleep at night, the bewitched woman ran about the streets. She had been heard screaming for the Lord Jesus in a tone described as more lascivious than devout. Though her Dominican confessor spoke appeasingly of hard trials imposed on her by marks of divine favor, it was widely held that Father Christian Roze, who was also a doctor of canon law, ought finally to initiate proceedings against her. Sin was shamelessly masquerading as penance. Small wonder, with such goings-on, that the plague hung on and on. And despite last year's potential harvest the prices of rye, barley, and oats were going up again.

Urged not only by the burghers of the Old City but also by his congregation at Saint Mary's in the Charter City, Roze first spoke to the Dominicans, then consulted Abbot Johannes

Marienwerder and Walrabe von Scharfenberg, the district commander of the Teutonic Knights. The dignitaries decided to pay a visit to the Old City swordmaker, who enjoyed the esteem of the patrician council since, far from participating in the insurrectionary folly of the guilds, he had exerted a moderating influence.

Because political events (the marriage of the Polish Jadwiga to the Lithuanian Jagello) required the commander to absent himself for a short while, the visit, though announced in March, could not take place until the end of April. Though the four dignitaries came on a Thursday, and though it was well past Lent, Dorothea—after they had questioned her and listened to her husband—served them Scania herring, which were to be had cheap at the fish market, because the city of Danzig had a *Vitte*, or trading post, in Falsterbo in the Scania district of Sweden.

The Dominican Nikolaus wore cowl and cord. Abbot Johannes Marienwerder came in travel dress. The massive commander Walrabe wore the white mantle of the order with the black Teutonic cross and did not take it off until he sat down at table. Roze's ample gown and velvet cap made him look more like a scholar than a priest.

Before the meal, the swordmaker confirmed the gentlemen in their knowledge that when a ninth child had been born, after three had been carried away by the plague and five more had died from one cause or another, he, Albrecht Slichting, on his wife's demand and in the presence of the Dominican prior, had pledged himself in writing never again to share the bed of his wife, Dorothea, whereupon she had been granted the special privilege of partaking once weekly of the Lord's body.

After a detailed report on their pilgrimage of the preceding year to Aachen and to Einsiedeln in Switzerland—he pushed back his woolen shirt to show them a scar on his right shoulder as evidence of an attack by bandits—Slichting testified to, and Roze noted, Dorothea's desire for a separation; she had wished to remain in Einsiedeln and formally sever relations with her husband and eight-year-old daughter, so as to be free for, and wholly available to, the Lord Jesus. Despite the widespread disturbances before and after the Battle of Sempach, she had thought Einsiedeln a "forecourt of paradise."

In him, on the other hand, the rasping dialect and self-righteous bickering of the Swiss had instilled a gnawing homesickness. He could never have borne the thought of dying and being buried in the mountains. And so, when she kept demanding her freedom day in, day out, he had decided to give in. After signing a statement, to which his age—he was sixty-six at the time—lent credibility, that their life together was without sin, they had declared their willingness to separate. But before the chapel altar, when they were asked to confirm, he his wish to be separated and Dorothea her renunciation of the eight-year-old Gertrud, he, Albrecht Slichting, had several times uttered a loud "no," which, he was well aware, gave them every reason to call him a fool complete with cap and bells. Then the three of them had left Einsiedeln, although it was midwinter and most of the passes were closed.

Then Dr. Roze and Dorothea's confessor cross-examined him about the particulars of the hard journey home: Was it true that he and his daughter, Gertrud, had ridden long distances on horseback, whereas his wife walked the icy roads in paper-thin shoes? Why, when the ice began to break up as they were crossing the Elbe, had he instantly reached out to save his daughter, but—laughing scornfully, what's more!—let his wife be carried away on an ice floe, so that she was saved only by God's help? Could he testify that during the sea voyage from Lübeck to Danzig, Dorothea had several times committed acts of lewdness with a carved wooden figure of Jesus? Had he, on the journey homeward or since their return, noticed anything to suggest that his wife was engaged in witchcraft? And more of the same.

In defense of his riding while she walked every day for four weeks, Slichting cited his age and Dorothea's indestructible good health. He confessed to the laughter, but attributed it to his own terror and to his fear for his wife when he saw her swept away on the ice floe. As for the acts of lewdness with the wooden Saviour, he denied them but owned that the sailors on shipboard had talked and made jokes on the subject. Nor could he supply any evidence that his wife had engaged in witchcraft. True, she stirred the ashes of burnt coffin wood into her Lenten soups, but this she did as a reminder of man's frailty before the Lord God. And when, as happened now and then, she seemed to be worshiping her little bottles of pus, she was undoubtedly praying the Lord to intercede in favor of the lepers at the Holy Ghost and Corpus Christi hospitals.

The commander said nothing. As though in passing, Abbot Johannes Marienwerder asked Slichting about his affairs. When the swordmaker groaned, the abbot, with a glance at the commander, held out the likelihood of new orders. Now that the Lithuanian Jagello was king of Poland, it would be necessary to prepare for war. Then he asked Slichting as though in jest whether, if another opportunity for a separation from Dorothea should offer itself, he would again be fool enough to cry "no." At this the swordmaker made no bones about calling his marriage a hell, his wife a sanctimonious bitch, and the possibility of getting rid of her the last hope of his declining years.

The dignitaries, including the commander, smiled. At their request, the impoverished Slichting displayed what products of his craft he still had on hand: an enchased dagger in a silver scabbard, two swords of different lengths with gemstudded handles and bird's-head pommels, and a crossbow covered with gold leaf, which the English nobleman Henry Derby had ordered on his way through but neither called nor paid for.

They comforted the swordmaker—the mad Derby would surely be back—and told anecdotes about the young earl, who took as much pleasure in the annual winter campaigns against the Lithuanians as in fox hunting back home in England. Then there was talk of founding—the matter had been under discussion for years—a Brigittine convent on the Swedish model. The body of Saint Birgitta, or Bridget, had lain in state in a chapel beside Saint Catherine's in Danzig, before being moved to the Wadstena Convent in Sweden. But Abbot Johannes Marienwerder held that what the country needed more than another convent was a saint born here, between rivers, nurtured in this flat farming country, and of proved piety. It wouldn't do to have all the miracles happening in Poland.

Then Albrecht Slichting was allowed to leave, and his wife was called into the long, narrow room, with its two tall windows looking across Bucket Makers' Court to the half-timbered cottages and mud huts of Carp Pond on the other side of the Radaune.

Clad in a coarse hair shirt, Dorothea of Montau entered the room. She was forty-one at the time and still beautiful in a way that can only—and not for want of a better word—be termed indescribable. Be that as it may, the room was transfigured by her entrance, and the four gentlemen corrected their posture as though taken by surprise. They pulled their hands with the gnawed fingernails—even Abbot Johannes nibbled—back into their sleeves and sat up stiffly, with their backs to the two windows. In front of them stood a massive table, empty except for Dr. Roze's writing materials.

Dorothea declined to be seated in the gentlemen's presence. Her tall frame tilted slightly forward, she stood looking with this eye and that eye out of this and that window, as though the April sky, which had been overcast for days, were clear and open. Then she gave the commander a compelling look and, speaking quickly, without emphasis, employing a strange word order, prognosticated woe. She knew the exact date of the battle the Teutonic Knights would wage at Tannenberg, and she knew of their defeat. Perhaps because the date was in the following century, the four gentlemen took refuge in manly laughter. After that the din of the bucket makers could be heard more clearly.

Breaking in roughly, Christian Roze made light of the dire prophecy and went on to castigate her outrageous conduct: What had got into her, giggling during Holy Mass and wagging her tongue in her open mouth like a lewd whore? If she burned moldy coffin wood, then why not the horns of the He-goat? What lover was waiting for her when she ran, laughing raucously, through the streets of the Old City to the Wicker Bastion? Was it true that she could hover two hands' breadth above the ground and walk over water? Is that how she had saved herself from the ice floe on the river Elbe? And to whom had she sold her soul in return for these gifts?

Her mouth twisting slightly and turning upward like that of a fish, Dorothea replied in chains of words that did not always form sentences, but with their end rhymes suggested poetic method.

"When Jesu cumeth for my mouth to kisse,
Our tongués meten in the orifice."
"Swet Jesus pain doth shrood my hed
And nary ash of coffin wud."
"When dark descendeth, than luv min hert rendeth

My Jesu swet I go to mete
His body is my soles delete."
"Always I risé from the glomby earth
When Jesu sucketh me with his swet mouth."
"My sol I yelde up to Jesu dere
Alwhan he cometh att me with his spere.
So lordlings, to your dishes.
Ichab ykookt four fishes,
Frish herrings for the bord
Of Jesu Christ, our Lord."

Abbot and commander, Dominican confessor and doctor
of canon law—all were moved by her answers. Surely it
could not be Satan who spoke so charmingly out of the poor
thing's mouth. That little tongue, which sometimes—yes
indeed, to be sure—fluttered rather provocatively, must have
been loosed by the Lord God. True, the boundary between
carnal lust and spiritual rejoicing was not always clear in this
all-rhyming Dorothea's word combinations, but her love for
the Lord and Saviour could not be doubted, as the abbot,
who was of Alemannic origin, observed with a distinctly
Swiss intonation that lent charm to his flat Low German. The
scholarly Johannes Marienwerder cited examples of Christian
mysticism and likened the words he had heard from
Dorothea's lips to the legends of the nun Hrosvita and the
poems of Mechthild of Magdeburg. And considering that
there is no incompatibility between mystical experience and
canon law, provided no heresy is involved, Dr. Roze made it
clear that he had no fault to find. The vicar of Saint Mary's
agreed, but for safety's sake went on to inquire about one
thing and another—the bottled lepers' pus, for instance.

Whereupon Dorothea again set her mouth on the bias and
established a connection between her "brestkins twain" and
"Jesues body of pain." As for the pus she had taken from the
lepers of Corpus Christi Hospital, she called it "honey from
Jesues iniurees," which just happened to rhyme with "heavens
littul bees." She dissociated herself from Satan, whom she reviled as "the Lord of Lies," which she rhymed with a reference to the shifty look of a tasty flatfish—"the Flunderes
skemy eyes."

In the end the doctor of canon law declared himself satisfied. Commander Walrabe von Scharfenberg, a man disinclined to open his mouth, sent Dorothea off to the kitchen to

161

prepare (at last) the promised and so charmingly rhymed Scania herrings.

As Dorothea of Montau withdrew her eyes from one and the other window, turned, and walked the length of the room to the door, the four dignitaries behind the table had the impression that she was gliding along two hands' breadth above the floor.

Alone again, they relaxed in their chairs. Roze, fired with enthusiasm, was first to say the word: "A saint. She is a saint." The others agreed. But the considerations that suddenly made Commander Walrabe eloquent were of a more practical character. Though perhaps a shade too somber—he began—the prophecy of the politically ignorant Dorothea would be fulfilled, but not to the disadvantage of the Teutonic Order. War with the now united kingdoms of Lithuania and Poland was imminent. Just because the Polish Jadwiga had succeeded in converting the pagan Jagello and metamorphosing him into the Christian Wladislaw, the people, even in Teutonic territory, were calling this power-hungry female a saint. Countermeasures were imperative. Dangerous, dangerous, the way those Polacks kept turning out picturesque miracles, whereas the piety of the honest, simplehearted Germans was too dull for words, and as for the Hanseatic shopkeepers, before they'd buy a miracle they'd count up the costs. "In short," he concluded, "I, Walrabe von Scharfenberg, will bear witness to this woman's holiness and pledge the support of the Teutonic Order, which rules this territory in the name of the Blessed Virgin. We must act quickly. War is hard upon us. In addition to arms and supplies, our imperiled country needs the protection of a tutelary saint. What's more, the man whose word is guided by such wheaten-haired beauty will fight better."

Johannes Marienwerder sighed and threw up his hands. Though for less warlike motives, the abbot agreed with the commander, but how were canonization proceedings to be initiated? The dignitaries could see no way, for there was one little difficulty: Dorothea was alive. And despite the many hardships endured on her pilgrimages, despite her racking penitential exercises, convulsive ecstasies, other kinds of absence, migraines, and protracted periods of insomnia, she was in excellent health; her strength was in no wise impaired by her frequent nosebleeds, which on the contrary seemed to purify her humors.

When Walrabe termed Dorothea's demise conducive to the welfare of the Teutonic Order and therefore a necessity, and offered in hardly veiled language to promote said demise, possibly with Dominican help, the monk Nikolaus managed a show of indignation: No no no! Out of the question! In a pinch Dorothea could be sent on a pilgrimage to Rome, where the Swedish Birgitta had met her death and been promptly canonized. The soil of the Eternal City, drenched as it was with martyrs' blood, and the unhealthy climate both gave ground for hope. And besides, the papal canonization commission tended to be favorably impressed when prospective saints chose Rome as their last dwelling place. Of course it would be necessary to wait for a jubilee year. And as far as the Dominican knew, there mightn't be one for some time.

The commander refused to be put off. Apparently, he remarked, the monk had no objection to being ruled by Polacks. The war, in any case, would not wait. And what if this indestructible Dorothea went to Rome and survived the feverish climate? No, not at all. He didn't suspect the Dominican brothers' loyalty to the Teutonic Order. Not for the moment, at least.

After a long enough pause to conjure up a more favorable view of the commander's project—the tin-jangling bucket makers could be heard again—Abbot Johannes promised to do his utmost. Since, as they all knew, Dorothea desired a hermit's existence and looked upon withdrawal from the world as freedom, it might, he thought, be possible to accommodate her in Marienwerder Cathedral. True, it was not the custom of the country to immure pious hermits and lady penitents, and elsewhere as well the custom was falling more and more into disuse, but with the support of the bishop it would no doubt be possible to make an exception. And once immured, her mortal envelope was bound to dissolve soon enough.

The four dignitaries had hardly finished discussing the possibilities and possible setbacks—What if she's caught practicing witchcraft?—when Dorothea, now properly setting one foot in front of the other on the floor boards, entered carrying the Scania herrings on a platter.

They can be used fresh, salted, smoked, or marinated. They can be boiled, baked, fried, steamed, filleted, boned and stuffed, rolled around gherkins, or placed in oil, vinegar, white wine, and sour cream. Boiled with onions in salt water, they went well with Amanda Woyke's potatoes in their jackets. Sophie Rotzoll laid them on strips of bacon, sprinkled them with bread crumbs, and popped them into the oven. Margarete Rusch, the cooking nun, liked to steam sauerkraut with juniper berries and throw in small, boned Baltic herrings toward the end. Agnes Kurbiella served tender fillets steamed in white wine as diet fare. Lena Stubbe rolled herrings in flour, fried them, and set them before her second husband. But when Dorothea had the four dignitaries at her table, she prepared Scania herrings salted down and shipped in crates from the Danzig trading post in Falsterbo—for which reason the crate makers and the sailors of the Scania fleet, though belonging to separate guilds, had joined forces to provide Saint John's with a Lady altar and silver utensils—in accordance with her usual Lenten rules. After carefully washing them in fresh water, she bedded twelve Scania herrings on ashes strewn over the coals, so that without oil, spices, or condiment of any kind, their eyes whitened and they took on the taste of cooked fish. Before setting the herrings down on the platter—side by side, alternating head and tail—she blew the bulk of the ashes off each one, but a silvery-gray film remained, so that no sooner had Dorothea left the room than the four gentlemen could not help asking what kind of wood the Lenten cook had burned to ashes.

After a short prayer, spoken at Johannes's request by Dorothea's Dominican confessor, the four gentlemen hesitated briefly and fell to. All agreed that Scania herring prepared in this way was singularly tasty. Not one of them wished to look more deeply into the origin of the ashes. All four, even the refined Roze, propped their elbows on the table, held their herrings by the head and tail, and ate them—the monk Nikolaus with rotting teeth—off both sides of the backbones, which they then set down in the original order, head beside tail, whereupon each one took his second and then his third herring off the platter. Only Commander Walrabe bit the crispy tips off his herring tails. Abbot Johannes ceded his third herring to the Dominican monk. As long as they were eating, all four were silent, except that the vicar of Saint Mary's muttered something in Latin between the first and second and the second and third herrings.

When at last the twelve backbones lay neatly side by side, the abbot, the commander, the doctor of canon law, and the Dominican returned to their subject. It was decided that on the occasion of the next jubilee—which Pope Boniface was not to proclaim until 1390—Dorothea would be provided with the pilgrim's pence and dispatched to Rome under the escort of Frau Martha Quademosse, a Dominican agent. Then they would wait and see whether the pilgrim survived the rigors of the journey and the unaccustomed climate. Frau Quademosse would send reports.

Dorothea did indeed fall seriously ill when shown the Veil of Veronica, the famous relic preserved at Saint Peter's in Rome, but she recovered miraculously in spite of Frau Quademosse's ministrations and was in the pink of health when, along with other pilgrims, she entered Danzig through Jacob's Gate on the Sunday after the Ascension.

With her aged husband's consent, the four dignitaries had decided that in the event of her returning alive they would announce his death and let it be known that the child Gertrud had been entrusted to the care of the Benedictine nuns in Culm. The house on Bucket Makers' Court had belonged to the Dominicans since Dorothea's pilgrimage, and the indebted swordmaker had to pay rent to the monks.

This, too, was done. Pronounced dead (an empty coffin was buried in the graveyard of Saint Catherine's), swordmaker Slichting was glad to be relieved of his debts and free at last from the cross of his marriage. Three days before Dorothea, surrounded by the throng of pilgrims announced by Frau Quademosse, paid her first visit to the Cathedral Church of Saint Mary, father and daughter moved secretly, with the help of the Dominicans, to Konitz, where Slichting joined the guild under another name and, since a war was on, became a wealthy man again, married Gertrud to a swordmaker, and lived to a ripe old age, old enough to take cognizance of the fulfillment of Dorothea's prediction that the Teutonic Knights would be defeated at Tannenberg.

Once the preparations decided on at table were complete, Abbot Johannes declared that he was now prepared to have the widowed Dorothea immured under her maiden name of Swarze in Marienwerder Cathedral.

This was done, after some delay (resulting perhaps from

Polish intrigues) in obtaining the bishop's consent. In a solemn ceremony, the pious penitent was removed from the world on May 2, 1393, in the presence of the four forward-thinking dignitaries, and lodged under the southern staircase, which led to the choir loft. Each brick was blessed. The wool of the divine lamb was mixed into the mortar. At last Dorothea had won her freedom. Only one small opening remained, through which she could breathe, receive small amounts of Lenten fare, pass out her meager feces, follow the Mass in the cathedral, take daily Communion, and confess her holy progress to Johannes Marienwerder, who proceeded to write her life story in Church Latin; but there was no possibility of publishing it until 1492, when it was printed by Jakob Karweysse, Danzig's first book printer.

The four dignitaries also swore over the platter where the backbones of twelve Scania herrings lay alternating head and tail in their original order, that in case Dorothea Swarze, known as Dorothea of Montau, should be immured, they would institute canonization proceedings immediately after her death—they gave her six months.

This, too, was done. But the immured woman lasted longer than expected. She died on June 25, 1394. Whereupon her cell, after numerous believers in miracles had looked in through the opening and gazed for a moment at the corpse stretched out on the floor, was sealed up tight. True enough, canonization proceedings were initiated without further delay, and Grand Master von Jungingen of the Teutonic Order communicated his special interest in a Prussian saint to the canonization commission. But unfortunately the disorders attendant on the Great Schism obliged the postulator to transfer the file to Bologna for safekeeping, and there it was lost. So nothing came of the proceedings. The Teutonic Knights didn't get their saint. And if, on the basis of the sparse evidence now available, the canonization proceedings resumed in 1955 should be carried to a successful conclusion, I doubt if anyone will derive real pleasure from this late triumph of Catholic infallibility except my onetime Latin teacher, Monsignor Stachnik, who has always taken a pious interest in Dorothea.

The four dignitaries soon left the swordmaker's house. No more work sounds rose up from Bucket Makers' Court. Now the swift-flowing Radaune could be heard. A Baltic twilight was falling. The four were of good cheer, for they felt sure that their manly good sense had led them to plan wisely. Roze expressed his conviction that the canonization of Dorothea would swell the collections for additions to Saint Mary's. Only Commander Walrabe von Scharfenberg expressed concern lest with Satan's help this woman, who might be a witch after all, live longer in her immurement than they had so carefully planned.

When on their way out the four dignitaries cast a last glance into the smoky kitchen, they saw the child Gertrud playing with moldy graveyard wood. Old Slichting sat by the fire as though forgotten. Dorothea was kneeling as usual on dried peas, which she was planning to cook, thus softened, the next day. They heard her praying:

> "What blissful pain thy spere
> Doth giv me, Jesus dere. . . ."

To Ilsebill

Dinner is getting cold.
I'm not punctual any more.
No "Hello, here I am!" pushes the accustomed door.
Trying to approach you indirectly,
I've gone astray—up trees, down mushroomy slopes,
into remote word fields, garbage dumps.
Don't wait. You'll have to look.

I could keep warm in rot.
My hiding places have three exits.
I am more real in my stories
and in October, our birthday time,
when the sunflowers stand beheaded.

Since we are unable to live
today's day and the bit of night
I offer you centuries,
the fourteenth, for instance.
We are pilgrims on our way to Aachen,

feeding on pilgrim's pence.
We've left the plague at home.

This on the Flounder's advice.
In flight again.
But once—I remember—
in the middle of a story that was headed
for some entirely different place, across the ice to Lithuania,
you found me with you: you, too, a hiding place.

My dear Dr. Stachnik

One who remembers Dorothea and sets out to record her
Lenten soups, or even to oppose a diabolical or High Gothic
antitype to the sublimity of the (still-uncanonized) saint, is
bound to come up against your more pious than secure erudi-
tion, can be certain of your criticism, and will have to reckon
with your Catholic indignation; for you have appropriated
Dorothea, every bit of her.

When you were still (with small success) my Latin teacher
and I a dull-witted Hitler Youth, you were already specializ-
ing in Dorothea of Montau and the fourteenth century, although the times (the war years) offered small opportunity
for escapism. After all, you had been the local chairman of
the Center Party (until it was prohibited in 1937) and its deputy in the Danzig Volkstag. As a tacit opponent of National
Socialism, you had to be careful. And yet Nazi persecution
followed you even to our musty schoolroom, though it hardly
made a dent in the thick heads of your students.

With your Latin rigor you remained a stranger to us
students, a freak who—let Stalingrad fall or Tobruk be
lost—didn't really care about anything but grammar. Only
when you indulged in a bit of naïve Catholicism, only when
you spoke (with discernible affection) of the blessed
Dorothea and her impending canonization, were you able to
win my heart and stir my imagination; at the age of thirteen,
in any case, I had a crush on a little girl who must have
resembled Dorothea—I remember blue veins in white
temples. Of course I had no tangible success. She had black

hair. But you and I are certain that Dorothea of Montau's hair was the color of wheat. Maybe we also agree that her beauty had no use value. And I join you in the belief that she was unfit for marriage, though you insist in your writings that Dorothea tried to be a good housekeeper and wife to sword-maker Albrecht Slichting. (You point out, for example, that she often washed the dishes when unable to sleep at night.)

In your last letter you write, "If I have come out strongly for our home saint, the patron saint of Prussia, and am still working in her behalf, it is because, as I am sure you recognize, Dorothea was an extraordinary creature. I regard her as intellectually, morally, and spiritually the most outstanding woman of Prussia during the period of the Teutonic Knights." Here I cannot follow you, for while I agree that Dorothea was extraordinary, I can find no trace of saintliness in her makeup.

In your letter you refer to testimonies presented to the canonization commission of the time. You cite Jungingen and other such ruffians from among the Teutonic Knights, build your case in part on Dorothea's biographer, Johannes Marienwerder, and recommend the study of his great trilogy, *Vita venerabilis dominae Dorotheae*. But it is not only my scant knowledge of Latin that turns me away from the onetime Prague professor of theology and later dean of Marienwerder Cathedral. Johannes was too deeply involved, too intent on producing a saint for the Teutonic Order. I prefer to rely— since I, like you, my dear Herr Stachnik, am at home in imaginary worlds—on my personal memories, on my own painful experience with Dorothea, for before, during, and af-ter the Black Death, I was the swordmaker Albrecht, eight out of nine of whose children died, whose bit of hard-earned prosperity was dissipated by Dorothea's openhandedness at church doors, who was the laughingstock of the gold- and coppersmiths, of whom, in short, she (the pious bitch) made a fool. Oh, if I had only consented to a separation in Ein-siedeln, when she wanted to throw me and her last child overboard like ballast.

Perhaps you will argue: what do my domestic troubles and years of sexual privation (because she stopped doing it, she wouldn't let me in) amount to, measured against Dorothea's ecstasies and illuminations; how insignificant was my squan-dered fortune weighed against what Dorothea gained each day by pleasing God with her (bloody) flagellation; what did the

169

loss of eight children (at a time of high infant mortality) signify if through the Lord Jesus (with whom she communed daily) she became a true child of God; and how could I think of demanding retribution for earthly trouble now that after almost five hundred years' patience the heavenly reward was at last on the point of being paid out—any day now!

If you look at it that way, you are right—my High Gothic family-man troubles shrink to nothingness in the light of your joyful expectation. Triumphantly you write, "As the relator general of the canonization commission recently informed me, the *'Confirmatio cultus Dorotheae Montoviesis, Beatae vel Sanctae nuncupatae'* will probably be announced before the year is out in an apostolic brief, so bringing the canonization proceedings to a successful conclusion."

That I am quite prepared to believe, for I am still Catholic enough to tremble at the power of the True Church to suspend time. I know that faith, however darkly it may err, outshines the pathetic lamp of reason. And yet I take the liberty of putting a different, more earthly interpretation on the impending canonization not only of your, but also of my Dorothea: Dorothea was the first woman (in our region) to rebel against the patriarchal tyranny of medieval marriage. Soon after her father's death, her eldest brother, without consulting her (she was then sixteen), married her to an elderly man (me). What did I do? I made the frail child one brat after the other, dragged my expensively dressed Dorothea to boring guild dinners, showed her what a coward I was through my half-hearted participation in a ridiculous artisans' uprising (what did I care about the interests of the brewers or coopers?), and beat her with my hard swordmaker's hand or—as on the return journey from Einsiedeln—threw stones at her because I hated her and her witching ideas of freedom.

Because that was all she wanted—to be set free. Free from the prison of marriage. Free from sexual duty. Free from domestic trivia. Free for what?

You, my dear Herr Stachnik, will say: Free for God! Free for the love of God! But when the case of Dorothea of Montau was debated before the Women's Tribunal in Berlin—you must have read about it in the papers—the presiding judge said: "Dorothea Swarze wanted freedom for herself. Religion and Jesus were only a means, the one permissible agency through which to press her demand for emancipation and escape the all-engulfing power of men. Since she had no other choice than to be burned as a witch or immured as a saint, she decided—for the sake of her freedom—to serve a halfway credible legend up to the dean of Marienwerder Cathedral. A case typical of the Middle Ages, but not without relevance to the present day. We women of today have every reason to look upon Dorothea Swarze as a precursor. Her attempt at self-liberation—bound as it was to end tragically—obliges us to take a sisterly view of her affliction, to evaluate her Godforsaken!—yes, Godforsaken!—failure as a call addressed to us, and to hold her name in honor."

I feel sure, my dear Monsignor Stachnik, that if all this feminist gush calls forth any reaction in you, it will be the stoical smile of the Latinist. And yet I beg you to consider my compromise proposal, halfway between the Catholic and the feminist positions.

I will never again—though I could furnish proof—call Dorothea a witch; you for your part will stop harping—though she had the makings of a saint—on her impending canonization. We both agree that Dorothea Swarze was an unfortunate woman who suffered under the servitudes of her times—more foolish than clever, tormented by insomnia and migraine, a slovenly housekeeper, yet remarkably efficient when it came to organizing processions of flagellants, a woman of gaunt beauty and ruthlessly strong will, despite her hours of convulsive ecstasy unable to think up appealing miracles, endowed with a slight lyrical gift, sluggish in bed but energetic with the scourge, a good walker, hence adept at pilgrimages, cheerful only in the company of wandering penitents and other nuts, rich in extravagant desires, but practical and innovative in devising her ego-related Lenten cookery: it was really good! Ah, her manna grits with sorrel! Ah, her Scania herring! Ah, her dried peas! Ah, her codfish roe on buckwheat cakes! Ah, her *Glumse* with herbs!

You have no doubt noticed, my dear Herr Stachnik, that like you (though without heavenly reward) I, too, loved Dorothea. But she kissed the Flounder, a matter on which her biographer, Johannes Marienwerder, wasted not so much as a word. To be sure, after that kiss (and her fornication with the fish, to be sure) her mouth slipped out of shape, but even crooked of mouth and slanting of eye she was still beautiful. The mass of her hair. Her scourged and bleeding flesh. I even liked her rhymes, her "herte" and "smerte."* And her habit of stirring ashes into all her soups. And she could really hover two feet above the ground—I saw her do it several times (and not only out of doors in the fog).

My Ilsebill, who sends you her regards, doesn't believe all this. Every day she cries out, "You with your historical excuses and your stories that are all lies!" Ilsebill only believes what she reads in the paper. You and I, however, know that stories can't help being true, but never twice in the same way. As my Latin teacher, you were a failure, but you infected me for good with the Dorothean poison. And so I write to you, in esteem and bitter doubt. After all, neither of us knows what Dorothea wanted. . . .

Surplus value

Or frozen jubilation
that I've collected, collected to look at.

The glasses on my shelf
like side light; all are not Bohemian.

Two each day are special.
So much love, ready for the dustbin.

Breath from afar, that hasn't shattered.
Thus, nameless, survive

air and its surplus value:
glass blowers, we read, did not grow old.

---

* *Smerte*: "pain," "sorrow."—TRANS.

The third month

~~~~~~

How the Flounder was protected
against aggression

When the Women's Tribunal met for the first time, four
working women rolled the Flounder into the courtroom in a
flat, roughly five-by-seven-foot tub. He was illumined by an
overhead light. It was the kind of tub that might just as well
have kept carp alive from Christmas to New Year's Day.

While the bill of indictment was being read, the Flounder
lay motionless on the bottom of the tub, as though the accusation—that he had served the male cause in an advisory
capacity since the late Neolithic, well knowing that his advice
redounded to the detriment of the female sex—did not
concern him. It was not until Ms. Ursula Schönherr, the
presiding judge, asked him if he wished to comment on the
indictment that his voice was heard over the loudspeaker, and
then only to say that he would say nothing as long as he was
obliged to lie in Baltic Sea water, which, in addition to being
disgustingly stale, was polluted with mercury. Ignoring his
court-appointed counsel, the Flounder declared, "This borders
on the only-too-notorious methods of torture practiced by the
modern system of class justice, which it is incumbent on all,
including the feminist movement, to combat. And moreover,"
he added, "this overhead light is an instrument of discrimina-
tion; I demand that it be switched off immediately."

The court was obliged to adjourn. From then on canisters

of fresh North Sea water were flown in daily via British Airways. The changes of water were supervised by Beate Hagedorn, one of the associate judges, who was employed as a marine biologist by the aquarium of the Berlin Zoo.

No longer illumined from above, the Flounder became co-operative. But before the court had finished debating the neolithic phase of the legendary fish and the three breasts of the reigning goddess Awa, the defendant in his zinc tub lodged a new protest—accustomed as he was to lying flat, he declared the zinc floor of his tub to be prejudicial to his health and well-being. It so happened that his soft and sensitive underside was allergic to zinc. How, under these circumstances, could he be expected to concentrate on the proceedings? Water was not his only element. He needed sand to bed himself in, and specifically, Baltic Sea sand. "That and no other," he concluded. "Until I am provided with an environment compatible with my needs, I cannot cooperate in this otherwise epoch-making trial. I regard the conditions of my detention as unacceptable. Is this a fascist court martial?"

Another adjournment. Baltic Sea sand was flown in. But during the next phase of the trial, from the Bronze and Iron Ages down to the advent of Christianity—the Wigga and Mestwina cases—the defendant had a further complaint: he was sick of being fed dried flies and prepared fish food like a goldfish, and "How do I know that I'm not being shamefully and criminally drugged? I need fresh food. If this is beyond the powers of our esteemed marine biologist, why not enlist the help of the fishery school in Cuxhaven or Kiel?" And he wound up, "I am asking no more than my rights."

Once the suggested contacts had been established, the Flounder was provided with algae, insects, and similar fresh food, and the trial went along smoothly until the case of the Lenten cook Dorothea of Montau was nearing its summation.

The probable reason for the agitation in the hall was that the defendant had managed to bring in certain particulars which, taken in conjunction with certain acknowledged facts, added up to a historical picture that mitigated his guilt (Dorothea's services as a spy for the Dominicans). In any event, some member of the public threw a fist-sized stone, which missed the zinc tub but might have hit it. The public was excluded from the hall. With the Flounder's consent, workmen (males) covered his tub with fine-meshed wire. The optical effect was unfortunate. The defendant could hardly be seen. The word "cage" kept cropping up in the news stories.

When the public was readmitted, further assaults were made. The public consisted mostly of young women, and when the Flounder set forth his cynical migraine theory in speaking of Dorothea of Montau, one of these young women threw a small bottle, which landed on the protective wire. The Flounder demanded to be informed of the contents, but refrained from any comment derogatory to the women's movement when the words "potassium cyanide" were pronounced.

Again the trial was adjourned; again the public was excluded. Specialists (male) required a whole week, first to seal off the zinc tub with a pane of bulletproof glass, second to equip the tub with an oxygen tank, and third to install an intercom system. When the trial started up again, the Flounder sounded weird, very much (to High German ears) as in the fairy tale that made him a popular legend: "Vot does she vont now?" He was evidently aware of the acoustic effect, for he occasionally sprinkled his usual exaggeratedly involved and old-fashioned sentences with Low German flourishes, charmingly vulgar expletives, and puns on the name Ilsebill. The intercom system seemed to amuse him.

But at the very start of the debate on the case of Margarete Rusch, when the Flounder had just admitted to the Tribunal that it was he who had advised putting little Margret in a convent, or, more exactly, right after the accused fish had illustrated convent life with a few anecdotes, and had imitated Fat Gret's nun's farts with a remarkable vocal virtuosity, someone in the public took aim at the Flounder and fired. The bullet—fired as it later turned out by an old lady, a librarian by trade—struck the hind end of the zinc tub. She had fired standing in the eleventh row. The bullet passed clean through the metal and came to rest in the Baltic Sea sand. But the hole was large enough to provide passage for a finger-thick stream of North Sea water. The prosecutor herself, Ms. Sieglinde Huntscha, tried to stop the hole with a Kleenex. The marine biologist was in despair. A plumber was called. The Flounder could be heard laughing raucously over the loudspeaker: "Hey, there, that's a new way to fart. That must have been a cowboy and no Ilsebill. Going after the poor Flounder with a Colt. Why not a cannon?"

Only a four-day adjournment was needed for the installation of a man-high tank of bulletproof glass, as long and wide as the retired zinc tub but filled to half its height with Baltic Sea sand. It goes without saying that the glass house was provided with the necessary technical equipment. The Flounder could now be seen much more clearly. One could even distinguish his archaic stony protuberances, except when he buried his whole flat body in the sand, showing only his crooked mouth and slanting eyes. But now no one could endanger his life by aiming stones or bullets at him or pouring poison in his water. His security had been provided for.

He was also safe from kidnapping (thanks to an alarm system). (Only a short while before, anonymous, presumably male threats had been made known: "They want to swipe him on us. Those male chauvinists stop at nothing.") The Flounder was pleased with the bulletproof-glass box. On request, he generously admitted photographers. Even a television crew was permitted, during a recess, to transmit his protected beauty to millions of tubes. The discussion of the cooking nun continued—almost without a hitch.

When I was her kitchen boy

The gleaming copper pan.
Her early morning voice. Here! I cried. Here!
and ran to her, as often as I tried
to run away from her pots.

At Easter I skinned lambs' tongues—Protestant
and Catholic—and my sinful soul as well.
And when she plucked geese in November,
I blew feathers, blew the down,
to keep the day in suspense.

She had the dimensions of Saint Mary's Church,
but there was never a mystical draft,
it was never cool inside her.
Ah, her box bed
that smelled of goat's milk
that flies had fallen into.

176

Captive in her stable smell.
Her womb was a cradle.
When was that?

Under her nun's habit—she was an abbess—
time did not stand still,
history was enacted,
the controversy over flesh and blood
and bread and wine was decided without a word.
As long as I was her kitchen boy,
I was never cold and never ashamed.

Fat Gret: a half pumpkin
laughs and spits out seeds.
I seldom saw her
stir beer into bread soup,
but then she peppered heavily: her grief
had no aftertaste.

Vasco returns

Who else, Flounder! Who else! Blacksmith Rusch, Franciscan
monk Stanislaus. Pracher Hegge, rich man Ferber, and Abbot
Jeschke. If during the lifetime of the abbess Margarete I was
one and the other and successively this one and that one—
her father, her kitchen boy, her opponents and victims—why
would it not be conceivable that far away from her but
wishing to help her by making pepper cheaper, I opened up
the sea route to India to Portuguese caravels? Consider that
the São Rafael dropped anchor off Calicut on March 28,
1498, at which time Kristin Rusch, an inhabitant of the
Wicker Bastion, was pregnant with Fat Gret.

At first I merely toyed with this question along with my
usual worries (Ilsebill), but then, when I'd started on my
trip, it became an obsession. Possibly it was fear of the foreign surroundings that made me look for a role. (How was I
to exist in Calcutta without one?) Or cursory readings in
Hinduism beguiled me into extending my Eastern European
rebirths to the Indian subcontinent; but I didn't want to have

been Lord Curzon or Kipling. I finally said to myself: the abbess Margarete Rusch must have had some reason for marrying her elder daughter, Hedwig, to a Portuguese merchant, whose intention of opening a trading post on the Malabar Coast in southern India was explicitly mentioned in the marriage contract. It was decided that with the viceroy's permission the couple would take up residence at Cochin, and from there, as stipulated in the marriage contract, ship suitable amounts of pepper twice a year, for the feasts of Saint Martin and Saint John. The rule dating from the days of Vasco and of Affonso d'Albuquerque that prohibited the entry of Christian women seems to have been relaxed, and the family struck root.

They settled in Cochin, where the merchant Rodrigues d'Evora and his wife, Hedwig, soon made a fortune in the spice trade—pepper, cloves, ginger, and cardamom—but the climate was too much for them. Along with four of their five children, they died before Margret Rusch, who, thanks to the stipulated spice shipments, was able to give Indian spices currency in Danzig and environs: tripe with ginger, millet curry, gingerbread, hare in pepper sauce, pepper with anything and everything. And because my travel schedule included a visit to the seaport town of Cochin in the Indian state of Kerala, I decided to travel unofficially as Vasco da Gama. While still at the Frankfurt airport, though with my seat belt already fastened, I wrote in my sketchbook: Vasco returns.

He arrives in a jumbo jet. Actually all he wants to do is visit the black Kali and see her stick out her red tongue.

Vasco has read all the statistics. Vasco knows what the president of the World Bank thinks about Calcutta. Vasco is supposed to deliver a lecture. As a precaution he has already written it down, in long and short sentences. "By a rough estimate . . ." says his speech. Well fed, Vasco suffers under the problem of world hunger. After many rebirths, Vasco is now a writer. He is writing a book in which he exists down through the ages: the Stone Age, the Early Christian, High Gothic, Reformation, and Baroque eras, the age of the Enlightenment, et cetera.

Immediately after the takeoff he quotes himself: Somebody ought to write a report on hunger down through the ages, comparing past, present, and future hunger. The famine of 1317, when there was nothing to eat but manna grits. The

178

meat shortage of 1520, when dumplings of many kinds were invented. Hunger in Prussia before the introduction of the potato, and hunger in Bangladesh. The gestures and language of hunger are in need of study. Behavior patterns induced by the anticipation of hunger. Evocation of past famines: the rutabaga winter of 1917; the soggy corn bread of '45. What it really means to be starving. We need a catalogue of hunger quotations, says Vasco to himself, toying listlessly with refrigerated and therefore tasteless Air India pâté.

The goddess Kali is looked upon as the female aspect of the god Shiva. Her power destroys. When in the mood she demolishes man's precarious structures. We are living in her era. (Vasco thinks in passing of his wife, Ilsebill, who likes to smash glasses and is a great hand at wishing.)

Even before the fueling stop at Kuwait his eyeglasses get broken. But he is not unprovided for. Because of the humidity in Calcutta, Vasco has bought cotton trousers, shirts, and socks in a tropical-outfitting store in Hamburg. Vasco is supplied with Enterovioform. Vasco has had cholera and yellow-fever shots. Vasco has thrice swallowed colored antityphoid capsules on an empty stomach. Vasco is carrying five pounds of statistics in his luggage. Vasco is the guest of the Indian government. This is known on board the jumbo jet. Vasco is really someone else and is known under a different name.

He ought to have spoken to his wool-gathering audience in Delhi about Kali and how she sticks out her red tongue, instead of citing roughly estimated figures replete with zeros, standing for protein deficiency, excess population, and mortality rates: abstract quantities worshiped only in footnotes, whereas the unfathomable Kali can be understood everywhere, but especially in Calcutta, on the Hooghly River. She who is hung with garlands of skulls and chopped-off hands. She, the playful, commanding, terrible, Dravidian Kali. (She can also be called Durga, Parvati, Uma, Sati, or Tadma.)

Still aboard the jumbo jet (without sleep), Vasco tries to construct a kinship between the neolithic goddess Awa, remarkable for her three breasts, and Kali, the four-armed strangler. He thinks up an uprising: oppressed by matriarchy, the men in the swamplands of the Vistula estuary band together. In a frenzy of procreative activity (advised by the Flounder), they try to introduce the patriarchate. But Awa

179

wins out and has a hundred and eleven men emasculated with stone axes. From then on she wears their dried penises strung on a chain around her vast pelvis, just as the Indian Kali decks herself out with chopped-off hands and skulls.

The moment he gets there, Vasco starts writing postcards. "Dear Ilsebill, everything here is strange. . . ." Then, wishing to gain a visual impression of the strange country, he has his glasses made whole.

Fourteen ninety-eight: Vasco knows that he lied to himself then, just as he deceives himself now. Men are always rubbing up their aims to a high polish: For the glory of God . . . To save endangered humanity . . . When what actually impelled him to find a sea route to India, the land of spices, was nautical ambition. It was other people, the "peppersacks," or shopkeepers, who made the big money.

At an evening reception (in his honor), some ladies who have studied in England question Vasco about the aims and motives of the women's liberation movement. Vasco tells them about a women's tribunal that is being held in Berlin but making headlines far beyond its confines. A captured Flounder, he tells them, is symbolically on trial; the Flounder embodies the principle of male domination; he is being tried in a bulletproof tank. Then Vasco suggests to the ladies that the liberation of Indian women be placed under the high patronage of the goddess Kali. (Mightn't Nehru's daughter, Indira, be an embodiment of her terrible aspect?) While pine nuts are being nibbled, his suggestion arouses interest, although the ladies, daughters of prominent Brahman families, prefer Durga, the mild aspect of the goddess; Kali, it seems, is more popular with the lower castes.

The next day Vasco doesn't feel like going to the museum; he wants to visit a slum. The slum dwellers look at him in amazement. He is intimidated by the cheerfulness of these poverty-stricken people and their unconquerable charm. The giggling of the ragged young girls who, because they have hips, show their hips. True, they beg with their hands and eyes, but they don't complain. (They're not starving, after all, just chronically undernourished.) It all looks so natural. As though that were how it had to be forever and ever. As though the growth of bigger and bigger slums were an organic process that shouldn't be disturbed, but at the most cured of its worst abuses.

180

Vasco (the discoverer) asks questions about work, wages, number of children, school attendance, family planning, intestinal flora, latrines. The answers confirm the statistics in his possession, no more. Then he is obliged to visit a large fortress (dating from his Mogul days) in which some units of the Indian army are now quartered. Looking down from the battlements at midday, Vasco tries to engrave a picture on his mind: five hundred ragged bodies lying in a flat field (whose grass covering has been eaten away by cows), looking as dead as if English machine guns, firing from the fort's embrasures, had mowed them down. Each bundle lies by itself. Dusty units. Corpses eager to rot. Their death-sleep warmed by the sun. Extras out of a colonial film, waiting for the next pan. A pity Vasco has left his 35-mm camera at the hotel. He makes a note of the word: death-sleepers. And I, he says, am supposed to have discovered this? In vain Vasco forbids himself to find these sleeping corpses, arranged by chance or some other law, beautiful. If he were tired and lay down among them, he would look awkwardly out of place.

The chairman of the planning commission fills out a Nehru suit and speaks past Vasco deep into the distance: We have, as you know, three thousand years of history behind us. We did not come into existence when that Portuguese discovered us by the sea route.

Vasco appears to be listening attentively while he tries in vain to recall the details of the 1498 landing at Calicut. (We sent a convict ashore to see what would happen.) The chairman of the planning commission explains that despite its infinitely various faces India is nevertheless one. No outsider can fully know us. Calcutta, he says, is indeed a problem, but there are many artists living in this fascinating city. And Bengali poetry . . .

The next slum has grown up (organically) beside the Delhi power plant, which uninterruptedly belches vast clouds of smoke. Across the slum stands the modern high-rise building of the World Health Organization, South Asia Section. The clouds of smoke and not the slums are reflected in the windows of the WHO building. Next door, lest there be anything missing, stands the pavilion of the Indian Council for Cultural Relations, which has invited Vasco to come, see, and understand that "we are a modern democracy."

In the slum Vasco speaks with women from Uttar Pradesh,

who have six or eight children but do not know how many rupees their husbands earn as sweepers at the power plant next door. This slum is reputedly clean. Vasco finds a doctor who, however, has never crossed the street to visit the WHO, just as the WHO has never called on the doctor. Of course we have cases of smallpox, he says. I report them. But they always vaccinate too late. I'm only a volunteer. I have no counterpart in other slum sections. The people here think I'm a fool to be doing this. This doctor doesn't speak English. In translation everything sounds plausible. Maybe he's only a medical orderly. Vasco puts a rupee on the table of the mud-hut dispensary for medicines. As he was leaving home, Vasco's children said: Don't go bringing us any presents. None of that crazy stuff. Give somebody the money. And on this occasion Ilsebill had no particular wishes, either.

Vasco goes to Fatehpur Sikri to see the sights from his Mogul days. Today he smiles to think how he tried to be tolerant in his spacious fortress apartments by including not only a Mohammedan but also a Hindu woman and a Christian lady from Portuguese Goa in his marriage contract. Only the Hindu woman bore him a son (who turned out badly). Nothing remains but fragments of carved red sandstone. Each column cut differently. But the desert said no. When the water ran out, the city had to be abandoned. All that tolerance for nothing. (When Vasco died in Cochin in 1524, Margarete Rusch, cook and nun, became abbess of Saint Bridget's, after which, as her fancy bade her, she took Protestant, Catholic, and seafaring men into her bed, and runaway monks as well. So tolerant she was, so spacious.)

Still in the state of Uttar Pradesh, Vasco visits a village school, built of clay like the huts and walls round about. Everything is mud-brown—the hard-stamped village street, the cows, the bicycles, the children, the sky. Only the women's saris are colorful, though faded. Once again poverty indulges in beauty. The teacher has light-brown eyes. He shows Vasco schoolbooks. In one little book, which tells the history of India in Hindi script, Vasco sees himself portrayed in simple lines, bearded under a velvet cap. In some wrinkle of his traveler's existence he is proud or touched, but he is also somewhat put out because he has made school history and become textbook material. (What do they actually know about me? About my restlessness. Always looking for goals beyond the horizons. Using my nautical skill as a means of reaching God. And my lifelong fear of Dominical poison. Everything has died away. But I'm still inwardly rich in figures. . . .)

Because it's expected of him, Vasco asks questions. The teacher complains about social workers who come to the village and use pictures without written commentaries as propaganda for family planning, as though addressing themselves to illiterates. And yet forty-five percent of the children attend school off and on. To prove it, the schoolchildren read aloud from the book in which Vasco has become textbook material.

In the left-hand niche of the temple the goddess dances, this time in her gentle Durga aspect. The right-hand niche discloses a monkey god. The cawing of the crows, the laughter of the children. The peasants' complaints about the price of wheat, which has suddenly doubled, are translated for Vasco's benefit. Most have sold too cheap. A third of the peasants are landless. Many move to the city. A rich peasant rents out his tractor. For fear of abduction (a common occurrence in the days of the Moguls) the women cover their faces as Vasco passes. In the midst of the dust an old man, who is chewing betel, gives him a carrot. Next day Vasco has diarrhea and has to take Enterovioform—three tablets daily. After a while it helps. But his shit is still mustard-blond and liquid. Bubbles in the soup. He looks for worms and feels disappointed because his stools refuse to turn black like those of the poet Opitz, who was carried off by the plague. That was in the days when the earth was a vale of tears. Opitz's cook was named Agnes. In his book Vasco gives her credit for feelings that she served up to the poet as diet fare. The plague, it was thought, had been brought in from India by the sea route.

While viewing the remains of his Mogul period in Sikri and visiting his tomb, he, like other tourists, ties a cotton wishing string (for which he has paid a rupee) to the battered filigree of his mortuary chapel. But he doesn't know what to wish for. Good God! This absurd *joie de vivre*. This splendid splendor. This screwed-up planning, O Lord! Why has thou piloted me to this place? (It was an Arab helmsman, who knew the way and knew the monsoon winds. Ahmed ibn Majid was in the habit of celebrating his nautical feats in verse.)

At the airport a wreath of flowers is thrown over Vasco's head. Flags everywhere (not on his account). The world-championship table-tennis matches, now being held in Calcutta, are viewed as a political event. The International Table Tennis Association has excluded South Africa and Israel, but the Palestinians have been invited. Only Holland protests. The Brazilian contestants lack a few inoculations and are quarantined. It has taken only four weeks to build the modern table-tennis stadium. The city government of Calcutta, with its three thousand slum districts, here called bustees, is proud of the achievement. Because of the table-tennis tournament all the hotels are full, so Vasco is housed in the guest apartments of the former viceroy's palace, since independence the residence of the provincial governor. Vasco's room is twenty feet high; the bed, under its canopy of mosquito netting, is in the middle. Two ventilators and three electric fans keep the air in motion. On the writing desk, two inkwells from Queen Victoria's day. Vasco jots down notes about the farm cook Amanda Woyke. Her correspondence with Count Rumford. Both wanted to combat world hunger with giant kitchens, she with her West Prussian potato soup, he with his Rumford soup for the poor. Vasco writes: But the Kashubians couldn't get used to potatoes, just as semolina is repellent to the rice-eating Bengalese, even when they are starving. So the Kashubians continued for a long time to eat too little millet, until at last they consented to fill up on potatoes.

The governor's palace is known as Raj Bhavan. On every side, quietly moving servants in slitted red coats under white turbans. They fold their hands when they greet Vasco. The soldiers in the corridors salute. The cook has been in the house for thirty-six years. He has cooked for Englishmen and their guests. At table four servants wait on Vasco. The aged cook calls his cooking European. At breakfast (ham and eggs), Vasco is served the newspaper with the latest word of the table-tennis matches. Through an aide the governor requests the honor of Vasco's company at luncheon. Vasco dreads the meal with the governor. (Good God! What am I doing here!) He wants to go home to his Ilsebill.

But Calcutta, this crumbling, scabby, swarming city, this city that eats its own excrement, has decided to be cheerful. It wants its misery—and misery can be photographed wherever you go—to be terrifyingly beautiful: the decay plastered with advertising posters, the cracked pavement, the beads of sweat adding up to nine million souls. People pour out of railroad stations which, like Vasco only yesterday, have daily diarrhea: white-shirted maggots in a shitpile with Victoria excrescences, a shitpile that dreams up new curlicues every minute. And on top of everything betel-reddened spittle.

On foot across the Hooghly Bridge and back. On the left side junk for sale: worn-out shoes, coconut fiber, school slates, faded shirts, primitive tools, kitsch from Hong Kong, native kitsch. The right-hand sidewalk is bordered by groups of peasants from the surrounding villages selling purple onions, yellow, sand-gray, or bright-red lentils, ginger root, sugar cane, molasses pressed into cakes, unhusked rice, coarse-ground wheat, chapatty. The bridge, which has no central support, vibrates under the two-way traffic of bare feet, trucks, rickshas, and oxcarts. Suddenly, in the midst of the crowd, Vasco is overcome with joy. He, too, wants to chew betel. But when he looks down from either bridgehead, there is nothing but misery; he is aghast at the sight of hollowed-out women and old men with shrunken heads, upon whom death has set its mark.

There are no separate slums, or bustees, in Calcutta. The whole city is one bustee, or slum, and neither the middle nor the upper classes can segregate themselves from it. High-school girls with their books can be seen plodding down the street among bundles of rags the same age as themselves, forming islands in the traffic, then merging again with the great, flowing mass. Wherever the traffic leaves a free space, there are people living in the roadway. Side by side with parks and run-down mansions one sees villagelike groups of cardboard and sheet-metal shacks. People flushed into the city by the last famine (just a year ago), those whom the bustees have expelled or found no room for stay on in such places. They come from Bihar; they are strangers among the Bengalis. At night they squat around fires outside the shacks and cook what they've been able to find in the garbage. The collecting instinct is all they have left. The fires are fed with cow dung or cakes of straw and coal dust. Here the Stone Age is staging a comeback and has already made deep inroads. The buses look like an archaeologist's dream. Vasco takes refuge in the governor's palace. The palace guard knows him by now.

On the program: tea with a film maker who is flying to Chicago tomorrow to show American students his Calcutta film. Smilingly we converse—two sophisticated producers. Vasco asks about the possibility of a film in which a reborn Vasco de Gama visits modern India, fears the goddess Kali, comes to Calcutta, gets diarrhea, and lives in the governor's palace. Then he talks about the cooks of his various time-phases; the neolithic Awa, the High Gothic Dorothea, the revolutionary Sophie, and the cooking abbess Margarete Rusch, for whose cookery a drop in the price of pepper was important. He mentions the Flounder and his activities since the Neolithic era. The film maker nods. Yes, he says, a similar fish in a similar function has been known in India since the Dravidian period, and this fish was hostile on principle, though ineffectually, to Kali.

Then the film maker talks about the next film festival and, in passing, about the dead bodies in the streets of Calcutta, which are collected toward morning. It has always been this way. In 1943, when he was a child, two million Bengalis had starved because the British army had used up all the rice stocks in the war against Japan. Had a film been made about it? No, unfortunately not. You can't film starvation.

Wherever he goes in Calcutta, at the film maker's, with Mother Theresa's nuns, at the governor's luncheon in his honor, everyone wants to know what his next book is about—as if that could make any difference to India.

Even on his visit to a bustee, the planner from the Department of Economic Planning asks him literary questions. Vasco explains himself in detail. The book deals with the history of human nutrition. It all happens in the region of the Vistula estuary, though actually it might just as well take place at the mouth of the Ganges or here on the banks of the Hooghly River. The goddess in his book is called Awa. Unfortunately he knows much too little about the Dravidian Kali.

Then Vasco takes refuge in statistical questions and gets answers he could have found in statistical tables. There are three thousand bustees in Calcutta. "We prefer not to call them slums." The population of the bustees ranges from five hundred to seventy-five thousand. That adds up to three million bustee dwellers. An average of eight to ten people to a room. Ten to twelve huts form an open square around a court. Excrement and kitchen waste flow down the main streets in open gutters. In this particular bustee the schoolroom holds some forty-five children. A social worker is in charge of it. The same cheerfulness: so proud to have a school. Vasco tries to imprint the stench on his memory. Hallmarks of misery; the usual injustice. Extortionate rents are paid to hut owners who also live in the bustee. Everybody shits where he can and must. True enough, Vasco writes, but compared to Frankfurt am Main, the people here are alive. Later on he wants to cross out this sentence.

The bustee dwellers come from the countryside. To clean up Calcutta, says the planner, you'd first have to clean up the villages. So Vasco goes to the villages: mud huts under coconut palms. He sees the round storehouses, mounted on trestles to keep out the rats, but empty. A smiling peasant woman with a cluster of seven children sends her eldest boy up a palm tree. Vasco drinks the coconut milk and remembers. There's not enough water in the fields for the young rice plants. The roadside canal has been drained; it's supposed to be dredged, no one knows when. The peasants are deeply in debt, mostly for their daughters' weddings. They pay forty percent interest. Untouchables are not allowed to help with the harvest. Men and women bathe in a number of pools where last month's rain water is fast evaporating. All bathe in their clothes. (Mohammedan puritanism followed by Victorian puritanism.) All the children have worms. Vasco agrees: a beautiful village. He likes the coconut palms, the banana trees, the mud huts, the wormy children, and the smiling women. But the village is sick and on its way to becoming a Calcutta.

China and Czechoslovakia are leading in the table-tennis matches. The newly built table-tennis stadium is almost empty, since the tickets are priced too high even for the middle class.

After his four servants have brought him the morning paper and served his breakfast (poached eggs), Vasco visits the former premier of the West Bengal People's Front government. He finds himself facing an elderly gentleman, bolt upright in a white cotton garment stirred by the draft. No, he doesn't belong to the Moscow-inspired party, he's a Marxist Communist. Without bitterness he names defeats. Vasco learns how the Naxalites have split off and regrouped as a revolutionary movement. So many intelligent young people, says the Marxist with regret, and adds ironically: Of good family. When they found they weren't getting anywhere—because all the stories about "liberated territories" were Chinese propaganda—the Naxalites started murdering their former comrades, some four hundred Marxists. No, says the old man, Maoism cannot be transplanted to India. Basically Naxalite radicalism is just another gesture of bourgeois impotence.

In this country, Vasco hears himself say, I'd be a radical myself. He decides (so many characters swarming inside him) to invent for his book a conversation between Lena Stubbe, cook at the Danzig-Ohra soup kitchen, and Comrade August Bebel, who happens to be on his way through (1895), in which they take up the question of whether working-class women should emulate "bourgeois" cookery, or whether they require a proletarian cook book.

The melancholy (Brahman) Marxist sits in a bare room and flexes his knees. From time to time a laconic telephone conversation. On the walls, side by side with three wooden wild ducks that pass as ornaments, a small picture of Lenin. Only last week there were two attacks on comrades. In front of the house is parked a black automobile, surrounded by the Marxist's bodyguards.

Next Vasco visits poets. They read one another (in English) poems about flowers, monsoon clouds, and the elephant-headed god, Ganesha. An English lady (in a sari) lisps impressions of her travels in India. Some forty people in elegant, spacious garments sit spiritually on fiber mats under a draft-propelled fan; outside the windows, the bustees are not far away.

Vasco admires the fine editions of books, the literary chitchat, the imported pop posters. Like everyone else he nibbles pine nuts and doesn't know which of the lady poets he would like to fuck if the opportunity presented itself.

Why not a poem about a pile of shit that God dropped and named Calcutta. How it swarms, stinks, lives, and gets bigger and bigger. If God had shat a pile of concrete, the result would have been Frankfurt. Calcutta airport is called Dum-Dum. The formerly British munitions factory there is still producing. Christian hypocrites used to say that the enormous holes made by the truncated, expanding dumdum bullets spared the victims the usual tortures (of belly wounds, for instance). The surviving Naxalites are imprisoned in Dum-Dum Prison. Hope has no place in a poem about Calcutta. Write with pus. Rip off scabs. . . .

A nun from Wattenscheid, belonging to the Order of Mother Theresa, takes Vasco to a lepers' bustee. A child is lying there, half dead. With her white hand, the nun shoos the flies away from the half-dead child. Vultures are perched on the tile roofs of the stinking slaughterhouse across the way. All you can do is walk through, step across, look away.

Vasco no longer knows where he is or has been. Now in a day nursery—so affectionate, these two-year-olds. Now in a school, where the children sing something Catholic with closed eyes. Now in a foundling home—a childless Brahman couple adopt the newborn son of an untouchable mother. Vasco wishes them well. Now milk is being distributed outside a dispensary—all so inadequate. A resolute nun keeps the crowd in order. Sister Ananda tells me what Mother Theresa says about the problems of Calcutta. "Maybe we're only a drop of water in the ocean," she says, "but the ocean wouldn't be full without us."

No, don't look. Step across. Stop your ears with lead. Practice glassy-eyed indifference. Leave pity in your suitcase with your shirts and socks, or stick a bank note in your guidebook at the place where it says "Calcutta." Or look. Stop. Listen. Feel moved and ashamed. Show your red tongue, because pity is small change and quickly dispensed.

Now in Kalighat, where the ragged bundles that are picked up off the street at night are (for once) given ample helpings of rice at Mother Theresa's home for the dying. Next door (at last) the temple of the goddess Kali. A priest explains, and Vasco pays him five rupees. In the sacrificial area blood covered with flies recalls the goats that were sacrificed this morning. Young women scratch little good-luck symbols in the blood-drenched clay. Close by there's a tree for mothers who wish for children, lots of children, another child, more children, more and more children, a child (or two or three) year in, year out. The mothers hang wishing stones on the tree. The tree is full of wishing stones, all signifying children, more children. Wherever Vasco looks, flowery madness and Catholic-type Hindu kitsch. The black Kali is hidden behind the crush of the faithful.

Vasco stands to one side. He wants to know why she sticks out her red tongue. The priest explains that after Kali had killed all the demons (and other counterrevolutionaries) she couldn't stop killing and only came to her senses after setting her foot on the chest of her recumbent male aspect, Shiva. Then Kali was ashamed, and for shame she stuck out her tongue. Sticking out the tongue has been regarded as a sign of being ashamed ever since. Nowhere has Vasco seen a minister, governor, Brahman, or lisping poet stick out his tongue. He has seen the pale tongues of cows grazing gently in garbage. He has seen how undernourishment turns children blond. He has seen mothers dipping their whining babies' pacifiers in brackish sugar water. He has seen flies on everything under the sun. He has seen life before death.

Vasco takes refuge in the newspaper. Side by side with a story about the strike of the food truckers he reads the latest about the table-tennis matches. The members of the Swedish team have the runs. After a short stroll around town they flee back to their hotel in horror. Now they talk of leaving ahead of time. And Vasco writes his Ilsebill, now in her third month of pregnancy, horrified half sentences on a postcard showing a glossy picture of the black Kali: "This place defies understanding. Reason won't get you anywhere. The lepers are worse than I thought. I've met a nun who believes with all her might and is always cheerful. The heat is something. Leaving tomorrow. Flying to the Malabar Coast, where Vasco da Gama landed . . ."

Send a postcard with regards from Calcutta. See Calcutta and go on living. Meet your Damascus in Calcutta. As alive as Calcutta. Chop off your cock in Calcutta (in the temple of Kali, where young goats are sacrificed and a tree is hung with wishing stones that cry out for children, more and more children). In Calcutta, encoffined in mosquito netting, dream of Calcutta. Get lost in Calcutta. On an uninhabited island write a book about Calcutta. At a party call Calcutta an example (of something). Rethink the Frankfurt/Mannheim area as Calcutta. Misbehaved children, women like Ilsebill who are never satisfied, and men who live for schedules—curse them, wish them all in Calcutta. Recommend Calcutta to a young couple as a good place to visit on their honeymoon. Write a poem called "Calcutta" and stop taking planes to far-off places. Get a composer to set all the projects for cleaning up Calcutta to music and have the resulting oratorio (sung by a Bach society) open in Calcutta. Develop a new dialectic from Calcutta's contradictions. Transfer the UN to Calcutta.

When Vasco de Gama, hardly able to remember his first landing, returned reborn to Calcutta, he decided to level the city with ten thousand bulldozers and rebuild it by computer. Thereupon the computor vomited up three thousand sixteen-story bustees, another vast slum, only deep-frozen and much lonelier, beyond hope of disaster and totally isolated, since all noise has been absorbed. And then Calcutta died, though the living standard had been raised just above the destitution level. Very little was lacking, only the things that matter. People who multiply as a form of self-assertion. All the same, says Vasco to himself, infant mortality has dropped. Or perhaps if all the existing statistical charts and tables were pulped, a new study could be financed on the proceeds. Let's not waste another word on Calcutta. Delete Calcutta from all guidebooks. In Calcutta, Vasco gained four and a half pounds.

Three questions

How,
where horror should cast us in lead,
can I laugh,
even at breakfast laugh?
How,
where garbage and only garbage grows,
am I to speak of Ilsebill because she is beautiful,
and speak of beauty?
How,
where the hand in the photo
remains forever riceless,
shall I write about the cook
and how she stuffs fattened geese?

The sated are going on a hunger strike.
O beautiful garbage!
It's enough to make you die laughing.

I'm trying to find a word for shame.

Too much

Between the holidays
as soon as it's late and quiet enough,
I read Orwell's utopian novel, *1984,*
which I read for the first time in 1949
in a very different frame of mind.

To one side, next to the nutcracker and the package of to-
    bacco,
lies a book of statistics,
the figures that maximize-minimize
the world's population—according to how it will be fed
or not fed up to the year 2000.
In pauses,
when I reach for my tobacco
or crack a hazelnut,
I am overtaken by difficulties
which in comparison with Big Brother
and the world-wide protein shortage
are slight
but refuse to stop snickering in private.

Now I am reading about interrogation methods in the near
    future.
Now I am trying to remember figures,
present infant-mortality
patterns in southern Asia.
Now I'm unraveling on the edges,
because, before the holidays, ebbed quarrels
were tied up in little packages: Ilsebill's wishes . . .

The ash tray is half full of nutshells.

Too much of everything.
Something has to be deleted: India
or Oligarchic Collectivism
or the family Christmas.

Esau says

Commuted to lentils.
Drown in a sea of lentils.
On my lentil-stuffed cushion.
Hope springs like lentils.
And what the prophets have always wanted is
a miraculous multiplication of lentils.

And when he arose on the third day
his hunger for lentils was great.

Beginning at breakfast.
Thickened till the spoon stands erect.
With marjoram-seasoned shoulder of mutton.
Or remembered lentils: once when King Stephen Batory
returned to camp from the hunt
Mother Margarete Rusch boiled up a (tough, year-old)
    pheasant
with lentils to make him a Polish-style soup.

With a bagful I walked without fear.
Since me, birthrights have been available.
Paid off, I live by lentil law.
My little brother has a tough time of it.

The last meal

First built in 1346 as a bastion to the High Gate and
subsequently enlarged as the need for prison cells, torture
chambers, and business premises increased, the Stockturm,

whose dungeon keeps were reputed to be dry, was rebuilt in 1509, when city architects Hetzel and Enkinger added two stories and capped the tower. Thereafter it stood empty and unused until King Sigismund of Poland, responding in April 1526 to the call of Mayor Eberhard Ferber, occupied the city, posted Counter Reformation statutes in the seven principal churches, and haled all the leaders of the uprising against the patrician council, except for the fugitive preacher Hegge, before a court of aldermen, which sentenced the six ringleaders to death by beheading, including the blacksmith Peter Rusch, whose daughter had recently been appointed abbess of Saint Bridget's—an imposing woman of controversial reputation who flattered the taste of all parties with her conventual cookery, took her cut on every transaction, and even in times of general ruin (war, plague, and famine) made a profit.

And because Mother Rusch was not without influence, she was able to obtain, if not her father's pardon, at least the right to cook one last meal for him. Highly placed persons accepted her invitation. Mayor Ferber, deposed and banished to his starosty in Dirschau by the rebellious guilds but now restored to office, and Abbot Jeschke of the Oliva Monastery repaired to the Stockturm in fur-trimmed brabant, quite willing to join blacksmith Rusch in spooning up his favorite dish. Executioner Ladewig was also invited, and came. The cooking abbess had put her full kettle on the hearth the night before in the kitchen of the executioner (and knacker), and the smell penetrated to every last dungeon of the now fully occupied Stockturm.

Who will join me in a dish of tripe? It soothes, appeases the anger of the outraged, stills the fear of death, and reminds us of tripe eaten in former days, when there was always a half-filled pot of it on the stove. A chunk of the fat paunch and the limp, honeycombed walls of the second stomach—four pounds for three fifty. It's the widespread distaste for innards that makes beef heart and pork kidneys, calf's lung and tripe cheap.

She took her time. She pounded the pieces and brushed them inside and out, as though some beggar's sweaty rags had found their way to her washboard. She removed the wrinkled skin, but she spared the belly fat, for tripe fat has a special quality—instead of hardening into tallow, it dissolves like soap.

194

When a last meal was prepared for blacksmith Rusch and his guests, seven quarts of water seasoned with salt, caraway seed, cloves, ginger root, bay leaf, and coarsely pounded peppercorns were set over an open fire. The limp pieces, cut into finger-long strips, were added until the pot was full, and when the water came to a boil the scum was skimmed off. Then the daughter covered her father's favorite dish and let it boil for four hours. At the end she added garlic, freshly grated nutmeg, and more pepper.

The time it takes. Those are the best hours. When the tough has to be made tender, but can't be hurried. How often Mother Rusch and I, while the billowing tripe kept the kitchen stable-warm, sat at the table pushing checkers over the board, discovering the sea route to India, or catching flies on the smooth-polished table top, and telling each other about the tripe of olden times, when we were Pomorshian and still heathen. And about older than olden times, when elk cows were the only source of meat.

Later on, after the daughter had cooked her father's last dish of tripe, she cooked for rich coopers at guild banquets, for Hanseatic merchants who cared about nothing but Öresund tolls, for fat abbots and King Stephen Batory, who wanted his tripe sour and Polish. Still later Amanda Woyke, in her farm kitchen, cooked up tripe with turnips and potatoes into a soup that she seasoned with lovage. And still later Lena Stubbe taught the patrons of the Danzig-Ohra soup kitchen to enjoy proletarian cabbage soups made with (cut-rate) tripe. And to this very day Maria Kuczorra, canteen cook at the Lenin Shipyard in Gdańsk, makes a thick soup once a week out of *kaldauny* (tripe).

When you are feeling cold inside—try the walls of the cow's second stomach. When you are sad, cast out by all nature, sad unto death, try tripe, which cheers us and gives meaning to life. Or in the company of witty friends, godless enough to sit in the seat of the scornful, spoon up caraway-seasoned tripe out of deep dishes. Or cooked with tomatoes, Andalusian-style with chickpeas, or à la Portugaise with kidney beans and bacon. Or if love needs an appetizer, precook tripe in white wine, then steam it with diced celery root. On cold, dry days, when the east wind is banging at the windowpanes and driving your Ilsebill up the wall, tripe thickened with sour cream and served with potatoes in their jackets will help. Or if we must part, briefly or forever, like the time I was a prisoner in the Stockturm and my daughter served me a last meal of peppered tripe.

Because the execution was to take place next day in the Long Market, in the presence of the king of Poland, of the seated and standing councils, of the aldermen and various prelates and abbots, the abbess of Saint Bridget's had invited the guests to her father's dungeon for an early evening meal. Torches on the walls provided light. A basin of coals under the barred window hole kept the pot of tripe warm. Margarete Rusch tasted for seasoning, and after that she didn't touch another mouthful. She said grace, appending a prayer for the condemned blacksmith, then served her father and his guests. But while the men were spooning up their tripe out of earthenware bowls, and while she was pouring black beer into mugs, she spoke. She spoke and her words passed over the autocratic head of the patrician, over the sleek, round head of the abbot, over the bald pate of the executioner, and over her father's head, which he had lowered into his bowl. She spoke without paragraphs or punctuation of any kind.

Margarete Rusch was known for that. When the soup was too hot, while the men were gnawing at goose drumsticks, before fish was served on Friday (mackerel bedded on leeks), but also over tables eaten bare, the abbess spoke to all those she cooked for, with a broad accent that brooked no interruption. She could reel off several stories (or instructive disquisitions) at once without dropping a thread. From sheep raising on the Island, from the sewage sludge in the Mottlau, she would ramble on to Councilor Angermünde's daughters, but without failing to bring in price increases that the Danes had clapped on Scania herring, to get the latest joke about Preacher Hegge off her chest, to mention the continued interest of the Brigittine nuns in certain Old City real estate; yet with it all she found breath to spin out her favorite topic— larded with pious invocations of all the archangels from Ariel to Zedekiel—namely, the necessity of establishing a pepper depot in Lisbon (with a warehouse on the Malabar Coast of India), spinning out every detail of the commercial law involved.

Regardless of whom she cooked for, her table talk was thrown in—a subliminal mumbling with subplots as intricate as the politics of her time. She spoke as if to herself, but loud enough for the bishop of Leslau, who was dipping his bread into Margarete's hasenpfeffer, or for Councilors Angermünde and Feldstadt, who were shoveling in her beef hock with millet, to detect the purpose behind her chatter, although it was never certain whether Mother Rusch favored the patrician council or the lower trades, whether she was agitating for the Hanseatic League and against the Polish crown, and whether or not she was outwardly Catholic but contaminated through and through with Lutheranism. And yet her table speeches captured all ears with their ambiguities. They put this one in the right, injected that one with doubt, supplied tactical pointers, and in the long run brought benefit only to the Abbey of Saint Bridget, which obtained profitable fishing rights (Lake Ottomin), indentured leases (the Scharpau, the sheep farms of Schiedlitz and Praust), and property in the Old City (on the Rähm, in Peppertown), and an episcopal letter safeguarding the abbey against Dominican snooping.

And so, when the abbess Margarete Rusch served up the last dish of tripe to her father and his guests, her tongue wagged as usual. That was her way. Always, along with her cookery, she apportioned her subtly balanced interests.

At first the men at the table sat silent. The only sound was the jangling of Peter Rusch's irons, for the blacksmith ate in fetters. And outside the barred window hole, the tower pigeons clamored. Guzzling and gulping. The executioner's Adam's apple bobbed up and down.

Yet it was not at all certain that the king of Poland had intended so harsh a sentence. Jeschke and Ferber had worked on the judge and on the aldermen. Ferber, who spoke first, admitted as much; law and order, he said, must be manifested visibly. True, the abbot conceded, the blacksmith might have been spared (and merely blinded) if Hegge, that minion of Luther, had not escaped. He had a pretty good idea, said the wealthy Ferber, bending over his tripe in his fur-trimmed broadcloth, who had helped Hegge escape from the blocked-off city. That, said the abbot, all the while plying his spoon, was known to all, though no one could prove it. Executioner Ladewig gave assurance that the scrawny neck of the escaped Dominican would have been far more welcome to him in the morning than that of a blacksmith. When Peter Rusch lifted his head out of the bowl and said, more in resignation than in protest, that he, too, was not unaware who had helped Preacher Hegge, spiritual head of the burghers' uprising, to escape from the beadles of the patrician order, Ferber said harshly, while holding out his bowl to the abbess to refill, "Then you also know whom you can thank for your death sentence." "Yes, indeed," said Jeschke. "Things have come to a pretty pass when a father can expect no mercy from his child. That's what happens when the pulpit is opened up to heresy." Here he threw in a bit of information, namely, that Hegge had apparently escaped to Greifswald and was going right on with his preaching.

Then Mother Rusch laughed so resoundingly, with every ounce of her flesh, that the walls expanded, and, pouring black beer, said casually: Yes, yes, she supposed all these insinuations were aimed at her. And maybe there was some truth in them. For one night in April, after it had pleased His Polish Majesty to occupy the city, she had seen a man in woman's skirts clinging to the town wall, in a place where it's low, not far from Jacob's Gate. Trying to climb over it, but he didn't have the strength. His misery had cried out for help, and she had helped. She had reached under his skirts, and when all her pushing and puffing had gone for nothing, had bitten off his left or right testicle. After that he had literally flown over the wall. Maybe the man had been Peter Hegge. But how could one be sure? Because, in her fright, she, Margarete Rusch, had swallowed this left or right ball. To tell the truth, she had been feeling pregnant ever since—this was the third month. But by whom? That was the question. If he was so inclined, Ferber could go to Greifswald, taking Jeschke with him, and they could reach between the still-eloquent Hegge's legs. Then they'd know more.

At that blacksmith Rusch and the bald-headed Ladewig laughed. Then, apart from the chains, nothing could be heard but the spoons in the bowls, the sound of chewing and swallowing, and the pigeons in the window hole. And when she saw the men so deeply immersed in their tripe, Mother Rusch started in again with her ambiguous mumbling; for the abbess spoke freely and frankly only in the refectory of Saint Bridget's, where at vespers and in the evening hours the nuns and novices forgathered around the long oak table.

In troubled times—everywhere monks and nuns were escaping from their cloisters to risk the perils of secular life—it was often difficult to hold pious girls to their vows. They fidgeted, they wanted out, they wanted a man in breeches, wanted to be married, to bear children by the dozen, to walk in silk and satin and try to keep up with the town fashions.

And so, while the sweet millet porridge diminished on the long table, the abbess told her little nuns, whose asses were itching for life, what life is and how quickly it crumbles away. She listed the freedoms of the nunnery and, in the debit column, the arduous duties of the married woman. While buckwheat piroshki filled with bacon and spinach were being enjoyed on both sides of the long table, the abbess explained the male build to her man-crazy women with the help of the vegetable course, buttered (and parsleyed) carrots, which with their varied shapes provided a graphic illustration of what a man is good for. How deeply penetrating he can be and how knobby. How soon he gives out and starts drooping pathetically. How brutal he becomes when he can't get it up. How unprofitable this quick fucking is to women. How all he wants is children, especially sons. How soon he looks for variety in other beds. But how his spouse must never wander, never lust for other carrots. How hard his hand strikes. How suddenly he withdraws his favor and gets his carrot cooked soft away from home.

But when the nuns, and especially the novices, kept squirming on their stools and persisted in seeing harder and more lasting promise in their buttered carrots, the abbess gave them permission to receive visitors through the back door of the convent, and also to range freely outside the cloister, thus acquainting them with the pleasures of the flesh and making them better able to resist the seductions of married life.

Before saying grace and dismissing her charges, the abbess gave them further bits of advice: Let no quarrel over a codpiece ever disturb their monastic tranquillity. Let them always remain good sisters to one another. Let them not content themselves with holding still, but ride with and against. A man's thanks should always be weighable in silver. And never, never, never, must they succumb to weepy, gushy love.

Though not yet thirty, Mother Rusch had been abbess of Saint Bridget's for over a year, having, as nun in charge of the kitchen, shown accomplishments of many kinds. And the accomplished abbess succeeded in holding her nuns, whereas the monks and nuns of the Dominican, Beguin, Franciscan, and Benedictine orders were running away to Luther. The consequence was unrest, uprisings of the guilds, iconoclast riots, alarums, and excursions, followed by little change or at the most by Royal Polish punitive expeditions. Preacher Hegge, to be sure, had managed to escape, but blacksmith Rusch and five other artisans, all poor devils, members of the lower trades, were condemned to death. And that is why a daughter served her father his last dish of tripe, which, since beginning to feel pregnant—most likely the work of Hegge shortly before his flight—she had taken to peppering excessively.

And after she had filled her guests' bowls for the third time, pepper kept cropping up in her talk.

That was her obsession. Fat Gret had a thing about pepper. It sharpened her wit, she thought, it did wonders. It tormented her to think that all the new sea-borne pepper—the overland pepper that traders had been bringing in from Venice as long as anyone could remember was so fearfully expensive—passed through Lisbon. True, the Augsburgers maintained a depot there, where they hoarded pepper to keep the price up, but the Hanseatic towns let the trade slip through their fingers. Which explains why for some years Mother Rusch was impelled, by political ambition as well as the normal concerns of the kitchen, to take a hand in international politics. Much as she hated the patrician Ferber, she was determined to harness the experienced merchant and still actively seafaring admiral to her plans.

After dishing out a third helping of tripe for her father and his guests, she let her table talk drift overseas. It wouldn't do to leave the New World to the Portuguese and Spaniards. The Dutch and English were already coming in on a large scale. The only bankers engaged in the pepper trade were the Fuggers. But the Hanseatic League was short-sightedly confining its operations to the lesser seas, squabbling to no effect (as it had done only last year) with the Danes over Öresund tolls and herring silver, spitefully competing with one another (witness Lübeck and Danzig), sticking to wood, cloth, grain, dried codfish, and salt, refusing to take over the pepper trade, and neglecting to fit out ships for the longer voyage, too small-minded to establish a trading post on the pepper coast of India, as the Portuguese had done in Goa and Cochin, and preferring to engage in divisive religious quarrels and chop off the heads of good men like her father.

She went on to discuss the principal pepper varieties most knowledgeably, their moist and dry weight, how stored and marketed; undertook, if an overseas expedition should be organized, to lure certain Arab helmsmen away from the Portuguese caravels; predicted spice wars between Spain and England; and even professed her eagerness—provided Jeschke would come along—to embark her own full weight on a vessel bound for India, there to propagate the Catholic faith, if only Ferber would consent to throw off his weariness, stop toadying to the Polish court, and at last start commissioning navigation charts.

But Ferber remained indifferent over his tripe. Jeschke only sighed: pleasing as such a mission would be to God, he feared the Indian climate. Blacksmith Rusch said nothing. Executioner Ladewig had other dreams. And when the patrician leaned back, after spooning up the last bowl of tripe, his answering speech was uncompromising.

He knew the world. He was a humanist and spoke five languages. Everywhere things were the same as in the Baltic area. Trading posts and warehouses in distant places could never be maintained for long; great losses were a certainty. Novgorod was giving them trouble enough. Falsterbo cost more than it brought in. Goa! It would cost the Portuguese dearly one of these days. As for the English, they seemed to have no inkling of what a burden India might well become to them. Trading posts in India. Ridiculous. Now, after last year's futile war, did we want to pay the Danes pepper fees along with their herring silver? Hamburg in a pinch could afford such an undertaking. To maintain colonies you need an open coast. Danzig's motto remained: Moderation in all things. No, he had no use for adventures. And speaking of his weariness: despite the ingratitude of the local rabble, he had earned the right to rest. Immediately after the morrow's execution, he would divest himself of his chain of office and retire to his starosty for a quiet old age. Yes indeed! He would collect paintings from Antwerp. Musicians would play the lute for him and sing Italian songs. If the abbess wished, she could follow him to Dirschau, but not—by God!—to India. What was to keep him from financing a branch of the pious Brigittines in Dirschau? There'd always be plenty of pepper for her kitchen.

Thereupon Mother Rusch, for the fourth time, filled first her father's bowl, then the bowls of the guests with tripe.

Even as she wielded the ladle, she cursed men for hopeless stay-at-homes. Then she fell silent, and the executioner spoke his mind. Ladewig complained about the wretchedness of his job. Luckily horse flaying brought in a little extra money. They wouldn't pay him to kill stray dogs. And the city was drowning in shit and piss.

Ladewig, whose meticulous, unhurried methods in the torture chamber allowed of no premature confessions, outlined an exemplary system of sanitation for the walled city, but only the blacksmith was listening. Here again Ferber was shortsighted, or he might have commissioned the executioner to keep the city clean, catch ownerless dogs, take measures against the plague, and, for suitable fees, clean out the sludge boxes of all premises adjoining the Mottlau (thereby anticipating the "Newly Revised Ordinance" of 1761 by a good two centuries).

Sensibly as Ladewig spoke and hard as he tried to win the patrician's approval, Ferber's mind, as he spooned up tripe, was already on his retirement in Dirschau. Still deeply immersed in his tripe, Abbot Jeschke dreamed himself and his benefices into a perfect world, undarkened by heresy. But though reacting with resolute silence to the cleansing of the city, Mother Rusch would not desist from Indian pepper. And because she was pregnant, her hope grew and grew.

It will be a girl! And a girl it was. She was named Hedwig, brought up by Fat Gret's aunts in the Wicker Bastion, and seventeen years later married the merchant Rodrigues d'Evora, a Ximines of the big Portuguese spice-trading family, who opened a trading post in Cochin on the Malabar Coast of India. Twice a year, for the feasts of Saint John and Saint Martin, the son-in-law honored the marriage contract (for Hedwig's body was beautiful, in a Baltic sort of way) by sending a keg of ginger, two bales of cinnamon, a ship's pound of saffron, two crates of bitter orange peel, a sack of almonds, a sack of grated coconut, specified amounts of cardamom, cloves, and nutmeg, five barrels containing Mother Rusch's weight (at the time of the marriage contract) in black and white pepper, and one barrel of moist green pepper.

After merchant d'Evora, his wife, and four of his daughters died of the fever in Cochin, the one surviving daughter, who later married the Spanish pepper magnate Pedro de Malvenda, is believed to have kept up the pepper shipments to Mother Rusch as long as she lived. Isabel de Malvenda lived in Burgos, then in Antwerp, from where, after her husband's death, she corresponded with Martin Enzesperger, the Fuggers' pepper agent, and established her contractors as far afield as Venice.

By then London and Antwerp had taken a hand in the trade. Hamburg, which like all the Hanseatic towns was hostile to anything foreign, maintained a pepper trading post for only a few years. Several spice wars contributed dates to history, and in one of them Spain lost its Armada.

Even when the bowls were empty for the fourth time, the blacksmith and his guests had not yet spooned up sufficient peppered and caraway-seeded tripe. Accordingly Mother Rusch ladled fifth helpings out of her deep kettle and poured black beer into mugs. She also went on mumbling her table talk: hints smothered in local gossip, threats stirred into her usual nunnish chatter. But if patrician Ferber and Abbot Jeschke had not been too stuffed to listen, they might have had something to think about, for Mother Rusch quite transparently detailed her plans for settling accounts with both of them. Which plans she also carried out, for three years later she smothered the rich Eberhard Ferber in bed under her double hundredweight; and fifty years later—for Fat Gret lived to a ripe old age for her vengeance—she fattened Abbot Jeschke to death: he died over a bowl of tripe.

Blacksmith Rusch may have gathered the gist of his daughter's projects from her table talk and understood how she meant to avenge his death, for the poor devil grinned broadly over his empty bowl. Indeed, something more than the warm feeling of having filled his belly one last time may have accounted for his satisfaction. He sang his daughter's praises, and there his talk became rather confused, for he brought in a fish, whom he referred to as the "Flounder in the sea," and thanked him for having advised him, at a time when his hair was still brown, to send his youngest daughter, whose mother was dying of the fever, to a convent, for there, so the Flounder has assured him, she would become shrewd and crafty, so as to manage her female flesh independently and have hot soup in daily readiness for her father in his old age.

Then he, too, fell silent, replete with tripe. After that, belches were accompanied only by an occasional word or

203

half sentence. Ferber dreamed of his life in the country; far from all strife, he would live in the midst of his art collection, culling wisdom from books. After eating so much tripe, Abbot Jeschke could think only of the tripe he hoped to spoon up in the future, peppered just the way the abbess did it. But by then Lutheranism would—by drastic measures if necessary—have been eradicated from the world. Executioner Ladewig anticipated several articles of the "Newly Revised Ordinance." He would have liked to place with the local coopers an order for the barrels needed to clean up the city. For every barrel emptied he would charge only ten groschen. Blacksmith Rusch, on the other hand, predicted that the patrician council would be faced forever and ever with unrest and insurrectionary demands on the part of the guilds and lower trades, and his prophecy came true in December 1970. The lower orders have never ceased to rebel against patrician authoritarianism and to risk their necks for a little more civil rights.

Then, full fed, the guests left. Ferber said nothing. Jeschke delivered himself of a Latin blessing. Ladewig took the five emptied bowls with him. The pigeons in the window hole were silent. The torches had almost burned down in their holders. Peter Rusch sat in his chains and shed a few tears for his last supper. Laden right and left with the kettle and the empty beer keg, his daughter resumed her mumbling on her way out: "You'll soon be out of your misery now. You'll soon be a lot better off. They'll give you a nice cozy place in the heavenly guildhall. And you'll always have plenty of tripe. So stop worrying. Your Gret will settle up with them. It may take time, but I'll fix them good."

Then Mother Rusch admonished her father to hold his curly gray head erect the next day and not to fling curses at anyone whomsoever. He should kneel unbowed before the executioner. He could rely on her vengeance. The taste of it would linger in her mouth like Indian pepper. She wouldn't forget. No, she wouldn't forget.

Peter Rusch did as his daughter had bidden. He must have had a goodly portion of tripe half digested in his innards when, next day in the Long Market, facing the Artushof, where the patricians and prelates stood as though painted around Sigismund, king of Poland, he (fourth of the six candidates) silently let his head be severed from his shoulders.

204

No bungling. You could count on executioner Ladewig. The abbess looked on. A sudden shower of rain made her face glisten. And addressing the Women's Tribunal, the Flounder said, "In short, dear ladies, vigorously as Margarete Rusch pursued her aims, perseveringly as she raked in her gains, slow as she was in settling her account—on June 26, 1526, when blacksmith Peter Rusch was executed along with the other ringleaders, a daughter wept for her father."

Tarred and feathered

She only liked me plucked.
Feathers—I write
about fights between gulls
and against time.

Or how a boy with his breath
wafts the down over
fences to nowhere.

Down—that means sleep and geese, priced by the pound.
To every bed its burden.
While she plucked between her stupid knees
and the feathers, as the saying goes, flew,
the ordained power slept downy-softly.

Poultry for whom?
But I blew, kept feathers in suspense.
That is traditional faith;
doubts tarred and feathered.

Not long ago, I found
some quills and
cut them for my use.
First monks, later town clerks,
today secretaries keep the lies flowing.

Fat Gret's ass

was as big as two collective farms. And if you sexual
sociologists, deep in worry blubber from counting flies' legs,
had been asked in as witnesses when, as she liked me to do
on Wednesdays, I came at her from behind but first, to make
it all soft and as wet as wept on, licked her asshole and environs like a goat (hungry for salt), which was easy to do
when Fat Gret offered her double treasure for worship, you
would have seen the archetype of Christian charity, our partner-oriented fervor; but my Ilsebill—who is sometimes adventurous on Thursdays—has never, no matter how devoutly I
get down on my knees to her, licked my ass, because she's
afraid her tongue would drop off with her last shred of modesty.

She's much too prim, always worried about disgracing herself. Sexy, yes, but so coy about it. And because she's perpetually forming the word "dignity" with curling lips, she has
puritanical lockjaw.

Yet Ilsebill reads books of all sizes in which the overcom-
ing of inhibitions is said to be the first requirement for a free
society. Never fear, I'll knock or teach these late-bourgeois
refusal mechanisms—"Somehow," she says, "I don't dare, I
still don't dare"—out of her, and I'll do it the way it says in
her women's lib books, with partner-oriented conflicting-roles
games, until on one of these Catholic Fridays—Believe me,
holy father!—she and her little tongue will see how nice it is.
For it can't be bought and paid for. It's within reach of all. It
has nothing to do with class. Old Man Marx didn't know
anything about it. It's a foretaste of beauty. As every dog
knows. Oh, to sniff at, lick, taste, and smell one another!

But when I say to my Ilsebill, "Tomorrow is Saturday. I'll
take a thorough bath, I'll smell of lavender all over," she
says, "So what!" Because we've lost the habit. Because we
only read about it. Because if we mention it at all we mean it
symbolically. Because we've discussed it, chewed the whole
thing over too often. Because we don't suspect what expectant rosebud lips an asshole is always making—all week long.

For our playing fields—yours, Ilsebill, and mine—have just the right proportions—no speculator, no concrete-crazed developer can divide up your meadow, no flaming-red party boss can grab my ass away from you (or yours from me). The ass is one thing that ideology is afraid to touch. Can't gets its claws on it. Can't read any idea into it. Therefore disparages it. Only gays are supposed to make use of it. A kick in the ass is nevertheless permissible, linguistically speaking. And with deplorable bad taste the asshole has been transformed into a term of opprobrium. Ass licking is looked down on, though the capitalist developer and the flaming-red party boss lick each other's asses, but without pleasure, for whether officially or unofficially they do it in trousers, their taste running to flannel, fifty percent worsted and fifty percent synthetic fiber.

No, Ilsebill! It's got to be bare. My meadows, your rolling hills. Our fields. I worship it, God's rounded idea. Yes, yes, ever since the partly cloudy Neolithic, when Awa's dimples were still unnumbered, the heavens for me have been festooned with asses. And when Margarete Rusch, the cooking nun, first let her sun rise for the runaway Franciscan monk—for me, in other words—I achieved an unveiled understanding of Saint Francis's hymn: devotion, jubilation, industry. Forget no dimple. Stop to rest beside country lanes. The hills ask to be gently grazed. Deep in dialogue. Entrance and exit exchange greetings. Where does the food go? Who's kissing whom? Insight gained. Soon I will know every bit of you. Ah, Ilsebill, now that you're pregnant and burgeoning all over, you ought, you ought to . . . Come on, it's high time, come on! Because it's Sunday and all week we've done nothing but talk around it and discuss the anal phase of infancy much too seriously.

When Fat Gret let a fart because I'd been licking her too meticulously, we both relished the breeze. After all, as usual on Wednesday, we had eaten beans with turnips and peppered pork chops; and anyone who is repelled by his sweetheart's farts has no business talking about love. . . . All right, laugh. Get that stuffy look off your face. Have a heart. It's funny, isn't it? Let me tell you about white beans and nuns' farts. How they argued about bread and wine and wine and bread, the right order in which to take the Eucharist; a quarrelsome century. Margret, Fat Gret, laughed herself healthy over it.

To cheer my Ilsebill, now in the third month of pregnancy, up a little—but she remained stony-faced and said I was "vulgar"—I had cooked white beans down to a purée and served them with roast pork and pepper sauce. We also had Teltow turnips, and the whole meal corresponded to the peppery menu which, in the spring of 1569, Mother Margarete Rusch served up to Abbot Jeschke, Johannes Kostra, the Danzig commandant, and Stanislaw Karnkowski, bishop of Leslau at the Oliva Monastery. The three dignitaries had met to straighten out some senseless discrepancies in a sheaf of Counter Reformation decrees. For though King Sigismund Augustus used the "Statuta Karnkowiana" as an instrument of the Counter Reformation, their actual purpose was to curtail the economic power of the city of Danzig, and incidentally to incite the politically impotent guilds against the patrician council. And because this idea, embedded in bloodcurdling antiheresy provisions, had sprung not from the heads of Jeschke, Kostra, and Karnkowski but from that of the cooking nun, I told my Ilsebill the story of Margarete Rusch; for Fat Gret is still imprisoned inside me, and now at last I mean to set her free.

In the year 1498 after the incarnation of our Lord, when, thanks to an Arab helmsman's knowledge of the winds and ocean currents, the Portuguese admiral Vasco da Gama finally sighted land and put shore in Calicut, thus opening the sea route to India with all its still-tangled skein of consequences, a girl child was born in the Wicker Bastion, the erstwhile Pomorshian settlement, by then a part of the Old City of Danzig, to the blacksmith Peter Rusch by his wife, Kristin, who then promptly died. The little girl was born on Saint Martin's Day, for which reason whole flocks of geese later grew cold under Fat Gret's plucking fingers.

Beginning at the age of twelve, Margret stood in the kitchen of Saint Bridget's Convent in the Old City, cleaning turnips, scaling carp, husking rye, and cutting tripe into finger-long strips, for the Flounder had advised blacksmith Rusch (or, in my then time-phase, me) to put this superfluous girl into a convent as soon as possible; for which reason the Women's Tribunal has asked the overbearing flatfish questions that he will answer elsewhere. In any case Margarete became a novice at the age of sixteen and took her solemn vows in the very year when, with sturdy hammer, the monk Luther nailed up his theses.

As a full-fledged nun who presided over the convent kitchen, Margret (known at an early age as Fat Gret) began to cook outside the house as soon as the widely ramified affairs of the Brigittine nuns called for her kitchen diplomacy. When Jakob Hegge preached Lutheranism on the Hagelsberg, she, at the foot of the hill, cooked Counter Reformation tripe and fish soups for the crowds that gathered there. And when I, the runaway Franciscan monk, became her kitchen boy and, when she so pleased, bed companion, we cooked for that archenemy of the guilds, Mayor Eberhard Ferber, sometimes in his patrician house on Long Street, sometimes on his Island farm, and sometimes in his starosty at Dirschau, where he took refuge, for so hated was Ferber by the coopers, drapers, dockers, and butchers that he often had to flee the city.

Just when Vasco da Gama the Portuguese viceroy was dying of plague, yellow fever, or Dominican poison in Cochin in southern India, Ferber was deposed as mayor. Led by blacksmith Rusch, Hegge's increasing following had risen up and taken over the city government, though for only a short time. The following year King Sigismund of Poland marched against the city with eight thousand men and occupied it without a fight. The "Statuta Sigismundi" were posted. Ferber was restored to power. A trial was held.

Before her father was executed, the abbess Margret Rusch cooked his favorite dish for him; then she moved in with the embittered Eberhard Ferber, who, no sooner reinstated as mayor, retired to his next-to-last dwelling place in Dirschau. Three years later—Fat Gret was still cooking for him—he died, leaving several pieces of Old City real estate, his sheep farm in Praust, and various properties on the Island to her convent. Altogether, the cooking nun Margret added so much to the wealth of the Brigittine order with her free-ranging outside cookery that she soon gained the stature of a true abbess, both respected and feared, even though she was widely reputed to keep a houseful of bedworthy kitchen boys and to be an out-and-out slut.

Because I was always with her. She took me in—me or one of the little Franciscan monks who kept running away from Holy Trinity—buried me in her flesh, and resurrected me, acclimated me to the warmth of the stable, covered me with her fat like a meat pasty, kept me as contented as a well-fed baby, and in quickly changing seasons wore me out. Whether the Reformers were on top in the outside world or whether the Dominican Counter Reformation was turning every poor sinner's words inside out, Margret's box bed preserved a sultry vapor that the Flounder, addressing the Women's Tribunal, characterized as "strictly pagan."

"If it is permissible," he said, "to call a revolution cozy, then one may say that the revolutionary doings in the bed of Abbess Margarete Rusch took place in cozily warmed areas of freedom." And I, too, proved to my Ilsebill that in those days only nuns could possibly pass for emancipated women, free from irksome conjugal duties, free from the state of childishness induced by male domination, never made fools of by fashion, always protected by sisterly solidarity based on their betrothal to the heavenly bridegroom, deluded by no earthly love, secure through economic power, feared even by the Dominicans, always cheerful and well informed. Mother Rusch was an enlightened woman and, in addition, so fat that her pregnancies went almost unnoticed.

She bore two daughters. While traveling, on the road, as it were. Some barn was always available for her confinements. But never was I permitted to speak of fatherhood, father's duties, or father's rights. "There's only one father," she said, breaking into a shattering laugh, "and that's our sweet Lord, who's supposed to be up there in heaven."

And she didn't care a bit if strait-laced Protestants or Catholics thought the two girls, both of whom were brought up in the Wicker Bastion by Fat Gret's sisters, showed a resemblance sometimes to Preacher Hegge, sometimes to the patrician Ferber, and sometimes even to a no-good Franciscan monk. As far as she was concerned, fathers were all ridiculous. She called the married women in their bourgeois stables "dressed-up mares" who had to hold still for their stallions, whereas she could make use of her little pouch as she saw fit. Moreover, Fat Gret did not hold still, but jounced so heavily on her soon exhausted bed companion that she often knocked my wind out. She really crushed me. When it was over, I lay there as white as chalk, like a corpse. She had to rub me with vinegar water to revive me.

She may well have stopped the autocratic Eberhard Ferber's breath the same way, smothered the old goat under her bed weight. For she was not content just to cook for her succession of males. She also had to have her fun, her play and entertainment, all of which may strike a puritanical mind as obscene.

And so Abbess Margarete Rusch solved the bitterly earnest question of the century, the question of how to serve up the bread and wine, the Lord's Supper, in her own way, to wit, bedwise, by acrobatically moving her twat into the vertical and offering it as a chalice, which was then filled with red wine. Bread demanded to be dipped. Or consecrated wafers. Here the question—is this really flesh and blood, or only its sign and symbol—did not arise. The paper quarrel of the theologians became irrelevant. Ambiguities were over and done with. Never did I take Communion more devoutly. How simple Margret made the oblation and transubstantiation for me. With what childlike faith I immersed myself in the great mystery. Luckily no Dominican eye ever spied on our bed masses.

Ah, if only this home custom had become practical religion for papists and Lutherans, Mennonites and Calvinists! But, torn by discord, they cut one another down. They let their quarrel over the right table arrangements cost them long-drawn-out military campaigns, pillage, rapine, and the devastation of lovely countrysides. But to this day they have gone on fighting and gouging one another, living without mutual affection, and with morose morality condemning Fat Gret's chalice as sinful. Yet Margret was pious. Even for the most fleeting pleasure she thanked God with a prayer.

Two years after the Peace of Augsburg, when His Polish Majesty Sigismund Augustus also proved willing at least to tolerate Communion in both kinds, the majority of the burghers of Danzig decided in favor of Luther's table arrangements, and from then on quarreled only with the Calvinists and Mennonites. Thereupon, after ruling for twenty-seven years, Abbess Rusch declared herself weary of office and asked her sisters of the Brigittine Order for leave to retire as abbess and once again to make herself useful outside the convent as a cooking nun.

So much humility was interpreted as contrition. The truth is that the old woman, vigorous within her fat, wished to regain her old political mobility. From then on she was always a step ahead of the vicissitudes of history. Under the veil of Catholicism she worked for the Protestant cause. She was no longer interested in the Eucharist but still and once again in the rights that were denied the guilds. After all, she had grown up in the Wicker Bastion. What had cost her rebellious father, blacksmith Peter Rusch, his head—democratic grumbling and incendiary speeches in every guildhall—now became the daughter's stock in trade, but she spoke softly, over simmered cod liver, hasenpfeffer, and thrushes, which she barded with bacon and stuffed with juniper berries.

In 1567, when Stanislaw Karnkowski became bishop of Leslau and under his aegis a second Counter Reformation began looking for appropriate table arrangements, the elderly nun was cooking for Abbot Jeschke, whose monastery at Oliva had always been a place of contemplative reaction. There, after milky fish soup, Fat Gret served either hasenpfeffer or beef hearts stuffed with prunes or peppered pork roast with white beans and turnips, which last dish induced eminently political farts in the conspiring clerics.

The cooking nun believed in the liberating power of the fart. With what unabashed gusto she let her intestinal winds blow! Whether cooking for friend or foe—in the midst of her mumbled table talk, she would let loose a merry succession of farts, usually setting a full stop or following a question as its answer, but sometimes also parenthetically. Echoes of receding storms. Solemnly spaced gun salutes. Dry broadsides. Or mingled with her laughter, because nature had given her cheerful disposition a twofold, double-mouthed expression: as once when she brought King Stephen Batory the key of the besieged city as the stuffing of a sheep's head stuffed into a pig's head, and subsequently made the king's startled dignity laugh and fart so hard that His Polish Majesty and retinue were carried away, as though dissolved in laughter and soothed by their nether winds. The king had no choice but to impose mild conditions on the city and turn a blind eye to the cooking nun's offense. For it was Margret who on February 15, 1577, incited the lower trades to rebel and (very much her father's daughter) put them up to setting the Oliva Monastery on fire.

When, immediately after the solemn Peace, Abbot Jeschke returned to the burned monastery to oversee the corvee of the peasants who were rebuilding it, he insisted—much as he knew she hated him—that Sister Margret take charge of his kitchen. Never had she cooked under duress. For her cookery had always been a labor of love. For three years she clothed her vengeance in stewed breast of beef, stuffed goose, sour aspics, or suckling pig, which she stuffed with shredded cabbage, apples, and raisins, never sparing the pepper.

What that man managed to shovel in. How long and hard his jaws labored. Why he couldn't leave anything over. How many had to go hungry to keep him belching-full. At last, by the summer of the year 1581, she had fattened Abbot Kaspar Jeschke to death. He died at table. More precisely: his sleek monk's head, with cheeks that had glowed with Catholic power for decades, fell into a bowl of the very dish that a lifetime before Fat Gret had cooked for her father, blacksmith Peter Rusch: peppered tripe. The cooking nun had forgotten nothing. And the Flounder also thinks that though stuffing an abbot to death is rather a drastic use to make of the culinary art, it was quite in keeping with the life style of the deceased.

Margarete Rusch died in 1585 from swallowing a pike bone, in the presence of King Stephen Batory, who by the recent peace treaty had confirmed not only the city of Danzig's rights to carry on trade and collect customs duties but the privileges of the patricians as well. Once again the guilds, the lower trades, and the sailors came off empty-handed. Patricians and courtiers feasted for days. More than a fishbone must have stuck in the aged nun's craw.

All of a sudden, when only leftovers remained of the roast pork with beans and turnips, my Ilsebill, with the stubborn persistence typical of pregnant women, wanted to know what, apart from the fact that she was born in 1498, the year of the landing in Calicut, Fat Gret had to do with Vasco da Gama. When I tried to answer with nunnish tales—how Abbess Margarete Rusch had traded her elder daughter to a Portuguese spice merchant for annual shipments of pepper from the Malabar Coast—Ilsebill got up from the table and said, "Aren't you clever! Or did the Flounder think that up? Trading her daughter for pepper! It's just too typical."

Delay

A pinch of Redeemer salt.
Another delay when my question—which
century are we playing now?—was answered
kitchenwise: when the price of pepper fell . . .

Nine times she sneezed over the bowl
where lay the hare giblets in their broth.
She refused to remember
that I was her kitchen boy.
Darkly she gazed at the fly in the beer
and wanted (no more delay)
to be rid of me no matter what. . . .

Soups in which the grit wins out.
When she praised hunger as if it were something to eat,
when she laughed quintessentially and not about turnips,
when at the kitchen table
she persuaded Death with dried peas
to grant a delay . . .

And so she sits inside me and writes her story. . . .

The Flounder's ideas about nunnish life

Possibly because I don't rightly know under whose name I
was connected with the abbess Margarete Rusch, and because
I remember my neolithic time-phase rather more clearly than
the confused circumstances of the Reformation period, the
Flounder's statements before the Women's Tribunal have
been termed contradictory. He claims to have advised me
first as little Margret's father, then as the patrician Ferber,

and later as the sleek abbot Jeschke. (He also hinted at far-reaching political responsibilities in other parts of the world. Allegedly he wanted to bring the price of pepper down, and for that reason sent a certain Vasco da Gama to India by the sea route.) But the Flounder left no one in doubt about his support of Margarete. Three days after the little girl's birth, blacksmith Rusch called him out of the stormy November sea: What was he to do with the brat? The mother had died of fever. Had to be fed goat's milk. Warm, direct from the teat. A plump little lass she'd be. O Lord, O Lord, would the Flounder please tell him what to do.

The blacksmith's desperation will be understood more readily if we recall that Peter Rusch belonged not to any guild but to the lower trades. The Flounder, in any case, introduced me to the Tribunal as a social phenomenon of the Middle Ages, a victim of the self-seeking policies of the guilds. "This Peter Rusch," he declared, "belonged to the lumpen proletariat of his day. Admitted to no guildhall, despised by the guild members among the journeymen, though they had no more political rights than he did and were just as much at the mercy of patrician highhandedness, and to top it all he was cursed with seven children. And as if that were not enough, no sooner had his wife, Kristin, given birth to his daughter Margarete than she died on him. And besides, he was in debt. In short, a natural-born rebel. Quick to draw his knife. Not very bright, but unswerving in his quest for justice. A poor devil who wanted my advice."

So this is supposedly who I was. And not the recurring runaway monk, kitchen boy, and bed companion? The Flounder must know. And if Margret hadn't on every possible occasion reacted to any mention of fathers and fatherhood with scornful farts, I'd gladly have been her father, I'd have been proud of my prodigious daughter, though all she ever gave me was pity and tripe soup. Anyway, the Flounder advised me to leave her with the pious nuns at Saint Bridget's as soon as she was weaned from the goat. He did it to help me. But when questioned in court, he gave other reasons.

"But my esteemed prosecutor and judges, please, please! Mere social sentiment—the desire to help the poor devil— would never have led me to dispense a piece of advice so

215

fraught with consequences. The truth is very different: I wanted to offer the little, but later so lusciously upholstered Margarete the best possible prospect of freedom by sheltering her in a convent. For what would have become of her otherwise? She'd have had to marry some unguilded boilermaker. Doomed to four walls and child raising, she'd have pined away in the Wicker Bastion. The marriage bed would have given her no sensual pleasure but only a dismal push-push, no sooner begun than over. The usual fate in those days. Yes, women had a rough time of it in the so-called age of the Reformation, whether they had to put their pouches at the disposal of Catholic or of Protestant husbands. The only free women were nuns, and possibly the little whores in Peppertown, because they had organized as efficiently as the nuns; in fact they elected their own abbess—later known disparagingly as 'the madame.' It wasn't the cantankerous married women, kept as they were in a perpetual state of jealousy, who practiced the solidarity which today is rightly demanded at feminist congresses and in feminist pamphlets; no, it was the nuns and whores. Without wishing to meddle in the affairs of the feminist movement, I must ask the High Court, before which I have the honor of being on trial, to concede that an astonishing degree of emancipation prevailed, if not in the brothels of the Middle Ages, then at least in the convents of the Middle Ages. As the career of the nun Margarete Rusch shows, my advice to an ignorant blacksmith gave the female sex access to areas of freedom from which at the present time—let's fact it—it is still—or shall we say once again?—barred.

"Permit me to cite certain facts in evidence.

"Margarete Rusch was never the property of any man, but a dozen men or more were obedient to her whim and pleasure. The allegedly so confining rules of her order—claustration, exercises, rule of silence—gave her leisure and enabled her to concentrate her thoughts, undisturbed by the bustle of everyday life. True, she brought two girls into the world—a painful business at the time—but child care never chained Fat Gret to any four walls. No paterfamilias imposed his law on her. No patriarchal thumb held her down. She was no domestic harridan with a bunch of keys jangling at her waist. She was free to exercise her physical and mental powers by cooking, by ordaining menus conducive to the pleasure

216

of the flesh, by contributing, not many, I admit, but all the same a few democratic bright spots to the male-dominated, oligarchic, power-oriented political life of her day. Permit me to remind you of the 'Statuta Karnkowiana,' which without Fat Gret's influence would hardly have granted rights to the guilds.

"In short, my advice accomplished all that. For if I hadn't saved the girl by sheltering her in the convent, she would never have grown up to be our Fat Gret. And as for this heavenly bridegroom the nuns were betrothed to, please believe me that the convents of the sixteenth century were free from High Gothic mysticism. Ecstasy was a thing of the past. Very little of the girls' passion went to the Son of God. Flagellation, barefooted asceticism, hysterical Saint Vitus's dancing—all completely out of fashion. No Dorothea of Montaus demanding to be immured and die to the flesh. Motivated by earthly considerations, the nuns of Saint Bridget's knew how to increase their wealth and make use of their power. True, there were nuns' quarrels and nunnish infighting. But as long as Abbess Margarete Rusch was at the head of the convent, the nuns formed a women's association that looked upon and practiced sisterly solidarity as the highest virtue. United, they were strong. The Dominicans kept their peace, though the whole town stank with their gossip about Fat Gret and her sinful goings-on."

To this harangue Prosecutor Sieglinde Huntscha replied promptly and with striking figures of speech. The Flounder, she contended, was trying to ingratiate himself with his claim to have promoted solidarity among women, though she admitted it could do with some promoting. He had brought forward a model, and what a pretty picture he had painted of that model. But if the truth be known, Margarete Rusch was nothing but a political opportunist. By advising the girl's father to put her in a convent, he, the Flounder, had been responsible for the cooking nun's misuse of her freedom. To call a spade a spade, she had simply prostituted herself the whole time. Take her dealings with Ferber. How can you call this nun's lecherous escapades a mark of emancipation? On the contrary, Abbess Margaret's alleged freedom was almost identical with the petit-bourgeois liberalism of a middle-class housewife who signs on as a call girl to make a little extra pocket money. In a pinch the sexual behavior of this nun could be characterized as protorevolutionary, although it was strictly self- and body-related, and therefore not transferable to other women and their narrow, dependent lives. At no expense to himself, he, the Flounder, after serving the male cause exclusively for three and a half millennia, was trying to publicize himself as a friend of womankind. But Mother Rusch wouldn't do as a model. How did nuns' farts contribute to feminine consciousness raising? And the misuse of the vagina as a chalice in the Christian ceremony of the Lord's Supper could only be regarded as an example of male perversion. "In sum, what execrable taste! And this I say as an atheist, not because I'm afraid of offending anyone's religious sensibilities."

In conclusion, the prosecutor suggested that a time limit be imposed on the accused Flounder. "We cannot afford to let our Tribunal, whose proceedings millions of oppressed women are following with hope and expectation, be misused for purposes of patriarchal propaganda."

The court-appointed defense counsel opposed this measure on formal juridical grounds. And a majority of the associate judges were unwilling to anticipate the verdict. The associate judge Ulla Witzlaff, ordinarily rather slow and often behindhand in her reactions, was positively outspoken: "Give him a fair chance. Can it be in our interest to take over the notorious practices of male class justice?"

And so—over the prosecutor's objection—all four of the affidavits that the Flounder through his counsel had commissioned from recognized historians were read.

The first affidavit characterized the activity of the medieval witches as a desperate attempt at female emancipation. A statistical evaluation of the fifteenth-century witch trials showed a surprisingly high percentage of nuns among witches burned at the stake, namely, 32.7 percent, whereas by the sixteenth century the percentage had fallen to 8 percent. The meager data available for the fourteenth century did not lend themselves to statistical treatment.

The second affidavit showed why conventual witchcraft had diminished in the century of the Reformation. An increase in the number of lay witches was symptomatic of the distress prevailing among uncloistered women, especially those of the artisan class. In convents, which on the surface had preserved their fidelity to the Catholic Church, the Reformation seems to have been a force for emancipation, since it opened the eyes of the nuns to earthly matters and fostered a new type of vigorous, hard-working, shrewd, and enlightened nun. Numerous lay women, on the other hand, could escape only into religious mania or eccentric witchcraft. A list of sources followed.

The third affidavit took up the political influence of the convents in the Middle Ages, under such headings as "The Convent Kitchen as Power Center," "The Convents and Their Kitchens as the Scene of Peace Negotiations," "Conspiracies and Debauches." The convent, it stated, had proved its worth as an institution where at least at times the woman's shortfall could be made good.

The fourth affidavit dealt with the broadening of the nunnish horizon since the discovery of the New World by Columbus, Vasco da Gama, and others. In particular, it confirmed the Flounder's contention that Abbess Margarete Rusch had in 1549 married her elder daughter, Hedwig, for trophopolitical reasons to a Portuguese merchant, who later established a trading post on the Malabar Coast of India. This merchant had solemnly undertaken to supply his mother-in-law twice annually with shipments of spices—pepper, cloves, ginger, cardamom. The author of the affidavit had no doubt that Fat Gret was in correspondence with the New World and that Portuguese merchantmen frequented the port of Danzig from the mid-sixteenth century on.

Then the Flounder spoke again. Modestly, barely exploiting the success of the affidavits, he spoke of his small part in emancipating and raising the consciousness of the young novice, then kitchen nun, and later abbess Margarete Rusch. He brushed in a picture of Fat Gret, exaggerating the comic aspect. Frivolous anecdotes alternated with grotesque episodes: how when Preacher Hegge incited the populace to smash images, she forced him to eat every crumb of a Saint Nicholas she had made of puff pastry stuffed with sausages; how when patrician Ferber's pecker hung its head, she made it stand up straight by piling silver guldens and Brabant talers into paradigmatically vertical towers; how after burning down the Oliva Monastery she fried pancakes for the poor over the monastic embers; how Fat Gret plucked geese while riding into the camp of King Stephen Batory on the back of a sow. And more tales, which made the public laugh, for after a short interruption—caused by the Advisory Council, which wanted to dissolve itself—the public had been readmitted.

Thus encouraged, the Flounder went on: "You see, dear ladies, who have managed to smile after all: that's the sort of woman the cooking nun Margarete was, heart-warmingly cheerful, because it was in nobody's power to oppress her. We might think of her as a sister of the parish priest of Meudon, François Rabelais, not only because they were the same age, but more because she shared his enlightened way of life. Ah, if only he had known her! I'm sure he would have conceived a female companion piece (and a worthy one) a Gargantua in the form of Fat Gret, and that she, too, would have grown into a stout volume. For literature is short on comic female protagonists. Don Quixote and Tristram Shandy, Falstaff and Oskar Matzerath—it's always a man who makes comic capital of our despair, while the ladies perish in unrelieved tragedy. Mary Stuart or Electra, Agnes Bernauer or Nora, all are in love with their tragedy. Or they pine and sigh over their sentimentalities. Or madness drives them to the moors. Or sin gnaws at them. Or a masculine power-hunger is their undoing—take Lady Macbeth. Utterly devoid of humor, they are handmaidens of suffering: saint, whore, witch, or all three at once. Or trouble turns them to stone, they are hardened and embittered, a wordless plaint. Sometimes their author allows them to go off their rockers like Ophelia and babble incoherent verses. Only the 'grotesque old crone,' far removed from all pleasures of the flesh, and the flighty chambermaid might be cited as examples of the female humor that is supposed to be 'imperishable.' But whether old and grotesque or young and flighty, only minor roles fall to woman's wit. And yet we need this comic female protagonist, we need her desperately! And the same goes for the movies. Why should it always be the men, the Charlie Chaplins or the Laurels and Hardys, who are privileged to supply the comic aspect of tragedy. I call upon you, dear ladies, to stage at long last the great feminine comedy. Let the woman comic triumph. Give the knight of the mournful countenance a woman's skirt and let her battle the windmills of male prejudice. I offer you the cooking nun Margarete Rusch. Fat Gret. Her laughter gave women scope, it gave them freedom in which humor—and now women's as well as men's—could explode its firecrackers and unleash its obscenities!"

Possibly the Flounder expected friendly applause or at least half-amused agreement. But his speech was followed by silence, then by throat clearing. Finally the prosecutor, more or less as an aside, as though preferring to minimize an unfortunate incident, said: "Doesn't it strike you as poor taste, defendant Flounder, to come here and crack literary jokes at the expense of the world's oppressed women? Yes, yes, we know the so-called lords of creation find our fight for equal rights amusing. We're used to that. But to us it is serious, not deadly so but objectively. We cannot sit idle while Electra or Nora is disparaged as just another tragic figure. There has been no shortage of quixotic women. Just stop offering us roles. Pretty soon you'll be wanting to sell us a female Dr. Faustus, or a Mephista in sparkling evening dress. But let's get back to the point! Considered in the light of her times, your cooking nun is important to us; we can't let you make her ridiculous with your distortions. Look. Margarete Rusch deliberately killed two men in execution of a long-matured plan. It was largely the fault of those two men that her father, the blacksmith Peter Rusch, had been sentenced to death on April 29, 1526, and beheaded. Three years later, in the course of coitus, she smothered Eberhard Ferber, the former mayor of Danzig, who had retired after the judicial murder. Margarete Rusch was then thirty, the same age as the prelate Kaspar Jeschke, abbot of Oliva Monastery, whom she fattened to death fifty-three years later. That, Mr. Flounder, is your oh-so-comical Fat Gret, your witty nun, your laughter-loving mountain of fat. No, she was a woman of serious and unflagging purpose. A woman who knew how to hate her enemies. And what, I ask, was your part in these two politically necessary acts? Did you prod Margarete Rusch's heroic memory with your voluble advice? We demand the truth. And nothing but the truth. No escaping into comedy."

Here the Flounder admitted that he had advised patrician Ferber and Abbot Jeschke as well. True—the Flounder assured the court—Ferber hadn't taken his advice. In his lecherous old age he had put himself in Fat Gret's power. Nor had the Flounder's advice prevailed on Abbot Jeschke. But it wasn't lust that had chained the old man to the aged Margarete; no, it was the gluttony and love of pepper so widespread at the time.

"Still," said the Flounder, "I did manage in '77 to persuade the old fool to escape, after telling him they had set fire to his monastery. But his gluttony—and he knew the nun had resolved to fatten him to death—was beyond the best-intentioned advice. I tried to prevent both murders, because I had no wish to see Margarete Rusch's impressive contribution to democratic progress darkened by this long-drawn-out vengeance. She worked hard and well—though in vain—for the powerless guilds. By guile and cookery she obtained a liberal peace from King Stephen Batory. And not least: for the cloistered nuns of the sixteenth century she won freedoms that even today seem worth striving for. On the other hand, she accomplished nothing by encompassing the deaths of two old men. The only worthwhile action is one that emancipates! And if, as I hope, the High Court wishes with this trial to help oppressed womanhood, I urge you to take note—even if you do not follow it—of my experienced advice. For aren't we all interested in seeing the shortfall of womankind at long last made good?"

The Flounder's plea was granted. And so one can read in the minutes of the debate on the case of Margarete Rusch how the accused Flounder advised the international women's movement to establish throughout the world feminist convents with exclusively earthly aims, so creating an economically powerful counterweight to the *Männerbünde* that are now everywhere dominant. Thus and thus alone, he declared, in a state of economic and sexual independence, would women be able to revive their forgotten solidarity and through it to usher in equality between the sexes. That and that alone would clarify the ambivalent structures of the feminine consciousness. The shortfall specific to the female sex would be overcome. And the consequences would be very funny.

What cannot be found in the minutes is that immediately after this session several members of the public seem to have applied for jobs as abbesses. The Tribunal adjourned.

Yes, yes, Ilsebill, suppose it happened; suppose first in ten, then in a hundred, then in a thousand places from Swabia to

Holstein, feminist convents sprang up, in which, say, five hundred thousand organized women rejected marriage and with it male-organized sexual intercourse; and suppose that in these convents you women were able to liberate yourselves in this respect and shake off your thousand-year-old dependence on male property rights and patriarchal customs, on the whims of the pecker, on household money, fashion trends, and in general on male high pressure; and suppose you succeeded, before you knew it, in creating economic power centers, either by building up a feminist consumer-goods industry or by gaining control of the consumer-goods market, which (though perhaps unwittingly) is bound to be woman-dominated in any case, wouldn't a first phase of the Flounder's project of setting up convents on the model exemplified by Margarete Rusch, abbess of Saint Bridget's, as counterpoles to the dominant male groups of today, have been realized?

For suppose, Ilsebill, that feminine solidarity should become the rule in more and more feminist convents and conventual workshops, so that woman can no longer be played off against woman in accordance with the rites of sexual competition or on the basis of a usually doll-like ideal of beauty such as men keep dreaming up in their need to cloak the unchanging dependency of women in ever-new disguises; suppose, Ilsebill, there were feminist convents all over the world and that these convents wielded economic power; suppose that traditional patriarchal marriage were observed only by a vanishing minority of the population, that children engendered by free choice but without obligation or paternity claims grew to adulthood in these convents, and that female reason, possibly abetted by a male intelligence aware of its own inadequacy, ushered in a new, nunnish matriarchy, and consequently that male-dated history would stop happening, that there would be no more wars, that male ambition and progress mania would stop sending rockets and super-rockets out into mindless cosmic space, that commodities would stop terrorizing mankind, that people would lose their fear of being inferior to one another, that from this time on no one would want to possess anyone, that the battle of the sexes, that time-honored drama, would lose its audience, that only tenderness would increase, that there would be no victors in bed, that the very meaning of victory would be forgotten, and that time would no longer be counted; suppose, Ilsebill, that

223

all this were possible, calculable, and demonstrable; suppose computers (superfluous at a later stage) could be programmed to spit out this New Order; suppose the Womens' Tribunal gave its wholehearted support to the Flounder who was only yesterday in the dock, and took his fish-mouthed advice; suppose, I repeat, that feminist convents, memorials to the abbess Margarete Rusch, sprang up on every hand, and that you (though more than two months pregnant—by me) were to enter such a convent tomorrow in order to be free, liberated, no longer subjugated or possessed by me or anyone else, would you then—supposing all this came to pass—let me, simply as a man, drop in on you for a little while?

Hasenpfeffer

I ran and ran.
At cross-purposes with the signposts, driven by hunger.
Down the hill of history I ran, slid, rolled,
flattening what was flat to begin with,
a messenger in the wrong direction.

Chewed-over wars,
The Seven and the Thirty,
the Norse hundred I took in my stride.
Stragglers who looked back out of habit
saw me vanish and double back.
And those who wanted to warn me—Magdeburg is burning!—did not suspect
that laughing I would run through
the still (but not for long) intact city.

Following no thread but only the incline.
Some, dismembered, put themselves together,
some leaped from plague wagons, some from the wheel,
and witches, escaped from collapsing pyres,
hobbled a bit of the way with me.

Ah, the thirsty reaches of year-long councils,
the hunger for dates,
until, breathless and ravaged, I ran to her.

224

She lifted the lid off the pot and stirred.

"What's cooking? What's cooking?"

"Hasenpfeffer, what else. I guessed you were coming."

Whoever wants to cook in her footsteps

Something stuffed, for instance. We're living in a state of expectation. Winter refuses to come. The fog moves everything too close, and already a family Christmas threatens.

"Our quarrel," says Ilsebill, "lies tender and juicy on our plates. We like the taste, but we don't know why, or what it's all about."

My last attempt to inject meaning is beef heart stuffed with prunes in beer sauce, such as Mother Rusch cooked for me, the runaway monk, without inquiring about my reasons. But our guests—two architects, a pastor—look for deeper meaning in everything that comes along.

The chambers of the heart lend themselves to stuffing and demand it. Buy the whole heart, slitted on one side only. Remove the clotted blood, cut out the web of sinews, make room, lift off the envelope of fat. Politely our guests let one another finish speaking.

"Soak the prunes in warm water," says Ilsebill, talking in Mother Rusch's footsteps. "but don't pit them." And suppose there were a meaning, what good would it do us?

For browning, we use the diced heart fat. "But there has to be a meaning," says the pastor tolerantly, "if only a negative one. How can we be expected to live from hand to mouth, without meaning?"

The heart, which has been stuffed and tied with white string, is browned on all sides over a high flame; then beer is added to cover. ("That, Reverend, must be obvious to a theologian.")

But the architects keep coming up with their pure Bauhaus theory. Simmer for a good hour, then add nutmeg and pepper, but less than Mother Rusch, in her time-phase and mine, thought expedient. Christmas means two more paid holidays for us. Though no meaning has been supplied, the pastor is desperately cheerful. And sour cream, which is not stirred in

225

but forms meditative little islands: in those days, Ilsebill, when Vasco da Gama in quest of God . . .

Maybe the Scandinavian high-pressure zone will bring in a belated winter after all and create meaning. Serve it with boiled potatoes, says Ilsebill, and be sure to warm the plates, because beef fat, like mutton fat, tends to form a film.

There were once forty-seven lambs which, along with eight hundred and sixty-three sheep and innumerable other lambkins, grazed on the Scharpau, a lush marsh owned and managed by Eberhard Ferber the future mayor. The only world these lambs knew was their pasture as far as the flat horizon, seen through the legs of the mother sheep. The taste of these meadows gave no indication of their owner's identity.

Up until 1498, when the sea route to India was discovered and the future abbess Rusch was born, Councilor Angermünde owned the Scharpau and gouged his tenant fishermen, peasants, and shepherds; but when, after a long-winded intrigue, the betrothal of Moritz Ferber to the daughter of the patrician Angermünde was called off, even though community of property had been stipulated by contract, the Ferber brothers became bishop of Ermland and mayor of Danzig. Both were pushed by the clergy and under obligation to the nobility.

Neither the sheep on the Scharpau nor the peasant serfs noticed much difference when the Ferber brothers succeeded in forcing the Angermündes out of Scharpau and the Dirschau starosty. Shearing and slaughtering, rent gouging and corvee labor went on just the same. In 1521, however, though the sheep and peasants continued unprotesting, the trades of the Old City and Charter City, as well as the unguilded artisans of the Wicker Bastion, rose up against Ferber and his Church Mafia. Candles were doused in the churches. Stones hit priests and Dominicans. Leaflets smelled of printer's ink. Songs likening drapers and tailors to Ferber's sheep went hobbling through the streets on one-legged rhymes, and angry men stamped out their rhythms in the guildhalls. In addition the zealot Hegge had begun to inveigh against priests and papism.

But on the Scharpau, in Tiegenort, Kalte Herberge, Fischer Babke, and in other spots where peasants were treated worse than sheep, lambs were unsuspectingly and hence peacefully putting on flesh for Easter. In honor of the bishop of Erm-

226

land, forty-seven of them were to be slaughtered and roasted over basins filled with glowing charcoal on the country estate of the patrician Ferber family. The kitchen nun of the Brigittine Order had obtained permission from the bishop of Ermland to cook the lungs and hearts of the Easter lambs in sweet-and-sour sauce for Good Friday.

Fat Gret had had no trouble convincing the episcopal palate that the innocent creatures' innards could hardly be characterized as meat, that lamb's lung preserved in all its purity the scent of the thyme that grew on the Scharpau pastures, and that the Lord Jesus Christ would be pleased to see the hearts and lungs of Easter lambs exalted to the rank of Good Friday fare. The kitchen nun, you see, was determined to give a liberal interpretation of the fast rules. "These little lambs," she said, "have never sinned. They've never been bucked by desire. How can you call that meat? Especially the innards." After cooking the whole lungs and halved hearts of the forty-seven lambs in a large kettle with anise and pepper until tender, Fat Gert had let them cool and chopped them up. Next she had boiled a sackful of lentils in the remaining broth but without reducing them to a puree, added vinegar to the chopped innards, bound the mixture with buckwheat flour, and stirred in raisins and prunes—for everything that came out of her kitchen required plenty of peppercorns, raisins, or prunes.

It was at that Good Friday meal that Mayor Ferber decided to sail against Denmark with six men-of-war. He further decided that on his victorious return he would, with the help of his richly rewarded sailors, crack down on the guilds and on all those town councilors who had been infected by Lutheranism. Nothing came of his plan. The ships returned in the autumn without spoils. It was announced that the costs of the war would be defrayed by new taxes. That led to unrest. Even the sailors deserted Ferber.

But once she had devised her Good Friday dish, the kitchen nun and later abbess Margarete Rusch stuck to it. Year after year she served her nuns and novices sweet-and-sour lamb's lung with lentils as an appetizer, a custom further encouraged by the fact that from 1529 on, the shepherds, peasants, and fishermen of the Scharpau were obliged to pay rent to the Convent of Saint Bridget, to drive Easter lambs into the convent kitchen, and deliver live eels in baskets.

Chemicals in the rivers have driven them away. Soapy

227

wastes have put reddish spots on their light-colored bellies, dorsal and tail fins, injured the mucus that protects them. The eel traps that can be seen at low tide on both banks of the Elbe are mere reminders. We pay high prices for eels from foreign waters; deep-frozen eels from Scotland are thawed out here and spring miraculously to life.

I know stories, Ilsebill: Spitted on branches they lashed my back. They were in all my thoughts. They slithered like me under cows' udders. They're as old as the Flounder.

"Why," says Ilsebill, "shouldn't the children see you kill eels and cut them in pieces? It'll be educational, as long as I don't have to watch."

Buy the eels alive. "No, children, they're really dead. Those are the nerves in each piece. That's what makes them thrash around. The head piece wants to go on living and sucks itself fast."

Now the children know what they're eating. Boiled *au bleu* in vinegar and rolled in flour, the pieces are sprinkled with sage. A neighbor sharpened the knives yesterday.

The sage bush used to grow in a garden, since destroyed by dredges, near the mouth of the Stör, where they are now building a dam equipped with locks and a big bascule bridge, which is supposed to change the course of the river and seal it off from the Elbe at times of spring tide.

We place piece after piece in hot oil and salt them lightly. There's still a bit of life in them; that's why they wriggle in the pan. Now the sage bush is growing in our garden. Our neighbor who helped with the transplanting is a free-lance slaughterer and still slaughters on Mondays for the village butcher. He fertilized the bush with hog's blood, muttering meanwhile in his coastal dialect.

The sage-sprinkled pieces are fried over low heat until crisp; they provide an appetizer that should be followed by a light main course. Let's hope the sage bush lives through the winter.

It anybody wants advice: don't buy big, fat eels; buy slim ones.

A crosswise incision just below the head is supposed to block off the nerves. We do not pull the skin off. I advise you, in cleaning eels, to watch out for the gall. If harmed, it will spill, make them bitter, depress us, and give us, wheresoever we turn, a fore- and aftertaste of sin and corruption— like Preacher Hegge.

Hegge! His sermons reduced me to silence. Nothing could stop his mouth. Nothing came easier to him than making words. Only Fat Gret could sling such a syllable stew. When he excoriated, "Hell's brew! Sin broth!," she spewed right back, "Inksquirt! Tongue-happy fizzlecock!" To all the ducks, quail, snipe, and wood pigeons she stuffed and spitroasted she gave the names of angels: Uriel, Ophaniel, Gabriel, Borbiel, Ariel; he, on the other hand, knew a devil's name for every sensual indulgence: there was wheedling Stauffax, bucking Bles, musty Haamiach, tit-loving Asmodaeus, silvery Mammon, and rutting Beelzebub. And while the cook glorified a wild goose stuffed with prunes and pork sausage as the angel Zedekiel, the goateed Hegge looked upon all pleasure of the palate as Belial's slobber.

At the very start of the Reformation, this Hegge, whom Abbess Rusch generally referred to as "the mangy goat," introduced the language of Protestant pedantry to Danzig. His father, a tailor, had come from the shores of Lake Constance. But his mother was said to have been a native of the Wicker Bastion, brackish, fishy, crooked-mouthed, with scales (or was it dandruff?) in her hair. In Jakob Hegge the garrulous waves of the Baltic mingled with the jibber-jabber of the Lake Constance Swabians. His verbiage made sins of thumb-sucking and even lesser pleasures. The alarmed burghers sent him to Wittenberg for six months. They wanted to be good Protestants all right, but Hegge's Calvinist zealotry threatened to throw too gray a pall over their life style. The guilds paid for his journey.

In Wittenberg Dr. Luther seems to have advised him to concentrate on the thirst of tormented mankind for consolations firmly grounded in the Bible, and to have his congregation sing hymns: "In Thy mercy grant us peace. . . ."

But Hegge didn't want to stop ranting and railing. In his heart the runaway Dominican monk was locked in a strange struggle with his paternal inheritance: Swabian clean-up compulsion. For all Luther's urging that he leave the good burghers a few colorful pictures and the familiar scroll-work, he wanted to create bare walls wherever he went. He may have brought a few of Dr. Luther's practical maxims back with him, but as soon as he was preaching again to his swelling congregation in the graveyard of Saint Gertrude's, the expletives burst out of him, swarming like maggots freshly expelled from the Devil's asshole, though Jakob Hegge never doubted for a moment that he was teaching the pure word of God. True, the effect was slightly attenuated by the shade of the graveyard lindens.

So it came about that soon after his return he thundered from the pulpit of Danzig's Saint Mary's Church, which offered plenty of room for a populace intent on murder, "The gray monks wear cords around their waists. Better if they wore them around their necks."

Words easily transposed into action: the next day several Dominicans were dangling from their cords. And Hegge let further phrases escape him, for fume as he might against all images, he knew the power of imagery. "I want," he cried, "to see all these churches cleared and whitewashed." And again the populace took him at his word, cleaned up Saint Mary's, Saint Catherine's, and Saint John's most radically, smashed pictures, statues, and carvings, disposed of altars as useless encumbrances, and, still not content, set out to clean up the Old City Church of Saint Bridget.

By the way of transposing one of Hegge's favorite phrases—"To the pillory with him!"—into action, some soapmakers had already dragged the wooden statue of Saint Nicholas out of Saint Bridget's, with the intention of placing the brightly painted saint in the town pillory, when Abbess Margarete intervened with her twenty-seven nuns and novices. The sisters fought with a will. Saint Nicholas was rescued. Hegge was seized and led away to the nearby Convent of Saint Bridget amid the laughter of his fickle following.

What happened to him during the night I don't know. The usual, I suppose. In the daytime, at all events, he was punished in accordance with the rules of Fat Gret's kitchen. Three hundred and eleven little cakes, which she herself had baked from lard dough, were coated with colored frosting and shaped into a Saint Nicholas closely resembling the wood carving, and the preacher was obliged to chew, rechew, and swallow him, from the wafer-thin halo to the bread-dough pedestal. To top it all, the nuns had filled this pastry Saint Nicholas with peppery blood sausages and tripe sausages, every last one of which had to be eaten.

For three whole days Hegge munched. He washed the pepper down with water. He rammed the little cakes down with raisin-flavored blood sausages and shoved in more little cakes after the marjoram-spiced tripe sausage. At first he seems to have listed all the devils from Ashomath to Zaroe. Then the battler with words fell silent. Later, his insides thoroughly greased and peppered, he seems to have shat in his pants. The blood sausages and tripe sausages, it was reported, came out unchewed, after which he invoked hell and the Devil with only moderate gusto.

The following year, when King Sigismund of Poland occupied the rebellious city with eight thousand men and ordered the rebels punished, Jakob Hegge fled, disguised in a woman's skirts. Abbess Margarete Rusch seems to have helped him get away. Hegge was thought to have found a haven in Greifswald and there to have lived a life of pure contemplation.

Every sixth of December since then, however, the people, both Catholic and Protestant, have baked up Saint Nicholas in plenty of lard—though smaller, much smaller, and without sausage filling—and in general Mother Rusch's cookery was adopted by the whole population both of the city and of the Kashubian countryside.

If you want to cook in her footsteps today, to cook fieldfare—for instance, the thrush with the ash-gray head—then bard the little birds with thin strips of lard, stuff them with the tiny livers and plenty of juniper berries, and roast half a dozen of them on a spit over glowing charcoal. But don't invite any bird lovers to dinner. I myself, the runaway Franciscan monk, felt sorry for the succulent little birds when Fat Gret stuffed them as an appetizer for King Sigismund's banquet, all the while imitating bird calls: the bleating of the snipes, for instance, because of which these swamp birds are also known as sky-goats.

But if you are counting on guests with an ear for tall tales, then brown the feet, halved heads, ribs, lungs, and liver of a hare in lean bacon, as Fat Gret did, throw in a handful of previously soaked raisins, and simmer briefly. Heat the whole with crushed black pepper, deglaze the pan with red wine, bring to a boil, and let the hasenpfeffer simmer for an hour over medium heat—or longer, if your guests are late, as happened once upon a time when on his way back to Oliva the bishop of Leslau lost his way in the trackless beech forest and was frightened by an apparition, of which he spoke with easy good humor afterward. Humming into the air but inwardly rich in figures, he had been riding through the forest when a hare had peered out of a cleft tree and, speaking in flawless Latin though with a Kashubian accent, had prophesied that before the day was out the bishop would meet a second hare, who would be steeped in wine. "Give him my regards! Do give him my regards!" the Latinizing hare had said, and to this request the bishop of Leslau acceded, before the prelates, over the steaming stew, embarked on their discussion of the grave political situation.

But if you want to surprise your guests as Fat Gret surprised Stephen Batory, king of Poland, on December 12, 1577, when inside a pig's head she served him a sheep's head from which, when it was cut open, fell the intricately webbed key of the besieged city, which had now surrendered, then take a short knife, bone a pig's head and then a sheep's head without injuring the fatty casing, sprinkle the inside of the pig's head with fresh marjoram, and insert the sheep's head. Your guests will get a good surprise if the incision has been carefully sewed up. When after an hour and a half the pig's head with the sheep's head in it emerges from the oven and is cut open, the guests must be expected to exclaim "Ah!," because something will shimmer and fall out, something strange, beautiful, hard, miraculous, and ambivalent, that may signify happiness and may signify something else—for instance, a little gilded box containing, folded small, a savings and loan association's home-construction loan, or whatever else my Ilsebill's heart may desire.

And if you still want to cook in Fat Gret's footsteps and have a reason such as she had when I, her bed companion at the time, became listless, lost all desire to partake of her flesh, and lounged about with my cock dangling, good for nothing but world-weary questions about the meaning of it all—then try the following recipe:

Take twelve to seventeen cockscombs, soak them in warm milk until the skin can be easily removed, wash them in cold water until the red pales to a surprising white, sprinkle them with lemon juice (Margret used pickling liquor), roll the cockscombs in beaten eggs, fry them briefly on both sides, and serve them, on rounds of celery root previously sautéed in butter, to any male who, as I did then, has trouble getting and keeping it up and displaying a cocky virility even when he has good reason to hang his head. For it wasn't easy living in her shadow. That cook had no use for lazybones. Time and time again, Fat Gret revived my bludgeon. You'll find it worth your while to cook in her footsteps.

That no doubt explains why, while the case of Margarete Rusch was being debated before the Women's Tribunal, I saw members of the public diligently taking down recipes. When tripe and chopped lung came up in the proceedings, only Associate Judge Ulla Witzlaff laughed, laughed all over as only Fat Gret could laugh, and pronounced a warning against excessive use of pepper, which, so she said, gave promise of more ardor than the ingester could supply and should have been left growing where it grows, for far from bringing out flavors it shouts them down, frazzles the nerves, and causes people, especially women, to be in too much of a hurry. . . .

An organist by profession, Ulla Witzlaff is as imperturbable as Mother Rusch. She comes from the island of Rügen and knows lots of island tales. One of her great-grandmothers, who once rowed a boat from the small island of Oehe to Schaprode, is believed to have told the painter Philipp Otto Runge the tale of the talking Flounder in Low German. Ulla also speaks the Low German of the coast. Slender as she is, I can see her in Fat Gret's clothes. "I'm bored," she says, for after twelve years of Protestant church services, the Sunday-after-Sunday hypocrisy stinks, so she says, all the way up to the organ pipes. She's fed up with the parish blackskirts, one of whom rants and wears a goatee like Hegge.

The other day, I fled, as I do now and then, from Ilsebill and her wishes, which renew themselves like chives—Christmas is coming—and escorted Ulla Witzlaff to her Sunday service in some Neo-Gothic church. After Ulla had played the prelude, the *Kyrie* had been sung, and the pathetic congregation had struck up the hymn "Open, O Lord, the door of my heart," we sat on the organ bench in the choir loft, talking in an undertone about the Flounder and his activities in the days of the abbess Margarete Rusch, for down below the latter-day Hegge had embarked on his sermon. Ulla was knitting something long and plain and woolly, while the ranting goatee poured forth his latest spiritual awakening for the benefit of seventeen old women and two pietistically inclined teen-age maidens: "Beloved congregation, the other day I was riding in an overcrowded subway train. People were pushing and shoving. Dear God! cried my inner voice. What has become of Thy love? And then of a sudden the Lord Jesus spoke to me. . . ."

At which point, Ulla said without preamble, "I wouldn't be

surprised if Mother Rusch in her convent had used a hymnbook with a preface by Luther."

I confirmed her suspicion: "On his return from Wittenberg in 1525, Jakob Hegge brought back a volume of the first edition of the Klug Hymnal and give it to Fat Gret. Possibly on the advice of the Flounder, who always kept posted on the latest printed matter. And every evening after that Mother Rusch would sing with her nuns, 'Rejoice, dear Christians all, and let us jump for joy. . . .' "

And Ulla said, "Maybe Mother Rusch had an organ, if only one with a single manual, maybe in Saint Bridget's or possibly in the convent chapel." Whereupon she dropped her knitting, moved over on the bench, pressed buttons, manipulated levers, pulled all the stops, and, playing with both hands and feet, made the organ literally thunder. Without regard for the struggling preacher down below and his interminable outpourings, she gave me a demonstration of the Klug Hymnal and its importance for the development of sixteenth-century music, at the same time letting—as Mother Rusch had done beneath her Catholic veil—her blaring, jubilant voice ring out with Luther's translations and Luther's original hymns. First: "With peace and joy I came." Then: "As we journey through this life." Then: "Salvation unto us is come." And finally, in the old setting, every verse of "A Mighty Fortress is our God," down to "And the Word shall stand forever. . . ."

By that time Ulla's jubilation had emptied the church, for it was more than either the latter-day Hegge or his faithful could bear. After a frightened "Amen" and a hurried blessing, the pastor, followed by his ladies in their chamberpot hats, hurried out into the cold December air.

Oh, bliss of empty churches! For a short hour Ulla Witzlaff played the organ and sang for me alone. With musical examples she showed how Abbess Rusch and her Brigittine nuns had been Catholic on the one hand and devoutly Lutheran on the other. While she was at it, she gave me a bit of elementary instruction in liturgy and hymnology.

When, after a concluding "Come, Holy Ghost," the organ breathed its last, the organist threw her arms around me. I wanted to respond right there on the narrow organ bench, but Ulla, perhaps in memory of Mother Rusch's stable-warm box bed, said, "Save it for later. We might as well be comfortable."

As it is written, we were one flesh. And we laughed and laughed over the sixteenth-century Hegge and the latter-day Hegge. And afterward Ulla served me leftover lentils and island stories with the Flounder out of the fairy tale swimming through them.

The cook kisses

When she opens her mouth
that would sooner hum than sing
and shapes it into a funnel for sticky porridge, mealy
    dumplings,
or with teeth created for this very purpose she bites
off a chunk of tender sheep's neck or a goose's left breast
and passes it on—rolled in her spittle—
to me with a thrust of her tongue.

Stringy meat prechewed.
Or if too tough, run through the grinder.
Her kiss is food.
So trout cheeks, olives,
nuts, the kernels of plum pits she
has cracked with her molars,
black bread afloat in beer,
a peppercorn intact
and crumbled cheese—
with a kiss she shares them all.

Broken in health, propped on cushions,
ravaged by fever, disgust, and thoughts,
I was revived (time and again) by her kisses,
which never came empty-handed and were never just kisses.
And I gave back
oysters, calves' brains, chicken hearts, bacon.

Once we ate a pike with our fingers,
I hers, she mine.
Once we exchanged squabs
down to the delicate little bones.

Once (and time and again) we kissed each other full of
    beans.
Once, after always the same quarrel
(because I'd drunk up the rent money),
a radish reconciled us after a turnip estrangement.
And once we had fun with the caraway seeds in the sauer-
    kraut,
and kept exchanging them, hungry for more.

When Agnes the cook
kissed Opitz the dying poet,
he took a little asparagus tip with him on his last journey.

The fourth month

~~~~~~

Inspection of feces

In the fourth month of her pregnancy (and therefore suddenly wild about hazelnuts), Ilsebill, who doesn't want to have been my kitchenmaid, whose thinking is strictly rectilinear, and who could easily be one of the Flounder's accusers, lost an upper-right molar made valuable by a gold crown and, taking fright as if a male toad were creeping up on her, swallowed it. All she spat out was the shell of the hazelnut, which, irony of ironies, had been empty.

"Well?" I said next morning. "Did you look for it? It's gold, after all."

But she refused to inspect her morning stools, let alone prod them with a washable fork. And I was forbidden to root around in her "excrement," as she contemptuously called it.

"That's because you were brought up unwisely and too well," I said. For our fecal matter should be important to us and not repel us. It's not a foreign body. It has our warmth. Nowadays, it's being described again in books, shown in films, and painted in still lifes. It had been forgotten, that's all. Because as far as I can think back and look behind me, all the cooks (inside me) have inspected their feces and—in all my time-phases—mine as well. I was always under strict supervision.

During her years as an abbess, for instance, Fat Gret made all the novices bring her their chamber pots, and every kitchen boy who came to her for employment had first to demonstrate his fitness by showing healthy stools.

And even when, as Albrecht the swordmaker, I was plagued with daily Lenten fare, I was subjected to *ex posteriori* inspections. So unyieldingly fanatical was my wife and meatless cook, Dorothea, about her ascetic way of life that, not content with setting a meatless and fatless table, she checked on my intake at other people's tables by poking through my feces for undigested bits of sinew or traces of bacon rind or tripe fiber, and compared my deposit with her own High Gothic and penitential stools, which were always dry and transcendental in their pallor, wheras I had sinned—at guild banquets, when suckling pigs stuffed with milky millet were carved for the smiths and swordmakers; or when, sometimes in the woods and sometimes at the lodge of the stonemasons then working on Saint Peter's in the Outer City, I cooked in secret with my friend Lud the wood carver: sheep's kidneys and fat sheep's tails grilled over an open fire. Nothing could be concealed from Dorothea. Many a time I gave myself away by swallowing cartilage or small bones, which came out the other end intact.

And when I was General Rapp, Napoleon's governor of the Republic of Danzig, it was the cook Sophie Rotzoll who, because I had disparaged her mushroom dishes as indigestible, spread my shit on a silver platter and served it up to me. I had a soldier's sense of humor; I put up with her impudence. And she was right: not a shred of mushroom skin, not a single mushroom worm to be seen. My palate grew keener and keener, and soon I was calling morels, milk caps, and egg mushrooms delicate. My taste developed to the point where I wouldn't even forgo the tasty though sandy Polish green agaric, although the sand would have shown up in my gubernatorial stools.

But what my last Napoleonic shit would have looked like if I had partaken of the special mushrooms Sophie added to her stuffed calf's head—which dispatched six of my guests, officers all, including three Polish officers and one officer from the Rhenish Confederation, into the other world—I hardly dare imagine, though the shattering effect of the poisonous sulfur tuft is well known.

All my cooks, I say, have inspected feces, read the future in feces, and in prehistoric times even carried on a pagan dialogue with fecal matter. Wigga, for instance, examining the

238

still-steaming shitpile of a Gothic captain who had been so ill-mannered as to relieve himself in the immediate vicinity of our Wicker Bastion settlement, read the inexorable destiny of the Goths, who were soon to embark on their migration. In our Old Pomorshian tongue (the precursor of present-day Kashubian), she oracled their division into Ostrogoths and Visigoths, into luminous Goths and sublime Goths: Ermanaric and the Huns, Alaric in Rome. How Belisarius would take King Vitiges prisoner. The Battle of Châlons. And so on and so on . . .

In the Neolithic, on the other hand, when my primordial cook ruled, the inspection of feces was a feature of the cult. We neolithic folk had entirely different customs, and not just in regard to eating. Each of us ate singly, with his back to the horde, not shamed but silent and introverted, immersed in mastication, eyeless. But we shat together, squatting in a circle and exchanging shouts of encouragement.

After the horde shit-together we felt collectively relieved and chatted happily, showing one another our finished products, drawing pithy comparisons with past performances, or teasing our constipated comrades, who were still squatting in vain.

Needless to say, the farting incidental to the rite was also a social affair. What today is said to stink and is crudely amalgamated with latrines and slit trenches—"It stinks like an army camp around here!"—was natural to us, because we identified with our feces. In smelling our turds, we smelled ourselves. These were no foreign bodies. If we needed food and enjoyed the taste, how could we fail to take pleasure in evacuating what remained of it? We looked upon each departing turd with gratitude, and with a certain sadness as well. Consequently, the horde shit-together, for which we assembled, nay, were obliged to assemble twice daily, was followed by a paean, a formula of thanksgiving, a hosanna or last tribute.

Because she was the horde cook, our priestess, Awa, inspected our feces, which had cooled in the meantime. Though she never established a fixed order of sequence, she strode around the circle, finding an exegetic word for each of us, even the meagerest shitter, for which reason this most human of institutions must be recognized as primordially democratic. All squatted in equality, none exalted above his fellows, for we were all her children. Anyone who had squatted unsuccessfully was reprimanded, and if he remained constipated over a period of days, he was punished—as is still customary—by being made to shit alone. And if even then he failed to squeeze out so much as a hard and undersized sausage, toads' eggs were funneled into him. Awa wielded the neolithic spoon, the ladlelike shoulder blade of an elk cow. That helped!

In our humanistic modern age political criminals, or "enemies of the people," are sometimes punished or tortured by being made to eat their own fascist, Communist, anarchist, or even liberal shit. We would not have felt humiliated by such treatment, because our attitude toward fecal matter was not only religious but practical as well: in times of famine we ate it, without pleasure but also without disgust. Today only babies have this natural attitude toward the end products of their digestion and toward the pleasurable process of metabolism for which adults have devised such coy euphemisms: Number two. Big business. To go where even the kaiser must go on foot. To disappear for a moment.

"You barbarians!" cried the Flounder when, more or less in passing, I told him about our maternally approved shit-togethers. "Pigs!" he screamed. "When in King Minos's palace they've already got flush toilets." He tried to talk me into a sense of shame. And soon, only two thousands years later, I developed one and shat alone like everyone else. The Flounder lectured me on culture and civilization. I listened, though I really never understood whether the individualization of the bowel movement was a cultural development or an advance in civilization. In the Neolithic, in any case, when we knew only the horde shit-together and our Awa twice daily struck up her vowel-rich paean, we were no strangers to hygiene: coltsfoot leaves. Never been beat.

(Ah, if only we had a collective toilet, a two-seater at least, if not the big family size.) Tell me the truth, Ilsebill, even if you didn't want to fish your gold tooth out of your excrement, and (like most people) you use the word "shit" exclusively and quite unjustifiably as an expletive. Admit it, Ilsebill, don't use your pregnancy as an excuse, admit that you, too, look behind you, though diffidently and much too genteelly. You like to smell yourself as much as I do myself. And I would gladly smell you, and gladly be smelled by you. Love? That's it.

And so the kitchenmaid Agnes Kurbiella, who cooked diet

fare for painter Möller and poet Opitz, inspected her lovers' feces each day and honored them in verses. Salutary words always came to her. And when the Black Death struck Opitz, Agnes recognized by the shit in his breeches that he was doomed to die, and lamented softly:

> "The Lord hath meant to give me the alarm:
> where shytte is black, beset with many a worm,
> the shytter soon must come to grievous harm."

Empty and alone

Pants down, hands joined as though in prayer,
my eyes right on target:
third tile from the top, sixth from the right.
Diarrhea.
I hear myself.
Two thousand five hundred years of history,
early insight and last thoughts
lick and cancel each other out.

It's the usual infection.
Brought on by red wine
or by quarrels on the stairs with Ilsebill.
Fear because time—the clock, I mean—
has chronic trots.

What afterdrips: breakfast problems.
No compact turd takes form,
love, too, flows thin and loose.

So much emptiness
is in itself a pleasure: in the crapper
with my own specific ass.
God state society family party . . .
Out, the whole lot of you.
What smells is me!
If only I could weep.

The burden of an evil day

In the sixteenth year of the war, when the Saxons were negotiating with the imperial forces and Silesia was about to fall for the second time, the eighteen-year-old Andreas Cryphius, whose native Glogau had been razed, went to Danzig, where he planned to defray the costs of his studies in history, theology, astronomy, and medicine by instructing the burghers' children, who lived behind newly remodeled façades that, with their flutings, ledges, and inscriptions, expressed the exuberance of life and gilded it with deep meaning.

Until recently the young man had written only heroic epics in Latin, but now, since becoming acquainted with a little book on the rules of poetics, he had taken to writing German verses, which in their first élan pushed the door so violently as to attract the notice of the author of the poetic rule book, who had settled in Danzig, where he was employed as Royal Polish court historian, by their voluptuous preoccupation with sorrow, their rage over the vanity of all things, their gushing sadness. For in a copy submitted to him by a friend, Martin Opitz von Boberfeld read:

"What , then, is mortal man? A house of bitter grief,
A plaything of false chance, an errant firefly,
A theater of stark fear and cruel adversity,
A quickly melted snow, a quickly fallen leaf"

and through their mutual friend the mathematician Peter Gürger informed the young poet of his desire to meet him.

At the age of thirty-eight, Opitz was shaken in health, sick to death of the interminable wars and of his unsuccessful efforts at diplomacy. Only the year before, when his father, the indestructible butcher from Bunzlau, married for the fourth time, he had taken stock of himself and written:

"My spirit burns no more,
No longer does it soar—
Disgust with the servility

242

Of friend and foe doth weigh
Me down above all else—
The burden of an evil day."

The meeting occurred on September 2, 1636, in the house
of the Reformed preacher Nigrinius, where Opitz lived in solitude—if we choose to disregard a strange kitchenmaid by the
name of Agnes who cooked half the day for him and half the
day for Möller the town painter. It is recorded in a letter
from Opitz to Hühnerfeld, his publisher, "Have just met a
new writer, endowed with a great gift of language, though
not versed in all the rules. His name is Andreas Gryph, and
he comes from Glogau. Everything about him offended me."

Opitz and Gryphius talked until the sky darkened. Outside
the windows the Baltic Indian summer lingered on. Occasional ringing of vespers bells. The kitchenmaid came and
went, barefooted on green-and-yellow-glazed tiles. Both spoke
with a slight Silesian accent that cannot be put into writing.
And sometimes they spoke like printed matter. That can be
quoted.

Gryphius had a round, boyish face that could suddenly
darken and sink as though devoured from within, and then
the voice that spoke from it was that of an angry archangel.
His prophet's mouth. His horror-stricken eyes. Despite his
rosy look, the young poet was of an atrabilious nature. As for
the older man, who sat stiffly in the Spanish-Flemish fashion,
his gaze was curtained by his eyelids, and whenever he spoke,
more to himself than to his guest, he peered into every corner
of the room like a beaten dog, or seemed at all events to be
looking for a way out. Evidently Opitz was sensitive to noise.
Outside the house barrels were being fitted with iron hoops.

At first Gryphius seemed embarrassed and addressed
studentlike quips to Agnes the kitchenmaid each time she
renewed the young poet's spiced wine and the older man's
elderberry juice, but received no reply. They talked about the
noise in this seaport town and about Silesia, now lost for the
second time. Gryphius told his host how the plague had carried off both sons of his Fraustadt patron Caspar Otto, whom
he, Gryphius, had been tutoring in Latin. Mutual friends
from Glogau and Bunzlau were named. Some irony still remained for the Fruitbearing Society, a Silesian literary club.

After mentioning the death of Prince Raffael Leszczynski,
the last protector of the Silesian refugees in Frauenburg and

Polish Leszno, Opitz, perhaps a bit too offhandedly, praised the bold though sometimes undisciplined prosody of certain of Gryphius's sonnets, but went on to deplore their immoderation: the unrestrained sorrow, the vale-of-tears tone, the condemnation of all earthly pleasure down to the most trifling as vanity and vexation of spirit. True, he, too, Opitz the restless seeker, could not help feeling personally concerned by the splendid line "How then shall man, that insubstantial bubble, endure," since he well knew the meaning of failure and had himself written equally disheartening lines in his time, but he could not find it in his heart to disparage all human endeavor as "dust, chaff, and ashes," waiting for the wind to blow them away. Some useful things had been done, after all. Enduring achievement often lay buried beneath ruins. The scattered seed would bear new fruit. Even unsuccessful effort bore witness to the courage of upright men. Nothing was ever lost. Swedish chancellor Oxenstierna had convinced him of the need for political action. The good could not be gathered ready at hand but had to be sifted out. And really Gryphius was too young to dispose of the whole world as a vale of tears and wish himself and his chubby-cheeked good health into the moldering grave. A life with all its weal and woe still lay ahead of him.

Thereupon young Gryphius drained his spiced wine, stared at the cloves and mace that remained at the bottom of his cup, glowered like an Old Testament prophet, lost all his inclination to address quips to the drink-renewing kitchenmaid, and, tapping the table edge rhythmically with his right forefinger, spoke in a steady flow, as though he had prepared his speech in advance.

First he acknowledged the debt of gratitude that he and his generation of poets owed to Opitz for his theoretical work. which had enabled them to spurn Latinizing affectation and commit themselves to German poetics. Then he held the finger, which only a moment before had been drumming, up to the lauded master's nose. He, the great Opitz, had squandered his strength in politicking; crowned and ennobled by the emperor, he, Opitz, had given to diplomacy what was owing to Poesy; for the sake of accented and unaccented syllables, he, Opitz the rule giver, had thrown a veil of verbiage over all man's misery; throughout the war, he, Opitz the busybody, had handled the dirty work of one prince after another, and even now, though at last in a secure haven, he could not desist, on the one hand from writing Wladislaw, king of Poland, letters of advice weighing one petty advantage against another, and on the other hand from sending Swedish chancellor Oxenstierna secret reports on the recruiting of Prussian mercenaries for the imperial armies. True, Opitz did all this out of concern for unhappy Silesia, once again under the Catholic heel, but also for the hard cash received from Poles and Swedes alike for his sinister double-dealing, his spying, and his weasel words. This is what had muffled his speech, though one would think that the all-destroying war and the crying distress of helpless mankind would lead a poet to speak out plainly and clearly. But he, the resourceful Opitz, had trimmed his sails to the winds of the day, served the Protestants but translated the Jesuits' antiheresy manual into German. He had knelt at Catholic Masses. When Magdeburg fell, he had gone so far as to write poems in mockery of that unhappy, God-fearing city—"Who always slept alone, the chaste old maid . . ."—for which reason he had been cursed in the Protestant camp. On his way through Breslau he had got at least two of that city's daughters with child, but had refused to pay alimony. And the flowery classicist hymns of praise that he, Opitz the sycophant, had penned, in strict accordance of course with the rules of poetics, for the bloodsucking Count Dohna—"Thou has exalted me, and set me wholly free. And from the burden of arms, saved me for Poesy"—were indeed masterful, as his little book on German poetics made amply clear, but they lacked the passion, the flaming word without which there can be no true poetry; they were lukewarm to the taste. And yet he, Gryphius, could recite poems by Opitz, the early Transylvanian ones, for instance, but also the one about the plague in Bunzlau, in which art did not posture, and the word did not conceal, but pointed inescapably to the vale of tears:

>   . . . What suff'ring as he lay
> Sick with the awful plague, ere he could pass away
> And cast his body off! For his infected blood
> like burning fire rose all upward to his head
> And seized upon his eyes, with raging fever bright.
> Speech had forsaken him, his throat was bounden tight.
> His lungs did heave and pant, th' entire frame was sick
> And losing of its strength. A nauseating reek
> As of a long-dead beast from out his gullet flowed.

His poor defenseless life upon the threshold stood
And looked this way and that, and looked beyond to see
If there be any balm amid such agony.

After an interval, during which Agnes the kitchenmaid passed through the room and set pewter plates on the table and the daily life of the seaport town went on outside—barrels were rolled—the elder man said to the younger, "Yes, yes, that's somewhere near the truth." He had indeed wasted his energies in the tangled business of war, always in harness, always traveling from place to place with petitions, appeals for help; Breslau's daughters had given him more fatigue than pleasure; true, he had been obliged to fear the Jesuits and curry favor with princes, and yet, like the eminently learned Grotius, with whom he had sat face to face in Paris "just as we are sitting now," he chose to regard himself as an irenicist, a man of peace, motivated by allegiance to no one party, but by a desire for universal tolerance, and that was why, though weary of struggle, he was still writing letters in the hope of persuading Chancellor Oxenstierna, now that the emperor was weak, to reinforce the army of Marshal Banér and enable him, with the help of Torstenson's cavalry and the Scottish regiments of Lesley and King, to prevent a junction of the imperial troops with the Saxon renegades; and indeed, seeing that the royal child was being brought up on perfectly insane principles by her mother in the castle at Stockholm, he was trying to bring about an alliance between Sweden and Wladislaw of Poland against the Habsburgs, all the more so since the king of Poland was still hoping to mount the throne of Sweden, for which reason he, Opitz, had only last year written a poem in praise of His Polish Majesty, in which to be sure he had lauded the king's love of peace and wise suspension of hostilities—"That thou, O Wladislaw, forsakest war for peace"—and yet he would always, to the detriment of poetics, grieve over the misery of Silesia, even though he had made his home in an unscarred city in the hope that he might still turn out some worthwhile verses. For, he said as though in conclusion, that was the one thing he really cared about. And then, looking Gryphius full in the face, he favored him with a little lesson. "Every verse is either iambic or trochaic; not that we take account of specific syllabic quantities in the manner of the Greeks and Romans; rather, we recognize by the accents and the intonation which syllable is to be considered strong and which weak."

Then, before Gryphius could discharge his thunders, the kitchenmaid, perpetually smiling but only around the corners of her mouth, brought in a boiled codfish on a silver platter. And now Agnes spoke across the table. In God's name, she pleaded, the young gentleman should stop quarreling and let her dear master, whose stomach was easily unsettled, enjoy the fish—which she had boiled in milk and seasoned with dill—in peace. With a little jingle, which she recited with her broad country pronunciation and misplaced accents—"To fight over cod is displeasing to God"—she obtained silence, for before falling gently off the bone, the fish, too, looked white-eyed at no one.

That wasn't their only reason for eating in silence. There was no more offending to be done. Only half words were left dangling. Everything had been said. Young Gryphius stuffed himself ravenously, holding his left hand under his chin, while Opitz poked about rather listlessly with a fork, the new-fangled table tool he had brought back from Paris years before. Gryphius sucked the larger bones and lapped up the jelly from the eye sockets. The two sightless orbs lay off to one side. Opitz ate none of the honeysweet millet porridge with candied elderberry blossoms, which Agnes served when nothing was left of the codfish but the clean backbone, the well-licked tail and dorsal fins, and the plundered head bones; but so early fatherless, so young and despairing, so homeless and Silesianly starved was young Gryphius that he proceeded as though braving a stupendous task, as in the fairy tale, to eat his way through the steaming mountain of millet.

At first only the smacking lips of the poet, who would soon be famous for his eloquent death-yearning and renunciation of all earthly joys, could be heard, then other sounds, the bubbling, gurgling, belching of Opitz's nervous and acid stomach, upset no doubt by the guest's presence. Behind drooping eyelids Opitz bore his misery. Only from time to time did he pluck at the Swedish-style goatee designed to give strength to his weak chin.

When the millet mountain had at last been razed, the young man injected a question into the silence: what was the master doing, what planning, what great work had he conceived, and, now that he had translated Sophocles so ably, what hopes did he nourish for a German tragedy? Opitz smiled, or, rather, he allowed the morose wrinkles of his ugliness to unfold into a grimace, and assured his visitor that his inner fire was spent and that no dense smoke could be expected. No use poking about for embers in a cold stove. He doubted if he would ever produce a well-turned essay on ancient Dacia, for that idea, conceived in his youth, was now choked with weeds. As for a German tragedy, only someone still in his prime like Gryphius could hope to write one. He was planning, however, to translate the Psalms of David with the utmost care, for which task he would have to study the Hebrew scriptures under learned guidance. Then he thought he would render Greek and Latin epigrams "into our tongue and have them printed here." He further harbored the intention of bringing certain Breslau treasures to light and acquainting the world once more with the long-forgotten *Annolied*, in order that it might endure. No more.

As though to justify himself, Opitz waved a hand in the direction of the depleted table and said, "Surely no one will take it amiss if we devote the time that many spend in overeating, futile babbling, and bickering, to the charms of study, and close our minds to things that the poor often have and the rich cannot buy."

With these words he may have been tacitly enjoining the young man to say no more, but to go home and study in the quiet of his room. In any case Gryphius stood up, showing by the look of horror on his face how pitifully drained he had found the still-revered master. And when Opitz—no sooner had the strange kitchenmaid, now humming in a monotone, cleared away the empty dishes—confided with an ugly leer that Agnes's warm flesh, though he was obliged to share it with the local town painter, had revived his affections of late, given him new life, and, belatedly to be sure and with only partial success, rekindled his desires, Gryphius, quite revolted, buttoned his jacket. He would go now. He would disturb the master no longer. He thanked the master for his instruction. He had stayed too long.

Already in the doorway, the young poet nevertheless had a request to make. Without any hemming and hawing, he asked Opitz to find him a suitable publisher. Though well aware of the vanity of publishing books and striving for posthumous fame, he would nevertheless like to see the sonnets he had written in this city of false glitter and illusory happiness printed, precisely because they excoriated such vanity. Opitz listened, reflected for a moment, and then promised to do what he could to dispose a publisher in the young man's favor.

Suddenly Opitz switched to scholarly Latin and, with the help of quotations, moved into an area of humanistic remoteness (after which Gryphius, too, switched to Latin). Finally, after a Seneca quotation of some length, the older man explained that he knew an imperial councilor who for reasons of ill health had retired into contemplative seclusion and took an interest in the arts. He hoped that the imperial title would not trouble Gryphius. Not everyone in the imperial party was evil. He would write a letter of introduction.

(And so he soon did. Gryphius moved to the estate of a certain Herr Schönborner, won his favor, instructed his sons, and in the following year, financed by the imperial councilor, had his sonnets printed in Lissa, that they might live after him.)

When, full of fish and millet but also replete with sadness, young Gryphius had finally left, Agnes the kitchenmaid lit two candles, laid out paper, and placed a freshly cut goose quill beside it. Then, within easy reach, she put down a small dish of caraway seeds, which Opitz liked to nibble while writing letters. He picked them up with a moistened fingertip. Caraway seeds were his little vice.

He wrote to the Swedish chancellor, imploring him at long last to set Torstenson's troops and the Scottish regiments in motion. To judge by the information he, Opitz, had gathered in this seaport town—"For Dantzik is the meeting place of all manner of agents and couriers"—it was necessary to move quickly and defeat the Saxons in Brandenburg before they could join forces with the imperial army. Both the distress of Silesia and the military situation made a decision imperative.

(In response to which, a month later, on October 4, 1636, the imperial troops were cut off from those of Saxony, and on a battlefield between forest and marshland near Wittstock on the Dosse, a tributary of the Havel, defeated by the Swedes under Marshal Banér, an engagement in which the Scottish regiments of Lesley and King played a decisive part. After uncounted losses on both sides, captured banners, cannon, and provender were counted. No more.)

After sealing his letter to Oxenstierna, Opitz sat quietly for a while by the candles, chewed the remaining caraway seeds, and far from all sound waited for Agnes the kitchenmaid, who soon came in and made up to him for all, or nearly all, his sorrows.

Turnips and Gänseklein

In November,
when the dishwater has been emptied,
the last colors wiped out
and the geese plucked,
just in time for Saint Martin's Day,
Agnes, who always knew
what to cook when, cooked
the neck in its limp skin, the gizzard and heart
and both wings: *Gänseklein*
with turnips and diced squash,
cooked them slowly over low heat, deep in thought
about a Swedish ensign, whose name was Axel
and who had promised to return:
soon, in November.

Into it went
a handful of barley, caraway seed, marjoram,
and a little henbane to ward off the plague.
All this—the gizzard was chewed, the wing gnawed,
the neck bones sucked by painter Möller
whom Agnes served while poet Opitz
spooned up the mild broth, the soft turnips,
spooned and found no words—
though everywhere in November
and in the cloudy soup there floated
a goose heart looking for something to be compared with.

Why the Flounder tried to rekindle two cold stoves

When the Women's Tribunal took up the case of Agnes Kurbiella, it was thought that adequate provision had been made for the accused Flounder's security, though some attempt at aggression (e.g., kidnapping, poisoning) was to be expected. In his tank of bulletproof glass, the flatfish spent most of the time buried in Baltic sand, so that his breathing could only be surmised: nothing but his bulging eyes and crooked mouth was discernible. But when the prosecutor moved that in view of the enormous quantities of material before the court, the discussion be limited to what she termed Agnes Kurbiella's "more relevant relationship" with the court historian Martin Opitz, the Flounder agitated his fins and stirred up his sand bed in protest.

"High Female Court! Such supposed time-saving would halve and thereby destroy all understanding, for young Agnes did not merely carry on a dual relationship; she was truly split, though not at all to her detriment. So spacious was her nature that she was able, as cook and mistress first to painter Möller, then to poet Opitz, and finally to both of them, to keep house for them, warm their beds, and—how shall I put it?—rekindle their stoves. I must own at the very outset that I advised both Möller and Opitz. They both called me out of the Baltic Sea at the usual place. I heard and helped. That day a land breeze was blowing from the northeast. But if the esteemed prosecutor is determined to save time at all costs—that is, to questionable advantage—then let her halve me along with Agnes. I suppose ruthless decisions of this sort are fashionable these days. Let us for once be unfashionable."

Ms. von Carnow, the court-appointed defense counsel, who cut a pathetic figure because the Flounder consistently ignored her, supported his countermotion. In a piping little voice she said, "If such things are done to save time, people might get the idea that this is a show trial, with the verdict

251

decided in advance. Women must never resort to such contemptible, typically masculine methods."

The ensuing disorder made it hard to determine where the public stood. After brief deliberation the judges decided to treat the case of Agnes Kurbiella in its dual aspect. Still, the Flounder was admonished to be brief and to abstain from prolix accounts of Möller's artistic travels and Opitz's diplomatic ventures, neither of which, it was pointed out, could be of much interest to the court. After all, town painter Anton Möller had been an old man of sixty-eight when he reduced Agnes, then just fourteen, to a state of dependency, and Opitz had been at least in his late thirties when Agnes, who had turned eighteen in the meantime, became his willing slave.

"You've spared me the need for explanations," said the Flounder. "As you say, they were both old, though one could have been the other's son, and thoroughly plucked, exhausted, and burnt out. That's why I gave the poor devils my advice. I felt sorry for them when first one, then years later the other, stood in the shallow water near Weichselmünde and cried out, 'Flounder, say something! My bed is always half empty. I'm cold inside and out. I'm clogged with slag and I smell of cold smoke.' My advice was, 'Take something young. Refresh yourself. Drink of the fountain of youth. Let the feminine principle warm you back to life.' For both Möller and Opitz needed inspiration, sensual encouragement, call it fire, in their cold stoves, if they were to wrest some late achievement, a last flare-up of youth, from their middling talents. Both of these moribund gentlemen were in need of spiritual mouth-to-mouth resuscitation. The proverbial kiss of the Muse. Knowing full well that here, under the critical eye of a female assembly that takes pride in its cold reason, I am likely to be ridiculed as old-fashioned, I confess that I recommended gentle Agnes as a Muse to both the painter and the poet."

The public was not alone in laughing at the Flounder. "It's too kind of you," said Ms. Schönherr in her capacity as presiding judge, "to grant, perhaps not to women in general but at least to this particular Agnes, a further function, in addition to those of cook and bed warmer: so now she's entitled to serve as a Muse, to give little kisses, to fertilize the moist, warm soil, and, by bestowing higher inspiration, to help burnt-out artists to mediocre achievements. What a blessing to the aging geniuses of our own day if the custom were revived! Why, these Muses could be tax deductible! But joking aside, what came of this division of labor?"

"Not much, I'm afraid," said the Flounder. "A few insignificant though rather nice-looking portraits of the nude and pregnant Agnes; for old man Möller did manage to produce a home-grown testimonial to the virility of his old age. But Opitz was unable to squeeze out a sonnet or an ode to Agnes. He couldn't even put her dill garden into iambics. He devoted himself rather peevishly to a new edition of his old poems. He kept himself busy correcting the proofs of successive new editions of *Arcadia,* a tear-jerker he had translated from the English. His translations of the Psalms of David were creditable but hardly inspired. The one thing he was really good at was commissions, the usual panegyrics to princes. Apparently, he didn't even succeed in impregnating Agnes, for when, three years after the death of her first-born daughter, she burgeoned a second time, the restless Opitz had again been absent for quite a while, in Thorn, Königsberg, Warsaw, and so on: Possibly painter Möller had managed once again to fan up a bit of flame from the ashes. No, esteemed Tribunal, neither Möller nor Opitz succeeded in producing an enduring work of art, a gift to the world, the real thing, a late-ripened panel painting—the long-planned crucifixion on the Hagelsberg with sinful Danzig in the background—or a shattering war, plague, and vale-of-tears allegory, comparable to Opitz's early poem about the plague in Bunzlau, although young Agnes, with her touching, always rather giddy-seeming charm, was well able to create the buzzing silence in which art can germinate. True, Opitz's eyes bugged out with visions when, looking as transparent as an astral body, Agnes stirred an egg into the chicken broth, but all that came of his visions was poetic first lines and hopeful stammerings that never settled into an iambic order. Quick sketches, yes, suggestive of grand designs, but never carried to completion. All in the realm of promise. In short, my well-meaning advice fired both painter and poet like tinder, but after a while both stoves went cold again."

After a pause, during which the Flounder probably listened for the effect of his half confession (the sounds of the public part of the hall were channeled into his bulletproof compartment), he observed, once again in a piping falsetto: "I hear

253

derisive laughter. You people never seem to tire of trying to be witty at my expense. And yet I'm quite willing to admit that I wasted young Agnes Kurbiella's gifts as a Muse. I was deceived by hope. I sincerely believed that a work of lasting value could be wrested from the talented Möller and from Opitz the brilliant theoretician. Möller was no run-of-the-mill town painter, you know. And without Opitz it seems unlikely that German poetry would ever have achieved proper rhymes and a regular succession of accented and unaccented syllables. I therefore ask the High Court to take cognizance of the scholarly comments on Opitz, a reading of which I have requested, and to authorize an illustrated lecture by way of showing an uninformed public how promisingly painter Möller started out, how soon he began to allegorize, and how pitifully his not inconsiderable talent went to the dogs. Only then will you be in a position to judge whether I, the Flounder so sternly accused by womankind, acted criminally, mistakenly, or, permit me to suggest, rightly, in providing these two just about washed-up artists with a Muse."

Despite protests from the public—"Now he's trying to sell us Muses' kisses!" "This Flounder is nothing but a shitty Germanist!"—the Tribunal decided in favor of the accused, largely because Ms. von Carnow, the defense counsel, threatened with wild gestures and fluttering voice to withdraw from the case. (She even wept a bit—effectively.)

First photographs of Möller's best-known works, *The Last Judgment* and *The Tribute Money*, whole and in detail, were flashed on the screen of the movie-house-turned-courtroom. Then examples of his more popular work: ladies of the Danzig bourgeoisie against a background of sumptuous Hanseatic façades, fishwives on the Long Bridge, a buxom lass or two, maidens on their way to church, all in the costumes of the day. An art historian from Holland lectured informatively about the unknown provincial painter: how the son of a Königsberg court barber had studied painting more in the Netherlands than in Italy; how his copies of Dürers had unfortunately been lost; why, despite the many influences discernible in his work, he could not be written off as an epigone; how hard it was for youthful talents between the declining Renaissance and early Baroque; why, despite all its little allegorical games, Möller's *Last Judgment* could be reckoned among the outstanding productions of the time;

254

how noteworthy a figure Möller had been before, roughly in 1610, his creative powers failed, and what high hope his talent had justified.

Next the affidavits of prominent literary critics were read. The court learned that on comparison with Gryphius and Hoffmannswaldau, Opitz was lacking in metaphoric power and formal refinement. Quotations were employed to show what skillful use Opitz had made of quotations from other authors. On the basis of his biography, the events of a varied, adventurous, but increasingly dubious existence, darkened by his activity as a double agent, were dated. Then came the regretful observation, "Little of this is concretized in his poems. Even in the love poems everything is coded, spiritualized, mythologized, or reduced to didactic epigrams. A pity that his opera librettto and Heinrich Schütz's undoubtedly far-superior music have been lost." A quotation or two was offered (". . . freedom demands to be oppressed, enslaved, contested . . .") by way of showing that a few of his lines had had staying power. "He was a man of compromise, who as a diplomat, sometimes in the Protestant, sometimes in the Catholic service, tried to mediate between the two warring religions: 'Force maketh no man pious. Force cannot make a Christian!' "

Another affidavit characterized the poet's political position as unchanged through all his seemingly opportunistic transformations. "In the very midst of the Thirty Years' War, Opitz was an irenicist. *Eirene*, which is Greek for peace, was his guiding star. Tolerance was his motto. And that is why we find no partisan passion in his writing, but, often to its detriment, a well-balanced artistry. The man was too intelligent, too committed to orderly reasoning, to turn out bold, exalted, beautiful, and in the last analysis stupid metaphors. And this explains his painful encounter, soon after his arrival in Danzig, with young Gryphius, the liberator of the German language, who attacked the esteemed master for the political activity that had consumed his energies, for his service as a paid double agent, for the pusillanimity that deterred him from candidly baring his soul and openly proclaiming his sorrow. Nevertheless, his influence on our literature has been considerable. Not so long ago a deserving Germanic scholar was able to prove that the account of the Battle of Wittstock on the Dosse in Grimmelshausen's *Simplicissimus* was at least inspired by the battle scenes in Opitz's translation of *Arcadia*.

255

Possibly young Grimmelshausen, while viewing the battle scenes from the top of a tree, compared them with the printed metaphors and so recognized their authenticity, since they presented all the palpable horror that literature prescribes, so demonstrating once again that nothing happens but what has first been prefigured by the written word."

But all the affidavits agreed that Opitz's true achievement was to be found in his theoretical treatise *Über die Poeterey (On Poetics)*. For the common tongue created by Luther had been fit only for jingles, but Opitz had purified it and made it into a medium of art. One of the affidavits went so far as to say, "Thanks to Opitz, high-level writing was set free from its centuries-long Latin captivity; he was an emancipator."

The Tribunal took note of all this and would probably have arrived at a mild verdict if Sieglinde Huntscha, the prosecutor, had not provoked the Flounder with barbed questions. This woman, who rose to heroic stature even when seated, jumped up, turn red to the roots of her hair, fortified her voice with contempt, pointed a gaunt forefinger at the bulletproof cage where the Flounder, possibly cheered by the affidavits of the literary critics, had brought all his fins into play several handbreadths above the bed of sand. Then, suddenly assuming a Saxon accent, she directed—no, fired—question after question at the accused flatfish. The effect was immediate. The Flounder drooped as though shot, burrowed into the Baltic sand, threw sand over his pebbly, age-old skin, and muddied the water of his glass house, which may have been secure against bullets but offered no protection against well-aimed questions. He seemed to have vanished, escaped, to be gone forever.

And yet the prosecutor's questions were no intellectual fish-hooks. The Flounder was not attacked as such. Simply and directly Sieglinde Huntscha asked: "If a woman can be a professional Muse, what about men? Are they, too, eligible? And if so, what men have functioned as Muses, what men, that is, have indirectly promoted art by helping to inspire well-known woman artists? Or does the defendant hold that the role of woman in art can only be one of passive, servile, manuring mediation? Are we only good for firing your burnt-out stoves? Is there to be an hourly wage for female Muse work? Maybe the Flounder will be kind enough to draw up a wage scale, or even found a Muses' union. And tell me this, defendant Flounder: can a woman keep a male Muse if she pays him properly? Or was the verbiage those experts of yours dished up just a smoke screen to hide your true meaning? Because here's what you really mean: Yes, yes, some of the girls play the piano very nicely and some do well enough in applied art or interior decorating, for instance, and when they go in for loving or suffering or Ophelia-like schizophrenia, they sometimes manage to write touching, absorbing, melancholy verses in heart's blood, cunt juice, or black bile. But Handel's *Messiah*, the categorical imperative, the Strassburg Cathedral, Goethe's *Faust*, Rodin's *Thinker*, and Picasso's *Guernica*—such summits of art are beyond their reach. Is that it, defendant Flounder?

The stirred-up Baltic sand had settled in the meantime. The Flounder had stopped thrashing his tail and lay still. Only rising bubbles showed where his gills were drawing breath. And his crooked mouth came to life. "Ye-es," he said, "I'm sorry, but that's how it is."

The public was floored, too weak even for indignation. The most they could summon up was one long sigh. Only Ms. von Carnow, the court-appointed defense counsel, spoke. "How awful," she gasped.

Then silence invited the Flounder to say more. "Without trying to attenuate my 'Yes,' I would like to praise woman's power to serve as Muse by telling you about Agnes. She was more than Möller and Opitz together. Not even a Rubens, not even a Hölderlin could have used all she had to offer. My mistake was to bury two worn-out talents under her superabundance. No, Agnes produced no art. But she was a source for all the arts: her fluid form, her epic silence, her thinking in which nothingness spoke, her ambiguity, her moist warmth. Only in her cooking was she creative, when she coddled Opitz's sick stomach with potted calves' brains and asparagus tips, all the more creative because she sang over her cook pots, always in one and the same tone, which was quite sufficient, because it was richer than any melodic development. Mostly she sang brief ditties in which the Swedes had forced all the horrors of war into rhyme. Here I must tell you that in the spring of 1632 Agnes, then thirteen, had been made a full orphan and used as a knothole on the Hela Peninsula by some Swedish cavalrymen belonging to Oxenstierna's occupation regiment, and that the experience had scrambled her wits. Sometimes she talked about someone

257

called Axel. He must have been one of the cavalrymen. He alone seems to have penetrated her lastingly.

"So much, esteemed court, for Agnes Kurbiella. Yes, I say, yes and again yes. Agnes had no need to produce, to create. She had no need to be creative. Because she was a creature—and perfect as such."

Though the Flounder's speech, gradually swelling to the old deep organ tones, was undoubtedly conveyed to the ears of the judges and of the public as well, the verdict went against him. He was found guilty of encouraging two worn-out old men to derive stimulation from their abuse of a child who was already addled as a result of male war crimes. Something was said of male pimping. In reading the court's opinion, the presiding judge smiled as though finding savor in bitter almonds and conceded that a certain indulgence was warranted in view of the defendant's limited male intelligence. "The lords of creation just can't help it," she declared. "They can't do without their monopoly on creativity. We women have to be creatures—perfect creatures, what's more. Thanks be to the Swedish cavalrymen, especially to the sinister Axel, for driving the childlike Agnes crazy in a manner so conducive to art. Slightly batty women make excellent Muses. We are looking forward to the next session, when the defendant will speak fishily on love."

When the Flounder's court-appointed counsel stood up to plead in his defense, a good part of the public walked noisily out of the former movie house. Nor was the Revolutionary Advisory Council interested in listening to Ms. von Carnow. I myself found her plaintive, whining, piping monotone hard to bear, even though Bettina—outwardly an attractive young woman, inwardly a plucked angel—may have resembled my Agnes: the curly, rust-colored hair, the steadily blinking eyes, the smile that nothing could efface, the high-arched, childlike forehead.

Only a few heard Ms. von Carnow's anachronistic plaint: "But is it not fitting and proper for a woman to be an artist's Muse, his cracked glass, his bed of moss, his primal form? Haven't all great things come into being in this and only this way, through the quiet influence of inspiring women? Are we women to walk out on this magnificent job and seal off the wellsprings of the arts? Is devotion not the best proof of womanly strength? Do we want to harden ourselves to the point of insensibility? And what, I ask you, what is to become of the Eternal Womanly?"

"OK, OK!" the Flounder interrupted. "Your little questions move even me to tears. But my dear lady, you're behind the times, and nothing worse can happen to a woman. I'm afraid you would even be capable, like little Agnes, whose case is here under discussion, of giving your love unconditionally. Good Lord! Nobody could put up with that in this day and age."

(Then I, too, walked out, much as Bettina von Carnow attracted me by awakening memories.) Oh, Agnes! Your boiled fish. Your meaningless smile. Your bare feet. Your sleepy hands. Your soporific voice. Your never-to-be-filled emptiness. There was always fresh dill in the house: your love, which always and always grew back. . . .

Late

I know nature
only insofar as
it shows itself.

With groping fingers
I see it in fragments,
never,
or only when luck strikes me,
as a whole.

What so much beauty, manifested
bright and early in my feces,
signifies or intends,
I do not know.

Therefore I go to bed reluctantly,
for dreams give objects fluidity
and talk meaning into them.

I try to stay awake.
Maybe the stone will move
or Agnes come,
bringing me what makes me sleep:
caraway seeds and dill.

Fishily on love poetry

He talked us men into it (and prescribed it for all
Ilsebills as a pacemaker). For in the beginning, when Awa
ruled, when all women were called Awa and all men Edek,
we didn't have love. It wouldn't have entered our heads to
single out any particular Awa as something special. We had
no chosen one, though we did have the Superawa, who was
later worshiped as a mother goddess and who, because I was
able to scratch figures with her proportions in the sand or
knead them in clay, always favored me just a little. But
crazy, mad about, in love with each other we were not.

By the same token there was no hatred. In the customary
life of the horde no one was pushed aside, except perhaps the
poor devils who were individually excluded and driven into
the swamps, for infringing on some taboo. Taboo, for instance, were garrulous group eating and solitary shitting. And
undoubtedly our Superawa would have sternly tabooed love
between two individuals—if such madness had ever cropped
up among us—and banished the offending pair. Such things
are believed to have happened—somewhere else.

Not among us. To us the individual meant nothing. One
Awa was as fat as another. And we Edeks were taken wherever we fitted in. Of course there were differences. Of course
there were little preferences. Don't go thinking we were a
shapeless neolithic mass. Not only age groups but also groupings based on the division of labor determined the sociological makeup of our horde. Some of the women gathered
mushrooms; in the beech woods they came into contact with
the male group that had specialized in hunting bear but
mostly speared badgers. Since I was numbered among the
fishermen—though I preferred to fish by myself, which was
not taboo—the women who plaited eel traps made more use

of me than did the mushroom gatherers. But this had nothing to do with love, not even group love. Still, we were buoyed by a strong feeling, which might have been called tender loving care.

When, no sooner had I caught him and set him free, the Flounder questioned me about my life in the horde, he was curious to know what three-breasted Stone Age women liked me best, whose pussy I serviced with Stakhanovite enthusiasm, which basket plaiter or otherwise occupied Ilsebill I tried to madden with love: "So tell me, my son, which of these women's heads have you turned?"

By way of an answer, I explained our system of horde care. "We care first for our mothers and mothers' mothers. Then we care for their daughters and daughters' daughters. Then, if any of our men have been eliminated by work accidents, for our mothers' sisters and their daughters and daughters' daughters. The products of our care—game, fish, elk cow's milk, honeycomb, nuts, berries, et cetera—are distributed by the mothers' mothers in accordance with the Superawa's instructions. So the products of our care-work revert to us in the end, for the old men are served first."

In accordance with this principle, no Awa or Edek is preferred, though our Superawa always pampered me a bit at the night feeding. If we loved anyone, it was her. And our horde supplied a clear and unmistakable answer to the Flounder's question "Look, isn't there somebody you love best if only symbolically, some person you love so much you could eat that person?" For when one day our Superawa died, we, each for himself, ate her up. Not for love, but because in dying she commanded us, not as was the custom to lower her into the swamp in a squatting position, but to eat every bit of her. She even (caringly) left us a recipe: she wanted to be cleaned (by me, incidentally), then stuffed with her heart and liver to which mushrooms and juniper berries had been added, wrapped in a thumb's thickness of clay, bedded on coals strewn with ashes, and covered over with ashes and coals. Thus indeed did we roast Awa, and toward evening she was done. The burnt clay was struck off, and then after caringly dividing her into portions, we ate her. I got a piece of the neck, the forefinger of her left hand, a bit of liver, and the barest morsel of her middle breast. She didn't taste especially good. Like a superannuated cow.

No, friend Flounder, we didn't eat her for love. A long, hard winter had covered the rivers and sea with ice, buried the mangels under the snow, and driven away the badgers, boars, and elks. We were all out of manna grits. Starving. Chewing birch bark. The women who suckled us were on their last legs. Only the old ones were holding out. That was when Awa offered herself. Not until later, much later, did it become the custom, even without famine, to roast each deceased Superawa according to the traditional recipe and eat her. Call it cannibalism if you will. Maybe it was, friend Flounder, but we never ate one another for love, requited or unrequited, never because we were lovelorn or love-crazed.

Even in the days of Wigga, or much later of Mestwina, love did not transfigure us, we didn't blush or turn pale at the sight of each other. True, I was and remained Wigga's charcoal burner, and Mestwina seldom exchanged me for a fisherman or a plaiter of baskets, but grandiose emotions that tightened or expanded the chest, the quickened heartbeat, the desire to embrace the world or at least the nearest tree, to give ourselves wholly, to fuse with each other, to become each other's thing possession chattel, to gnaw on the same little bone, the absurd desire to die in each other's arms—this whole giddy, warbling romanza was alien to us, and I don't believe we hankered after it in secret, either.

Not that we were altogether lukewarm. Though Wigga ruled us men with a sternness carried over from the Stone Age, she could be affectionate when we bedded down, and even playful after cooking pike dumplings. And when we were old and knotted with gout, and flesh no longer tempted us, we often sat in silence outside our hut, watching the sun set behind the forest. Maybe after all we had a kind of old folks' love, that trembling holding of hands and muttering of do-you-remember.

I'd have liked to live the same way with Mestwina. We didn't own each other, and when spring came she took to lying where she listed, but we had got into the habit of wintering together. Since love had never smitten us, we were not smitten with jealousy. When March came, she didn't begrudge me my capers, nor I her cavortings.

All this changed when Bishop Adalbert turned up with the cross. In any event, the Flounder claims that when Mestwina started cooking for the holy man and, soon thereafter, sharing his ascetic bed of leaves, her gaze clouded over and she often showed a drawn, melancholy smile.

"Believe me, my son," he said after the saint's death, "she loved him even if she did strike him dead. Or she hit him with the cast iron because she loved him and he wouldn't give up his love of the Lord God. It was unrequited love that drove her to drink—mead and fermented mare's milk. In any case, love seems to divert women from their natural supremacy. They humble themselves, they want to be humbled, they come crawling, and their love turns to homicidal frenzy only when their offer of unconditional servitude is rejected, or, as in the case of Saint Adalbert of Prague, misinterpreted as satanic temptation. In short, love is an instrument that demands to be handled with care. We will practice that, my son."

And then the Flounder developed his theory of love as a means of putting an end to the domination of women. Love would unleash feelings. It would set a standard that no one could live up to. It would suckle but never appease a lasting dissatisfaction. It would invent a language of sighs, the poetry which at once illuminates and obscures. It would go into partnership with falling leaves, swirling mists, the worm in the woodwork, the melting snow, and the lusting little leaves of spring. It would give rise to supernaturally colorful dreams. It would paint the world in rosy colors. It would beguile women into compensating for their lost power by voraciously escalating their demands. It would become the everlasting plaint of every Ilsebill.

Then the Flounder ordained that love be made to provide an ideational superstructure under whose sheltering canopy practical marriage as guarantor of property might develop. For marriage has nothing in common with love. Marriage makes for security; love makes only for suffering. Not only would this be demonstrated in moving poems; unfortunately, it would also result in crimes. How many times would "the other woman" be poisoned, strangled, punctured with knitting needles!

On the other hand, the Flounder went on, love could be so distilled, spun so fine as to implicate third and fourth persons, as to take up three or four exciting acts in a play, to be set to music or filmed, and, just incidentally, to show women the way to complicated psychological disorders. (Here the Flounder listed all the disorders, from loss of appetite to migraine and raving madness, that have since been honored by medical insurance as bona fide afflictions.)

His disquisition, which was bolstered by quotations of poetry from the troubadours to the Beatles and anticipated the latest in pop songs and advertising slogans, concluded with the programmatic sentence: "Only if we succeed in persuading woman by subtle suggestion that love is a saving power and the certainty of being loved the supreme happiness, and if concomitantly man, even though loved to the point of adulation, steadfastly refuses to love or to guarantee the longevity of his little love affairs, so that the woman's dependence on the never-attained certainty that he loves her, still loves her, loves her and nobody else, becomes a lifelong anxiety, a humiliating torment, and an oppressive servitude—then alone will matriarchy be defeated, will the conquering phallic symbol overturn all vulvar idols, will man illuminate the prehistoric darkness of the womb and perpetuate himself forever and ever as father and as master."

Yes, Ilsebill. A lot of women were indignant when the Flounder began to shoot his mouth off in court recently. At the very start of the proceedings, the prosecutor had considered bringing up the Flounder's theory of love in connection with Dorothea of Montau, but because Dorothea did not love and worship the swordmaker, Albrecht Slichting, but on the contrary I, fool that I was, in defiance of the fishy theory of love, fell in love with the witch, the prosecution reserved this hybrid topic until the case of Agnes Kurbiella should be debated.

In any case, love brought me no freedom, but only long-haired misery. True, the Flounder had advised me never to marry a woman I was capable of loving, but I married my pale-faced bride of Christ, and if I'd been brought up at court I'd have written love songs to her in the chivalric fashion of the day: "Ah, lady swet beyond compare . . ." For the pining and sighing of the troubadours dragged on into my High Gothic time-phase. Disgusting slobber that turned our otherwise coldblooded Teutonic Knights into moaning, lisping mollycoddles. Even the most buxom peasant girl was seen as a little Madonna. Our good old mating games degenerated into sinful fornication. Only what was forbidden turned people on. Ballad-making love—"for all min lyfe is luv"—promised eternal chastity, but then two stanzas farther on, once the key to the chastity belt had been found, the poet wallowed in the usual meat salad. Yet our ladies—my Dorothea in the lead—kept sanctimoniously aloof, casting down their eyes if anyone so much as mentioned a codpiece. And we men dangled from the string with which, on the advice of a loquacious fish, we had tried to bind our women to the marriage bed.

Dorothea! Lord, what didn't I do to coax a little love from that cold-blooded bitch. But even when she made her body available, she withheld it. I could whimper, I could babble, I could turn somersaults like the queen's dwarf—she turned away in boredom and went on with her elaborate penitential exercises; only heavenly love could get a rise out of her. Enslaved to her sweet Jesus, she crushed me, reduced me to a miserable rag. That, Ilsebill, is what love did to me. That, Mr. Flounder, was your contribution to the emancipation of men. If things had only stopped with Awa Wigga Mestwina and their loving-caring rule—all that unvarying warmth and bedding down, all that moist mossy bottom. Awa and her priestesses never destroyed us with love.

It wasn't until Fat Gret started cooking for us that the pressure let up. In the meantime the custom of property-securing marriage had become so engrained that women, weary perhaps of chivalric effusions and threadbare chastity games, were positively dying to get married; power over household, keys, and kitchen was power enough for them. They were faithful and cozily devoted to their husbands. And because housewifely infidelity was severely punished, by whip, pillory, or casting off, husbands and fathers could rely on their women to bring up the children. At last the Flounder's fishy theory of love was reflected in home-grown practice: how stingily the ladies pinched pennies, how neighborly they clucked, gossiped, made matches, quarreled, and gradually developed into hags or matrons. Only whores and nuns refused to join in—and first of all Fat Gret, who could have run a whorehouse if she hadn't been an abbess.

Whereas Dorothea rebelled against marriage by daily opening the back door of her Lenten kitchen to her heavenly bridegroom, Margarete kept clear of agonizing situations from the start. As a nun she was betrothed in heaven, but the solid flesh demanded earthly love. Thus as an abbess she taught her young nuns to let no man—be he monk or straying paterfamilias—bamboozle their hearts. Just as the Flounder had taught us men to make women pant for love but never—or only away from home and with due caution—to lose our heads over love, so Fat Gret advised her free-ranging Brigittines to believe no man's whisperings. "Don't aggravate me," she would say. "You're married already." Yet two or three nuns ran away from Saint Bridget's (because the Reformation was on) and succumbed to the unrelieved misery of married life.

Mestwina may have worshiped Saint Adalbert; and possibly Ilsebill has me in mind when she looks for her ignition key. Fat Gret—I'm certain—loved no man, caringly as she cooked for her dozen men. At the most she gave me, the runaway Franciscan monk, something on the order of mother love. Margret was a vigorous thirty at the time, and I a seventeen-year-old novice. With me she had no need to disguise her feelings. I hardly counted. Her constantly changing kitchen boys. There were so many uprooted monks running around, looking for shelter and warmth, her motherly sheltering fat. Margarete Rusch had plenty of that. And she gave to everyone she fancied. A few men (I, for instance) may have mistaken that for love.

Agnes, the gentle, barefoot diet cook, was the first grandly loving woman, a type that the Flounder may well, with fishy calculation, have thought up. For Agnes Kurbiella loved me without reserve, me Möller the town painter and me Opitz the poet and diplomat in the service of the king of Poland loved me so thoroughly in accordance with the rules of the Flounder's theory that her love can be qualified by all those epithets and phrases that later became clichés: devoted, self-sacrificing, humble and uncomplaining, with all her heart, beyond the grave, unselfish, unquestioning, uncomplaining. And withal, she was not loved. Opitz was too wrapped up in himself and his stomach trouble, too much involved in too many political intrigues to be capable of concentrated feeling; painter Möller loved only food and drink. But Agnes loved us without asking to be loved in return. She was our handmaiden. She was the bucket into which we vomited our misery. She was the cloth that absorbed the sweat of our anguish. She was the hole we crawled into. Our pillow of moss, our hot-water bottle, our sleeping potion, our evening prayer.

Maybe she loved Opitz a little more than Möller, though

for six years, without so much as turning up her nose, she changed Möller's breeches every time he shat in them. All the same, stingy as the poet was with his money and feelings, she was more deeply attached to him. When the plague carried him off, she clung to the straw he had died on and his sweat-soaked bed sheet. The constables had to beat her to make her let go. She loved totally. When Hoffmannswaldau, another poet from Silesia, came to Danzig for the deceased Opitz's posthumous papers (and quarreled over them with Herr Roberthin, whom Simon Dach had sent from Königsberg), Agnes Kurbiella appears to have fed the kitchen stove with the final version of the Psalms translation, a whole sheaf of poems in rough draft, the unfinished manuscript of the *Dacia antiqua*, which Opitz had been working on intermittently ever since his years as a young teacher in Rumanian Transylvania, and his correspondence over a period of many years with the Swedish chancellor Oxenstierna. She wouldn't even give Hoffmannswaldau Opitz's goose quills. (Would you, Ilsebill, be capable of oiling and dusting my old portable typewriter someday and holding it more or less sacred?)

In the Flounder's opinion, so much undeviating love was just another form of domination and not at all what he had suggested. Agnes Kurbiella's unrequited love, he maintained, hadn't caused her so much as an hour's unhappiness. Never had she chewed a handkerchief to bits; on the contrary, she had radiated unclouded joy, and it would be no exaggeration to say that, far from making her dependent or servile, love had given her strength and blown her up to more than life size. "Even if this kitchenmaid's triumph wasn't what I originally intended," said the accused flatfish, "I can't deny that I respect her: so much indulgence, devotion, resignation."

And at the Women's Tribunal, when the prosecution at last took up his theory of love, the Flounder declared in self-defense: 'Easy does it, my dear ladies. I have already owned that early on, when men were maintained in a state of dependency and one might reasonably have termed them 'oppressed,' I conceived of love as a counterforce which, by way of compensation, would make for male privilege and female dependency. But then, by following the example of Agnes Kurbiella, quite a few women succeeded in transforming my—to cite the prosecution—so craftily devised instrument of oppression into a symbol of eternal womanly greatness: What self-conquest! What selflessness! What fortitude! What overflowing, uncontainable feeling! What fidelity! Think of all the great loving women! What would literature be without them? Without a Juliet, Romeo would be a nobody. To whom, if not to his Diotima, could Hölderlin in his hymns have poured forth his soul? Ah, how moved we still are by the love of Käthchen von Heilbronn! Or by the death of Ottilie in Goethe's *Elective Affinities*.

"Our Agnes's love had this quiet, sometimes melancholy, always effective, but never aggressive strength. Of course I can't help seeing that the ladies of this esteemed Tribunal choose to be different and have to keep step with the times, that Ms. Huntscha, for instance, undoubtedly has feelings but makes sure to rationalize them before putting them into words, but I nevertheless beg you to show just a little sisterly comprehension for a poor child surrendered, by me I admit, to the mercies of two worn-out wrecks. I have spoken of Agnes's talents as a Muse but have been unable to convince the High Court of the existence and dignity of this exclusively feminine quality. But perhaps Agnes, sparing as she was of words, succeeded in speaking for me. By transforming my dirty trick, the love that enslaves, into pure feeling, she enabled womanly love to win out in the end and to make men small, so small."

In conclusion, the Flounder pleaded with the presiding judge, the associate judges, the prosecutor, and the entire Revolutionary Advisory Council of the Women's Tribunal to harden their hearts no longer, but to follow the example of Agnes Kurbiella and let their whole being reduce itself to love: "That and that alone is your true strength. No man has it. Not your intelligence—shrewdly as it has seen through me, exposed, refuted, and discredited me—no, it is the power of your love that will someday change the world. Already I can see the beginnings of a new tenderness, a new sympathy embracing every man and every woman. Love will glorify the whole world with its radiance. Millions of wishless Ilsebills. Shamed by so much meekness, men will renounce their power and their glory. Love alone will remain. As far as the eye can see . . ."

At this point the Flounder was interrupted. The intercom in his bulletproof-glass house was cut off. Even though Ms. von Carnow, the court-appointed defense counsel, burst into tears in protest and the Revolutionary Advisory Council (once again) split—it was then that the faction later known as the Flounder Party first made its appearance—the Women's Tribunal nevertheless refused to acknowledge the love of Agnes the kitchenmaid as a contribution to the emancipation of women. The court was adjourned. Affidavits—counter-affidavits. Factional struggles.

But the subject of love was often discussed after that, if only as a marginal topic. When, in the course of the trial, the case of Amanda Woyke was argued and her letters to Count Rumford were qualified as love letters even though both sides of the correspondence dealt with nothing more romantic than potato growing, slow-combustion stoves, soup kitchens, and Rumford soup for the poor. As for the cook Sophie Rotzoll, though the Tribunal evaluated her life as a revolutionary experiment, the Flounder held that it was marked from first to last by tragic love. Had she not been obliged at the age of fourteen to surrender her passionately beloved Fritz—condemned to life imprisonment for membership in a secret society—to the fortress of Graudenz? Had she not resisted all male temptation for forty years? For then at last he had returned, in pretty bad shape. "Yes, my dear ladies," said the Flounder. "This you must recognize as love. Love worthy of Agnes."

Nor was the Flounder inclined to minimize the love factor in the cases of Lena Stubbe, who cooked for the poor, and of Sibylle Miehlau, Billy for short, who wanted so tragically to be different, and of the still-unconcluded case of Maria, the cook at the shipyard canteen. At every turn, love broke through. It pulled strings. It outlasted hunger, plague, and wars. It refuted cost accounting and all economics. It ravaged and, in the case of Lena Stubbe, was a silent torment. Captive to love, Sophie remained a spinster down to her delicately wrinkled old age and never stopped hoping. Billy looked for it elsewhere. Amanda encoded it in letters. And most likely, since love can also harden, Maria will slowly turn to stone.

"No!" cried the Flounder, wholly embedded in sand as he addressed the Women's Tribunal. "I regret nothing. Without love there'd be nothing left but toothache. Without love, life—and this I say deliberately, speaking as a fish—wouldn't even be beastly. None of our Ilsebills could get along without love. And if I may briefly return to the cook Agnes: by cooking with devotion for painter Möller's swollen liver and poet Opitz's delicate stomach, she imparted tender meaning to the silly proverb 'The way to a man's heart is through his stomach.' Ah, her oatmeal gruel! Ah, her soup chicken!

"Hard-boiled ladies, if you will lend me your ears for just another moment, I should like to conclude with a few lines from one of Opitz's lost poems:

"Is love to be all passion, a flaming, blazing hell?
Ah, dearest, let us hasten, or else the bland, white
    fish
Thou hast in milk transfigured will cool off in the dish.
Is't not for love thou wishest the fish to make me
    well?' "

Agnes remembered over boiled fish

Upon the codfish which today
I simmered in white wine
while musing about the days
when codfish was still cheap,
I laid—when his eyes had turned milky
and white fisheyes were rolling over
the feverish Opitz's blank paper—
strips of fresh cucumber
and then, removing the broth from the heat, added dill to it.

Over the boiled fish I strewed shrimps' tails,
which our guests—two men who didn't know each other—
had toyed with, conversationally
concerned with the future, while
the fish was cooking.

Ah, cook, you watch me
as with a flat spoon
I help the tender flesh: willingly it gives up its bones
and wants to be reminded, Agnes, reminded.

By then the gentlemen knew each other better.
At our age, I told them, Opitz died of the plague.
We talked about the arts and about prices.
No political excitement.

Afterward sour cherry soup.
Pits from the old days got counted, too:
when we played rich man poor man beggarman thief. . . .

It seems his name was Axel

No, no, Ilsebill, it's not like that at all. Love isn't just something the fairy-tale Flounder dreamed up. No, it exists, the same as rain exists. It can't be turned off, it doesn't smell of fish, it's playing in all the movie houses, it finds opportunities that don't always make much sense. For instance: somebody likes buttermilk; funny, so do I, and there you have it.

And here you are in your fourth month of pregnancy, because we were looking for a way of expressing love. So something palpable has to come of it. It can't just be an era in itself! But love is more spacious than a double bed and grows without regard to time: everywhere it languishes, utterly dispersed, divided, and yet whole.

So it wasn't hard for Agnes to make soup for Opitz by adding fresh dill to the boiled fish that Möller had left over. And you, too, if I left leftovers, would put them to tasty use somewhere on the outside, where there's no phone to come between us. Why wouldn't we be able to meet in reverse motion, at the Green Gate, for instance, which in Dorothea's day was called Koggen Gate? Agnes is just coming from the market; she has bought an unplucked chicken for painter Möller, while I (engaged in negotiations with King Wladislaw), am inwardly rich in figures and quotations from other authors. She's pregnant, and the scene is wintry. She's plodding through the slushy snow. Her waddling gait. She turns onto Beutlergasse. Let's hope she doesn't fall. . . ."
"All a lot of subterfuges!" you say, looking sternly out of the window into the present January. But how do you expect us

to live without subterfuges! You yourself are a subterfuge. That's why Agnes never closed doors. Always left them ajar. No hesitations between her comings and goings. Often she was there, but I noticed only myself, whereas someone else (Möller) noticed her even though she was with me. Her love was placeless. That's why I was never able to perceive her presence: what I missed was there. And even the Flounder, for whom everything, like his backbone, tapers down logically to a tail fin, couldn't understand that what she never ran out of was dill. He thought love must work like a mousetrap and that she must have fallen for Möller and me. Actually it was one of the four or five Swedes whose regiment was occupying Putzig, and they'd only wanted to go for a ride and hunt rabbits in the dunes, where they came across Agnes, who was sitting curly-haired in the beach grass. She was tending her geese, and all of a sudden she had all four on top of her, one after another, it didn't take long. But only the first really counted. He was closer to her than Möller and Opitz later on. It seems his name was Axel. And it seems his downy boyish beard was blond. And his brittle, commanding voice lingered on. He never came back, and he was always near her while I, sitting over blank paper as Agnes passed through the room, traveled to Zlatna, where in my days as a young teacher in Transylvania I was surprised on a straw pallet by a kitchenmaid who never cooked for me—just as you always listen when I'm with you to see if someone else is coming. When actually I've been gone for ages and I'm just smoking.

My subterfuges—yours. I suggest that we meet where the Striessbach flows into the Radaune and the Radaune flows into the Mottlau and the Mottlau flows into the Vistula and all these rivers empty into the Baltic Sea. And there I will tell you how it was with Agnes, whom I also have in mind when I come to you and absent-mindedly—which always makes for a fight—call you Agnes.

When Agnes Kurbiella came to the city from the Hela Peninsula, where the Swedish occupation troops were garrisoned, Möller, the aged painter who had taken to drink years before, saw her playing like a child with sea shells, the only things she had brought with her from the Hela beaches. The Swedes had taken her father, her mother, and all her geese. (Later she could never say exactly whom or what first.) Struck by her way of carrying her head—tilted as though in thought—Möller took her to his home on Carp Pond, where she put herself to work in the kitchen.

After Agnes had posed for the town painter for three years as a market girl, as a grave-faced braid maker, or as a dressed-up burgher's daughter and (despite his fondness for fat) cooked light food for him, the hem of her apron began to rise; she became a pregnant model.

After quite a few competent red-chalk sketches, Möller, shortly before her confinement, as though to confirm his impending fatherhood, portrayed himself in colored chalk on the rounded belly of his kitchenmaid; a mobile likeness, for whenever the unborn child modified its position or tried its limbs, some part of the presumptive father's taut image would bulge. He had the look of a peasant with laughing eyes, a goodly number of puffy cheeks, and a reddish beard around his mouth.

Next Möller did an oil painting that faithfully portrayed the ultrapregnant Agnes carrying his healthy physiognomy before her, but left an empty space on the right side of the canvas. Immediately after the confinement—the little girl died when less than a year old—he first sketched himself in chalk on the young mother's sunken belly, then, taking up his oils, transferred Agnes with his bilious countenance to the empty space on the canvas, beside the hopeful belly (with his joker's face on it): chubby-cheeked father and peevish father.

Painter Möller saw himself in double. To him everything was an allegory. A pity that the successful picture, appealing for all its mannerism, has not come down to us; for after little Jadwiga's death Möller is thought to have scratched, punched, and cut the canvas to pieces, murdering it—as far as he was concerned—twice over.

Along with other horrors-turned-paper, statistics tell us that European infants, with their specially prepared food, consume nine times as much protein, carbohydrates, and calories (or barely peck at them and let the rest spoil) as is left for the infants of India. Agnes Kurbiella knew nothing of protein or vitamins. True, Erasmus of Rotterdam had strongly recommended (in Latin) that all mothers suckle their own babies, but since after a few days her milk dried up and Möller was unwilling to pay a wet nurse, she fed the already sickly child first on diluted cow's milk, then on oatmeal gruel, and finally on such prechewed foods as chicken with millet, calves' brains with turnips, herring roe with spinach, lambs' tongues in purée of lentils. Painter Möller's leavings.

And in a later day, when my Ilesbill went off on a trip (the Lesser Antilles), I, too, fed our child prechewed food—out of labeled jars, costing 1.50 to 1.80 marks apiece, with vacuum caps that go pop when you open them. Also boiled beef with egg noodles in tomato sauce. This dish contained 3.7% of protein, 3.0% of fat, 7.5% of carbohydrates, 82 calories per 100 grams. Net weight of jar 220 g; meat content 28 g.

In the course of the week's program—creamed spinach with fresh eggs and potatoes, turkey with rice, ham with mixed vegetables and egg noodles—the figures varied in such a way as to produce a balanced diet. The label of the codfish in herb sauce with potatoes indicated 5.4% protein and 93 calories. The fish content came to 49 g. In addition, as long as my Ilsebill was away (strolling across white beaches, blond among dark-skinned people, as in the travel folder) I daily dissolved instant semolina out of a sealed package in boiled water. This preparation contained milk, vegetable fat, durumwheat semolina, honey, and sugar. It was (as the package assured me) enriched with vitamins. At 6:30 A.M. and at 12:00 noon I also gave our child a bottle containing enriched powdered milk dissolved in water (by me), having first, in accordance with Ilsebill's instructions, sterilized the nipple in boiling water. (Ah, if only I had paid Frau Zenlein next door to suckle my Agnes's baby!)

Taking care of baby is no longer a problem for the grass widower, because everything is right there: absorbent disposable diapers all ready to use, salves and powders, sedative suppositories when needed, and for emergencies telephone numbers that give promise of a male or female doctor. There are also paperbacks with instructions and diagrams showing you how to do everything you might possibly have to do. You'll soon be able to rely on a man. Soon he'll be able to manage by himself. Soon he'll have learned to husband his warmth. Soon he'll be more motherly than he was designed to be. . . .

"You needn't worry. Why, it's child's play. It won't take me any time at all. Why shouldn't a man be able to manage by himself? What makes you think that only a woman can? Have a good fight, Ilsebill. And don't forget us. And love me a little off and on. And take care of yourself. There are supposed to be sharks down there. And drop us a line from your island. We'll get along fine."

When Dorothea went off on pilgrimages to Finsterwalde and Aachen, leaving me with our remaining four children, including the twin girls who were not yet a year old, things were more difficult. In Calcutta I saw mothers who prechewed as I did when Dorothea High Gothically left me at home as Agnes chewed turnips and breast of chicken for her daughter Jadwiga. (Möller, who stingily refused her a wet nurse, made sketches of her chewing.) But the baby didn't want it, took less and less, couldn't keep it down, shat hard balls, shat undigested liquid, whined and whimpered, aged fast, and languished—fed to death.

That's how it was in those days, as retrospective statistics have calculated everywhere, except among the Outer City tanners and the peasant serfs. Teensy-weensy Martha or Anna, pocket-sized Gundel. Stine, Trude, Lovise. So many of my children by Dorothea, Agnes, Amanda, died on me, I had so much suffering behind me, that when I gave our baby its sterile bottle or opened the popping vacuum jars with their precisely measured contents, or when I dissolved instant semolina in boiled water and saw the well-digested results— how well fed they smelled!—in the disposable diapers, I became positively euphoric and sang paeans of praise to the Central European baby-food industry, though well I knew that our child and millions of other sweet little babies eat so much every day as to deprive the infants of southern Asia of the barest essentials. And worse: it is now known that our vitamin-enriched powdered milk is positively fatal to many infants in the less industrialized countries, so that the advertising of a leading concern that is trying to develop a market for powdered milk in Africa can only be termed criminal. (Undermining the African mother's faith in her own milk.) For which reason the Flounder, when infant nutrition was being discussed at the Women's Tribunal, could say with profound, mellifluous concern, "At this point, my dear ladies, I would recommend a little female solidarity. If you must persist in your disposable wastefulness, then at least do something to help your sisters in Africa, for instance, by boycotting the handsomely packaged products of a certain company. After all, you wouldn't want to solve the problem

275

of overpopulation by increasing infant mortality. Or would you?"

But the female public protested loudly; all were unwilling to give up their powdered milk. The Revolutionary Advisory Council came out strongly in favor of prepared baby foods in vacuum-sealed jars. Was the Flounder nuts? Advising mothers of all people to cut down on consumption! Especially working mothers. Anything that lightened the housework was a force for emancipation. Solidarity, yes, but some things you can't do without. They'd send telegrams of solidarity to Africa. Of course what the company was doing there was unspeakable. (And a resolution was voted by an overwhelming majority, given weight by the signatures of the public, and cabled out into the world. . . .)

Soon after the death of her child, Agnes wanted another. But not by painter Möller, who had refused her the wet nurse.

When Martin Opitz, who also called himself von Boberfeld, entered the Royal Polish service and took up lodgings in Danzig, he was not yet forty, while painter Möller was over sixty. Soon after his arrival the poet fell in love with a girl of patrician family who could recite Latin poems but was already engaged to the son of a local merchant. Agnes, who, thanks to the good offices of Pastor Niclassius, was now cooking for Opitz as well, obliterated the silly thing—her name was Ursula—with her mute, barefooted presence. And yet he sighed for Ursula and probably couched his sighs in Latin verses.

More subterfuges. He never made it—not for any length of time. Agnes was the first woman who regularly slept with him. His father, the butcher, after the early death of his first wife, took a second, third, and fourth, and got all four with child after child. So there wasn't much left for his son to do. Just little flirtations, mostly at one court or another. One or two intrigues with burgher women in Breslau, bringing pecuniary consequences, whereupon he took flight again. When he was a young tutor in the service of Prince Bethlen Gabor, a Dacian servant girl seems to have horrified him by really showing him how it was done. Even the war, which lasted all his life, didn't give him what it gave every Swedish cavalryman (Ensign Axel). Always over books and parchment, alone and ugly on straw pallets or in bed: his receding chin.

Nothing but poems and epistles of thanks to successive princes. And so, when little Ursula was not to be had, Opitz, weary and drained, fell to Agnes Kurbiella and her apron.

Agnes, who had plenty, didn't want to have anything, but only to give. For three years she sheltered him with her warmth. But assiduously as he wrote his agent's letters hither and thither for double pay, all he was able to put on paper in the way of poetry was rhetorical flourishes and inky speculations; even the new quill pens that Agnes brought him when she had plucked a goose for Möller were no help, whereas I can always think of something to say about my Ilsebill; she has only to state her wishes, as in the fairy tale. Ilsebill wants this. Ilsebill wants that.

Luckily, I've been able to write her into her sickbed. (I can do that.) Behind my back the door to the next room has been left ajar. From there her cough comes to me, demanding to be heard and put down in line drawings. Choker knots and softly outlined nests (around the shoe) form settlements on my paper. The rubbing lotion contains 60 mg of camphor. The wind is blowing from the west. And light heating oil is getting more and more expensive. (Let her cough this thing out of her, damn it!) For even in weather like this, Agnes turns up and brings herself along.

We and the kitchenmaid Agnes Kurbiella, said the Flounder, were a classical triangle—all corners taken. So it's conceivable—or true—that as Anton Möller I painted the pregnant, by me impregnated, Agnes, although (somewhat later) I was the Opitz who tried in vain—shortly before my miserable death—to transpose the same Agnes into Baroque language. After her child had wasted away, I was obliged, as the Flounder ordered, to prove my mettle: between unsuccessful stanzas I knocked Agnes up without asking who she was thinking about at the time; it seems his name was Axel.

The painter, the poet. They didn't like each other. Opitz thought Möller crude; Opitz, in Möller's eyes, was all spindly-legged theory. But Agnes had to think up a menu for both of them, dishes good for Opitz's delicate stomach and the drinker's swollen liver. I wanted to be painter and poet at once; casually wielding red chalk, pedantically counting iambic measures.

What drew us to Agnes was her allegorical emptiness. You

could read whatever you pleased into her; she admitted of any meaning. (Her features were indistinct; she could look more or less like.)

And every day there was millet cooked in milk, sweetened with honey, and made wholesome for both of them with hazelnuts. Agnes knew what was equally inoffensive to the innards of poet and painter: broth made from beef bones with spinach-stuffed dough pouches floating in it, breasts of chicken with green peas, or beer soups seasoned with nutmeg and cinnamon.

But Möller demanded, insisted on, clamored for smoked bacon and fat mutton rinds. And Opitz nibbled caraway seeds. He became addicted to them, for too many caraway seeds act as a drug: hopeful daydreams, in which the vale of tears became livable, a place inhabited by nymphs and Muses singing verses that had never been written, where peace and peace alone was always victorious.

Agnes let them both make wrecks of themselves, the one with his rich food, the other with his addiction to caraway seeds, until the one's stomach turned inside out and the other's liver swelled to the size of a fist. Then her diet fare was again in demand: boiled fish that fell off the bone, millet cooked in milk, buckwheat cakes. The drunken Möller, the peevish Opitz: carefully as Agnes cooked for both of them, they looked for a very different taste, and found it with deadly certainty.

The door is still holding. But when it crashes, you will bring me war or make me look for coins with your question "Got two mark-pieces for a slot machine?" But then the door opened gently and Agnes came in, bent over me and my scribble-scrabble, and said play words.

I can think of nothing better than to endure this fear or hope and—while the door still holds—draw my little men. Here I can be found, though never entirely. And you, too, come in only briefly, and you're gone before you've come. Once upon a time and long ago, earlier still and earlier than early, you came and stayed for a short lifetime; neither of us knows why.

And once you came—it was probably Agnes—and wanted to hear me scribble for just a little while. Think back. My name was Martin. I came from Bunzlau. The man with the rules of poetics. But you didn't want to know why I'd stayed on so long in the Catholic service and never again collaborated on secular operas with the pious Schütz. All you wanted was to hear me scribble. But I wanted to die and escape from the vale of tears, as naked as I came.

If only I knew whether you died of the fever after me, in giving birth to your daughter—Ursula was her name, Ursel for short. It was another plague year, and all sorts of things were possible with so many people passing away.

As I lay dying because in my niggardliness I had made a beggar give me change for a silver gulden, no one opened the door. Only Niclassius, the preacher at Saint Peter's, was there. Later on he bowdlerized my deathbed in Latin verses. Or can it be that you came and I didn't hear the door open?

In the summer of the year 1639, after Martin Opitz gave a silver gulden to a beggar who held out his hand at the door of Saint Catherine's, and, stingy by nature, demanded copper in return, he acquired the Black Death along with the change. Before he became incapable of doing anything, he wrote letters to Oxenstierna, the Swedish chancellor, and to Wladimir, king of Poland, and ate a little of the codfish that his kitchenmaid served him in dill sauce. (Agnes shook out his pillow. Agnes daubed away his sweat. Agnes changed his bed sheet when he shat black in it. Agnes heard him breathe his last.)

Immediately after his death, before the straw he had died on could be burned and the house fumigated, someone broke in and robbed the poet's room. Some of his papers are missing (to this day), including the Dacian material and all the political correspondence. A Swedish colonel accompanied by two mercenaries is believed to have seized the depositions of Generals Banér and Torstenson, Oxenstierna's letters, and the Polish letters acknowledging Opitz's reports, and secreted them in a safe place. We do not know the colonel's name, but kitchenmaid Kurbiella was long suspected of being an agent of the Swedish crown, of having been in contact with this officer, and of having made off with documents on previous occasions. But nothing was ever proved against Agnes. And before the Women's Tribunal the Flounder had only his usual obscurities to offer. "My dear ladies who always want precise information: we know too little. True, the rape of the thirteen-year-old Agnes Kurbiella by calvarymen of the Oxenstierna regiment may have imprinted her at an early age, leaving her with an undying attachment for one of the four debauchees—it seems his name was Axel—but the circumstances attending the poet's death nevertheless show neither rhyme nor reason. The one thing we know for sure is that his kitchenmaid gave birth to a daughter soon afterward, and that both lived for many years to come."

Excrement rhymed

Steams, is examined.
Does not smell strange, wants to be seen,
to be known by name.
Excrement. Metabolism or bowel movement.
Shit: what settles in a ring.

Make little sausages! the mothers cry.
Early modeling clay, knots of shame
and leftover fear: what has gone into the pants.

Recognition: undigested peas, cherry pits,
the tooth that was swallowed.
We look at one another in amazement.
We have something to say to one another.
My waste—closer to me than God or you or you.

Why do we part behind a bolted door
instead of admitting the guests
with whom, sitting noisily at the table the day before,
we predestined beans and bacon?

From this time on (per decision) we will each eat singly
and shit together,
thus neolithically fostering insight.

All poems that prophesy and rhyme on death
are excrement that has dropped from a constipated body
in which blood meanders, worms survive;
thus did Opitz the poet,
whom the plague incorporated as an allegory,
see his last diarrhea.

Only one was burned as a witch

And yet witchcraft was carried on in kitchens if any-
where, in all kitchens. All cooks knew and handed down recipes for purées, soups, and broths which were thick, ash-gray,
or cloudy, one that bloated, a second that physicked, a third
that induced numbness. From the very start (Awa), henbane
had its uses, ergot was mixed into things, and fly agaric
(dried), grated to a powder, steeped in milk, or imbibed with
mare's urine, was good for a journey into succubine transcen-
dence. We men were as dependent on Wigga, who raised
mandrakes along with other roots, as if she'd bewitched us.
Mestwina ground amber into fish soups for us. (And Ilsebill,
too, I'm sure, adds, mixes, stirs this into that.) I've always
lived among witches. Don't go thinking there weren't any; it's
just that the wrong ones were burned. None of those shorn
herb-women, virgins, and matrons on the quickly burning
woodpiles were real witches, even if they confessed under torture to such abstruse rubbish as broomstick riding and misuse
of church candles.

Naturally there were no witches' sabbaths, no goat-legged
cavaliers, no Devil's spot or evil eyes, but let's not doubt the
existence of witches' kitchens and witches' brews. Why, didn't
I see Dorothea fry slimy toads' eggs in the fat of stillborn
baby boys, which she got from Corpus Christi Hospital, moist-
ening the mixture with holy water from Saint Catherine's.
Why, you could smell it all over the house when that pale
witch, alone in the kitchen, burned the hoofs of a kid to
ashes. Why, everybody knew that she stirred not only the
ashes of rotten coffin wood into her Lenten soups but horn
ash as well. It was rumored that she carried the dishwater
from the pesthouses, where, with her pious air, she came and
went as she pleased, straight to our kitchen. It was rumored
that she filled little bottles with lepers' scabs and the sweat of
women dying of childbed fever. And it was rumored that, before the Teutonic Knights went campaigning in Lithuania,
she boiled their mail shirts in virgins' piss. But only rumored.
She was never put to the question. Others were burned:

plain, dull-witted neighbor women who had always cooked dutifully for their husbands but had hairy birthmarks on their buttocks or breasts. (I am sure that Dorothea, whose body was without blemish, gave her Domincan confessor little hints, for poor women and patrician ladies came to her in shamefaced secrecy, asking for ointments against warts and moles. With maybe a magic spell or two thrown in.)

And Fat Gret, too, knew witching recipes but wasn't burned. Who doesn't remember how, when Mayor Eberhard Ferber lost his manhood on laying down his chain of office, she perked him up again with herring milt and the semen of runaway Franciscan monks; how she fuddled the memory of the aged abbot Jeschke—who had too much political information—by taking a spoonful of his excrement, kneading it into a dough with peppercorns, poppy seed, wild honey, and buckwheat flour, and baking it into spicecakes for Advent; and how she bewitched me, too. I don't know what with. For she mixed everything with everything. She never cooked for taste alone. She stirred raisins into goose blood, made beef hearts stuffed with prunes in beer sauce. When I turned up and became a long-term guest in her box bed, she often fed me carrots that she had anointed with her pussy. And what all else, without a shred of shame! Everyone knew she sent away to far-off places for more things than Indian spices. Everyone knew—though details remained in the dark—that witchcraft was practiced when she sat down at table with her nuns and that she offered up heathen sacrifices. She and her free-ranging Brigittines were said to have nibbled pastry figures (with an intimation of three breasts?) and sung from the Wittenberg hymnal, "The house that God hath never blest . . ."

But no wood was piled for her. Not Dorothea and not Margarete Rusch, but gentle Agnes was destined to burn. True, I prefer to believe that soon after the plague carried me away, Agnes, still in the bloom of her youth, died in childbirth, but the Flounder has testified that she didn't die until fifty years later, by then an old hag, and moreover that she went up in flames.

No, I'm not going to tell you how the wind suddenly died down, a cloud sprang a leak, rain fell, and a miracle almost came to pass. As we all know, the Women's Tribunal accepted the Flounder's version, according to which Agnes Kurbiella, long after the poet Opitz died of the plague, went running through the streets talking dementedly to Ursel, her likewise demented daughter, and quoting the dead poet's works in both Latin and German, until, early in the summer of 1689, she met another poet, Quirinus Kuhlmann, the so-called Cool Monarch.

Kuhlmann was also introduced to the Women's Tribunal in affidavits by Baroque specialists. The Flounder called him a precursor of Expressionism. But the prosecution had no use for his eccentric genius. Kuhlmann, it was pointed out, had unscrupulously fed Agnes Kurbiella's confusion with his speculations, day after day indoctrinating her with his hubris. He, too, had exploited her as a Muse. He had manifested dangerous phantasms and gone to his death, drawing the old woman with him.

The accusing feminists were only too pleased to hear how Agnes Kurbiella fell victim to male exaltation, how she followed Kuhlmann from Danzig via Riga across the vastnesses of Russia to Moscow, how she became his handmaiden and served as his medium at séances of the Boehmenist community, how on trial and under torture she still went on mumbling Opitzian rhymes and Kuhlmannian verbal cascades, how she was burned along with her mad Ursel while Kuhlmann and two other male heretics were burned at nearby stakes for blasphemy and political conspiracy against the tsar's rule. The statistics show that men, too, were acceptable to the flames. And yet, in the opinion of the Women's Tribunal, the Inquisition and its witch trials were typical instruments of male domination, calculated to crush women's persistent strivings for freedom. The prosecutor's exact words were "The so-called witch was a male fiction, at once a wish dream and a projection of fear."

Maybe so. Yet Agnes, who did not want freedom, was nevertheless sent to the flames as a witch, whereas Dorothea of Montau and Margarete Rusch, both of whom strove for freedom and took liberties, were not elevated on pyres. It was the slight poetic confusion of her brain that equipped Agnes for activity as a Muse; only persons hostile or indifferent to the Muses called Agnes crazy, possessed, bewitched, Belial-ridden. Even her little dill garden was under suspicion, and that as early as Möller's, as Opitz's day. They had to protect the poor child from Catholics and Lutherans alike, for when it came to burning witches, the zealots of both religions joined forces in less time than it takes to pile up faggots and logs.

And even Amanda Woyke, who knew recipes, and definitely Sophie Rotzoll, who was familiar with every variety of mushroom, would have met the Christian gentlemen's requirements for fuel. But by Amanda's day and Sophie's, the revolutionary housecleaners had thought up other victims—so-called counterrevolutionaries, who were guillotined in the name of reason.

The Flounder, who seemed to be hovering in mid-water above his bed of sand, said to his judges: "As a fish whose tasty relatives are stewed and fried, I know whereof I speak when the purifying power of fire is under discussion. Thank your stars, my dear ladies, that nowadays witchcraft is more likely to be subsidized than punished. Modern man longs for a telekinetic dimension. But what if you had lived in one of those time-phases, my dear ladies? I don't know! I don't know! When I let my eyes rest on you and look you over as you sit there on your dais, judging me—so much concentrated earnestness, so much power-generating intensity—I hear a spiritistic rustling. Now forceful, now soothing glances strike my pebbly skin. And yet, each face taken individually has a beauty of its own. Eleven defiant egos. Fleeting, twisted smiles. Twinkling connivance—at what? Eleven heads of hair—mown to stubble, Afro-crinkled, or witchily windblown and easily ignited. In short, I see you all burning. The esteemed presiding judge, the chorus of associate judges, you, too, my dear Ms. Paasch, I see you all penned into knackers' carts, forced into nettle shirts, while the medieval populace gape, monks mumble their Latin, and the children pick their noses. On expertly constructed pyres, I see you, too, beautiful Ms. Simoneit, and next to you Ms. Witzlaff in all the splendor of the flesh, first swathed in smoke, then clad in flames. Those whispered screams! That clustered ecstasy! Elevenfold desire stilled and freedom at last. Even Ms. von Carnow, my court-appointed defense counsel, so well meaning and yet so helpless, would like to go up in poetic flames, though she's as innocent as the dill in kitchenmaid Agnes Kurbiella's garden. I see you all burning, the whole lot of you. And the majority of the Revolutionary Advisory Council are fit for the fire, too. But not Ms. Huntscha—not my prosecutor, who shows too sisterly a resemblance to the Lenten cook Dorothea of Montau. She in her supernatural beauty and pallor was too mystically world-removed, too emaciated to require such physical purification as poor Agnes. . . ."

(When, after a brief shower of rain, she finally took fire, nothing political could be gleaned from her mumblings, only bland-diet poetry; whereupon Axel Ludström, the Swedish ambassador to the tsar's court, sent instruction to Stockholm to close the Kurbiella file.)

What about you, Ilsebill? Would you prefer birchwood to the beech logs customary in those days? I'd get you ready for the fire. I'd be the gentle Dominican father Hyazind, who came from Cracow with his special instruments in tool chests with silver fittings. I'd approach you, closer and closer, with the flexible iron rods. Carefully, forgetting no limb, I'd make your ball joints jump out of the sockets where they were imprisoned; they'd be beside themselves. So much skin, from the shoulders down, all along the blond back. Ah, the thoughts! Uttered at last. My embarrassing questions cloaked in kindness. Your naked confession. For it's to loosen your tongue that I've come from far away. This is something we want to hear. Softly murmured. Read from the lips curled in pain: Yes, I did. Yes, several times. No, not alone. With another Ilsebill. And later a third one joined us in the fog. We did. Yes, at night, but every day, too. At the new moon and on Saint John's day. With our menstrual blood. Made little marks on objects and name plates. On the abutments of bridges and industrial installations, in the field where they're planning to put up a nuclear plant, on freshly programmed computers and several typewriters. Yes, we made the mark on yours, too. Inside, under the "I" key . . .

When at last my Ilsebill burned, but to the very end refused to relinquish her beauty, I wept under my hood. I was sorry, Flounder, to have given her that freedom.

Immortal

Having in all directions,
pushed open the promised windows,
I was certain that once
dead I would see nothing.

But gazing over the flat,
neatly settled countryside
and across the street into open windows
with old men and women looking out of them,
and at the partly cloudy sky,
I saw starlings in the pears,
schoolchildren the bus had brought,
the savings-bank building,
and the church with its clock:
it was half past one.

An answer came to my complaint:
such afterlife was usual
and would soon stop.

Already my old neighbors are greeting me.
They claim to have really
seen me from all those windows.
And there, overloaded, comes Ilsebill,
back from her shopping.
Tomorrow is Sunday.

The fifth month

~~~~~~

What potato flour is good for (and against)

When, early in February, the Women's Tribunal took
up the case of the farm cook Amanda Woyke, the Flounder
immediately launched into a lecture (based as usual on affidavits) about the relations between famines, army movements, and epidemics, quoted relevant literature—the plague
in London, the plague in Venice—and pointed out that we
owe the *Decameron* and its form, the elaborate frame narrative, to the plague in Florence. For the first time, he accepted
the help of his court-appointed counsel, Ms. von Carnow,
who quoted, "It began, both in men and in women, with
lumps in the groin or armpits, varying in number, some at-
taining the size of a common apple, others that of an egg;
they came to be known as buboes." Then the Flounder went
on to speak instructively of leprosy, yellow fever, typhoid,
cholera, and the venereal diseases. Pictures were flashed on
the screen.

Ever since 1332, when the plague trickled into Europe
from India by way of Venice, it had been a frequent visitor
to my part of the country. In no time at all, it carried off
three of my daughters by Dorothea. The maid who left Danzig with me and little Gertrud died in Konitz of spotted pul-
monary plague, which is also called the Black Death because
the skin takes on a bluish color; whereas my little daughter's
skin remained as fair as ever, and she still had a long while

287

to live. But one of her daughters, Birgit, was laid low by the pestilence that traversed the length and breadth of the country with the Hussites—like them a scourge of God.

And when, in 1523, Abbess Margarete Rusch rescued me from Trinity Church (next door to the Franciscan monastery) during the Vespers service, she transferred me just in the nick of time from my little group of officiating monks to the safety of her box bed; for in the following year all the other brothers and the abbot as well were carried off by the bubonic plague.

And when, in the year 1602 after the incarnation of our Lord, the straw death pallets of 16,919 sons and daughters of man were burned in the streets of the rich city of Danzig, the plague took many of the models that I, the town painter, needed for my mural of the Last Judgment, which was to adorn the Artushof of the niggardly patricians and merchants and, both as an admonition and as an offering, serve to ward off the constantly recurring pestilence.

The picture was quite successful, and yet I lost more models twenty years later when the plague returned, stayed a few months, went away, and came back as if it had forgotten something, carrying off nine thousand people the first year and seven thousand the second. Though the Dominican market and the Corpus Christi procession were prohibited, though the beer and brandy cellars were closed, corpses were carted from houses in every street and buried in big holes behind the Hagelsberg.

Later the plague came hesitantly, as though just passing through, but still later it occupied the city and took my drinking companions and buxom lasses. Only young Agnes was left to serve as my kitchenmaid. She watched me growing older with my drinker's liver until that Opitz fellow came along, and then she cooked for him, too, and got attached to him in other ways as well. In 1639, when the plague caught up with the poet, who was sickly to begin with, I died with him; Agnes left me without so much as looking behind her, as though I, the allegorical painter Möller, had gone to the plague pit with that long-winded, vale-of-tears Opitz. Actually it was senile decay. I still liked my drink, but I'd long been as good as dead. It didn't take any plague to carry me off.

They were all immune. Neither Dorothea, nor Fat Gret, nor Agnes, not a single one of the cooks was stricken by God or his diabolical partner with buboes, black spots, or any of the more recent epidemics. And when, after the second partition of Poland, Amanda Woyke helped to popularize the Prussian potato, she truly believed (and wrote as much to her pen pal, the widely traveled Count Rumford) that in potato flour she had found a safeguard against cholera; for after the Seven Years' War, when several crop failures made starvation universal among the lower classes, and rats, cooked up into emergency soups, sold for a good price, cholera (along with other plagues) ran rampant.

On the Royal Prussian State Farm at Zuckau, not only the hired hands, maids, journeymen, cottagers, and old folks, but the administration as well, took the precaution of rubbing their whole bodies with potato flour in accordance with Amanda's instructions. As long as the epidemic lasted, the death wagons made the rounds of Danzig and Dirschau twice a day. There were cases in Karthaus, too. Here in Zuckau the death knell was no busier than usual. We rubbed ourselves with flour and believed in it. Let the city gentlemen smile. Count Rumford, in his ever-so-rational letters, also doubted the medicinal and preventive properties of distillate of potato juice.

Later on, Amanda rubbed in potato flour for everything conceivable, applied it as a poultice, ladled into sacks that she hung up in the cupboards, and strewed it over thresholds. If the cows didn't want to calve, funneled-in potato flour made them. Daubed on fences, it frightened ghosts away. And when, in accordance with Amanda's prescription, I put a little sack of potato flour under the pillow of my Ilsebill, whose pregnant cantankerousness is dragging into the fifth month, and mixed a level teaspoonful into her powder box, she treated me most amiably for a whole week, had next to no wishes, was astonishingly free from migraine, and even sang silly songs while loading the dishwasher: "Lott is dead, Lott is dead, and Yul is gonna die soon...."

Told while pounding acorns, plucking geese,
peeling potatoes

A good deal has been written about storytelling. People
want to hear the truth. But when truth is told, they say,
"Anyway, it's all made up." Or, with a laugh, "What that
man won't think up next!"

And after a long story about the effectiveness of old wives'
remedies in cases of toothache, lovesickness, constipation,
gout, and Asiatic cholera, which I had told while the potato
soup was being spooned up to the point of couldn't-eat-
another-bite (and even Ilsebill enjoyed it a little), one of the
guests said, "Such things can't be invented. A character like
that—your farm cook, I mean—wouldn't come to you out
of the clear blue. Was there really such a person? Really and
truly, I mean? Or is it just something that might have happened?" And Ilsebill said, "Tell that to the Marines. Not
to me."

But retold, Amanda's potato peelings are the winding road
to do-you-still-remember, late memories of my umbilical
cord, which, uncoiled, leads to her as she sits at her kitchen
table. Her potato knife knew how the story would go on. I
could see by her peelings, and still can, what curling, thinly
peeled tale would slide over her thumb: a tale about the hunger of the peasants in the sandy Tuchel Stolp Dirschau
region, when earthworms became food and babies crawled
back into the earth like worms. Of the seven daughters I had
begotten upon her during the war (between campaigns),
three died and became abysmally sad stories named Stine
Trude Lovise, and all ended up with the sweet Lord in
heaven.

For making soup she preferred sprouting winter potatoes.
The peelings kept falling, always meaningfully and always in
a different way. And when I decided to leave, to clear out of
that dump and go to Saxony or still farther, Amanda, who
had wanted to go with me, turned around with her pack basket by the potato-top fires and said, "I'd better stay with the

spuds." That way, whenever I came back, each time downer at heel, she could tell me over her potato knife about all the things that had gone to pot in the meantime.

She herself had had few adventures (and those without traveling). Amanda Woyke, born a serf in 1734 at Zuckau-the-Cloisters when it was still Polish, died in Preussisch-Zuckau, a serf of the state farm, in 1806. But adventures came to her: I with my seven war years, nine scars, and twenty-three battles; the crazy Count Rumford, who couldn't stick it anywhere for long and always had to invent something useful. Bent with gout, the aged king came to Zuckau and (like me, his old campaigner and inspector) listened to her while she peeled potatoes. For Amanda knew that stories can never end, that there will always be a thief running across the fields with the stolen church silver, that tales about the last plague of mice will be told during the next one, that the Premonstratensian nun who died years ago will search the flour bin for her string-mended spectacles forever and ever, that the Swedes or Cossacks will come around time and again with their goatees and mustaches, that calves will always talk on Saint John's Day, and that stories will demand to be told as long as there are plenty of potatoes in the basket.

Mestwina had no potatoes. She told stories while making flour by pounding acorns (previously soaked in lime water) in a stone mortar with a wooden pestle. We stretched our bread dough by mixing in pea and acorn flour.

Margarete Rusch the cooking nun told stories while plucking geese under the beech tree, under the lime tree, in the convent yard, or in the barn. She would pluck nine or eleven geese in one afternoon for a guild banquet.

While pounding, while plucking. Mestwina knew tales about Awa: how Awa brought fire from the sky, how Awa invented the eel trap, how Awa was eaten by her starving children and so became a goddess. Mother Rusch told funny stories: how a merchant's son who lusted for her flesh was fobbed off with a sow that had been slaughtered the day before; what she stuffed the sheep's head in the pig's head with; or how she had helped Preacher Hegge over the city wall when he was obliged to run away from the Catholics. And other stories that did not feed on myth like Mestwina's, but drew their substance from the earth.

During the winter Mestwina pounded acorns into flour, which she mixed with barley groats and baked into flat-bread. Abbess Rusch plucked geese from Saint Martin's Day to Epiphany. In the spring and summer no stories were told. But after the farm cook Amanda Woyke had succeeded in making potato growing a Prussian virtue, she peeled potatoes all year long. Even in the spring and fall, when potatoes were served unpeeled with whey, she peeled old potatoes for her all-year-round, inexhaustible, at all times warm potato soup; how else could she have filled the farm hands' bellies?

Actually I had no intention of telling stories (to my guests and Ilsebill); I'd been meaning to cite figures and at long last drain the swamps of Kashubian legend with statistics—how many peasants were made serfs after the Thirty Years' War; how much corvee labor was performed in West Prussia before and after the partitions of Poland; at how early an age the children of serfs were put to work; how the mismanaged lands of the Zuckau Convent became profitable under the Prussians; by what devices the East Elbian landowners (and the managers of the state farms as well) flouted the decrees and made a sport of seizing the peasants' lands; how the Prussian landed gentry treated their serfs as chattels, won or lost them at cards, and swapped them at will; why in Holland and Flanders crops were already being rotated and fallow fields sown with clover and rape, while in our region the strict enforcement of the three-field system admitted of no innovation; why rural life was praised in treatises on agronomy and bucolic idylls, though the peasants and their cattle were both reduced to starvation when the millet ran out in March; at what date people began to smoke English tobacco, drink coffee from the colonies, and eat off plates with knives and forks in the cities of Danzig, Thorn, Elbing, and Dirschau, while in the country time stood still on one leg. But for all the figures I line up—showing yield per acre, amounts of salt tax and other taxes levied, the horrific infant mortality rates, the disastrous exodus from the rural districts, the corresponding increase in uncultivated acreage, and the ravages first of the plague, then of typhoid and cholera—conscientiously as I comb the eighteenth century for facts and figures, they still don't add up to a convincing picture of the times. I am obliged to sit as though spellbound beside Amanda's basket and watch her potato knife as I did then. "In the old days," she said, "there was nothing but grits, and when there warn't no grits, we had nothing at all. Then Ole Fritz sent us this dragoon with potatoes, and we started growing spuds. . . ."

"I want to know all about it," says Ilsebill. "How much farm produce requisitioned? How much corvee labor? How was the Prussian Chamber of Crown Lands organized?"

But stories live longer than figures. Passed from mouth to mouth. Mestwina's great-granddaughter Hedwig, while weaving baskets, still told of the forced baptism in the river Radaune, just as her great-granddaughter Martha, while baking bricks for Oliva Monastery, told of Saint Adalbert's death, so that after her great-grandchild Damroka had married swordmaker Kunrad Slichting and moved to the city, she was able, over her spinning, to tell her grandchildren how Adalbert had been struck dead, the Pomorshians baptized, the fishermen of the Wicker Bastion compelled to bake bricks for the Cistercian monks, how the wars went on and on and the Prussian raids never stopped, one damn thing after another, but there were miracles, too, that fiery apparition in the marshes, the Mother of God telling stories as she picked cranberries, for which reason, as the Lenten cook Dorothea later told her children while picking over peas, the Parish Church of Saint Mary was built on that very spot.

And the story of the Flounder was handed down in the same way. A true story told differently each time. First the fisherman wanted to have him cooked and eat him, but the fisherman's wife, Ilsebill, said, "Let him talk." Then Ilsebill wanted to put him in the pot, but the fisherman wanted to ask him a few more questions. Another time, the Flounder wanted to be stewed—"liberated," as he put it—but the fisherman and his wife kept having more wishes.

And once when Mestwina, while pounding acorns, told the story of the Flounder, she came close to the truth. "That," she said in Pomorshian, "was when Awa lived here and only her word counted. The Sky Wolf was angry, because Awa had stolen the fire from him and made herself powerful. The men were all devoted to her. They all wanted to sacrifice to the Elk Cow, and not one of them to the Wolf. So the old Sky Wolf turned himself into a fish. He looked like a common flounder, but he could talk. One day when a young fisherman threw out his line, the Wolf in the Flounder bit. Lying in the sand, he made himself known as the old wolf god. The fisherman was afraid, so he promised to do whatever the Flounder commanded. Thereupon the Wolf said from inside the Flounder, 'Your Awa stole my fire, and the wolves have had to eat their meat raw ever since. Because Awa has won power over all men with fire, you must give a masculine nature to the fire that people use to cook and warm themselves and bake clay pots. The hard must be melted and grow hard again when it cools.' The fisherman relayed all this to the other men, and they began to break rocks of a special kind. When they heated the lumps of ore in the fire, the iron in them melted and made the men into mighty smiths. Because the Wolf in the Flounder so commanded, they pierced their Awa with their spearheads. And I, too," said Mestwina whenever she pounded acorns to flour in her mortar, "will be killed by a sword forged in fire."

It seems, however, that when the Flounder of Mestwina's story heard of Awa's death, he turned himself back into a ferocious Wolf and brought war into the land with forged iron. For which reason Amanda Woyke always concluded her stories about Swedes Pandours Cossacks or Polacks with the words "They were like wolves. They wouldn't leave anything in one piece. They even ripped up the children."

(But the text of the story that the Flounder communicated to the painter Runge, the poets Arnim and Brentano, and the Grimm brothers had already been established and made ready for the printer, whereas the unpublished storyteller always has the next, entirely different, very latest version in mind.)

While pounding acorns into flour or letting potato peelings grow over their thumbs, Mestwina and Amanda told tales of the old days, but always as if they had been there: how men pierced the body of Awa, the primal mother, with iron spears, how Swedes raided Kashubia from the base in Putzig and were so intent on searching for silver gulden that they even cut open the bellies of expectant mothers.

Only Margarete Rusch never told of remote times, but always of herself and her life as a nun. How, on April 17, 1526, His Polish Majesty decreed an end to all heresy, occupied the city, closed all the gates, threw all the rebels (including her father, blacksmith Peter Rusch) into the Stockturm, ordered a trial, and had the "Statuta Sigismundi" posted on doors of all seven parish churches. How Preacher Hegge, in a lamentable state, sought refuge with the Brigittines, and the nuns had their pleasure of him by turns until Fat Gret took pity, dressed him most laughably in a woman's skirts, dragged him out of the convent in the dead of night under an eighth of a moon, through the sludge and ditchwater and squeaking rats of Paradise Street to the cesspit behind Jacob's Hospital, where the pallets of the dead smoldered day and night, and tried to lift him over the city wall, which is low at that point. But heave and push as she might, Hegge couldn't summon up that last saving burst of vigor. Maybe the sisters at Saint Bridget's had been too hard on him. He hung down the wall like a sack. The Royal Polish watch were making their rounds; already they could be heard approaching from nearby Peppertown, jangling their iron weapons and singing hymns to Our Lady in their drunkenness. Thereupon Fat Gret reached under the skirts of the once so hurried preacher and mangy goat, lifted him up by the thighs, higher, still higher, until his balls were dancing right under her nose—for he had nothing on under his skirts—and cried out, "C'mon, pull, you mangy goat, pull!" He managed to grab the top of the wall, appealed to every devil from Ashmodai to Zadek, and gave vent to two farts and any number of sighs, but not even the approach of the bawling litany of the royal watch sufficed to drive him over. Already the sliver of moon was throwing glints of light on reeling helmets. And then Fat Gret, after calling him a shit and a flabbycock, concentrated her rage and concern, snapped at the preacher's scrotum, and bit off his left ball.

It's true, Ilsebill. Men are terrified of being bitten that way. There are theories to the effect that all women have a secret wish to bite off the balls of all men—their cocks, too. "Snapping Cunt" and "Penis Envy" are chapter headings in avidly devoured books. The *vagina dentalis* is a well-known symbol. There are more men running around with one ball than show up in the statistics: emasculated heroes, pipsqueaks, hypersensitive eunuchs, village idiots, and obese tomcats. The female of the praying mantis, who slowly devours her mate right after the sexual act, might well be the heraldic animal of all Ilsebills. How cuttingly they smile, how they show their teeth, eager to nibble something more than carrots. "Fear for your lives, men!" cried the Flounder before the Women's Tribunal. "You're all at their mercy. Since prehistoric times they've been lusting for vengeance. Verily I say unto you: when I questioned the black widow, a rare specimen among the exotic spiders, about her husband, she, dangling from a long thread, spoke of his vices, which, so she said, had consumed him, consumed him entirely. . . ."

Abbess Margarete Rusch, however, was free from atavistic lust for vengeance or any secret desire to castrate, even though she tried to encourage but perhaps only frightened poor Hegge and other runaway monks with cries such as, "I just feel like biting something off you!" It was only necessity and desperate concern, because the danger was coming closer and closer, that made her bite down and off, whereupon Preacher Hegge was over the wall before you could say Jack Robinson, screaming for all he was worth as he ran through the New City woods. (He ran as far as Greifswald, where he preached again and attracted a new following.)

Sometimes, when Margret told this story while plucking geese, the feathers flew so merrily that she offered a supplement. A moment later, it seems, the Royal Polish watch broke off their litany and addressed her roughly, demanding an explanation for the screams on the other side of the wall. The drunken louts would have killed her if she hadn't answered. So what could she do but swallow the preachers' left testicle?

The many geese, incidentally, that Fat Gret had to pluck from Saint Martin's Day to Epiphany were for the guild banquets of the coopers and anchor makers, for the patricians of Saint George's Bank, or for dinners given at the Artushof by the town council in honor of Hanseatic delegations or of the visiting bishops of Gnesen, Frauenburg, or Leslau. And while they lived, she also plucked geese for Ferber's son Konstantin and for Jeschke at the Three Pigs' Heads manor and at Oliva Monastery, and always had stories to tell while doing so. How she filched fifty-three sacks of powder from a Brandenburg gunner, leaving fifty-three sacks of poppy seed in their place—and this the day before the storming of the city. How for the sake of better seasoning she arranged for a musketeer to shoot grainy black pepper, which her daughter had sent from India, into some marinated haunches of venison. How on a bet with the Dominicans she rolled down the Hagelsberg (laughing) in a barrel. And time and again, how with a bold

296

snap of the jaws she helped Preacher Hegge over the city wall.

Amanda Woyke, on the other hand, who never spoke of herself as an outstanding woman casting shadows in all directions, but only spoke of others and their hardships, knew stories that drew threads from earliest times but were nonetheless found as big as walnuts in the potato fields of the Royal Prussian State Farm in Zuckau. For when those fields were plowed (still with wooden plows to which, for lack of oxen, Polish day laborers were harnessed), the plows uncovered pieces of amber so cloudlessly pellucid as to suggest that in the beginning, long before Awa, the Baltic Sea had devoured the Kashubian forests, leaving only these tears of resin, which in time had become amber.

Actually a much later date could have been assigned to these astonishing finds. As the potato peelings piled up imperturbably, Amanda told how, and exactly when, amber had suddenly found its way to the hills of Kashubia. On April 12 of the year 997 after the incarnation of our Lord, a Bohemian executioner avenged the murder of Adalbert, bishop of Prague, by beheading the Pomorshian fisherwoman Mestwina. His sword stroke not only separated her head from her trunk, but also cut the thin waxed string around Mestwina's neck, whereupon all the threaded pieces of amber fell off and flew inland from the scene of execution, where the Radaune empties into the Mottlau; for when Mestwina asked leave (since the day was drawing to a close) to kneel facing westward, her request aroused no suspicion on the part of the executioner or of the other Christian converters.

Amanda related all this not in the Kashubian tongue, which I did not understand, but in the broad Low German of the coast. It seems that even as the pieces of amber were flying over the hills of the Baltic Ridge, the holes in them had closed of their own accord, out of grief for Mestwina.

Every time Amanda Woyke set forth for historical explanation for the amber found in the potato fields of Zuckau, one of her daughters had to go and get the bright-colored cardboard box which I had brought her filled with Saxon candy after the capitulation at Pirna, and in which the pieces of amber with their insect enclosures now lay bedded on cotton.

One spring day, much later, when Amanda had grown so

deaf that she could no longer hear the potatoes bubbling in the big cook pot, when potato bugs invaded us for the first time, bringing crop failure and a new famine, the cardboard box was empty. While Amanda was telling about earlier famines in comparison with the present one, she threw out little hints which gave us to understand that she had taken the pieces of amber back to the potato fields and dug them in. And true enough, the plague of potato bugs let up for a while.

A good deal has been written about story telling and narrative style. There are scholars who measure the length of sentences, pin down leitmotifs like butterflies, cultivate word fields, excavate language formations as if they were strata of the earth's crust, and take psychological soundings of subordinate clauses. They are suspicious of all fiction and at pains to expose all tales of the past as escapism, flight from reality. But speaking of my Mestwina's evocations, of Fat Gret's undammed flow of speech, and of Amanda Woyke's mumblings, I must insist that in every case (for all their reprehensible attachment to the past), the style was determined by work being done in the present.

For example, the act of pounding acorns in a stone mortar imposed its rhythm on Mestwina's delivery and so made her couch her mythical evocations of Awa in succinct telegraphic sentences. Breathlessly she reported the uprising of the men against the matriarchy: "Spears tipped with iron. Sharp sharp sharp. Light on metal—gives them a kick. The din of their forges. Dance to the jangling of their weapons. Cut holes in air, clouds, prospective enemy. Stand planted on hills. Looking for a target. Awa presents herself: All strike at once. Straight to the heart. Cut her open, disembowel her, divide her up, eat her raw, catch her blood in cup-deep wolf skulls, drink it down! Prove manhood by murdering mother!"

With Margarete Rusch it was very different. Her plucking of geese gave her an airy, feather-light style. "Hmm, I thought, so the fellow thinks he can stick his money-grubbing fingers in my pussy without forking over his twelve Scania talers, his stinking herring silver. He takes me for a sow in a pig sty, and that's just what he'll get, I says to myself, the one that was slaughtered yesterday. So I fill her up with hot bricks, dress her in my nightgown. And there she was all ready for him when he hopped into bed with his cock at the ready!"

And on the lips of the goose-plucking Gret, the horror of the young merchant Moritz Ferber when he discovered that he had poured his seed not into the nun's flesh but into a warmed-up sow, became a narrative blowing of feathers. "So he screamed and yelled and broke out in pimples between the legs and jumped out of bed like a bee had stung him. And that wasn't the end of it. He could never quite get his patrician pecker up after that. It just hung its head. So after a while he went on a pilgrimage to Rome, renounced the flesh, and was rewarded for his piety with the fat benefices of Erland bishopric—the sow's bridegroom!"

And potato peeling, that work process interrupted only by the digging out of eyes, also fosters a style, an even flow—interrupted by compassionate exclamations like "It would break your heart!"—of country tales, stories in which plagues of mice, drought, and hailstorms reduce the peasantry to chewing tree bark, in which pillaging Swedes are always followed by the plague and marauding Poles by cholera, and which always end (provisionally, for Amanda's stories go on and on like potato peeling) with the ultimate triumph over the lifelong hunger of the peasant serfs: "When King Ole Fritz's dragoons brought us a few sacks of potatoes, nobody knew what to do. And I said to myself: Into the ground with them. And when they came up and flowered, but yielded nothing better than bitter little apples, I said to myself: Oh my, oh my, now what? But when the bad weather came in October and the boars came out of the woods in Ramkau and rooted around in the plants, I said to myself and Erna and Stine and Annchen and Lisbeth: Now go look at the spuds. And there were plenty. And they lasted through the winter. And they tasted good, too. And the sweet Lord be praised."

Later on, when Amanda Woyke entered into correspondence with Count Rumford, inventor of the slow-combustion stove and of the poor man's soup that bears his name, a change occurred—not in her style, for she still told all her stories while peeling potatoes, but in her tenses, for now she anticipated the future. She told of giant kitchens that would feed the whole world. From the reality of the farm kitchen she derived a utopian West Prussian potato soup that would be dispensed the world over. In her giant kitchen there would always be enough. Her pots would always have room for seconds. She would drive hunger from the world. She spoke with loving concern of well-fed "Moors and Mamelukes." Her giant kitchen would be just the thing even for Eskimos and the savages of Tierra del Fuego. and with the earnestness of the technician—here the influence of the inventive Rumford was discernible—she detailed the qualities of the future potato-peeling machine: "Won't be nothing to it. You'll empty a basket like this in no time flat."

But what will become of remember-the-time-when and one-fine-spring-day? Our guests, who had enjoyed Amanda's potato soup until the pot was empty, shared my opinion that work norms and conveyor belts do not admit of storytelling. Even if Mestwina were semiautomatically packaging wheat flour, even if Fat Gret were employed in a poultry-processing factory, vacuuming the last feathers off scalded, hormone-fed geese while the hooked conveyor belt carried them past, even if Amanda Woyke were alive today, deftly imprisoning (at union scale) uniformly peeled potatoes in tin cans, there wouldn't be time during packaging, vacuuming, canning, to tell the necessary stories in all their length and breadth, not even to relay the latest gossip (and anyway, to whom?).

"That's true!" said Ilsebill. "But we women will never again consent to pound acorns into flour. I prefer to buy my geese already plucked. And the few potatoes we eat are no trouble at all to peel; I can even smoke. You'd like to see us sitting at spinning wheels, wouldn't you? Nostalgic for the treadle sewing machine, aren't you? I guess you're tired; I guess you miss the old stove bench."

At that she fell into a resolute silence. And I wandered off into the next story.

Plaint and prayer of the farm cook Amanda Woyke

When all three of her babies—
their names were Stine Trude Lovise—
died on her because
the stalks had been rotted by rain, battered by hail,

gnawed by drought and mice,
so that nothing was left after threshing,
no millet grained, no gruel stuck to palates,
no porridge was sweetened nor flatbread soured.
Before two March dusks had fallen
they died all three. Also because the goat
had run afoul of a Cossack's knife,
the cow had been led away by foraging Prussians,
no chickens scratched the yard, of the pigeons
nothing remained but pigeon droppings,
and on top of it all the man with the twirly mustache,
who with his tool had made her—nothing to it—
those little babies Stine Trude Lovise
because Amanda spread her legs for him every time,
was gone again for the enlistment bounty
to Saxony, Bohemia, Hochkirch
because the king, the king had called.
So when the three rag dolls
named Stine, Trude, Lovise
went limp in her arms,
Amanda wouldn't believe it
and wouldn't let go.

And when the little girls,
pale, blue and gnarled with hunger,
cranky old women in arms—
just born, barely weaned, and Lovise would
have been wanting to walk soon—were laid in a box,
nailed shut, and shoveled over,
Amanda complained aloud,
sustained a tone that was something more than a whimper,
a trembling wail,
a long-threaded sound somewhere between *euhhh* and *euühh*,
yet admitting of sentences
(such things as people say in grief):
More than a body can bear;
The devil himself could weep;
Who'll speak of justice now;
How can the sweet Lord stand it;
I'll scream and yell forever;
There is no sweet Lord,
no matter what the Book says. . . .

Three whole bright-blustery days in March she screamed,
till, finely sifted, her plaint reduced itself to *eeeee*.
(And in other cottages
in Zuckau, Ramkau, Kokoschken,
the mourners screamed *eeeee*. . . .)

Nobody paid attention.
As if nothing were wrong, the elders burst into bud.
Buckwheat and oats filled out.
Plenty of plums to dry.
Gathering mushrooms was worthwhile.
And leading a cow on a rope, the twirly man came back
from winter quarters, this time as usual invalided.
Since Zorndorf he'd had two fingers less,
after Torgau he'd come home one-eyed, laughing.
Now after Hochkirch there was a scar on his crown
that made him dopier than ever.
But all the same, because she lay still,
he readied his tool
to make her—nothing to it—baby girls
who were named Lisbeth, Annchen, Martha, and Ernestine,
and lived.
So that the sweet Lord was good for a prayer again:
He must have had His reasons for so much suffering.
He had His cross to bear forever and ever.
He rewarded toil
and had so much love, heavenly flour bins full of it. . . .

There was lots of kingdom and power in it,
later a handy rhyme for potato flower—
and just a grain of hope
that Stine Trude Lovise were angels by now, and
getting plenty to eat.

Ole Fritz

Patata, *potato, tartuffel*, pomme de terre, *spud . . . Raleigh*
or Drake is supposed to have brought them to Europe.
But since they come from Peru, it must actually have been

Spanish contemporaries of the abbess Margarete Rusch. Shakespeare must have known them as objects of religious awe, for he makes Falstaff say, "Let the skie raine Potatoes!"—though here it needs to be pointed out that Shakespeare was thinking of the sweet potato, a delicacy that was already being sold for high prices when our common potato, like all exotic *Solanaceae* (tomato, eggplant, et cetera), was still under suspicion, put to the question by the Inquisition, condemned, burned at the stake, and even despised as cattle feed.

First to plant them were the starving Irish. Parmentier gave them to France, whereupon Queen Marie Antoinette decked herself out with potato blossoms. Count Rumford taught the Bavarians to grow them. And who helped us Prussians?

Today we eat mealy boiled potatoes, grated raw potatoes, parsley potatoes, or plain potatoes in their jackets with cottage cheese. We know steamed potatoes with onions or in mustard sauce, buttered potatoes, potatoes au gratin, mashed potatoes, potatoes boiled in milk, baked in aluminum foil, old potatoes, new potatoes. Or potatoes in green sauce; or mashed potatoes with poached eggs. Or Thuringia, Vogtland, or Henneberg potato dumplings in cream sauce, with bread crumbs. Or sprinkled with cheese in flameproof-glass pannikins, or, as the Nostiz brothers made them, dotted with crayfish butter and baked. Or (in wartime) potato marzipan, potato cake, potato pudding. Or potato schnapps. Or my Amanda's mutton with potatoes, when (on holidays) she browned flank of mutton in kidney fat, added quartered potatoes, filled the kettle with water, simmered until the broth was soaked up, and only then moistened with dark beer. Or her potato soup, which the domestics of the Royal Prussian State Farm at Zuckau spooned up evening after evening, as the sky poured forth its ink and the forest moved closer and closer.

That was after the second partition of Poland. The farm was expected to become different in every way, more orderly, more profitable, in short, Prussian. The mismanaged conventual estate (founded in 1217 by Mestwina's daughter Damroka) had been secularized and turned into a state farm. This was termed progress, and progress had to be inspected and supervised—by Him in person.

When He came to Zuckau, it was raining. It had been raining for days, so that the potatoes had to be got out of the ground. The royal farm hands chopped, dug, gathered the potatoes in baskets, carried the dripping baskets on their backs to the edge of the field—sad giant crows, among whom common crows sought their share, while the king's clay-encrusted, springless four-horse carriage, though ready for retirement and already a legend, was nevertheless approaching. This time it came on the highway from Karthaus, limped over potholes, turned off to the right, stumbled along the cart track leading to Zuckau, where the farm hands were stretching their limbs in the rain-soaked fields as the royal vehicle appeared between the birches, vanished in a sunken lane, reappeared looking bigger—an event!—and stopped in a chain of mud puddles. Behind the steaming horses the right-hand door of the carriage was opened from within, and, preceded by his hat, which everyone knew, feared, and saluted, the old king, Frederick II, Fredericus Rex, His Majesty, Ole Fritz, with his cane hung on his coat, as he would later be painted in oils, alit and plodded into the potato field; his aide-de-camp and I, August Romeike, veteran of his wars and therefore his inspector, plodded behind him.

As everywhere, he came to Zuckau unannounced. He kept his visits secret to avoid petitions, garlands, maids of honor, and the representatives of the provincial estates. He didn't care for fuss and bother. He had his legend to live up to. And so, though racked with gout, he plodded across the fields with his cane, enjoined the farm hands with short barking noises not to gape but to go on digging and piling, and did not stop until he reached the baskets full of spuds. His first words: observations about the sandy soil of Kashubia, which he compared to the soil of eastern Pomerania. Instructive stuff, gleaned from informative treatises on crop rotation and the benefits of clover that had been translated (for him) into French from the English and Dutch. The aide-de-camp took notes in the rain. I, the inspector, was obliged to reel off yields per acre. He wanted to hear precise figures that would demonstrate the increasing trade in seed potatoes. When I didn't know how many gulden-pfennigs more the Dutch varieties (among them the ancestors of the present-day *"bintje"*) cost at the Hanover market, he hit me with his cane. That, too, became an anecdote, though later on a different reason was given for the royal beating.

Then, glistening under the Kashubian rain, he asked for a

certain woman who had set the new Prussian provinces an example with her pioneer work in potato culture, whereby she had demonstrated not only the hunger-stilling power of the potato but its tastiness as well.

I led him to Amanda. She was sitting as usual on the stove bench in the farm kitchen, peeling potatoes for the daily soup. Not in the least surprised, she said, "So here's Ole Fritz after all."

By then she had invented home-fried potatoes. Potato pancakes were also Amanda's invention. And she seems to have made the first potato salad, into which she mixed cucumber, onions, finely chopped lovage, and sunflower oil—food for the gods. She imparted diversity to the daily potato, lending it more and more new tastes with caraway seed, dill, mustard seed, marjoram, and parsley. But fundamentally Amanda's potato soup with bacon rinds remained true to itself, for she kept peeling and adding day after day; the pot was never empty.

She should just go on peeling, was the king's order, and he made himself at home on the footstool beside the potato basket. He was dripping wet, and a puddle formed at his feet. Amanda's daughter Ernestine lit tallow candles, for it was already getting dark in the farm kitchen. Amanda wore her spectacles while peeling potatoes. First Ole Fritz examined the peelings for thickness and apparently found the waste minimal. Then, while his clothes dripped and Amanda's daughters, Lisbeth, Anna, Martha, and Ernestine, gaped, he tilted his old man's head and listened, for, setting her knife in motion, Amanda began to tell of former days, when there had been nothing but too little millet and buckwheat, and her stories were as long and circular as the potato peelings that curled over her knife blade.

First the old hunger stories. She lamented the death from starvation of her babies Stine Trude Lovise. After listing means of combating potato bugs (amber dug into the fields, et cetera) and claiming that rubbed-in potato flour helped to keep cholera away, she addressed the king directly: good that he'd finally come, too bad about the rain, but that was part of it, would he like a pair of dry socks? Then she came to the point. He'd done right, she said, in confiscating the run-down convent—she herself as a girl had been made to embroider chasubles with tulip patterns, and there'd only been four, five nuns left, no use to anybody, and they'd have died soon anyway—and turning it into a decent state farm; but what she couldn't understand was why Ole Fritz had let the inspector, the dope, take the last bit of land the peasants owned as well as the fields they had leased from the convent, all of which had lain fallow ever since and were overgrown with nettles. So naturally the peasants weren't going to work for nothing; they'd gone off to Elbing and Danzig and waited for the administration and this prize dope that called himself an inspector to get some sense into their heads. So then (but not before) they'd taken her advice—for she, Amanda, knew what was wrong—and divided up the land around the cottages and given it to the serfs at a low rental in return for a written promise to grow only potatoes on their lots, same as on the state farm, which they tilled for nothing. And indeed they'd grown nothing but spuds for the last four harvests, except for a bit of oats and barley for porridge. But unfortunately this lout, who had the gall to call himself an inspector—here she pointed her potato knife at me—had thought up a rotten scheme, and Ole Fritz had better hear about it, because they were doing it all in his name. The inspector and the rest of the so-called farm administration, especially the old colonel in his armchair who couldn't get warm even in August, had decided to join all the lots together again, because that way the land could be administered more efficiently. That's why the peasants had been expressly forbidden to grow anything on their own. That's why there were no more self-supporting peasants in Zuckau, but only bonded serfs. And to make matters worse, hereditary serfs. Surely that couldn't have been what Ole Fritz wanted. Yes, she cooked for the whole lot of them. Not just for the Polish day laborers and brickmakers. For the children, too, and the old folks and the old colonel in his armchair. Seventy-eight mouths. Which also had its advantages, because, as Ole Fritz must know, a big kitchen like that saved fuel; she could reckon up the exact amount of peat consumed and the exact saving in cordwood, if he wanted her to.

The king listened and signaled his aide-de-camp, by glancing at him in his own special way, to make a note of certain remarks relating to the savings at the farm kitchen and the possibilities of community kitchens in general. Amanda's method of making potato flour was recorded, and the aide also put his pen to work when Amanda made a laughingstock of me (and even more of the king) by referring to "the inspector's carcass" as a picture book in which all the battles the king had fought for his glory were inscribed in the form of scars. For in addition to the eye he had lost at Kolin, the inspector had contributed a finger or two on either hand to the treasury of Prussian history, with the result that, no longer able to pick his nose and meditate, he was getting stupider than ever, for which reason he tormented the poor and made dopey speeches. He could distill potato schnapps for his cronies, and that was about all he was good for.

Then Amanda spoke again of hailstorms and plagues of mice and told again how three out of seven of her children—all of whom Romeike had pumped into her quick-quick between glorious battles, when she was still a stupid girl—had died on her and the Lord had shown no mercy. Because in those days there'd been no spuds, just too little millet and not enough buckwheat.

Finally, when the basket was almost empty and the potato peelings formed a pile as jumbled as my cerebellum, when Amanda's daughter Lisbeth (begotten after the Battle of Burkersdorf) had cut the washed potatoes into the big, gently boiling kettle on the kitchen stove, when Annchen (begotten after the Battle of Leuthen), now pregnant by an itinerant schnapps dealer with the future Sophie Rotzoll, began to fry chopped onions glassy in beef fat, and Marthchen (begotten after Hochkirch) rubbed majoram off its stems into the soup, while Ernestine (begotten between the capitulation of Saxony at Pirna and the Battle of Kolin) scrubbed the long farm-hands' table, when finally and meanwhile the king's clothes had dried, for he was sitting close to the stove, Amanda called on Ole Fritz to fight no battle but potato battles from then on. She mapped out a country of the future, extending from the March of Brandenburg through Pomerania and Kashubia to Masuria, all planted with potatoes and promising from harvest to harvest to supply community kitchens after Amanda's heart: "There won't be any more hunger then. Everybody will be full, and the sweet Lord will love Ole Fritz." (If Amanda had known more than the know-it-alls of her day thought they knew, she would have talked to the king about carbohydrates, protein, vitamins A B C, and about the minerals sodium, potassium, calcium, phosphorus, and iron, all of which are contained in the potato.)

It is not true, as was later bruited about in anecdotes, that the old king wept when the farm cook told him he had fought enough bloody battles and he should finally conquer hunger. It is true, however, that after the last potato had been peeled, diced, and dropped into the big soup kettle, she commiserated with him over his loveless childhood: "and nobody to pet and mother the poor little tyke." With an all-understanding glance she appraised the drenched king, now drying in her kitchen. With genuine tenderness she called him "my little Ole Fritz" and "my little tyke," for Amanda was a good head taller than His Shrunken Majesty.

A king who kept taking snuff, as though in response to an order from within. With dripping, watery eyes he sat listening to her warmhearted words of cheer. We heard her whisper to him as to a child, "You'll feel better soon. Don't you worry. Come on, Ole Fritz, you'll get some nice hot soup. It's good. It'll cheer you up."

For a good Kashubian hour (which in terms of normal time is more than an hour and a half) she mothered him as the soup kettle bubbled. She even removed a few snuff spots from his coat with cold malt-coffee. Maybe he dozed off for a while as she was chopping parsley, toward the end. The old cottagers along the walls and in the adjoining feed kitchen whispered among themselves, aware that this was a historical hour. Each was holding his spoon. And with their tin spoons they knocked softly on the wood of the kitchen table. The soup basins were ready on the long farm-hands' table, seven dishes to a bowl, one bowl to every seven farm hands.

Then the king spooned up Amanda's potato soup with all of us—for at nightfall the hands had come in from the fields. A dish of his own was set before him. He sat beside Amanda, a prematurely aged man who trembled and splattered himself with soup. From time to time he transformed his reddened, dripping eyes into big blue king's eyes (recorded in later portraits). Since everybody slurped, his slurping attracted no attention.

I was sitting too far away to hear what the two of them were mumbling between spoonful and spoonful. Supposedly he complained to Amanda of the Prussian landed gentry, who weren't carrying out his edicts. At the very least, he is supposed to have said, serfdom should not be hereditary. They should stop grabbing the peasant's lands. How could

308

you keep an army in decent shape when the country people were treated like cattle? For Prussia had many enemies and needed to be always in arms, always on its guard.

In reality—as Amanda told us later while peeling potatoes, and also wrote to her pen pal, Rumford—Ole Fritz merely wanted the recipe for her potato soup, which was wholesome, he said, and soothed his gouty bones, though he wished it could have been peppered to his taste. That couldn't be done. The farm kitchen of the Royal Prussian State Farm at Zuckau was without pepper, either crushed or in grains. Amanda seasoned her food with mustard seed and caraway seed, and with herbs such as marjoram or parsley. (Of course sausage can be boiled with the soup or bits of fried bacon stirred in. Sometimes Amanda cooked carrots in the soup, or leeks and celery for seasoning. In the winter she put in dried mushrooms, or a few handfuls of greenies and morels.)

When the king rode away in his springless carriage, it was still raining. I, Inspector Romeike, was given no snuff-box. Amanda found no ducats in her apron. No hand was laid on the heads of daughters Lisbeth, Anna, Martha, and Ernestine. No chorale was sung by the still-drenched farm hands. No spontaneous edict did away with serfdom. No miracle of enlightenment occurred under absolute rule. Nevertheless, the date of the historic encounter was handed down by the aide-de-camp. On October 16, 1778, immediately after the king's departure from rain-drenched Zuckau, an edict was promulgated declaring Amanda Woyke's potato soup to be the king's mainstay, whereupon it became a universal stand-by far beyond the confines of West Prussia.

And because the case of Amanda Woyke was taken up at carnival time, the Women's Tribunal, instead of the usual Women's Mardi Gras, staged a special women's celebration in costumes of Amanda Woyke's day, and Associate Judge Therese Osslieb, who might well have directed a farm kitchen, cooked Amanda's potato soup in her pots, which were more accustomed to Czech seasonings. Everybody, including the whole Revolutionary Advisory Council and even the court-appointed defense counsel, was invited to the Osslieb tavern, rechristened "Ilsebill's Barn" for the occasion. Not we men, of course. It seemed that Helga Paasch dressed up as Ole Fritz. Ruth Simoneit came as August Romeike. Ms. Witzlaff wore a wreath of marjoram and parsley. Naturally

Therese Osslieb was done up in potato color as Amanda. And after the soup, the women seem to have danced the polka with one another.

Speaking of weather

All of a sudden nobody wants the right of way.
Where are we going, anyway, and what's the hurry?
It's only in the rear—but where is the rear?—
that they're still pushing.

Is it the right thing
to prevent those many people
in distant places who are starving
but otherwise attract little attention
from starving? The question
is often asked in conversations.
Nature—the Third Program will tell you as much—
will find a way out.

Be realistic.
There's so much to be done at home.
All these broken marriages.
Systems decreeing that two times two is four.
In a pinch something about the civil-service law.

At day's end we note with indignation
that the weather forecast was wrong, too.

How letters were quoted in court

I found them in the bright-colored cardboard box which, along with other loot, I had brought home filled with Saxon sweets after the capitulation of Pirna. Later the box contained pieces of amber from the sandy fields of Kashubia.

And later still, after the amber had been dug back into the fields to combat a plague of potato bugs, Amanda Woyke put Count Rumford's letters into the box and laid her spectacles on top of them. Then she died, while I was in Tuchel on a tour of inspection.

The first letter was written in Munich on October 4, 1784. The last is dated Paris, September 12, 1806. Up to the summer of 1792 all the letters are signed "Your sincere friend, Benjamin Thompson"; thereafter, having been made a count of the Holy Roman Empire, he signed "Sincerely, Count Rumford."

In all I found twenty-nine letters in Amanda's cardboard box. And since exactly twenty-nine letters signed by Amanda in purple ink were discovered among the papers of Rumford's daughter Sally after her death, we may assume that not one thought was lost, especially as the letters connect up perfectly, each relating to the last. In the revolutionary year 1789, when Rumford (still under the name of Benjamin Thompson) wrote from Munich, giving a detailed account of the newly laid-out English Gardens and of the light-hearted atmosphere at the opening ceremonies, Amanda inquired in her answer how big the gardens were, and whether the soil was rich or clayey, and the ensuing letter cites the figure of 612 acres of untilled land. "Good pasturage," Thompson wrote. "Here, apart from the public park, we shall breed bovines from Holstein, Flanders, and Switzerland on a model farm, thus improving the now wretched quality of Bavarian livestock and setting the whole world a veterinary example."

After my death as Romeike the correspondence was lost and has never come to light. No biography of Count Rumford mentions Amanda Woyke. And out of jealousy or stupidity, Sally Thompson also helped to suppress her father's exchange of ideas with a Kashubian cook, though Sally cites in her memoirs certain ideas her father imparted to Amanda, such as "registration forms to be filed with the police will help us to keep track of foreign visitors."

All this, Ilsebill, must now be revised, for the lost correspondence has been found. In Amsterdam, where everything comes to light. A secondhand-book dealer unearthed it. At the very start of the trial, the Flounder made inquiries. (He has his agents, you know.) As a result, quotations from letters played a crucial role throughout the deliberations on the case of Amanda Woyke. I was mentioned only marginally, although, on the Flounder's advice, I had perpetuated serfdom on all the state farms under my supervision by interpreting the king's edicts and the liberalized provincial law in my own ingenious way, abolished hereditary serfdom only in rare cases, and preferred to issue new regulations that restored it in its older form. In short, I had been a hard-hearted inspector, hated throughout Prussia. Even Amanda had died a serf.

The Flounder admitted in court that he had used me as an instrument of reaction. The East Elbian rural populations, he maintained, were not ripe for reforms; considering themselves members of a big family, the serfs felt sheltered, secure, and hence relatively happy. The Polish day laborers were a lot worse off, except in the harvest season, when if nothing else they had enough to eat in Zuckau and elsewhere. And the Tribunal could hardly deny that despite the lack of freedom characteristic of her times, the farm cook Amanda Woyke had been capable of grandiose ideas, which to be sure found their public expression in Munich, London, or Paris, that out of naïve affection she had made use of a certain Benjamin Thompson as their channel. He, the Flounder, so he declared, knew more than was on public record or thought fit for schoolbooks. Therefore, with the help of the recovered letters, he wished to erect a monument not only to a certain Thompson, but also and in equal measure to the farm cook Amanda Woyke.

"A female biography," said the Flounder, "that, I believe, the feminist movement should take as an example. Amanda Woyke not only gave taste to our potatoes; with her big farm kitchen she also provided a harbinger of the future, already burgeoning Chinese world food solution. ("And when they really get it working," I said maliciously to Ilsebill, "where will you be with your wishes?")

The said Benjamin Thompson was born in 1753 in the British colony of Massachusetts. His father died when he was still a child, and was replaced by a stepfather—or, as Thompson wrote to Amanda, "by my poor mother's tyrannical husband." While apprenticed to a merchant, Thompson became interested in methods of storing and shipping salt fish. (In addressing the court, the Flounder did not deny that he had advised the young man—"directly or indirectly; after all, I'm at home in all seven seas.")

Boston just then was aboil with anti-British sentiment. While tinkering with fireworks designed to celebrate a victory of the American colonists over the colonial administration— the Whigs had just defeated the so-called Stamp Act in the British Parliament—Thompson suffered an accident. From that time on he sided with the colonial power, became a spy for the British, and as such tested his latest invention, an invisible ink that showed up after a certain lapse of time.

After his burns had healed, he studied at Harvard College during his spare time and became a schoolmaster at Concord, New Hampshire, which had previously borne the name of Rumford. A rich widow soon took the young teacher as her husband, an event that seems to have had the effect of another premature explosion of fireworks, for he enlisted in the army, was appointed a major in the second New Hampshire regiment, wore a scarlet coat, and looked upon himself for a short time as the father of his daughter Sally. Then, despised by his countrymen, he fled, was arrested by the so-called Minutemen, tried by a Concord court, and released, though still under suspicion of having served the British as a secret agent and written the British governor coded letters in his invisible ink.

On the outbreak of the Revolutionary War, Thompson took the last ship out of besieged Boston. Before the Women's Tribunal, the Flounder justified this flight on the strength of youthful ambition. Thompson, so he claimed, had sought broader fields for his talents. In the Old World, strange to say. In London he was appointed secretary of the colony of Georgia. Regrettably, Thompson had been responsible for suggesting the use of Hessian mercenaries; he had also recruited them and organized their crossing. Still, his election to the Royal Society shows that he had engaged in scientific activity as well.

To which the prosecutor replied, amid general laughter: "Scientific activity! Let's call it by the right name. Mr. Thompson improved the construction of muskets by figuring out the best place to put the vent. From childhood on he had a thing about gunpowder. When he grew up, he still wanted to play at war. He set up a regiment in New York, though the war was already lost. And let me tell you about his one act of heroism: building a fort in the graveyard at Huntington. Do you know what he built it with? Tombstones. Even the oven was made of tombstones. Later on the incised names of the departed—Josiah Baxter, John Miller, Timothy Vanderbilt, Abraham Wells, and so on—would be read in raised mirror-writing on the freshly baked loaves, so bearing witness to Colonel Thompson's scientific enterprise. In recognition of this grandiose achievement, he was pensioned for life at half a lieutenant colonel's pay the moment he arrived back in England. When they wouldn't let him play war games in India, he crossed over to the continent in the hope of European wars. He had his riding horses with him. As ridiculous as ever in a scarlet uniform. Went to Vienna via Strassburg and Munich. Cut a figure wherever he went. But nothing came of the war against the Turks. After getting himself knighted in England, he entered the service of Maximilian, elector of Bavaria, and settled in Munich as Sir Benjamin.

"So much, defendant Flounder, for the early life of your magnificent protégé Mr. Thompson. A hidebound reactionary. A spy. An adventurer and a charlatan. A conceited fop. A morose philanthropist, morose because he'd been deprived of his war games; not untalented, quick to learn languages, for by the autumn of his first year in Bavaria he wrote the farm cook Amanda Woyke a stilted letter asking for advice: how, he asked, might the benefits of potato culture, as exemplified in Pomerania and West Prussia, be conferred upon the people of Bavaria?" The prosecutor quoted: "'I, no, the world knows of your agronomic achievements, thanks to which war-sick Prussia has recovered so admirably.'"

Believe me, Ilsebill, it wasn't the Flounder, it was I who gave Thompson Amanda's address. But since the Women's Tribunal recognized only my particular incarnations and not my obstinate survival, I was not allowed to appear as a witness. Too bad. I'd have told the girls a thing or two. They wouldn't have cut me down to manikin size. Why, it was me with my dragoons who brought seed potatoes to the state farms in West Prussia at the king's orders. Whereupon I (as a nine-times-wounded veteran) was appointed inspector. I invigorated Prussia with potatoes. I organized the transportation and marketing of the surpluses. I brought order into the Polish economy. My balance sheets were mentioned with praise at the Chamber of Crown Lands. I traveled widely; why, I went as far as Hanover. And at meetings with fellow veterans I discussed Thompson's experiments with gunpowder to measure recoil and muzzle velocity and determine the best place to put the vent in the common musket.

So I wrote to the Royal Society. (Or a soldier friend who knew English wrote.) And Thompson answered from Munich. Promising precise data on vents for Prussian muskets, he asked in return for information about potato culture in Kashubia after the partitions of Poland. So then, in addition to pointers on farm management, I was so foolishly kind as to send him Amanda's address. By return mail he told me how to improve our musket. Their high-and-mightinesses in Potsdam failed, however, to act on his advice—a bit of negligence that was to be dearly paid for at Jena and Auerstedt. But nobody would ever listen to me. They all ran to her. She knew. She remembered. She prophesied. She saw the future. She had visions.

Unfortunately, I lost all my baggage, including Thompson's letters, after a solid night's drinking in Leipzig, where I had gone for the Fair. Only his letters to Amanda and her answers were quoted before the Women's Tribunal. When asked to account for this correspondence, the Flounder explained that through intermediaries he had sent Sir Benjamin a detailed account of the king of Prussia's October 1778 visit to the state farm at Zuckau. That was how the British American in the service of Bavaria had learned of the memorable conversation between the Kashubian farm cook and Frederick II of Prussia. Indeed, Thompson speaks of the meeting in his first letter to Amanda: "It has come to our attention, honored friend of the useful potato, with what admiration His Majesty has spoken of your accomplishments. In the document before me, the Great Frederick writes, 'A Kassubian female cooks a potato potage, which should make peace delicious for our peoples.' But what amazes me, dear friend, is how quickly you have succeeded. How were you able in so short a time to move the countryfolk to grow potatoes? Here superstition and Catholic fears prevail. Our beneficial tuber is said to induce rickets and consumption, leprosy and cholera. Can you perchance advise me? By the elector's favor I am in command of a cavalry regiment consisting of young peasants impressed into military service. They are lying about on garrison duty, doing nothing, for since the curious War of the Austrian Succession, here known as the 'Potato War,' nothing has happened in Bavaria; only the curse of beggary has increased."

Addressing the Tribunal, the Flounder was able to prove that Amanda's advice, as adapted by Sir Benjamin Thompson, had provided the impetus for the introduction of potato culture in Bavaria. The land donation wrested from the Crown Lands Administration (and from me), the leasing of plots of fallow land to the landless serfs of the Zuckau farm on condition that they grow nothing but potatoes—presents I later took back—all these ideas were adopted by Thompson, who divided the wasteland that was later to become the English Gardens into military garden plots. Every private soldier and corporal, during his period of service, enjoyed the use of 365 square feet of potato field. The harvest belonged to him alone, and every discharged peasant returned home with sacks full of seed potatoes, to the amazement of his fellow villagers. (When I took the serfs' plots away from them so we could plant on a large scale, Amanda said, "The sweet Lord won't like it.") She also communicated her panacea for plague, cholera, and leprosy—rubbing the whole body with potato flour—to her pen pal, who must have smiled.

Late in the summer of 1788, Thompson was appointed Bavarian minister of war and police, made a member of the Privy Council, and promoted to the rank of major general. After listing these titles, the Flounder declared to the Women's Tribunal: "That kind of thing probably doesn't mean much to the ladies. I can already hear you saying, 'A typical male career!' Maybe so. Thompson's ambition sometimes went to ridiculous lengths. And yet his correspondence with the farm cook Amanda Woyke made a great change in him, the kind of change that is ordinarily produced only by love letters. It is indeed my contention that Amanda, then a sturdy forty-five, and our American, some ten years her junior, were impelled by passionate reason to write each other love letters revolving around the problems of human nutrition. For once no soul music, no sob stuff, no pens dipped in heart's blood. Listen to what he wrote to Zuckau:

" 'To you alone, esteemed friend and benefactress, I owe the great, the crucial insight that no political order can be truly good unless it redounds to the common weal. I have undertaken to combine the interests of my regiment with those of the civilian population and to make our military might serve the public welfare even in time of peace, by seeing to it that every garrison in Bavaria maintains soldiers' gardens and therein, apart from the estimable potato, cultivates not only rutabega but also, by way of crop rotation, clover for cattle feed. I take the liberty of sending you, my friend and benefactress, a few seeds and young rutabaga plants by the same post. This highly nutritious root plant has, not without my help and advice, been bred from rape. Rest assured that only my diplomatic tact deters me from proclaiming to the Bavarian people what my heart knows full well, to wit, that they are indebted to an estimable Prussian woman not only for the potato, but for the potato dumpling as well. In conclusion: do you know of a rational way of eradicating the plague of beggary with which Munich is now afflicted? A mere police action would accomplish nothing.' "

Here I must interpolate the fact that thanks to Thompson's express package, rutabaga took hold in West Prussia and soon gained popularity under the name of *Wruke: Wruken* with *Gänseklein,* flank of mutton with *Wruken*, tripe stewed with *Wruken*. But also, in the rutabaga winter of 1917, *Wruken* cooked with nothing at all.

Of that the Flounder made no mention before the Tribunal. But Thompson's great achievement—suddenly arresting all the beggars in Munich, registering them, and moving them to a workhouse—was celebrated in quotations from letters which made it clear that the minister of war and police had derived his inspiration from Amanda. For this is what she wrote Thompson: "My dear Sir: If enny tramps or beggars turn up here in Zuckau, they haff to chop wud and unravvel nitted yarn in the junkroom if they want enny of my potato soup."

This little hint sufficed to start Thompson off in the right direction. He replied: "Ah, dearest friend. If you could see how ubiquitous the crime of beggary is here. Parents put little children's eyes out or maim their limbs so as to arouse pity by exhibiting them. The situation is generally thought to be hopeless. Thoughtful persons have come to regard beggary as an intrinsic feature of our social order. It is widely held that wicked persons must first be made virtuous before they can be made happy. But why, in response to your excellent advice, should I not attempt to reverse the order? Made happy by work, my sinners will become virtuous."

The rest is known. Thompson requisitioned a run-down Pauline monastery in the suburbs and transformed it into a military workhouse with shops for turners, smiths, dyers, saddlers, and so on, as well as dormitories, a refectory, and a community kitchen with a masonry cooking stove that Amanda later had copied (from Thompson's blueprints) for her farm kitchen: horseshoe shaped with numerous openings and fire grates. He then established welfare committees in Munich's sixteen districts, put up a sign in gold letters over the gateway of the workhouse saying, "No alms accepted here!," and finally, on January 1, 1790, arrested twenty-six hundred beggars in a sweeping roundup, had them registered on previously prepared blanks, and sent them to the workhouse the following day.

In a letter to Amanda, Thompson wrote, "We are making footstools, horse blankets, and uniforms for the whole Bavarian army. We wind yarn and spin wool. Fourteen hundred permanent inmates are industrious and happy. Even the little children help. It is to be hoped that my success will encourage others to follow my example."

What was discussed before the Women's Tribunal, however, was not the successful police action but the accused Flounder's contention that by advising Thompson to give the beggars and other paupers work, wages, and food, a farm cook, who was not only a Kashubian but a serf as well, had prevented the French Revolution from spreading to Bavaria.

Protected by his bulletproof glass, the Flounder said: "If such advice had been given to an able Frenchman, if the French mob had been provided with well-heated workhouses and ample community kitchens, if they had been guaranteed full soup kettles with smiling eyes of fat floating on top, there would have been no revolution, the guillotine would not have had to function many thousands of times, no Robespierre, no Napoleon would have become known to us; instead, enlightened princes would perforce have resolved to promote the public welfare. As it was, Amanda Woyke's advice benefited only the Bavarian people. While elsewhere the Furies raged, the beggars of Munich were made over into useful citizens."

You're right again, Ilsebill: carrot and stick. It would be easy to imagine Ms. Huntscha, the prosecutor, taking a strictly materialistic approach and demolishing the Flounder's speculations—"If the dog hadn't shat, he would have caught

318

the hare," and so on. But she adopted an entirely different tone. "Excellent reasoning," she said. Then she dissociated herself from "male revolutionary rites," expressed her horror of Robespierre and Napoleon, exposing the one as a hypocrite, the other as a little man who wanted to be big. After that, she wound up for a haymaker:

"But what, defendant Flounder, became of your enlightened princes' alleged achievements? A few years later Thompson's workhouse, with its rudiments of self-government, had become a common jail where the prisoners were bullied and beaten. And on the state farm at Zuckau serfdom was maintained until well into the nineteenth century. Nay, more: your great genius, your friend of the people Thompson, was chucked out by the Bavarian estates. And Amanda was obliged to look on as an ambitious inspector drove the serfs of the state farm from their individual potato plots. That's right, with whips. Her little talks with the sweet Lord didn't help one bit. And as for Thompson, who'd been made a Holy Roman count in the meantime, the best this Count Rumford could do, even in his late years in London and Paris, was to rush into more and more new ideas which, as the defendant has succeeded in proving, were kindled in a Kashubian farm kitchen and exploded in Rumford's brain.

"We concede that by their division of labor the Woyke-Thompson correspondence tandem were productive—we owe them the slow-combustion stove, the steamer, and the soup kitchen—but what part did the Flounder play in this often pioneering collaboration? He claims to have been the *Weltgeist*. He claims to have coupled the ambition of a delinquent upstart with the public spirit of a farm cook rooted in her native soil. He tried to play God for Amanda Woyke and to embody social progress in the interest of Count Rumford. A scheming matchmaker, that's what he was. It's beginning to look as if he'd sold the Tribunal a bill of goods, as though we feminists had fallen for his flimflam about equality, as though his belated monument to the farm cook had turned us into a lot of gaping fools, as though he, in his Floundery way, were contributing to our emancipation. But let's not be deceived by appearances. His version simply doesn't make sense. The intention is too obvious. Here's what the Flounder is really saying: in the hands of a man, the naïve invention that this dear little woman managed to arrive at over her homely cooking stove—West Prussian potato soup, for instance—becomes social and political achievement, namely, Rumford soup for the poor, which was spooned up for a whole century in Munich, London, Geneva, and Paris. In other words, the defendant wants us to praise, glorify, and perpetuate the inventive little woman's humility, the admirable inner freedom of a lifelong serf, subservience misrepresented as equality. There's Flounder morality for you! What a stinking, fishy trick! I move that we rule out all further quotations from letters!"

The motion was overruled. (The Flounder faction in the Revolutionary Advisory Council had already become a powerful enough minority to force majority decisions.) Then the Women's Tribunal adjourned, because the Flounder claimed to be, or really was, feeling faint; in any case he left his sand bed, showed how his steering mechanism had failed and cast him helplessly adrift, reeled, threatened to capsize and float belly up, and just under the surface of the water whispered over the intercom system: "What deplorable, what painful suggestions! So much injustice almost strikes me dumb. When what I really wanted—ah, me!—if I hadn't been so gallingly insulted was to elucidate Count Rumford's ideology by the example of the Chinese Tower in Munich's English Gardens. But—ah, me!—all I get is vilification, and I'm too weak to insist on my right of rebuttal and on further quotations from the letters. Ah, me! Ah, me! Has it ever occurred to this feminine and therefore stern court that I, too, the Flounder, the detested male principle, might be mortal?"

Don't worry, Ilsebill. Naturally the flatfish recovered. And the trial took its course. Further quotations from letters were admitted as evidence. The recipe for Rumford soup for the poor was read: "Dried peas, barley, and potatoes are boiled for two and a half hours until they form a mash; then soured beer is stirred in; then diced stale bread is fried crisp in beef fat and added; then the whole is seasoned with salt." Amanda's violent reaction to this mushy perversion of her potato soup was quoted: "I wouldn't feed such pap to the Devil himself."

After Rumford's embittered departure from Munich, his activities in London, his move to Paris and marriage had been discussed rather briefly, and the father's conflict with Sally, his daughter beyond the seas, had been allowed to flare up in quotations from letters, Rumford's political creed, his

320

belief in Chinese beneficence from above, complemented by Amanda's concern for her Kashubian farm hands, became the storm center of the court proceedings.

A single sentence of the Flounder's—or, rather, his rhetorical question "Is it not clear that with their utopian descriptions of cultural mass movements and of community kitchens feeding entire populations, Count Rumford and Amanda Woyke foreshadowed Maoism?"—unleashed a tumult and would have broken up the Tribunal if Ms. Schönherr, the presiding judge, had not found words of appeasement. "Defendant!" she shouted into the rising storm. "I assume that by your conjectures you have merely meant to say that the ideas of the great Mao Tse-tung have long lain dormant in the minds of the peoples, but have often, as in Rumford's case, been absurdly misunderstood and, as in Woyke's case, been too narrowly confined to the agrarian sector to move the masses to revolution, and that consequently they did not find relevant expression until the present period."

The Flounder hastened to corroborate the presiding judge's assumption. Quickly he cited pertinent passages from the letters. "Listen, if you please, to what Amanda has to say about it: 'And someday there won't be nothing but farm hands and farm hands' kitchens.' And listen to Rumford: 'Just as today the sons of peasants are impressed into military idleness, no later than tomorrow armies of peasants will be in a position to till and at the same time defend the fields.' They both had quite a gift of prophecy, though they could hardly foresee that this High Court would for the first time attach to their letters the importance that I, too, for all the skepticism of which I am capable, believe to be their due."

Who would have thought it possible. The Flounder Party in the Revolutionary Advisory Council gained new support. (You too, Ilsebill, are hesitating.) Those clever girls let the Flounder sell them an image of Rumford as a "restlessly questing spirit" and of my good-as-gold Amanda as a "sand-colored potato heroine." Even the prosecutor withheld her barbs as the discussion of the Amanda Woyke case neared its positively touching conclusion. There were stirrings of pity for Rumford, whose beastly wife, widow of the guillotined physicist Lavoisier, drove him half mad with her turbulent social life; yet even Amanda's purple-inked warnings—"a quarrelsome devil she is for sure, a living Ilsebill, a powder-puffy bitch"—had been powerless to talk him out of the rich match. Even Rumford's opportunism met with the prosecutor's understanding; his move from menaced England to Napoleonic France was justified as evidence of scientific neutrality, though Amanda expressed herself on the subject in no uncertain terms: "And speaking of Napolyon, I wouldn't keep no soup warm for that man."

After the controversial condemnation of the Flounder in the case of Agnes Kurbilla, the Women's Tribunal had resolved to make a show of objectivity. It was conceded that the accused had meant to serve the cause of the Enlightenment. The count and the farm cook, for example, were termed pioneers in the field of equal rights; the final summation even made mention of the "pre-Maoist component" in their thinking, and no objection was raised to the fable woven by the Flounder as a funeral wreath for Amanda. Immediately after the disastrous battles of Jena and Auerstedt, so his story went, Count Rumford, seized with foreboding, had left Paris and traveled to West Prussia via Munich. He had had the good fortune to reach the Kashubian hamlet of Zuckau before the arrival of Napoleon's marauding army (and the siege of Danzig). And before dying in his arms, the desperately weary Amanda had been able to tell one last time her dream of community kitchens that would conquer hunger the world over. The dying cook seems even to have forgiven the count for his repulsive, stomach-gluing Rumford soup. Not a blessed word about me, the one-man funeral procession who buried Amanda in the former convent graveyard after my hurried return from Tuchel. Only a touching holding of hands up to the reason-transfigured end.

The next day the *Tagesspiegel* commented on the atmosphere in the courtroom. The Women's Tribunal, according to that worthy organ, had shown indications of deep emotion. The gaze of the usually cold-eyed prosecutor had clouded over. The public, consisting for the most part of women itching to mount the barricades, had actually sobbed. More solemnly than triumphantly, a small group, later joined by the majority, had intoned "We Shall Overcome." But then the Flounder, though deeply embedded in sand, had sent up a last speech balloon: "After Amanda's death darkness descended on Europe."

That was in November. Three months later, on February 24, 1807, when the Prussians had been defeated at Dirschau and the flames of the pillaged city could be seen as far as Kashubia, French grenadiers belonging to the army of Marshal Lefebvre occupied the Zuckau state farm and gobbled up our seed potatoes.

Why potato soup tastes heavenly

When Amanda Woyke died, she took nothing with her but her spectacles. She looked all over heaven for the sweet Lord. He had hidden, for he was afraid of Amanda, who wanted to give him a piece of her mind about the lack of justice, and what kind of a sweet Lord was he anyway, and maybe he didn't even exist. In the halls of heaven she met lots of old friends from Zuckau, Viereck, Kokoschken, and Ramkau. None of them had the slightest idea where the sweet Lord was keeping himself, and they were all standing around looking pretty anemic, because all they had to live on was memory. It wasn't till she got to the heavenly flour bin, which, however, hadn't a bit of flour in it, that Amanda found her three girls Stine Trude Lovise, who had died of starvation on earth because King Ole Fritz had kept up his war for seven years, and Pandours, Cossacks, and Prussian grenadiers in turn had eaten the bit of buckwheat and oats grown in Kashubia straight off the stalk.

Stine Trude Lovise, who had turned to meal worms in the heavenly flour bin, cried out, "The bin is empty. Nothing here. Oh, bring us oatmeal, Mother dear!" So Amanda clapped the lid of the flour bin shut and, pushing it ahead of her with a terrible din, went looking for the sweet Lord in all the halls of heaven.

Oh her way she met King Ole Fritz. He was playing with brightly painted tin soldiers. He still had plenty of ammunition, for he had brought a little sack of black peppercorns with him from down below. With the fingers of his left hand he flipped the peppercorns off the palm of his right hand, hitting Pandours, Cossacks, and white-enameled Austrian foot soldiers until he had finally won the Battle of Kolin. Amanda was furious. "It's high time you made peace!" she cried and threw all the tin soldiers and the black peppercorns into the empty flour bin, where the three little meal worms Stine Trude Lovise now had company. Then she harnessed the king to the bin like a draft horse. And so with a terrible din, he pulling, she pushing, they continued on through the overpopulated but seemingly empty halls of heaven looking for the sweet Lord.

On the way they met Count Rumford, who in the meantime had died of a sudden fever in far-off Paris. He was glad to see Amanda and showed her his latest invention: a tiny, shiny, softly purring machine. Pointing to the fiery-red gate of hell, he said: "Just imagine, dear friend, I've finally succeeded, with this little machine, in storing up hell-fire, the primal heat, that shameful waste of fuel, compressing it into tablets, and making it available for beneficial use. Down with superstitions! Now at last we can carry out your pet project and set up a giant Kashubian farm kitchen here in the halls of heaven. Now, with the help of hell-fire, dreams will become reality. You and I know what the world needs: the maximum within the minimum. Let us, you and I together, get to work on world nutrition. Unfortunately we still lack the ingredients of your excellent soup, first and foremost our belly-filler: the potato."

Amanda thought they ought first to ask the sweet Lord's permission; maybe in return for a moderate amount of corvee labor he'd lease them a few heavenly acres. She'd be glad to dig potatoes. She put the hell-fire utilization machine and the first dozen heat tablets into the flour bin along with the three little meal worms Stine Trude Lovise, the brightly painted tin soldiers, and the black peppercorns, harnessed Count Rumford to the bin alongside of Ole Fritz, and, they pulling, she pushing, they moved on through the halls of heaven with a terrible din, looking for the sweet Lord.

On the way they met me, war veteran and Inspector of Crown Lands August Romeike, who in between the battles of the Seven Years' War had made Amanda seven children, three of whom had died of starvation and now as meal worms had company in the flour bin. When Napoleon's Grand Army, returning sorely battered from Russia, reached Kashubia, a gang of looting grenadiers from whom I was trying to save our seed potatoes shot me dead. All I could bring with me to this other world was one sack of spuds, on which

I was sitting when Amanda, with Ole Fritz and Rumford harnessed to her flour bin, caught sight of me and started right in chewing me out: "You stupid, scurvy no-good!" But she was pleased with the rescued seed potatoes and a few little bags of seeds, among them chervil, mustard, caraway, parsley, and marjoram, that I'd happened to have in my pocket. And Ole Fritz and Rumford also exclaimed, "Superb!" and "Splendid!" I had to heave the sack into the flour bin, taking care not to hurt the meal worms Stine Trude Lovise or the tin soldiers, and most especially not to damage the diminutive hell-fire utilization machine. Then between king and count, I was harnessed to the vehicle, and off we went with a terrible din. Now there was no need for Amanda to push.

And so we looked for the sweet Lord throughout the halls of heaven, until we came to a body of water that made little waves like the Baltic and smelled the same, too.

"Sweet Lord! Sweet Lord!" cried Amanda over the Baltic-green sea. "Where ya hiding. Come on out! Come on out!"

But the sweet Lord didn't show himself, for he didn't exist. Only a flatfish jumped out of the sea and gave them a slanting look. It was the Flounder out of the fairy tale, and he said with his crooked mouth, "Since the sweet Lord doesn't exist, I can't very well be your sweet Lord. But I'll be glad to help if something's wrong. What's wrong?"

And then, before the three men harnessed to the flour bin could speak, Amanda told the Flounder first her earthly, then her heavenly woes: how she had put up with everything and in spite of plague, famine, hunger, war, and long-lasting injustice always stood by the sweet Lord, how she'd been looking for him in heaven, but all she'd found was King Ole Fritz, his dopey inspector, and her old pen pal, the well-known inventor of the slow-combustion stove, and she'd harnessed them to an empty flour bin in which were assembled her meal worms Stine Trude Lovise, the king's tin soldiers and peppercorns, the dopey inspector's sack of potatoes, a few little bags of seeds such as marjoram, chervil, mustard, caraway, and parsley, and the pen pal's hell-fire utilization machine along with some heat tablets: "So what's to happen now? If you can't be our sweet Lord, then be our sweet Flounder, and help us."

Thus flattered, the Flounder said, "What you could not do

325

on earth, you shall do here in heaven. Your sweet Flounder will provide as if he were the sweet Lord."

Thereupon he vanished into the Baltic-green sea. Instantly the halls of heaven were transformed into proper Kashubian sandy acres—gently rolling, already fertilized and plowed, hedged around with gorse and blackberry bushes. Out of the flour bin jumped King Ole Fritz's tin soldiers, and they began to till the soil like peasants, planted the seed potatoes out of the dopey inspector's sack, and put in an herb garden off to one side. And Count Rumford set to work building for Amanda an enormous heavenly kitchen to feed the world's hungry. As fuel he used the compressed heat tablets, three of which were spat out each second by the hell-fire utilization machine.

In the meantime the meal worms Stine Trude Lovise were growing up to be dear little girls, as pretty as pictures and so clever besides that Ole Fritz didn't have to govern any more, or Count Rumford to invent, and the dopey inspector didn't have to bully anybody, for there in the heavenly Kashubia Amanda and her three laughing daughters took care of everything. Each day there was plenty of potato soup, for herbs and turnips were soon growing, pigs were grunting miraculously, and even onions were taking heavenly root. While peeling potatoes, Amanda told her old sweet-Lord stories, but now they'd become sweet-Flounder stories. And the children weren't the only ones who knew Amanda's sayings by heart. For instance: "Marjoram and parsily, good for the whole family"; or "Equal as the spuds we be—only the kingdom of heaven is free."

So day after day they all spooned up the same soup, and only King Ole Fritz's peppercorns lay around unused and dangerous, for they were as big as cannon balls, until one heavenly day Amanda rolled them down to hell, whereupon the fires burned even better than before.

But the Flounder, who told this fairy tale before the Women's Tribunal by way of exculpating himself, said in conclusion, "In short, dear ladies, I took the liberty, in heaven at least, of creating Kashubian Maoist conditions. I won't say yes and I won't say no, but if you choose to conjecture that I am Amanda Woyke's sweet Lord, go right ahead."

Starvation

Always the flour bin has spoken
words of consolation out of an empty stomach
and snow has fallen as if in corroboration.

If starvation were limited to Holy Week,
fasting would be a pleasure, eating
flatbread with nothing on it;
but starvation covers my region like a pall
all winter until March
while elsewhere the granaries are sly
and the markets glutted.

Much has been written in defense of hunger.
What beauty it confers.
How free from slag its concept.
What dullness comes of three square meals.
And always there have been Swiss
doing good in the eyes of God
(or someone else): only
the indispensable has been lacking.

But when at last there was enough,
And Amanda Woyke went out to the potato fields
with basket, hoe, and daughters, some gentlemen somewhere
    else
were sitting around a table, worrying about the falling price
    of millet.

Ultimately, said Professor Bürlimann,
everything's governed by demand,
and he smiled a liberal smile.

The Great Leap Forward
and the Chinese world food solution

Toward the end of February, after buttered potatoes in their jackets with cottage cheese and caraway seed, in the course of one of the few after-dinner walks Ilsebill has brought herself to take since she became pregnant—I had just come back from a congress at which the future of socialism was discussed point for point—on a clear, sunny day with a foretaste of spring (shortly after 2 P.M.), my Ilsebill leaped, despite my shouts of "Please, please, don't jump! Don't, don't!," across one of the many ditches known as *Wettern* that serve to drain the lush Wilster Marsh, the pasture land between the Elbe and the Geest. Despite her bulk she managed to clear the roughly five-foot ditch but landed on her face, though on soft ground, to be sure.

Later, the question of guilt came up: I had allegedly provoked her leap with my obsessive insistence on slow, gradual, deliberately procrastinating change.

As we crossed the marshy meadows, there had been talk of the socialist congress and its resolutions. (What might have been if the opposite hadn't happened.) When I said: "The Prague Spring probably came too suddenly and seems, in the days preceding the Soviet occupation, to have had a certain erratic character, a failure to take account of the overall development in the Eastern bloc or of the premature expectations of the West, with the result that one more long overdue, but nevertheless ill-timed attempt to reform state Communism came to grief because it took the form of a Great Leap Forward, the immediate consequence being the all-too-familiar limping lag . . ."—after, more to myself in mulling over the congress than with any intention of provoking Ilsebill, I had said these words, she replied: "Go on! You with your snail philosophy. How's there going to be any progress if we have to crawl all the time. Look at Mao and China. They weren't afraid to take a Great Leap Forward. They're ahead of us. They're over the hump."

Already my Ilsebill had her eye on that ditch. She took a run; a concept had hurried on ahead and she leaped after it. Despite my shouts of "Don't!" she, by then close to five months gone, leaped. In defiance of all reason she leaped and, turning her belly to one side, fell on the rain-softened ground. I jumped after her, no distance at all, and said, "Hurt yourself? Why can't you listen? What a childish thing to do. In your condition."

For the first time during a persistently contentious pregnancy we were worried about the baby. I palpated. I listened. But there was nothing wrong. She'd only turned her left ankle. In three shakes we were fighting again. ("You and your shitty snails!" "You and your shitty leaps!") Ilsebill had to lean on me, which she doesn't like to do. Step by step, I limped her home.

When we got there, I was still worried. I made vinegar compresses, listened again, palpated some more. The child in her womb—"My son!," as Ilsebill said—made knocking movements. "It could have been worse. What if a stone had been lying there. Or some other hard and pointed object. Besides, you're wrong when you attribute the achievements of the Chinese to Great Leaps. Look how they've bloodied their noses with their endless Cultural Revolution. These things can't be done in a hurry. Think of Amanda Woyke. It took years and years for potatoes to take the place of millet. And even longer to abolish serfdom. Always relapses. After Robespierre Napoleon, then Metternich . . ."

After that I told my Ilsebill—as she lay there at my mercy—about the developments at the Tribunal. To cheer her up, I mimicked the Flounder's arrogantly curled lip when Amanda's utopia, the world-wide farm kitchen, was being discussed. I ridiculed his trick of affecting benevolent understanding for everything, even the sheerest nonsense. Then I parodied his manner of speaking: "'But my dear and gracious ladies! Of course I was glad my contention that the Rumford-Woyke world food center points the way to an egalitarian solution of the food problem has found supporters in your midst, but these things can't be done helter-skelter. It will first be necessary to set up working groups that will— thoroughly and knowledgeably—research the basic foodstuffs of the past and present. A number of questions arise. What role was played in times of famine by the manna grits obtained from wild grasses? Or: what position shall we take on the protein shortage and hence on the soybean problem? Or: is the European millet shortage before the introduction of the potato comparable to the rice shortage in China before the onset of the Mao Tse-tung era? But if you wish to approach the Chinese world food solution on the basis of the Central European experience, then I must beg you to lose no time in advancing from theory to practice, in other words, to revive Amanda Woyke's West Prussian soup. To the best of my knowledge, Associate Judge Therese Osslieb operates a successful restaurant. Couldn't an experimental kitchen be installed there? Mightn't that be a good place in which, slowly, with deliberate procrastination and phase lag, in slow motion as it were, to initiate the Great Leap Forward?' "

"So then what?" asks my incapacitated Ilsebill. "Did the girls fall for that? Are aprons in demand again? Good God! Do they expect to emancipate themselves with cooking spoons?"

When the nunnish freedoms of the cooking abbess Margarete Rusch were under discussion and the Flounder (more or less playfully) suggested the establishment of feminist convents, first a loose, then a more structured group began to form, drawing its first members from the various factions of the Revolutionary Advisory Council, but then enlisting certain of the associate judges. While the case of Agnes Kurbiella was being debated, the group, far from gaining in definition, stagnated, but when Amanda Woyke's farm kitchen was held out as an example, it crystallized into a faction which was widely decried as revisionist and which, first in the press, then among the public at large, became known as the "Flounder Party." Restaurant owner and Associate Judge Therese Osslieb passed for its spokesperson. Ulla Witzlaff and Helga Paasch were members. Ruth Simoneit supported it with reservations. Ms. Schönherr, the presiding judge, was said to have expressed herself in private as a sympathizer. And even Bettina von Carnow, the court-appointed defense counsel, tried to ingratiate herself with the Flounder Party.

This development, which split most of the groups, especially the liberals and Spontaneous Revolutionaries, led to constant conflict with the explicitly ideological groups, and all the more so as heresy had raised its head even among the Marxists. Group discipline became more severe. Anyone who had signed up for the working groups of the so-called Flounder Party was expelled or rejected. And yet those feminists who had unjustly been classified as "moderates" gained more and more influence, for the Flounder Party was very hard on the Flounder, and Therese Osslieb gave him a really rough time. Just as Amanda Woyke had berated Inspector August Romeike as a dope or a bully, so Osslieb flung such titles as "flathead" and "super-Hegel" at the Flounder.

She took a critical view of the Flounder but opposed a blanket condemnation. The prosecution, she said, would have to acknowledge that his enlightened bourgeois approach had been relatively progressive at the time. The Tribunal, after all, had him—and his protégé Rumford—to thank for illuminating material concerning the pioneering function of the farm kitchen. The present world food situation—more than half of mankind being undernourished—called for the radical elimination of the family kitchen and reconsideration of historical forms of the large-scale kitchen. This thesis of the Flounder's, Osslieb went on, defied argument and should definitely be taken into the program of the feminist movement. While justly deploring his male arrogance, the Tribunal should be grateful to him for his fruitful ideas. As associate judge, she, Therese Osslieb, would put the egalitarian, or as the Flounder called it, the Chinese world food solution into practice. This she would do on her own premises. Let the men jabber about the Great Leap Forward if that amused them; the women, at long last, would actually make it.

Now Therese Osslieb's restaurant in Kreuzberg was rather a fancy sort of place, where eccentrics hung out and the cuisine was explicitly Czech; Therese's maternal grandmother seems to have been a Viennese of Czech descent. The owner, however, soon managed to drive away most of the geniuses to gain an empathetic understanding of Amanda Woyke's farm kitchen and to popularize, along with West Prussian potato soup, other simple dishes: manna grits boiled with bits of bacon rind; sorrel cooked like spinach; millet cooked in milk; potatoes in their jackets with curds and caraway seed; oatmeal sausage on mashed potatoes; naturally, potato dumplings, Bavarian as well as Bohemian; and fried potatoes accompanied by one thing and another: herring, fried eggs, meatballs, jellied pork.

Up until then the restaurant had borne an esoteric name;

now, as the meeting place of the feminists, it became "Ilse-bill's Barn." The imperial Austrian décor disappeared; now freshly whitewashed walls were graced with just a few rustic ornaments. Few of the old patrons stayed on. But soon the prices started going up again, for each evening Therese Osslieb's husband, who was quick to adapt, put on a program for the entertainment as well as the enlightenment of the public: "Sir Walter Raleigh and the Potato." "The Potato in Shakespeare." "The Introduction of the Potato as Precondition for the Industrialization and Proletarianization of Central Europe." And, breathtaking in its timelessness, "Potato Prices Yesterday and Today."

Associate Judge Helga Paasch of the Women's Tribunal, owner of a nursery garden at Britz, promised to grow organic potatoes for Ilsebill's Barn on a half-acre plot which, moreover, would be open to educational visits. The children of committed women were invited to take part in a painting competition, and soon the restaurant was decorated with potato motifs. Songs in praise of the potato were written, set to music, and sung. A back room was set aside for the production of potato prints. Diners who wished to could sit in a circle, chatting and peeling potatoes for themselves and others. The name Amanda was conferred for life on several female babies who had been born while the case of Amanda Woyke was under discussion and whose mothers (and fathers) were among the steady customers of Ilsebill's Barn.

And yet, despite all the playfulness—a few young women wore necklaces of (sprouting) winter potatoes—the earnestness of the original intention was maintained: working groups discussed the nutritive value of the basic foodstuffs, the protein-rich soybean, millet, rice, the exemplary character of the farm kitchen, the necessity of combating hunger on a global scale, the ultimate goal, the Chinese world food solution, and over and over again the Great Leap, which was said to have already begun. We are already in mid-Leap. Seen dialectically, the Great Leap is not a precipitate action, but a continuous process, unfolding in several phases. A Permanent Leap.

I shouldn't, when Ilsebill was taking her run, have cried out, "Don't! Don't jump! Please! Don't! Don't jump!," because then she had to jump and so prove herself in the light of the, to me, unfathomable law that governs her actions—to prove herself if only for the time of a quick leap, which to me, when I suddenly saw her and her arching belly in a state

332

of weightlessness, seemed to stretch into several leap-phases. I saw my Ilsebill after the takeoff, while my cry of "Don't jump!" was still quivering in the air, saw how she detached herself miraculously from the heavy, wet soil, saw her rise a scant two feet, then, propelled by her momentum, cover forty inches without loss of altitude, and finally, after a distinct downward bend, drop. She just made it over the ditch.

But before I concern myself with Ilsebill's fall, I would like for an extended moment to celebrate her at the zenith of her leap. She was beautiful, though her leap accentuated the awkwardness, not to say ungainliness of her condition. Her defiant goat face, as if the whole world had offended her. I'd have liked to engrave her in copper as a leaping *Melencolia* (freely adapted from Dürer). In Knossos the Minoan maidens (in honor of Hera and to spite Zeus) jumped over a charging bull. And when Awa our mother discovered her shadow and wanted to get rid of it, she jumped over the rivulet Radune—just as Dorothea, on our return home from the pilgrimage, crossed the river Elbe by jumping from ice floe to ice floe. For at the sight of Ilsebill leaping, I carried myself backward, I saw Awa, I saw Dorothea in mid-leap, I fled to the late eighteenth century, where Amanda Woyke, a serf bonded to the state of Prussia, was sitting with her whole sedentary being beside the stove in the farm kitchen, serenely peeling potatoes, and a hundred years later I visited Lena Stubbe's working-class lodge (at Brabank 5), where I found immemorial poverty entrenched as a social problem. Only then did I attend the congress at Bièvres, on the outskirts of Paris, which tried to do something about the future of democratic socialism.

Some Czechoslovak refugees had invited me. A French Communist, risking explusion from the party, met me at the Orly airport. I had hardly checked into the hotel when I bought a postcard to send to my Ilsebill, scribbled full of sentences such as: "Take care of yourself! Please don't overdo it. Your condition permits of no leaps. The congress promises to be interesting. About a hundred revisionists . . ."

They sit at a long table and have that refugee look. Sparse beards matted with vestiges of the last and next-to-last revolutions, which have become part of them in the meantime. In among the veterans sit young, inexperienced beards, in which the future nests, giving hope of hope.

This congress at Bièvres (it seems there used to be beavers here) has been well prepared, with reports that go on and on and leave no historical aspect untouched. Mimeographed copies of the speeches in French translation are made available. Each orator addresses the toiling masses as though speaking to a large crowd, as once he did on public squares, in factory halls, at the now celebrated party congress. Words listen to words with approval. Stalinism condemned in absentia. Determination to remain a socialist, come what may. Appeals to reason. The lament of the enlightened.

Those not speaking draw box constructions or hairy twats. In the translators' booths emancipated women confidently translate the speeches of errant men into English, German, Czech, and Italian. Outside the windows that can't be opened, February claims to be March. They've come from everywhere. (Only the comrades from Chile haven't come.) An old Trotskyist marked by four party splits takes the minutes (in Spanish): his posthumous papers.

Cover your eyes and forehead with your palm and your joined fingers until emptiness sets in: a new promise. Now that reason and the potato have triumphed over superstition, it must be possible to . . . Now that we know so much, at least the most glaring hunger must be . . . If we, the whole lot of us, are not to perish, then at last the Great Leap must . . .

All of a sudden I want to be sitting outside in my overcoat on a bench for old folks and sparrows, eating cheese off my knife and drinking red wine out of a liter bottle, until I'm too demoralized to withstand the claims of time and absolutely without hope, or until I meet some of the other veterans I sat with in Amanda Woyke's farm kitchen, discussing every battle from Kolin to Burkersdorf back and forth over potatoes with caraway seed and *Glumse*.

The next man has the floor. Off to one side a resolution is born. On a motion by the Italians. About the Prague Spring: it doesn't want to be over.

(No no no! I mean it. That was foolish. Even if we were lucky.) By twisting her belly to one side as she fell and landing on her elbow, she got off lightly—once again. Dutifully I leaped after her. But for quite some time, while I was saying my little sentences—"You were lucky, damn it. But what an irresponsible thing to do!"—the veterans' meal in Amanda's

334

farm kitchen dragged on (and the congress of European revisionists stuck to the agenda point for point). For right after the Peace of Hubertusburg I was made inspector of crown lands on the strength of my services. My comrades of the regiment found some sort of livelihood, mainly in the school system. And Amanda had no objection if once a year, after the farm hands had been fed, we sat around the much-too-long table and drank potato schnapps until we were drowning in blissful battle memories: "Ah, comrade, when I think of Torgau . . . Remember the time we found all that tobacco and chocolate in the Saxon baggage train. . . ." (And during the intervals between conferences in Bièvres, a few political jokes that were new to me were told: Brezhnev and Nixon meet Hitler in hell. . . .) And after her fall I said to my Ilsebill, "It could have turned out worse, my dear. When Amanda was pregnant with her youngest daughter, Annchen, the one Romeike made her after the Battle of Burkersdorf just before the end of the war, she jumped across a brook while gathering mushrooms in the woods and fell on some mica rocks, which brought on labor pains prematurely."

Annchen got born all the same. And her daughter Sophie got to be cook later on for Napoleon's Governor Rapp. And when we former corporals celebrated our reunions, little Sophie served potatoes in their jackets with *Glumse* and caraway seed (with linseed oil), which are today coming into fashion again.

Recently, when last the spirit carried me off to Berlin—Ilsebill's sprained ankle had mended in the meantime—Ruth Simoneit took me along. We managed to talk Sieglinde Huntscha, who just on principle says the Barn is "shitty," into coming with us. We sat at a table with Ulla Witzlaff. After the manner of restaurant owners, Osslieb sat down with us now and then for a brief chat. Considering I was the only man in the place, I wasn't treated too badly. Ulla Witzlaff was knitting (knit one, purl one) a man's sweater. (The girls are better natured than they put on.) When I talked about my hopeless socialist congress, they actually listened. Only Ruth Simoneit, who had ordered a double potato schnapps the moment she arrived, bristled: "Licking your wounds, eh? That's the one thing you men are good at. When you're not brutes, you're crybabies."

But then things picked up. Helga Paasch joined us with a

big hello. Osslieb served potato soup. Ulla Witzlaff filled the deep dishes to the brim. Until late into the night the future was evoked: the great crisis and the collapse of all (masculine) systems. Everyone looked forward to the impending Chinese world food solution. I treated them to a few rounds of potato schnapps. "Here's to the standardized swill of the future!" Then Paasch treated. Naturally Ruth Simoneit was plastered. Witzlaff sang, "Our Flounder is a Maoist! Our Flounder is a Maoist!" And Sieglinde Huntscha tried to make a pass at Osslieb. They were getting really chummy.

Too bad my Ilsebill wasn't there. But she just had to jump over that ditch. I could beg, I could plead—"Don't jump! Don't! Please don't jump!"—she jumped all the same; she wanted to fall. There she lay in the mud. I jumped after her. She was lying on her ass. I yelled at her. She yelled back, "It's my belly, and I'll jump when and where I please with it!"

"It's not just your child; it's going to be our child!"

"I refuse to let you tell me when to jump and when not to jump."

"You should have thought about it sooner if you don't want the child."

"Shitty ditch! I'll never do it again."

"Swear to me, Ilsebill, that you'll never again."

But forswear the Great Leap, promise never to leap again—no, not my Ilsebill.

Boiled beef and historical millet

Me and the cook inside me—we spare each other nothing. Ilsebill, for instance, has a cook inside her—that must be me—and fights him. Our quarrel from the start: who sits like a complex, plump or lean, inside of whom, inspiring new dishes or old ones that have come back into style, since we started cooking with historic awareness.

Now, while five pounds of beef shank simmer over low heat and I helpfully and haphazardly clean vegetables, she is reading a book with lots of footnotes, dealing with, among other things, millet as poor man's food, festive fare, fairy-tale motif, and chicken feed.

I keep quiet, thinking up story after story that may have sweetened the porridge of the Zuckau farm hands in the days of serfdom: when the flour bin was empty and the heavens rained millet grains as big as peas, and everybody was miraculously replenished. . . .

Her voice passing over my fairy tale and cutting through it, Ilsebill says: "The author has just plain forgotten about *us*. It's always the males. When it's the women's doing that beginning in 1800 the surface planted with millet dropped from 53,000 to 14,877 hectares, thanks to the rapid expansion of potato culture, especially in Prussia. Nowadays you'll only find millet in health shops, along with pine nuts, couscous, and soybeans. If you spoke of 'a bad millet year,' nobody would even know what you were talking about."

I say: "And long ago, before the potato defeated millet in Prussia and elsewhere, a bride had to cook a brimming potful of millet in milk the morning after her wedding night, to make sure the seed took inside her. She'd smack a helping of this millet porridge into the hands of the poor weavers' children with a wooden paddle; they'd shout for joy and pass the blob from hand to hand, until it was cool enough to be tasted."

"You and your stories," says Ilsebill. "They only take people's minds off reality. Trying to talk me deaf and blind." She slaps the book with historical footnotes shut. "In the old days millet made us women stupid. And today? What about today?"

I lapse into a timorous silence. She's right, damn it, right. (And yet Amanda Woyke, the farm cook, learned so well how to write, from watching Inspector of Crown Lands Romeike, that she could soon correspond more intelligently than he with the famous Count Rumford and was able to read to the farm hands out of the latest gazette what Mirabeau had said about the price of bread and the principles of the revolution.)

The cook whom Ilsebill keeps inside her, if only to fight with, obeys her implicitly. She decides that no potatoes (which are getting more expensive) will be peeled today, that instead historical millet will be scalded in a good quart of bouillon and placed in a covered pot on top of the kettle with the simmering beef: and now the millet swells as tradition demands, while I continue to clean vegetables.

"Don't cut up the carrots! And keep the salsify whole, too. Typical man! Wants to boil everything together until nothing tastes like itself."

While I try to take flight down the stairs of history, she screams, "Oatmeal gruel! Barley grits! Millet porridge! That's what you've kept us down with for centuries. But from now on it won't wash, hear? Now it's your turn. So get to work and stop dreaming."

Obediently I halve the cabbage and celery root. I leave the carrots, onions, salsify, kohlrabi, and three cloves of garlic whole. Ah, to be condemned to see what beauty a cabbage displays in cross section: what structures, what system, so labyrinthine, the endless line . . .)

"How about the rutabaga?" she says from inside herself, not I from inside her. And instead of boiling the hell out of them as a typical male would, Ilsebill puts all the vegetables I've cleaned, plus a fist-sized chunk of rutabaga, to simmer with the meat that will soon be done, under the swelling millet.

Then our guests came. They praised our historically aware dish and asked for more; and more and more.

When the guests had gone and I had loaded and unloaded the dishwasher, later, much later, I lay beside Ilsebill and dreamed: A mountain, and I have to eat my way through it. But when at last I have the millet behind me, there's a mountain of boiled, still-steaming potatoes ahead. I've begun to munch my way through them as resolutely as can be, I've already gone halfway, when I'm overcome with fear that beyond the sweet millet and the steaming boiled potatoes there will be a high-piled mountain of raw rutabaga between me and the Promised Land.

Both

He doesn't say *my*, he says *the* wife.
The wife doesn't like it.
I'll have to talk that over with the wife.

Fear tied into a knotted necktie.
Fear of going home.
Fear of admitting.
Frightened, they (both) belong to each other.

Love complains and makes its claims.
And then the usual little kiss.
Only memory counts.
Both live on bones of contention.
(The children notice something through the keyhole
and decide on the opposite for later.)

But, says he, without the wife I wouldn't have so much.
But, says she, he does what he can and then some.
A blessing, a curse, and when the curses become law.
A law that becomes more and more welfare-minded.
Between built-in closets paid for in installments
hate forms
knots in the carpet: hard to keep clean.

When sufficiently
estranged, they discover
each other only at the movies.

The sixth month

~~~~~~

Dresses from India

Going into her sixth month of pregnancy, she'd had
enough of compressing her belly, lacing it in, forcing it into
an ideal mold; she stopped covering the mirrors, stopped
outraging her nature with pills, and, while looking for the ignition key, finding senseless pretexts for a fight. Because the
child, now under her navel, was knocking in protest, she began taking things more calmly and presenting her belly,
wherever she went, as an object worth admiring. No more irresponsible leaps. Rare outbreaks of primally bubbling man-
hatred. Moments of gentle cow-eyedness. First acquisition of
baby clothes. And after the leap over the ditch, when everything could have gone wrong, she made herself a so-called
maternity dress, some sort of shit-brown smock that I termed
impossible.

So we went to one of those Indian boutiques which in
Hamburg and elsewhere are cheap and crammed full from
floor to ceiling. Streets of dresses and avenues of blouses. So
much to choose from. You only had to reach out.

Taking, no, grabbing five or seven dresses—roomy at the
waist, laced under the bosom, and more or less simply cut—
Ilsebill escaped with her prey into one of the little curtained-
off dressing rooms. Then at brief intervals she appeared five
or seven times in Indian cotton or silk: embroidered, decorated with little mirrors around the swollen bosom, or corn-
yellow and mystic-green, or all of red bunting.

A show just for me. I nodded, expressed misgivings, praised what I disliked, carped at what I wanted to see her wearing, stuck to my role, and considered myself halfway victorious when she finally decided, if not on the wide-sleeved corn-yellow one or, despite a moment's hesitation, on the mystic-green silk one, at least on the simple, roomy one all of red bunting, with red embroidery only over the bosom. A floor-length dress with spacious sleeves. The ample folds, just the thing for the swelling belly, festive yet casual. A bargain at eighty-five ninety, no problems up to the eighth month, and possible to wear even after the delivery. Already I saw her slender, with company at parties, in discussion groups, traveling.

"It's not so bad here in the West," said Ilsebill. "I mean rummaging, trying on, not wanting to buy, being free to pick and choose." Guilty conscience expressed itself only in an aside: "Of course the things are so cheap there's got to be exploitation. That cheap labor in Pakistan, India, Hong Kong, and so on." In red bunting, she flung these words of accusation in my face. As her husband, I have to answer for every male misdeed perpetrated in historical times or the present. "Can you tell me, for instance, what the fat bosses down there pay their seamstresses? Take a look at this. All hand-sewn!"

During her five or seven Indian acts, I was surrounded by women who rummaged, briefly tried on, rejected, or selected. A few of them were also pregnant. Or may have been. Asian kitsch in glasses, on straw dishes, in brightly colored cardboard boxes. Unneeded for moments at a time, I relapsed into my obsessive daydream of having been Vasco da Gama and discovered the sea route to India: all of a sudden, the Malabar Coast—palm trees, everywhere palm trees—lies ahead of us, palpably close. We send a convict ashore to see what will happen, and he comes back unharmed, telling of wonders. Napoleon, in whose time lived Sophie Rotzoll, the prettiest of all cooks, is thought to have had military designs on India. But when I was still Vasco da Gama, full of unrest and inwardly rich in figures . . .

The smell of musk did it. Bittersweet smoke arose from several little bowls. Music from somewhere, packed in cotton batting, made everything still cheaper. The salesgirls, though all of the Hamburg build, moved like temple dancers in their first year of training. Soft-spoken empathy. "The pale-blue one with the white braid is also being worn a good deal." Ilsebill settled on the red bunting.

"I feel entirely different now," she said. "No, not Indian, of course not. Just somehow different."

I said, "We owe it all to Vasco da Gama and his successors. He brought down the price of more things than pepper."

We promised the salesgirls to come again in the eighth month. "By that time," said the long-suffering cashier with the blue eye shadow, "our summer collection will be in. Really delicious stuff."

In paying, I put one mark ten into the "Bread for the World" collection box. Outside, in spite of a halfhearted March sun, it was too cold for the red bunting, which changed color in the daylight: Ilsebill shivered in her fly-agaric-red acquisition. I helped her on with her coat.

Sophie

We seek
and think we find;
but it has a different name
and belongs to a different family.

Once we found one
that didn't exist.
My spectacles clouded over.
A jay screamed,
we ran away.

It seems that in the woods around Saskoschin
they looked each other over.
And because the egg mushrooms
were still recognizable
the others laughed at them.

Mushrooms mean something.
It's not just the edible ones

that stand on one leg
at attention for metaphors.

Sophie, who later became a cook
and political as well,
knew them all by name.

The other truth

In the fall of 1807—the farm cook Amanda Woyke was
dead, French troops were billeted all over the place, Sophie,
Amanda's granddaughter, still in a revolutionary frame of
mind, was beginning to cook for Napoleon's governor, and
mushrooms were plentiful in all the forests—the brothers
Jakob and Wilhelm Grimm met the poets Clemens Brentano
and Achim von Arnim at the Oliva forester's lodge, to discuss
a publishing venture and exchange ideas.

In the previous year von Arnim and Brentano had published a collection of rare and precious folk songs and folk
poetry under the title *Des Knaben Wunderhorn* (*The Boy's
Magic Horn*). Since the general misery brought on by the
war increased people's need for sweet-sounding words, and
since fear sought refuge in fairy tales, they had come to this
quiet spot, far from the city's bustle and from the political
quarrels that had become the stuff of daily life, to compile a
second and third volume from their still-unsorted hoard of
rare treasures, hoping at long last, after so much cold Enlightenment and classical rigor, to give their people some consolation, if only the consolation of escape.

Two days later, the painter Philipp Otto Runge and Clemens Brentano's sister arrived, he from Hamburg via Stettin,
she from Berlin. The forester's lodge had been recommended
to the friends by Pastor Blech, deacon of Saint Mary's
Church in Danzig, through Friedrich Karl von Savigny, with
whom he corresponded; and besides, the young people were
drawn to secret meeting places in the heart of nature. Only
the old forester and a Kashubian woodsman with his wife
and four children lived in the wooden house, situated, as
344

though outside of time, between woodland pool and deer meadow.

The friends found the silence hard to bear. When Brentano, whose wife had died and whose second marriage, concluded a few months before, was off to an unhappy start, wasn't sulking, he was offending the others, especially the sensitive Wilhelm Grimm, with his strained wit. His sister was still full of her travel experiences; that spring she had actually met Goethe, with whose mother she corresponded. The dialogue between the two women was to lead quite naturally to a book of jottings about the great man's childhood.

Jakob Grimm and von Arnim, who had moved to Königsberg immediately after the disaster of Jena and Auerstedt, spoke bitterly of the recently concluded Peace of Tilsit, which they termed a shameful *Diktat*. Von Arnim had decided by then to confine his activities to the management of his estates. Jakob Grimm was trying to decide whether to accept the post of private librarian to the detested upstart king Jérôme Bonaparte at Schloss Wilhelmshöhe near Kassel. (He did.) Wilhelm, who had just completed his study of law, decided that in such evil times it would suit him best to be an independent scholar. All spoke of their hopes and plans. Only painter Runge remained silent (though full of inner discourse) and aloof from the happenings of the day. He had come from Hamburg, stopping on his way at his native city of Wolgast and the nearby island of Rügen, where, some years before, he had heard an old woman, now dead, speaking in the Low German dialect of the coast, tell a number of tales, a few of which he had written down. A man with side whiskers, bulging eyes, and a constantly worried forehead, who in another three years would die of consumption, cut down, as they say, in his prime.

The forester's lodge was a good hour's walk from Oliva, and though its attic rooms, in which the friends dreamed away their happiness and slept away their sorrows, were narrow and low-ceilinged, the kitchen, with its long table on a floor of beaten earth, offered room enough for agitated pacing, impassioned harangues, rebounding laughter, and far too many sheets of neatly penned manuscript or correspondence with publishers. The brick stove, at which the forester's wife, who answered to the name of Lovise, was permanently busy, maintained a pleasant warmth. There was always a pot of hot malt-coffee on the stove, and in the breadbasket a big loaf of rye bread from which the friends broke off chunks because it was fresh-baked and made them ravenous. Only seldom was a whimper heard from one of the four children, all of whom, from the six-month-old infant to the six-year-old Amanda, were fed from Lovise's breast. This the friends saw with surprise and some misgiving. Only Bettina was delighted. "That's life!" she cried. "Simple and authentic!"

Then they remembered their work. The next volume of *The Boy's Magic Horn* must be even more splendid than the first. For the moment they disagreed only on the guiding principle. While Arnim wanted to preserve German folk poetry by presenting it in its original form, unfalsified, as it welled from the mouths of the people—"For when treasures have endured this long, we have no business taking a file and trying to polish them"—Brentano wanted to improve on the old songs, tales, and fables, and teach the voice of the people to speak more artistically: "The artist's hand is needed to ennoble the crude stone, magnificent as we find it uncut." Jakob Grimm was more scientific in his enthusiasm; he wished to proceed with method and put order into the super-abundant material: "We are dealing with a linguistic river; like other rivers it has its source, which we will search for and question with regard to origins." Only the sensitive Wilhelm thought they should listen in all humility but with meticulous ear to everything said or sung around the hearth or spinning wheel, and preserve it by taking it down without embellishment. "That alone would be enough for me," he said. (And later on, to be sure, he patiently collected folk tales and gave them to the world as a household treasure.)

Violently as they argued, Fräulein Bettina managed, strangely enough, in her childlike yet precocious way, to agree with all of them. She favored unfalsified folk poetry, the art fairy tale, the search for the sources of language, and the humble transcription of fireside stories. And when painter Runge spoke haltingly and obscurely of primordial forces, of unformed matter, of the breath of chance, of gossamer and transience, all of which he held to be the very texture of life, and proceeded from image to image, Bettina agreed with him, too; in her eyes the friends were all splendid. Each one was right. There was room enough for all their ideas. That's the way nature was in its beautiful disorder: spacious. All these thoughts could be set before the reader in their wild luxuriance; little order was needed. The reader would know what to do with them. "And then," she cried, "you can go on with your research!"

Thereupon painter Runge said: "I'm glad to say that *The Journal for Hermits* has accepted one of the tales I've taken down in dialect, 'The Juniper Tree,' but the other, which was also told me years ago by an old woman on the island of Rügen and which I took down in two versions, because the old woman, who was strangely obstinate, kept shifting from one to the other and back, this tale of 'The Fisherman and His Wife' is still unpublished, though Zimmer the book dealer recommended it a good two years ago to Messrs. Arnim and Brentano for inclusion in their *Boy's Magic Horn*. Our meeting here gives me an opportunity to bring the story up again, and I'm going to submit both versions. That's why I've come all this way at the Messrs. Grimm's request. Because I ought to be at work on my painting. It's called *Morning*, and it simply refuses to get finished."

Thereupon painter Runge laid the two versions of his dialect tale on the long, paper-littered table. The one is the tale as it has come down to us; of the other, there is more to say.

Because, you see, the old woman, who lived on Oehe, a small island between the thin, elongated island of Hiddensee and the large island of Rügen, but who, when the wind was right, came rowing over to the main island on market days to sell her sheep's-milk cheese in Schaprode, told painter Philipp Otto Runge two different truths to take down in his sketchbook. The one made Ilsebill the quarrelsome wife credible, how she wants to have more and more and more, to be king emperor pope, but finally, when she wants the all-powerful Flounder to make her "like God," is sent back to the old thatched hut, called "pisspot" in the story. The other truth dictated to painter Runge by the old woman showed a modest Ilsebill and a fisherman with immoderate wishes: He wants to be unconquerable in war. He wants to build, traverse, inhabit bridges across the widest river, houses and towers reaching to the clouds, fast carriages drawn neither by oxen nor horses, ships that swim under water. He wants to attain goals, to rule the world, to subjugate nature, to rise above the earth. "But now," he says in the second tale, "now I want to fly, too. . . ." And when at the end the fisherman, though his wife, Ilsebill, keeps advising him to be content

("Now suppose we stop wishing and let well enough alone"), wants to rise up to the stars ("I must and will fly up to heaven"), all the splendor, the towers, the bridges, the flying machines collapse, the dikes burst, drought parches, sandstorms devastate, the mountains spew fire, the old earth quakes, and in quaking shakes off the man's rule. And cold blasts usher in the next all-covering ice age. "And there, under the ice, they've been sitting to this day." So ended the tale of the Flounder who granted every wish of the man who kept wanting more and more, every wish except the last—to fly beyond the stars to heaven.

When painter Runge asked the old woman which of the two tales was right, she said, "The one and the other." Then she went back to the market to sell her sheep's-milk cheese, for she wanted to be on her island before nightfall, "with some sweet stuff and a bottle."

As for painter Runge, he returned to Wolgast, where he lived in his father's house. There he copied both tales, the one and the other truth, out of his sketchbook in his best calligraphy, without changing a single word.

When the Grimm brothers, the writers Arnim and Brentano, and Brentano's sister Bettina had read the one and the other manuscript, asking what certain words meant because they didn't know much Low German, they all praised the tales for their moral substance and originality, but each in a different way. Arnim wanted to put both of them right into his *Boy's Magic Horn;* Brentano wanted to cleanse them of dialect, transpose them into verse, and fashion them into a great epic; Jakob Grimm delighted in their free and easy grammar; and Wilhelm Grimm resolved to publish these tales and others in the future. Only Bettina took a dark view of the one version in which, so she said, Ilsebill was painted too black. If the tale were published in that form, it would be easy for men to say: That's how you women are, greedy and quarrelsome, all alike. "When actually," she cried, "women have such a hard time of it!"

"I, on the other hand," said her brother Clemens, "cannot approve of the other tale, which so cruelly demolishes man's strivings and dreams of greatness. None of the things we hold sacred, our rich and complex history, the glorious empire of the Hohenstaufens, the towering Gothic cathedrals, would exist if men had dully contented themselves with what they had.

348

To publish the tale in this form, so suggesting that all men's striving leads to chaos, would soon make a laughingstock of male authority. And besides, women are undoubtedly more immoderate in their wishes. Everyone knows that."

After that, brother and sister argued across the long table, and soon the other friends also began to quarrel. Even the scientific-minded Jakob Grimm thought the greedy Ilsebill more plausible than the overweening fisherman. He knew other tales (from Hessen, from Silesia), about women (always women) who wanted more and more. The sensitive Wilhelm took the contrary view. It was common knowledge, he contended, that male lust for power was a source of tyranny and oppression. Consider Napoleon—or Caesar. Hadn't the Corsican wanted more and more? As general under the Directory, to be consul; as one of three consuls, to be first consul; as first consul, to be emperor; and hadn't he gone on as emperor to subjugate all Europe? And wasn't he planning, at this very moment, to invade India; didn't he hope to break the world dominion of Britain and perhaps even, like Charles XII of Sweden, to penetrate deep into Russia?

The friends, who were all stricken by the misfortune of their fatherland, agreed. Only Bettina would hear no slur on the greatness of her undersized hero. Hadn't she heard Goethe in person, himself a great man, praise Napoleon in no uncertain terms? Whereupon Arnim poured abuse on Goethe and waxed loudly patriotic. (Later on, during the War of Liberation, he was to show bravery as captain in a Landsturm battalion.)

To all this Runge said nothing, though he had his own grounds for bitterness against the great man of Weimar, who, when viewing Runge's *Achilles's Combat with the River Gods* at a competitive exhibition, had thought it "not classical enough." Once, to be sure, though no one heard him, Runge informed his friends that the old woman had said both tales were true.

When Brentano now declared the quarrelsome, greedy Ilsebill from the one tale to represent the very essence of womanhood, in support of which judgment he cited some revolting anecdotes drawn from his recent but already foundered marriage to a certain Auguste Busmann, Bettina (who after the Revolution of 1830 was to become a militant champion of women's rights) was furious with her outspoken brother: "Haven't we women been humiliated enough?"

Then, with a glance at the silent Kashubian woman at the stove (and her frightened children), she put an end to the angry quarrel: "Friends, let's stop and think this over quietly. Our dear Lovise tells me the woods are full of mushrooms. Let's entrust ourselves to nature and gather into our baskets what it has to offer us. It's still early afternoon. The autumn sun will give us a golden light. Where, if not in the forest cathedral, will our quarrel give way to appeasement? And besides, our dear Lovise has announced her cousin's visit for this evening. She is the local governor's cook and moreover an expert on mushrooms."

So they went into the forest, which they saw in different ways. Each carried a basket. For fear of getting lost, they arranged to remain within calling distance of one another. Oliva Forest, consisting mostly of beeches, merged with Goldkrug Forest and the hilly woods of Kashubia farther inland. Brentano was soon overpowered (as though rehearsing his subsequent conversion to Catholicism) by a feeling of profound yet exalted, all-embracing yet concentrated piety. Sobbing with *Weltschmerz* as, holding his empty basket, he leaned against a smooth beech trunk, he was found by the sensitive Wilhelm, whose consolations were so ineffectual that he, too, burst into tears; whereupon they threw their arms around each other, and so they remained until their sobs died down and, moving like blind men, they finally gathered a few mushrooms: for the most part inedible members of the argaric family, more sulfur cups than honey tufts.

Meanwhile Arnim and Bettina (who were to marry some years later and have eight children) had met as though by chance at the edge of a clearing by the side of a dark pond. They showed each other what they had gathered in their baskets: Arnim was proud of a few specimens of butter fungus and numerous chestnut mushrooms; the playful Bettina called attention to a few moss heads and begged indulgence for the fly agaric she had gathered. They were as beautiful as fairy tales, she said. They emanated enchantment. She knew that fly agaric, even if one ate only a little, induced dreams, suspended time, freed the self, and reconciled the most glaring contradictions. Thereupon she peeled the skin from the cap, broke off a morsel, took some for herself, ate a piece, and gave some to Arnim. Then they stood silent, waiting for the effect. It soon made itself felt. His fingers and hers wanted to play together. Standing eye to eye, they looked deep into each other's souls. They spoke words clad in purple that found their mirror image in every pool of water. Bettina compared the nearby pond to the sorrowful eye of an enchanted prince.

When the effect of the fly agaric wore off a little—the sky had already begun to darken—Arnim reached into his trouser pocket and found a peasant knife, which he had bought for next to nothing while on a trip to the Rhineland with his friend Brentano. With it he cut into a beech trunk, as smooth as the one Clemens and Wilhelm had wept by, the word "forever," and under it the letters "A" and "B." (Thus they made the clearing and the dark pond significant. Much later a stone was placed there, which remembered them with a hewn inscription.)

Meanwhile Jakob Grimm and Philipp Otto Runge had managed to carry on a serious conversation, though they had passed any number of honey tufts and a few ceps. Runge was not only a painter but also a theoretician; he wrote about colors, for which reason a work entitled "The Color Globe" was found among his posthumous papers; whereas Jakob Grimm studied the laws of phonetic change, the mythological background of all reality, and vast realms of words, for which reason we still refer to the dictionary that bears his name.

At length they got around to the two versions of the fairy tale about the Flounder. Jakob Grimm said he would be glad, at his next opportunity, to publish the first version, in which the greedy Ilsebill is sent back to her pisspot. (And indeed, a year after Runge's death, the tale of "The Fisherman and His Wife" was included in the Grimm brothers' *Kinder- und Hausmärchen.* The other version, however—as Runge himself finally agreed—would have to be withheld, because of its apocalyptic tone. "It would seem," said the painter with some bitterness, "that we humans can tolerate the one truth and never the other."

The elder Grimm brother wondered if it might not be possible to rewrite the tale, stressing the ethical aspect, to convert it into a political attack on Napoleon, and so make it serve the unhappy fatherland. (And in 1814, to be sure, such an attack on the tyrant was published in High German; but by then Napoleon had already been defeated.)

And now, as dusk descended on Oliva Forest, the friends

called out till they found one another, but they didn't know the way back. They were just beginning to be afraid—even Runge and the elder Grimm brother were troubled—when the forester appeared from the depths of the woods. He must have heard their cries. Without a word, as though there were nothing to say, he led them all home.

At the forester's lodge, beside the pond and the already dark deer meadow, the woodsman's Kashubian wife's cousin had by then arrived with fresh-baked bread from the governor's kitchen. Lovise called her cousin Sophie. And when the pretty but noisy young lady began to sort the mushrooms that had been gathered, saying, for instance, "This is a sulfur tuft, it's poisonous," Brentano remembered sorrowfully that Sophie had been the name of his wife who had died a year before.

And Sophie Rotzoll—as the French governor's cook continued to be called—cleaned the good mushrooms and fried them in a big pan with bacon and onions till they gave off juice, which she peppered and at the end seasoned with parsley. The friends ate of the dish at the long table, and there was enough for Lovise and Sophie as well. The old forester and the Kashubian woodsman, whose name was Kutschorra, sat on the stove bench, dipping chunks of the bread Sophie had brought into bowls of beer soup left over from the day before. And the friends also broke off chunks of bread. In the bedroom beside the kitchen, Lovise's children were no doubt dreaming of spice cookies with anise baked into them.

How merrily the friends talked. How cleverly Sophie the cook answered their questions. When the conversation suddenly went back to the Flounder and his truths, Sophie and Lovise said that they, too, had heard such tales. But only the one truth was right. It was the men and no one else who wanted more and more and more. "They're to blame for all the trouble!" cried Sophie, slamming her fist down on the bread.

That would have provoked more quarreling at the long table if the sensitive Wilhelm hadn't suddenly said, "The moon! Look at the moon!" They all looked through the little windows and saw how the full moon shed its light on the pond where the swans were sleeping and the deer meadow where the deer were grazing.

So they went out in front of the forester's lodge. Only the

forester stayed on the stove bench. But while they were all looking at the moon and thinking up pretty names to call it by, painter Runge returned to the house, came back with a brand he had taken out of the stove, and set fire to a sheet of paper with writing on both sides.

"All right, Mr. Flounder," said Runge when the manuscript was consumed. "There goes your other truth."

"Good Lord!" cried the younge Grimm. "I only hope you've done the right thing."

Then they all went back into the house. And now I must write and write.

Beyond the mountains

What would I be without Ilsebill!
the fisherman cried
contentedly.

My wishes clothe themselves in hers.
Those that come true don't count.
Except for us everything's made up.
Only the fairy tale is real.
Always, when I call, the Flounder comes.
I want, I want, I want to be like Ilsebill.

Higher, deeper, more golden, twice as much.
More beautiful than imagined.
Mirrored ad infinitum.
And because the concepts of life and death no longer.
And have a chance to invent the wheel once more.

Not long ago I dreamed riches:
everything I could have wished for,
bread, cheese, nuts, and wine,
only I wasn't there to enjoy them.
So then my wishes went off again
and searched beyond the mountains for
their double meaning: Ilsebill or me.

Gathering mushrooms

It was easier to tell us apart by our shoes, which were found later—those are Max's, those Gottlieb's, those Fritzchen's—than by our faces before; the three of us with our round heads could be confused as readily as the mushrooms in the woods around Zuckau and Kokoschken, where we went with Sophie, who, after we had once again managed to get lost, called all the mushrooms and us, too, by name.

That must have been in the fall of '89, because seven years later, when after a good many things had happened we found our way out of the woods, Fritz Bartholdy wanted to proclaim the republic right away; and Sophie, who brought home baskets full of chestnut mushrooms and lordly ceps, agreed with her Fritz.

That's how big the forests were in those days: if you got lost in them as a child, you were older by the time you got back. Almost grown up, and with his mouth full of determination, the gymnasium student Friedrich Bartholdy declared, when we met in the attic of his father's town house at Beutlergasse 7, "Freedom must be won by violence!" Sometimes he quoted Danton, who was dead, and sometimes Marat or Robespierre, who were also dead. But because we'd been gathering mushrooms repeatedly and for so long, the idea had stuck with us. It was as beautiful as a solitary cep. And when Sophie read aloud what the latest gazette had to say about General Bonaparte, Fritz said, "Maybe this Napoleon is the idea for our time."

Since then I've gathered mushrooms time and time again with Sophie, Ilsebill, and whoever. Names I've shouted in the woods. My terror when no answer came. And sometimes I, too, have found, I, too, have been called, and I've answered too late.

Last fall, before we made the baby after mutton with beans and pears as though it were an idea, Ilsebill, while gathering mushrooms in Geest Forest near Itzehoe, found a solitary cep, which was so big that we long looked in vain for something to compare it with, until Sophie, in the adjoining forest but just two centuries earlier, found an even bigger one that was beyond compare. Like all mushroom forests, those I've gone into with Ilsebill, Sophie, and whoever are twined and matted with ferns and seamlessly upholstered with moss; I never knew who actually found the biggest cep—which in Sophie's day was known as the imperial mushroom—when or where.

Ilsebill found hers at the edge of a clearing, while on a bed of pine needles some distance away I found, clustered close together, enough orange agaric for a whole meal. (Fried in butter, they taste like meat.) Gathering mushrooms is worthwhile. True, you lose time—how often Sophie and I strayed farther and farther apart while calling each other—but some, not all, of the years lost in this way will be found again as long as there are forests. Ilsebill wouldn't believe me when I told her that. She thinks every mushroom she finds is the first and last. That there's never been anything comparable. And that never again will an imperial mushroom stand singly on such a stem, so luxuriantly hatted, in a bed of moss, and—while the hand still hesitates—make someone happy, incomparably happy.

For seven years, while beyond the woods the Revolution was going on and the guillotine was being celebrated as humane and progressive, we gathered mushrooms and had a beautiful idea. We lay under parasol mushrooms. Uprooted, the stinkhorn with the lacquer-green head ran after us. Anise agaric stood in a magic circle. We didn't know yet what fly agaric can do in addition to shining red. Sophie wore a funnel-shaped miller mushroom as a hat; its imposing stem rose heavenward, looking like my father's cock when with open breeches he climbed the stairs to my mother's room to beget me, his son Fritz.

Much later, when Ilsebill sat still for me under the miller mushroom and I with a soft pencil drew a picture out of which Sophie peered gravely, she no longer looked like a child. By then she knew everything. No more curiosity. That's why she never let Governor Rapp, imperiously as he wanted to, bury his stinkhorn in her moss. Sophie stayed closed.

Of course we were never really lost. A jay screamed, showing the way. Ants were our pacemakers. Across clearings, through chest-high ferns, between smooth beech trees we went down and down until we came to the river Radaune, which flowed to Zuckau, where Sophie's grandmother would be sitting on the front porch, reading the latest news of the Revolution to Inspector of Crown Lands Romeike; those terrifying words: September murders. When she had finished, Amanda Woyke the farm cook would inspect our haul, mushroom by mushroom, and tell us about the imperial mushrooms she had found in the woods around Zuckau in times of famine, when there were no potatoes yet.

Max, who gathered mushrooms with us, emigrated to America later on. Gottlieb Kutschorra, who came from Viereck, married Sophie's cousin Lovise, who also gathered mushrooms with us. He became a woodsman, and she kept house in the Oliva forester's lodge. And later on, because Sophie's mother, Anna, had married a city man after Danzig became Prussian, Sophie Rotzoll, who took her name from her stepfather, a journeyman brewer, came into daily contact with the gymnasium student Friedrich Bartholdy, who was making his final preparations in his father's house on Beutlergasse.

When, with a few sailors and raftsmen, some longshoremen, and a corporal of the former city watch, which four years before, on Holy Thursday 1793, had tried with disorganized rifle fire to stop the Prussians from occupying the city, gymnasium student Bartholdy founded a Jacobin club and, taking an example from France, decided to proclaim the Revolution and with it the Republic of Danzig, Sophie Rotzoll, who since the brewer's death had been selling flounders, smelts, and lampreys at Hawkers' Gate with her mother, was fourteen, and because she was in love with the seventeen-year-old gymnasium student, she was also wild about all things revolutionary. She had known Fritz since they were children, for his mother was a staunch believer in family excursions to the country. Fritz and Sophie were both to be seen with the Zuckau children at raspberry-picking time; they had caught crayfish in the Radaune, helped with the potato harvest, and gathered mushrooms in the fall.

In Sophie's eyes Fritz was a proclamation of freedom if not freedom itself—in gangling, freckle-faced form. Hopelessly as the boy stuttered at the family board, he read revolutionary proclamations with loud abandon to his little group of conspirators and cited Danton or Marat with perfect fluency. Sophie's presence oiled his vocal cords.

For Fritz and his group she sewed rosettes of tricolor ribbon. For the Jacobin Club she stole four pistols from the old arsenal at Leege Gate. For her Fritz Sophie would have done more; she'd have done anything. But fortunately, April 17, 1797, when the conspirators were arrested on Beutlergasse, was a market day; Sophie was selling smelts.

The elder Bartholdys did not long survive the conviction of their only son. Divested of his citizenship, the merchant moved to Hamburg, where he and his wife soon died of cholera. Fritz Bartholdy, the corporal, four sailors, three longshoremen, and two Polish raftsmen were sentenced to death for seditious conspiracy; but only the sentences of the corporal and the two raftsmen were carried out to the full. Pastor Blech, the deacon of Saint Mary's, appealed to the highest authorities, and the sentences of Fritz and the others were commuted to life imprisonment. The sailors and longshoremen died in prison or perished as cannon fodder, for when Napoleon's forces besieged the fortress of Graudenz, they were posted to the outermost communications trenches. As for Friedrich Bartholdy, however, it was as an inmate of the fortress that he experienced the defeat of Prussia, which gave him hope, Napoleon's rise and fall, which he as a patriot suffered and celebrated, the Congress of Vienna, and the Carlsbad Decrees, whereby his sentence of life imprisonment was confirmed. Finally, after thirty-eight years in the fortress, he was released. Sophie had never stopped petitioning the successive rulers for his pardon.

It was a morose man who returned home in wooden shoes, bringing a bad cough with him. He had kept his stutter. Fritz Bartholdy could no longer be fired with enthusiasm for anything but pot roast and red cabbage. But since he lived for another ten years, and with old Fräulein Rotzoll to cook for him recovered his strength, the two of them could often, in the early fall, be seen leaving their cottage in the sand pit at the foot of the Bischofsberg and setting out with baskets over their arms to gather mushrooms. The neighborhood children shouted mocking jingles after the mushroom woman and her wood goblin. (Wasn't it strange, if not suspicious, that the two old people brought specimens of the useless fly agaric home with them along with the edible varieties?)

I've long refused to have been Friedrich Bartholdy, Sophie's Fritz, and yet I see myself, old and burnt out, on the other side of Schiedlitz, where there were still woods at the time, gathering mushrooms because Sophie wanted us to. There under the beeches, in the mixed forest, on a floor of moss and pine needles, time hadn't happened. The milk caps and egg mushrooms were still the same. And the imperial mushrooms still stood solitary and beyond compare, as though the idea lived on in undiminished beauty.

Hopefully as she questioned me, I never, not even in the woods, spoke to Sophie of my years in the fortress. She kept looking for something in me that I seem to have been when we were young and went gathering mushrooms and played at getting lost. To her the imperial mushroom was still an idea. And when she wanted to remember freedom, to experience freedom, the otherwise useless fly agaric helped her; it grows where the imperial mushroom is often to be found.

Sophie Rotzoll, who got off scot free at the trial of the Jacobin conspirators of Beutlergasse, liked to sing. That may have helped to predispose her in favor of the Revolution, which gave birth to so many new songs. Even when Fritz Bartholdy stayed and stayed in the fortress, she kept faith with the Revolution and its songs, which soon became kitchen songs. Since the Year One she had been cook and housekeeper to Pastor Blech, who not only preached at Saint Mary's, but also taught history at the Royal Gymnasium. There he had instructed young Bartholdy and, with historical examples, aroused his enthusiasm for the Republic and the virtues of Reason.

At first Pastor Blech had spoken up for the Revolution, though coded in Old Testament terms. When Queen Marie-Antoinette was guillotined, the ideal of liberty and equality lost an in principle Enlightened champion. Nevertheless, and because he had recently welcomed First Consul Napoleon as a force for order, he tolerated Sophie's rousing kitchen songs. He gave the young lady a few French lessons, which made her singing more expressive, but for the most part Sophie sang in the seaport dialect which she stylized for the sake of the rhymes and enriched with her new parsonage culture.

Sophie kept pace with the times. She, too, celebrated the savior of the Revolution, and in her songs rhymed putrid aristocrats with pickled sprats, the Republic with princes in aspic, equality with mushroom fricassee, triumphant cannonade with pepper marinade, and (it goes without saying) the latest hero Napoleón with Revolutión. To her Fritz, languishing in the fortress, she sent calves'-liver sausage made in accordance with a recipe of her own and honey cake into which, besides a certain special ingredient, she had baked encouraging little slips of paper inscribed with her rhymed barricade songs. In the dismal light the prisoner read:

"Mushroom soup in the harvest moon,
Napoleon will spring you soon.
Orange agaric we mince,
head and neck has many a prince.
Kings are trembling, cannons booming,
soon, dear Fritz, we'll go mushrooming.
I saw an imperial mushroom today.
Let freedom come, *la liberté!*"

And when Fritz had eaten of Sophie's honey cake, he recovered a little and scarcely felt the damp cold of his dungeon.

Meanwhile Sophie went to the woods alone and was not afraid. There, too, she sang, and rhymed what went into her basket. Nearsighted as she was, she always found what she wanted. Or else honey tufts, egg mushrooms, butter fungus, and broad-topped parasol mushrooms ran after her.

And just as she did while gathering mushrooms, so Pastor Blech's cook also sang while stirring, rolling, beating egg whites, washing dishes, or stuffing thickened blood or chopped calves' liver into sausage skins. Some of her dishes that were served up at the parsonage were given the names of Napoleon's victories: cabbage with *Gänseklein* à la Marengo, for instance. But when Sophie named her ragout of veal after the double disaster of Jena and Auerstedt, Deacon Blech remonstrated. "My dear child," he said, "though it may look as if only the king had lost these two battles, this war and its miseries will soon overtake us all, just and unjust alike. Already Stettin has capitulated. Already our forces here in Danzig are putting up palisades around the bastions. Already, after a brief stay in our threatened city, the royal family have again taken flight and established themselves in distant Königsberg. And already the garrison here is being reinforced. Two field regiments and two grenadier battalions arrived yesterday. Some fusiliers are due tomorrow. Even Cossacks are expected. You just have no idea, my child, what

359

this means. After all the sieges our city has undergone, sieges in which Teutonic Knights, Brandenburgers, Hussites, King Stephen Batory of Poland, Russians, Saxons, and time and time again Poles and Swedes have distinguished themselves, the French are about to give us a demonstration of their skill as besiegers. This is no time to be singing sans-culottish hymns to freedom or indulging your kitchen wit."

It was then that Pastor Blech, who was me in my Napoleonic time-phase, began to write his chronicle, which later appeared in two volumes under the title *History of Danzig's Seven-Year Sufferings* and met with a divided reception. Blech did not spare the collaborationists among his fellow citizens. (But concerning Sophie's dual role I confined myself to hints.) At any rate Sophie stopped singing in the kitchen, in the stairwell, or over the crinkled parsley in the parsonage garden. She dispatched her housekeeping duties in sullen silence. Day after day she served bread-and-beer soups with dumplings, though the woods were full of greenies and honey tufts and one could hope to find a last few solitary imperial mushrooms. No more searching for happiness. Only bad news brought Sophie cheer. In mid-November the suburbs were evacuated. The hamlet of Neugarten was razed. The Church of Saint Barbara became a hay barn, then an emergency hospital. Already the Kashubian countryside was infested with Polish insurgents. In the new year, to be sure, successful engagements, especially the victory at Preussisch-Eylau, gave new hope; in mid-February a solemn *Te Deum* was sung at Saint Mary's, but then Dirschau fell, and on March 7, Praust.

Two days later the French under Marshal Lefebvre, the Poles under Prince Radziwill, and the Badeners commanded by the hereditary prince were firmly established in Sankt Albrecht, Wonneberg, Ohra, and Wotzlaff on the perimeter of the city. The ring around the city had only one opening, across the sand spit at the mouth of the Vistula, and here Count Kalckreuth, the newly appointed commander of the garrison, was able to make his entrance. At length the Cossacks arrived and were much gaped at.

All that was no help. The sand pit was sealed off; the ring was drawn steadily tighter. The Russians lost the Holm. An English corvette bringing in ammunition was lost. Thereupon, after heavy losses on both sides, a first parley was held at Oliva Gate. The capitulation of March 24 provided for the honorable withdrawal of the garrison, but the local population had once again to put up with unwanted guests: Marshal Lefebvre marched in with the French regiments, Saxon and Badener troops, and Polish uhlans. Homes had to be evacuated wholly or in part. The parsonage was soon short of space. But Sophie sang once more in the kitchen, in the stairwell, and in the herb garden, for she thought freedom had been billeted on the parsonage.

In June the one-time general, then consul, now emperor Napoleon Bonaparte rode through the High Gate under a braidless hat, trotted across the Long Market reviewing his victorious troops, then moved into Allmond House on the Long Garden, which had been requisitioned for his use. And when, on the following day, he imposed a "contribution" of twenty million francs on the merchants and town councilors who had been summoned to pay their respects, Sophie, along with several other kitchenmaids, was called in to serve at the reception.

And so it came about that she saw the emperor (standing as solitary as an imperial mushroom). He spoke in terse commands. His gestures wiped everything imaginary off the table. At every turn he had to create facts. Comical to see how he treated those little merchants. His knowledge of the city's finances was staggering. His gaze, addressed to all, including Sophie. While serving the restless man—he ate standing up—canapés of smoked Vistula salmon, she curtseyed and begged mercy for her imprisoned Fritz, whereupon the emperor uttered a sharp command, and she was taken aside by General Rapp, his aide-de-camp.

Rapp, who had just been appointed governor of the Republic of Danzig, gave Sophie his promise—he would look into the matter quickly. He tried his Alsatian wit on her, was pleased with her replies, salted as they were with seaport wit, and offered to put her in charge of his, the governor's, kitchen. That, he intimated, would make it so much simpler to help her Fritz.

From then on Sophie cooked not for Pastor Blech but only for Rapp (who, however, was also me) and for Rapp's guests. And because Rapp was wild about mushrooms, she gathered mushrooms for Rapp alone when the summer egg mushrooms sprouted and later when the autumn chestnut mushrooms and greenies shot up in mounds and the imperial mushroom stood solitary. But in among beech trees or

361

on the pine-needle floors where she found puffballs and orange agaric, Sophie thought fondly and exclusively of me, her Fritz.

Our love, Ilsebill, all the things we've whispered with tightened throats, tucked away in letters, trumpeted down from towers or over the telephone, outroaring the sea or stiller than thought, our love, which we've fenced about so securely, packed up so secretly in hatboxes with all sorts of trifles, which was once as conspicuous as a missing button, and incised under varying names in the bark of every tree, it, our love, which only yesterday was palpable, an object of daily use, our all-purpose glue, our slogan, our bathroom motto, our flickering silent film, our evening prayer spoken as we shivered in our nightshirts, our love, a push button that would play our sweet pop song over and over again, our love, which ran barefoot through the quaking grass, our love, that (almost intact) brick in a ruined wall, our love, which we lost while housecleaning and looking for something else, and found among the usual justifications disguised as a pencil sharpener, our love, which never expected to die, is no more, Ilsebill. Or it consents to be possible (or to exist) only under certain conditions. Or it still exists—but somewhere else. Or it never was and for that very reason is still thinkable. Or suppose, like Sophie and me, we go gathering mushrooms again and look for it deep in the woods. (But when an imperial mushroom stood solitary, beyond compare, and was found by you or you, you never had me in mind.)

So much has been written about it. They say it hurts. They say it tinges everything blue. They say it's the one thing that can't be bought. Where it's lacking, there's a hole, a heart-shaped hole. No one can deliberately turn it on or off. It's always undivided. But Agnes the kitchenmaid loved me and also me. And when Mother Rusch sapped Preacher Hegge's strength, she seems to have had me, too, in mind. While Ilsebill recognizes herself in my High Gothic Dorothea or mistakes me for her wishes. But Sophie, whom I loved as Pastor Blech and as Governor Rapp, loved only and undividedly me, her Fritz, who spent his life in fortress arrest, faraway and unerodable, while Sophie went gathering mushrooms for others (first for Blech, then for Rapp), always with freedom, the beautiful idea, in mind when she found, announced or betrayed by fly agaric, the imperial mushroom standing solitary.

From the early summer of 1807 to the fall of 1813, Sophie Rotzoll cooked for the governor of the Republic of Danzig and his numerous guests. (In the meantime her grandmother had died, and shortly thereafter her mother, of grief, so it was said, at hearing her daughter decried as the governor's whore.)

This is what Pastor Blech, deacon of Saint Mary's, had to say of Jean Rapp, his rival for Sophie's affections: "A young man of about thirty, a child of fortune who like his master had risen quickly from the obscure middle class to a high military rank, sporting several medals on the costly uniform of a general and an aide-de-camp, he almost led me, with his smiling face and not unfriendly gestures, to mistake him for a benevolent spirit. But just as his good qualities were not grounded in sound principles of virtue, so his faults did not emanate from an inherently evil nature; all his faults and all his virtues were, rather, those of an impetuous weakling, a plaything of circumstances and conditions, moods, fancies, and passions. Hence his easily wounded pride and his increasing love of ostentation; hence his tendency to lend ear to every wretched purveyor of gossip and make sudden decisions that have brought untold harm to many an innocent; hence the thoughtless mockery with which he often receives the most just complaints; hence the abandon that has often led him to make the most sacred promises and fail to keep them; hence, finally, his lechery, which he has not always shamed to display in public . . ."

When I think of myself today as Rapp, I cannot help agreeing with what I, as Pastor Blech, said about him. Oh, how that generous and at the same time rapacious man, now playfully gallant, now bestially lecherous, tortured poor Sophie over the years with his constantly reiterated promises to help the imprisoned Fritz; how often his love, rather touching in itself and made more so by his awkwardness and bashfulness, became brutal and importunate; and how often his cynical abuse of power and contempt for the common man's aspiration to freedom offended Sophie's still-childlike faith in the beautiful idea, with the result that, as the French occupation went on, she began first to suspect, then to dislike, and finally to detest everything connected with Napoleon.

And when, after five and a half years, history went into reverse and the Grand Army was decimated in Russia, when Rapp, who on the emperor's order had taken part in the campaign, tried to compensate with ill humor for the frost damage he had incurred, Sophie had grown up to be his enemy who, when gathering mushrooms, considered not only the edible varieties but also those that can be politically effective.

In January 1813, hard pressed by Cossacks, the Grandjean, Heudelet, Marchand, and Cavaignac divisions took refuge behind the city walls. The garrison was reinforced by Polish legionaries, Westphalians from the Rhenish Confederation, a regiment of Bavarians, three regiments of Neapolitans, and a certain number of French chasseurs and cuirassiers. By the time the warehouses on Warehouse Island were freshly stocked with provisions, the bastions were equipped with additional cannon, and the Russo-Prussian siege army had at last closed the ring around the city, Sophie's plan was ready; but then, at the beginning of March, there were no suitable mushrooms.

After daily skirmishes and foraging expeditions up to Schiedlitz and onto the Island, after the first utilization of Congreve rockets, after extensive fires and epidemics, when, after six months of unremitting hunger, the midsummer floods surpassed all bounds, because heavy rainfall had so swollen the Vistula that the dikes from Schwetz to Montau Point burst in seven places and the lowlands were under water as far as the city bastions, that all the outworks, Fort Napoleon, and Fort Desaix were cut off, that palisades went drifting through the flooded streets along with household wares, and fish could easily be caught in large quantities by anyone with a net—a miracle that fed the whole population—when, in short, the midsummer floods had completely fouled the military plans of besieged and besieger alike, and peasants fleeing from the Island managed to pass through the siege ring and into the city by water, foodstuffs that had become rare, such as fruit, vegetables, eggs, and *Glumse*, reappeared in the half-starved city; and early in September Sophie began to hope that certain mushrooms she had ordered would be delivered. Her hate had boiled down to a recipe.

Yes, Ilsebill. We, too, know that. When we wear love with the lining on the outside. When at last we cut holes in, and therefore see through each other. When everything and its opposite narrow down to a single point. When we—repairing to the woods again—look no longer for the incomparably beau-

364

tiful idea but for its opposite, which also has its beauty—hate disguised as a mushroom stands on a moss floor and under oaks—quite unmistakable.

And incidentally the Flounder, called by Rapp when the midsummer floods reached the city, is believed to have warned the governor of the dying Republic of Danzig, "My son! Careful at the table. All calf's-head stuffing is not equally wholesome."

Searching for similar mushrooms

A litter of puffballs
successfully found,
close by.

When I was proved right,
I gave up everything else
for lost.

This hat fits
a head shorter
to a T.

Take it diffusely;
even the light
will swindle its way through.

True, they are puffballs,
but the wrong ones
exactly.

Hidden under sorrel

One March evening, though a northwesterly wind, blowing in squalls of up to hurricane force, was battering at the house, we had invited guests, failing to suspect that the ferry service across the Stör might be suspended. Only when the village siren reminded us of wartime and we saw the volunteer firemen bucking the wind, when the openings in the dikes, including the big gate leading to the ferry, were closed, when the old-timers in Kröger's store said high tide might bring something as bad as in '62, when under low-racing clouds the village cowered behind the dikes, because the wind squalls were rising to hurricane force, making the light flicker and cutting the electric stove off for minutes at a time, only when one of the young birches in the garden snapped, did my Ilsebill realize that we had put on three plates too many.

Already she was making a face as though behind closed shutters. Already, as a feminine answer to nature's apocalyptic mood, a house-filling migraine, a shattering of glasses, seemed to be in the offing. New, hair-thin cracks in the plaster. Our guests phoned to say they couldn't come. Storm warnings on the radio. Road cut off at Wedel. Damn shame. They'd been looking forward.

We'd been going to have potatoes and rutabaga with flank of mutton, a dish into which Amanda Woyke (and later Lena Stubbe) liked to stir diced sweet-and-sour squash at the end. Crushed pepper, allspice, fresh marjoram, and three cloves of garlic go into this one-dish meal for damp, cold days.

Already feeling very lonely among the gleaming plates, I consoled myself—or was it the Flounder who spoke to me? "Come on," he said. "Stormy weather and migraine are only half the story. How often the Vistula used to flood. Why shouldn't the Elbe and the Stör? Let your Ilsebill lie in a half-darkened chamber and shroud herself in gloom. Even without ferry service, guests come from afar. In Awa's day the women of the neighborhood came with honeycombs and dried morels. When Wigga cooked manna grits for the Goitches, as you used to call the Goths, until they were fed

366

up and shoved off on their so-called migration. And when the Bohemian prelates and Polish knights were treated to wild boar with cranberries. When Dorothea served Scania herring to the four dignitaries, though it wasn't Friday. When Sophie seasoned the meal she prepared for the governor's guest with political mushrooms: what a feast! Not one of the guests left as he had come. Just keep open house, my son, for new guests will come, even if the ferry isn't running. Stiff-legged, with creaking sound effects, they are leaving mass graves, archives, and altars. Pleasantly hungry they are, and fat with stories. Mother Rusch has just roasted seventy-nine Easter lambs from the sheep farms of Schiedlitz and Scharpau over charcoal for Ferber the rich patrician, who has invited abbots, Polish nobles, and others. You'd better warm the plates, because mutton fat leaves a film in cooling. But quietly, so as not to disturb your Ilsebill in her torture chamber . . ."

He talks in pious adages. "Guests," he says, "are nothing more than stretched soups, spice of sorts, the unavoidable extra helping; it's the stupider ones who come too late."

Thinking up guests: historical, contemporary, future. When Agnes cooked for Opitz, and the Silesian refugees sat starved at his table, babbling vale-of-tears poetry. One time Amanda cooked a mountain of mashed potatoes for me and my last remaining war comrades and sprinkled bits of bacon out of the pan over them: a meal for old soldiers. And one day (without exactly consulting Ilsebill) I will invite Associate Judge Griselde Dubertin of the Women's Tribunal for a mushroom dish. And in our present situation the manna grits of famine days might come in . . .

Outside, the hurricane squalls began to lose heart. The wind shifted to the west. March rain. Warm with schnapps, the volunteer firemen came from the dike gates. My Ilsebill doffed her migraine, clothed herself festively in fly-agaric red, and said: "Let's eat by ourselves. What do we need guests for? Can't we manage, just you and me? Does there always have to be a big crowd, followed by two full dishwashers? Those neurotic city slickers. With their everlasting marriage and tax problems. Let 'em stay in Hamburg. I'd rather you told me about Sophie."

This was her plan: to serve up a calf's head stuffed with mushrooms. She was famous for her stuffed calf's head. And over the years Governor Rapp's regular guests had come to trust the dishes she made with honey tufts, millers, egg mushrooms, milk caps, and imperial mushrooms. Unsuspectingly they spooned up dark mushroom soups with rabbits' innards and even abandoned the precaution—after all, they were deep in enemy territory—of having the domestics taste their food for them.

Sophie got the calf's head from the allied Westphalian troops, whose stables were situated in Kneipab, beyond range of the Prussian batteries and protected by the Bear and Renegade bastions. The quartermasters never protested, for the governor's kitchen squad was entitled to requisition from army units as well as from the civilian population. After all, Westphalian and Polish officers were among the regularly invited guests.

It was more difficult to bring wild mushrooms into the besieged city. The midsummer floods helped. Since the Russians were still allowing fugitives from the flooded Island to pass through their lines into the Lower City, Sophie was able to make an arrangement with the Kashubian raftsmen. Coming from Petershagen by raft, the fugitives had to pay five Prussian ducats each, half of which went to the Russian outposts, while the French commander of the Gertrud Bastion demanded one ducat a head. In return for the governor's written authorization of this refugee trade, the (in principle) neutral Kashubians supplied, for money or confiscated English cloth, what the cook Sophie Rotzoll required: in the early fall, partridges, hares, deer that had been shot in the woods between the lakes for the governor's table, little baskets of cranberries, plums, and edible mushrooms. Until one day Sophie, having made her plan, sent her cousin Lovise at the Oliva forester's lodge a secret message, asking for special mushrooms. The usual shopping list—fresh butter, pullet's eggs, *Glumse*, sorrel, and dill—included certain old Kashubian words.

Eighteen thirteen. A mushroom year. Like Sophie, her cousin knew all the edible, unpalatable, and poisonous varieties. She knew where they grew on moss or pine needles, in clearings or in underbrush, singly or in magic circles. As children we had often gone mushrooming, with Sophie in the lead. When her grandmother Amanda Woyke was still alive. Out on the front porch she taught Sophie and Lovise to recite the names of all the mushrooms.

This is the dark horn of plenty. It grows under beeches and

tastes good. This is the broad-brimmed hawk mushroom; it loses its bitter taste when blanched, and it's very good for you. This is a greenie, but it has other names. These are tree mushrooms; the trunks of alders and poplars are sometimes full of them, and they're good for flavoring soups. This is the cep, also known as the imperial mushroom. It stands alone. And it's good luck to find one. (The fly agaric shows you where to look.) This thin one is anise agaric; Grandmother used to pickle them in vinegar for the inspector of crown lands. This is orange agaric. They have crumbly, hollow stems, they grow under young pines, and they taste like veal. This beauty is a parasol mushroom. Everybody knows them. Fairy tales happen under their umbrellas. They protect you from the evil eye. If you eat them raw, they taste like nuts. This is the honey tuft; they grow in clusters. They don't come up until late fall, and they don't agree with everybody. Ink caps (very tasty) grow in the rubble along the monastery wall. Greenies are sandy and need to be washed thoroughly. And these here are morels; we string them like beads or spit them on thorny branches to dry, and then we flavor our winter soups with them. And these are the political mushrooms: the names are sulfur tuft, panther cap, destroying angel, and deadly amanita.

Autumn 1813. Sophie knew the time had come. For years she had been including revenge for her imprisoned Fritz in her evening prayers, just before the amen, but it took her a long time to decide what special ingredients she should add to the mushroom stuffing of her calf's head to be sure of the effect. The panther cap wrecks the nervous system, often with fatal results. The sulfur tuft contains the poison muscarine, and so does the destroying angel, but in stronger concentration. The deadly amanita, which has a faint, sweetish smell and tends to grow under oak trees, destroys the blood corpuscles, but not until twenty-four hours later, when it has long been digested, or so one would suppose.

Sophie decided to use them all. Along with a basket of magnificent, almost maggotless imperial mushrooms, her cousin Lovise at the forester's lodge sent her the requested varieties wrapped in a knotted cloth. And because fly agaric acts as a stimulant, she put in two young, still bulb-shaped specimens. In addition, the Kashubian raftsmen, who were still carrying fugitives from the flooded Island to the besieged city, brought a basket of otherwise unobtainable sorrel and fresh parsley. As for the Westphalian calf's head, the kitchen squad had requisitioned it the day before. (All the butter, eggs, and *Glumse* had been taken by the Russians.) The calendar read September 26.

During the day the Prussian batteries in Aschbude and Schellmühle had set the Dominican monastery on fire with red-hot cannon balls and Congreve rockets. Advancing from Ohra amid light musket fire, the Russians had attacked the outworks of the star redoubt. But Major Le Gros, who was one of the invited dinner guests, had thrown the Russians back with canister shot before they could reach the palisades.

Always when Sophie prepared a calf's head for Governor Rapp and his guests, either to be stuffed or to be served in sour herb jelly, she obtained as a by-product soup for her special boarders. Behind the governor's house on the Long Garden, standing white in the late summer shade of lindens and maples, beyond range of the allied batteries, the hungry children of the Wicker Bastion came crawling through the bushes, rattling their bowls.

After removing the cushions of skin, the fat cheeks, the embedded eyes, the ears, and the soft mouth from the bone with a short, sharp knife, after detaching the tongue, spooning the brains out of the split skull, stuffing the boned calf's-head casing with the precooked tongue, the brains, the chopped onion, and the mushrooms cut in slices, and sewing it up, Sophie boiled the removed bones, in other words, the calf's upper and lower jaws, with barley and lovage until the bones were bare and flat, deep-rooted molars as well as the long front teeth of the lower jaw were easily pulled. They looked nice. And with the thick barley soup, which she poured over the fence into tin bowls, Sophie gave the Wicker Bastion children long, fat calves' teeth, which were good for earache, gave you sweet dreams, protected you from flying lead, gave strength to your first, second, and third wish at the time of the full moon, and in general made for happiness.

Many years later, when old Fräulein Rotzoll was buried in the graveyard of Saint Barbara's, the mourners included several sedate ladies and gentlemen who still carried those calves' teeth as good-luck charms in their handbags or tobacco pouches. During the siege, they said—though none of the children wanted to hear about the siege—when hunger had settled in every neighborhood, when after the dogs the rats were eaten, when even human flesh (Cossacks who had gone astray on patrol) was sold in the market as pork goulash, a pound for twelve groschen, while horse meat was selling for eleven groschen, an angel—yes, an angel, though the city women called her "Rapp's whore"—saved us from starvation with her thick soups.

Sophie never gave the governor or his guests any calves' teeth. Every day Rapp had guests at table, sometimes few, sometimes many. In the years before the siege he received quite a few celebrities, such as Murat, Berthier, Talleyrand, the future prince Bernadotte. But he also invited selected city notables, to whom, after dinner, he served up the bill for their "contribution." On several occasions Pastor Blech had been the governor's sole guest. The two men got along nicely as long as the conversation revolved around the ifs and buts of the revolutionary years, Sophie's cookery, or most knowledgeably, the growing of roses.

After dinner Blech always submitted a petition for the pardon of his former pupil Friedrich Bartholdy, who by then was well into his second decade as a prisoner in the fortress of Graudenz. But Rapp rejected all petitions, alleging that Europe must first be at perfect peace. As long as England failed to knuckle under, as long as Schill's bands were fomenting insurrection, as long as the emperor was being defied in the mountains of Spain and elsewhere, a pardon was not to be expected, for law and order must be demonstrated incontrovertibly. Rapp also gave the pastor to understand that the virginal pride of his cook, Sophie—since it was on her behalf that the pastor wrote his petitions—forced him to be hard. Yes, yes, why not admit it, he was mad about the obstinate creature; no fort had ever resisted him like Sophie. He didn't expect her to love him as she loved her imprisoned Fritz. But a man of his stamp couldn't be warmed by her everlasting "no." If she wanted her man back, she should just open up a bit for him, the governor. What he asked was only natural and would be fun for both parties.

Pastor Blech never came to dinner again after that. And Sophie, who wanted to keep her virginity for Fritz, stopped putting in her petitions. But it was only when Rapp had returned from Moscow and recovered from his frostbite, when the city was encircled and besieged by Prussians and Russians, when the people of the city were gouged, humiliated, exposed to the outrageous demands of the *commissaires* and (within plain sight of the still-banqueting French) to merciless hunger, that she made up her mind. In the early fall she wrote to her cousin Lovise and soon received, buried in sorrel, the desired ingredients: mushrooming hate.

Here's how we see her: still girlish, though, with her thirty years, old enough to be a matron. Head slightly tilted over the imperial mushrooms. Her peat-brown hair, plaited into a kind of bird's nest. Eyes close-set. Two vertical creases in her forehead underline her determination. An acute angle. Her nose. Her small mouth whistling kitchen songs. Now she cuts an imperial mushroom into slices from stem to cap. Not a one is discolored. How lovely they are. Silence in the kitchen. The whistling has stopped. Now she puts on her spectacles. Produces something from under the sorrel.

On September 26, when Sophie stuffed a boned calf's head with mushrooms in such a way that it resumed its full-rounded form, the guests were the heroic French major Le Gros, a Saxon merchant by the name of Zetsche, and three Polish officers, one of them being a young uhlan, the son of General Wojczinski. The company was in high spirits and made a great fuss over Le Gros, whose cannoneers had repulsed a Russian attack on the star redoubt. The first course—in view of wartime shortages—was a simple sorrel soup with flour dumplings. Then Sophie served smoked Vistula salmon, which was always available because the midsummer floods had driven pike, salmon, and perch into the ditches and gutters of the besieged city. Then, emerging crisp from the oven, accompanied by the saffron rice with which the Neapolitan allies were constrained to supply the governor's table, came the calf's head, whose stuffing Sophie, by way of avenging the betrayed revolution, the years of tyranny, the insults to her virginal pride, and her imprisoned Fritz, had seasoned with four definitive arguments. (A small amount of fly-agaric juice may have been stirred into the sorrel soup as a stimulant.)

Actually she felt no loathing for Rapp. It would be more accurate to speak of indifference and vicarious hate. He wasn't the worst of them. He kept the looting within limits. He punished the depredations of drunken soldiers severely. For a few months—while Rapp was in Russia with Napoleon—the citizens had longed for his return. At least—and here Pastor Blech agreed—Rapp kept order. That he, too, confiscated a fortune, that he had a hand in the general profiteering and traded through middlemen (among them the merchant Zetsche) in confiscated English contraband (mostly cloth), that before the siege he had kept mistresses on country estates in Langfuhr and Oliva and beset the wives of leading citizens with his spicy Alsatian wit—all this would not have sufficed to decide Sophie in favor of her sure-fire calf's-head stuffing; something must have happened to release the catch.

Though he doesn't mention it in his journals of the French period, Pastor Blech later expressed the belief that shortly before the siege, when the road to Graudenz was still open, Sophie had crawled into the governor's bed in the hope of obtaining her Fritz's freedom. But Rapp hadn't been up to it. Couldn't convert his frantic desire into action. Couldn't bend nature to his will. The standard male calamity had struck. His private just wouldn't stand at attention. Possibly it was Sophie's innocence that disarmed this eminently virile man. In any case, so the story went, she left the governor's couch still a virgin and doubly offended.

Rapp wouldn't admit his defeat; he put all the blame on Sophie (her heroic coldness) and was quite unwilling to compensate with an act of chivalry for the bit of pleasure he had missed. So Fritz remained a prisoner of the French. And when Graudenz fell into Prussian hands, a royal decree lost no time in confirming his status as prisoner. The systems changed without a hitch. Petition after petition—Pastor Blech remained indefatigable—failed to set the poor fellow free.

But maybe there's nothing in the whole story; probably Sophie never crawled into Rapp's French bed; conceivably there wasn't any male calamity, and what she did wasn't for Fritz at all but for the sake of something much bigger, of freedom itself, for, Jacobin as this kitchenmaid may have been in her younger days, the lasting presence of the French turned her into the most German of patriots, and when she'd been cooking a while for Rapp, Sophie's sans-culottish songs, after a brief period of Napoleonic enthusiasm, took on a fatherlandish tone. Maybe the four sure-fire mushrooms were dedicated to the variety of diffuse freedom that lasts only as long as a song in several stanzas supplies a cramped soul with air. In any event, the Flounder's "personalist" interpretation was contradicted before the Women's Tribunal. Sophie, as Associate Judge Griselde Dubertin, concurring with the prosecution, declared, acted not out of childish love, but for the sake of freedom. For reasons of principle.

After the soup the company was already in high spirits. Over the smoked salmon jokes passed around the table. The stuffed calf's head was easily cut in slices. Rapp served his guests. All ate; only the general held back. Ah, how beautiful life was! The Polish uhlan praised the stuffing. The Westphalian colonel asked for a second helping. Le Gros gobbled and for the third time related his morning victory over the Russians. Dressed in English cloth from top to toe, Zetsche the Saxon merchant talked and talked with his mouth full. Rapp didn't want to overtax his stomach at the evening meal; after the soup and salmon, only a spoonful of saffron rice and the barest morsel of the crispy calf's muzzle. He encouraged his guests to eat their fill and join him in drinking to the emperor, to France, and to this bounteous mushroom year.

When Count Wojczinski pressed him to take a little something, he helped himself from the top of the dish to a calf's eye, a traditional delicacy. Vivats and flowery phrases followed. Already voices were rising. Merchant Zetsche praised the Continental Blockade as if a shrewd Saxon had thought it up. The Westphalian had started talking more than he meant to. The Poles had begun to sing. Le Gros was quoting himself and other heroes.

And knowing the governor's guests and their liking for riddles and charades, Sophie, before putting the stuffed calf's head in the oven, had incised the date of the Revolution, the present date, and, in tiny letters, the initials of her friend Fritz in each of the fat cheeks, and tinted the incisions with saffron. Crisp-roasted skin announced the date at which the youth of Europe had conceived hope. Some of the gentlemen, who knew Sophie's undiminished esteem for the heroes of the Revolution, joked, but within tactful limits. Young Count Wojczinski even delivered himself of an enthusiastic speech in praise of Mirabeau. Another of the Polish uhlans countered with sayings of Robespierre. Danton and Saint-Just were cited. Gironde and the Mountain, the Convention before and after the September murders, argued over minimum and maximum. And Marat proclaimed the despotism of freedom.

But while, stimulated by the fly agaric in the soup, they were still re-enacting the Revolution with argument, counterargument, and mimed reminiscences of the guillotine, at the same time trying to guess whom the initials F. B. incised in the calf's head might stand for—Rapp, who had a strong suspicion, kept aloof from the conversation—muscarine, the mushroom poison specific to the sulfur tuft and the destroying angel, began to take effect. A slight twitching of the facial muscles. Dilated pupils. Outbreaks of sweat. Zetsche and the Westphalian had their eyes crossed. Fuddled hand movements. Glasses were knocked over. Le Gros's heroic stutter. Then the panther cap induced quarrelsome agitation—in everyone except Rapp. At first the remarks about the relationship between the Committee of Public Safety and the guillotine had been rather good-natured, but now national antagonisms erupted. Poland accused France of betrayal. Saxony called the Rhenish Confederation a shame and a disgrace. Since words could no longer be uttered and weapons were absent from the table, the patriots brandished bottles and the carving knife. Chairs fell backward. No sooner had the Saxon contemptuously spat out the words "fat slob," than the beefy Westphalian was at his throat. Aghast, Rapp moved out of the way but neglected to summon the watch. Nevertheless, he grabbed a heavy silver candlestick to defend himself with, for suddenly, after Le Gros had cut down one of the Polish uhlans with the carving knife, Count Wojczinski tore some ornamental cavalry sabers off the wall. The Westphalian released the strangled Zetsche and impaled himself on a saber Le Gros had picked up. Next the heroic colonel struck the second uhlan down. Then, staring into empty space, Le Gros and Wojczinski, their nervous systems shattered and their tongues paralyzed, dispatched each other—pierced and tattered, they lay clutching each other in a last convulsive embrace.

Only Rapp, with his candlestick, was still standing. The flames died down. Not the faintest stirring of life. The deadly amanita, which ordinarily takes effect the following day, would have no occasion to destroy any red blood corpuscles.

Then at last members of the house staff appeared, among them Sophie. The orderly officer summoned the watch. Rapp made a first report: six dead, including one civilian. By pure chance he himself had come off unharmed. What had started out as an innocent little quarrel among officers had ended tragically. Women, gambling debts, offended honor, especially the effrontery of the civilian, had lashed them—see for yourself—into a frenzy.

Then the governor tersely ordered a clean-up. The remains of the calf's head and stuffing were removed. The bodies were lined up and covered with cloths. Rapp left it to the orderly to supply the watch with further details. When Sophie's weeping threatened to look incriminating, he led his cook to the open terrace overlooking the garden and put his uniformed arm over her shoulder. She let him, possibly giving him some happiness.

A moonless night lay over the besieged city. The crackle of sporadic musket fire could be heard from the direction of Schellmühle. Just to annoy, the Prussian batteries were firing from Ohra, doing little damage. In the Old City, not far from Bucket Makers' Court, two houses were burning, throwing a side light on the Church of Saint John. Wind in the lindens, wind in the maples. The first leaves were falling. The garden smelled of autumn. Now Rapp, too, was in tears. While they were standing on the garden terrace, the governor of the Republic of Danzig, whose name is still borne by an avenue in Paris, advised his cook to take a few weeks off. The terrible scene, all that young blood, the lifeless rigidity of the twisted corpses, Wojczinski hacked to pieces—all that must have been a shock to her. An investigation was inevitable, and he didn't want her to be further tormented. Even if she, dear child, were innocent in a higher sense, they were likely to question her very severely. She could always count on his affection, even if she regarded him as an enemy and would not accept his love. Yes, he knew what had happened, and all things considered he was sorry he hadn't tried the calf's-head stuffing. A voice—Rapp wouldn't say from where—had forewarned him. Ah, if only he were her Fritz, imprisoned in the fortress. He hoped she, Sophie, would forgive him. He was only human. "Go now. I shall miss you."

And so it was that Sophie Rotzoll went underground. Pastor Blech knew a safe place for her. Soon the warehouses on Warehouse Island went up in flames. The blaze was believed to have been started not by enemy fire but by terrorist action. Rapp had few dinner guests after that.

Afraid

Shout, shout in the woods,
Mushrooms and fairy tales
are overtaking us.

Every bulb sprouts new terror.
Still under cover,
yet the funnels of fear round about
are already full up.

Someone has always been here.
Demolished bed—was it me?
My predecessor left nothing intact.

We distinguish tasty,
unpalatable, and poisonous mushrooms.
Many connoisseurs of mushrooms die young,
leaving well-filled notebooks behind them.

Milk cap morels destroying angels.

I gathered mushrooms with Sophie
before the emperor went to Russia.
I lost my spectacles
and used my thumb;
she kept finding and finding.

Three at table

No single one of them could ever hold me. I had dealings with them all, even with Helga Paasch when she was still selling the vegetables she raises in Britz from a stand at the Berlin weekly market, and for a whole season I got my rutabaga and carrots for practically nothing. My affair with Ruth Simoneit turned out badly, but it's not true that she started swilling first cognac, then cheap vermouth, on my account. With Sieglinde Huntscha I can do it any time. It's an old established habit, and I never dream about it. But one day when we were young and absent-minded, Bettina von Carnow and I almost got engaged, because of a damp, cold autumn mood. Hardly anything happened between Therese Osslieb and me, though I can well imagine a lingering fried-potato relationship. My esteem for Ms. Schönherr hasn't diminished over the years, even if she doesn't care to remember that night in Bielefeld (or was it Kassel?): "You must be mistaking me for someone else. Men with the collector's instinct are always doing that." Of course Ilsebill's suspicions are exaggerated, but I admit I like it best with Ulla Witzlaff. She keeps me stable-warm. Nothing is missing. Everything is possible. Her laughter would make a stone calve. We're happiest sitting in the kitchen. I must have been out of my mind the other day when I started something new—or, worse, warmed up something old.

We got to talking during a recess in the trial. Yes, yes, it's the case of Sophie Rotzoll that brought us back together. We behaved as if there were a possibility of starting up again, as if it were not completely over and done with. A pharmacist by trade, she, too, is an associate judge at the Women's Tribunal. Though a few years older than Ilsebill (who's just a bit matronly), Griselde will be girlish for years to come. Two or three more wrinkles around the eyes, a touch of bitterness at the corners of the mouth; otherwise she has hardly changed.

We've known each other since the days before the Wall. (When I was still more or less going with Sibylle Miehlau.) Though she thought me too solid in a masculine kind of way and therefore insensitive, we got along nicely for a time. Her periodic speeches of dismissal ended with sound observations such as "You've always got to be protective, carry suitcases, light cigarettes, the fatherly act." Unfortunately she's drawn to weak, inhibited types. So she shook me off and heroically sacrificed herself for a punk who was only interested in her drugstore and bank account, and who dropped her soon afterward to study theology at government expense. Then my affair with Billy foundered. And something else, I forget what, went wrong at the same time. Anyway, the whole thing had receded into the dim past, all I remembered was a vague misunderstanding, and then suddenly, when the case of Sophie Rotzoll was taken up, something in me began to tick. And Ilsebill, who always had a good nose for these things—Witzlaff was the only one she failed to suspect—flew into a rage: "First Simoneit, then Huntscha, with me pregnant, and I mean pregnant! And now this! That's why you're always going away. Back and forth, back and forth. I want a talk with her. Right away. Woman to woman. To get things straight. See?"

Resistance was unthinkable. "All right. We'll invite her. I'll cook something. Big three-way discussion. If she'll come. Ridiculous, this jealousy! When you know I'm always thinking of you . . ."

And so, because Ilsebill badgered me and wanted to get things straight "once and for all," I invited Griselde Dubertin (a Huguenot family from way back) to join us in a jellied calf's head: "Oh, come on. I'll pay for the plane and the train, too. You'll have to get acquainted some time." While I was at it, I should have crowded the whole lot of them around our table, Osslieb and Helga Paasch and even Ms. Schönherr and—so Ilsebill could finally get everything straight—Ulla Witzlaff as well; the expense be damned. I said as much to Ilsebill: "Why just Dubertin? That's water under the bridge. Why not Carnow and Paasch? All in the same dishwasher, Ilsebill! So you'll finally get it all straight!"

But she wanted to keep it intimate. We were three at table. Griselde came over the weekend. Just that Friday she had pronounced the Flounder guilty as a traitor and counterrevolutionary. Whereupon he once again played dead and (belly up) forced an adjournment of the Tribunal. The Flounder Party protested and demanded affidavits concerning the admissibility of special mushrooms as political weapons in the struggle for emancipation.

I asked Griselde to come in mystic green, because Ilsebill could be expected to wear fly-agaric red. I was looking forward to the discussion. And I was determined to make my jellied calf's head "à la Sophie" something special. But to tell the truth, I'd rather have hidden away in the kitchen with Witzlaff, within earshot of her serenely clicking knitting needles (knit two, purl two). Or concealed myself behind her church organ and had a real good cry, while she cut loose at the keys: "Out of the depths to Thee I cry. . . ." Or her voice—Lord, what a voice she has!—might have carried me over the Jordan: "Bitter tears and sorrow's breath, anguished yearning, fear and death . . ." For the business with Ruth Simoneit is still on my mind. Maybe she did start swilling vermouth on my account. And all I do with Griselde is talk and argue about the old days. And with Ilsebill, too, things are getting more and more difficult—these daily quarrels! The pleasure she takes in demolishing the man she loves. Her fury that redoubles after a brief pause, and all because she couldn't manage to get pregnant by herself without male help). And yet, as far as I'm concerned, now and forever, there's no one but Ilsebill Ilsebill. . . .

And then we were three at table. (As a present for Ilsebill, Griselde brought a whole pile of women's lib books: instructions for the new pecking order. For me she brought potholders: "For the cook!")

Much as I'd been looking forward to it, I did not enjoy that meal. The two of them hit it off on sight. They harmonized in color and voice. Before I brought on the jellied calf's head in its bowl and unmolded it unharmed onto a platter— how it shivered, how it shook!—the two of them had agreed that I never gave any more than a small fraction of myself. I could never fully make up my mind. I always had something else in view. "Subterfuges. His everlasting subterfuges! Right now, for instance! He's at it again!" cried Ilsebill. "Just look at him, Griselde. That snotty look in his face! He's not here at all. He's miles away. He's always got company in the back of his mind."

Nothing's allowed. Strict supervision. Stick to the point, don't digress, don't go into quick motion. But I refuse to sit here forever, in the present or immediate future. I've been invited to clear out, to chuck all this monetary crap, or, as Ilsebill puts it: "I guess you want to split again. To take a powder. I guess you're sick of me. And look at Griselde, who's taken this long trip just on your account; I guess you've had enough of her, too. I guess you've got a yen for something or somebody else."

The siege of the city, as Sophie wrote me in the fortress of Graudenz, where I had been imprisoned for sixteen years, had ended on November 29, although the occupying troops were staying on for another four weeks as a point of honor. Consequently the encirclement would also continue. But the most urgent necessities—syrup, potatoes, bacon, and manna grits—were being smuggled in at outrageous prices by way of the Prussian advance post on the Zigankenberg. Unfortunately the mushroom season was over. Yes, she'd been cooking for Rapp again lately, though without enthusiasm. After that dreadful massacre—even now no one could say what the fight had been about—she'd been pretty badly shocked at the sight of so much blood. ("Such young fellows they were.") So she'd given notice and gone to live in the Wicker Bastion. A little later all the French stores had caught fire. Exactly 197 warehouses had gone up in flames. An amazing sight. And a rumor was still going around that it was not enemy guns but patriots that had kindled the fire on Warehouse Island. She, too, Sophie, was under suspicion, but they had no proof. Evidently Rapp didn't want to lose her (as his cook). She was making big dinners again. The negotiations for the capitulation and the resulting festivities had brought Russian and Prussian officers to the house. Friend and foe were as gay as if 12,640 howitzer shells, Congreve rockets, and canisters of shot had been exchanged for the fun of it, as if half the garrison had not been carried off by epidemics or bullets. But since she often made jellied calf's head for these banquets, they yielded plenty of rich, meaty soup for the children of the Wicker Bastion. If only there were mushrooms. She'd have been only too glad to serve Rapp a last portion of good stuffing.

Then Sophie told me not to give up hope, for as soon as the city was liberated from the French, she would write a petition with her heart's blood: May the queen, who has known suffering, be merciful and release her dearly beloved Fritz from the damp, cold fortress where he's already been missing out on his youth for sixteen years, for he has long since repented. It was all a childish mistake. They'd been thinking of an entirely different freedom. . . .

But I was obliged to spend many another mushroom season in that damp, cold hole. (In the meantime I'd forgotten what for.) And to Griselde Dubertin I said, "I've cooked this jellied calf's head in honor of Sophie Rotzoll and let it gel all by itself, without gelatin." (No, no! I don't want to have been her conspiratorial Fritz, condemned to life imprisonment in the fortress.) To Ilsebill I said, "This Sophie was a really interesting case. Worked with mushroom poison, as the Flounder was able to prove." (I'd rather be Governor Rapp, who survived the stuffed calf's head and kept order to the end.) The pharmacist in Griselde now spoke. She expatiated on bacterial, vegetable, and animal poisons, so-called toxins: "Especially the mushroom poison muscarine, a small quantity of which is also present in fly agaric . . ." (Anyway, Rapp survived. And Pastor Blech wrote: "On January 2, the departure of the Poles was followed by that of the French, Neapolitans, Bavarians, and Westphalians. Still 9,000 strong, with 14 generals. Over 1,200 sick remained in the city. The officers kept their swords and equipment. At Oliva Gate the Bavarians, Westphalians, and Germans stepped out of the ranks and begged leave to return to the fatherland, there to fight against the common foe, which was granted them. . . .") And speaking (past me) to Ilsebill, Griselde repeated what she had said at the Women's Tribunal: "The Flounder betrayed Sophie. Rapp would never have survived the *Amanita phalloides*. The amanita toxin specific to it destroys the liver, kidneys, and red blood corpuscles, attacks the heart muscle. . . ." No, I don't want to have been Rapp, either. I'd rather just be Sophie's fatherly friend. When the terrible French period was over, she cooked for Pastor Blech again, cooked for him for twenty-five years, until the deacon died of old age. I wasn't Rapp (the traitor). And after Sophie had served me (the kindly pastor) jellied calf's head with tongue, sweetbreads, and capers, I wrote in celebration of a special day, "On March 29, the Royal Provincial and Municipal Court was established here; its first promulgation was an edict abolishing Napoleonic law."

We were three at table. Two women, one in her middle, the other in her late thirties, sat facing each other on the long sides, while I, after picking up the bowl and unmolding the jellied calf's head onto a platter, seated myself at one narrow end. (A triangle situation, they call it.)

Once the two of them had smilingly appraised each other and exchanged their first remarks about me, it became evident that I had (once again) bitten off more than I could chew. Where I sat there was obviously nothing, or possibly a hole, or, if you prefer, an exemplary something, which bore my name but was discussed for an hour and a half as

382

an anonymous "case," now with kindly forbearance—"It must have been the war years that brutalized him so"—now with severity—"He really belongs in an institution!" Every time agreement was expressed, mystic green and fly-agaric red harmonized, Griselde and Ilsebill touched fingertips or exchanged glances as though exchanging mother-of-pearl buttons. No loud effusions, but quiet, affectionate solidarity. How fervently they spoke: "Oh, how well I understand you! You've taken the words out of my mouth." "Oh, Griselde, your words are balm to my soul." "Oh, Ilsebill, how strong you are in your pregnancy."

Only cider and black bread were served with the calf's head, which was praised, to be sure, but without direct mention of the cook. I refilled the glasses, dished out, and kept silent, busy with thoughts of Sophie, of how her room under the eaves of Allmond House became a little temple to her hero Napoleon, where she worshiped him as she had previously worshiped Reason and Universal Enlightenment. (I had some difficulty in repressing a wish that Paasch might be sitting, peevish but just, across from me, or Witzlaff with her knit-two-purl-two stocking.)

I had made my dish with a halved calf's head, the calf's tongue and sweetbread, seasonings, and a special spice. In the cupboard I found two young, dried specimens of fly-agaric mushrooms left over from the previous fall. These I placed in a mortar and pounded to a powder, meanwhile lisping wishes, spitting out curses, and running in a zigzag (down the stairs of history): You won't destroy me, no, not me. . . .

When they had finished trying me, as it were, in absentia, the two women started in, both at once, on child rearing and the inadequacies of their dishwashers. Ilsebill called hers a bad buy. Griselde had (and expressed) her doubts about all pedagogy. I kept silent in thoughts of Sophie, who never stopped loving me, her Fritz, for immediately after the War of Liberation (which did nothing for me) she started petitioning for my pardon and kept sending me little packages of honey cake, into which she had baked finely ground fly agaric to cheer me up.

Then I served Ilsebill and Griselde another helping of quivering jelly. They agreed that though their dishwashers undoubtedly had their faults and though they'd obviously been had by the manufacturers, they would never, under any circumstances, go back to washing dishes by hand. They further agreed that anti-authoritarian methods of child rearing must, in principle, be retained. For one thing, there were no more authentic father figures. "How true!" That was my contribution, which went unheard.

No vinegar had gone into my jellied calf's head, only lemon. I boiled the halved head for a good two hours, the tongue for almost an hour and a half, and the sweetbread for just half an hour over medium heat. Only at the end, after detaching the meat from the bone, dicing it along with the tongue and sweetbread, and stirring capers, dill, and lemon juice into the broth, did I mix in the powdered fly agaric: an old Siberian recipe, known also to the Indo-Iranian conquerors of Dravidic India and to the Vikings. (Soon after the Mestwina period, for instance, the Varangians, before attacking the Prussians on the Hagelsberg, drank mares' urine after mixing fly agaric with the beasts' fodder; this is believed to have helped them to think up myths while the battle was still in progress; and similarly, the Indian Vedas were written under the influence of Soma, the mushroom of immortality, for fly agaric encourages travel, suspends time, removes all inhibitions, and makes us more real than we thought. . . .)

After the dishwasher as such and pedagogy in general had been disposed of, I again became a topic, though without being mentioned by name. It was always just "he." What he had done again. He always wants to. He thinks he's the only one who can. He regards himself as irresistible. He must, he is, he will, his big mistake is, he lacks all . . .

They put down my talent—which they did not question—to a congenital failing (and extenuating circumstances): "It's none of his doing. Something just keeps coming out of him. Even if it's only ironic or cockeyed. You should hear him talk about nature. Just no feeling for it. As far as he's concerned it's a catastrophe. And when something goes wrong—the other day we were out of toilet paper, for instance—he thinks it's the apocalypse. Just like a man."

Then my political work was judged: all the projects I (he) had bungled despite the best of intentions. Which was only natural since I (he) could never make up my (his) mind; it was always on the one hand and on the other hand. My (his) absurd dislike of ideology had become an ideology with me (him). "Too bad. You know, Griselde, one really can't help feeling sorry for him, the way he shilly-shallies and doesn't know how or what, and casts about helplessly for excuses, mostly historical. If I, for instance, say 'dishwasher,' he says, 'But in the fourteenth century . . .' "

After that they agreed that because of my talent on the one hand—"He's always got to be doing something!"—and my political excursions on the other—"He was always away, on the road somewhere!"—his (my) children were neglected, always had been. Then for the first time (when the fly agaric had gently dispatched me on voyages) they both began charging me with long-past crimes, holding me responsible for the Baroque poet Opitz's illegitimate brats (the unpaid alimony) and for the death from starvation of the farm cook Amanda Woyke's babies during the Seven Years' War. "No wonder," said Griselde or Ilsebill, "that he got to be interchangeable as a male partner. The nun, for instance, only tolerated him in her bed and kitchen as a visitor who'd have to take flight any minute."

When the two of them had reconstructed their and other women's present and past elations with me, Ilsebill said, "He hasn't changed much." And Griselde Dubertin, who had known me longer than Ilsebill likes, said, "He'll never change."

That's a fact. It's that early imprinting. Anyone who has learned fear from Dorothea of Montau, anyone who has been immersed in Fat Gret's stable-warmth will fear for all time, will look for all-embracing warmth, if only in the chaotic kitchen of an otherwise well-tempered organist.

My jellied calf's head was also the consequence of early imprinting—by Sophie Rotzoll, who cooked it for me to build me up when at last I was released from the fortress of Graudenz in the early summer of 1835. I was still in my fifties, but already an old man. Fräulein Rotzoll on the other hand, was still in many ways a young girl. And like Sophie I seasoned my jelly with capers, gherkins, dill, and lemon, and with a bit of powder made it—for we now know what fly agaric can do—deeply meaningful and hallucinogenic. You observe yourself. Wide awake, you lie side by side with yourself. You are sheltered in Awa. And around you moist and warm the cavern arches. . . .

Was it Ilsebill or Griselde who first brought up my mother complex? (Or was it Paasch who peevishly, Osslieb who sleepily, Huntscha who snottily, Ruth Simoneit who drunkenly butted in, as though invited to share in the calf's head?) Anyway, Ilsebill said, "He's got one, all right. It's gilt-edged."

After Helga Paasch (with Iron Age arguments) had uncovered this aspect of my existence, Griselde Dubertin—at variance with Witzlaff, who had said, "So what!"—disposed of me once and for all: "In any case, just about everything in his character can be laid to his extreme mother fixation. Just look at him. He's getting wrinkles, but he's still the same breast-fed baby."

Ulla Witzlaff, supported by Osslieb and Helga Paasch (and wasn't Ms. Schönherr also on the table?), pointed out that my undeniable talent necessitated a neurotic hang-up of this kind. Bettina von Carnow listed artists with similar complexes: "The great Leonardo was suckled by a goat!" Ruth Simoneit babbled, "Aren't we all sucking babes?" But Ilsebill and Sieglinde Huntscha cried, "He's still attached to his umbilical cord! It's got to be cut!"

And then this Griselde Dubertin, in whom I had foolishly looked for my Sophie, blabbed what I (like an idiot) had said to her in confidence: "Him? He'll never go to a psychiatrist. He told me so last week. He was foaming at the mouth: 'He'll never get me on his couch. Nobody but me is going to cash in on my mother complex! I'm going to put that in my will. I mean to die uncured. And on my tombstone they can write: Here lies So-and-so with his mother complex!'"

Everybody at the table laughed at me. Typical, said Ilsebill. Witzlaff smiled because she knew more. Dubertin said, "Why not, if that's what he wants." And Ms. Schönherr, who, I'm sure, was enjoying my special jellied calf's head, spoke for the lot of them (I know, because Osslieb and Witzlaff nodded) when she said, "A common case of arrested development."

Then I spoke up. The Devil in the form of fly agaric must have got into me, for suddenly I broke the silence that had been imposed on me and said, more to Ms. Schönherr than to Griselde Dubertin, though I was thinking of Witzlaff, even if I looked my Ilsebill square in the eye (and under the table fished for Ruth Simoneit with my left foot, to which Osslieb responded): "Actually, dearest Ilsebill, Sophie Rotzoll, to whom I am indebted for our jellied calf's head, never gave up. Year after year, whenever she could get permission, she went to Graudenz and pleaded with her Fritz to stick it out.

She sent gingerbread and honey cake with love letters baked in. She sent petitions to Queen Luise. She pleaded on bended knee, she did everything in her power, until at last he was free. And then she cared for me and went mushrooming with me, as in our early youth, when I still had an idea. . . ."

I don't believe the far too many women at the table were listening. Still laughing at me—"There *is* something lovable about his childishness"—they confirmed one another in their opinions: He's always kidding himself; his dread of conflict keeps him from working out his conflicts; that's why his stomach is starting to rumble again; he's always making part payments, never the whole amount; now the poor fellow has again bitten off more than he can chew (Griselde); he can't bear to lose anything or any one of them (not even Ruth Simoneit), he wants to keep them all, even Helga Paasch, same as those glasses he collects; in short, he's impossible, a typical male.

Then, as sisterly as could be, they drank my health and, this time mentioning the cook by name, praised my jellied calf's head; it was really something special, they agreed.

By way of enriching the potato-fixated Amanda cult, Therese Osslieb promised to add jellied calf's head à la Sophie to the menu of her restaurant. At that Ilsebill asked the assembled associate judges of the Women's Tribunal for the latest news of the Sophie Rotzoll case: "He only tells me the parts he figures in. Couldn't you give me a little inside dope? I'm so curious. Tell me, Griselde, will the Flounder get his comeuppance this time?"

Although she has children by her husband, from whom she lives separated by the distance between two different neighborhoods of the same city, and although she has had a succession of short-term affairs with other men, there is something virginal about her. That's why I felt called upon to look for Sophie in her, not the childlike Sophie (grave face under mushroom hat), but the slightly wrinkled kitchenmaid after her return to the parsonage. Sophie was then in her early thirties, unhinged by her experiences of the French period; there was often a look of dread in her eyes, as though she kept seeing horrible things, and in that she resembled Griselde Dubertin, pharmacist and associate judge of the Women's Tribunal, who had also been terrified (by some private experience), for which reason she often lost the thread and now fed Ilsebill's hunger for information with contradictory statements, which were interrupted by Helga Paasch and Ruth Simoneit.

She was talking about the poisonous sulfur tuft and the deadly amanita. On the one hand she firmly rejected political murder by toxins as a means of female emancipation; then, in the next breath, she recommended a politically effective mushroom dish as an instrument of feminine self-liberation. "But not in the hands of a bungler like Rotzoll," Sieglinde Huntscha carped. And Ruth Simoneit snarled, "I'm for firearms. Out in the open! Bang bang!"

When Paasch called Sophie a silly goose with nothing in her head but her Fritz, Griselde stared at me as though seeing me in the governor's uniform and cried, "Poison's the only way! If I had a Fritz in prison, I'd take up mushroom lore myself. But I wouldn't bungle!" And then she protested that despite this Sophie's patent servitude, her act had advanced the cause of freedom. "Why, even the Flounder doesn't deny that; in fact, he takes all the blame on himself. The rotter!" To avoid worse disasters, he had caused the Jacobin Club on Beutlergasse to be raided. "The traitor!" And at his instigation, Pastor Blech had informed the town constables.

"There you have it," Paasch put in. "He hates childish playing at revolution."

Possibly Bettina von Carnow thought she was distributing good cheer when she said, "But after forty years of fidelity our dear Sophie got her Fritz, all the same."

Before Griselde could resort to violence, Witzlaff appeased the rising tumult. "Not a word against Sophie and Fritz. Think of those two old folks waddling out to gather mushrooms. What a touching pair they must have been!"

You kept tugging at my sleeve. But our time was past. True, the mushrooms seemed to be growing for us alone, but the idea, had gone by, or it had a different name; it no longer stood on one leg but was mounted—there was talk of the *Weltgeist* on horseback. We never met him in the woods. Only ourselves. That's why we gathered fly agaric. They're special. They make for images. They pay back time. Without removing the skin or stems, you cut them into slices and pound them into a powder that you stir into soups, cake dough, or meat jelly. Or you don't pound anything into a

388

powder, but keep the tough, leathery, fingernail-sized slivers, take one from time to time in the morning or evening, and chew it until images come, until time pays itself back, until Sophie and I go gathering mushrooms again like children, go gathering mushrooms deep in the woods and get an idea.

Old Fräulein Rotzoll and I made a living from the mushrooms we gathered, dried, pounded to powder, and pickled in vinegar. Not far from Hawker's Gate, where Sophie had sold flounders as a child, we were authorized to keep a stand twice a week. Strings of greenies and dried morels found purchasers all year round. From nettle cloth left by Sophie's grandmother, I made little sacks (I had learned to sew in Graudenz) in which to sell dried ceps and orange agaric. And from early summer until November, we picked baskets full of table and soup mushrooms and sold them. We did all right financially, for we had mushrooms to offer at all times, either fresh or dried. Our clientele—students at the gymnasium, lieutenants of the Body Hussars, and liberal schoolteachers—were lovers of travel and fireside escapism. And of course there were also shriveled old people, like Sophie and me, who took some of our fly agaric—which also had its beauty—because they wanted their time paid back in images.

Then, as three of us (but along with many more) ate my jellied calf's head, Griselde Dubertin (and the other associate judges) reported the day-to-day happenings at the Women's Tribunal. Tales of the feminist movement's internal tensions were told out of school. The Flounder Party was vilified, and increasing collusion, possibly a conspiracy, between the accused Flounder and Sieglinde Huntscha, the prosecutor, was hinted at. Once again strife was in the cards. At issue (between Griselde and Osslieb) was the Flounder's assertion that Sophie Rotzoll and her friend Friedrich Bartholdy had all their lives been addicted to fly agaric, and moreover that Sophie had done a thriving trade—even by mail and through middlemen—in powdered fly agaric.

This assertion had provoked a tumult at the Tribunal. The Flounder's testimony about Sophie's "trips" had been corroborated by a special affidavit on "The Stimulating Effects of Fly Agaric"; and this affidavit would have been publicly read but for the objection of Ms. Schönherr, the presiding judge. "Schönherr was perfectly right," cried Griselde. "Fly-agaric trips might have become fashionable. The bourgeois press is just waiting for us to lay ourselves open. And I'm sure Sophie would have been against it, too."

Then they all got together and concentrated on me. They agreed that I'd been neither Sophie's Fritz, nor Pastor Blech, nor Governor Rapp; no, I—"the shit!"—had actually been Sophie's father, an itinerant schnapps dealer, who had cheated the poor Kashubian countryfolk and in passing, so to speak, knocked up Amanda Woyke's youngest daughter. "The heel!" I was the one and only villain. "Hateful! Worthless! Lousy! Superfluous!" And Dubertin shouted, "Let's show him! Let's show the bastard!"

Already the girls were assuming menacing postures. Already I was invaded by fear. Already all escape was barred. Already I was expecting to be drawn and quartered. Pins and needles in the groin. (Didn't Simoneit cry out, "Quick, the carving knife!"?) And then I was saved by fly agaric.

For in the meantime, thanks to the special ingredient, our meal for three had taken on a new dimension. Not only were the complete Flounder Party—so it seemed to me—and Schönherr, the personified authority of the Women's Tribunal, sitting at the table along with Paasch, Osslieb, and Witzlaff; in addition, Agnes Kurbiella and Amanda Woyke, Mother Rusch, Saint Dorothea, and Sophie Rotzoll had escaped from their time-phases. The morose Wigga sat facing Paasch. My Mestwina was comforting Ruth Simoneit. All had their doubles and vice versa. The table had grown. And, miraculously multiplied, my jellied calf's head filled several bowls. And always there was more. Time-suspending talk. Witzlaff's laugh mingled with Mother Rusch's laughter. And somewhere, no, everywhere, was Awa, the three-breasted principle, just as Ms. Schönherr was everywhere with her tender loving care. It was she who saw to it that no harm befell me. She allowed no quarrel to rise among the women, though the air still crackled alarmingly where Huntscha and Dorothea were sitting side by side. Only a moment before, Sophie or Griselde had been about to assault if not me, then gentle Agnes or poor Bettina von Carnow. Hadn't I seen scratch marks? Weren't there tufts of hair—blond, peat-brown, curly, waved—lying between the half-empty plates? (Witzlaff and Mother Rusch stood there like flaming Furies, determined to protect me.)

But then, after a few tears had flowed, female solidarity won out. Sisterly chitchat about potato prices in one epoch or another. They bemoaned the high price of Scania herring and the perpetual shortage of millet. And they tested their wit on me, the kindly paterfamilias, the dope, the provider, the eternal braggart. And suddenly an organ, or better still a kitchen–living room harmonium, was there beside the table. And Witzlaff was pulling the stops while Mother Rusch sang with Agnes and Sophie, "King of heaven, we welcome Thee." My Mestwina was passing amber charms around. And the Flounder was there, too. Splashing in the kitchen sink, beside the dishwasher. Nasally pontificating: "In short, dear ladies, before male hegemony, which has seen its day, is replaced by female management . . ."

Time paid itself back. Images flowed free. Awa bowed down. And I, the male, the priceless individual, was sheltered in loving care. I lay in the bosom of my pregnant Ilsebill and sucked at her big breasts; sated, at peace, safe, happy, wishless as never before. . . .

But when the fly agaric withdrew its effects, when happiness had lost its afterglow, when from our respective time-phases we relapsed into the flat present, when we sat shivering in the real world and all our dreams were spent, nothing was left of the jellied calf's head. In a bad humor again, my Ilsebill (in red) wanted nothing but a hot bath. Griselde Dubertin (in green) looked severe and spinsterish. Again they talked past me as if I'd been nothing, though they were referring to me when they said, "He's thought it all out, but he's got another think coming. He wants to cook us all up in jelly. We'll have to keep a tight rein on him. A little reminder, that's what he needs. We'll make him pay for all this. And no shilly-shallying. The first of every month."

When I tried to conclude the meal with a little conciliatory speech—"My dear sisters of one century after another, I've really enjoyed cooking my special calf's head for you and . . ." —Ilsebill coldly cut my thread: "If cooking gives you such fiendish pleasure, you can load the dishwasher, too."

So I loaded the dishwasher. There were more than three plates. More than a dozen knives and forks. No end of dishes. And thirteen glasses with small amounts of cider swishing around in them. Griselde gave me token help. The dishwasher was almost full. (Incidentally, I died before Sophie, in the revolutionary year 1848, without knowing which freedom it was all about that time.)

Nothing but daughters

When, toward the end of the debate on the case of Sophie Rotzoll, because Associate Judge Griselde Dubertin had maintained that Sophie had died a virgin, the Flounder was questioned by Ms. Schönherr, the presiding judge, more in jest than in serious quest of information, concerning the difference between the sexes, the flatfish, without stirring from his sand bed, replied at length:

"It's an old story, dear ladies. Women conceive, bear, suckle, rear, see one out of six children die, get stuck with a new one before they know it, bear it with the usual pain, suckle it with this breast and that breast, teach it to say 'Mama' and to walk. Then after a while the girls—and for the moment I'm thinking only of the daughters—spread their legs for some man and as always conceive something that only a mother can bring into the world.

"How poorly men are equipped by comparison. All they can conceive is absurd ideas. And all they can bear is arms. The fruits of their labor are things like the Strassburg Cathedral, the diesel engine, the theory of relativity, Liebig's bouillon cubes, the gas mask, the Schlieffen Plan. Thousands of these famous achievements are known to us. Nothing has been impossible for their lordships. The north wall of the Eiger had to be conquered, the sea route to India discovered, the sound barrier broken, the atom split, the tin can and the breach-loading rifle invented, the ruins of Troy and Knossos excavated, and nine symphonies finished. Because men cannot conceive and bear naturally, because even their blind and frenzied acts of impregnation spring from a dubious momentary caprice, they have to do clever little tricks, climb icy north walls, break sound barriers, pile up pyramids, dig Panama Canals, dam up valleys, experiment obsessively until everything on earth is synthetic, have to keep asking about the ego, about being, meaning, the why, whither, and wherefore in images, words, and tones, have to run themselves ragged on the treadmill known as history to make it spit out certified male products such as dated victories and defeats, church schisms, partitions of Poland, records, and monuments. Mark my words, dear ladies: Mr. Nixon will have to resign soon. A little man by the name of Guillaume made history the day before yesterday. And in Portugal generals keep deposing one another.

"The affairs and achievements of today: Calcutta. The Aswan Dam. The pill. Watergate. These are men's ersatz babies. Some principle has got them with child. They are pregnant with the categorical imperative. At least the military art, which they alone master, enables them to antedate death as birth into the unknown. But what they give birth to—whether creation or monstrosity—will never learn to walk, never be able to say 'Mama.' Unsuckled, it will waste away or reproduce itself only on paper: children born of desk-ridden males. Culture? Yes, if you will. Or should we speak of a morgue? Dusty old books in libraries. Canned music. Crumbling Gothic brickwork. In air-conditioned museums art has forgotten its origins. And the secret archives in which the monstrosities born of men live on in sinister, softly rustling dossiers. Already there are data banks. Already human beings are computerized; terrifyingly, their punch cards can be pulled out at any time. In short, extraordinary things are being done. We speak of epoch-making achievements. We say: Even in failure he was great. We look with emotion upon tragic proofs of existence, but nature plays no part in them; how impoverished they are in comparison with nature, and, because they were achieved by unnatural effort, we are bound to evaluate them negatively. Women, on the other hand, even if they have studied, even if they have emancipated themselves, even if they have been able to perfect the computer, increase profits, modernize the armaments industry, and put their imprint on government, will always—even with the fanciest hairdos—be nature. They menstruate. They give life even when they draw nameless seed from sperm banks. Milk wells promptly from them and them alone. Yes, they are mothers in a fundamental sense, even if they are not, or are not yet, or possibly never will be, even if they remain virginal all their lives like Fräulein Rotzoll.

"Women have no need to worry about immortality, because they embody life; men, on the other hand, can only survive outside themselves, by building a house, planting a tree, doing a deed, falling gloriously in battle, but after first begetting babies. Persons who can't give birth to children are at best presumptive fathers; nature has not done well by them."

When the Flounder had finished saying all this and worse— for he predicted that women, along with increasing equality, would develop an increasing predisposition to male-type baldness—he left his sand bed (in apparent triumph) and disported himself with his fins, while the associate judges of the Women's Tribunal condemned his differentiation of the sexes as "one-sidedly biological" and "hopelessly conservative."

Griselde Dubertin shouted, "He is and remains a reactionary." And before summing up the case for the prosecution, Sieglinde Huntscha quipped, "Those poor little menfolk. Not even allowed to have babies. My ass bleeds for them." After what seemed like liberating laughter on the part of the female public, she said drily, "In any case the revolutionary Sophie Rotzoll died childless and unmarried."

Except for her, they all bore me children, even Billy. In every case I was at least a possible begetter. But fervently as I've longed for sons ever since patriarchy was put through, much as I longed to see myself, my name, and my possessions perpetuated by sons, they all gave me nothing but daughters.

My friends made fun of me, called me a cracksman, recommended tinctures, pills made from mouse droppings, strenuous pilgrimages, but after every confinement I was shown the characteristic Parker House roll; no watering can ever consented to fill me with paternal pride. Even the Flounder didn't know what to do. When Dorothea gave birth to her fourth daughter and I went to him with my trouble, he spoke darkly of maternal counterforces. The mother goddesses, he whispered, Demeter, Hera, Artemis, the Pelasgian Athene, the three-breasted Awa, had all been defeated, but continued to wield a subliminal power. He, the Flounder, could only attribute the failure of certain individuals to beget sons to the vengeance of the mother goddesses—that was the price we had to pay.

Every time I begot a child from then on, the Flounder's suppositions were confirmed. Nothing but girls ever came of it. I'm not speaking of Awa, Wigga, or Mestwina. To them the concept of fatherhood was long unknown, and after that a mere joke. But when as a master swordmaker and member of the guild, with two journeymen in my employ and good hope of leaving a little something behind me, I got my Dorothea with child nine times, I think I might have been rewarded with at least one son. And even the fact that eight of the nine girls died (five of the plague) can hardly be regarded as a consolation, for Gertrud, the survivor, also had nothing but girls (four or five), among them Birgitta, who went off with the Hussites and came to a sad end at the siege of Bautzen.

I repeat: daughters, nothing but daughters. Mother Rusch was delivered of daughters—twice. Never any mention of fathers. Hedwig, the first daughter, was married to a Portuguese merchant who set up a trading post on the Malabar Coast, and Katharina got a local butcher for a husband. Hedwig and her Portuguese died (along with three out of their four daughters) of Indian swamp fever; Katharina's surviving daughters (three out of six) married local butchers, to whom they bore daughters, nothing but daughters. (And by the way, my Ilsebill has two sisters. Griselde Dubertin comes of a so-called three-girl family. And Witzlaff never speaks of any brothers, either.)

It was and remains a spooky business. Apart from the boy (by painter Möller) who wasted away, we know that Agnes Kurbiella gave birth to a little Ursula soon after the poet Opitz died of the plague. And the best Amanda Woyke could do for me was seven daughters. Stine Trude Lovise starved to death in infancy. The others lived out their lives as Kashubian serfs, all except Anna, the youngest daughter, who was bought free and went with her illegitimate child to live in the city, where she married the journeyman brewer Christian Rotzoll and was widowed when her daughter, Sophie, was nine years old. It only remains to be said that during her first and second marriages Lena Stubbe bore and nutured four daughters, Billy's daughter grew up with her grandparents, and Maria's twin girls are now four years old.

One of the things I liked about Sophie was that she kept shut and even as an elderly spinster still had a virginal glow. When her case came up before the Women's Tribunal, the fiendish pleasure she took in arousing men and letting them dangle and fret filled the public with enthusiasm. A color poster (closely resembling Associate Judge Dubertin) was made of her as she was presumed to look, or perhaps as she was sketchily described by the Flounder, and marketed as a feminist relic. It showed Sophie dressed as a Danzig market girl standing on a barricade. With her left hand she was clutching the Flounder by the tail fin and with her right brandishing a kitchen knife. Her narrow, scowling face. Her peat-brown hair, piled high and tied with a tricolor ribbon. Her small mouth, open and rounded, apparently singing something revolutionary. And at the foot of the barricade uprooted mushrooms, clearly suggesting that an unmanning massacre had taken place.

It is safe to assume that Sophie Rotzoll as political poster served, along with similar graphic works (for posters of Dorothea and Amanda were also on sale), to decorate the walls of rooms in old houses and new; and I, too, bought a freshly made print for five marks, because the Sophie I remember is all too split a personality.

It took the poster to simplify the prim spinster whose father I am supposed to have been. I had never seen her so explicitly—a daughter, never a mother. And, addressing the Women's Tribunal, the Flounder maintained that Sophie's virginity could be viewed as an essence, though the circumstance that her childhood friend the revolutionary schoolboy Friedrich Bartholdy spent a good forty years of his life in fortress arrest undoubtedly helped her to remain true to her essence.

When the verdict was announced, when the Flounder—thanks to the intervention of the Flounder Party—was declared only "ideationally" guilty and the Sophie cult had replaced the Amanda cult, the flatfish left his sand bed to speak a final word in honor of the revolutionary Sophie Rotzoll. As though to shame the predominantly female public, he cried: "This much is certain, dear ladies: Sophie let no one get near her! While Saint Dorothea of Montau conceived and bore nine times, while the abbess Rusch, in contravention of her vow of chastity, bore, it is true, only two children, but familiarized a good three dozen men of various religions with her flesh before, between, and after her confinements, Sophie Rotzoll kept closed without taking vows, even if it amused her to throw kisses at Polish uhlans, for which reason the burghers and burgheresses of Danzig regarded her as a whore. Ah, dear ladies, if only you, who sit so sternly in judgment and condemn the male cause, were closed like Sophie. If only each one of you were sealed up for good. Wouldn't it be in your power to put an end to all conceiving and bearing? Isn't it high time to give up intercourse, to dispense with sons and daughters, to stop having babies, and to grant humanity a thoughtful demise? I have statistics here that give me hope. They speak of two-child, then one-child, then zero-child marriages. No more history. No more growth rate. A gradual aging, then a quiet, uncomplaining fade-out. Nature would owe you a debt of thanks. Our planet would have a chance to regenerate. How soon the earth would be reclaimed by steppe forest wilderness. Once again, at long last, rivers would be allowed to overflow their banks. Once again the oceans would breathe easy. I'm saying this off the cuff, apart from my legend, speaking as a plain fish."

But when I listed all the daughters of the cooks inside me to Ilsebill, mentioned a few daughters' daughters, reeled off the story of Sophie the exception, reported the Flounder's suggestion as my own, and called it "at least arguable," she countered with an assurance rooted in her pregnancy: "I still say it'll be a boy this time."

Continuous generation

A thought depopulates.
Ratless it rolls
off to one side.

The counterwitness appears.
Bottom wants to be top.
Not no order; no, the other order.

The mushroom stands
umbrellawise,
lays bare its root.

For when the final lopping off?

Yet you, too, remain
astounded and open.

Beget—bite off.
But so far
it's only a dangerous game.

The seventh month

～～～～～～～～～～～～

With Ilsebill, too

you can go through fire and water. Now in her seventh
month and conspicuously pregnant, she wants to prove it,
even if you're not in the mood to go through fire or water.
"I'm your best pal, somebody you can count on if the going
gets tough."

She longs for emergencies. She provokes emergencies. A
pioneer woman on a wide screen, dreaming of danger on
horseback. Go west! Danger on the prairies. Wind in her
skirts. Wind-blown hair. Unblinking eyes take possession of
new lands.

But we aren't new settlers. The house is threatened neither
by Indians nor by desperadoes. Not even by mortgages. (Yes,
yes, the recent flood, when the dike gates were closed and the
ferry didn't run. But the waters subsided, and the insurance
covered the storm damage—a couple of broken windows.)

But my Ilsebill can't live without danger, which she faces
or averts or invents. Since the oil crisis made everything more
expensive, she has been saying first thing in the morning, "It
doesn't scare me. We'll just have to stick together, stick together."

She always wants to go through thick and thin with somebody, with you, with me, come what may. She protects you
against undesirable relatives, but also against your best
friends, whom she qualifies succinctly as "bad company"; in
fact, she'll protect you against life and all its horseflies.

399

"Those crooks, those spongers! All they want is your money; anyway, they've got something up their sleeve."

Ilsebill lies vigilantly across the threshold, scaring all temptations away with her bark. If you're in a sweat, she casts a spacious shadow around you. Whenever you climb into seven-storied abstractions, she stands watch. When garishly painted, wildly tattooed doubts start creeping up on you, she lets out a warning whistle. She lets her golden hair down into deep dungeons to save you. When you torture her curiosity, she keeps quiet. She never betrays the fact that you've been betraying her for quite a while. She keeps her mouth shut, closely shut: no view allowed into imaginary distance.

She never complains. My heroine suffers in silence and is painted in heroic stance against a black sky (the children to the right and left of her). Woman amid ruins. The Gleaner. The Always Pregnant One. Dame Care. Filching coal. Bartering the last of the family silver for beet syrup. Staunchly at her post when all is lost. By sheer force of will compelling sick people to live, and no back talk. She makes you sick so she can sacrifice herself in caring for you. Once you're sick, she perks up. If you wanted to die, she'd play the whore with death to get a postponement and still another postponement. Nothing can hold her back. If necessary, she'll run through all your money, just to show you that poverty brings out the best in her. She'll let you fall off a precipice just for the pleasure of teaching you, ever so gently, to walk again (on crutches). It's only when you're suffering—and she'll help you do that, too—that you'll appreciate the full measure of her sympathetic love. ("Can I help you? Isn't there something I can do? You're sure to need my help someday. Desperately. And then it may be too late.") When she puts your eyes out, you can be sure she'll guide you (even through heavy traffic).

In a word—you can rely on Ilsebill. She has perjured herself for me. When I was caught running out on the check, she ransomed me. She transfigured my leavings, many little piles of dirt. She always saw to it that my picture hung straight and dustless over the sofa. Thanks to Ilsebill, I am remembered: "Otto, oh yes, he was really a great guy." Otto was my name at the time. And my Ilsebill, who protected my reputation so fiercely, was called Lena.

Lena Stubbe had me twice as a husband. And it took enemy action to free her from both marriages. In the Franco-Prussian War, after I had been shooting my big mouth off for twenty-eight years, French shrapnel put an end to my bragging. And when in the winter of 1914 the Landsturm was called up to stop the Russian invaders, I died a second soldier's death at Tannenberg after fifty-five years of uninterrupted boozing. Lena put up with me throughout the one and the other marriage and would have survived me a third time.

Lighthouse, bulwark, haven, the thick-and-thin woman. How she put up with my beatings in silence, knowing them to be bungled caresses. How with her kindly encouragement she helped me, ordinarily a failure in bed, to achieve little weekend successes. How when I robbed the strike fund, she made good my theft by working as a toilet attendant at the Hotel Kaiserhof. How she translated my socialist Sunday talk into workaday action. How, when they were going to expel me from the party, she spoke to the comrades and wouldn't let them speak any harm of "her Otto." How she went to the police station for me. And all the times she washed my vomit off the floor. And took a knife and cut me down from the nail where I was dangling. You could always rely on Lena. You could go through fire and water with Lena. Same as you could with Ilsebill.

But I don't want to go through fire and water. I don't want to be saved. I like being led into temptation. And most of all, I like going astray. No sense in her sacrificing herself for me, no matter where; it doesn't pay. Tomorrow, in a pinch, as a favor to Ilsebill, I could be a little sick, weak, fragile, pathetic, a sad case, just barely rescuable. I could lie still and cry "Mama" in my sleep. But if Lena hadn't mothered me so mercilessly, hadn't maintained me so deliberately in infancy with her mumbling of "Now, now, it's all right; you'll be better soon," I'd never have become a soldier and (out of sheer fear) a hero.

Lena dishes out soup

Out of deep kettles
with limp cabbage or barley floating in them
or potatoes and rutabaga cooked to a mash
and the barest rumor of meat—

unless some tripe had come her way
or a horse had passed on and the price was right—
Lena ladled mealy peas
boiled down to the husks
and gristle and small bones
which had once been a pig's foot,
and which now in the kettle, when Lena stirred deep, clinked
as those standing in line before the kettle
clinked with their tin bowls.

Never blindly, or fishing about with her ladle.
Her way of dishing out soup was famous.
And when she stood upraised behind her kettle,
with her left hand lining up tally marks on the blackboard,
with her right hand stirring, then ladling exactly half a liter
into bowl after bowl
and out of her wrinkled winter-apple face looking
not into the kettle,
but, as though seeing something, into the future,
one might have hoped, hoped for something or other.
At the same time she saw behind her,
saw herself ladling past soups,
before, after, and during wars,
and lastly she saw herself young beside the kettle.

But the bourgeois,
as they stood off to one side in their overcoats
and saw Lena upraised,
were afraid of her enduring beauty.
They therefore decided
to give poverty a higher meaning:
there lay the answer to the social problem.

A simple woman

As the Flounder testified before the Women's Tribunal:
"Often as this Lena Pipka, whose married name was Stobbe
and whose remarried name was Stubbe, found herself at the
center fo regional events, she was and remained a simple,

though not simple-minded woman. If the High Court regards the career of Lena Stubbe as exemplary and therefore resolves to examine it here in the presence of a select public, my share in this proletarian destiny will prove to be slight; for since the Great Revolution, history has confronted me with gigantic tasks, transcending all regional boundaries; the era of world politics has dawned. Controversial issues, whichever way you look. Freedom, equality, and so on. Because my services have been everywhere in demand, I've been able to give the Baltic region only routine attention. Since my recent promotion to the rank of *Weltgeist*, the demands made on me have sometimes overtaxed me as a Flounder (and principle). I seldom find time to examine individual cases like the one now under discussion as carefully as they deserve. Still, it will give me pleasure to answer the knowledgeable questions of the esteemed prosecution, all the more so as Lena Stubbe, perhaps by reason of her very simplicity, was a significant woman: the early history of the German Socialist Movement would be unthinkable without her, though her name is nowhere recorded, though no street, avenue, or obscure square has been named after her."

When the presiding judge read the biographical data of Lena Stubbe, née Pipka, the impression made was one of long-drawn-out monotony, for apart from her conversation with August Bebel in May 1896 and a train trip to Zurich, the only noteworthy feature seemed to be her biblical age—she lived to be ninety-three. Twice married. One child by her first marriage. Three children by her second marriage. And yet the events of her life just happen to run parallel to the history of the working-class movement. Third daughter of a brickyard worker, born the year after the Revolution of 1848 in Kokoschken, Karthaus district, found work at the age of sixteen at the Danzig-Ohra soup kitchen, married the anchor maker Friedrich Otto Stobbe a year later, soon became, like him, a member of the German Workers' Association, joined the Social Democrats after the so-called unification congress at Eisenach, was widowed for the first time in 1870 at the very start of the Franco-Prussian War, ran the soup kitchen on Wallgasse for ten years, married the anchor maker Otto Friedrich Stubbe soon after the promulgation of the Socialist Laws, took charge of the strike fund when the workers struck the Klawitter Shipyard in the fall of 1885, supplemented her earnings by serving meals on Saturdays, received a visit from

403

her party chairman a few years after the abrogation of the Socialist Laws but found no publisher for her "Proletarian Cook Book," exhausted her savings on a trip to Zurich in the summer of 1913, was widowed for the second time at the very start of the war that broke out in the following year, worked in various soup kitchens all through the war, after the war at Workers' Aid kitchens, then in a settlement-house kitchen, then in a Winter Aid kitchen, then in an emergency kitchen set up by the Jewish community, and, lastly, ladled out soup in the kitchen of the Stutthof concentration camp. She outlived not only her husbands, but her four daughters as well.

After reading this bare summary and praising Lena Stubbe as a passive, but for her time exemplary heroine, the presiding judge of the Women's Tribunal called on all those present to rise in her honor; the Flounder, too, left his sand bed and with a gentle motion of his fins kept himself for one minute hovering in mid-water.

Then the prosecutor spoke. She reproached the Flounder for having, in his (to be sure, more and more neglected) capacity as adviser to the male cause, failed to keep either Friedrich Otto Stobbe or Otto Friedrich Stubbe from beating Lena when drunk. Perhaps, she intimated, he had even recommended beatings. One could easily imagine the male *Zeitgeist* of the nineteenth century speaking out of his mouth: his pertinent quotations from Nietzsche, his master-of-the-household attitude. His ironic references to the weaker sex. His pedagogic jokes. The male folk-belief that women thrive on beatings.

"Only the other day," said Sieglinde Huntscha, "a man had the gall to sing that song to me. Listen to what the swine said: 'You want me to sock you, don't you? I can tell by looking at you. Square in the face. Maybe you'd like me to give you a black eye to show around. Well, I'm not going to. Not if you beg me on bended knee. You want me to act like a typical male, that's what. You need it for your emancipation crap—the incorrigible male brute.' And this fine gentleman—I'm not mentioning any names—is sitting right here in the courtroom, putting all his trust in the Flounder: 'He'll talk us men out of this. He knows that beatings have always been necessary. He has always been in favor of striking arguments. We can count on the Flounder.' And the guy calls himself a liberal."

404

After the public had let off steam with shouts of "Boo!" and glared at the few men in the hall (including me) with knowing hostility, the Flounder, now back on his sand bed, spoke. "Esteemed prosecutor, you know as well as I do that corporal punishment has always been an expression of male weakness. Disappointing as your personal experience may be—you speak of a man steadfastly refusing to give you a beating you had provoked—at that time, in Lena Stubbe's day, the female sex was maltreated with an abysmal lack of restraint. In all classes. Not excepting the nobility and the bourgeoisie. But working-class women were beaten more regularly, every Friday to be exact, because the workers knew of no other way to bolster up their insecure egos on payday. Yes, yes, even the organized workers, even the members of the Socialist Party laid it on with a heavy hand every Friday. So it needn't surprise you that Friedrich Otto Stobbe and Otto Friedrich Stubbe beat their Lena, especially if you bear in mind that, rousing agitators though they both were, their vigor and dash were all on the outside; around the house, in their suspenders, they didn't amount to much. Lena, the punctually beaten Lena, was always, even when suffering in silence, the stronger. She'd have worn out ten strongmen. She accepted beatings in the dismal knowledge that a man's tenderness often goes too far. She never defended herself, with the poker, for instance. She knew that when it was over her Friedrich Otto or Otto Friedrich would be an exhausted, humiliated little man, contrite and tearful. And if, esteemed Ms. Huntscha, this anonymous gentleman in the audience who recently refused you a beating had lived in Stobbe's or Stubbe's time, he would undoubtedly have laid it on with a heavy hand. I know the gentleman and his pathetic demonstrations of love."

Weak, the way I stood beside her or made faces in her shadow, the way, still fastened to her umbilical cord, I kept escaping, weak though rebelling against her flesh, rich in excuses when I was caught, open-handed at her expense, always in her debt, always confident that she'd see me through when I hit rock bottom, hit rock bottom again, weak the way she wanted me and made me, the way she found me right for her love, though she didn't rule, but, strong as she was, bent down over the weak man, anticipating my failings and enveloping me in loving care. She led me where she wanted, she

405

helped me into my trousers and out of my shoes, she always knew where I'd passed out, what crowd I'd got stuck in again; and as for my dreary love affairs—even the neighborhood women were mad about me—she just stirred them into her soup, mumbling the while, "Oh well, oh well. I know you don't mean no harm. You've promised so often. Sure, it would be nice. But go ahead, don't mind me. I wonder . . ."

It was only when she caught me in the kitchen necking with Lisbeth, her eldest daughter (the one by Stobbe), who was barely fifteen, that Lena, who had just come in with the dustcloth, flew off the handle, the same as today Ilsebill gets mad over the telephone when (exhausted by her) I've cleared out for a while: "Just don't do it again. You've really got to stop this childishness. Running off without a word. When will you ever grow up? What? A social worker from Wedding. An associate judge at the Tribunal? Erika? Don't make me laugh. Just for the weekend. A little trip to Paris! You ought to be ashamed. That's right. This minute. No, take the next plane. I'll meet you in Hamburg." And when I went off to Berlin with a waitress from the Hotel Kaiserhof and we ran out of money, Lena wrote in her fine Sunday handwriting: "Dear Otto, I am sending you your return ticket. I had better not send any cash money. Just come home and get some sleep. Then we will talk it over. I will make you soup with dumplings, that has always helped. And don't do anything foolish. You know what I mean. Take the 12:03. I will meet you at the station."

So she kept after me, and I clung to her. The fortitude with which she endured my infidelities and brutalities had its equal only in the weakness that obliged me to prove myself by beating her. I wasn't sure of myself as I am now, when my Ilsebill or Sieglinde Huntscha can try all day to provoke me with women's lib slogans and I still don't take a poke at them. I prefer to roll myself a cigarette and say, "No, Siggie. It's no go. I am not going to hit you. You'd like me to, wouldn't you? You think we'd have more fun in bed afterward. So you can call me a 'typical male.' Try it on the Flounder some time. He dotes on silly slogans."

Over the intercom system of the Women's Tribunal—which for the past week had been giving its attention to the case of Lena Stubbe, to her special achievement, the "Proletarian Cook Book," and the brutality of her two husbands—the Flounder said: "Esteemed High Court, here's the way it was. Lena ruled. Her husbands were nothing but jumping jacks. Both with their everlasting love affairs. Dragging their incapacity from bed to bed. And by contrast Lena's inexhaustible love, which resembled the never-empty soup pot in her kitchen–living room, because Lena never let the beef broth she made from cheap bones run out or get cold, for she was always making provision for even poorer days. While her Friedrich Otto and Otto Friedrich spent and squandered until nothing was left, empty husks both of them, flabbycocks, barely good enough to shout hurrah. No use my giving them any advice.

"The most I could do was turn contemporary history to Lena's advantage by making use of first one war, then the other. When the French war started up in 1870, Friedrich Otto Stobbe, a strapping young fellow with a twirly mustache, ran down to the Baltic Sea at East Neufähr and shouted: 'War! Hey, Flounder, heard the news? War! At last things are moving! No more woolen socks home-fried potatoes sewing box apron strings. The First and Second Body Hussars have moved out. So have the West Prussian Field Artillery. Only the Fifth Grenadiers are still here, on garrison duty. Flounder, what should I do? Go on being an anchor maker and keeping my Lena warm? That can't be the whole story. That's not enough to fill a life. I'm still young.'

"So I advised him to go with the Fifth Grenadiers, whereupon he promptly—after two or three acts of bravery—died a soldier's death at Mars-la-Tour.

"In 1914, when the First World War, that masterpiece of European manhood, began simultaneously on several fronts, Otto Friedrich Stubbe, who at fifty-four thought of himself as a still-vigorous man, came running to the harbor mole in Neufahrwasser and shouted over the Baltic Sea: 'Flounder! The Russians are coming! They've invaded Masuria. Murdering and burning. The fatherland is in danger. Every manly hand is needed. What use am I here? A foreman in the anchor shop. They're recruiting for the Landsturm. We socialists have no right to stand aside. At a time like this the kaiser knows no parties. Should I, Flounder? Should I go and fight the Russians?'

"And him, too, High Court, him, too. I encouraged. At Tannenberg, where German arms triumphed under Hindenburg, he, quite logically, died for the fatherland. Two exemplary men.

"Ah, High Court, how sick I was of the male cause even then! How fed up with this incorrigible forward-mentality. What was I to do when every male folly was so quick to involve international complications. Participating more with negative than with positive advice, I soon became aware that the male principle was manifesting itself more and more incompetently in bed and more and more monstrously on the stage of history. And so, at the turn of the century, when women—Lady Pankhurst and her daughters—took to the streets for the first time, I was favorably disposed toward them and tried to make contact. Unsuccessfully, I regret to say. The suffragettes rebuffed me. My offer came too soon. Time would be needed. Male madness hadn't yet reached its apogee. I could only look on as it rose to unprecedented heights. But it will not have escaped the High Court that I at least succeeded in liberating our Lena Stubbe from her increasingly useless husbands. After the heroic death of her second husband, she was an emancipated woman; in the war winter of 1917 Lena Stubbe spoke loudly, while ladling out cabbage soup at the Wallgasse soup kitchen, against the war credits, and was far to the left in all other questions as well."

Is that right, Flounder? Is that why you twice sent me to the firing line? Had I been written off so soon? Had you begun even then to change sides, to turn traitor?

When the Tribunal was adjourned—affidavits were needed concerning proletarian cookery in the nineteenth century—I went out (in a strictly private capacity) for a beer with Sieglinde Huntscha. Then she (as usual) led me up four flights to her attic apartment, where we first talked about the Tribunal in general and then picked Ms. Schönherr and all the associate judges to pieces. When that was done, Siggie directed her attention to me. "You know what, you may not think so, but you've got a Stobbe or Stubbe inside you. You'd like to, but you don't dare. You know what I mean, slap batter punch. Poke me or your Ilsebill in the jaw. And say, wasn't the little Nöttke girl looking kind of weepy yesterday? Your doing, I bet. Playing the he-man. Bim-bam. Keep women in their place. All right! Go ahead. I need it. I need it, I tell you. So let loose, and don't stand there like a hypocrite."

But I refused (on principle) to deliver blows. I never wanted to be Stobbe or Stubbe again. "Look here, Siggie. That's all over and done with. We can make love without it. You just want me to react typically again. But you don't need it. We don't need it."

And true enough, we did all right without it. It was strictly private, and we were both affectionately *distraits*. (And I straightened out the business with Erika Nöttke: "That's more of a paternal thing. She's been crying for entirely different reasons. Overworked and so forth. The Tribunal has also been a strain on her. She's just too young for it, I tell you, much too young.")

Afterward Sieglinde said, without poison in her fangs, "You probably want to, at that. Even now. You just force yourself to be rational. But then I don't always know what I want, either. Why don't you caress me? Go on! Quick! Caress me!"

Then (as usual) we took a cab out to Steglitz. She led me into the former movie house with her key. But this time she wanted to be present when I talked to the Flounder. He had no objection. He rose with animation from his sand bed and gave us a demonstration of fin play. He welcomed the change and paid Siggie old-fashioned compliments. Then we talked about my time-phase with Lena Stubbe. He reminded me of a few dismal love affairs that still set my teeth on edge. Then he mentioned what had only been hinted at in the court proceedings: my theft from the strike fund and Lena's nail-and-rope soup. I promised to write about all that. All of a sudden he said: "Oh yes, the book. Is it definitely going to be called 'The Flounder'? I insist. And you, too, Sieglinde—may I call you Sieglinde?—I want you to make sure he keeps this simple title, as the Women's Tribunal would wish. We are gradually approaching the great historical accounting. My son, it's time you drew up a balance sheet—take a special chapter for it. When you've finished with Lena Stubbe's death, have them all die again in their time-phases: Awa, Wigga, Mestwina, the High Gothic Dorothea, and, gruesomely, your Fat Gret. Agnes died horribly, Amanda peacefully, Sophie quietly and alone. . . ." Then he gave me literary advice. He told me to write at length about "Nail and Rope," then about "Bebel's Visit." "But don't forget, my son: no complications. Don't lose yourself in socialist theory. Even when writing about revisionism, always keep it simple. Like Lena Stubbe. She was no Clara Zetkin. She was a simple woman."

Sometimes late at night she goes to the station restaurant, which is still open, and eats a jellied cutlet. It's not yet certain whether Margaret, Amanda Woyke, or Lena steps through the revolving door. She doesn't want to be a cook any more, seasoning soups, rolling dumplings, sizzling herrings in skillets, head next to tail, always pondering what to put in last. She no longer wants to inspire praise and comparisons in her guests—in rich man, poor man, beggarman, thief. She no longer wants to flatter any palate. Nor does she want ever again to force children to eat spinach. She wants to chastise her palate. Never again cook for any man, let the kitchen fire go out. She wants to take her distance from herself as she sits inside me or as, expressed by me, she becomes history. Her dated recipes: hasenpfeffer and *Gänseklein,* codfish in dill sauce, beef hearts in dark beer, Amanda's potato soup, Lena's pork kidneys in mustard sauce. None of these are obtainable nowadays, they are obsolete; in a station restaurant that's open late at night she wants to apologize (as though palateless) to a jellied cutlet with its chemical freshness.

Lena, Amanda, Fat Gret? There she sits in her skimpy coat and cuts herself piece after piece. Late trains are called out. (Rhenish, Hessian, Swabian voices.) In the station restaurant of Bielefeld, Cologne, Stuttgart, Kiel, or Frankfurt am Main, regardless, she motions to the waiter, who slowly, as though wishing to delay her century, appears between the empty tables and finally (it's me) gets there.

A second jellied cutlet without potato salad, bread, or beer. (Could it be Mother Rusch, cleverly disguised?) Questioned, I tell her the name of the preservative. She cuts, spears a piece with her fork, and shovels it in, as though driven to discharge a debt or fill up a hole or destroy someone (still Abbot Jeschke?) who has disguised himself as a jellied cutlet of the quality served in station restaurants that are open late at night.

I'm not sure whether I'm waiting on Amanda or Lena. The only one I would recognize (with dread) is Dorothea. Sometimes in serving I try to catch her with words like "sweet Lord" or "nail and rope." But she doesn't hear me: she just goes on cutting her meat. When Lena or Amanda comes to our restaurant and gives her order, I get sensitive: I notice the draft that makes all food-serving waiting rooms wide open and timeless. There she sits alone. A simple woman who has seen plenty of trouble (including repeatedly me).

I bring Lena a third cutlet trembling in gelatin—there's no shortage—and zigzag between the empty, spotted tables, in order that she, entirely outside me, may have time to see me coming, each time by a different itinerary. (When we were young and apples crunched under our bite. When without a word she let me march off with the Fifth Grenadiers. When they struck the Klawitter Shipyard. When she caught me in the kitchen with Lisbeth. When I beat her every Friday with my razor strop. When I hung from the nail and the rabbits were so scared that . . .)

Before we have to close—because even station restaurants close some time—she'll want a fourth jellied cutlet without garnish, wrapped in a paper napkin to take out—where to? When she leaves in her skimpy coat—how round her back is—and vanishes into the revolving door, I wonder why she never gives me a tip. Can it be that Lena respects me in spite of everything that has happened and is yet to happen?

All

With Sophie,
so my poem begins,
I went gathering mushrooms.
When Awa gave me her third breast,
I learned to count.
When Amanda peeled potatoes,
I read the progress of my story
in the flow of her peelings.
Because Sibylle Miehlau wanted to celebrate Father's Day,
she came to a bad end.
Actually Mestwina wanted only to love
Saint Adalbert, just to love him forever.
While Abbess Rusch plucked Polish geese,
I mischievously blew downy feathers.
Agnes, who never slammed a door,

was always gentle and only half there.
The widow Lena attracted distress,
that's why her place smelled of cabbage and rutabaga.
Wigga, the haven I ran away from.
Beautiful as an icicle was Dorothea.
Maria is still alive, getting harder and harder.
But—said the Flounder—one is missing.
Yes—said I—beside me
Ilsebill is dreaming herself away.

Nail and rope

I've eaten apples with all of them, on the garden bench,
standing face to face at the kitchen table or under a tree,
made tipsy by the fermenting windfalls—with Agnes before
the plague carried me off, with Margret when Hegge came
back from Wittenberg and tried to teach us religious fury,
with Sophie when, still childlike, we played at revolution. We
crunched the apples, exchanged significant looks as we bit,
looked past each other (Dorothea and I on our pilgrimage to
Aachen) in biting, or bit standing back to back, at which
time Amanda, who was built like a guardsman, overtowered
me by a head.

Sometimes we crunched our apples in adjoining rooms—
Lena in the kitchen, I in the parlor. But wherever and however we were placed, in whatever century, a comparison
always followed. By matching up our apples, bite against bite,
we tested our love.

Other methods—dangerous ones—are known. Ours was
harmless, and I can recommend it. By the imprints of our
teeth we recognized how different, in spite of everything, we
remained, what strangers to each other. I held the apple with
the stem pointing heavenward and bit down toward the small
end; Sibylle Miehlau (later called Billy) held the apple, before biting, by both ends. That way we blunted our teeth.
That way we bore witness. That way cocooned feeling was
made manifest. The surface: love; the inner lining: hate.
Crosswise and lengthwise we bit, and heard ourselves biting.

It had to be quiet in our kitchen or in the garden. At most

412

the beef-bone soup simmering in the kettle. Or wormy apples falling with a dull thud on rotting apples in which wasps were getting too much sweetness. We never bit into apples as we lay on the creaking bed in the dark, and never while the clock was striking. Never did anyone watch us at it. Often we delayed our comparison until her bite and mine discolored, until our teeth marks turned significantly brown. But without words. Love tested.

So Lena and I were standing in our little garden behind the tarpaper-roofed workers' houses and rabbit hutches on Brabank, across from Strohdeich, on the opposite bank of the Mottlau, with the port and shipyard behind us. But no riveting hammers. Because we at the Klawitter Shipyard had already been on strike for four weeks. Lena, now six months gone, was standing under our Boskop apple tree. That morning I'd been agitating and distributing leaflets, which was forbidden, outside the rifle factory in the Lower City. Lena's early-socialist soup-kitchen face. Though the harm was already done and couldn't be undone, though the theft was already behind me, I looked her full in the face while I bit and heard her bite.

Quickly discoloring, our apples lay bite to bite on the pile of driftwood that Ludwig Skröver and I had rafted from the Dead Vistula at night. Lud was my friend. Boskop apples are the most suitable. After testing our love, which was strong in spite of it all, Lena said, as though suspecting nothing, "I'll take some of these windfall apples and make us pancakes and put on a little cinnamon." Or maybe she noticed something? I tossed my bitten apple in with the windfalls in Lena's apron. In the autumn of 1885, at a time when Bismarck's Socialist Laws were in force, the workers struck the Klawitter Shipyard. Otto Friedrich Stubbe, a dashing young fellow and a rousing agitator, was a member of the strike committee, while Lena Stubbe, because she had formerly been a cook at the Wallgasse soup kitchen, was drafted, despite her advanced state of pregnancy, to cook cabbage and barley soups in an unused laundry for the hundred and seventy-eight striking shipyard workers and their many-mouthed families. At the same time, she took charge of the strike fund.

The usual incidents. Fights with scabs outside the shipyard gate in Strohdeich. Mounted police joining the melee with their clubs. The injured—bruises and abrasions, for the most part—were all workers. Socialist meetings, at which not only speeches but also leaflets in bold-faced type called upon the sawmill workers in the timber port, the stevedores on Warehouse Island, the well-organized printers and typographers at the Kafemann Print Shop, and the bakers at the Germania Bread Factory to join in a solidarity strike, were broken up by the police, who confiscated the leaflets.

When work stoppages nevertheless occurred in the port, in the railroad-car factory, even at the rifle factory and the Imperial Naval Shipyard, eleven party functionaries were arrested and—as the laws provided—exiled. A few, among them Otto Friedrich Stubbe's friend Ludwig Skröver, emigrated to America. But the strike went on and might possibly, after six or seven weeks, have forced the introduction of the ten-hour day and a reduction of the work load if, during the fourth week, the strike fund had not been robbed.

Lena Stubbe immediately reported the theft to the strike committee, promised to replace the stolen sum—seven hundred and forty-five marks were missing—but expressed no suspicion, though there were some who in whispers suspected Lisbeth, her sixteen-year-old daughter by her first marriage, and though Lena knew perfectly well that her Otto, who accused and thrashed all the children, had laid hands on the strike fund. Immediately after Lena's confinement in November, the newborn girl child (Martha), the five-year-old Luise, and the five-year-old Ernestine were given over to Lisbeth's care. Lena took a job as toilet attendant at the Hotel Kaiserhof. And in the spring of the following year, when Otto Friedrich Stubbe was brought up on charges though more than half the stolen sum had been worked off, Lena went to the comrades, spoke in defense of her husband, and got the charges withdrawn. "I know my Otto," she said. "He'd never do such a thing." The comrades apologized to Comrade Stubbe.

But hard as Lena tried to hush up the theft, to fill the hole in the strike fund by nightwork, and to make her Otto think she suspected nothing, he knew she knew. And because he was humiliated by her forbearance, he got drunk on potato schnapps every Friday and beat her regularly every Friday in the presence of the whimpering children. Lisbeth would run out of the house. And every time Otto Stubbe beat his Lena with a heavy hand or with his razor strop, he cried about himself, and Lena, who didn't cry, had to comfort him. And how, indeed, could she have stood there with her hands folded while a grown man cried his eyes out as if he had nothing but his suspenders to hold him up.

It had been the same with Friedrich Otto Stobbe, her first husband. Stobbe, who barely had time to get her with child (Lisbeth) before enlisting in the Fifth Danzig Grenadiers to fight against the French (in the Franco-Prussian War) and falling at Mars-la-Tour, also, like Otto Friedrich Stubbe after him, drank rotgut and beat his Lena every Friday. Stobbe, too, was a weepy type, needful of consolation. Lena had a penchant for strong men with weak characters.

At the time when she was being beaten regularly once a week by Otto Stubbe, who like her first husband was an anchor maker, and obliged to comfort him afterward, she was in her mid-thirties, he in his mid-twenties. Consequently it wasn't hard for Lena to be the young man's always willing wife and all-forgiving mother. Never, during either the whopping or the comforting, was the robbed strike fund mentioned. The weekly ritual was more on the silent side, if we choose to disregard Lena's motherly mumblings—"Now it's all right; you'll feel better soon"—and Otto's invariable announcement of "I'm going to hang myself. I'm going to hang myself." People say those things without thinking. Lena was familiar with such talk from her first husband. And yet Friedrich Otto Stobbe had died quite normally of a bullet in the belly. So all Lena could say was "Oh, Otto, you wouldn't go doing yourself a harm for nothing."

But one day, a good year after the strike was called off— Lena was pregnant again, the stolen money had been repaid—Otto Friedrich Stubbe was hanging from a nail over the doorway in the rabbit hutch behind the house—in his socks, for his wooden shoes had fallen off. Lena, who was sweeping the yard because it was Saturday, heard the crashing of the stool and the wooden shoes, heard the drumming of the terrified rabbits, dropped her broom, thought of Stobbe and Stubbe both at once—also probably of apples I had eaten with her to test our love—put all the blame on the accursed potato schnapps, thought no more of the beatings than if they had never happened, grabbed the knife she used to kill rabbits with, and cut the dangling Otto down from the nail in the lintel. The ordinarily dashing anchor maker soon regained consciousness, but for a good week he had to wear the collar of his blue shirt turned up.

Men with neatly parted hair are standing all about, and they mean me when they ask "Why?" To the question why, when there's so little time, I spend such an extravagant amount of it drawing hand-forged nails with a soft pencil or an English steel pen, I, who collect odds and ends out of pure passion, knew no answers; for the three bent nails mean enough, have left purpose behind them, no longer recall their occasions or the wood they were driven into once upon a time, when each nail stood straight and may have made some sense.

But since the question why is still standing at order arms, and since nothing but stories can fatigue the stern questioner and his voice that always goes straight to the point, I tell dispersed stories in which the cooking nun Margret has hung just-killed and still-warm geese on the first nail to drip into a bowl for black pudding, while on the second nail Sophie's dried mushrooms (greenies, morels, ceps, and milk caps) hung in linen sacks. But on the third nail (the most recent in my hatchwork drawing) I hanged myself, because social conditions were what they were, because I dealt blows when drunk, because I'd got drunk on potato schnapps, because I was a brute, because I'd never done more than threaten to hang myself, because nothing could undo my assault on the strike fund, because I couldn't stand Lena's pity, her way of understanding everything and putting up with it in silence, because I couldn't stand the knowledge she kept to herself, all that merciless kindness and selfless forbearance any more, because my last vestige of pride, my cock, refused to bestir itself, and because I'd been constipated for days; in vain I pushed, in vain I gulped down castor oil; nothing came out. So I took a calf's tether. And I already knew about the nail in the lintel. The only thing that worried me was my rabbits. Maybe it would scare them if I did it in the doorway of the rabbit hutch. . . . But Lena, who kept having to save me, who was never without hope, who knew recipes for and against everything, who was reliable, hellishly reliable, cut me down in time. Oh, God! When will it all end?

Then she made me a soup out of beef bones, in which she boiled the nail and the rope, noose and all, for an hour. At the end she stirred an egg into the broth and didn't ask "Why?" as, with slight pain in swallowing, I spooned up the soup.

Never again did Otto Friedrich Stubbe hang himself. But that soup, made from beef bones, a blacksmith's nail, and a calf's tether, with an egg stirred into it for strength, which Lena from then on served up every Saturday as a preventive, soon acquired a reputation among the suicide-prone. Potential dangling men would knock at her door, shyly introduce themselves, and invite themselves to dinner. They got used to the faint taste of hemp. They came again and again. And Lena didn't ask "Why?" but cooked a family-sized potful of nail-and-rope soup for her Saturday table, and got pretty well paid for it.

In addition to her Otto—who was unable, after the usual whopping and whimpering, to drop his Friday announcement of "I'll hang myself one of these days!"—Herr Eichhorn, a Royal Prussian department head, Herr Levin, sole owner of a flourishing sugar refinery, Götz von Putlitz, a lieutenant in the first regiment of Body Hussars, and Karlchen Klawitter, the shipyard owner's son, would be sitting at her kitchen table.

Besides these habitués, there were casuals from all walks of life. Occasionally even Herr Wendt, one of the elders of the Sankt Jakob Church congregation, would attend. And there were some whom Lena served free of charge, poor devils like Kabrun the porter and a hypertense young man by the name of Paul Scheerbart who dreamed of a crystal world of perfect transparency.

Good cheer prevailed at her table. Even political arguments ended in backslapping and brotherhood. Hanging and bullets through the brain were seldom mentioned, and then in jest, as, for example, when Herr Levin told the story of how, after looking in vain for a suitable rope, he had finally, to punish his unfaithful Klothilde, tied several of her pearl necklaces together. But when he kicked the chair away, the high-priced rope snapped in several places. "For two solid hours I picked and threaded before the damage was repaired. Because you can't fool with my wife."

Yes, along with its aftertaste of hemp, there was something about Lena's soup that lifted people's spirits. From then on the lieutenant bore his major-size debts more lightly; later on, he left the Body Hussars to look after his run-down family estate in eastern Pomerania. The Prussian department head replaced his first wife, who had died young with a second wife, who some years later left him again a widower; but thanks to Lena's nail-and-rope soup, he also managed to survive his ailing and short-lived third wife and to enjoy himself after working hours. Even Karlchen Klawitter succeeded (while spooning up three dishes of soup) in seeing his father, the stern shipyard owner (who, after all, had launched the first Prussian steam-powered corvette), in perspective, as a ridiculously little man. When, later on, Hermann Levin strangled his unfaithful wife with a pearl-embroidered silk scarf, he refused to have his murder represented in court as an act of despair (which might have given him the benefit of extenuating circumstances) and spoke instead of liberation. Sentenced to life imprisonment, he wrote Lena affectionate letters from prison, all the more so because for many years (until the time of his death in 1909) she brought him a dinner pail of her life-affirming soup on visiting days at Schiesstange Prison. Its heartening substance remained unchanged, but the flavor-contributing ingredients varied.

Lena Stubbe knew how to provide her free and paying guests with variety. True, she always cooked the same original nail, consecrated by her Otto, which she had bent slightly in pulling it out of the frame, but which if straightened would have been as long as a good-sized human pizzle. She also stuck to calves' tethers, which she bought cheap in lots of sixty from a dealer in farm produce on Milchkannengasse; Otto had to tie each one of them expertly into a noose before it was lowered into the foaming broth. But Lena's menu was not limited to beef-bone soup with an egg stirred in at the end. She cooked (with the above-mentioned additions) neck of mutton with beans, smoked spareribs with caraway-flavored sauerkraut, *Gänseklein* with rutabaga, even tripe cut from a cow's paunch and boiled for four hours, sour dumplings, West Prussian potato soup with garlic sausage, pigs' feet, dried peas with salt pork; and on festive occasions (at a small extra charge) she cooked nail and rope with tender calves' tongues, which she flavored with white wine, garnished with cooked turnips, and served with mayonnaise made of sunflower oil and egg yolks. Or she would stuff a suckling pig with rope, nail, and prunes.

It was at a festive meal which took place on January 18, 1891, that Herr Levin, who was to strangle his wife shortly thereafter, joined department head Eichhorn in toasting the twentieth anniversary of the German Empire, while Otto Stubbe and Karlchen Klawitter, the radical-minded son of shipyard owner Klawitter, drank to the recent abrogation of the Socialist Laws and to Bismarck's dismissal as well. But the hypertense Paul Scheerbart was deep in his vitreous visions of the future. While the ex-lieutenant and by then rural Junker Götz von Putlitz, wishing for liberal and therefore vague reasons to celebrate neither the foundation of the German Empire nor the belated triumph of the socialists, lauded the recent establishment of the Schichau Shipyard as a great economic achievement that would prove beneficial both to the Empire and to the simple worker, for without economic progress—as sugar manufacturer Levin and anchor maker Stubbe must realize—there could be neither capital gains nor social progress. He then pointed out that he had always been opposed to Bismarck's policy of protective tariffs, whereas the Sozis in the Reichstag had supported them on several occasions.

Otto Stubbe and Karlchen Klawitter proceeded to argue without bitterness, more for the fun of it, about the true road to socialism. Lena Stubbe tried to reconcile them with quotations from Bebel. The debate revolved around sordid practice and sublime principle. And thus, attenuated to be sure by the nail and rope sewn up in the suckling pig, the revisionist controversy of the late nineties was prefigured on a festive occasion. Karlchen Klawitter represented the revolutionary wing. Otto Stubbe had misgivings on the one hand and intimations on the other. Both cited Engels; only Karlchen cited Marx, and none too often. Meanwhile, unmoved, Paul Scheerbart dreamed his glass-blown utopia. And while serving the dessert—stewed Boskop apples with whipped cream—Lena Stubbe, who did not sit at the table but waited on the men as a simple matter of course, quoted from her favorite book, Bebel's *Woman and Socialism*. In conclusion she said, "All you men do is talk. But there's got to be action, too."

In any case the party ended happily with effusions of brotherly feeling. Karlchen Klawitter and the ex-lieutenant fell into each other's arms. The department head, Otto Stubbe, and the manufacturer Levin sang *"Heil dir im Siegerkranz"* and "Arise, Ye Prisoners of Starvation!" Lena patted the bemused Scheerbart and was happy because nothing was left of the suckling pig. In among prune pits and gnawed bones the slightly bent blacksmith's nail and the calf's tether in noose formation lay grease-coated and shiny. For all their exuberance, the guests, before taking their leave and drinking a last toast of cider in water glasses to friendship, progress, and life, did not neglect to cast a thoughtful glance at the rope and nail, each in his own way assuming a meditative attitude. (Afterward the well-boiled rope went into the garbage; the nail, however, was washed, dipped in linseed oil to keep it from rusting, and enshrined and locked in an ebony casket, which porter Kabrun had made with his own hands and donated in token of his gratitude for free meals, there to remain until the following Saturday.)

And so it went for many years, for Stubbe—now an anchor maker at the Schichau Shipyard and up to his neck in the (to this day unabated) revisionism controversy since the Erfurt party congress, where he as a delegate had voted now against Kautsky and now against Bernstein—was still a risk, as were all the other men, regardless of class. Under his Lena's consolations, Otto Friedrich never ceased to mumble: "I'll take a rope. I'll find me a nail. And that'll be the end. And this one won't break. Through with the whole business. Too much for one man. All by myself it's out of the question. What do you mean, why? Ain't it enough? No no no. I refuse to be mothered. I'll do it if it kills me. Wash my neck first, that's it. With a calf's tether I'll do it. And I know a good reliable nail. No later than tomorrow, if not . . ."

Against which, as we know, Lena Stubbe had a recipe. And when shortly before Chairman August Bebel came to Danzig—that was in May 1898—she finished collecting the recipes that would make up her "Proletarian Cook Book," she had clearly described the preparation of all her dishes and accompanied them with class-conscious commentaries (omitting the nail and the rope, however), for Lena was opposed to bourgeois cookery and its "take-a-dozen-eggs" ideology. In her introduction she wrote, "Such pretentious extravagance confuses the cooking workingman's wife, encourages her to live beyond her means, and alienates her from her class." Her reason for not including her nail-and-rope soup in her collection of proletarian recipes was probably that this dish was dedicated to the desperate of all classes and walks of life.

But on the day when she received Comrade Bebel in the parlor and submitted her class-conscious cook book to him in manuscript after her proletarian festive meal—pork kidneys in mustard sauce—she served him, before the main dish, a broth made from beef bones, in which she had (secretly) boiled the bent nail and the rope with a noose at the end, for at that time a rumor was going around that the chairman of the Social Democratic Party was feeling tired. People were saying that his never-ending struggle for just a little more justice had exhausted his store of hope, that he no longer had an answer to the question why, that he was profoundly depressed by the inner-party conflict between the reformist and revolutionary wings, that he often stared unseeing or muttered fatalistic words. That doubt was becoming a principle with him. And that, short of a miracle, the worst was to be feared . . .

Home-fried potatoes

Mine with lard.
It's got to be old ones with curling sprouts
that have wintered on a dry wooden rack
in a cellar where the light
is never more than a far-off promise.

Long ago, in the century of suspenders,
when Lena was almost six months gone and still
carrying the strike fund under her apron.

With onions and remembered marjoram I
would like to make a silent movie in which Grandfather,
I mean the Sozi who fell at Tannenberg,
curses before bending over his plate
and cracks each one of his finger joints.

But only with lard and in cast iron.
Home-fried potatoes with
black pudding and suchlike myths.
Herrings that roll themselves in flour
or quivering meat jelly in which diced gherkins
keep their natural beauty.

For breakfast, before he went on
the morning shift at the shipyard,

Grandfather Stubbe ate a whole plateful.
The sparrows outside the casement curtains
were class-conscious proletarians even then.

Bebel's visit

Not another word of table eloquence. No argument, no counterargument. Never again disruptive, irrelevant talk over the heads of the stiffly attentive comrades. Because the pigs' feet in the big kettle, with every little bone still embedded, have boiled for two hours in their broth with bay leaves, cloves, and crushed black pepper, with onions (but without nail and rope), because they are done at present and reduce us all, who have talked everything and the future as well to tatters, to silence.

In deep soup dishes, broth that has been seasoned at the end with vinegar. For each guest a halved pigs' foot split between the toes and up to the cartilage of the hock. On the edge of the plate a dab of mustard. Rye bread to dip in the sauce. No knife, no fork. With soon jellied fingers, with teeth that remember long and still longer ago, that remember Lena Stubbe's special pigs' feet, we sit between and across from strangers, the old comrades, who quarreled and talked themselves apart until nothing was left but faded, blue-tinged hope, and who are now gnawing bone after bone bare, biting into the cartilage, tugging at sinews, lapping up marrow, chewing away on the soft, rubbery skin, and are needful of a second, a third half pig's foot. Without a word, each for himself as though alone at the table, eyes narrowed to sight slits between propped elbows, everything taken back, until, united by sounds, we are restored to our old solidarity.

Pigs' feet have always been cheap. Right now three pounds for one fifty. Now we're full, holding our beer glasses with sticky fingers. The silence is fenced around with sighs. We're sitting in jelly. Sucking gaps between teeth. Belches rise up and the first fuzzy words: "Hey, that wasn't bad. Brings back the old days." We chat, we agree with one another. Determined to be reasonable, for a change. And to stop snarling. A simple meal, all it takes to bring peace. We see one another with friendly eyes. Great piles of bones. Ah yes, there were dill pickles on the side. Someone—probably me—wants to make a speech and praise the socialist cook Lena Stubbe, who silenced all the contentious comrades of her day with a kettle full of pigs' feet, defeated them for the time of a brief kindness, for which reason she included "halved pigs' feet with rye bread and dill pickles" in the "Proletarian Cook Book," which she submitted to the unforgettable Comrade Bebel when party business brought him to our part of the country and he called on Lena one afternoon in person.

On the northern edge of the city, not far from the port and shipyard area, where the Old City merged with the New City and poverty put its stamp on children, there was a row of workers' houses, one-storied structures of unfaced brick with tarpaper roofs. They belonged to the Schichau (formerly the Klawitter) Shipyard, and each house had always been occupied by two shipyard workers' families. The Stubbes had long lived next door to the Skrövers, until Ludwig Skröver and his family had been served with expulsion notices and emigrated to America. Ship's carpenter Heinz Lewandowski and his wife and four children then moved into the Skrövers' dwelling, the door of which, side by side with the Stubbes' door in the center of the elongated house, was painted in the same green. The hallway led to the kitchen–living room with its window and French door, which opened onto the adjoining yard, outhouse, and garden. The parlor with its two front-facing windows branched off from the passageway on the right (on the left at the Lewandowskis'). Likewise to the right and left, but smaller than the parlors, the bedrooms adjoined the kitchen–living rooms of the Stubbes and Lewandowskis. There was no room for closets under the flat tarpaper roof. In the backyard there were rabbit hutches leaning against the house. The tile stoves had to be stoked in the parlors, but through the partition walls they also heated the bedrooms of both families.

The kitchen was the warmest place. The water pump in the yard was intended for the use of both tenants. It would never have occurred to either the Lewandowskis or the Stubbes to convert the little-used parlor into a bedroom for the children. So the three small children from Lena's second marriage slept in two cots alongside the big marriage bed, at the foot of which was placed a narrow bed where Lisbeth, Lena's daughter by her first marriage, slept until she was eighteen, when, thoroughly instructed in the ways of matrimony, she married a worker in the railroad-car factory, became pregnant, and moved to Troyl, whereupon the narrow bed was taken over by twelve-year-old Luise. Lisbeth, Luise, Ernestine, and Martha experienced Otto and Lena Stubbe night after night: their snoring, creaking, groaning, farting, weeping, their sudden silence, their talking in their sleep. The children learned in the darkness and forgot nothing.

The parlor remained a place of mystery, virtually unused except on the high holidays, until 1886, when, shortly after the strike at the Klawitter Shipyard and her husband's attempted suicide, Lena began setting a Saturday table in the kitchen–living room for possible suicides and, since a few of her guests belonged to the upper classes, took in considerable extra money, a good part of which she spent on books and subscriptions to magazines. The parlor then became Lena's study. If she hadn't mislaid her spectacles in the kitchen, they were sure to be under a sheaf of papers in the parlor. There Lena read *Die Neue Zeit (The New Age)* and *Das Neue Frauenleben (The Modern Woman)*; there she lined up recipe after recipe for her "Proletarian Cook Book," and there in her Sunday handwriting she wrote the party chairman two letters full of questions about his book *Woman and Socialism*. An answer came in which he soft-pedaled his utopian ideas on free choice of profession, unsaid a little of his "state as educator" program, and taking an interest in Lena's class-conscious cookery, announced his visit.

In Kiel with shop stewards: "Look, fellow worker. Why do you write such complicated stuff? It's no good for us workers because only the privileged bourgeoisie can understand it." A turner (today we call them lathe operators) speaking. "It's too highfalutin for us. When we get home from work, we're all in, no good for anything but the tube. If you want to talk to us, it's got to be simple and exciting—like a crime thriller."

As if sleep-work-goggle-at-the-tube were a smooth-running process. As if the lathe were ever switched off and you didn't have quiz flicks running through your sleep. As if the rationalized work process weren't interspersed with reels of film, films run in reverse, protests from the back benches, and cost-efficiency figures, so that the lathe shavings get inextricably mixed with private refuse and suchlike nonsense. As if the workshop didn't have veto power while the quiz master varies his jokes. As if there were no other film uncoiling, running on, breaking off, starting up again, repeating itself, flowing right on from your dream through the early work shift, through your shop contacts, even while your wife, that permanent stranger, is taking up so much room—a film running on without intermission or time clock, as if there were no such thing as a wage scale, only hit music in the ear, warmed-up red cabbage, and the whole thing, even the black-and-white parts, in color.

"But fellow workers, that's just what I do. I write compressed time, I write what is, while something else, overlapped by something else, is or seems to be next to something else, while, unnoticed, something that didn't seem to be there any more, but was hidden and for that reason ridiculously long-lasting, is now exclusively present: fear, for instance."

"That's it, fellow worker. That's the way it is. We can't turn it off. And usually there's something else running at cross-purposes. And the kids who won't ever keep quiet. And always something else besides. Not exactly fear. Just a kind of feeling. But your long sentences, fellow worker, are no help. By the time you're through, you've lost me. Can't you make it simple?"

"I can, fellow worker. I can."

One Monday in 1885, when the workers of the Klawitter Shipyard were on strike and Lena Stubbe, one of the many cooks who are inside me and want to come out, was running the soup kitchen that fed the whole lot of them and their families and taking charge of the strike fund, she noticed that seven hundred and forty-five marks were missing from the fund, but she said nothing to her Otto, who always started clobbering the moment he was caught at anything, and kept her peace when Otto beat first the girls, who all wore pigtails, and then her, his Lena, with the heavy hand of a father, husband, socialist, and anchor maker until he was exhausted and reduced to tears, because Otto didn't want to be as I've described him in another overlong sentence, and would rather have been a class-conscious model of working-class solidarity. For only recently Otto Stubbe, addressing the comrades at Adler's Beer Hall, had inveighed against the beating of proletarian children and early-worn-out wives: "As Bebel says, we don't want to bring up no subjects, but independent-minded Germans."

And the comrades of those days all nodded and said "Right!"—just as you, too, fellow workers of the Kiel local group, nod and say "Right!" when I try to explain why complicated sentences are short and simple ones are long. Now here, for instance, is a short sentence: The spy in the chancellor's office is said to have been an eminently reliable Social Democrat in the daytime. But you refuse to read my short and long sentences, because a few leftist sons of rightist families have written you off as underprivileged illiterates, stigmatized you as stupid vulgarians, wife-beating Ottos. But the cook Lena Stubbe in her day knew several books that helped to shape the history of her times. After cooking pigs' feet until tender for the comrades, who were often at logger-heads, to gnaw at, she read sentences and paragraphs from the already classical work *Woman and Socialism* aloud, while the men munched.

And when the chairman of the Social Democratic Party came to Danzig in '96 to reconcile the warring factions among the comrades—even then the point at issue was revisionism—she discussed the proletarian cook book, which was still both lacking and needed, at length with her party chairman. They were sitting in the parlor. At first Otto Stubbe was there, too. The children in the adjoining room could be heard trying to be quiet. The Lewandowski children in the apartment next door were noisier. Outside it was May, lilacs were blooming between the houses. Otto had suggested killing a rabbit in Bebel's honor. But Lena Stubbe cooked pork kidneys in mustard sauce. They, my dear fellow workers, tasted good.

When August Bebel stepped into the Stubbe family's apartment in the workers' house at Brabank 5, Lena led him into the parlor, whose furnishings, unlike those of other parlors, included a desk with many drawers and, on top, several piles of books with slips of paper inserted in them. Also on the desk, next to a small ebony box in which Lena kept a wrought-iron nail, stood a framed picture of Bebel, standing up to Bismarck in the Reichstag. And now the famous man with so much past behind him was actually present, standing frail and most respectably dressed beside the sofa. Yet he stood there as though absent, at a loss for a first sentence. He sniffed: "Ah, so we're having something pungent?" For crossing the corridor from the kitchen–living room and seeping through the door of the parlor, an unmistakable smell announced the pissy, not yet attenuated bouquet of the main course.

Only recently Lena had said to her Otto, "We're through, I tell you, through!" after he hadn't just beaten her as on every Friday. "Go on like this and we're through for good."

But this announcement, that she might be through with him one of these days—and for good!—was not provoked by the usual clobbering. The most she said about that was "You're only hitting yourself in the face." Far worse, he'd been turning up his nose at her pea soup of late, and all he had to say about her pork kidneys in mustard sauce was that they tasted pissy. "Then you'll see who's willing to cook for a shit like you. And it'll be too late when you start sniveling that Lena's kidneys were the best. You'll go down on your knees, but it won't do you no good. A hundred times I've said: He can't help it. Always has to make a big noise and bang his fists on the table. Afterward he's sorry. Gets all weepy. Well, I ain't going to say it no more. All right, cook him a couple of kidneys cut up small so they give up their juices, that's what he likes. And put in mustard at the end. 'Cause that's the way he likes them. Aw, go on, he dribbles. Make some more kidneys in sauce. 'Cause when they're done, I put in pepper, I grate fresh horseradish into them, and put in five tablespoons of mustard, and I stir and I stir over a low flame so it doesn't boil. But that's all over now. I'm through. Always talking about solidarity with his big mouth. All right, if he's got to clobber, let him. It doesn't bother me. Even if he gives me black eyes. But I don't let nobody run down my kidneys. Why should I cook and slave for him! And boiled potatoes to go with the sauce. And a couple of allspice berries for seasoning. But it's not good enough for him. I 'spose he'd like me to soak them in water or milk to get rid of the piss. And if you could get any taste back into them after that. That'll do, I say. That'll do. He can go somewhere else. Maybe he'll find somebody that'll soak them in water or make them all mushy with milk. But they still won't be right for him. And he'll pine and sigh for Lena's nice kidneys. But then it'll be too late."

Lena Stubbe said all this time and again, and from then on

she soaked her pork kidneys in water for half a day before cooking them until they were first hard, then soft. But in her cook book she wrote something entirely different. And for the master turner, commercial traveler, agitator, party chairman, street-corner orator, and Reichstag deputy, she soaked her kidneys neither in water nor in milk, for which reason the smell penetrated to the parlor.

After the beef-bone soup (with one or two special ingredients), Comrade Bebel relaxed a bit. At first he seemed depressed or perhaps only tired from the relentless obligations that went with his functions. More to Lena than to Otto Stubbe he lamented, though with manly self-possession: how many friends he had lost in the course of these last embattled years, what staunch discipline the party had shown in spite, or perhaps because, of the burdensome Socialist Laws, and how flabby yet quarrelsome the party membership had become with increasing success; how difficult it was to accustom the party to legality without letting it succumb to the compromises encouraged by this indispensable development, how far the Socialist Movement still was from the goal despite its increasing success at Reichstag elections, and how, now that victory was within reach, the goal seemed hazier than ever before.

Bebel expressed doubts and spoke corrosively of himself: he had been too cocksure in predicting the revolution and the downfall of the capitalist system; how often he had aroused false hopes by going so far as to date the impending collapse of the state. True, he had been misled by Marx's prognoses, which had been wrong even with regard to England. As to the pauperization of the masses, Bernstein had been right. It had to be admitted that capitalism was capable of adapting itself and not devoid of ideas. On the other hand, the concept of socialism would be lifeless without the hope that a radical transformation would soon usher in a new society. And actually there was good reason to believe that the present system, with its exploitation and mismanagement, would soon collapse. Revolution was a distinct possibility, though one shouldn't say so out loud, because the party advocated the strictest legality.

While Lena Stubbe waited serenely (confident in her special ingredients) for her beef broth to take effect on the profoundly depressed man, and as long as Bebel, overcast

428

with doubts, was postponing the revolution to a hazy future, Otto Stubbe squirmed restlessly in his chair; but as soon as the chairman, thanks to Lena's beef broth, perked up and flashed signals for the future out of bright, commanding eyes, the easily swayed anchor maker was fired with enthusiasm. Boldly he delivered himself of revolutionary phrases with anarchistic overtones and took on such a now-or-never expression that Bebel was obliged to remind him of the decisions reached by the Erfurt party congress and firmly, though without severity, call him to order.

By that time Lena was serving her pork kidneys in mustard sauce with boiled potatoes. A glass water pitcher full of dark beer, which the Stubbes' daughter Luise had brought from the tavern on Bucket Makers' Court, was already on the table. During the meal, the Lewandowski children made so much noise they seemed to be right there in the room, while the Stubbes' own little ones, though only a few feet away, were hardly audible. Bebel praised the simple yet so tasty dish. Lena told him about her daughter Lisbeth, whose consumptive husband probably didn't have long to live. Now at his ease, taking a warm interest in the details of their family life, the chairman stopped pulling out his gold pocket watch (as he had done frequently at first). Thus encouraged, Lena, no sooner had the dessert, her famous cinnamon-flavored Boskop applesauce, been spooned up, sent her Otto, who was getting too obstreperous anyway, out of the parlor with a mere glance (backed up by her battered authority). Otto explained dutifully that the children seemed restless and in need of attention, and that perhaps Lena and Comrade Bebel had best be left alone, since he knew nothing about the political implications of cookery. Of course he was able to appreciate good plain food, but the theory of it was beyond him. That was Lena's department. But once things started up, on the barricades and so forth, he'd come running. Comrade Bebel could bank on that.

When Otto Stubbe had gone, there was silence in the parlor. It went on for a while. There weren't even any flies. The chairman lit a cigar and remarked that it was one of a lot inherited from Engels. Then a bit of a joke: yes, old Friedrich had been first and foremost a manufacturer to the end, but in the last years of his life, possibly because he was no longer under pressure from Marx, he had developed into a useful Social Democrat. Then more silence. Lena looked for her specs, found them, and without a word set her neatly written manuscript before the cigar-puffing chairman. Here reading, there skipping, Bebel leafed through the "Proletarian Cook Book."

Some of the cooks inside me would be unionized today. Amanda Woyke undoubtedly. Possibly Fat Gret. Sophie Rotzoll with her militant left-wing orientation. But most certainly Lena Stubbe.

At a congress of the food and hostelry workers recently held in Cologne, delegate Lena Stubbe addressed canteen cooks, cooks of the Vienna Woods restaurant chain, cooks for the canning industry, and others. Naturally there were also waiters, waitresses, butchers, industrial bakers, et cetera, in the hall. At the beginning of her short speech on "The Cookery of the Oppressed Classes," Lena said, more in fun than provocatively, "Fellow workers, what's the sense in quick cooking? To hell with convenience food. Even if it saves time, I ask you: time for what and whom?"

She got only a sprinkling of applause. And the few cooks who supported her attack on the frozen-food industry, peppered with examples of poor quality, were those stigmatized as "élitist" because they worked in luxury hotels (Rheinischer Hof, Hilton, Steigenberger, et cetera), where they were faced with supposedly international demands: breast of pheasant on sauerkraut with pineapple. The majority were loud in praise of frozen foods—"That way the common man can afford beef tongue in Madeira sauce"—and one delegate went so far as to speak of "progress in a spirit of trade-union solidarity."

"In that case," cried Lena Stubbe, "you should also sing the praises of pea sausage. Remember that just before the War of 1870, one of our fellow workers, a Berlin cook, reinforced the Prussian army by inventing pea sausage." (Applause, laughter.) "And why not give honorary membership to Count Rumford, who early in the nineteenth century tried to solve the social problem by inventing a stomach pap that was named after him, Rumford soup for the poor. It consisted of water, potatoes, barley, peas, beef fat, stale bread, salt, and flat beer, cooked until it was so sticky that it didn't fall off the spoon." (More applause and laughter among the delegates.)

But when, drawing on early socialist experience, the former cook of the Wallgasse and Danzig-Ohra soup kitchens larded her brief exposé with historical references, when she insisted that the proletarian cook book, the need for which was felt even then, remained a necessity here and now, when Lena Stubbe tried to prove that for lack of class-conscious cook books the working women of the early capitalist era had turned to worthless bourgeois books—Henrietta Davidi's and worse—thus becoming alienated from their own class and infected with petit-bourgeois cravings—"Your beef tongue in Madeira, for instance!"—when Lena maintained that the labor movement and within it the unions had neglected to teach the young female industrial workers class-conscious cookery—"They just shut their eyes and reach for a can!"—the majority of the delegates protested. "What's the matter with quality canned goods!" and "Sounds like the old class-struggle crap!" And somebody shouted, "Leftist ravings!"

Nevertheless, the cook from the nineteenth century had the last word. "Fellow workers!" she shouted at the cooks. "Your cooking lacks historical awareness. Because you refuse to recognize that for centuries the male cook was a product of the monasteries and courts, in other words of the ruling class. We female cooks, on the other hand, have always served the people. In those days we were anonymous. We had no time to work up fancy sauces. In our ranks there are no Prince Pücklers, no Brillat-Savarins, no famous chefs. In times of famine we stretched flour with acorns. It was up to us to find ways of varying the oatmeal porridge. It was a distant relative of mine, the farm cook Amanda Woyke, and not Ole Fritz, as you might think, who introduced the potato into Prussia. While you men—all your ideas have been extravagances: boned partridge Diplomat-style with truffled *farce*, accompanied by goose-liver dumplings. No, fellow workers! I'm for pigs' feet with black bread and dill pickles. I'm for cheap pork kidneys with mustard sauce. If you haven't got the historical taste of millet and manna grits on your tongue, you have no business coming here and shooting off your mouth about grilling and sautéing!"

The cooks were furious. "Come to the point!" they cried. Then the discussion turned to the next round of wage-price negotiations in North Rhine–Westphalia.

Meanwhile the chairman of the Social Democratic Party had been looking into Lena Stubbe's draft project for a proletarian cook book—not very deeply, but enough to form an impression. He praised the undertaking and agreed that young workingwomen, most of whom came from the country and were used to living in self-sufficient farming communities, were at sea in urban surroundings and in need of class-conscious guidance in matters of housekeeping and most especially of cookery. He was well aware of the enormous amount of sugar consumed by working-class families, to the detriment of their health. And he was convinced that the alcoholism so prevalent among the workers was not unrelated to their unreasonable eating habits. Bourgeois temptation, he realized, began at the shopping stage. And he conceded that his book about women ought to have had a chapter on the subject. Perhaps not only he, but also the labor movement in general, should have turned their minds to these mattters from the start and developed a class-conscious sense of taste. After all, everything couldn't be left to reason. There was something dry and theoretical about the demand for justice. It lacked flesh and blood. That was why, shrewdly as socialists could analyze situations, they were short on robust humor. So such a work was long overdue, and he could only congratulate Comrade Stubbe on her commentaries and historical references, for instance, to the meat shortage in 1520 and the resulting development and dissemination of dumplings, both sweetened and unsweetened. He also agreed with her that the introduction of the potato in Prussia had brought about more changes than had the glorious victories of the Seven Years' War. He could only second her opinion that the triumph of the potato over millet had been revolutionary in its implications. All this was good Marxist thinking, although Marx, probably because of his bourgeois upbringing, had failed to recognize the importance of proletarian eating habits. Socialism, like capitalism, had had a puritanical streak from the very start. Moreover, he admired Comrade Lena's knowledge and regarded her as a model of the self-educated working-class woman. He, too, as a turner's apprentice, had learned what he knew by reading, without adequate formal preparation.

So thoroughly had she convinced him that August Bebel thereupon pressed Lena's hand for a long moment and cried out, "What an unforgettable day!" But when Lena, arguing that as a woman, and an unknown one at that, she would be unable to find a publisher, asked him to write a foreword to her book, Bebel was assailed by doubts. Were the comrades intellectually mature enough to recognize the political necessity for their party chairman's writing a foreword to a cook book? Wouldn't he be making himself ridiculous and so harming the good cause? Not to mention the reaction of the bourgeois public, for in the enemy camp they were only waiting for him to lay himself open. Unfortunately. Yes, unfortunately.

And Bebel also regretfully rejected Lena's suggestion that at least essential parts of her cook book—even without mention of her name—be included in small print as an appendix to his successful work. Comrade Stubbe, he could see, was a regular reader of *Die Neue Zeit*. So she must have followed his controversy with Simon Katzenstein on the woman question. He was being urged to include Katzenstein's critical article and his answer in the new edition, so—most unfortunately—there would be no room for excerpts from her cook book. Besides, it would be a shame to abridge her excellent work. No, no. He couldn't do such a thing to Comrade Stubbe.

When August Bebel took out the gold pocket watch that Willy Brandt, the chairman of the SPD, carries today on festive occasions, Lena removed her spectacles, cast a watery look at the plundered table, and said, "It don't matter." He said: "I own that I was depressed when I came; but I leave you in good spirits. For now unfortunately I must. The comrades are waiting for me at Adler's Beer Hall. That *is* the name of the place on Tischlergasse? Revisionism is on the program again. This eternal bickering. I'd much rather stay and hear a little more about your great-grandmother, the farm cook Amanda Woyke. Yes indeed. If it weren't for the potato ..."

When, surrounded by the Stubbe family, August Bebel left the workers' house at Brabank 5, a large crowd was waiting outside; they cheered him and wished him well, for they believed in the good cause. Workers' songs were sung. He had to shake many hands. Men and women had tears in their eyes. The May evening donated a sunset. A police lieutenant who with his men was keeping an eye on the crowd said, "They're more excited than if it were the kaiser in person!" And a workingwoman, Frau Lewandowski from next door, answered the lieutenant: "He is our kaiser."

The trip to Zurich

started on Friday at the main Danzig station, after the news of August 13–14 had appeared in Thursday's *Volkszeitung.* True, the local leadership had immediately decided to hold an appropriate memorial service, which was well attended when it did indeed take place at the headquarters of the Citizens' Shooting Club on Saturday, but the comrades also wished to send a delegate and were all the more pleased to do so when Comrade Lena Stubbe, who years before had had an animated talk with the party chairman, decided then and there to take the long trip at her own expense. The local party district donated a laurel wreath with a white ribbon on which were inscribed in red letters the words "Farewell!" and "Solidarity!" Otherwise her luggage, apart from strictest necessities in a straw suitcase, consisted of a loaf of bread, a jar of potted pork, and a string bag full of apples. A special passport was made out for her, and she received it just in time.

Otto Friedrich Stubbe took Lena to the station. He saw her off with manly self-possession but deep emotion, though the day before he had advised against the expensive trip, which would use up all Lena's savings, saying, "There'll be enough of a crowd."

Though I can indicate the approximate time when the express left for Berlin (shortly after 11 A.M.), and though that August 1913 is clear in my mind in other respects as well, the present time eludes me almost entirely. Only a few days ago the present chairman of the SPG resigned as chancellor merely because the Communists had put a spy in his office. It's beyond me. "Those swine!" I fume. I call equally bewildered friends on the phone, I sit down, because running around doesn't help, and over and over again I lament, "It can't be! It can't be!" And to revive the past I write about August Bebel: What would he have done in a similar situation? What would he have said about the spy problem? and for and against whom would Bebel have decided when

434

on April 22, 1946, the CPG and the SPG of the Soviet-occupied zone met at a unification congress and voted to fuse into the Socialist Unity Party? On that solemn occasion the Social Democrat Grotewohl applauded when an aged comrade handed the Communist Pieck a wooden staff, which Bebel himself had turned, and with which he had pounded the table for order at the turbulent Erfurt Party congress of 1891.

But the symbolic import of that staff was not sufficient to save several Social Democrats from Bautzen Prison (soon after the unification congress); nor could anything stop the ruling Communists in the German Democratic Republic from spying on one another and everybody else, including Bebel's successor.

Naturally the master turner hadn't thought of that when—still for love of his trade—he turned a handy staff with which to give emphasis to his authority when the comrades started arguing too violently about the true road to socialism. (Or had Willy resigned because he was disgusted with power?)

At 7:30 P.M., when Lena Stubbe arrived at Berlin's Friedrichstrasse Station, she had to change to the Stadtbahn, because the 10:13 express to Zurich via Halle, Erfurt, Bebra, Frankfurt, Karlsruhe, and Basel left from Anhalt Station. So flat was the Pomeranian countryside that from Schneidemühl on she had slept imperturbably in her corner seat. On the platform, which was lined with wreath-bearing comrades from other local sections and districts, she ate an apple. Later, after luckily finding a window seat in her compartment, she cut two slices from her loaf of black bread and spread them with potted pork out of her jar. This she washed down with one of the bottles of Aktien beer that Otto Friedrich had thoughtfully put into her carryall.

Since his only daughter had married a Zurich man and was living there, the chairman, whose activity as a writer of books had proved profitable, had built a house on the Zürichsee for his old age. When August Bebel died, at the age of seventy-three, Lena was sixty-four. The woman comrade across from her must have been in her early forties. In addition there were three men in the compartment, only one of whom, however, was going to Zurich for socialist reasons. Though pure chance had brought this Herr Michels, who lived in Turin, where he was an instructor of economics at the university, to

Lena's compartment, he was on familiar terms with the other woman. Soon after the train pulled out, he spoke to her on so radical a note that though it wasn't far to Halle, where they were getting out, the other two gentlemen changed compartments, in the course of which move one of them, much to the amusement of the two women, spoke of "Communist riff-raff."

They were doing Robert Michels an injustice in more than one sense, for the young man came of a Rhenish merchant family. True, after a brief interlude as a Prussian officer he had taken up with revolutionary socialists, but, repelled by German Social Democracy and its law-abiding ways, he had made friends with French and Italian Syndicalists. Influenced by Sorel, he detested the petit-bourgeois reformism of the socialists, and yet, though disappointed in Bebel, Michels, because of his longing for true authority, was also fascinated by that son of a career sergeant. Which explains why he was on his way to the funeral of the chairman of a party that he, in his headlong development, had long left behind him. He regarded himself as far to the left of Frau Rosa, who belonged to the left wing of her party. In Lena Stubbe, who offered him and everyone else in the compartment apples, he saw nothing; and how, indeed, could he have understood this white-haired woman who crossed herself as the train pulled out and re-enacted this sin against the spirit of enlightenment at every station?

The two younger passengers discussed the general strike as a revolutionary weapon, and their dialogue became more and more impassioned. Michels, too, favored the great strike, but criticized Rosa for having feared to overstep the limits of legality, for submitting to Bebel, the "notorious majority-politician," and for not daring to take her left-wing faction out of the party. "You with your democratic talk. The masses are a blind power. They need a guiding will to drag them forward. All the people ever want is a few pfennigs more on payday and free beer. Your Social Democracy stinks of bourgeois decadence. All you can think of is statutes. No feeling for the anarchic power that sweeps away the dust of the centuries with an iron broom and at last makes room for true freedom."

She, too, wanted true freedom, said Rosa. But freedom couldn't be commanded from the top down. It had to grow up from the base—though organization could help. "Of course the compromise solutions they're now suggesting are out. The Bernsteins and Kautskys have to go. Now that the Old Man is dead, younger leaders will rise up. We've got to find our way back to spontaneity. Against the party, if need be."

They talked like this as far as Bebra. As darkness fell outside, Lena spoke: To tell the truth, she wanted to sleep a while. But there was something that needed to be said. What Comrade Luxemburg was saying—she'd read pretty much the same thing in the party press. And on paper it was true. Freedom from the bottom up—she was all for it. And as for Comrade Michels, whose writings she was sorry to say she hadn't read, he talked mighty big, sounded almost like her Otto Friedrich shooting his mouth off in Adler's Beer Hall when he was carried away on his radical Sundays. But people live on Mondays, and every day of the week. Comrade Bebel had said that time and time again. Too bad he wasn't chairman any more. What would happen now if no one could put just enough left-wing and right-wing truth into sensible sentences? Because too much truth was dangerous. Pretty soon you'd talk the party's unity away. Comrade Luxemburg should think about that. And as for Comrade Michels, who was so learned and such a glib talker, he should take care that his talk didn't carry him too far to the left, because then he'd come out on the right. She knew people, take Karlchen Klawitter, for instance, who'd changed beyond recognition in only a few years. The only thing that didn't change was the real world, its poverty, for instance.

Then, after again offering her apples, Lena Stubbe pulled her coat over her face and slept, while the express sped through the bright morning, making every effort to get there on time, for the engineer and fireman, as well as the relays of conductors, were all comrades. They knew exactly whom they were taking where, and knew that their regularly scheduled train was becoming more historical from mile to mile.

Lena's words—at one point she had called Rosa "child" and "my lass"—had made Rosa Luxemburg and Robert Michels rather thoughtful. And yet, because socialism is like that and habit is habit, they had to argue the principle of the thing for another hour, though in a considerate undertone, until they, too, were tired.

Of course Rosa didn't want to split off from the party (as

she did later on, with dire consequences). Of course the radical son of the bourgeoisie didn't want to end up in the camp of reaction after an eccentric career (and yet soon after the First World War—then imminent—he became a Fascist in Italy, where he was a professor, and remained an enthusiastic and radical Fascist to the end). All in all, a good deal of future was traveling in that train to Zurich: Ebert and Scheidemann were riding in a first-class carriage, and Plekhanov, whom Lenin was even then excoriating as a revisionist, was also on his way to speak beside Bebel's grave in the name of the Russian comrades.

Unfortunately, there are some things that no one can foresee. For all his jokes about sons of the bourgeoisie, Bebel had held the brilliant young man in high esteem: his (liberal) scientific attitude, his (colorful) style. While with Brandt, Guillaume's reliability and even disposition had become a soothing habit. Traitors have their special charm. It was rather flattering, in fact, for even in their betrayal Michels and Guillaume always managed to speak respectfully, the one of Bebel, the other of Brandt. No one reading Michels's obituary of Bebel, even the critical passages, can fail to see how dearly he must have loved the old man. And if Guillaume should some day present us with the "Memoirs of a Traitor," I am sure he will draw a neat distinction between his political employers' cause and his own private feeling. After all, one can only betray what one loves; though Lena Stubbe, who all her life obeyed only necessity, remained single-minded even in her love.

Punctually at 3:30 P.M. the express pulled into the Zurich Central Station. The Workers' Association had prepared lodgings for the new arrivals. As usual, the arrangements went off without a hitch. Lena—who had taken leave of Rosa with a motherly "Take care of yourself, lass; and try and write something sensible about us poor womenfolk," and of Michels with a good-natured slap on the back—went to spend the night with the Loss family, to whom she had been assigned. For supper there was café au lait with a Swiss variant of home-fried potatoes known as *Röschti*.

Old Man Loss, who had worn out shoe leather as a postman until he himself was worn out, told her how the comrades among the Swiss and German post-office employees had

438

worked together at the time of the Socialist Laws, to smuggle *The Social Democrat*, which was printed in Switzerland and forbidden in Germany, across the border.

Lena Stubbe told her hosts about the strike at the Klawitter Shipyard, and how Bebel had come to their place on Brabank for a visit. Though mentioned only in passing, her cook book, for which she had found no publisher, aroused the interest of Mother Loss, who was about Lena's age.

Then they all went to bed. The bells of Zurich woke them. A fine summer day gave the impression that the whole world was sparkling bright. Money was going to church. God was keeping his finances secret. Bebel's death had thus far gone unnoticed.

It was May when Willy resigned. On the sixth I had spent the whole day drawing pictures of myself with gulls' quills: aged and worn, but still blowing feathers as I'd done as a boy (when airships were in vogue) and even before that, as far back as I can remember myself (B.C., Stone Age), three, four at once, the down, the wishes, the happiness, lying, running, blown them and held them in suspension. (Willy, too. His amazing second wind. Where he got it from. The Lübeck recreation yard.) My feathers—some were his—are getting limp. It so happens that they fell in the usual pattern. Outside, I know, state power is puffing up its cheeks; but no feather, no dream will dance for it.

The funeral ceremonies were scheduled for two o'clock Sunday afternoon. As Comrade Loss belonged to the organization committee, Lena was favored with an admission ticket to the municipal cemetery at Sihlfeld, which she picked up at the Workers' Association on Stauffacherstrasse. Until Saturday the body had lain in state in the auditorium of the Volkshaus. From there the dead Bebel was transferred to the house of his widowed daughter on Schönbergstrasse. That was where the funeral procession formed. In the lead the Konkordia band. Then more than five hundred wreath bearers, among them Lena Stubbe, who had not wanted to delegate her wreath. Then came the hearse, followed by several carriage loads of flowers, the carriage bearing the bereaved family, and two more occupied by persons too frail to walk. The bearers of the traditional banners were followed by delegations from Germany (including the Reichstag fraction), France, England, Austria, Switzerland, and other groups. Then came the Harmony band, followed en masse by the political organizations of Zurich and environs. The trade unions brought up the rear. Even the *Neue Zürcher Zeitung*, always ready to sneer at the labor movement, was amazed at the size of the crowd and wondered why.

Bound for Sihlfeld, the procession made its way down Rämistrasse, across the Kai Bridge, down Thalstrasse and Badener Strasse. The churches remained silent except for the Jakobskirche, where the bell ringer was evidently a comrade. Thousands of people lined the sidewalks. Most of the men wore flat straw hats; the women's hats were adorned with artificial flowers. Not all the men removed their hats as the hearse passed. A year later straw hats of the same type were photographed when many-headed crowds gathered all over Europe to cheer the declaration of war, although only recently the Socialist International, meeting in Basel, had passed a resolution opposing all war, on which occasion Bebel had made a speech denouncing the armaments race and the general war mongering, and concluded as usual with an appeal for action: "So now let's get to work. Forward! Let's go!"

At the cemetery in Sihlfeld, Lena Stubbe saw Comrade Rosa only briefly but caught several glimpses of Comrade Michels, who was acquainted with all the delegations and on terms of special intimacy with the French and Italians. Such was the press of the delegations that Lena could not get into the little Greek temple, which would have been hard to identify as a crematorium. She was barely able to hand over her wreath, and later to hear a word here and there of the speeches. The speakers included Hermann Greulich, a member of the Swiss Nationalrat, the Austrian Viktor Adler, the Belgian Vandervelde, the Reichstag deputy Legien, the Russian Plekhanov. Unfortunately Jean Jaurès was prevented by illness from attending. Names that became famous only later were Otto Braun, Karl Liebknecht, Otto Wels, Friedrich Ebert, Philipp Scheidemann. Clara Zetkin spoke in the name of the socialist women of all countries. She called Bebel the man who "awakened millions of women." She said, "No one has ever fought with a more sacred fury than you against all the injustices and prejudices that have plagued our sex. . . ."

His ashes were interred beside those of his wife, Julia. At

the end, as August Bebel had requested in his will, the Grütli male chorus sang Gottfried Keller's song about Ulrich von Hutten:

"Thou luminous shadow, we thank thee. . . ."

Since she had made the trip, Lena stayed on for another three days as the Losses' guest. But she saw the mountains only from a distance, in the foehn wind, from the shore of the Zürichsee. For Frieda Lewandowski, her neighbor on Brabank, she bought a cowbell. It was only on the last day that she grew sad and that everything seemed strange to her.

When Comrade Loss took her to the station, she gave her a round loaf of bread, a piece of Appenzeller cheese, and a small jug of light wine from the Herrliberg. In the express to Berlin she sat with strangers. But after a while she took her diary out of her carryall. She found her spectacles in a black silk bag, in with what money she had left, her passport, a few hair clips, and a tube of bicarbonate. She wrote down the recipes that Comrade Loss was accustomed to cook by, such as onion tart, deep-fried cheese balls, sliced liver with *Röschti*, and a soup made with browned flour. And so Lena rode back to her Otto Friedrich, whom, when the war started taking its toll, she would soon survive.

Where she left her specs

Under potato peelings, in the flour bin, in among the bacon rinds that Amanda Woyke set aside for rubbing pans.

Any number of still lifes with spectacles: I could put Lena Stubbe's string-mended frames in front of the crooked nail and on top of the rope with a noose at the end.

While chopping onions and doing what all else, they didn't take off their specs. When picking over lentils, when my Ilsebill studs a leg of mutton with garlic, when sewing up the apple-stuffed Saint Martin's Day goose, over Lena Stubbe's spice box, in which marjoram was never lacking, when Sophie Rotzoll went gathering mushrooms.

Her lost specs would be found again in the flour bin, under potato peelings, and where all else: weeks later at the very bottom of the earthenware jar of goose fat, in the stuffed (also with prunes) beef heart that Margarete Rusch served up to the wicked Jeschke at Oliva Monastery; and the specs that Sophie lost while gathering mushrooms were found exactly a century later right beside the liver of a newly bought codfish when Lena Stubbe cut it open because it was Friday.

How many pairs of specs did they wear, mislay, and sometimes find again? Thirteen. The last was broken on Father's Day 1962, when Sibylle Miehlau, Billy for short, and her glasses were run over by motorcycles.

Maria checks prices with the naked eye. Agnes, who could neither read nor write, didn't wear specs. After her immurement the Lenten cook Dorothea could have done with a pair of specs when scribbling her confessions of sins by the light of a tallow candle; her Dominican confessor had taught her High Gothic letters. The Flounder claims that Wigga and Mestwina were also nearsighted. But who—and not only because her image belongs to the Stone Age—can conceive of Awa in specs?

And so Sophie, who had once again mislaid her specs, sorted with clouded eyes the basket of mushrooms that had made its way to the city in spite of the siege, which had consequences, whereas Lena Stubbe, with no spectacles on her nose, cut her Otto down from the nail before it was too late.

They wiped their specs with woolen sleeves or whatever came to hand when their vision was obscured by cooking steam, grease spots, fog, or fly shit.

Mother Rusch, who had inherited her specs from the patrician Ferber, wiped them with the tail feathers of a duckling. Before addressing a fresh petition to the commandant of the Graudenz fortress, the elderly spinster Sophie Rotzoll took a hare's paw to clean her specs with. Billy borrowed my handkerchief. Amanda Woyke rubbed her misty lenses with a silk kerchief that Count Rumford had sent her from Munich, London, or Paris. And before sitting down at the writing desk in the parlor, Lena Stubbe, who like Amanda and Sophie had ruined her eyesight at an early age reading works of an educational, revolutionary, agitational, or strictly scientific character, wiped her specs with a red scarf that had once been worn by her dashing first husband.

Clever women, the whole lot of them, who inscribed their household accounts on slates and lined paper, in copybooks, or on slips cut out of blue sugar-bags, wrote letters, petitions,

442

recipes, and careful footnotes. Before copying it out in her Sunday handwriting, Lena Stubbe wrote the first draft of her "Proletarian Cook Book" on the backs of old leaflets and strike proclamations.

They used their specs when immersed in the newspaper, in the almanac, in the Klug Hymnal, when searching children's scalps for lice—and where all else?

In the toilet, for inspecting their own feces, the diarrhea of their respective menfolk, and the children's little sausages; for reading aloud from the Bible, as Mother Rusch and Amanda Woyke did while lambs' tongues, tripe, pigs' feet foamed in their broth; for learning about me and my vicissitudes from the letters of their daughters and daughters' daughters—I wrote seldom, or only when in my flights I had once again got myself into trouble and debt.

To bone up on Bebel, Lena Stubbe put on her specs as she sat beside the bubbling kettles of the Ohra and Wallgasse soup kitchens or her own family pot. Here's how I see her: anxiously devoted to progress, which she viewed through nickel frames that kept slipping. But when dishing out soup-kitchen soups with her half-liter ladle, Lena took off her specs, and her light-blue eyes, rather watery in later life, peered into our future.

An obituary for Lena

Some time or other, our Awa died. The story is that we ate her half raw and half cooked, because hunger drove us to it. Wigga died of blood poisoning. She who was always warning us against the Gothic fire eaters wounded herself with a rusty roasting spit, left behind by the Goths on the alluvial soil of the Vistula estuary.

Mestwina was first baptized by force, then beheaded, because she had killed Bishop Adalbert with a cast-iron spoon.

When Dorothea of Montau had herself immured in Marienwerder Cathedral, the space for the last brick was left open. To this gap in the masonry we owe closely scribbled papers, wildly ecstatic outpourings, sweet-Jesus rhymes, and coded messages in which, mingled with obscene prayers, shot through with screams for freedom, and connected by words of abject repentance, were inscribed recipes for the dishes that Dorothea wanted to be served to her in her cell, until the day when she ceased to accept food, ceased to evacuate even the scantiest waste, and lay stiff in her vestigial corporeity.

The ex-abbess Margarete Rusch choked on a fishbone on February 26, 1585, when King Stephen Batory of Poland concluded a peace treaty with the city of Danzig and celebrated the happy occasion over a fish dinner (pike) with the patricians.

When the poet Quirinus Kuhlmann, the merchant Nordermann, the kitchenmaid Agnes Kurbiella, and her somewhat crackbrained daughter, Ursula, were burned under the open sky in Moscow on October 4, 1689, the men as conspirators, the women as witches, Agnes, still in pursuit of a fish recipe (her pyre had already been kindled), was said to have quoted from the poems of Martin Opitz: "His dearest love am I for all eternity. For fish and pleasure he depends on none but me. Come, dearest, come, let us at table stay. In sumptuous repose and pass the time away."

And when Amanda Woyke expired peacefully in the arms of her enlightened pen pal, Count Rumford, she is believed to have beheld a vision of giant atomic-powered kitchens the world over and to have proclaimed the end of human hunger.

And Sophie Rotzoll, who lived so dangerously and kept death in the form of mushroom recipes in readiness for her enemies, died quite normally of old age in the fall of 1849. (Later on there was some argument as to whether her last words had been "Long live the Republic!" or "Venison in aspic!")

And Lena? Lena Stubbe went on living for several years, though she would have preferred to die immediately after her chairman, August Bebel, or at any rate right after his funeral in Zurich.

And then came the war, then there was hunger, and then there were strikes. Then the Revolution was proclaimed. Then everything turned out entirely differently. Then there was more hunger. Then came the League of Nations. Then the Free City was proclaimed. Then the hunger let up a little. Then the money lost its value. Then new money was printed. Then Lena became a great-grandmother. And still she dished out soup. Her always fair measure. Almost a century. Already a monument in her lifetime: the woman with the soup ladle.

For just as Lena Stubbe had dished out soup in soup kitchens during the four war years, and just as during the inflation she had cooked and dished out cabbage and barley soup for the Workers' Aid in the Red waterfront suburb of Neufahrwasser, in Ohra, and in Troyl, so she continued to ladle soup when, in compliance with the Winter Aid program, the SA, the League of National Socialist Women, the National Socialist Welfare Organization, and the Hitler Youth distributed pea soup with bacon at field kitchens on so-called one-dish Sundays. At these ceremonies, which became more and more popular after 1934, the Free City police band, conducted by Kapellmeister Ernst Stieberitz, played march music and merry tunes so blaringly loud that just as a certain three-year-old boy, pounding furiously on his tin drum, could not make himself heard above the noise, no one could hear the almost ninety-year-old woman who cursed into the air between ladleful and ladleful, yet dished out fairly and without so much as a glance at anyone's coat collar.

It wasn't noticed or reported until considerably later that, just to be helpful, Lena Stubbe was cooking kosher soups at the emergency kitchen of the Jewish community on Schichaugasse for poor East European Jews, who since April 1939 had been waiting in vain for visas to America and various other places. And when, after the start of the Russian campaign, Lena made flour and bread soups, the ingredients for which she had begged or saved out of her own rations, for the Ukrainian slave laborers, when as though in defiance the old woman, like the hungry workers from the East, wore a big cloth patch with the letters E A S T painted on it, when at the age of ninety-three Lena Stubbe grew childish and started speaking her mind openly, she was arrested at her home on Brabank and sent without a trial to the nearby Stutthof concentration camp. For reasons of public welfare, as her granddaughter Erna Miehlau was told in answer to her inquiries. (Lena's great-granddaughter Sibylle was then twelve years old and still playing with dolls).

In Stutthof, Lena Stubbe continued to dish out soup. For exactly a year she ladled blue-green barley soups into tin messkits. All the prisoners, and not just the politicals, trusted her. The ladle was never out of her hands. She couldn't help being fair. Her half-liter measure. Born in '49. A century of watery hope. Her way of ladling. How her memory remained serviceable to the end. How she always and only had good things to say of her husbands, killed in two wars. How she told tales about earlier soups. How, in dishing out soup, she quoted from the writings of the man who, as though no time had elapsed, was still her chairman.

Died on December 4, 1942, of old age. According to a different version, a kitchen *Kapo*, who as a common-law prisoner belonged to the privileged class of inmates, beat Lena Stubbe to death when she tried to stop the *Kapos* from pilfering the already meager kitchen rations of margarine and beef fat. With a beech log. Two political prisoners, who knew Lena from her Workers' Aid days, found her battered body behind the latrines. They had to shoo the rats away. Her string-mended specs lay beside her, in pieces.

When the Second Soviet Army occupied Danzig and the tarpaper-roofed workers' houses on Brabank burned down, Lena's "Proletarian Cook Book," which had failed to find a publisher, burned with them.

Apart from Amanda and Sophie, so much violent death: the poisoned blood, the starved body, the burnt flesh, the stifled laugh, the headless trunk, the slain tender loving care. Ugly realities that can't very well be glossed over. Totted-up losses. The violence account.

My Ilsebill, who's not out of the fairy tale but comes from Swabia, likes to settle accounts with men. "The one thing you're good at is starting fights. Your eternal Waterloo. Your heroic defeat."

And now the Flounder has made out my account: "Let's have a look at your balance sheet, son. It's not a pretty sight. I'm afraid you're in the red."

Those words were spoken after the Tribunal had wound up the case of Lena Stubbe. Sieglinde Huntscha had (secretly, at night) let me in to see him again. (She stayed in the box office: "Don't mind me. Just talk talk talk!") He rose from his sand bed and seemed to be in high spirits from top to tail fins, though he's sure to be convicted soon and his health has suffered visibly from long confinement: his pebbly epidermis has paled, and his bone structure stands out as though he were trying to prove his credibility by becoming transparent.

When I tried to read him my next chapter, the story of my poor Sibylle, he interrupted me: "There's been enough dying!" Then he started bandying clichés like "ultimate audit" and "hour of truth." Once again he reviewed his mission, from the neolithic Awa to the early-socialist Lena. He listed his achievements—patriarchy, the state, culture, civilization, dated history, and technological progress—and went on to deplore the sudden turn from grandiose to monstrous action. "I gave you knowledge and power, but all you wanted was war and misery. Nature was entrusted to you, and what did you do, you despoiled, polluted, disfigured, and destroyed it. With all the abundance I made available to you, you haven't even succeeded in feeding the world properly. Hunger is on the increase. Your era is ending on a sour note. In short: you men are finished. How can there be order with so much waste motion? In capitalism and Communism alike, everywhere I find madness impersonating reason. That's not what I wanted. It's no use advising you men any more. The male cause is bankrupt. Time to knock off, my son. To abdicate. Do it with dignity."

Then he suggested that I end the book named after him with the case of Lena Stubbe, and after the Women's Tribunal handed down its verdict, let him say the last word: "You can blame me for Alexander and Caesar, the Hohenstaufens and Teutonic Knights, even for Napoleon and Wilhelm II, but not for Hitler and Stalin. There I disclaim responsibility. Their crimes were none of my doing. The present is not mine. My book is closed; my history is done."

At that I cried, "No, friend Flounder. No! The book goes on, and so does history."

Ah, Ilsebill! I dreamed the Flounder was talking to you. I heard the two of you laughing. Smooth was the sea. And there you were, working out the future. I was sitting far away; I'd been written off. Present only in retrospect. A man and his story: Once upon a time . . .

The eighth month

~~~~~~~~~~~~~~~~~~~~~~~~~~~~~~~~

Father's Day

On Ascension Day, which is a holiday, we celebrate
Father's Day. Innumerable men, gaunt ones, all bone and
sinew, fat ones, who have cushioned themselves against everything, men with laughter lines, men with scars, shriveled men,
foursquare men, men weighed down by their appendages, a
whole nation of men, men and only men, are on their way to
the open spaces: in festooned carriages, on bicycles decked
with pennants, in club strength, in horse-drawn wagonloads,
in motor vehicles old and new.

From early morning, beer-tipsy hordes are on the move,
crowding into subway and elevated trains. Double-decker
buses are jam-packed with singing men. Swarms of teenagers
on motorcycles: leather-jacketed, swathed in their noise. Here
and there a resolute footslogging loner. Veterans of the last
wars, frenzied half shifts from Borsig and Siemens, employees
of the municipal waterworks, garbage men, truck drivers,
post-office clerks, the management of Schering & Co., whole
shop committees, fans of the Hertha and Tasmania teams,
bowling clubs, credit unions, skat clubs, stamp collectors, embittered pensioners, exhausted heads of families, young shop
clerks, pimply apprentices—men, all men, wanting to be
among themselves, without Ilsebills, without skirts or curlers,
far from the breast and cunt, far from all knitting, the dishwashing, the hair in the soup; they want to go wild and to the
country, to Tegel and Wannsee, to the Teufelsberg, Krumme

Lanke, Britz, and Lübars, to the shores of the Griebnitzsee, Schlachtensee, Grunewaldsee, with bottles and sandwiches, cowbells and trumpets, in stripes and checks, to the woods, to sit under trees on moss or pine needles, or fat-assed on bandy-legged camp chairs, to let loose the monstrous inner pig, to be great and glorious, disumbilicated from Mama.

So when Ascension-Father's Day came around, Sibylle Miehlau also wanted to celebrate. Dead set on it! Her friends, whose names were Frankie, Siggie, and Maxie, called her Billy or Bill. All four considered themselves a different breed, though as I well know, all four could be quite different from different, for in the early fifties Sibylle and I had wanted to get married. Big plans, we were engaged. There are photographs of us on the Piazza San Marco, us at the foot of the Eiffel Tower, us atop the chalk cliffs of the isle of Rügen. Cheek to cheek. Hand in hand. We were just right for each other. In every situation. And our child . . .

Billy—I still say so—was a remarkable woman. She had her law degree. Men were crazy about her. She passed as a vamp and wore stiletto heels. She slept around. That's why nothing came of our projected marriage, which we regretted, for Sibylle had a domestic side, which later, when she decided to be different, was actively indulged. She took Maxie (with her duffel bag full of old junk) to live in her apartment, which, with its children's room and a double bed, was actually our apartment.

Maxie looked like a menstruating boy, flat and frail, while Sibylle had the proportions of an all-American pinup. Siggie and Frankie also lived together, but their relationship was flexible; they were both as restless as three-year-old stallions and always looking around. For all their male affectations— always in trousers, their voices dropped to cellar pitch—they were four intelligent and normally high-strung girls, who fled to their own sex after too much experience with idiotic boys or boring men (like me). Now they wanted to be different, different at all costs. Though all of them would have done it with me. And on the whole Sibylle and I were great in bed. My sexual relations with the cool Siggie were perfectly normal, and as far as I know she never complained. And I took a shot at Maxie, too, when she started up with Billy. Only Frankie, who had the soul of an old wagoner, never appealed to me.

One day, in any case, all four of them began to act crazy. "No more of that stuff. It makes us sick. It's so crude; we won't take it any more. Our way of loving is entirely different. All you want is in and out and finished. Love 'em and leave 'em. That won't go down with us, not any more. Get someone else to service you. We just happen to be different. Well, all right, we didn't use to be, but we are now. What happened before doesn't count. Something we had to get behind us, definitely. A phase. But we can still be friends. Drop in now and then, for a schnapps or something."

They drank schnapps, all right, and beer straight out of the bottle. And there were two bottles of schnapps rattling around in an ice bucket and two cases of beer in Frankie's open (fifth-hand) three-wheeler, when all four of them, Siggie in the driver's seat, drove up Hundekehle and Clayallee, meaning to celebrate Ascension-Father's Day by the Grunewaldsee along with ten thousand, no, a hundred thousand men.

Billy was wearing a top hat, Frankie a derby. Siggie had put on her Hell's Angel cap. An oversized, shapeless fedora was pulled down over Maxie's ears, and she had to hold on to it in the wind. Figures in a film where hats defined roles. (Later they exchanged lids. And Billy's top hat was tragically abandoned.)

And the ten thousand men bound for the open spaces had also, according to their own roles, hatted themselves in peaked caps, straw hats (known as circular saws), paper helmets, and genuine steel helmets, some spiked and dating from the First World War. And someone had covered his bald head with a small checked handkerchief, knotted at the corners.

All for the hell of it. Ordinarily they went bareheaded and seldom or never wore hats or caps. Now that she was through with being a vamp, Sibylle's curls had been hacked into a boyish bob. Frankie had always gone in for a man's haircut, died blue-black. Siggie's ash-blond hair hung down in a shoulder-length pageboy. One Sunday when there was nothing else to do, Billy had given Maxie a crew cut; it stood up crisp and stiff as a brush.

And true to the movie, Frankie smoked a pipe, Siggie chomped morosely on a cigar stub, Billy had a hand-rolled cigarette dangling from her lower lip, and Maxie chewed gum while all four rumbled toward the Grunewaldsee in a three-wheeler decorated with paper rosettes and surmounted by a yellow-and-blue garden umbrella. Wedged between an open Mercedes full of simpering fraternity students in full regalia and a one-horse carriage bearing three elderly gentlemen who never seemed to tire of singing "In Grunewald, in Grunewald, they're auctioning off the woods. . . ."

High good humor. The weather was magnificent and promised to remain so. Midmorning, shortly after ten o'clock. The political situation tense, as usual. The Wall had been finished for a year. West Berlin was an island, but inhabitable. Real-estate prices were falling, but the economic situation wasn't too bad. Frankie, in particular, had nothing to complain about: lots of people were moving, the trucking business was thriving. And Billy's law office had plenty of divorces to handle. "Dumb clucks, they go right on hoping and they get the short end every time." In Sieglinde's kennels, pedigreed shepherds were reproducing and little lap-and-lick dogs were selling like hot cakes; Sieglinde had studied law to the dry and bitter end, but then she'd lost interest. (Ten years were to pass before she would manage, in the course of a public trial, to make use of her hard-crammed legal knowledge: "I accuse.")

Typically of the times, they all worked for a living, except Maxie, who was still studying (at Billy's expense): ecstatic barefoot dancing and classical ballet. Anyway, they were competent, full of life, and not without ambition. Doing men's work, though not to be confused with those lousy males who masturbate even when they're fucking. Or those silly females with their day and night creams, their permanent waves, their fourteen pairs of shoes, their artificial pearls, their slip covers, squeeze-out tears, porcelain collections, handbags full of junk, and mortal terror of getting fat. No, not just of pregnancy. Of hanging bosoms and spare tires. That scream before the mirror because wrinkles snicker, veins are blue, and Mother's tendency to a double chin is breaking through. The dread of becoming old, no longer desired, felt up, kneaded, clutched, invaded in every hole by a man's asparagus tip; because that's what it's all about—that worn-out chunk of feel-up flesh with a hole in the middle—extra big for somebody's hard-on. "So don't bother me with this soul-mate partnership stuff!" cried Billy, when I ventured a word about Sunday.

No, not with us. Nothing doing. Free-wheeling fathers, that's us. Always on the road. Unattached. Natural-born hunters. Childless and happy. It's true that Frankie (under the name of Franziska Ludkowiak) has two little girls from her earlier married and cookstove life, whom she ceded along with her share in the construction business to her former husband, the perpetually worried daddy, and their new mommy, who never has a thought for herself. But that doesn't count. And Billy's long-discarded daughter (by me) was growing up with her grandmother.

Down with diapers! Shitty brats! We don't give each other any. And as for our chicks—because Maxie, too, insists on having her private life—we don't knock them up; we have other ways of making them dependent. As if we didn't have our crises and domestic worries. Our constant jealousy and where were you yesterday? All so petty and nerve-racking. Having to make up lies for every fart. As if there were no bigger, higher, why not say it, more spiritual problems, the kind that challenge a man's very existence and make him productive. Oh no, just perpetual scenes and petty quarrels. Siggie's chick has attempted suicide twice. Frankie has to maintain discipline with her fists. Billy, to tell the honest truth, is disappointed: she'd thought Maxie was entirely different, more stable and reliable, but Maxie does it with men off and on or lets men watch while she's doing it with some chick. They're all pretty mixed up. Their tragic pasts. They've all had ghastly experiences. Siggie claims her father felt her up when she was twelve. Billy talks about early imprinting because she was only fourteen, though already plump and fully developed, when the Russians came, so three, sometimes she says five, Russians raped her, one after the other. Frankie says her mother was a bareback rider (or a ventriloquist) with a circus. And Maxie never wanted to play with dolls but was made to. (And so many other possibilities: the milk that was too hot, the ghoulish uncle, Grandpa's mustache holder, and a cousin from Stolp who could piss his name into the snow . . .)

But this is Father's Day. Today all chicks and imprinting episodes from the past have been left home. All by ourselves, we're off on a trip. Surrounded by a hundred thousand faceless men, we four voluntary, conscious, and therefore supernatural men are purposefully on our way: we're doing fine without the appendage, we're free, the new sex. Nature has taken us to her bosom. In every Prussianly signboarded forest, around trash cans on every lake shore, at every sylvan snack bar, we stop off, take a leak, settle down, and call one another from group to group: Hi, fellows! Cheers! It's good for us to be here. Let us here make tabernacles. Out here we're by ourselves. With no one to bother us. Blessed peace. No women quarreling and wishing for things. No Ilsebills far and wide. Nothing needs to stand at attention. Relax, friends. And let's have a drink. To what? To fathers. To all tired, broken-down, floppycock fathers. To all of us under Prussian pine trees, at scrubbed beer tables, in among the lake-shore garbage. Whichever way you've come: on foot, on bicycles, in carriages or cars. That's right, a nation of brothers, as it says in the song, all men together. On this Ascension Day let all men celebrate the Father on high, the Father who has exceeded all norms. And you guys on the gleaming motorcycles—"That's right, you over there on the opposite shore!"—who don't know yet what to do with your strength, who've wrapped yourselves in leather, black, rivet-studded angels, wtih your easy, springy stride and unerring flair, film figures all. Lanky, lurking wolves. And one who has brought a trumpet blows aggressive signals. Yes, let us celebrate Father's Day, celebrate Father's Day. . . .

On the shore of the Grunewaldsee, in a place where the forest has been thinned, under a clump of pale mottled pines, on a floor of sand, pine needles, quaking grass, Frankie and Siggie put down the cases of beer and the ice bucket with the schnapps. Maxie carried the food basket with the steaks and lamb kidneys. When they had unloaded the spade, the poker, and the iron grill, Billy hauled two stones from nearby and set them down as a fireplace. As though at the end of a long journey, of mythogenic wanderings, she said, "This place is fabulous. This is where we cook."

(Long years ago, on our retreat. Dispersed in the Masurian marshes. And after the Battle of Wittstock, when with the help of Torstenson's cavalry and the Scottish Lesley and King regiments we had defeated the imperial troops and stopped to roast twelve spitted oxen over . . .) Make a fire. Gather wood. Dead wood, washed ashore and now as hard as bone. Break branches over knees. Crate salts. Once contained sprats from Kiel. Snap brittle branches off bushes for which it is still winter. Pick up gnarled pine cones that burn like mad. And what else? Your feelings and suchlike kindling. My crumpled papers with their iambic meshes of hate. All ideas are born of flame. We who rub together and take fire. The old quarrel that heats the house. My arguments burn better than yours. Your love only smolders and dies away. Your morality has never yet struck a spark. It leaves us cold! Cold cold cold!

"No, Maxie. Oh, why didn't we leave you home!" said Billy as she piled kindling on crumpled paper between two stones. "These hordes of men—it's just no good for little girls like you. You and your begging; I could kick myself for giving in, giving in once again. Oh, please take me, oh, please let me come. I'll never forgive myself. What if those vulgar boys over there notice who's here! What I'm talking about? You're not going to stand there and tell me you're not a little girl any more. Don't make me laugh. Hear that, Frankie? Little Maxie doesn't want to be Papa's darling any more, she wants to be a he-man like us. No more feminine frills, everything simple and straightforward between men. Did you ever hear anything so ridiculous?"

By then the wee little flame was rising voraciously. No one laughed. Only a few gnats from the lake. And more to herself than to Siggie, Frankie said: "Our Billy doesn't realize that when you come right down to it she's our darling butterball; that's why Maxie gave her an oversized bra for her tits on Mother's Day. Actually our Billy should have stayed home like a cozy housewife, doing crossword puzzles or darning Maxie's socks. I could have sent my Bettina and a couple of Siggie's chicks to chat with her and nibble pretzels. Our butterball is completely out of place here, don't you agree?"

At that Billy, who had once been my Sibylle, kept silent like a man (obstinately, sullenly) and busied herself with the fire. By then it was sending up proper flame symbols. And at other cooking sites in Grunewald and Spandau Forest, in clearings between the trees of Tegel, wherever it was forbidden to cook, light matches, play with fire, men had piled wood between stones like consummate Boy Scouts and were cheering the rising flames. The mounted police patrols could hardly ignore them. "We haven't seen a thing," they said. "But be careful, guys, even if it is Father's Day."

This is what distinguishes the male. Wherever he goes and describes his circle, he will set up a fireplace, test the wind, gauge the situation, and comply with the regulations. This he knows from the beginning, the moment he starts out. His passage is marked by traces of fire. That is how men give evidence of history.

They took the spade and dug a ditch around their campfire. "Didn't you ever hear of forest fires?" Siggie watched the flying sparks. Frankie stared at the flames as if to read messages in their secret script. Maxie jumped three or four times over the fire, which was gradually burning down to a bed of embers. Only Billy kept a purpose in view; off to one side, where she had deposited spices, pepper mill, and other accessories, she smacked the foot-long, inch-thick steaks down on a breadboard. She rubbed bacon rind over the four-legged iron grate, which showed signs of encounters with numerous beds of coals. Then she cut green peppers into strips. Sleeves rolled up. Sturdy forearms. Cleaver the Cook, to whom all things are hamburger. Then she cut the kidneys open, releasing their pissy smell.

Close to the fire, Billy's face was shining. All that stupid talk; she tried hard not to listen. You shits! What do you know! Cooking over an open fire has always been man's business. Ever since the Stone Age. And later, those spitted oxen. It was the men who scoffed at pots and pans and made steaks and sheep kidneys sizzle over naked coals. On winter campaigns through the swamps of Lithuania. On the still-burning timbers of razed convents, I roasted piglets, lambs, and young geese. . . . When the Hussites got as far as Oliva . . . And after the Battle of Wittstock . . .

But Frankie continued to despise all cookery as woman's work. "What delicious tidbit is Mommy going to make for us now? Tattooed bulls' balls? Little boys' peckers? Ah, what would we do without our mommy. We guys just stand around like dopes, talking about the nuclear deterrent and the grave political situation, but she takes care of us, she works and slaves without a question or thought for herself. Nothing's too good for us."

Maxie only said, "Don't mind her. You're OK, Billy. We appreciate you."

But that's something my Sibylle never knew. When I took up with her in May 1950, she had just come over from the

456

freshly baked Democratic Republic, specifically from Hoyers-werder, where her parents, refugees from Danzig–West Prussia, had settled and whence they regularly sent their only child plum butter and crumb cake. In those days Billy was a curly-blond law student, voluptuously rounded, sometimes hard-working, sometimes moodily lazy, who had really wanted to study something entirely different, I don't remember what.

We considered ourselves engaged. And during the first four semesters she actually did things my way. Then she suddenly and deliberately turned vamp, and I was only allowed to fuck her before or after. Intermittent fits of weeping. That early imprinting. Five or seven Russians. In the cellar. On empty potato sacks. Made her want to give up her studies. And do something entirely different, something normal, start a chicken farm or just be a housewife, have children (five or six) or emigrate to Australia and start from scratch.

While casually preparing for her exams, she drained and dropped at least a dozen men, including two or three exotic types. I stayed within reach and said my little piece: "Look here, what do you really want? Look here, can't you finally make up your mind? Look here, must you always go on wanting something different? Look here, how many wishes have you got left?"

So quick as a flash, because I thought it would help, I made her a child. But the kid was in the way and got turned over to its grandparents quick as a flash. Motherhood nauseated Sibylle. And her vamp phase was petering out. She lost weight, began to look like a skinny old maid. She wouldn't let me or anyone else near her. Just talked about existentialism, that kind of thing. And when she'd finished clerking and opened her own office in Schmargendorf, she started making friends with divorcees whose cases she had argued successfully in court; one of them was Frankie.

But once her decision—"I'm different and that's that"—was more or less definite, she let me in now and then. We got along much better than before. (You have to expect these contradictions.) Our daughter even got to visit the monkeys and seals with us once a month at the zoo: we looked (in photos) like real parents, a little family.

It wasn't until the summer of 1960—Sibylle had made a big thing of her thirtieth birthday—that I was definitely through. Maxie had come into the picture and refused to be satisfied with half the cake. ("You can go on being friends. But that's all.") At first I had thought or hoped that Maxie would be just another chick like the others. It's just an act, I thought. And Billy will gobble up this spindly-legged kid the same as she'd been gobbling up men, rare or well done. And for quite some time Billy did think she was wearing the pants. But meanwhile she was filling out and softening up; she'd gone crazy about keeping house, with a built-in kitchen and a dishwasher and fancy furniture from Knoll's. Her standard sentence (preceding a long speech about cookery) was "If I only had the cook book my great-grandmother wrote before the Nazis killed her in the concentration camp."

Oh well, she'd always liked to cook, and there was no change, either during her vamp phase or when she went different. (Her Rhenish sauerbraten, her Hungarian goulash, her saltimbocca, her coq au vin . . .)

Anyway, it wasn't long before Maxie had the say. Maxie decided when and with whom they'd take vacations on Elba, Formentera, or this year on Gotland. Maxie decided which Godard film, what Beckett or Ionesco absolutely couldn't be missed. Maxie had the wall-to-wall carpeting ripped up. Maxie said, "The television set goes here." Maxie slept around. Maxie ran up debts, and Billy paid. And Maxie had said, "On Father's Day you'll kindly stay home."

What a scene. It took a two-hour crying jag, six broken champagne glasses, and a handkerchief chewed to pieces to bend Maxie's will. So when Siggie interceded with "And who'll do the cooking? Frankie, I suppose?," Maxie had said, "OK, let her come, just this once. But no scenes, see? None of your fuss and bother and bickering and wishing this and wishing that. I won't stand for it. I simply won't stand for it."

And when, all over Berlin, Father's Day began with a mass exodus, a painstaking search for suitable spots, and the ritual of fire making, Billy tried her level best not to behave like an offended crybaby or a moody femme. Taking care of the fire helped. And Frankie, Siggie, and Maxie were so Father's Day crazed and busy with themselves that Billy's state of cozy-warm inner conflict probably escaped them.

There was plenty to do. Like all the ten thousand, no, hundred thousand men on the lake shores, between the trees, outside refreshment stands, at scrubbed tables, Siggie (sprawled out), Frankie (standing), and Maxie (walking restlessly back and forth) were guzzling beer. The fifth and sixth bottles had already been sloshed down. When the pressure became overwhelming, the boyish Maxie did something terrific; instead of relieving her bladder in the usual squatting position, she unbuttoned the fly of her jeans, spread her legs, took out a pink pecker with a deftness suggesting long practice, brought it into a horizontal position, and began, in time-honored male manner, to urinate against a pale mottled pine tree.

Evidently the appliance, made from some synthetic material, was efficiently fastened over the piss hole by a rubber suction cup, for Maxie pissed at length with deceptive verisimilitude (seen from a distance, of course) against the tree trunk. In so doing she looked past the tree and across the lake at the hordes of male Father's Day celebrants on the far shore. (If it had been winter, Maxie could easily have pissed a big M into the snow.)

Laughter and amazement. Frankie wanted a chance at the marvelous thing; she wanted to touch it, fasten it onto herself with the suction cup, and give it a try. "Boy oh boy! Where'd you get it? Denmark? Only nineteen marks eighty? I gotta have it. I gotta!"

Frankie stood like a man, her masculine gaze lost in hazy, faraway prairies. No more penis envy. Never again that humiliating female squat. Like thousands and thousands of men facing thousands and thousands of other pine trees, Frankie pissed erect, sending a gently slanting stream against upstanding Prussian trees. Yes sirree!

When it was Siggie's turn, she held a bottle of Schultheiss to her lips up top while pissing down below—like a real man. Her Hell's Angel cap pushed back over the nape of her neck. "Father's Day! Father's Day!" she roared, and the stags of the neighboring male groups, among them fraternity students in full regalia, responded with rutting cries.

But when Billy left the fire and her growing bed of coals and said, "Me, too. Let me try it!" she got nothing but fatherly words. "You're going too far, child. Enough is enough. We can't just go on wishing all the time. Our little butterball promised to behave. How about something to eat?" Frankie bellowed, "I'm hungry!" And Maxie began to sing: "One two three! We are hungaree. . . ."

This left Billy, my poor insulted and so tragically imprinted Sibylle, no choice but to smooth out the accumulated coals with the poker, set the four-legged grate over them, dispose four enormous steaks previously rubbed with ground pepper, thyme, and oil, and six halved sheep kidneys into which she had pressed quartered cloves of garlic, close together on the grate, till they hissed, sizzled, and discharged their fragrance, which mingled with the resinous Grunewald air and the musty smell of the lake.

Billy was as busy as Cleaver the Cook in the Swedish camp, as busy as if she'd been called upon to tend twelve spitted oxen at once. "Cooking over an open fire is man's business. You can't tell me different. It's a primordial instinct. Nature wanted it that way."

After turning the steaks and halved kidneys, Billy thrust the strips of green pepper between the pieces of meat, which, though shrunken, retained their juice. Only the fluid from the kidneys was dripping into the fire. When Maxie, supported by Frankie, gave a repeat performance of the hunger song— "One two three!"—Billy shouted, "Just a minute, you pigs. It's almost ready."

Four women eating. But if you saw them chewing their oversized bites, their teeth not nibblingly concealed but brazenly bared, you'd have said it was four men eating.

"Hm," said Frankie, chewing. "That was before the Battle of Wittstock. A bouncing lass; she was wearing women's clothes when we caught her, but there was a young boy underneath. We'd have to put him to the question. But already the bloody battle was . . ."

"They couldn't keep watch over me in the confusion," said Maxie, chewing, "so in the first alarm I escaped up a tree. And there I read line after line of a book I'd swiped from the provost. And that book told me in pictures and in words exactly what was happening on the battlefield."

"That's how it is with reality," said the chewing Siggie from between terrifying incisors. "Whatever is, has already been written. And us sitting here chewing steak, that, too, has happened before; it happened right after the battle, after we'd driven the imperial troops across the Dosse and into the swamps. Am I right, Billy?"

"Right," said Billy, chewing. "That's when I was the cook in the Scottish Lesley regiment. And we didn't have steaks; we had spitted oxen. And when the slashing and gouging were over, our Maxie, whom we'd caught somewhere in women's clothes, climbed down from the tree with her book in which everything had been written beforehand, and we gave the kid a chunk of beef because he was so skinny, but he was lively and talked in phrases plucked from the lips of the people—a little scamp from the baggage train, a simple fool, as it says in the book. Always putting on an act. Gets ideas while standing on his head. Why, the kid has ears like funnels."

I've told you how it was. Maxie drove me out. That skinny kid, inappropriately christened with the gentle name of Susanne. The skinny kid whom nothing, on pork cracklings, no boiled beef, no roast goose, no greasy, hot mutton could fatten. Nothing could upholster her collarbone, cushion her spinal column. Now that Maxie was moving away from ecstatic interpretive dancing and concentrating on classical ballet drill, we called her body emaciated and her soul bulimic.

That's why Sibylle drove me, who had the gall to be a man, out of our shared apartment. No, it was Maxie who drove me out, took my place, took my desk and my wellworn chair. As for my bed—the bars of which had been affixed as though for all time to the frame of Sibylle's bed—she sawed it off, snip-snap, with a metal saw.

I was present. Ostentatiously amputated. Severed from board and bed. My bed was thrust aside, reviled, cursed, and spat upon. Pillow, feather bed, sheets, bolster, springs, and mattress were handed, along with a tip, to the garbage man: 'Throw the bastard out! What do we need him for? Anything he can do I can do with my little finger."

Only then did Maxie send for some metal workers, who from the skeleton of my orphaned bed fashioned a long, round bar, the ends of which were bent into handles and sunk in the masonry. The remains of my bed had become Maxie's ballet barre. Converted to an ascetic function. Divested of all memory of Sibylle as we lay (when times were good) in our double bed and were one flesh. Nothing left but severe discipline. Classical beauty. Sweat-raising exercise. Maxie wanted to go on the stage and do solo or at least group dancing. Susanne Maxen, known as Maxie, was thought to be talented.

And Billy, too (my Sibylle), thought herself destined, if not to play other roles, then at least to portray herself. Often after meals, and so likewise when Father's Day was being celebrated all around them, and the steaks, still red within and salted only before serving, as well as the juicy sheep kidneys, had been done away with—there was unbuttered black bread with the meat and sheep's-milk cheese afterward—Billy said, "My whole life is a movie."

For which reason the Grunewald Father's Day, which Billy and Frankie, Siggie and Maxie celebrated to the gruesome end in the midst of a hundred thousand men, forming on the lake shore a group among other groups, must now be viewed from varying perspectives: prone in the trampled grass, from the branches of climbable Grunewald pine trees, from bushes, from the unruffled lake. And let there also be cameramen with the other ninety thousand and more men in Spandau, Britz, and Tegel Forest, at beer tables and around other lakes, and keep at it, keep at it. Everywhere camouflaged microphones, lest any talk be lost. Now! Now! During the noonday break . . .

After replete belching a few words are said. (We'll keep them in reserve and cut them in later on.) By the Griebnitzsee, a bank clerk in his mid-forties announces over a schnitzel that isn't there any more, "But life is like that." At a gathering of the Harmonia Choral Society under beech trees in Britz, a pensioned schoolteacher says to his fellow members after jellied pig's knuckle with cabbage and puree of peas, "Song is the only pleasure left." Immediately after the third *Bockwurst* on the banks of the Teltow Canal, a foreman bricklayer sums up the situation: "Now the world is OK again." And one of the black-leather boys who are keeping their motorcycles ready to take off—his name is Herby—says (after the bags of French fries have been emptied), "A day like this with no fucking is a total loss." While, almost simultaneously, Billy contributes her significant sentence: "My whole life is a movie."

After that, bemused by the buzzing midday stillness, they pursue their own thoughts. The hour of Pan. A few high-pitched gnats. Hats and caps put aside. Billy, Frankie, Siggie, Maxie lie, each by herself—Billy on a camel's-hair blanket—smoking, chewing blades of grass, with Maxie trying, as thousands are trying in Spandau and Tegel, to wear out a piece of chewing gum. The thoughts the four of them are pursuing this midday are thoughts of the kind that lead, in a classical Western, to conflict between heroes.

Maybe Siggie, maybe Frankie, anyway, one against many. Maybe Billy, maybe Maxie: back to back they shoot their way out of the trap. Quadriune thoughts unite the four of them—the victorious four. They caress the loneliness that goes with superiority. They despise the crowd. Their indolent, self-assured gait. For in thoughts they're always quicker on the draw. They cross the dusty square. Their eyes narrow; the saloon empties at their approach. All four at the bar. That thirsty ride. Weighted down with the saddles of dead horses. The way they shoot, period. In any position. Even funny ones. The way Siggie (after a long ride through the alkali desert) sits in the bathtub with soapsuds up to her neck, yet through the towel takes care of the lurking enemy bang bang.

And always there's a milk-faced boy who makes trouble, who's in the way, who stands dreamy-dopey in the field of fire and whom Billy has to rescue, though the Smith Brothers (Frankie and Siggie) have already tightened the noose around the trembling kid's (Maxie's) neck. But in thoughts and films that never tear, the rescued kid always turns into the scrawny, stubborn, and comically angular girl in pants. This comes out in thought and fact when the gunshot wound has to be cauterized, or the arrowhead extracted: small breasts under the gooseflesh. Our Maxie's name is Susanne. But Billy staunchly forgoes a fuck in the bushes. The leavetaking is gruffly affectionate, no more, a good-natured smack on the boy-in-girl's taut ass: "So long, Susie. Take care of yourself."

Then more loneliness in the saddle or walking beside the rickety nag through desert and prairie. Vultures describing smaller and smaller circles. Skeletons all about. Plagued by horseflies or gnats. Gold, money, thinks Frankie. Revenge, thinks Siggie. Only Billy yearns to go straight, not to have to kill kill kill any more, to raise cattle in the wide, billowing pasture land and back home in Kentucky—"You come, too, Maxie!"—and break in horses.

But Frankie jumps out of the film to the shore of the Grunewaldsee, where Father's Day lies dozing, and shoots from the hip with both index fingers: Bang! Bang! "You curs! You wuthless curs!"

But Westerns aren't the whole story. Billy, my Sibylle, whose life is a movie, stars in other pictures as well. Under the name of Bill, she has gone to sea and hauled codfish to Iceland. A hard life.

And in war films, Billy has taken an active part in several campaigns. In the Thirty Years' War she claims, if not as cook in a Scottish regiment, then as a colonel under the Swedish general Banér (immediately after the Battle of Wittstock), to have reconquered Silesia, driven out the Catholics, and as Chancellor Oxenstierna's courier gone to Danzig, where she met the poet (and double agent) Opitz, for whom a kitchenmaid cooked diet fare and whose later years she sweetened.

Or in love films: Sibylle Miehlau has at all times been irresistible as a man. She claims to have taken the place of sweet Jesus in the bed of the High Gothic Dorothea of Montau on the first night of the journey to Aachen, when the pilgrims stopped at the Jug in Putzig. A wandering student he was at the time, and they did it over and over and then some. Naturally Maxie has to play the part of the frail Dorothea in ecstasy.

And Billy also has the starring role in a picture called *Father's Day*, which begins with a hundred thousand men going to the woods and shows how on foot, in carriages, and in cars they go looking for places, make fires, drink beer, piss against trees, cook, chew pieces of meat, rest after lunch, and pursue thoughts that are all filmed.

Suddenly a breeze. The Prussian pines were clearing their throats. Under the ashes of the campfire the coals were beginning to look hopeful. The lake ruffled its forehead. Seven, eleven crows flew up into the air—messengers from the black-leather angels on the far shore. Pine trees stirred elsewhere, by the Schlachtensee, by the Griebnitzsee. The oaks in Spandau Forest and in the mixed forest of Tegel remembered keenly. Smells moved from place to place. Paper napkins bloomed at lakeside cafés. And near the village of Lübars, where the German Democratic Republic marks its border with barbed wire, the breeze—which came from that direction—knew only one Germany. As though the sweet Lord had decided to suspend the noonday peace of this Ascension Day, which in Berlin and elsewhere is celebrated as Father's Day, with a "We-e-ell" more sighed than spoken.

And Billy, Frankie, Siggie, and Maxie were also shaken out of their thoughts and exciting adventure films. They jumped to their feet. Maxie was wearing sandals. Frankie sported paratroopers' boots. Siggie and Billy were wearing plain though sturdy shoes. All four flexed their knees. They shook off tatters of thoughts and prairie dust. They cracked their joints. They hopped about like sparring partners or sprinters before the start.

And on the far shore, as on the shores of faraway lakes, male limbs were picked up, shaken, stretched: Let's see what we can still do. Give the old Adam a chance. We can't just laze in bed all the time, letting sweet dreams melt in our mouths. Hell no! Gotta get back into action. What price the world?

"Hey, Siggie, what's wrong with you today? Hey, Maxie, do something! Put on a show! And what about Frankie? Can this be our good old Frankie? The wagoner and hellhound. The man with the iron claw. Let's go, boys. You, too, Billy. Didn't Billy promise to pull out the stopper? Hell, this is Father's Day, Father's Day!"

And then on all sides the great, the unprecedented male competition began. What made it really worth seeing was that the contestants were amateurs, but professional class. The rules? It's simple: everyone shows what he can do. That's how it's always been, as you can see recorded in Old Man Homer and Old Man Moses, in the *Nibelungenlied* or *The Struggle for Rome*. Not just the young people; Grandpa can join in, too, grabbing hold of a café chair by the bottom of one leg and lifting it high into the beech leaves.

Lots of people can chew up beer glasses and swallow them. Anybody who's been in the army can volunteer to do a hundred knee bends while holding a jerrycan of gasoline (only half full) out in front of him. Walking on hands still earns gasps of amazement. And what else?

Wherever men have gathered in dispersed order: Bavarian finger wrestling, all-German tug-of-war, East Asian free-style wrestling. All demonstrate strength, courage, and dexterity. And that's the mark of a man: dead serious about his merry games.

On the far shore, the black-leather motorcycle boys—"Boy, you'd think they'd suffocate!"—were throwing switchblade knives at one another, aiming well for a bare miss. The silly fraternity students nearby—they, too, still in full regalia—hadn't been able to think of anything better than bottoms-upping their beer while standing stiff and straight (with increasing difficulty), and snarling Old German and Latin toasts. A bald man in his mid-fifties, his head protected by a handkerchief knotted at the four corners, the eternal loner who always has his own little act, was squatting by the lake shore in the left foreground, fishing leeches out of the Grunewald sludge and placing them on his dismal, old-looking legs.

Why not? Why shouldn't he, too, have his fun? Isn't it a free society? Isn't each one of us free to apply as many leeches as he pleases?

And then, availing herself of her freedom, Maxie decided to climb one of the straight and staunch Prussian pine trees. She tossed off her sandals, stationed herself at some distance, and took her measure of the chosen tree in the midst of the group. But she didn't leap at it; no, she approached with a slow, spring step, playfully spreading and hooking her fingers as the big cats spread and hook their claws, and paused near the tree for a few seconds of meditation, perhaps to say a brief prayer; for Maxie, who had been raised a Catholic, had learned to appeal to Saint Anthony for help in drastic situations, for instance, when about to climb a pale mottled pine tree, because it looks easier from below than halfway up, where Maxie stopped to rest; foot after foot and hand over hand, scraping the skin off the edges of her feet and the palms of her hands, with no other reward for her trouble, danger, and pain than the resinous fragrance of the sticky bark. She was helped by the shouts of her friends Frankie and Siggie, whose jingle—"Stiff and straight, stiff and straight, like a soldier on parade!"—did more than spur her on. At first it only made her sad, but then, just before the knobbly-tousled top of the phallic pine tree, it brought on an honest-to-goodness surge of desire, for which reason Maxie, in a state of supreme exaltation, had to pause again and press close to the vibrant wood, until a very natural and decidedly feminine moan came pouring out of her: ahahahah. . . .

After that Maxie had some difficulty in negotiating the remaining four or five feet. But she made it in the end. Her friends were far away. Applause from below. Those comical figures in absurd foreshortening. Naturally they'd noticed something; they were crackling silly jokes. Maxie was just a bit dizzy but happy all the same in the swaying treetop.

"So what!" came the cry from above. "Just jealous. You can do it, too, if you want to. There's no shortage of trees. Come on, Billy. Old sourpuss. Lift your fat ass. Get a little tree between your thighs. Rub yourself up. Come on, come on. You going to be a stupid chick all your life, a crybaby bedwetter mama bigtit, a lie-still-and-take-it cunt?"

At that my Sibylle tried to fight back the tears, but they seemed to well up of their own accord, while high overhead the exalted Maxie did gymnastics, let out Iroquois war whoops, demanded full freedom to be different, reduced everything that was, is, and will be woman to a hair-haloed hole, and belittled men as stoppers: "I, Maximilian, am the new sex!" And from high in the treetop Maxie shouted into the well-advanced Father's Day, "I will beget a son, beget a son. And shall call his name Emmanuel. Em-ma-nu-el!"

That sounded good down below, though kind of grisly and ripe for the nut house. "Come on down!" cried Frankie, and busied herself with the two stones that Billy had positioned as a fireplace. While Maxie slowly, cautiously, testing her footrests, descended from her Ascension pine tree, Frankie hauled the two stones, one under each arm, to the lake shore and there shot-put first one, then the other amazingly far out into the water. With consummate technique. Frankie, the man with the broad back and narrow hips. Splash and splash again went the Grunewaldsee, and put forth two circles, which grew and intersected until they may have represented roughly what Frankie had in mind—God knows with whom; for if Maxie seemed to be self-sufficient, Frankie still needed a partner: two stones, still hot on one side, wrenched away from the fire that had meanwhile burned down, that went splash splash and intermingled their waves.

The phallic pine, the splashing stones. "You two and your symbolic shit!" said Siggie, and she spat out her chawed cigar butt. "Now tell me, what does this mean? Here you see a trouser button. And here you see needle and thread. Good housewife, is that it? A screw loose somewhere? A button looking for the right buttonhole? Just a little patience. All honest and aboveboard. I'll show you. Just keep quiet."

And with even, parallel thrusts from the outside in, through all four little holes, Siggie, without a tremor or a moment's hesitation, sewed the common trouser button to her left cheek. Not a drop of blood flowed. No jokes were cracked, not even by Maxie. Billy sweated with excitement,

467

while Frankie stared at the sewed-on button as though more than a trouser button had come to rest on Siggie's left cheek.

"There!" said Siggie after biting off the thread that protruded between her large, regular incisors. "Well? How does it look? Button on cheek. Doesn't mean a thing. It's not symbolic; it's gratuitous, so to speak. Or would somebody like to tell a thoughtful little tale of love's labor lost?"

Since in all situations Siggie (as did the feminist prosecutor Sieglinde Huntscha later on) displayed a face of strict classical beauty—Greek nose, high cheekbones, large hawkeyes under boldly delineated eyebrows and chiseled forehead—the button on her narrow, tapering cheek did not look funny but seemed, rather, to intimate that her beauty (without a button) was perhaps excessive.

"Not bad," said Frankie. Maxie pleaded, "Sew one on me. Please, please." But when Billy cried, "Marvelous!" and produced a pocket mirror from somewhere—"Look; look how becoming it is!"—Siggie rejected this bit of feminine frippery. "I know what I look like. Nothing to get so excited about. A little joke among friends. So now I'll wipe it off. OK, Billy, what have you got to offer?"

So then my poor Sibylle, who had always done everything wrong, decided as Billy to do something especially forceful and masculine. She suggested, seeing they were all friends, that they build a pyramid of friendship. She would be the bottom man, the base. On her right and left shoulders she would gladly support Frankie and Siggie. The athletic Maxie was invited to stand, balancing herself as she had learned to do, on Frankie's left and Siggie's right shoulder, so crowning the pyramid. And maybe Maxie could do a handstand on top. But first they would have to practice in a halfway position, that is, without Billy as bottom man. And oh yes, would they kindly do their climbing with bare feet. And maybe they could ask the solitary bald-headed leech-man down by the shore to snap a few souvenirs of the once completed friendship pyramid with Billy's foolproof cameramabubble. Because it would really be good. Something they'd like to look at later on. No, she'd manage all right as bottom man.

And, with interruptions and incidents, they did it. Maxie practiced her handstand on Frankie's left and Siggie's right shoulder until they had it down pat. Billy looked on while Frankie and Siggie took their boots and shoes off. Maxie trotted down to the lake and asked the solitary bald man if he'd mind snapping a few pictures. He said he'd be glad to, and pulled the last leeches off his legs. With taut thighs and rock-hard calves, Billy stood still while, with Maxie's help, Frankie and Siggie climbed up. But then, suddenly capricious, Maxie refused to crown the pyramid. It was all a lot of nonsense, some shitty idea. Besides, Maxie wasn't going to take orders from a femme. That would be the end. She'd rather climb the big, tall pine tree again.

So Frankie climbed down from Billy's left shoulder, while Siggie stayed in position on the right. "Do as you're told," cried Frankie, "or you'll catch it."

"I ain't takin' orders from you," Maxie whined. "I do my own thing."

Whereupon Frankie gave it to Maxie in the face, one, two, left and right. "How about it? Not yet? Bim bam. Better now? Or would you care for a little more? OK, then."

In the end Maxie stood weeping on the shoulders of Frankie and Siggie, who were both standing on the shoulders of my poor Sibylle, who was crying because she felt sorry for the slapped Maxie. Frankie and Siggie were looking grim. Maxie didn't dare do her handstand. But even so, the picture, which the helpful baldy took after spoiling two exposures by jiggling the camera, was a success. Later on, when she had given up dog breeding and was free-lancing, Siggie had the picture of the pyramid of friendship blown up to enormous size and pinned it to one of her attic walls.

"Damn it all!" said Prosecutor Sieglinde Huntscha when asked about the meaning of the large, coarse-grained photograph. "It's just a part of what our Billy had to put up with."

Naturally, since the pyramid of friendship, with Billy as bottom man and Maxie, standing on the shoulders of Frankie and Siggie, as crown, was erected (and snapped) on Father's Day, it was not only seen by the neighboring group of fraternity students in full regalia, but also attracted attention on the far shore of the Grunewaldsee, where the black-leather boys had stopped playing with their sharp knives and wanted at last to be doing something.

I don't know if the boozing students belonged to a so-called dueling fraternity, whether the name of their club was Teutonia, Saxonia, Thuringia, Rhenania, Friesia, or just plain Germania. Nor have I any desire to read up on the subject and find out what tasks, duties, and rights fell to freshmen and full-fledged members. These boys had no dueling scars. Round faces and long faces, some with glasses. Anyway, they came closer while the pyramid was still standing and the pictures were still being taken. And the black angels from the far shore sent two motorized scouts, who took up positions on the lake-shore embankment, but too late; by then the pyramid had broken up. Never again would those four form such a tower. Never again would their friendship find so sturdy a bottom man. (Ah, Maxie, what has become of you? Giving physiotherapy treatments somewhere—in Wiesbaden, I think. And Frankie? High up in the real-estate business in Hamburg. And Billy? Ah, Billy! Only Siggie is still accessible to me, with her immoderate accusations. . . .)

But befuddled as they were from their bottoms-upping, the Teutonia or was it Rhenania brothers were still coming closer, whereas the black angels, on their motorcycles that lacked no accessory, kept as still in their seats as if they'd been turned to stone. The Saxons talked and talked. The black-leather boys didn't say one word.

"Marvelous! Amazing! Sensational!" cried a Teuton in glasses.

Another shouted, "Encore! Encore!"

Then all the fraternity brothers wanted to see the pyramid of friendship rebuilt. "Gentlemen, if it's not an imposition, we would be so delighted to witness your uncommonly extraordinary feat again."

But Frankie waved them off. "Nothing doing. Show's over. Beat it, kids. We want privacy."

Was it instinct, was it insight? Had my curvaceous Billy opened their eyes? Suddenly the tone changed. "Why, they're . . . This is too much! What insolence! Females! Common, vulgar females! Degrading Father's Day with their obscenities!"

And a fat freshman in glasses thrust himself into the role of spokesman. "Ladies—or whatever you are. Your presence in general, and most particularly in this area, which today is reserved exclusively for the celebration of Father's Day, inspires horror and protest in us, I repeat, protest. It would be no exaggeration to call it scandalous. We have here a monstrous infringement on ethical norms. Not that we are declared enemies of women. On the contrary. Very much on

470

the contrary. Women, said Goethe, are silver plates upon or into which we men lay, as it were, golden apples. But today—with all respect for your acrobatic feats—that does not apply. Your presence here is an offense against all principle. It is our duty to put our foot down, and in no uncertain terms. We expect you to leave the area at once, but first we demand an explanation."

Frankie, Siggie, Billy, and Maxie took a defensive stance. Frankie grabbed the poker. Siggie turned around her signet ring, which had a short, blunt knob on the palm side, transforming it into a knuckle-duster. Maxie armed herself with the four-legged iron grill. Only Billy stood facing the superior power of the fraternity brothers with bare hands, though well-armed tongue. "What's this I hear? Throwing *us* out! Don't make me laugh! Men? You bandy-legged curs call yourselves men? Queens with complexes, that's what you are. Mamas' darlings. Mass-produced Oedipuses. What's the matter? Mommy take her breast away? Didn't she let you suck enough when you were little? Did she leave you lying in your piss, screaming yourselves blue in the face? Did she give you too few strokes and too many clouts? And you, young man! Yes, you! Were you standing there in your nightshirt, peeking through the crack in the door, while Mama and Papa were doing awful things? Did a puppy ever lick you or you? And you over there! Was your big brother or your ugly little sister in the way, always in the way? Speak up. Let's swap complexes. I've got plenty."

They retreated. With and without glasses, they withdrew. No signet ring, iron grill, or poker drove the fraternity brothers from the field; no, what drove them was Billy's direct discourse, her expostulation: "Jerks! Jerk-offs!"

And when my Sibylle suddenly turned around, peeled down her tight-fitting jeans, and showed the Teutons her Venus-white ass, whence a fart instantly escaped, the Saxons and other Germani were seized with panic terror. In full regalia, they withdrew, losing two or three pairs of glasses and a book of student songs, out of which Maxie later on sang "*Gaudeamus igitur*," et cetera. . . .

What laughter! Frankie's neighing wagoner's laugh. Siggie, in laughing, showed two rows of clenched teeth. Maxie gasped, held her sides, and pressed her thighs together like a

471

little girl who is having trouble holding it in. Billy stood straddle-legged, hurling volleys of laughter after the enemy. (Thus, in their days as Teutonic Knights, had they laughed in the winter camp at Ragnit while hunting down the heathen Lithuanians and Prussians. Thus, as Swedish cavalrymen, had they laughed at the fleeing imperial troops at Wittstock, before the papists, every last man of them, croaked in the Brandenburg swamps. . . .)

A dry, infectious laugh. And the contagion of the four heroes' laughter seems to have carried a long way, for tatters of laughter blew across the lake from the far shore. And there was laughter on the shores of other lakes, under trees, and in club strength at tables, though for other reasons. Humor was the order of the day. Hearty male laughter. Slapped chests and thighs. Unrestrained belly-laughter. Don't choke, old man. I could die laughing. At jokes. Rip-roaring men's jokes. Heard this one? What's the difference between . . . ? Little Fritz goes to the goat barn and sees his father. . . . Count Bobby has an inflamed eye. . . . Moishe runs into Abie at the whorehouse. . . . Hitler and Stalin meet in hell. . . . So little Fritz says . . . Why, Moishe, says Abie. . . . Oh, cries Count Bobby, if it were only my eye. . . . Well, the difference between a coffee bean and . . . Oh, says Hitler to Stalin, if I'd only known. . . . But the goat isn't to blame, says little Fritz's mother. . . .

But loudly, softly, heartily, and tearfully as the ten, no, a hundred thousand men demonstrated their Father's Day humor, the two black angels, who witnessed the big laugh astride their overbred motorcycles, were disinclined to join in the merriment, to laugh, to put on so much as a fleeting smile. In them no punch line released a catch. Nothing, but nothing whatever, struck them as funny. Not the slightest joke occurred to them. Seriousness was written all over their faces. Attentively, as though doing their professional duty, the two in black leather had registered the altercation with the fraternity brothers—every incendiary word. Those incredible insults. Those kicks in the ass of male dignity. Billy's bare behind, which had put the students to flight, imprinted itself like a seal or a brand, deep on the minds of Herby and Ritchie, as the two black angels were called.

And no sooner had the laughter died down—only Maxie was still gasping—than the two motorcycles started howling chugging buzzing. After an ostentatious loop across the lake-shore meadow and impressive slaloming in and out of the Prussian pines, the witnesses roared away to make their sensational report on the far shore.

"Hey, kids!" Billy shouted after them. "What's the hurry?"

But when the men all around the Grunewaldsee, on the Wannsee, in the forests of Spandau and Tegel, had shown themselves and others what they could do (glass eating, stone putting, tug-of-warring, up-and-downing trees, bearing pain, lifting heavy weights overhead), when on Father's Day, which falls on Ascension Day, achievement-proud male laughter had reached its climax, when all had laughed their fill in Lübars and Britz, in woods and meadows, and even Maxie could laugh no more—Frankie stationed himself in front of a chaste birch tree—one of several birches among the pines—and laughed, battering everything, yes everything, even himself in his absolute greatness, with laughter, until he had laughed the chaste birch tree bare. The old wagoner and veteran of all wars (he'd been at Tannenberg, Wittstock, and Leuthen) could laugh birch trees bare.

Frankie stood ten paces away, so that the tree was full in his line of fire, and shot off volleys of laughter both aimed and scattered—his great cynical laughter act. (Nothing was sacred to him.) He commanded the fresh, May-green leaves to fall as in November, and when Billy, Siggie, and Maxie shouted "More! More!" he defoliated the rest of the birches roundabout, the last one only half, for in the meantime the laughter between Spandau and Tegel and on the shores of the Grunewaldsee had shifted, as it does so often, to male mourning. From one extreme to the other.

Everything, even the monumental feat that only a moment before had aroused wonder and demanded to be photographed, rose up in a bitter belch. Even the recent, undeniable triumph of seeing Mama's little fraternity darlings put to flight had the sour aftertaste of absurdity. The void shone through. Father's Day hangover turned the flushed cheeks of the men, wherever they had established themselves in the greenery, ash-gray. Leaden melancholy mingled with every swallow of beer. Nausea. Existential belches, bitter as gall. Sighs rose from bottomless depths, climbed stairs, forced their way to the light: pallid, alcoholic ghosts, which, unable to bear the sharp scent of the Prussian pines for long, burst, dis-

473

persed, and fell all about like mildew, which didn't make our Father's Day men any more cheerful.

Still, tongues were loosed. Men unburdened themselves. The misery of the centuries—just among men, after all—was avowed. ("Be honest for once, old boy. Why pretend? Out with the truth, the whole, unvarnished truth. It's the only way.") All the defeats, historical and present, notched on a long pole. Coiled omissions that, when uncoiled, yield thread enough to embroider a shroud for the male and his categorical greatness.

"The truth," said Siggie, "is that we're through. Completely washed up and useless. We men just don't want to admit it. From the standpoint of history, the one thing men were good for, we've failed. Or politically speaking, all we are these days is custodians of bankruptcy, trying to postpone the crisis and prevent the worst. The atomic deterrent. And what about the Wall? It stinks. Everything stinks!"

And Frankie's analysis—"Since the end of the Stone Age, when the future started with copper, bronze, and iron, we men have done nothing but build shit!"—rose up into the air like skywriting. "Failures! We're failures!" Even Maxie confessed that she'd come to the end of her masculine rope. "Sometimes I wonder if it was right to take full responsibility for everything, for every little problem. The strain has been too great. Down through the years. On every man jack of us. Why shouldn't the women once in a while? They'll see what it is to have to take the rap for everything. Anyway, I'm sick of it. No more ideas. I could use a rest. I wouldn't mind being dependent for five or six centuries, as long as I'm taken care of. Has its points, playing the little woman and nothing else. Nothing to do but flicker my eyelashes and hold out my cunt. Get a kid now and then. Look forward to Mother's Day. Read trashy novels and run the dishwasher when I'm in the mood. Wouldn't that be a ball!"

"All right, Maxie," said Billy. "You can start right in. Complaining won't get us anywhere. The dishes are still lying around unwashed. OK, get going. With sand and lake water. Ugh, they're all full of ants. Never mind, I'll give you a hand. I'll dry." Billy had even (with tender loving care) put a checked kitchen towel into the food basket.

But Maxie wasn't in the mood for anything. And certainly not for dishwashing. Or not yet. Not in this century. "Leave the ants be. They'll do it. They've cleaned bigger dishes than these. Besides, I've got to think. Well, about this and that and the meaning of it all."

But when Billy insisted on the dishwashing and said, "You can think later, my son," Frankie awoke from well-deep melancholy and said with a certainty grounded in equal depths, "What do you mean, 'my son'? If any of us is Maxie's father, it's me. And to make myself perfectly clear, let me add: my son does not wash dishes. And certainly not on Father's Day."

"Exactly," said Maxie to Billy. "My daddy's name is Frankie, and you're just a femme. So get going! Wash up the shit yourself. And don't bother us."

"But," said Billy, again on the verge of tears, "you can't push me around all the time and treat me like a maid. I cook and clean and slave. But why only me? I'm not your dishrag. I demand equal rights. I have my pride, too."

Here Siggie broke in. "Like women. Fighting just like women. I thought we'd left all that behind us. It's either all four of us or none. I say, let's celebrate Father's Day. In peace. Get me?"

"Exactly," said Frankie sternly to Maxie. "Hear that, my son?"

"But then you have no right to treat me like a femme," cried Billy, sobbing.

"But that's what you are. A femme and a weeping willow," cried Maxie. "Sob sob! Drip drip!"

"You're hopeless," said Siggie, giving Maxie a swift one-two in the face. Whereupon Frankie bellowed, "Nobody clouts my son but me, nobody!" and kicked Siggie in the shins. Whereupon Maxie—while Siggie was aiming a straight right at Frankie—spat in Billy's tear-stained face. Whereupon Billy dug both hands into Maxie's crew cut. And already the melee was exactly the same as long years ago when, after the Saxons capitulated at Pirna, the spoils were being divided and Frankie fought with Siggie over a box of sweets in which the farm cook Amanda Woyke was later to keep her correspondence with Count Rumford—the nut. (And on another historic occasion—at the very start of the migrations—there had been another argument over nothing, until only fists . . .)

From a certain distance—a stone's throw—the students in full regalia were watching. And two black-leathered scouts on motorcycles were again within earshot. Maxie's nose was genuinely bloody. Siggie gave Frankie a shiner. Frankie twisted Siggie's arm out of joint. But it was Billy who took the most punishment, for when Siggie, Frankie, and Maxie had made up and were wiping one another's noses, putting the arm back in joint, and cooling the shiner, the butterball was still weeping for all she was worth, and the news was carried around the lake by the two motorcycle scouts. (As the police reported the next day, harmless roughhouses but also serious fights were taking place in other spots, wherever Father's Day was being celebrated: a hundred and twelve calls went out to police cars. Property was damaged. Eighty-seven injuries were enumerated, among them nineteen serious cases and one death. . . .)

Oh, ye warriors for the cause. Ye dreamers, dreaming of the great day. Ye heroes always ready to antedate your death. Ye battlers for justice. Ye victors over life. Attackers and defenders. Ye death-despising men.

And then a great weariness descended on the warriors. And elsewhere as well, the ten, the hundred thousand men thought they'd take a little nap because they'd pretty well knocked themselves out. Frankie was snoring first. Then, lying on her belly, all four limbs outstretched, Siggie fell asleep. But when Billy couldn't stop sobbing, Maxie sat down beside her and said: "All right, butterball, just go to sleep. We mussed you up pretty bad, didn't we? Why did you start in with that stupid dishwashing business? You should have brought paper plates. But really, there's nothing to cry about. Oh my, oh my. Still a few tears. Just go to sleep. Or say: They can kiss my . . . Or think of something pleasant. Or I'll tell you a story to put you to sleep. A story about prehistoric times when all the women had three tits. Or something else. The story of the Flounder, for instance . . .

"There was once a butterball. Her name was—hey, what was her name?—Ilsebill. She had a man, and his name was Max. She sat home all the time, painting her nails with green polish. He always went fishing on weekends, off the harbor mole. And while Max fished and fished, his butterball wife would paint her fingernails green, and then she'd lie all alone in her pisspot, wishing this, that, and some other guy into her bed.

"So one afternoon when Max was fishing off the mole, a

476

Flounder bit. That's a flatfish. His popeyes are out of line with his blubbery mouth. He happens in a fairy tale, so naturally he could talk, and he said to Max, 'Set me free and you can make a wish.'

"So Max took the Flounder off the hook, threw him back into the sea with a splash, and said: 'Oh, Flounder. My Ilsebill is just a cuddly little wife; all she wants to do is kiss and cuddle, fuck and be fucked, by this one an that one and that one and this one. With me she's never satisfied. She always wants to be banged by some guy that's not me. She thinks my stinkhorn stinks. What should I do, oh, what should I do?'

"'So what kind of a guy does she want to do it with?' asked the Flounder, giving him a crooked look from the water.

"'Well, with a fire chief in uniform, for instance,' said the fisherman, looking out over the smooth sea, 'cause he was fishing in the Baltic.

"'You're a fire chief already, with braid and buttons,' said the Flounder and dove under.

"So Max in uniform climbed into bed with his Ilsebill and fucked her so hard that his buttons popped. And he kept it up until Ilsebill had enough of the fire chief and her legs went stiff and she started to fidget and moan, 'Oh, if only I could have a judge in there.'

"So then Max called the Flounder out of the slightly ruffled sea, and the Flounder turned Max into a judge in robes and horn-rimmed glasses and a black barret. And when Ilsebill was fed up with his stinkhorn and wanted an extra-neurotic anarchist between the sheets, the Flounder put Max the Terrorist into her bed with stocking mask, ticking bomb, and all. By that time the Baltic was making little short-winded waves.

"That was a big success for a whole week, because Ilsebill found this character 'terribly interesting.' But when she finally realized that even anarchists have only two balls, she said: 'What's so remarkable about him, I'd like to know. Right in the middle he starts thinking about something else and shoots his mouth off about politics. What I want now is a stinking-rich bank president, just to tide me over while I'm shaking off the habit.'

"So with the wind blowing at gale force five-to-six, Max called the Flounder, and the Flounder made him president of the Bundesbank, and he pulled up at Ilsebill's in a silver-blue

Mercedes. This bank president's hair was graying all over, even around his cock. So when Ilsebill, in her cuddlesome way, had finished off capitalism, she wanted, after only a brief interlude, to be screwed by a beer-assed trade-union functionary and then—by this time squalls were making the Baltic dangerous—at last, at long last, by a wiry movie star, and what's more she wanted the cameras shooting and bright lights.

"When he heard that—the wind was blowing at gale force ten—the Flounder cried, 'Looks to me like your Ilsebill will never get her hole full. It's always more! More and more!' All the same, though without much enthusiasm, he turned the trade-union boss into a regular Belmondo, who, while the camera hummed, leaped (from the wardrobe) into our Ilsebill's bed, where he immediately performed terrific disrobe-bite-fuck scenes with fade-ins of similar scenes from other films.

"But when Ilsebill had milked him so dry he was really comical, she wanted still more and cried out, 'Now I want an orchestra conductor with his baton in there!' And she trumpeted the destiny motif.

"So, leaning against the hurricane, Max called the Flounder, who heaved a sigh but turned him one-two-three into a top-flight maestro who could conduct anything under the sun without a score. But when, after three encores, Ilsebill had finished him off, too, our butterball wept several big tears and moaned, 'Always interpreters. Never an original creator. Everything second hand. Now I want ole Beethoven to fiddle me front and back.'

"But when the exhausted Max reported to the Flounder, the flatfish cried from out of his unleashed element, 'Enough is enough. Now she's going too far. Hands off our classics! From now on and forevermore, like it or not, she'll have to make do with her Max. Every Saturday after fishing.'

"Then and there the storm stopped. In half a sec the sea lay smooth and calm. And big feather-bed clouds went sailing across the sky.

"So Ilsebill had to content herself with Max. From then on she lived entirely on memories. But they were pleasant. . . ."

That was the story Maxie told Billy, who under his words fell asleep. Her tears had left a little salt train behind them.

478

Frankie was still snoring like a Canadian logger. Fallen—a fallen angel—Siggie lay prone. Maxie cuddled up to the luscious butterball and, just before dropping off to sleep, decided, "I'm going to make her a baby, make her a baby, make her a baby. . . ."

On the sand hill between Prussian pines, two black-leather boys sat astride their motorcycles, looking gravely down at the peaceful scene.

What thumps in deep sleep. Dreams in the dragnet. Everything is surreal and all action is delayed. Only recently I dreamed I was a woman in an advanced state of pregnancy who outside the main portal, just under the towers of Cologne Cathedral, in the afternoon rush hour, gives birth to a little girl—my Ilsebill—who is also pregnant—and right after me gives birth (a difficult breech presentation) to a little boy, who, however, has the head of a Flounder, crooked-mouthed, exophthalmic, and slant-eyed. People with shopping bags approach on High Street and from the railroad station, form a circle around our double birth, and cry: A miracle! A Catholic miracle! Whereupon my daughter's Flounder-headed son speaks from out of me to the people. He explains the meaning of life, the world political situation, the fluctuations in the prices of staple foods, and the need for tax reform. "In short," he says, "we are living at the expense of . . ."

Frankie woke up; it was Maxie's cry—"I will beget a son!"—that had shaken first Frankie and an instant later Siggie out of their Father's Day naps; for Siggie and Frankie, like Maxie, had dreamed the great, the unmistakable dream of procreation, which crowds out all subplots and holds the stage alone, which thumps more deeply than anyone can imagine, and whose abysmally stupid power erects itself where nature planned nothing.

But oblivious of their constitution as were all three in their dreams, it was only from Maxie that the outcry for a son to be begotten emerged from sleep into the afternoon light. As Frankie and Siggie awoke, they cried out in their procreative frenzy, "Yes! Yes!," while Maxie woke himself up with his strident trumpet blast. Yet Billy, the cuddly-soft angel, continued to slumber unsuspecting, though all three, Frankie the wagoner, Siggie the hero, and Maxie the steel spring, wanted to be fathers by her: she was the nurturing soil. Her ringlet-shrouded cunt was to be thrice entered, her flesh over-shadowed. It was the butterball they had in view. It was in Billy they wanted to invest their capital. To multiply in her. Upon her body was founded threefold hope for a son: yes yes yes.

Maxie had been first to cry out, and of course wanted to be first. And while the two belated yes-criers were still arguing with Maxie about who should have priority in the great procreative act (and while in every forest and on every lake roundabout Berlin men were winding up their naps and waking from deep-thumping dreams of procreation), Billy went on sleeping like an angel and dreaming on feather-bed clouds of a volunteer fire chief with a conductor's baton, of a black-robed judge with a terrorist inside him, of Beethoven making a flying leap into her bed, of more and more quickly going and coming gentlemen visitors, of the very latest attractions, of wishes that all came true.

Frankie and Siggie let Maxie have the first thrust. "Give the kid a chance. He's got to sow his wild oats."

While the two fathers, waiting their turn, cast their shadows, the young would-be father—"Take it easy, my son," Frankie admonished—peeled the jeans and panties off Billy's deeply sleeping flesh, so diffusing a pentecostal fragrance.

Oh, stupid omission of nature! When the jeans of the first procreation-frenzied father were dropped and nothing made manifest, Maxie was obliged to gird herself with plastic. Oh yes, everything was within reach. Vaseline and all. That's what distinguishes man (or woman) from the beasts. For everything that's lacking under the sun we find a substitute. Where there's a will there's a way.

Billy lay on her camel's-hair blanket ringed around by bushes, and breathed in dream rhythm. None of the bespectacled or unbespectacled fraternity brothers saw a thing. They were much too drooping-drunk in their regalia to take an interest. The sole witnesses were the black-leather boys on their motorcycles. Looking down from the sand hill, they saw will and faith enact a first procreation inside of Billy.

How tenderly the young stallion did it. How easily nature lets itself be fooled. What vast possibilities an open-air theater offers. You improvise a little and imagine the rest. True, our existence is full of holes, but with wonder-working ideas you can plug them. By force of faith and without batting an eyelash, you can give reality to what has none. For if a wafer can be the flesh and a swig of undistinguished wine the blood of our Lord Jesus, then an artfully conceived stopper (much more nobly shaped than the usual stinkhorn) can bring salvation or at least a bit of redemption. Ah, ye rams bulls stallions, how stupid nature has made you! Ye drakes and cocks, what one-tracked minds you have. Ah, ye natural fathers! What, when you shoot your jism, do you know of that surreal act of procreation that requires only the barest intimation of nature?

After Maxie had proved herself in the abstract, it was Siggie's turn. And Billy still clung to her dream. Looking down from the sand hill, the black-leather boys continued to etch on their minds what they saw: this act of unprecedented, monumental swinishness. This artificial fuck. This insult to all Mr. Cleans on this Father's Day of days; for when Siggie invaded the sleeping Billy, both boys took alarm for the chrome-pure innocence of their motorcycles and covered the twice three headlights of the 500-cc machines with their leather jackets. Similarly shamed, the crows on the nearest pine tree moved to the next to nearest. Such doings were bad enough unseen.

So neither the crows nor the motorcycles saw Frankie drop his trousers and gird himself with the imposing plastic organ. But this time the sacrament didn't work; no sooner was it introduced than Billy woke up. Gone was her dream, and the reality was Frankie. She tried to shake him off. But he went on bucking. Billy didn't want him. "No! No!" she screamed. Siggie and Maxie had to hold her left and right and crucify her a bit. Because to stop in the middle wouldn't have been fair to Frankie—the old wagoner.

"Shut up!" cried Maxie. "It won't be long now!" Siggie assured her. And after a few more thrusts, beneath which Billy whimpered softly, Frankie felt he'd begotten the superson. He went limp for a moment and then, getting down off Billy, said, "That does it. What's all the noise about? That little fuck sure gives me a lift."

Naturally Billy cried after what they'd done to her. She wept to herself, and she didn't want any tears wiped away by Maxie. "Vile," she said. "You're vile. My God, how vile you are."

Sobbing, she pulled on her panties and jeans and zipped

the zipper. The crows came back. The two boys on the sand hill unveiled the headlights of their motorcycles and were all in leather again. An evening breeze blew up from the lake. Now there were plenty of gnats.

Maxie said comforting words: "You just looked too sweet in your sleep. So innocent. We couldn't resist. We were gentle. You wouldn't have noticed a thing if Frankie hadn't come down on you like a load of bricks. Come on, be nice. I'll help you with the dishes. We'll make 'em shine. And if you still want one, you can have a new dishwasher for the house, with all the gadgets."

And Siggie also spoke up: "It had to be. Now it's really Father's Day. Let's drink on it. Come on, Billy. Take a swig."

Frankie popped open a beer bottle and, with a "Cheers" to nature, drank the health of the thrice-willed son.

But Billy didn't want to be nice. And she didn't want to wash any dishes with Maxie. She didn't want to drink anyone's health. Slowly, as though still weighed down with sleep, she stood up, took a few uncertain steps, and then said firmly, "I'm leaving. I never want to see any of you again. I didn't want that."

And looking each one full in the face, she said, "When I want that, I'll take a real man. It's better. I'm saying that as a woman. See? As a woman."

As though to get a different, fresher, more precise view of things, Billy put on her glasses, which as a rule she wore only at work. Then she walked away, without looking back through her horn-rimmed glasses. Verifiably, she took step after step. The crows followed her from pine tree to pine tree. The motorcycle boys saw what direction she took and started their motors, to carry the latest news around the Grunewaldsee.

Maxie, Siggie, and Frankie looked after Billy as she vanished step by step. They were pretty well disheartened, even though Frankie said lightly, "If they want to travel, let 'em."

After that the three drank beer and schnapps and schnapps and beer, so keeping Father's Day on its feet until dusk. Elsewhere the conversation may well have hinged on football, the state lottery, the income tax, and expense accounts; our three remaining heroes, however, recollected where and how often they had demonstrated their procreative powers in past centuries. Possibly the schnapps helped them to suspend time.

Maxie related how throughout the long Thirty Years' War, now here, now there, when Magdeburg burned, in Westphalian Soest, before Breisach, immediately after the Battle of Wittstock, and during periods of inaction in garrisons and winter quarters, he had tossed his pennies into hundreds of slots. "That was when my name was Axel Ludström of the Oxenstierna regiment. We were camped on the Hela Peninsula. Swedish cavalry, youngsters with hardly a bit of fuzz on our cheeks. It was May when I laid a Kashubian chick by the name of Agnes in a hollow in the dunes. The other boys took a quick turn at her, too. . . ."

As for Siggie, he saw himself as a Polish uhlan and painted a colorful picture of how the heroic young Count Wojczinski met Napoleonic Governor Rapp's prim little cook deep in the forest, where she was gathering mushrooms for the governor's table. "But naturally, when I got down off my horse, kissed her hand, and made her a few flowery compliments, she couldn't resist. We lay on a bed of moss. Around us grew morels, egg mushrooms, puffballs, and big parasol mushrooms. Ah, how they smelled! How we took our fill of being one flesh. What a delight! Only the ants were a bother. Sophie was her name. Later, the patriotic little vixen poisoned the whole lot of us with a stuffed calf's head. Only Rapp escaped. But I have no regrets. . . ."

Finally, Frankie related at length how as a Prussian dragoon in Ole Fritz's day he had taken care of a farm cook between battles. "Good old Amanda. After Rossbach, Kunersdorf, Leuthen, or Hochkirch, whenever I stopped with her to heal my wounds, every time it took. After seven years of war, I had begotten exactly that many sons, for which reason I was appointed inspector of crown lands. Oh, Kashubia! That wonderful, sandy soil! Whereupon, with hard discipline, I implanted the potato in Prussia. My sons helped me in my task, all seven of them. . . ."

And more such feats, until Siggie said, "She's just hypersensitive. I don't know. We shouldn't have let her go like that. Maybe she'll get into trouble. There's nothing but drunks running around at this hour. Guys you can't fool with."

"OK, time to pack!" cried Frankie, and gave Maxie, who didn't want to get up, a kick in the ass. Quickly they stowed the iron grill, the unwashed plates, and camel's-hair blanket, the empty bottles, and everything else that was lying around—only Billy's top hat was left behind—in Frankie's three-wheeler and drove off to look for Billy. (The fraternity brothers shoved off at the same time, singing, "High on the yellow chariot . . .")

Aboard their three-wheeled crate, their fifth-hand heap, their handy little pickup for quick deliveries and small removals, in Frankie's thick-and-thin, antediluvian, Stone Age, pre-fashionable vehicle, barely and perhaps for the last time tolerated by the new motor-vehicle code, Siggie and Maxie sat in the trailer with the Father's Day paraphernalia, the rolling beer bottles, the unwashed plates, which now proceeded to shatter one by one, while at the wheel Frankie the wagoner steered a sinuous course—"We'll find you! We'll find you, Billy!" Over sticks and stones they drove in their indestructible, all-purpose vehicle, around the Grunewaldsee, which lay still and reflected the sunset, to the hunting lodge, and back to the lake, past departing Father's Day groups, hemmed in by the caterwauling of a thousand half-drunken and totally drunken men. Maxie whimpered softly; only Siggie rasped angry words between thin lips: "Just runs out. Leaves us flat. Can't take a joke. Goes off in a huff . . ." And then, on a sand road made bumpy by uncovered roots, they dimly, in the failing light, saw a shapeless something, which in the beam of the headlights proved to be a pair of bunched-up jeans.

"Those are Billy's," cried Frankie, Siggie, or Maxie. (Off to one side lay her blue-and-white-striped sweater and her bra.)

Alone and forsaken, she had gone off through the trees, deeper and deeper into the woods. Because at the lake, in the clearings, outside the refreshment stands, men shouted abuse: "Look at the chick!" "What's she doing here on Father's Day!" "I guess she's got the itch."

Just to be alone. And undo it all. She cocooned herself in loneliness. It, too, can warm you and keep you company. She felt (so she mumbled to herself) as if the scales had fallen from her eyes. "It took those bastards to buck some sense into me."

What a new feeling: to be a woman. Even if she was

hopelessly alone. But her mind was made up. No going back. Burn bridges. Form forward-pointing sentences: "I come of a family of fugitives. All I went through even as a child. I know what it is to make a fresh start. Through with that stuff, through with it for good. Start again from scratch. From where I left off. I won't leave Heidi with her grandparents any longer—I'll go and get her and give her a real home. A child needs a mother's warmth and affection. I've got plenty of that. Ridiculous. As if I couldn't afford a dishwasher of my own. What do I need *her* for? Stuipd mistakes we all have to get behind us. But now I'll . . . A woman and nothing but. I'll . . ."

Through mixed forest and bushes, on sand roads and paths, over pine needles and moss, deeper and deeper into the woods, Billy carried her beautiful Father's Day illumination. Loudly she offered the weaker sex. Jubilantly she cried, "I'm a woman, a woman, a woman!" Triumphantly she flung out the bait: "A butterball, a butterball"

And they bit. They hadn't lost sight of her for a moment. Inveterate trackers. Advancing from treetop to treetop, the crows helped. And the seven black-leather boys ran her to earth. Came jogging along over roads and paths on their still-unlit motorcycles. The motors hummed rather good-naturedly. Just a game, after all. The real thing for a change, just to see what it was like. Suddenly flashing light from three times seven headlights, they drove Billy, the woman, the cuddly butterball, the by now well-frightened rabbit, ahead of them, this way and that way, into sheltered hollows, where only sandwich papers and beer bottles still bore witness to Father's Day.

Billy still protested: "Hey, kids. Stop the nonsense. Come on, we'll have a couple of drinks at the Roseneck or someplace. . . ." But already the circle had closed. Snap! went the trap. The old, familiar script. In this movie there was no escape. The end was set in advance.

"Clothes off!" said one, very softly. The motors had stopped humming. As under a shower, Billy stood plump and cute and awkward in the converging beams, her hair falling resplendent over her shoulders. She did as she was told but kept on her panties, shoes, and socks. That was as far as she would go. ("You don't seriously think . . .")

The rabbit broke loose. "You guys must be nuts!" she

485

screamed and ran in zigzags when seven motors resumed their good-natured hum. She ran into a thicket, curved around tree trunks, broke crackling through underbrush, ran and ran until at last she fell on a soft bed of pine needles, with all seven around her again. "Please, boys, please . . ."

They said nothing at all, or only "Slut! We'll show you, you slut!" or "You're going to get fucked, you slut!" Already they had their leather trousers open. One after another, as though by command, had a hard-on. And they lined up for Communion. And found the whole thing perfectly normal. And one after another shot their gook into her, until she was overflowing. And kicked her with their big boots before they and after they: "Take that, you slut!"

And one of them, when they had all finished, shoved a jagged pine cone into the wound. "All right, you superslut, now you can run. Go on, run."

But Billy couldn't wouldn't. Tears were all she had left. And a gaping emptiness that opened like a last wish: Oh. With their throttled-down motorcycles they nudged, pushed, bumped Billy—"Go on! Get moving!"—until first one, then another gave full throttle and ran over her legs and belly. Then, because all seven were doing the same thing, they did it over and over again. With dead-serious thoroughness.

That was how Frankie, Siggie, and Maxie found their Billy, mangled, mashed, no longer human, on a bed of pine needles off to one side of the thicket. Beside her, broken, her glasses. Not the least shred of beauty left. All life had gone out of her. The one thing to do—and Frankie did it—was say "Shit!" Maxie vomited against a tree. Frankie hammered herself with her fists: "God damn it!" So Siggie had to keep cool. "We'll have to leave her here. And phone on the way back. There's nothing we can do right now."

So they drove their three-wheeler for quick deliveries and short removals out of the thicket over sand tracks and roads, leaving the dead Billy in the woods. Sharing Clayallee with the returning Father's Day traffic, they drove to the Roseneck, where Siggie got out and went to the phone booth by the bus stop. Frankie stayed at the wheel, cleaning her pipe. Maxie was out of chewing gum. Siggie said into the phone: "You turn right from the Clayallee, that's it, then right again, then left and again left, then another right turn

486

into the thicket. Take fifty steps, turn left, take a few steps more, and there you'll find a naked woman. Dead. No, it's the truth. Right. You said it."

After that, life went on.

The ninth month

~~~~~~

Lud

Capable of friendship—that's the way we men are. From Ludek to Ludger and the prelate Ludewik, from Ludwig Skriever the woodcarver to Ladewik the executioner and the Swede Axel Ludström, from my old crony Ludrichkait and Bavarian Captain Fahrenholz to Ludwik Skröver, who went to America, and Frankie Ludkowiak, the old wagoner—we stuck together through thick and thin. Friends! Blood brothers! Oh, yes, and Jan. Jan Ludkowski. They shot him in the belly, which was full of boiled pork and cabbage. I miss Lud. How I miss Lud!

My friend Ludwig Gabriel Schrieber died recently. Whether he was coaxing form from inert plaster or laying fillets of smoked fish on grilled rounds of celery root and topping the whole with scrambled eggs (for himself and me), or sitting silent behind his glass and dipping his little finger for a drop to cool his forehead with, or relating his war experiences, as unchanging and familiar as a litany ("On the Arctic front, when the Ivans came creeping up in white parkas . . ."), or gnashing his teeth in anger, or caressing an uncarved stone—Lud was always and unmistakably the same: man, boulder, bull, activist, angel fallen in sin.

And so it had always been. When he fashioned the hand ax into a symbol. When he was a prelate and came with the Bohemian Adalbert to bring us heathen the cross. Later, when he carved the (High Gothic) altar for the Church of Saints Peter and Paul, and, just for the fun of it, a cherrywood Madonna who looked like my wife, Dorothea, and stared at a distant point with her inlaid amber eyes.

Usually he died after me. But now, while I'm telling the tale of "The Fisherman and His Wife" in an entirely different version and my Ilsebill is nearing her confinement, he has died on me. And so I must sing a memorial for Lud, my friend in every time-phase. And then Ludek the fisherman, whom the neighboring horde looked upon as their artist, sighed when he saw my ceramic knickknacks. And then Comrade Ludwig Skröver, who lived next door to us on Brabank and later, under the pressure of the Socialist Laws, had to emigrate to America, dragged driftwood out of the Dead Vistula with a long hook. And then Colonel Axel Ludström, who had served on Hela as an ensign with the Oxenstierna regiment, squeezed a lemon over the white-eyed codfish that Agnes, my kitchenmaid, served up to us. And then it so happened that Ladewik the executioner was obliged to sever the head of his friend the blacksmith Peter Rusch, whose last supper of tripe he had shared the night before. And then with one blow Frankie Ludkowiak hammered the nail into the table. And after scowling at his students' clay figures, the sculptor Schrieber, who died recently, spoke of himself and the Hittites, of Mycenae and of Minoan serenity, and with cool rigor of form.

Lud knew all that. He was always present as a sculptor, or simply as the man carrying a bull calf. The neolithic Lud and his hand-sized fertility idols. Those big Pomorshian mother goddesses, hewn from glacial boulders, that were dug up by Polish archaeologists near Oxhöft are all the work of his hands. When Lud became Christian at an early date (converted by Saint Augustine), he never portrayed the suffering of Christ on the cross, but always the triune principle. And when the swordmaker Albrecht Slichting visited him on his building site (next to the Church of Saints Peter and Paul), where he had carved a terrifying wooden Madonna after a likeness of my Dorothea, Lud cooked sheep's kidneys in their envelopes of fat over a bed of coals.

Afterward, with tallow-coated tongues, we talked about everything and nothing. He was dissatisfied. At odds with the times. He gnashed his teeth. He could easily, as sculptor Schrieber did later, have felled one or more of these shits with

490

his famous edgewise chop. When shortly thereafter the guilds rose up against the patricians, Ludwig Skriever the wood carver was with them. First it was about beer from Wismar, then about the rights of the guilds. Naturally the uprising was crushed. Lud escaped and was outlawed. I didn't see him again until two centuries later, when they started the big clean-up of the churches.

Though a coppersmith by trade, Lud, who now called himself Ladewik, got bored with art. It wasn't for Calvin, but entirely to suit himself that he became an iconoclast, one of Hegge's crew. With his own hands he smashed a copper baptismal font that he had (allegedly) fashioned in the dimensions of Mother Rusch and elaborately enchased. And then he lost interest again, became executioner in the Stockturm, and was obliged to behead me, his friend.

What was Lud against? He was against curlicues and filigree, against colorful donors' altars, against pomp and circumstance, against all images, against the word, against himself. With a heavy hammer, with well-aimed edgewise chop, with the executioner's sword. That was Lud: violent. Slash and thrust. Primordial phonemes in his roar. Couldn't help crushing the Devil in every petty Nazi.

But after Ensign Axel Ludström came to the Hela Peninsula with other cavalrymen of the Oxenstierna regiment and assaulted the still-childlike Agnes, she long remembered his voice. It went through and through her. It was archangelic, no longer earthly. For when, steeped in all the horrors of war, Colonel Ludström, along with Thorstenson's cavalry, wrought Swedish-style havoc in Saxony, he helped out by singing the tenor part—"Naked came I out from my mother's womb"—when, on February 4, 1636, a Requiem Mass was sung for Count Heinrich von Reuss; the long-drawn-out war had left Court Kapellmeister Schütz few musicians or singers.

As a Swede, Lud was a handsome man. His gentle earnestness. His cool zeal. His sternness, his anger. But when we met again at the start of the war in the next century, Lud had come down in the world. Now he was known as Ludrichkait (His Slovenliness). Everybody laughed at him. Except me. We always had a supply of brandy. War makes for comradeship. Through thick and thin. For seven years. We were at Leuthen and Hochkirch together. Toward the end, he lost a leg at Burkersdorf. But he always hobbled back to Zuckau, where the good Amanda always had *Glumse* with potatoes in their jackets and linseed oil to spare for us veterans.

It may have been Lud who as a Bavarian captain under Napoleon's Governor Rapp was downright heroic when, during the siege of Danzig, the Cossacks caught Sophie Rotzoll foraging, and with her in tow he hacked his way through. I didn't know Fahrenholz. (I was at Graudenz under fortress arrest.) Beyond a doubt my good old Lud was the revolutionary socialist shipyard worker who proclaimed the strike at Klawitter Shipyard and the Germania Bread Factory, in the timber port, and at the Kafemann Print Shop. Ludwig Skröver and Otto Stubbe were friends. Many a time, the two of them, unbeknownst to Lena, cooked a rabbit over the fire in the Saspe woods. Later the strike fund was robbed. After receiving an expulsion order, Skröver, with family, bag, and baggage, took a ship to New York. No letter came, only a postcard. He is thought to have been active as an anarchist in Chicago.

Up and down. Time and again. Lud was never humbled. In time of need, Lud would turn up. When there was a tricky job to be done, Lud knew how. Without Lud nothing worked. Even when in his present time-phase he became a teacher at an art school and began where he had left off in the Middle Ages (as an iconoclast), Lud was a center. People met at Lud's. Getting drunk with Lud. The legend of Saint Lud. For though he was sometimes harsh and sometimes brutal, he was always pious, especially when drunk. No one could stare at an empty glass like him, at the same time singing (with what was left of his archangelic voice) something Catholic and looking back through the bottom of his glass to where, as a Bohemian prelate and (soon after Adalbert's death) bishop of Pomerania, he ordered the forced baptism of all Pomorshians. As a self-portrait in bronze suggests, he saw himself as a prince of the Church or an abbot or a martyr: unapproachable, withdrawn, legendary, and soon to be canonized.

Describe him? Lud looked like a man buffeting a strong wind. Bent grimly forward when entering a closed room, such as his studio full of pupils. Prominent forehead and cheekbones, but all finely modeled. Hair light-colored and soft. Eyes red, because the wind was always contrary. Delicate mouth and nostrils. As chaste as his pencil sketches.

I miss Lud. How I miss Lud! And even when we quarreled

. . . Even when with our fists . . . Lud and I—a strenuous friendship . . .

As during my friendship with Ludek, when Awa and Ewa swapped us back and forth. And when Ludger took me with him on the migration, his horse kicked me. The prelate Ludewig tolerated my little three-breasted Madonnas. I don't know if Dorothea sat for Skriever the woodcarver; some of my daughters were by him. Before executing me, Ladewik praised my sturdy neck. When the plague snatched me away from this vale of tears. Colonel Ludström, in the name of the Swedish crown (and with the help of Agnes the kitchen-maid) carefully sorted my papers. With Ludrichkait I drank away my money (and my soul). I'm not sure Sophie thanked the Bavarian captain with only a kiss. When the strike fund was robbed, I'd have been glad to go fifty-fifty with Ludwig Skröver. It's only about Frankie the old wagoner that I choose to say nothing. And when I went to Berlin with Lud . . .

That leaves only Jan. Yes, Jan Ludkowski, with whom I was friends, who like me had a way with words, Jan, who belonged to Maria, is dead as Lud. Jan was different. So was Lud. With Jan you could talk over bread, cheese, nuts, and wine. With Lud, too. We sang until late into the night and were desperate. We clung fast to our dream. Men are like that; they can stay friends. Ilsebill can't understand it.

Late

Ilsebill's out.
I am not here.
Actually I'd been expecting Agnes.
Whatever else is going on—the clatter of plates—
belongs to Amanda: her daily dishwashing.

Lena has been here.
Maybe we just forgot
to appoint an exact time.
I met Sophie while the bells

of all the churches were ringing for vespers.
We kissed like at the movies.

Cold stand the leftovers, chicken and so on.
A sentence, begun, hangs fire.
Even the strangest things don't smell new any more.
In the wardrobe a dress is missing, the one with big flowers,
intended for feast days with Dorothea,
who always went in rags.

As long as there was music,
we, together, could hear the same thing differently.
Or love, a snapshot: Billy and I
aboard the white steamship, which was named *Margarete*
and sent up black smoke between the beach resorts.

Of course I'm behindhand.
But Maria wouldn't wait.
Now the Flounder tells *her* what time it is.

Why she vomited

I'm related to Maria. Her father is my mother's cousin.
As early as Amanda Woyke's day, there were Kuczorras in
Kokoschken, Ramkau, and Zuckau. And one of her grandchildren, Lovise Pipka (Sophie's cousin), married a Kutschorra, who came from Viereck (today Fiorga). So Maria's
descent can be traced back to Lena Stubbe, whose maiden
name was Pipka, and to Amanda Woyke, while the fact that
my maternal grandmother was by birth a Kuczorra (though
her mother started life as a Bach) indicates that (like Maria)
I, too, am related to Amanda and Lena. Since there are
several Kurbiellas or Korbiellas in Maria's maternal line,
since my mother had an uncle Korbiella (who emigrated to
America), and since poor Sibylle Miehlau remembered a
great-aunt Korbiella (the sister of her maternal grandmother)
who seems to have sold darning cotton, buttons, and
Güterman's sewing silk in Karthaus, I could easily conjure up
a kinship with Agnes, the diet-fare cook, especially as there is
494

reason to believe that Agnes's mother, who like her father was killed by the Swedes on the Hela Peninsula, was by birth a Woyke or a Gnoyke. (It also seems worth mentioning that Katharina, the younger daughter of the abbess Rusch, married a butcher by the name of Kurbjuhn and that the mother of Dorothea Swarze, commonly known as Dorothea of Montau, was by birth a Woikat.)

After all, we Kashubians are all related by way of a country lane or two. There was only the Goldkrug Forest near Bissau, the raspberry bushes outside of Zuchkau, the road to Karthaus, the Vistual River, the rivulet Radaune, and four, five centuries between us: the time before and after the potato, history that passed over us. Maria knew nothing of all that.

She's blond. Before she learned to be a salesgirl at the co-operative store, her curls fell as they pleased. Then her girl friend went to hairdressing school. Except for one of my uncle's brothers, who moved to the West in '45, the Kuczorras live either in Gdynia or in Wrzeszcz, a suburb of Danzig that used to be called Langfuhr. They live with Maria's two younger sisters in a two-and-a-half-room apartment on Ulica Lelewela, which used to be called Labesweg. (They still own a one-and-a-half-acre plot of potato and garden land in Kokoschken.)

In 1958, when I obtained a visa for the first time and went back with out-of-focus memories, Maria was nine years old and laughed when she saw me in my Western clothes. And so she remained: blond, giggly, wild about dancing, quick at mental arithmetic, an efficient salesgirl, rather boisterous in the company of boys, never knowing more than what was going on at the moment. I was the uncle from the West, who turned up every few years, brought records (the Beatles), and could speak neither Polish nor Kashubian, and concerning whom she formed a picture both lovely and mistaken.

But I also formed a picture of Maria. (That's what comes of forgetting your language.) What happened then was worse than anyone I had imagined. I should have made up a different story for Maria. A happy story with a little sorrow around the edges and a nice wedding present. But the times were against it. Maria did not remain a salesgirl at the cooperative. A job became available elsewhere. She was bent on getting ahead. Yet Maria wasn't cut out to be a cook. (She could have sold costume jewelry at a souvenir shop on

Frauengasse, and worn it; it would have gone well with her hair.)

Pomorshian currency. The small change of the coast. Long beaches. Rich. The dowry of wandering dunes. What the Baltic Sea paid back. The Phoenicians came sailing first from Sidon, then from Carthage by way of Cornwall, where they bartered purple cloth for tin, fist-sized ingots of which they traded to us for seed (barley and spelt). And when Mestwina was beheaded, the amber of her necklace scattered far into the back country. And when Maria gave me a piece of amber as big as a walnut, I recognized it, the old story began all over again, I saw Maria in a new light, a different Maria became possible.

At that time she was still learning at the cooperative. She had found the amber while digging potatoes in the bit of land they had left in Kokoschken. A fine piece: from a crusty yellow edge of shell, the transparent drop shapes itself into a dark globe enveloping a fly.

You shouldn't have given me that amber. Now I'm going to tell the whole story. How you became more real in a different way. How you stopped laughing. How you turned to stone.

Starting in the summer of 1969, Maria Kuczorra, who had first been a salesgirl at the cooperative store and then a cashier, worked as a cook at the canteen of the Lenin Shipyard in Gdańsk. There she made a hundred and twelve zlotys more than at the cooperative. Since she had no cooking experience, she only helped out at the kettles, but because of her knowledge of prices and quality she was charged with making wholesale purchases and inventorying the canned goods.

Her efficiency and cheerful disposition made for quick success. In her dealings with the bureaucracy, her experience at the cooperative helped her to obtain special authorizations. It was she, for instance, who acquired the big freezer. (And through black-market connections, she also traded spare tractor parts for fresh vegetables.) The menu at the shipyard canteen became more varied. But when Maria began to do some of her purchasing via the free port, and bananas and oranges suddenly made their appearance in the canteen, she found herself at odds with her friend Jan, a basically timid young man, despite his bold ideas, who worked in the publicity department of the shipyard, writing prospectuses for the export trade, and had helped Maria to obtain her job at the canteen.

Jan had studied shipbuilding, but his passion was early Pomorshian history. At night he wrote poetry. He had published in the *Baltic Almanac* an article on the love poetry of Wiclaw of Rügen. Along with some favorable criticism, his epic cycle on Prince Mestwin's daughter Damroka, first abbess of Zuckau Convent, had, because of its numerous erotic metaphors, provoked a protest on the part of the Kashubian Cultural Association. Holding to the controversial thesis that the general who defeated and destroyed the Kashubian prince Swantopolk was Fortinbras, prince of Norway, who in the last scene of *Hamlet* claims to have just come from victories in Poland, Jan was projecting a sequel to Shakespeare's tragedy. But he never had time. By day he wrote publicity for the Polish shipbuilding industry, which was translated into English, Swedish, and German and thought to be effective; in the evening Maria would be waiting for him to take her dancing or to the movies.

He had met her at the cooperative. They quarreled from the start. He had brought back a can of putrid peas and held it under the nose of cashier Kuczorra. When they met in the evening in the now public gardens of Oliva Monastery, Jan told Maria that with her corkscrew curls she reminded him of the Kashubian princess Damroka, a sister of his hero Swantopolk and cousin to Wiclaw of Rügen. This Damroka (Jan explained) had founded the Zuckau Convent on the banks of the Radaune because of the wild raspberries that grew there. And he quoted from his long poem. Jan's historical comparisons appealed to Maria. She let him call her Damroka. They were soon in love.

But what about me? I'm not Jan. I'm Maria's second cousin. But she calls me Uncle. She gave me a piece of amber, that's all. With an insect enclosure. I'm the enclosure. In case of doubt, I, late-enamored and kept in reserve. Beside me: I. Outside me: I. Foisted on me like a hoax, the obedient but grumbling I. Always escaping, fleeing the times, devious. Where a slat in history's fence is missing. Listen to me, Maria. It was when Mestwina wore a necklace of amber pierced by me. Sambor, Mestwin, Swantopolk, and Princess Damroka are descended from her daughters and daughters'

daughters. No, it was I who caught the talking Flounder. I in the guildhall when the guilds rebelled. I in the Stockturm, spooning up my last tripe. And when the plague greeted me in passing. And when the potato triumphed over millet. The great cook who stirs all things stirred me at cross-purposes with time. How she (to this day) clarifies me with the skimmer, how fairly she dishes me out. How tender I am to her taste, once marinated. Lovage and caraway seed, marjoram and dill. Seasoned am I. I, Maria, am Jan, as per your recipe.

And when Maria Kuczorra had been purchasing fresh vegetables, canned goods, and (illegally, to be sure) bananas and oranges for the Lenin Shipyard canteen for a year, when asked by her boy friend, whom she still loved and who (evenings in the dark movie house, whispering in her ear while dancing) called her Damroka, when, finally, because Jan so desired, she stopped taking her curly hair to the hairdresser's, when autumn came and the newspapers were full of treaties ready to be signed, when in Warsaw Gomulka and Brandt affixed their names for Poland and Germany, so—as people said—making history, when winter came and preparations for Christmas got under way, Maria, seeing there was too much talk about the priority of national tasks, said it was time to buy provisions in a hurry. The newspapers were stuffed with sublimities about the great historical hour. Not a word about consumer goods. That was a bad sign. "They're going to raise the prices," said Maria to Jan.

Which is just what happened. By decree. Sugar, flour, meat, butter, and fish. On December 11. And they'd been planning to marry on the fourth Sunday of Advent.

There were good economic arguments for it. Everything can't be subsidized. Even a Communist government can't afford it. If the market doesn't regulate prices, government regulation comes too late. But when prices get out of hand, so do other things, and sometimes the whole shebang.

When the prices of staple goods were raised between thirty and fifty percent on Friday—they had thought it was clever to take account of the weekend—Jan said it was a historical fact that on several occasions the rise in the price of Scania herring and the importation of cheap beer from Wismar had united the quarreling guilds and incited them to rebel against the patricians. Then he speculated at length on the drop in

498

the price of paper during the Reformation and the simultaneous meat shortage in Central Europe, due to a falling off in the marketing of cattle.

Maria said, "Maybe you have to expect such things under capitalism, but they shouldn't happen in a Communist state. Why, we learned that in school. And if the union doesn't do anything, we'll take action without the union. And if the men have no spunk, the women will just have to wake them up." No, she was in no mood for the movies. He, Jan, should go and organize. She, Maria, would go and see the women at the cooperative and talk things over. She knew them. They knew all about prices, too. They'd smelled a rat long ago. And you could count on them.

And because all the women had steamed up their men (as Maria had steamed up Jan)—"And don't show your face in my kitchen until the prices are back down again"—the harbor and shipyard workers of the Baltic coast, of Gdańsk and Gdynia, of Szczecin and Elblag went on strike the following day. The railroad workers and others, even the girls in the Baltic Chocolate Factory, joined in. Since the local trade-union leadership held aloof, strike committees formed spontaneously, and workers' councils were elected. They demanded not only the rescinding of the price increases but also worker management of the factories—the old, deep-rooted, foolish, beautiful, indestructible dream of self-determination.

At the canteen of the Lenin Shipyard in Gdańsk, new supplies were brought in before the police could start checking. It was done at night. Next morning workers and housewives came in from the suburbs, from Ohra and Troyl, Langfuhr and Neufahrwasser, maybe fifty thousand strong. They marched past the Central Station and assembled outside the Communist Party headquarters. There, since there wasn't much to make speeches about, they sang the Internationale a number of times. What discussion there was centered on Jan (who had been swept away form Maria in the crush), for Jan was overflowing with historical comparisons that he couldn't keep to himself. As usual, he began with the early Pomorshians, Sambor, Mestwin, Swantopolk, and Damroka of the beautiful hair. At that point the shipyard workers were still listening, but when Jan got longwinded, lost himself in the labyrinth of medieval guild regulations, and compared the demands of the trades for seats and voices in the seated and standing councils with present demands for worker management of the factories, the workers turned a deaf ear.

Then the crowd sang the Internationale again. Only Maria, who had been pushed to one side, saw her Jan agitating—historically aware, without listeners, imprisoned in a balloon. She held her head slightly tilted, her lips moving slightly, on the verge of a smile.

They've all tilted their heads that way, just a bit frightened, but at the same time amused at so much talk and virile enthusiasm. Thus, but already poised for mockery, Abbess Margarete Rusch watched, and listened to, Preacher Hegge when on the Hagelsberg he conjured up eternal damnation and all the devils from Ashmodai to Zaroe. Thus alarmed, but with a smile bordering on melancholy, the kitchenmaid Agnes Kurbiella looked over the poet Opitz's shoulder as, wordless, but inwardly rich in figures, he sat over blank paper. It was with just such an expression that Wigga, the Iron Age wurzel mother, received me when, sore of foot, I came limping home from the migration. And Lena Stubbe looked at me with similarly tilted head on Fridays, when I'd whopped her again with my razor strop and as on every such occasion looked for the rope and failed to find the nail. Dorothea smiled and tilted her head differently, scornfully, when I started talking guild business or counting up small change. Sophie, on the other hand, was full of tender concern as she tied up a package of gingerbread into which she had baked stimulating fly agaric, finely ground, for her Fritz, who was under fortress arrest. And my Mestwina smiled in the same way when she saw Bishop Adalbert spooning up her fish soup. And after giving me (the stupid lummox) my extra feeding, Awa tilted her head, grave with ever-loving care, yet smiling in the certainty that there would never be enough, that hunger springs eternal and there would always be grounds for care.

Maria tilted her head when she saw her Jan wedged in the crowd but agitating unheard. For she said to herself: In a minute he'll feel cold, all alone with his talk. In a minute he'll look for me, to unload on. Because when I'm not with him, it's only fear that makes him talk. In a minute I'll say: Jan, you're right. We must take a historic view of this. It never stops. Not even under Communism. It's always the bottom against the top. In those days the bosses were called patricians. They made Scania herring expensive. They raised the price of pepper though there was plenty of it. They kept saying: The Danes are to blame. They've raised the Öresund tolls. Everything is going up. That's the way it is. You've got to accept it. The party says so. And the party is right, always right. And the party says it's too soon for freedom.

When Jan found his Maria again in the crowd, she said, "Come on. We'll go to the shipyard now. There we'll be safe. They've got everything. So we'll wait. No matter how long it goes on. So the wedding will be after Christmas, and just as much fun."

It was only when the crowd began to disperse that there was fighting with the police. Some of the railroad-station windows were smashed. Some newspaper stands went up in flames. Later the party building was set on fire. Morale, in the main, was high. The workers had seen what a big crowd they were. Some were arrested, whereupon a part of the crowd marched to the Schiesstange Prison, where gasoline was thrown in through the windows. A boy was run over by a tank. But so far there was no shooting.

It wasn't until the next day—when the workers of the Lenin Shipyard withdrew to the shipyard grounds, posted guards at the gates, and, in case the army occupied the shipyard, made preparations to blow up essenital installations and send several unfinished ships down the ways; when units of the People's Army came rolling from Warsaw, and the police closed its ring around the shipyard area; when pork and cabbage with caraway seed was cooked for more than two thousand men in the shipyard canteen; when outside the main entrance to the shipyard a few young workers tried to start a discussion with the police, and Jan Ludkowski, speaking through a megaphone, first outlined the historical background of the strike, from the uprisings of the medieval guilds to the insurrection of the sailors and workers of Petrograd for the Soviet system and against the party bureaucracy to the present rise in prices and the strike committee's demands for worker management of the factories; when finally Jan quoted from the *Communist Manifesto* and raised his full, mellifluous male voice, to which only the cause lent a note of harshness, till it carried as far as the Old City—that the police fired, wounding several workers. Five fatally. Among them Jan.

There was also shooting in Gdynia, Szczecin, and Elblag.

The most numerous fatalities (over fifty) seem to have occurred in Gdynia, where the police lobbed mortar shells into the crowd and fired machine guns from helicopters. Then, in Warsaw, Gomulka was toppled. The new man's name was Gierek. He rescinded the price increases on staple foods. The workers thought they had won and called off their strike, although their demand for worker management of the factories had remained unanswered.

When Jan was shot by the police, he was hit in the belly, which was full of boiled pork and cabbage, and not, as he had wished in poems (after Maiakovsky), in the forehead. In midsentence he was dead. Maria couldn't help when the dead and wounded were carried into the shipyard grounds. Just then she was taking delivery of a load of canned fish, which had been donated by the crews of two Soviet freighters then in drydock. Later she threw herself on the dead man, whose mouth was still open, and shook him as if in anger: "Say something just this once. Say it's right and logical. Say the facts speak for themselves. Say history proves. Say Marx foresaw. Say the future will. Say something, say . . ."

After Jan's death, Maria didn't stop working at the shipyard canteen. As long as the workers were negotiating with Gierek, the new man—an agreement of sorts was arrived at—plenty of supplies were delivered. The dead were buried quickly and quietly at various cemeteries in Emaus, Praust, and Ohra. The families were not admitted. Jan is thought to lie in Emaus. The other four dead were Upper Silesians, whom no one really knew. Their families in Katowice and Bytom were notified much too late. That brought protest. Regret was expressed in high places.

But such deaths don't really amount to much. Traffic accidents account for more. And the social services take better and better care of the widows and orphans. All were shot in the abdomen. The police had aimed low. Though this was recorded for later reference, none of the guilty parties was mentioned at any trial. It's perfectly true: life goes on.

The actual funeral service was held between Christmas and New Year's on the shipyard grounds, in the open, because the canteen was too small. A cold, windless day. Maria sat in black beside other women in black, facing the speaker's desk,

502

the flowers, the flags, the music, the oil flame. The speakers (nearly all the members of the strike committee) repeated that these dead would not be forgotten. They said solidarity had brought victory, though all the workers' demands had not yet been met. Two ships were on the slips nearby, manned only by gulls. (Big orders for Sweden. They'd been sent down the ways unfinished if the police had stormed the shipyard.) Jan had been working on prospectuses in which progress was illustrated by photographs of ships' hulls. One of the speakers mentioned Jan's work, which he called imaginative. (Not mentioned was Jan's loudly and frequently repeated suggestion that newly built passenger vessels should be given Pomorshian names such as *Swantopolk* or *Damroka*. After all, Stephen Batory hadn't been a Pole but a Hungarian from Transylvania, and a ship had been proudly named after him.)

When at the end a party representative spoke, he apportioned blame but mentioned no names. Someone in the standing crowd of shipyard workers cried out, "Kociolek!" Maria didn't cry, because something was stuck in her throat. The other women in black cried. Between speeches they cried louder, Some of the men cried too.

After the speeches the shipyard band played first solemn, then militant music. The gulls rose from the tankers on the slips and settled down again. After that an actor recited a poem that Jan had written about death. True, the poet who "lived himself to death" in this poem was the Baroque poet and court historian Martin Opitz, but in the setting of the funeral, and thanks to the actor's interpretive emphasis, the line "And with his halted blood his words, too, ceased to flow" related exclusively to Jan. This line was repeated in every stanta.

After the poem, Maria, who had something in her throat, threw up. Two men from the workers' guard led the still-retching woman in black past the speakers, flowers, and flags, past the oil flame and the band, to a place between two sheds, where she finished vomiting. Before the funeral, Maria had gone to the hairdresser's.

Later, in the canteen, after drinking tea, she was taken with a craving for dill pickles. But there weren't any left. And as the families of the slain were sitting over tea in the canteen, one of the weeping women, Jan's mother, who had come from Konitz, said to the other weeping women in black, "That's from my son. They were going to get married. Maybe it'll be a boy."

But two girls were christened with the names of Mestwina and Damroka. They will soon be three, and they are acquainted with a photograph of Jan. It's standing on the living-room cabinet next to a historically faithful cog in full sail. But Maria, to whom I am related and who gave me that piece of amber from the potato field with the fly enclosed in it, Maria, who had a reputation for laughing—at the cooperative, in the shipyard canteen, everywhere—Maria turned to stone. A harshness has come into her speech.

Vestimentary preoccupations, feminine proportions, last visions

They refuse to say anything about Maria. Divided among themselves like the Advisory Council behind them, but agreed on this point. There they sit, cooking up a Last Judgment. When the Flounder also declined responsibility for the cases of Sibylle Miehlau and Maria Kuczorra, housewife Elisabeth Güllen and biochemist Beate Hagedorn walked out of the former movie house in protest. On conclusion of the Lena Stubbe case, Ms. Hagedorn had cried out: "Fuck the past. Repression is going on today. Everywhere. In Poland, for instance, even if it is some kind of Communism they've got there. It wasn't just the rise in prices that made them strike. It wasn't the usual household worries. No, it was something more. And it's still going on. What we need is action, something big. Get out on the streets and yell. And refuse our services. Not just in bed. Total noncooperation! Till everything stops. Till the men come crawling. And we take over."

The verdict is expected soon. All through May, while the last evidence was being heard and the worst was being once again recorded, the Flounder was undergoing a visible change. Whenever he left his sand bed, he struck us and the representatives of the press, who were on the lookout for indications that prolonged confinement had impaired his health, as more and more transparent, more and more glassy. A while ago you could trace his bone structure. Now his digestive tract is discernible. You can identify his milt, the proof of his masculinity.

This is no doubt why the Advisory Council has been urging the court to finish up, to pronounce a sentence and carry it out. The Advisory Council (without Hagedorn and Güllen) has set a definite time limit. Once again I consider them all, consider them with love, hate, or indifference, as (from the public benches) I see them. Sieglinde Huntscha, for instance: always in jeans and frayed leather jacket. Built, I would say, like a sportswoman, if I didn't know that she has flat feet, for which reason the prosecutor hardly paces at all, but mostly stands still while pleading (with a slight Saxon accent): "Since in the case of Lena Stubbe as in those preceding it the Flounder's guilt can hardly be contested . . ."

Likewise slender but with ballooning bosom, the court-appointed defense counsel wears embroidered blouses, which she likes to fasten with bows. Although Bettina von Carnow hunches her back when sitting and never quite knows how to turn her overlong neck, she reveals the proportions of a model as soon as she stands up or risks a step or two.

Quite otherwise, among the associate judges towers the sitting giant Helga Paasch. Here we have a person in her middle forties who, unconcerned about her frame, wears two-piece suits that overemphasize the squareness of her build. She can't open her mouth—"Man, are you finicky"—without sweeping invisible objects off the table.

Equally stately, though delicately proportioned and clad in a maidenly small-flower print, sits Griselde Dubertin, as straight as an exclamation point. Sometimes in culottes. The sharpness of her interruptions. The bitterness of her random comments. Always ready to pounce, always disagreeing and expressing herself too forcefully, she offers a contrast to Therese Osslieb, whose soulful phlegmatism communicates itself without needing words and appeases sudden squalls (quarrels with the Advisory Council).

Osslieb wears jumpers, wraparound skirts, and lace-trimmed, ancestral hand-me-downs. And yet she droops as tragically as her friend Ruth Simoneit, who, when not staggering drunkenly about on the podium, wishing everything (and herself) underground, is a pleasure to behold in her firm, sculptured beauty, from which, along with amber, too much Asiatic, African, Indian, or other exotic jewelry is always dangling.

Beside her the social worker Erika Nöttke has a hard time of it. Overworked as she is, worry has clothed her in fat, which as a rule billows most unbecomingly gray on gray in sweaters and expands pleated skirts. Though she is the youngest of the associate judges, she nevertheless speaks like Dame Care. Her piping voice keeps her professional jargon—"resocialized integration"—from sounding authoritative. No one listens to her. Her overlong tirades are drowned out by Griselde Dubertin's interruptions or Paasch's heckling or the protracted outcries of the public, although Erika Nöttke, more than any other member of the Advisory Council, tries to stick to the point.

A very different matter is Ulla Witzlaff, who for every historical incident finds private parallels, which are always listened to: "Back home, on a little island by the name of Oehe, there was an old woman who kept sheep. . . ." Ulla is the handsomest of the lot, though no part of her is pretty. You could fall in love with her hair. Usually she wears long, shabby skirts, and then, when you least expect it, she'll make an entrance as a lady, in a black evening dress. The public applauds. The presiding judge is obliged to demonstrate (imperceptibly) her authority.

Ms. Schönherr is believed to be in her mid-fifties. But since this recognized ethnologist dresses timelessly (in good sports clothes or Scotch plaids), one never gives a thought to her age. She emanates serenity. She never shows partisanship. Even when passing judgment she remains ironically ambiguous. All the associate judges—whether they belong to the Flounder Party or to the opposition—are convinced that Ursula Schönherr is on their side. Even the Revolutionary Advisory Council keeps quiet when she demands, nay, commands feminine solidarity.

For nine months she has guided the Women's Tribunal over all trip wires and has so worn herself out with loving care that in the always correctly dressed Ursula Schönherr I feel justified in surmising my neolithic Awa, as she cuts across my dreams.

Awa, however, was corpulent—no, fat, positively ungainly. Her ass hung down to her knees, but that fell in with the neolithic ideal of beauty, which like everything else in those days was decided by women. Thus the cult of shortleggedness determined the original form of the vase, for Awa's head was relatively small, perched on great rounded shoulders that left little room for a neck. Flesh overflowed its banks. Everywhere richly upholstered nests, nooks, and crannies that seemed ready to grow moss. Where today the tyranny of sports imposes a boring tautness on the female thigh, Awa's thighs, which between knee and vulva allowed themselves a fabulous wealth of bulges and swellings, were correspondingly rich in dimples, the hallmarks of primordial beauty. Dimples all over. And where the back resolved itself into a rump, densely populated fields of conglobulation were discernible.

If Awa's proportions were repeated anywhere, it was in the abbess Rusch, who cultivated her envelope of fat—possibly for the sake of the warmth she liked to dispense, possibly to provide an adequate sounding board for her laughter. It will be worth our while to list all the parts of Fat Gert that wobbled and formed folds whenever her sudden laughter erupted, gurgled, bubbled, and uphove her vast body: her four-times-vaulted chin, her primary, secondary, and tertiary cheeks, her breasts that reached out like mighty bastions and merged with her dorsal cushions of fat, her belly, which as though perpetually pregnant burst the seams of any cloth, her downy-blond forearms, each of which was as thick as the High Gothic waist of Dorothea of Montau.

But before I compare Dorothea with Sophie—the one as though blown of glass, the other scrawny and flat, but both equally tough—let me recall that Amanda Woyke was in every respect close to the potato: bulbous, firm of flesh, conveniently sized. Likewise compact but smaller in stature was Mestwina, while Wigga at an early age gave in to her powerful bone structure and set more store by the frame than by the flesh. Lena Stubbe, on the other hand, who started out as fresh as an apple, remained true to herself; at a high old age she still made one think of an apple—a shriveled one, to be sure.

Dorothea was weightless. Lighter than air. A sad case, because her beauty was so objectless. She was so meagerly endowed with flesh that she had the spectral look of a goat in March when the winter feed runs out. While cushions of fat can be palpably described, the only way I can resurrect the scant flesh of Dorothea of Montau is to measure the spaces it

507

occupied. Her ample garments that magnified every movement. The costumes she borrowed from the lepers—many's the time she came home from Corpus Christi Hospital in rags or cloaked in sweat-drenched winding sheets. But though her flesh was weightless, not so her hair. Pale-blond, it hung down to her knees. Wind in her clothes and wind in her hair, she took up space, strode through emptying streets, shook with ecstasy, lay, a quivering bundle of sackcloth overflowed by hair, with the beggars of Saint Mary's, or spooked through the ground fog outside the city gates, lusting for visions.

Even where for other reasons no man could have lost himself, Sophie was narrow. Flat, angular, charmingly boyish, with legs made for hopping and skipping, a tough, supple, but also cutting willow switch. Sophie's measurements. Apart from her voice, which required space, only her springy step, always ahead of itself, counted. And when she became an old spinster, there was very little of her, though enough, in concentrated charge, to blow the kitchen sky-high and make good the still-current demand for the women's rights that were lost long, long ago.

And Agnes? She didn't weigh. She didn't look. She could be seen only in the pictures that painter Möller painted and destroyed. She seems (Opitz intimated as much) to have been curly-haired. I remember her bare feet. Sometimes, when the door opens softly, I hope it's Agnes—but it's always Ilsebill, bringing herself along.

Now she fills my mock-up, which is in low country. A plate with the sky over it. Low rain clouds and suchlike slumgullion. My eyes roll from edge to edge. Since Agnes evades my grasp, I lay the hugely pregnant Ilsebill down on the Island between Käsemark and Neuteich, where the Vistula and the sky are conducive to aerial photography, or here, between Brokdorf and Wewelsfleth, on the walled-in Wilster Marsh.

There lies my Ilsebill, always with the river behind her. Sluggish jetsam with feminine proportions. Her dimple-strewn flesh supported by her right hip, so that her upended pelvis blocks off the sky. Her crooked elbow rests on the exact spot where men with brief cases full of experts' reports have planned to build the nuclear power plant. She obstructs all their plans. One of her breasts hangs over the dike. Her right foot plays with the Stör, a tributary of the Elbe. Bedded with all her weight, as though forever. Below her, at the bend of her left leg, high-tension pylons traverse the country in long strides: whispering power, the old rumors, the amber legend, once upon a time.

Around Ilsebill scurry the stick men who have planned, developed, sanitized, welfared everything to death. Above her, jet-propelled in oblique flight, local NATO maneuvers, which never stop rehearsing the real thing. So she lies, fallen from all time. Where the Vistula and the Elbe flow, or try to flow, into the sea. Her wandering shadow: history that has never been written but is enduringly there. Roads that are supposed to pass around her. Screens to shelter her from sight. Warning signs that deny her existence. A double-meshed fence to protect her. Leaping males all about. Measured brevity. Achievement trying to catch Ilsebill's eye. To strike her dumb with wonder. But when the mood takes her, she rolls her flesh to the other side, We call that exercise. With her dimensions she confutes male-administered power. Already Ilsebill has become landscape, closed to all interpretation. Let me in! I want to crawl into you. To disappear completely and recover my reason. I'm sick of running away; it's warmth I want. . . .

But when I tried to enter my Ilsebill, she said: "It won't be long now. It's starting to tug. It's going to be a boy. He shall be called Emmanuel. What else do you want? Always the same thing. I don't need it any more. Beat it! Beat it, I say. Or tell me what the Flounder is up to. . . ."

The Womenal

That's what the Flounder called the Women's Tribunal during the last session of his trial. He stopped saying, "But my dear and esteemed ladies!" No patriarch tried to ingratiate himself with "You are my beloved daughters, after all." Never again did he try to establish superiority with irony, by speaking of "assembled Ilsebills," or to ridicule with mock pathos the "High Long-haired Court." Instead, he reduced the assembly that was trying him to the one word "Womenal." Let the Womenal judge. Let the verdict be what it may, only the Womenal can decide. Other than the Womenal he recognized no superior authority.

Since, during his long captivity, he had grown transparent and lost all color from head to tail fin, it was in glassy terms that the Flounder formulated his admission of guilt, which, however, was also a program, opening up new horizons: "The punishment you are about to impose will put me under obligation to the Womenal for all time." To make his meaning clearer and amplify his neologism, he spoke of the "Last Womenal," and for that (so unsure of themselves were these emancipated women to the very end of their confrontation with the flatfish) he was once again suspected of irony.

And yet, what injustice! What had these bitches done to my Flounder! How pale he was! And could that be his voice? No fatherly advice was poured into his son's ear. No gripes, threats, commands. Where had his scintillating arrogance run off to? No longer did any Ilsebill, no longer did anyone call forth his cynical comments. Gone the cavernous laughter that had stirred up his sand bed and the bottommost depths of the psyche.

Whereas at the beginning of the trial, when Awa Wigga Mestwina were on the agenda, he had whispered primordial phonemes and taken refuge in mythological chitchat, involving the god Poseidon, among others, whenever the prosecution had become too captious for his liking, now he simply laid himself bare: "Just look at me. I am transparent. See through me. Let nothing remain hidden from you."

And whereas, while the cases of Dorothea Swarze, Margarete Rusch, and Agnes Kurbiella were being debated, every historical fact—the Council of Constance, the Battle of Wittstock, or whatever—had opened up to him an escape route into further facts, he now abandoned all prevarication and, conscious of his guilt, spoke to the point. No Dominican prior (in the shape of a Flounder) wanted to spout canon law. Never again would he be heard quoting nasally from the charters of the medieval guilds. No more inquisitorial showing of instruments. Not a word from the *Malleus maleficarum*. No vale-of-tears tone, transposing plague, hunger, the long-drawn-out war and my Baroque time-phase into iambics, was audible when the Flounder now spoke: "I did . . . I am . . . Never again . . . In the future I will . . . It serves me right."

Oh, God! How they have crushed you! He didn't even

510

want to weigh and balance any more, to consider in historical perspective, though apt parallels had brought him considerable advantage while the cases of Amanda Woyke and Sophie Rotzoll (and I in relation to them) were under discussion. Never again did the Flounder introduce an interminable speech with the little words "In short." Never again did he display his wide reading. Nevermore did the Church Fathers or the heretics speak from his lips. He had understood that in prosecuting him, the Womenal was also prosecuting Saint Augustine and Saint Thomas. Hadn't all the intellectual giants, from Erasmus to Marxengels and even—while the case of Lena Stubbe was under discussion—good old Bebel, been accused? Weren't three thousand years of history being condemned with him? Might not the Flounder, in his concluding statement, have let his voice ring out once more, have sung the swan song of his epoch, drawn up a deep-thundering balance sheet, writing off the male cause and with it civilization as a failure, yet at the same time illustrating its tragic grandeur, populating it with rhetorical figures, showing it ascending the grandiose staircase of cultural progress, and celebrating its demise, if not with a hymn then at least with a richly orchestrated symphonic poem, whose basses spoke of enduring achievement (the Strassburg Cathedral, the diesel engine), its high notes of guilty entanglements (the moon rocket, the splitting of the atom), and its middle register of the man in the street and his troubles (a family to support, tax bills)?

But he pulled no stops. Though his final statement was termed interesting and left what is known as a lasting impression, this was no longer the old Flounder I knew so well, but a new Flounder, a stranger. He, the jester, the concocter of droll anecdotes which had brought smiles even to the refrigerated faces of the ladies here assembled, he, who had found everything, even the death of poor Sibylle Miehlau, laughable, had become dead serious, though I'm sure he was snickering somewhere in the fishy depths of his existence.

Be that as it may, the Flounder tilled word fields in which only morality gave promise of harvest and bread. He, the talker, the master of digression, he, the slyboots versed in every dodge, laid himself bare, as if he had been vulnerable. When the prosecution attacked him for the last time, he didn't even take refuge in his sand bed. Though as transparent as glass, he nevertheless exposed himself; every word struck home. Fragile, he hovered in his tank. No longer palpable and yet (as photographs have shown) all there. Wholly at the mercy of the Womenal, the many Ilsebills.

They had dressed up for the occasion. Exotic silver jewelry dangled; feathers and flowers were stuck in their hair. Ruth Simoneit sat wrapped in a shawl. Ulla's hair pinned high to display gold earrings. Even Erika Nöttke wore jewelry, a pearl necklace. Jangling bracelets lent emphasis to each of the prosecutor's statements. Sieglinde Huntscha called the Flounder "Spirit of violence. Father of war. Instigator of all wars." She cried out, "We know you. You are the destructive, life-negating, murderous, male, warlike principle!"

To which the Flounder replied: "Yes. That's how it is. That's how it has been up to now. I declared war to be father of all things. On orders from me, positions, from Thermopylae to Stalingrad, were held to the last man. Relentlessly I said: Hold out. Time and time again I commanded death for one thing or another—the greatness of the nation, the purity of some idea, the glory of God, undying fame, an abstract principle such as the fatherland—my invention, incidentally—and exalted death as the essence of life. The balance sheet is known. In killing and in counting the dead, men have been thorough. Almost everywhere in Europe, as vacationing motorists can see by their road maps, far-flung military cemeteries, most of them charmingly situated, have become part of the landscape. Mass-produced crosses bear witness to the First and Second World Wars; in village churches one can read, incised on slabs of marble, the names of men who fell in one or the other war. What were they fighting for? Even I, the prime mover, am not sure. Of course I hoped that after the wars—what? That men would come to their senses? Transvalue all their values?

"The peace that broke out in 1945 has admitted only of limited conflicts; this much, thanks to the balance of nuclear terror, the Great Powers could promise one another. But these limited conflicts also brought millions of deaths, even though—since the advent of global politics—the counting has no longer been done with the old European precision. I am referring to the war in Korea, the war in Vietnam, the decimation of a people in the so-called Biafra conflict, the war of annihilation against the Kurds, all the wars in the Near East down to the most recent Yom Kippur War, the wars between

India and Pakistan, and, a relatively minor example, the never-ending-war-in-peace situation in Northern Ireland. And last but not least: in December 1970, the Polish People's Police fired on the striking shipyard workers. Deaths! Deaths! In two, four, six digits.

"Who is responsible? Who drives people to destroy one another? Can one speak of human reason when an appreciable percentage of the product of workers' toil is invested in a more and more highly perfected technology of destruction? What secularized Devil furbishes your portraits of the enemy so bright that in the midst of declared peace the nations, groaning under the burden of their armaments, confront one another eye to eye, deluded, dead sure? Can it still be Beelzebub? Or the so-called death wish? Or is it I, the Flounder out of the fairy tale? The warlike and therefore masculine principle?

"As the Womenal has rightly recognized and aptly stated, all this, this living toward death while parroting peaceful intentions, is pursued with resolute seriousness, with pragmatic know-how and moral pretensions, by men and women alone. With the blessings of the priests of this and that religion, all this has been planned and efficiently executed—in spite of a breakdown now and then—budgeted and endowed with meaning by men and men alone. I know whereof I speak. Peace and war have been my doing. My program was as follows: Men will make history. Men will resolve conflicts. Men will stand and fall—to the last man. Men will fear the day of wrath—and dream of it. Men will be trained to the hilt for premature death. Men will be buddies with death. And the rifle, to cite an old saw, will be 'the soldier's bride.'

"And this is how it will be as long as I keep at it, squandering my advice. As long as historiography sets dates. Grandiose in their exaltation, men, heroes out of stupidity, masking their fear of death with contempt, will continue to press forward—forward over graves. Permit me to remind you of Lena Stubbe's husbands: they got theirs at Mars-la-Tour and Tannenberg. Two run-of-the-mill heroes.

"But wars aren't the whole story. Every revolutionary process known to us has served up orgiastic rites of death, massacres drawing their justification from some masculine purity-principle or other. The guillotine was celebrated as humanistic progress; the Stalinist show trials met with the blessing of the knowing and the unknowing; in the Nazi

513

concentration camps re-education for death ceased to be anything more than a bureaucratic, administrative measure—in every case it was men, males, who with cold passion sprung from faith, with devotion to a just cause, with eyes fixed on the ultimate goal, with the chilling single-mindedness of archangels, have antedated the deaths of fellow humans—pious, self-assured males, far from their wives and families, but in love with the instruments of death, as though killing were the continuation of sexuality by other means. You have only to look in at the dances of marksmens' associations, watch young ruffians punishing one another, go to a soccer game, or mingle with the crowd when Ascension-Father's Day is loudly celebrated here in Berlin: that dammed-up aggression looking for an outlet. That fierce, destructive lust.

"Of course there have always been apostles of peace and men who have risked a bold and quotable word against war. Permit me to remind the High Womenal of the poet Opitz, who during the Thirty Years' War—how vainly, we know—attempted to foment peace. Or Old Man Bebel's antiwar speech. That was in the spring of 1913, and the Socialist International cheered him. We know that in religious songs and philosophical treatises peace has been sung, longed for, spun into allegory, and meditated upon *ad nauseam*. But since no one ever tired seriously to resolve the conflicts of human society while forswearing the categories of masculine thinking, nothing was ever accomplished beyond protestations of peaceful intent and sophistical distinctions between just and unjust wars. Crusaders have always managed to massacre people in the name of brotherly love. Wars of liberation are still very much in vogue, and the principle of the free market has meant undernourishment for millions of people: hunger, too, is war.

"And because history presents itself as an inevitable alternation of war and peace, peace and war, as though this were a law of nature, as though nothing else were possible, as though a supernatural force—take me as a captive example—had imposed all this as fate, as though there were no other way of discharging aggression, as though peace could never be more than a brief interval during which men prepared for the next day of wrath, this vicious circle must forever remain unbroken—unless it is broken by those who have hitherto made no history, who have not been privileged to resolve notorious historical conflicts, whom I have subjected to male history, to whom history has never brought anything but suffering, who have been condemned to feed the war machine and replenish the human material it consumes—I am referring to women in their role as mothers.

"But can this be? How uncomplainingly—as was recently brought to the Womenal's attention—the farm cook Amanda Woyke let herself be got with child after child between the battles of the Seven Years' War, without ever asking: What for? And the mothers, wives, sisters of the men engaged in murdering one another—haven't they always kept silent, turned to statues, stone embodiments of female suffering, or even allowed themselves to be honored as the mothers of heroes?

"It is my hope that the Womenal, upon whose mercy I cast myself, which has manifested my guilt, and to which I offer my desire to make atonement, will not only judge me, but will also bear in mind that power will henceforth fall to women. No longer will women be compelled to stand silent and look on. The world is at a turning point. Today history demands a female imprint. Already the male is hanging his head, neglecting to play his role. Already he is unwilling to will. Already he is beginning to relish his guilt feelings. He's finished, and he knows it. The world awaits a sign from the Womenal, a sign that will put the future back in business.

"And yet we wonder: Why only now? Why have hundreds of millions of mothers, sisters, and daughters looked on unprotestingly while men made their wars? To this day, women who have suffered irretrievable loss cling to the consolation that their husbands, sons, brothers, fathers—all those heroes who have died in the Volkhov marshes, in the Libyan desert, on the North Atlantic, or in air battles God knows where—have died for something and not in vain; that the deaths of sons, brothers, fathers, and husbands have had meaning and purpose. Given the male view of morality and power—for the one follows from the other—men have always been able to supply logical proof that their cause is just, that the enemy attacked first, that they themselves misjudged the situation but acted in good faith, that they want nothing so much as peace, but that conspicuous weakness, pacifism, and suchlike childishness only provoke aggression, that, suffering and sorrow notwithstanding, it is pleasant and noble to die for the fatherland or for an idea, sprung in all likelihood from a male mind, and finally that we can't expect to live forever.

515

And another thing: since the surviving males have been taught to be chivalrous, they never neglect, after won or lost wars, to bow respectfully to the mothers and widows. After victory parades, heroes dead or alive are honored. Days of national mourning are always a big hit. No danger that the dead will protest. And what do the mothers say?

"On the sideboard stand, over the sofa hang, the photographs of young men in dress uniform, some with an innocent smile, others with a look of earnest concentration, whose earnestness or smile never got beyond the stage of promise. In drawers and portfolios lie school diplomas, letters from the front, their last written words—'I am well and happy here'—and black-bordered newspaper clippings, which after the terse announcement once again list all medals and decorations. A millionfold inheritance without political consequences. Did the women voters say a massive 'no' when —the ruins were still there for all to see—rearmament was decreed? Not at all; they resigned themselves to the perpetuation of this male-ordained madness. And even when women have gained political influence or power, they have always— from Madame Pompadour to Golda Meir and Indira Gandhi—conducted their politics in the Procrustean bed of the male historical consciousness, and that, as I have shown, means war. Can this be changed? Ever, soon, at all?

"The Womenal will have consequences. Our time-phase bears the imprint of the women's liberation movement. Women have been politicized. They have organized; they are fighting, refusing to be silenced. Already they have registered partial success. But—I ask myself with misgivings—will women's striving for social equality end by shattering the male ethic? Or will equality between the sexes merely intensify the male striving for power?

"I am almost inclined to fear that womankind lacks counsel, sustained, reliable, or, to put it plainly, supernatural counsel. But as an embodiment of the guilty male and—as has been demonstrated—warlike principle, am I fit to advise the female cause, and henceforth the female cause alone?

"I want to. I could. I already know how. Let the Womenal judge."

Just as my Ilsebill always wants both at once, to free-lance and to hold a regular job, to live in the country and to enjoy the scenario of city life, just as on the one hand she strives for the simple life (baking her own bread), but on the other hand requires certain conveniences (most recently an automatic clothes dryer), for which reason her wishes, violently as they conflict, are constrained by force of will to run along in pairs—so, after the Flounder's peroration, when a verdict was at last to be pronounced, was the Women's Tribunal (or Womenal) torn. Strictly speaking, death would have been fitting punishment, if his advice (as expiation) had not been needed.

Taken as a whole, the Tribunal wanted both; its parts wanted this or that. While the Flounder Party raised objections to the liquidation of the accused, opposed the death penalty on principle, and contemplated at the most a symbolic punishment, after which the Flounder would be taken on as a repentant adviser and restored to his element, the radical minority were determined to forgo his advice and expunge the Flounder.

Prosecutor Sieglinde Huntscha demanded death by electrocution. Griselde Dubertin wanted to add daily-increased doses of mercury to his drinking water. Ruth Simoneit was for cooking him alive. And as for the court-appointed defense counsel, while on the one hand she demanded acquittal, on the other she pleaded for humane punishment, that is, confinement and psychiatric treatment.

No clear-cut verdict was arrived at. Since both the Revolutionary Advisory Council and the associate judges were divided, a majority could at most have been found for postponement of sentencing. Silent and deathly pale, as though he had decided to become an astral body, the Flounder waited.

And then, at the prompting of Associate Judge Ulla Witzlaff, Ms. Schönherr, the presiding judge, suggested a compromise for which my Ilsebill might have voted, since it promised to satisfy both wishes, the wish for harsh punishment and the wish for prolonged expiation. She proposed that in the Flounder's presence, under his obliquely set eyes, impossible for him to ignore, at a long table—which would make it necessary to remove three rows of seats from the former movie house—at which the associate judges, the Advisory Council, the prosecution, the defense, and a few representatives of the public would be seated, an ostentatious, memorable, ritual, solemn, and grandiose flounder dinner be held. Ms. Helga Paasch undertook, through her connections

517

with the Berlin wholesale trade, to deliver the required number of flounders to the kitchen of Therese Osslieb's restaurant, where nine or, when Erika Nöttke expressed concern that nine would not be sufficient, eleven good-sized specimens ranging from four-and-a-half to nine pounds each (at wholesale prices the bill came to 285 marks) were promptly sautéed in tarragon butter, deglazed with white wine, covered with stock, simmered, seasoned with dill and capers, and finally, along with the roe and milt, which are well developed in June, placed in preheated serving dishes, covered with aluminum foil, and (along with boiled potatoes and cucumber salad) conveyed to Steglitz by cab.

In the onetime Stella Cinema the table, forming a horseshoe around the Flounder in his tank, had been festively set. Candles had been lit. Lemon slices had been bedded on lettuce leaves. Chilled Riesling stood in readiness. The steaming dishes were brought in. The Womenal seated itself. After a short but, despite the solemn occasion, whimsical speech, Ms. Schönherr served first the court-appointed defense counsel, then the prosecutor. The flounder dinner began.

I had better explain how I came to have the honor of attending, although, so soon before her confinement, I should have stuck it out with my Ilsebill. The representatives of the public were chosen by lot. And when I drew one of the lucky lots, giving me the privilege of being the only man present among fifty-four women, Ilsebill had no objection. "Don't miss it on my account. I'll be all right. It's sure to be a couple of days more. I'll send you a wire if necessary or get someone to page you in your harem."

I sat between an old lady, a librarian by profession, and a young schoolteacher who refused to touch the milt though I called it a "delicacy." She said she abominated male organs but would like some of the female roe. I was glad Ulla Witzlaff was sitting across the table from us, with her head slightly tilted. (She took some of the milt.)

Far away, behind the convicted Flounder's tank but recognizable, sat Griselde Dubertin and Ruth Simoneit. Hagedorn and Güllen were also provocatively present. I was so excited I made faces. (Let's hope they don't start fighting.) So be extra gentlemanly. Bridge gaps in the conversation. Help to carve and serve the flatfish. How easily the white flesh let itself be removed from the backbone. Deftly I served the

518

ladies. "I recommend a few drops of lemon juice. The cheeks, I assure you, are delicious. Would you care for a slice of the tail piece, Ms. Nöttke? Just a little more broth and some capers? How strikingly the dill enhances the taste. And don't forget to save the boiled white eyes. Flounder eyes bring luck and make all our wishes come true."

So I made myself useful to the ladies. I refilled wine glasses, filleted deftly, offered "Another potato?," and even called the girls of the Advisory Council by their first names. I joked with Ilona, smiled at Gabriele, had a kind word for the always gloomy Emma, and was almost of the same opinion as Alice. I livened up the conversation by dissecting a turbot head with anatomical acumen and cracking jokes, but always at the proper moment resumed the gravity required by the solemn occasion. I praised the wise verdict, called the Flounder's peroration "artfully forthright," characterized the Womenal as an epoch-making institution, quoted from the well-known ancient Greek feminist play, spoke in passing of my Ilsebill's impending confinement—"She wants a boy so badly"—but added at once that I, the father, would be equally overjoyed with a girl, distributed good-luck charms—fisheyes—raised my glass in a toast, and, when nothing remained of the flounders but eleven sets of ravaged heads, fins, skin, and bones, took the liberty, as the very onliest man present, of making a little speech.

Witzlaff laughed encouragingly. Erika Nöttke begged me to make it short. The old lady on my right turned the hearing-aid button behind her left ear. When I tapped my glass with my fish knife, the young schoolteacher hissed, "Some nerve!" But Ms. Schönherr, from the center of the horseshoe-shaped table, nodded a friendly permission.

I first thanked the assembled ladies for the honor of letting me attend. I praised the culinary art of restaurant owner and Associate Judge Therese Osslieb. A little joke about Helga Paasch's expense-saving connections with the wholesale market. Then I came to the point.

In owning that the Flounder's admission of guilt and antiwar speech had moved me deeply, I gained my first opportunity to introduce myself in my changing time-phases. "As early as the Neolithic . . ." I said. "When we were finally converted to Christianity . . ." "There can be no doubt, to cite Friedell, that some good came of the plague. . . ." I quoted myself as Opitz from his "Poem of Consolation

Amidst the Horrors of War." I was at Kolin, Leuthen, Hochkirch. I opened the door when Comrade Bebel came to see me and my good Lena on Brabank. To spare Sieglinde Huntscha, I made only the barest allusion to the Father's Day death of poor Billy. Then I went into current politics: "Even now it's as if the canteen cook at the Lenin Shipyard in Gdańsk had been turned to stone. They shot Jan in the belly. Yes, the police fired on the workers. And that in a Communist state. Yes, wherever men have their fingers on triggers. And that's how it has always been. The language of arms. Mechanized warfare. Attack to defend. Scorched earth. The Flounder did that. His advice was: Kill! His word signaled violence. He was the source of evil. We are gathered here to punish him. Here, Flounder! Here! Look and see what's left of you. You dealer of death, you enemy of life!"

I lifted up a bare backbone with the ravaged head attached and showed it to the Flounder in his glass tank. Whereupon Griselde Dubertin and Ruth Simoneit, Huntscha and Paasch, but also Elisabeth Güllen and Beate Hagedorn, who had hitherto been silent, obstinately silent, each grabbed a backbone, and other women grabbed the remaining bones, heads, tail fins, and showed them to the Flounder, so that he was forced to see. And several women cried, "You're mortal!" Others went further. "The fact is, you're dead!"

I was overcome with rage. I went to him and threw a backbone down on the platform in front of his tank. "There!" Without delay the women threw down the remaining bones, heads, and fins, until all eleven carcasses lay in a heap and the Flounder was forced to see what was left of his fellows. "There! There!" And we all wiped our fingers and tossed our paper napkins onto the pile. And we all spat on the bony garbage, in which crooked mouths gaped in sightless heads.

But the pallid Flounder, who seemed to have been blown from glass, remained in his hovering position and did not take refuge in his sand bed. Ah, how grievously he suffered. Ah, how right it served him.

Then Ms. Schönherr said: "Punishment has now been dealt. The day after tomorrow the Flounder will be set free to expiate his guilt. All arrangements have been made for transportation. The Womenal is therefore disbanded. Sisters, I thank you."

With that the dinner party broke up.

On Møn

When the sentence had been announced, it was arranged that Associate Judge Ulla Witzlaff should take charge of its implementation. Even before completing his long peroration on the warlike character of men and on women's capacity for suffering, the Flounder, because someone, Ruth Simoneit, I think, was talking some sort of rubbish about the end of the world, had illustrated with examples how prone to catastrophe the earth was and dated the next ice age as "any day now." But while still engaged in spiriting ten thousand years away in a twinkling, he could be heard, in an aside, expressing the wish that he, the evildoer, conscious of his guilt and bowing to his sentence, might, to enable him to expiate most usefully, be set free in his favorite body of water, namely, the western Baltic. There, he informed the court, he knew an island the east coast of which consisted of steep chalk cliffs, from the top of which on a clear day one could with the naked eye see the similarly shaped island where the tale of "The Fisherman and His Wife" was put into circulation. "Two picturesque spots that are connected geologically and in other ways as well," said the Flounder, and explained that immediately after the last glacial age—"which really wasn't so long ago!"—the floor of the Baltic had formed between these islands. Flint could be found at the foot of the cliffs and interesting petrifactions as well, such as sea urchins and the tentacles of octopuses: "For the space of a cosmic half hour, the young Baltic was characterized by a Mediterranean warmth." That was where he wished to be set free. With that as a base he would get on with his new duties—for the advancement of the female cause.

"He means the island of Møn," said Ulla Witzlaff to her fellow associate judge Helga Paasch, who was sitting beside her. Ulla had spent her childhood on Rügen and attended the School of Church Music in Greifswald before crossing over to the West when the Wall was built in Berlin. Thus she was eminently suited to carry out the Womenal's sentence and set the Flounder free in the place he had chosen, particularly

521

since Ulla was able to assure the court that the mercury content of the Baltic Sea was minimal at that spot.

Because the authorities of the German Democratic Republic refused permission to cross its territory by train or Volkswagen bus to Rostock-Warnemünde, whence a ferry ran to Gedser in Denmark (the officials never mentioned the Flounder by name, but merely designated him as a "subversive element" or "reactionary individual," for the republic of workers and peasants lived in fear of the flatfish), it was necessary to fly the condemned Flounder to Hamburg in the strictest secrecy and under close guard, to forestall terrorist acts by Griselde Dubertin's radical group.

From there he was taken to Travemünde by car. From there the party crossed over to Gedser by the regularly scheduled ferry. There Danish feminists took charge, and the party traveled via Vordingborg to Kalvehave and thence across the bridge to the island of Møn. As it was late afternoon when they arrived, the party stopped for the night at an inn not far from the chalk cliffs.

The Flounder in his special traveling tank had come through the journey in good shape. As though in anticipation of the joyous event, he had lost some of his transparency. His pebbly skin had got back some of its color. Yet despite his cheerful fin play, he remained mute.

And I was there. (Naturally Ilsebill was furious at my wanting to prolong my absence so soon before her confinement. "You don't give a hoot about the child!" she screamed when I asked for permission over the phone.)

After Ulla Witzlaff, Therese Osslieb, and Helga Paasch had approved my request to travel with them, I was accepted as a helper. In addition to the women already mentioned, our party included Erika Nöttke (the gray mouse) and Ms. von Carnow, the Flounder's court-appointed counsel (all in sky-blue silk). Allegedly Sieglinde hadn't wanted to come. Ms. Schönherr thought her presence at the execution of sentence not absolutely called for.

We had good reason to ask the Danish delegation to take security measures that night and the next day, for Ruth Simoneit had joined Griselde Dubertin's radical opposition group, and both of them had spoken up (before the verdict) in favor of the death penalty, so that obstructive action if not actual violence was to be feared during the release of the Flounder. The seventh and eighth associate judges of the Womenal, the full-blown housewife Elisabeth Güllen and the biochemist Beate Hagedorn, who reminded me remotely of my Sibylle and Maria Kuczorra, were thought to be radical and suspected of terrorism, especially since they had been absent from the proceedings during the final pleas; only at the great flounder dinner had they been silently present.

The next morning the Flounder had to be carried on foot through a beech forest to the coast. The task fell to me. The tank hung from my neck by two straps like a peddler's tray. Looking through the glass wall of the tank, I could see the Flounder trying with deft fin play to compensate for my uneven gait. First we took a dirt road, then a narrow path through the woods. Ahead of me (and the Flounder) went the Danish delegation and the few newspaperwomen who had been authorized to accompany us. Behind us, Witzlaff and Osslieb, Helga Paasch and Erika Nöttke. Ms. von Carnow had pronounced the walk too much for her and stayed behind at the hotel.

Of course I attempted a last conversation with the Flounder. As soon as the women ahead of us and behind us were far enough away, I whispered, "For God's sake, Flounder, say something. Anything, just a word. Is it really all over between us? Have you really written me off? Aren't you going to advise anyone but those stupid women? Flounder, what's to become of me? Flounder, say something! I'm completely at a loss!"

But the Flounder's silence remained unbroken. I carried him as if, along with my burden, I were carrying myself and my historic mission, the male cause, to the grave. Before and behind me the women were chatting merrily. How airily their dresses with their large-flower prints took in the breeze. A Dutch television team shot us for the news. Erika Nöttke gathered a bunch of flowers. There was flint all about, and Paasch picked up a few handy-sized pieces to keep as souvenirs. Ulla Witzlaff, with her clarion voice, sang a Christian hymn, "This day so full of joy . . ." And in a spirit of sisterhood, Osslieb joined in.

When we came to the unprotected edge of the cliff and were able, since the weather (as promised) was fine, to make out the chalk cliffs of the isle of Rügen, the temptation rose

523

up in me to unbuckle the Flounder in his glass tank (my peddler's tray) and hurl him down onto the flinty beach (three hundred and fifty feet below), or, rather, I was tempted to leap to my death from the cliff—after all, I'm done for!—with the Flounder still buckled to me, if possible, crying aloud, "Long live the male cause!"—or perhaps just to fling myself alone, sparing the Flounder and the future, or pulling perhaps not Osslieb but then Ulla with me— lovingly united in death.

But already Erika Nöttke was anxiously at my side. "I'm worried," she said. "Don't you think the sudden change may be too much for the Flounder? For nine months his water has been changed frequently, he has been adequately provided with oxygen and fed regularly, in other words, safeguarded against environmental hazards. Don't you think the Baltic, with its pollution and supersaturation with algae, might be dangerous for him? In the last few weeks, it's true, we've tried to prepare him by gradually increasing the chemical adulteration, but it will be a shock all the same, possibly too great a one. Think how he has changed in captivity. Look how pale he is, how transparent, almost glassy. Oh, I do hope the Flounder outlives us."

Helga Paasch was worried, too. But Osslieb reassured Erika Nöttke, saying the change wouldn't hurt the Flounder, he was a tough customer, sure to live through the next ice age. A few blobs of tar and a bit of mercury wouldn't mean a thing to him, he'd adapt: if only for the principle of the thing, he'd go on living. "Just look at him!" cried Ulla. "He's getting his color back. He'll soon be in the pink!"

After we had all enjoyed the splendid view for a while and posed for the television crew—fillers were needed—we started down through a wooden gully embedded in the chalk cliffs. For tourist use, yard-long logs provided natural steps. By holding my peddler's tray in both hands, I tried to spare the Flounder excessive jolting in my passage from step to step, but it was pretty bumpy even so. Seeing me bathed in sweat, Erika Nöttke wanted to relieve me. Manfully I declined. (Damned if I let them take my Flounder away from me. He used to be my Flounder. I'll stick it out to the bitter end. I'll keep faith with my history.)

When we got to the bottom, there wasn't much time for a breather. A glance up the face of the cliffs revealed the grim reality, the danger we were in. Up top stood the bitches of the radical opposition—the Revolutionary Advisory Council —clustered around Griselde Dubertin and Ruth Simoneit. I recognized Elisabeth Güllen and Beate Hagedorn. "Christ!" cried Paasch. "Huntscha is with them!"

When the first stones were thrown down, I thought I recognized the court-appointed defense counsel among the infuriated women.

"Good God!" I cried. "Look who's gone over to the enemy!"

"Where is she?" Osslieb asked. "Where?"

"There!" I cried. "There!"

But Bettina von Carnow didn't show herself again. Besides, the hail of stones kept us from getting a good look at the traitor or snapping her picture. It was easy later on to make out Huntscha, Hagedorn, housewife Güllen, and Griselde Dubertin in the newspaperwomen's numerous photos and in the pan shot taken by the Dutch television team, but not Ms. Carnow. I saw her though, the stupid bitch.

Most of the stones missed us. Poor Erika Nöttke was hit on the head and bled profusely. There was flint all over the isle of Møn, and that's what they were throwing. Two members of the Danish delegation, an English newspaperwoman, and the Dutch camerawoman were slightly bruised. A piece of flint struck the Flounder's tank, but no damage was done. In trying to dodge a fist-sized stone (flung perhaps by Griselde Dubertin), I fell on the stony beach and cut my left knee through my trousers. Thank the Lord, I had put the Flounder and his tank down a moment before. Lying thus prone and slightly befuddled with pain, I found a tiny petrified sea urchin, so corroborating the Flounder's contention that the Baltic had been an almost tropical sea right after the last ice age. (I kept my find. I expect it to bring me luck and protect me from my Ilsebill. Who knows what the future may bring?)

While cries—most likely of "Treason!"—came down from above, Paasch and Osslieb cursed back like fishwives. Meanwhile Ulla Witzlaff took off her shoes and stockings, opened the Flounder's tank with the key that had been entrusted to her care, reached under the white belly side of the flatfish with both hands, lifted him out of the tank, showed him to us, to the photographers, to the television camera, and to the cursing, catapulting women on the chalk cliff, then carried him step by step across the sandy beach until she stood knee-deep in water. Then she proclaimed in her singing voice, "I hereby carry out the sentence pronounced by the Women's Tribunal upon the Flounder. Henceforth he shall be available to us alone. We shall call him! We'll call him, all right!" Then she put him in the water, and all was still. Only the clicking of the photgraphers and the whirring of the television camera.

Witzlaff reported that he had swum straight out to sea. Then we had to attend to the injured Erika Nöttke. In the meantime the radical opposition had evacuated the cliff. It was a hard climb, but Ms. Nöttke declined to be carried. She was still holding her bunch of flowers. Helga Paasch threw away her collection of flints. I'd have liked to spend a few days on Møn with Witzlaff, but at the hotel there was a telegram for me: RETURN IMPERATIVE. BABY IMMINENT. NO EXCUSES PLEASE. ILSEBILL. I made it home just in time.

Conversation

In the first month we were not sure,
and only the oviduct knew.
In the second month we argued about
what we had wanted and not wanted,
said and not said.
In the third month the belly changed palpably,
but our words only repeated themselves.
When in the fourth month the new year began,
only the year was new; our words were still tired.
Exhausted but still in the right,
we wrote off the fifth, the sixth month:
It's moving, we said ummoved.
When in the seventh month we bought roomy dresses,
we were still cramped and quarreled
about the third month, the one we'd missed out on.
Only when a leap over a ditch
became a fall—
Don't jump! No! Wait. No. Don't jump!—
did we begin to worry: stammering and whispering.
In the eighth month we were sad,

because the words spoken in the second and fourth
were still being paid for.
When in the ninth month we were defeated
and the child, quite unconcerned, was born,
we had no words left.
Congratulations came over the phone.

What we wish for

A she or a he. If it's a girl, we'll name her after my
mother; if it's a boy, he will, like me, gather from garbage
dumps the feathers the sky loses and raise them lightly,
barely breathing, then blowing, then with gusts of wind, and
hold them in suspense, falling, reeling, and then another up-
draft. It's flying, flying! we hear Emmanuel calling. . . .

One more child screamed at 10:15 A.M., and no sooner
had the umbilical cord been cut, was given its name, which
had never been open to argument. Sex, length, weight. It
already looks like, will soon, will later on, being Ilsebill's
daughter, but with a different walk, prouder, more self-
assured, walk straight ahead and take what's there, so that
no further wishes are left hanging, never aired, in the closet,
till the moths get them. One more girl with a crack that
stayed open when our beautiful view was nailed shut.

To the wish stated before the Womenal in the form of a
demand—"Why always us! Let the men for a change open
their legs, conceive, and bear!"—the Flounder had known an
answer. "Look, my dear ladies: even the moon lies mirror-re-
versed in a pond. How are we going to straighten that out?
How, I ask you, how?"

When Ilsebill was delivered, her daughter came as a disap-
pointment. Just another cunt, another twat, the goal of all
men who are homeless and unsheltered and want to get rid of
themselves, over and over again. (And the mother hissed at
me, "You cracksman!")

Not all Ilsebill's wishes consent to come true. Since I was
allowed to be present at the birth of our daughter, I tried (in
a green coverall, gauze mask, and sterile shoes) to console her.

527

"Honest, Ilsebill. Girls are much better off nowadays. In former times, when I stupidly believed in the right of inheritance, I always wished for a boy. But Dorothea, Agnes, Amanda, Lena—not one of them gave me anything but daughters; and even the abbess Rusch bore only girls. But when canteen cook Maria Kuczorra gave birth to twin girls—their names are Damroka and Mestwina—the workers of the Lenin Shipyard in Gdańsk, seeing that Maria's Jan was dead, gave her a double baby carriage and two pink pisspots to avoid any complexes later on. . . ."

Ordinarily it would have been a difficult delivery, because the breech presentation makes for complications. So we decided on a Caesarean, which is guaranteed painless because everything up to the navel is anesthetized. The size and position of the baby were first checked by ultrasonic means, but the coarse-grained picture didn't show the sex.

The obstetrician made an oblique incision in Ilsebill's abdomen where it arched above the shaved groin; he cut through the skin, the fatty envelope, the muscular tissue, and the peritoneum, all of which Ilsebill, whose head lay far in the distance, behind a screen, did not see.

I saw, because it's supposed to be good for fathers to see the womb laid bare in the gaping belly and opened with a scalpel. The obstetrician tore the amnion to let out the fluid. Watery blood. Absorbent cloths stuffed into the cavities. Veins clamped. Then he reached in with his gloved hands, and, ass first, our daughter emerged into the world, showing—hallelujah!—her little Parker House roll, while in the delivery room of the municipal hospital soft music from hidden loudspeakers made the whole affair pleasant, inoffensive, friendly, entertaining, and absolutely banal. The up-to-date hospital director, who is open to all reasonable innovations, does not want his young interns engaging during the Caesarean (because they have nothing else to do) in private conversations with the Korean student nurses about cars, politics, weekend delights, so depriving the mother, whose hearing, since she feels no pain, is particularly acute, of important small experiences; that is why he has decreed that, apart from the sound of the instruments and the obstetrician's soft-spoken instructions—"Clamp, please. Swabs, please"—only sweet music should be heard.

"And this," said the obstetrician through his mask for my edification, "is the Fallopian tube. . . ." (I also saw how yellow, like chicken fat, Ilsebill's belly fat is. A piece of it crumbled off and I could have fried two eggs in it.)

After being shown to her mother, our daughter (whose umbilical cord had already been cut) was screaming on the other side of the room, where she was weighed, measured, and secured against mistaken identity by a tag on the wrist or ankle. Ah, my babykins, my bawling chickabiddy, my lambkin, my daughter . . .

When Ilsebill's womb, which immediately contracted, and her belly had been sewed up again, and the scalpels, clamps, swabs, and absorbent cloths had concurrently been counted on a side table, one metal clamp was missing. They were going to undo the stitches and search the abdominal cavity, but luckily the clamp was found in the bucket with the afterbirth, where it didn't belong. But what I, the father, who was watching, wished into Ilsebill's belly stayed there, was sewed in; namely, big stones, and I'm not giving them away.

Oh, my secret thoughts! As though I found nothing worth wishing for. As though a quickly twining gourd-vine arbor or a wing chair to deafen me to the sufferings of the world were everything. As though my longings—"Yes yes, Maria, I'm coming; I'm coming soon"—were nothing but easy ways out, loopholes that ought to be plugged up. Oh, how I need rest, distant places, new wallpaper, a plane ticket to a better timephase. Ah, how I need a far-off century. Ah, how I thirst for death and eternity.

But my wishes have never counted. It's always hers, damn it, that I . . . And take all the responsibility, oh yes! And pay and pay! And feel guilty for everything and nothing.

What fault (after all) is it of mine that it's turned out to be a girl again. I'm not a slot machine that spits what you pick. At least, on the day when my daughter was born, the representatives of the one and the other German state signed a treaty extending the privileges of the Lübeck fishermen, which have been in force since the emperor Barbarossa's writ of 1188, to the territorial waters of the German Democratic Republic; and that, you'll agree, was long overdue.

At a snack bar around the corner from the municipal hospital, when I first took a schnapps or two with my beer, then ordered one, then another *Bockwurst* with bread and mustard, they were running the quarter finals on television.

Poland was leading. Chile had been eliminated. And it kept on raining. The world-championship soccer matches transformed me into an onlooker among other male onlookers, who like me drank schnapps, dipped *Bockwrust* in mustard, took bites, washed them down with beer, had that absorbed look, and may well have all been fathers, worried about their daughters.

The owner knew his clientele. The name of his bar was The Happy Father. He said, "No boy again? Don't let it get you down. Girls are cheaper now that they've done away with dowries. They're all emancipated nowadays. Nowadays they wish for entirely different things."

Yes, I assure you. You'll have everything. Your father will provide. Your father will attend to it. Your father is still something of a stranger to you, because he has no womb. Give him time for a schnapps or two and a walk around the block. Your father has his share of the restlessness that makes the world go round. Your father is on the track of something. Your father has to go away for a while, to see where he came from. Where it all began. There's a Maria up there whom he's related to. She gave him a piece of amber with a fly caught in it. Don't be afraid. Your father will be back. He'll come back and tell you stories in which feathers are blown and children who go looking for mushrooms manage to get lost and flies spend the winter in pieces of amber. And I'll tell you about the Flounder, too, when I get back. . . .

Man oh man

Stop it, will you.
Cut it out.
You're finished, man, still horny but that's all.

Say once again: Will do.
Once again press button and make puppets dance.
Once again show your will and its flaws.
Once again pound the table and say: That's mine.

Once again list how often you and whose.
Once again be hard, so it sinks in.
Prove to yourself once again your great, your proven,
your all-embracing ever-loving care.

Man oh man.
There you stand, present and soon to be present.
Men don't weep, man.
Your dreams, which were typically masculine, have all been
    filmed.
Your victories dated and listed.
Your progress caught up with and measured.
Your mourning and those who enact it weary the playbills.
Your jokes are too often varied; Radio Yerevan has gone off
    the air.
Enormous (even now), your power cancels itself out.

Man oh man.
Once again say "I,"
Once again think penetratingly.
Once again look through.
Once again be right.
Once again be profoundly silent.
Stand or fall just once more.

No need to clean up, man; just leave it all be.
By your own rules you're washed up,
dismissed from your own history.
And only the baby boy in you
has leave to play with building blocks for another short
    while.
What, man oh man, will your wife say to that?

Three meals of pork and cabbage

*Maria took two tin spoons and a full dinner pail with
her when we rode out to Heubude on the streetcar to sit in
the dunes in view of the sea.*

It can be proved that as early a cook as Amanda Woyke was acquainted with our common cabbage, which she shredded, stored in barrels, and made into sauerkraut, or cooked into a thick mash with potatoes and pork ribs and served to the farm hands on holidays. Since cabbage bloats, it seems unlikely that Agnes Kurbiella set potted or stuffed cabbage, let alone pork and cabbage, before painter Möller or poet Opitz; our easily digestible cauliflower didn't exist yet. It had to wait for progress. I have no recollection of Abbess Rusch preparing our present-day varieties of cabbage, but Chinese cabbage (pe-tsai) was occasionally imported in her day. It wasn't until later that kitchens smelled of *Wirsing* and *Kapuster*, as we called the common cabbage. Lena Stubbe saw us through the winter with rutabaga and cabbage. Since Dorothea of Montau did not know the green cabbage that is common today, she seems on Holy Thursday to have cooked the wild varieties, such as colewort or the slightly bitter sea kale, with nothing else. And just as Dorothea put up sorrel in a wooden barrel, so Amanda Woyke and Lena Stubbe shredded cabbage heads (after cutting out the cores) with a cabbage shredder, piled the shreds in barrels with cabbage leaves at the bottom, poured on salt, pounded the shredded cabbage with a pestle until there was juice to cover it, spread more cabbage leaves on top, and fitted the barrel with a wooden lid that had to be weighted down with a large stone.

And in time it fermented, so that pork and cabbage, such as Maria brought to the dunes in a dinner pail, could be made not only with fresh cabbage, but also sweet and sour with sauerkraut, caraway seed, and juniper berries. Pork ribs are suitable, or smoked spareribs, if you prefer.

And once, after Maria had started buying for the shipyard kitchen, I ate pork and cabbage with Jan Ludkowski in the canteen of the Lenin Shipyard. I had obtained permission to visit a few of the workshops, the then unused drydock, and an unfinished ferryboat on the slips. Since what they showed me is illustrated and described in several languages in the prospectus, it's not worth the telling. The work sounds of a Communist shipyard are no different from the work noise of capitalist shipyards. I politely took notes, which were later abandoned unused at the Hotel Monopol; still, it was interesting to see what the Poles had made of the Schichau, Danziger, Klawitter Shipyard, which at the end of the war was partly destroyed, partly dismantled by the Russians. Jan said, "Our orders from the West . . . That's where we get our hard currency. . . . Obviously, we have to sell to the Soviet Union at bargain prices, floating fish factories, for instance, that process the catch right there on the fishing grounds, the latest thing. . . ."

Lunch hour was over at the canteen. A flat-roofed two-story building, through the plate-glass front of which gulls could be seen stunt-flying. Only a few clerks in white smocks were still there, occupying two or three tables at the other end. For them, for us, there was leftover pork and cabbage, consisting of pork ribs, fresh carawayed cabbage, and potatoes, all cooked together. Our beverage was buttermilk. Jan, who generally looked after visitors to the shipyard, addressed me as if I had been a large delegation. Not to be turned off, he spouted production figures, boasted of large Swedish orders, and pickled his technocratic Communism, as one might pickle cabbage, with fatalistic salt: "That's the way we Poles are. . . . We know in our bones that something somehow will go wrong with our progress. . . . Regimentation just doesn't work with us. . . . But somehow we manage. . . . We know our history. . . ."

Still gnawing at his pork ribs, Jan Ludkowski was off on his thing. Since the ferryboat (which I had been authorized to visit) was to be named after some king of Poland (one of the Batorys or Wladislaws) and not after a Pomorshian prince (Sambor or Swantopolk), he, conscious of his Kashubian heritage, had submitted one petition after another—in vain, though anyone ought to recognize that Mestwina and Damroka are attractive names for ships.

Jan saw historical episodes in detail, as if he had been there. And since I, too, had lived in several time-phases and left someone lying around in every century, we found no difficulty over pork and cabbage with lumpy buttermilk in re-enacting the decisive battle in which Duke Swantopolk not only trounced the Norwegians, but with his victory over General Fortinbras also provided a sequel to Shakespeare's *Hamlet*.

Jan and I agreed to make a play out of it. Somewhere in the midst of the Kashubian water holes the armies stand facing each other. Swantopolk and Fortinbras taunt each other:

533

Kashubian swine! Norwegian swine! And then Hamlet appears as a ghost between the armies and expresses himself in obscure, ambiguous pentameters about many controversial matters: naturally about Shakespeare and his doubles. Naturally about Communism and capitalism. And why not an allusion to the Flounder: how he treacherously advised the one and the other hero and sent them to their doom.

"Why not?" said Jan. "And maybe after the battle Hamlet's ghost could appear among the dead. . . ."

"Naturally," I said. "But what happens after the victory?"

"The victorious Swantopolk," said Jan, "might be assailed by self-doubt. He shillies and shallies. . . ."

"Until," said I, "the Teutonic Knights, who don't know the meaning of doubt, get there and clean up. Ruthlessly, inexorably."

We didn't get beyond the first act of our sequel to *Hamlet*. Maria came in from the kitchen and said, "Shooting the shit again?" Coming in with her corkscrew curls, she was Mestwina's daughter Damroka. And it occurred to me that Jan loved her both in her historical and in her present time-phase. Stocky, round of head and belly, he became slender when he said "Marysia." But when the canteen cook of the Lenin Shipyard in Gdańsk wasn't laughing (from inside, over nothing), she liked best to talk about prices and bottlenecks in the supply system: "All we need is a cabbage shortage. Want some more pork and cabbage? There's plenty."

Jan and I wanted. Maria brought and left. And there was fresh lumpy buttermilk in our glasses. But we had no further ideas about Swantopolk and Fortinbras.

What is history? No one knows exactly when our common cabbage (*Brassica oleracea*), as important an innovation as buckwheat, millet, potatoes, rutabaga, was first planted on a large scale; for as far back as Mestwina's time the Pomorshians gathered the seeds of the early, wild varieties. Undoubtedly the Ems Dispatch set a good deal in motion, but the sugar beet far more. If Prince Hamlet (as ghost) had invited Swantopolk and Fortinbras, the Kashubians and the Norwegians, to a meal of flatulent pork and cabbage, history would have taken an entirely different course. I said as much to Jan. But when, in the following year, shortly before Christmas, a rise in the prices of staple foods was announced in Poland, when all along the Baltic coast the workers went on strike, there was plenty of pork and cabbage at the canteen of the Lenin Shipyard, yet history did not take a different course, but the usual bad one.

They shot Jan in the belly. On December 18, 1970, they shot Jan in his bellyful of pork and cabbage. The police of the People's Republic of Poland shot, along with other workers, the naval construction engineer, employee of the publicity department, trade-union and Communist League member Jan Ludkowski, aged forty-three, in his belly, then full of the pork and carawayed cabbage that had been dished out to upward of two thousand striking workers in the canteen of the Lenin Shipyard. Just in time, just before the shipyard was cordoned off by the police, Maria Kuczorra, who was in charge of provisioning the shipyard canteen, had managed to divert to the shipyard a truckload of cabbage intended for the army. Deep-frozen pork ribs were already on hand. And there has never been any shortage of caraway seed in Poland. He died instantly.

With Jan you could sit and talk. About mouth-blown glasses. About poems. Even about trees. We talked about Gryphius and Opitz, just as they may have talked about heaven knows what. About the burden of an evil day. How things were bad and sometimes got a little better. About iambic hexameter and internal rhymes. About politics, too, in the wider and narrower sense. Once we drove into the hills of Kashubia in Jan's old Skoda and sat down beside a water hole. Crayfish skittered away and hid under the rocks. A brimstone butterfly. Larks over the fields. It was so still that Jan was frightened after he said, "I've given up hope." And once we went down to the beach, looking for amber. We found a few crumbs. Sometimes Maria was with us. It was nice when she disturbed us. Of course we each saw Maria differently. I saw her more distinctly. The three of us went to the movies. I held Maria's other hand. In the film, Polish cavalry rode to their death against tanks. One horse was called Lotna. Maria cried. Afterward we went to the Rathauskeller. There Maria laughed again. She was pregnant when Jan was shot in his bellyful of pork and cabbage. And once, when I had told him about the Flounder—that was in March, and the sea was whipping up foam—Jan said softly,

535

"I know him. I know him well. . . ." And Jan also knew the story about Ilsebill.

Ah, Flounder! Where have you swum off to? It's so still, and nothing is decided. What's to become of us? We're worn out, our quarrel has dozed off, it's only talking in its sleep. Little words hang on. Apples of discord roll across the table. You have. You are. I want. I will. Our child will. Your daughter already has. What I'm entitled to. What I haven't got. My needs. Your interests. The second residence. The additional insurance. Travel folders. Wish for this. Wish for that. Go ahead, it's all right with me. It's perfectly all right with me. But it's expensive. Expensive and nothing else. So beat it. So why don't you beat it.

Ah, Flounder! Your story has a dismal ending.

Three months after the birth of our daughter, when she had begun to smile—"Look, she's smiling!"—and the sweet peas on the fence were still in bloom and the swallows were flying high and the summer lingering on and Ilsebill's belly was whole again and everything had been paid for (and nothing more had been heard of the Flounder), I said to my Ilsebill, who was slender and again full of unrest: "Pork and cabbage! That's something you can't understand. Just plain pork and cabbage. In his bellyful of pork and cabbage. I've got to go back. I've got to go back there again. That's where I came from. That's where it all began. That's where my umbilical cord was cut. We're shooting a film there. No. No actors or actresses. Just a documentary for TV. About the reconstruction. How the Poles have gone about it. All the streets and the churches. All the Gothic claptrap. More authentic than before. And how much it cost. What do you mean, pleasure trip! Of course I want to see her. Naturally. Why not, we're related. . . ."

After saying that (and still more) to Ilsebill, who wanted to go somewhere entirely different (Lesser Antilles), I took an Interflight plane from East Berlin across Kashubia to Gdańsk, where the Third Program television team was already inspecting shooting sites and storing up cutting copy, had already been to see the municipal conservator, had had a little trouble with customs (about their equipment), and were waiting for me with an old Pharus map of the Hanseatic Free City of Danzig.

The Charter City was now called Glowne Miasto, the Long Market Dlugi Targ, Brotbänkengasse Chlebnicka, and Jopengasse, its extension, Piwna. We shot on Hawkers' Street (Straganiarska) and in the ruins of Saint John's. From Warehouse Island (Spichlerze) we shot the reconstructed line of narrow-chested houses and brick-red gates along the Mottlau (Motlawa). We shot up or down Long Street (Dluga), according to the position of the sun. In the Charter City Rathaus we shot Anton Möller's painting *The Tribute Money*. Pan Chomicz, the conservator, recited his explanations, which disregarded costs. Suddenly the current went off. While we were waiting for the house electrician, Prince Philip of England paid a semiofficial visit to the Rathaus. And other incidents. And constant sunshine. Perfect shooting weather. Tourists. And sometimes when we stopped to rest, I sat down on the perron of the Gothic, gabled Writer's Club building on Frauengasse (now called Mariacka), because I had often sat there with Jan, talking of this and that; after a while Maria Kuczorra came by with her plastic shopping bag.

Of course she's more beautiful than ever. But she doesn't laugh any more. And right after her daughters were born, she cut off her corkscrew curls. She still works hard at the canteen of the Lenin Shipyard. She's saving up for a car. She has sold Jan's old Skoda.

With short-cropped curls, in sweater and jeans, Maria came by as I was sitting on the Frauengasse perron, drinking my gritty coffee, and (inwardly rich in figures) waiting for Agnes Kurbiella or fearing Dorothea Swarze, who at this time of day (vespers) often had her visions at Saint Mary's.

I called her—"Marysia!"—as Jan would have called her. She didn't want to join me for coffee; she wanted to get away, to go somewhere else. I paid and gathered up my papers. Notes on Opitz. What Hegge brought from Wittenberg. Extracts from the King Hymnal: "Oh, God in heaven, now look down. . . ." Extracts from the regulations of the Scania mariners' guild. The names of Napoleonic generals at the time when the Republic of Danzig was being besieged by the Russians and Prussians . . .

We made our way between perrons to Our Lady's Gate and the Mottlau. Frauengasse is a street that takes a lifetime to walk down. I'd have liked to buy Maria an amber necklace in one of the many shops on the perrons. She said she didn't wear jewelry any more. We went to an old barge tied up near the Long Bridge (Dlugie Pobrzeźe) that operated as a snack bar and, standing at narrow little tables, ate fried codfish from paper plates. I asked to know more of Maria's daughters than just their names. The girls, she told me, were staying with Jan's mother. She had pictures on her. When she asked the name of my daughter, I lied and said Agnes. I had no pictures on me. Maria went to get paper napkins. There'd been a dollop of ketchup with the codfish. The Mottlau smelled stronger than the fried fish. Not a word about Jan. But when we had left and were arranging to meet the next day, Maria said suddenly, "He came from Warsaw. His name is Kociolek. He gave the order. So then they fired. He's out of the country now. In Belgium. In charge of the embassy there."

At last it was all confirmed. Fairy tales only stop for a time, or they start up again after the end. The truth is told, in a different way each time.

Next day we shot Saint Bridget's, the Radaune, a muddy little river, the Big Mill, and the pinnacles sitting on blocks and waiting to be mounted on Saint Catherine's. For forty seconds I spoke sentences to end the film with.

In the late afternoon I called for Maria at the shipyard gate. In her plastic bag she had a dinner pail full of pork and cabbage. It was still warm, she said. She had also brought spoons. They rattled. The square outside the shipyard showed no sign of anything. In passing, Maria pointed to an undistinguished part of the asphalt roadway: "That's where he lay, over there."

We took the streetcar to Heubude, a fishing village now called Stogi that is still a popular bathing beach, equipped with bathhouses. We rode along the Outer City Ditch, across the Old Mottlau, Warehouse Island, the New Mottlau, through the Lower City, turned off to the left after Island Gate, crossed the Dead Vistula, and didn't say one word until we got to Heubude.

Of course that sentence isn't true. Heubude was the last stop. We walked through the shore woods on sandy paths. It was one of those early-September days when the light becomes ambiguous. We walked side by side, then in single file, first Maria, then me. From then on, her back: unfriendly, round.

Once out of the woods, Maria took her shoes off. I took mine off, too, and my socks. That was something I knew—

walking barefoot through beach grass in the dunes. We heard faint waves lapping against the beach. To the west, you could see the installations of the new oil port. On the last dune, which sloped gently down to the shore, Maria stood still. The beach was deserted except for a few figures receding in the distance. Maria let herself slip down into a hollow and took off her jeans and panties. I dropped my trousers. She helped me until my member stood erect. I don't know how long I took, or whether she finished. She didn't want any kissing, just the one thing, quickly. As soon as I came, she tipped me out and pulled on her panties and jeans. The distant figures on the beach had receded still farther.

After that we took the tin spoons and ate the lukewarm pork and cabbage out of the dinner pail. Maria chattered about her daughters and about the car she'd made a down payment on, a Fiat. The pork and cabbage reminded me. When the dinner pail was empty, Maria jumped up and ran across the beach to the sea. I stayed behind and saw her running: her back again.

The sea lay smooth, licking the beach. Maria went in up to her knees in her jeans. After standing there a while, she shouted a Kashubian word three times and held out her arms like a bowl. And then the Flounder, the flat, age-old, dark, wrinkled, pebbly-skinned Flounder, no, my Flounder no longer, her Flounder, leaped as though brand-new out of the sea and into her arms.

I heard them talking. I heard them both talking. They talked a long time, she questioning with strident emphasis, he fatherly and reassuring. Maria laughed. I understood nothing. Time and time again the Flounder. I could guess at those categorical finalities. She who never laughed was laughing, laughing up to her knees in water. How deserted the beach was. How far away I was sitting. Good that she was able to laugh again. About what? About whom? I sat beside the empty dinner pail. Fallen out of history. With an aftertaste of pork and cabbage.

It was starting to get dark when Maria finished talking with the Flounder. And when she had given him back to the sea, the evening breeze ruffled the Baltic. She stood for a while, showing me her back. Then slowly she came to meet her footprints. But it wasn't Maria who came back. It must be Dorothea, I thought with alarm. As step by step she grew

539

larger, I began to hope for Agnes. That's not Sophie's walk. Is Billy, my poor Sibylle, coming back?

Ilsebill came. She overlooked me, overstepped me. Already she had passed me by. I ran after her.

About the author:

GÜNTER GRASS, Germany's most famous contemporary writer, is a creative artist of extraordinary versatility, a poet, a dramatist, novelist, and also a graphic artist of considerable achievement. He is the author of *The Tin Drum, Cat and Mouse, Local Anaesthetic, The Diary of a Snail,* and various collections of plays and poems, the most recently published of which is *In the Egg and Other Poems.*